Valerie Georgeson has be
ANGELS, JULIET B
JONNY BRIGGS and S
as well as the phenomenall
Her three earlier novels, THE TURNING TIDES,
SEEDS OF LOVE and WHISPERING ROOTS, are
also published by Futura.

Praise for Valerie Georgeson's novels:

- 'Full of real people, a book to settle down with'
WOMANS WORLD

- 'A most enjoyable saga, rivalling Cathering Cookson's work'
LIVERPOOL DAILY POST

- 'Powerful emotional stuff'
WEEKEND

- 'Most enjoyable . . . very well written'
WOMAN'S REALM

Also by Valerie Georgeson

THE TURNING TIDES
THE SHADOW OF THE ELEPHANT:
VOLUME 1 – SEEDS OF LOVE
VOLUME 2 – WHISPERING ROOTS

VALERIE GEORGESON

The Shadow of the Elephant
Haunted Tree

Futura

A Futura Book

First published in Great Britain by
Macdonald & Co (Publishers) Ltd
London & Sydney 1989

This Futura edition published in 1991

Copyright © Valerie Georgeson 1989

The right of Valerie Georgeson to be identified as author of
this work has been asserted by her in accordance with the
Copyright, Designs and Patents Act 1988.

Printed in Great Britain by
BPCC Hazell Books
Aylesbury, Bucks, England
Member of BPCC Ltd.

ISBN 0 7088 4475 8

Futura Publications
A Division of
Macdonald & Co (Publishers) Ltd
Orbit House
1 New Fetter Lane
London EC4A 1AR

A member of Maxwell Macmillan Pergamon Publishing Corporation

ACKNOWLEDGEMENTS

My thanks to Gavin H. Brown, my husband, for his assistance in research, particularly with the geological and scientific background, and for his invaluable help with travelling arrangements. Without his encouragement this book would never have been finished.

Also thanks to George Pearce, Public Affairs Officer, Kirtland AFB; The Los Alamos Museum; Byron A. Johnson, Curator of History, The Albuquerque Museum of Art, History and Science; Buddy Bregman, U.K. Communications Inc. (Hollywood); The Academy Library, Beverly Hills; and to all friends in San Francisco, who showed me round the town. Thanks also to Ursula Stuart Mason, Public Relations Officer, National Maritime Museum, Greenwich; Betty Brittain, Ex - WREN.

Thanks also to Philip Ardery for invaluable background information in his book, *Bomber Pilot*, A Memoir of World War II, University Press of Kentucky 1978.

Extracts from, *Book of the Hopi*, by Frank Waters, reproduced by kind permission of Viking Penguin Inc.

Wizard of Oz copyright © 1939 Loew's Inc. Ren. 1966 Metro-Goldwyn-Mayer Inc. Extracts reproduced by kind permission of Turner Entertainment Company.

42nd Street copyright © 1933 Warner Bros. Pictures, Inc. Ren. 1960 UNITED ARTISTS ASSOCIATED, INC. Extracts reproduced by kind permission of Turner Entertainment Company.

Thanks to the Post Office for permission to use extract from 'London can Take it': Quentin Reynolds (1940).

Here Come the British. Words by John H Mercer, Music by Bernard D Hanighan, (©) 1937 Bourne Inc. Reproduced by permission of Chappell Music Ltd.

BEATTIE FAMILY

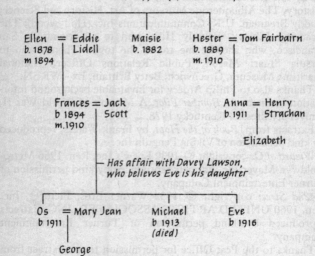

George Beattie m 1865 = (1) Jane Lovely

Harriet May
(Father unknown)

m 1871 = (2) Adeline
(No issue)

m. 1877 = (3) Jane Ridley

Ellen = Eddie   Maisie   Hester = Tom Fairbairn
b. 1878 | Lidell   b. 1882   b. 1889
m 1894   m.1910

Frances = Jack   Anna = Henry
b 1894 | Scott   b. 1911 | Strachan
m.1910

                                    Elizabeth

— *Has affair with Davey Lawson,
who believes Eve is his daughter*

Os = Mary Jean   Michael   Eve
b 1911 | b 1913   b 1916
                  (died)

George

RIDLEY FAMILY (USA)

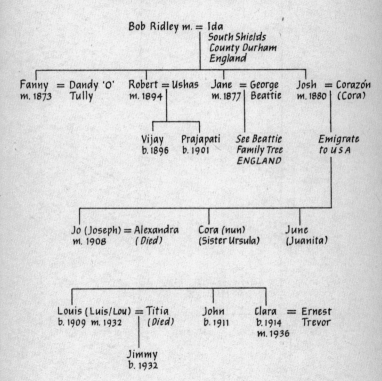

PART ONE

September 29th 1938

'That is the Sun. You are meeting your Father, the Creator, for the first time.'

Hopi legends

CHAPTER ONE

The dark was intense. There was no sound, save the inhaling and exhaling of heavy sleepers. Sharp, like reveille, a cock crowed and Jimmy Ridley stirred, opening his eyes onto the bald window of his room. He got up and stood on a chair, to watch. Suddenly, a spear of light thrust into the darkness, rising like a grey banner over the distant mesa top. The cock crowed again, and a flurry in the yard below made Jim look down to see the cock chase the hens from the fallen sunflowers, seeds sprawling in the dust. The little boy laughed and was surprised by a sudden release of perfume on the air. Then, dimly remembered through the chasm of the dark night, he knew what it was; sweet, sultry as a tropical garden after rain, the perfume Eve had daubed on him the night before.

'I shan't see you in the morning,' she'd said, 'so I'll wish you happy birthday right now!' Then she'd kissed him, and giggling, splashed him with the scent, before running downstairs to share the joke with the rest of Jim's family. Eve, the English cousin. Jim didn't know what to make of her. She wasn't like any other adult he knew. 'Contrary', Aunt June called her. Maybe it was with her being English. After she'd gone down, there'd been a row; something about the station wagon. Eve'd wanted to borrow it. She'd wanted to go somewhere very important to her,

11

but not to anyone else. He could hear them shouting about it last night, and he could hear her now, up early, banging in the kitchen below. She was talking to Ella, Jim's Indian nurse. But Jim didn't want to go down just yet. He stared on at the dull mesa through his bedroom window. Then, crimson, the sun lanced into the day, and the stone ridge of the mesa sang with orange, pink and red, a cliff of fire, hanging over the ranch, the empty expanse of dried earth and brittle rabbit brush, the raw beauty of New Mexico. He watched without blinking, unwilling to miss a single second till, suddenly, downstairs, a door banged. There was a shout, then an engine started like gunfire at the house side. Looking down, Jimmy watched the station wagon rock across the stony yard. Was Eve at the wheel? No, Uncle John was with her. That was surely *his* reckless driving! And now, Jim's father'd wakened. He was stumbling angrily down the stairs. He crashed out into the yard, shouting at the truck, as it careered away towards the road.

'Come back here! God blast you! Come back here!' He stared at the cloud of dust, like it was two fingers in his face, then went back in the kitchen to kick the table. 'God damn them! They've gone and taken the darned thing, spite of us!' In the silent land-scape, the engine faded then fired again, rattling off into the distance.

Then, Jim heard Aunt June's heavy steps on the creaking stair. At least, Jim called her 'aunt'. She wasn't really; she was his grandpa's sister. And, from across the passageway, he heard the old man grunt his thanks at the morning coffee, and June's voice yell,

'Well, Eve's gone, whether we like it or not! I don't know what's wrong with that girl. She must have a death wish or some-thing, going off in that rusty old thing!' Old Jo cackled, and slurped up a mouthful of coffee. He wiped his mouth on the sheet, and said, too low for Jim to hear,

'Know what she told me last night?'

'No,' June answered patiently.

'Told me the whole story.'

'Uhuh?' June encouraged.

'Told me, years ago, back home in England, she found her father, drowned in his own vomit. Drunk as a lord, he was. Dead

12

drunk! And then, when she went to find her mother, she surprised her in bed with another man!' June whooped with glee. 'And that's not all!' Jo yelped. 'Her ma went on to explain that the man she was in bed with was Eve's father, and not the other poor, dead sucker that had brought the kid up at all!' June was clapping her hands together like a seal.

'And there was me thinking the English were so prudish!' June honked.

'Told me not to tell anybody.' Jo grinned.

'You old confidence trickster! Why, I bet you made that up to spite her! That poor little girl!'

'She asks for it,' Jo grumbled. 'Calling me "Pa" the way she does. Don't know who the hell she is, if you ask me.'

'Ain't her fault, Jo. I don't wonder she left home, if what you say's true.'

'Pa!' Jo spat out the coffee grounds and smiled maliciously at his sister. 'I have it in mind to spring a surprise on that "poor little girl"!' Their laughter rattled across the landing like distant machine guns.

Downstairs, in the kitchen, Ella pulled out a chair for Lou to sit in, trying to comfort him about the loss of the wagon.

'Eve said it was her "big break",' she said, then hesitated, as June came back, smiling, from upstairs. What was she smiling about? Unable to think of an answer, Ella went on, 'Eve said it could make her a star. She had to get there somehow, Lou, now didn't she?'

'Well,' Lou murmured absently, wondering, like Ella what the mysterious smile could be, 'I only hope the engine don't die on her!'

'If the bottom don't drop out of the old can first!' June's smile broke into conspiratorial laughter and Lou sighed as the source of his comfort, the Indian nurse, went towards the door.

From his bedroom window Jimmy watched Ella come out into the rosy morning. She crossed the yard to the outhouse where the corn was drying. This was a special morning. Not just because it was his birthday. Not just because there was to be a family gathering in his honour. No. There was more. Out there in the vast silence something waited. Then Ella emerged from

13

the outhouse, dried corn leaves in her hands. She glanced up at Jim's window, before going back into the house. Excited and afraid, Jim scrambled from the chair, to drag on his clothes. Should he wash first? He glanced unwillingly at the jug of water, then at the huge red sun. Better safe than sorry. He reached for the soap. With any luck, he'd wash off the scent.

When Ella came back into the kitchen, Lou was growling at her.

'D'ye call this coffee, Ella?' He was picking grounds out of his mouth and smearing them on his plate.

'June made the coffee this morning,' Ella replied calmly. She was starting a corn dolly, plaiting the leaves by the light of the window.

Louis called over to his aunt at the stove. 'Aunt June, this is disgusting! Is this the kind of coffee you serve up at the restaurant?'

'Now, don't you start on me, Louis Ridley!' June volleyed right back. 'Just because you're mad with Eve!'

'I'm not mad with Eve!' Lou snapped. 'Why should I be mad with Eve? It's my brother John I'm mad with!'

'Why be mad with John?' June prevaricated. 'She put him up to it.' All the time Ella was calmly plaiting the corn dolly and the light was growing at the window.

'He's done it to spite me,' Lou spat.

'They're two of a kind, John and Evie.' June liked goading Louis. It got the day off to a smart beginning. 'Know your problem, Louis?' He glared at her, waiting for the insult. 'You're jealous.'

'Crap,' Lou snarled dangerously. Washed and dressed, Jimmy Ridley had come downstairs and was hovering in the kitchen doorway. Catching sight of him, Lou softened his tone.

'Hallo, son,' he said. 'Happy Birthday.'

'Thanks, Dad.' Then Lou's nose wrinkled. He sniffed.

'What's that pong?' he asked. But it was June, grasping the chance of another dig, who supplied the answer.

' "Evening in Paris",' she told him. 'You liked it when Eve was wearing it!' Satisfied, she turned to the birthday boy. 'Happy Birthday, Jim,' she said. Jim took her present, felt it and smiled, as he slowly pointed the gift wrapped gun at her. 'Look at him!' June whooped. 'He knows what it is alright!' The toy gun panned the room, ending on Ella, then it dropped, and the Indian face spread into a smiling moon.

'Happy Birthday,' she said and held out the corn dolly. Jim put down the gun, took the dolly, then the hand, and allowed himself to be led out into the sunrise.

Soon as the kitchen door was shut, June turned on Louis, whispering fiercely, 'What's this pagan crap Ella's cooked up now? I don't know how you can stand it, Louis!'

'Everything's crap to you, June.' Louis picked up the gun. 'Hell, it's only a belated kind of christening!'

'Christening? She ain't even Christian!' June hollered.

'That Indian woman's been like a mother to my son, since Titia died,' Lou said carefully. 'Pagan or no pagan, she's a deal more Christian than most people I could mention. And if she's got something special lined up for my boy's birthday, it's alright by me.' He unwrapped Jimmy's present. 'Anyway, what do you want to go giving him guns for? Ain't he going to learn soon enough?'

Clutching the corn dolly, Jimmy watched Ella sprinkle the corn-meal path east across the yard towards Red Mesa. She was singing the song to Taiowa, Father Sun. When she had done, she returned to the child, and taking the dolly from him, held it up.

'This is Corn Mother,' she said.

'Ella, where *is* my mother?' Jim asked.

'The Corn is your Mother, and she comes from the earth, so the Earth is your Mother too.'

'No, but I mean my real Mother,' he insisted.

'She is your real Mother. Your first Mother.' Ella passed the doll over him four times. 'I name you Little White Eagle,' she said.

'I won't always be little,' Jim objected.

'When you're big, you'll be Big White Eagle. O.K.?'

'Am I a real Indian papoose now?' Ella put her finger to her lips.

'This isn't a game, Jimmy. Come on.' She took the boy's hand and led him gently up the cornmeal path towards the red light. At the end of the path, she picked him up and held him high. 'I

15

give you to Your Father Sun. Father, here is your child!'

'Pagan crap!' June turned from the window in disgust.

Louis was pulling on his boots. 'It's just play acting, Aunt June.'

'So you say,' June snarled. 'By the way, hope you've not forgotten your own sister Clara's coming today, all the way from San Francisco! How're you going to fetch her from the railway station, with no wagon?'

'In the buggy. Ain't got no choice.' Lou stood, sighing.

'I don't know what your Pa's going to say about this darned play acting!' June warned, glancing outside again. Right on cue, a window opened upstairs, and the old man's voice screeched down into the yard,

'Enjoy your meal!' Ella was shooing the invading hens from her cornmeal path.

'Well, I guess it's one way of feeding them!' June cackled. 'You get down here and get your breakfast, you old reprobate!' she yelled up at her brother.

'When're you going to give the boy his present?' Jo yelled back.

'Later on, Pa,' Lou shouted.

'We got you something real special, boy!' Jo told the child in the yard. Then he slammed the window shut and Ella, wounded, retreated to the kitchen garden. White man and Indian had retired behind their respective palisades, leaving Jim, clutching his corn dolly in the no-man's-land between.

Eve and John were singing at the top of their voices as they hit the Albuquerque road. 'Come on and Hear, Come on and Hear, Alexander's Ragtime Band', Eve's feet pounding out the rhythm on the wagon floor.

'Hey! Stop that!' John shouted at her. 'You want to kick the floor out?' Eve laughed and pounded all the harder. 'This rusty old tank'll leave us sitting in the middle of the road, if you go on like that, girl.'

'What's the matter with you?' Eve asked. 'I got a real break at last! You should be glad for me!'

'Give me your autograph one day,' John sneered. 'Louis' not glad. He's real mad.' Eve looked slyly at John, and he grinned.

16

'You know, Eve, I don't think Lou wants you to be a film star. I wonder why?'

'The hell with him!' Eve swore recklessly. The wagon pinked.

'On second thoughts,' John said, 'keep dancing! There's a blockage in the fuel system.' Eve launched into a punishing tap routine, and the old van spluttered back to life. 'That's my girl!'

'You know this film job I'm going to Tucson for . . . ?' Eve said slowly.

'Yeah . . .'

'There's only one problem with it . . .'

'And what's that?'

'It isn't a dancing part!'

'Hell, it's a film, isn't it? It's a start!'

'Yeah,' Eve sighed. 'But, I'm not an actress!'

The van juddered to a halt at the Albuquerque airfield. John was well known at the field. He might be a loud-mouthed, small-time journalist from 'Frisco, but he was a big spender, all the same, and his flying was pretty hot for a mere amateur. So, there was a plane ready and waiting for them. Eve was breathless with excitement. What an entrance she was going to make on the film set, she thought; a real star, in a chauffeur-driven plane. She was a heroine in her own movie. The focus went fuzzy and the voice in Eve's head spoke over the top . . .

'She strapped on her hat, pulled down the goggles and waved. Then they were off and making for the sun. Soaring high over Albuquerque, over Laguna and Grants, the adventuresome pair were surely making history. Plucky Evie Lawson spoke up; "Oh, this is terrific! What a sensation. Do you think *I* could learn to fly, John?" '

The voice over faded. They were passing over the Lawe Top Ranch. John looked down and saw them, standing in the yard, hands shading their eyes.

'Hold on tight!' he warned. 'The heroine' screamed.

'Oh, my God! I'm upside down here! Help! Help!'

'I like a girl who knows which way's up,' John laughed. 'Now will you stop screaming? You're giving me earache!' He turned the aircraft right way on again, and Eve gathered her wits, looking out of the window.

'Hey, is that the ranch down there?' she asked.

'You betcha!'

'Looks really small from here,' Eve observed, surprised. Then the plane revolved again and she hung on, teeth clenched. She'd like to get used to this way of enjoying herself, because it scared her so much, she was sure it must be fun!

As the plane buzzed across the risen sun, Ella lowered her eyes. It was like a fly buzzing across the face of God. She went into the outhouse. They were nearly out of corn, and Louis loved his muffins. But June stayed, shading her eyes to watch the tiny plane, turning over and over. She was all ready for the long walk to Grants and her job at the restaurant. Usually she got a lift in the van; but not today.

'There goes Eve,' she said. 'On her way to stardom.'

'Show-off,' Lou murmured. June looked round at him, surprised. But he wasn't talking about Eve. 'Look at him. He'll kill that girl. Hell raiser! Why can't he do anything just normal?'

'Are you going to write me up in your newspaper?' Eve shouted over the drone of the engine.

'Why? What're you going to do?' John replied dryly.

'What do you mean, "What am I going to do?" '

'Come on! Starlets are two a penny! You'll have to do better than a two-bit part, if you want to get into the *San Francisco Independent*!'

'Be a sport, John,' Eve coaxed. 'You know you like me.' John said nothing. 'Come on, you do! Otherwise, why would you put yourself out, flying me all the way to Tucson?'

'I already got you an agent and a radio show, what more do you want?' John's lips were tight.

'I want everything. And I want it now!' Eve shouted out.

'I can relate to that!' John laughed, in spite of himself.

'Is Tucson far?'

'Yeah. Why don't you shut up and learn your lines?'

'I haven't got any.' Eve shrugged. John gave her a look.

'Then just shut up,' he said. He liked Eve, but she talked too much. Always demanding attention, like all women.

'*Is* it far?' Eve dared to ask. 'I don't want to be late.' John looked right at her.

18

'If there's one thing I hate,' he said, 'It's a nagging woman.'
Then he started dive bombing the Santa Fe railroad. She
screamed her head off. He'd got his own back. He'd shown her
who was in the driving seat!

But, on the set, John found himself relegated to the back. No one
was interested in him. He kicked at a clod of earth. It was baked
dry. What a place. What a hell hole. Why would anyone want to
come and farm here? Those early settlers must've been crazy!
And as for this film, it had him bored out of his hide already, and
he'd barely seen a shot. The director picked up his tannoy.

'Roll it!' he yelled. Eve adjusted her costume, and they went
onto script.

'Overhead a lone buzzard soared, looking for meat. The bodies
of a man and his children lay stacked against the smouldering
walls of the shack they had once called home. There was
nothing, no one, as far as the eye could see, only the bare rocks
and the ghostly arms of the saguaros, pointing at the cloudless
sky. A woman stood alone, exposed to sun and heat. She looked
dazed, hopeless. Thirst blistered her tongue. Dust and smoke
stung her eyes, or was it the memory of the horrors of the night?
On the distant horizon something moved. Was it a mirage, rising
out of a sea of heat? Or was that a horseman riding towards her?
Hope sprang in her heart, only to be followed by a new fear.
Suppose it was an Indian? She strained her eyes to see, as the
rider came ever nearer. No use hiding now. He must've seen her.
Terror gripped her heart. And then . . . ' What the hell was that?
Behind her, very close behind her, Eve heard the ominous rattle
of a snake! Dare she move? Should she run away? There was no
choice. She was on camera. 'The woman stayed her ground,
paralysed by fear and loathing. It *was* an Indian. The moment of
her death had come. He rode down on her, and swept her up
onto the back of his horse and . . . '

'Cut!' the director bellowed. The Indian sighed, and rode up to
the director's chair, letting Eve down at his feet. 'Who the hell
gave the rattlesnake?' the director asked. John grinned and
held up a baby's rattle. 'Suffering cats! Who let that joker in
here?'

'I thought it was a real snake!' Eve groaned. 'I was terrified out
of my wits, you bastard!'

19

'Get the hell out of here, mister,' the director said. 'We've gotta go again. Come on everybody. Move it!' It was with an uneasy feeling Eve watched John slope off. She heard his hire car start up and go. But she had to stay, to do another take. The Indian had disappeared over the horizon in a cloud of dust. 'O.K. Get ready. Roll 'em!' But, this time, all Eve could think of was how on earth she was going to get home without John.

'The rider drew nearer. He was an Indian. Terror gripped her heart . . . ' Or, at least, it should've done.

'Cut!' The director strode out and stood at Eve's side. He put an arm round her shoulder. 'You did it so well, on the last take. There were real tears in your eyes. I saw them. And that's what I want. Tears. Real ones. Come on. Let's have it good this time.' He strode back to his chair. 'O.K. We're going again.' The Indian rode off towards the horizon. He disappeared in a cloud of dust. 'Roll 'em!'

'The rider was getting nearer. Was it an Indian, or . . . ? Terror gripped her heart . . . ' Why couldn't John've said where he was going, or, at least, if he was coming back? Supposing she was stranded?

'Cut!'

Clara wasn't best pleased to be picked up in the horse and buggy, when the train stopped at Grants.

'I can't sit in *this*, Louis!' she complained. 'I've come all the way from San Francisco! My rear's sore from travelling! What happened to the station wagon?'

'Loaned it to your everloving brother John. You don't mind, do you?' John was the apple of his sister's eye.

'Oh well,' she said, getting into the buggy. 'I'm sure John had his need.'

'Taken Evie to Tucson, to do some filming or other.'

'In the station wagon?!'

'No. Station wagon only took him far as the airfield. Borrowed a plane when he got there. Any excuse to fly. You know John!'

'He's a man of many talents, Lou.' Clara smiled warmly.

'Evie's pretty talented too. Neat little dancer, so I've heard!'

'So! She's got a film part at last!' Clara took a sideways look at her brother. 'You know what, Louis? I think you've got a fancy for her.'

20

'Me? No!' Lou thought a bit, then added, 'Even if I did, hell . . . she's going to be a film star! She won't have anything to do with me, then!'

'I do hope, when Eve's famous, she won't give up that radio part John got for her in the serial,' Clara said anxiously. 'I'm getting really interested in that. I listen in most weeks. You know Eve sounds so English on the radio. Tickles me!'

'She *is* English!'

'I know. But she sounds more English when she's acting. She's got that funny "northern accent", most of the time. What's that accent called?'

'Geordie,' Louis reminded her.

'That's it. Kind of sing-song. Hey, the serial's on tonight! Don't let me miss it, will you?' They were driving down Grants' Main Street, past the restaurant where June worked. She came out and waved.

'Hi there!'

'Hi, Aunt June!'

'Why don't you come on in?' June asked them. 'I'll cook you kids some breakfast. Things ain't half quiet around here. Could do with the company!' Louis pulled in and June went to light the gas.

'This place's like a ghost town,' Clara said, as she got down from the buggy. 'What's happened to the lumbering trade? Hah! So much for President Roosevelt's New Deal!'

Lou shook his head sadly and said, 'Even the President can't make the trees grow again, honey!'

By noon, the sun was high in the sky and hot over the ranch, and the little foal that was Jimmy's special birthday present sought shelter under its mother. Jimmy watched it cowering in the meagre shade.

'When are you going to break him in for me, Grandpa?' he asked.

'Not for a while, yet,' Jo told him. 'Too young. He'll be broken in about the time you're old enough to ride him, and not before.' Jimmy nodded slowly. 'Not said if you like him yet, huh?'

'Sure do, Grandpa!' Jimmy grinned.

'That's fine. That's just fine. Yes!' The old man straightened up and took a deep breath. 'You're going to be the saving of this

21

ranch, boy!' he said.

Jimmy looked from the foal to the old man. Was there a catch, then? 'Me? How can *I* save the ranch, Grandpa?'

'You got the brains, boy. Your Dad and me . . . we got muscle but no brain. All the brain went straight through me, past your Dad and on to your Uncle John. And what's he doing with it? Writing newspaper articles and messing about in planes!'

'Oh.'

The boy and his grandpa started walking towards the farm in silence. The sage and rabbit brush crackled under foot. Overhead, the white lines of a cloud formed a huge eagle, flying across the vast sky. There was something out there . . . something beyond Jim's understanding. But his heart beat in tune with it, with the raw landscape and the blistering heat of late September. He loved this land, hard as it was. He loved it so much, it hurt.

'Yup! Going to need brains to lick this land into shape!' Jo was saying. 'Brains. And that's what you've got!' He looked at Jim. He was staring up into the sky, in a different world. 'You listening to me, boy?'

'Yes, Grandpa. Look! A white eagle!'

'Where?' Old Jo's rifle was pointing up at the sky. 'Where? I can't see no eagle!'

'There!' Jo followed the line of Jimmy's finger. 'The cloud!' Jo looked puzzled, staring into the blue yonder. Then he relaxed his grip on the rifle butt and shook his head. They were in the yard. Ella was singing in the outhouse, grinding corn. The old man grimaced.

'Brains! Don't let that Indian addle them! Do you hear me?'

'Yes, Grandpa.'

Jo went to saddle up, then rode out, rifle at his side, checking fences.

> Ki-tana-po, ki-tana-po, ki-tana-po, ki-tana-po!
> Ai-na, ki-na-weh, ki-na-weh,
> Chi-li li-cha, chi-li li-cha
> Don-ka-va-ki, mas-i-ki-va-ki
> Ki-ve, ki-ve-na-meh
> Hopet!

22

Jimmy put his head round the outhouse door. Ella looked up from her grinding and stopped singing.

'If you want to come in here, better take your shoes off first,' she said.

Jimmy left his shoes at the door and sat at a respectful distance. 'What were you singing, Ella?' he asked.

'Song of the Flute Clan,' she answered.

'What's it mean?'

Ella shrugged and resumed the steady rhythm of her grinding. 'Don't know. Nobody knows now. Not even Flute Members. Like with lots of things, the meaning gets lost.'

Jimmy watched the stone rise, drop and slide down the sloping base, over the yellow corn. It was mesmeric. Rise, drop, slide . . . 'Are you a member of the Flute Clan, Ella?' Jim asked.

'No. I'm a Snake,' she told him.

'Does that make me a Snake now, too?' Ella looked at him, then bent her head again, to her work.

'The Flute song's a very ancient song,' she said at last. She stopped grinding, and there were tears in her eyes. 'It was first heard at the dawn of the fourth world.'

'The fourth world!' Jim's eyes almost popped out of his head. 'What were the others?'

'God destroyed the first world by fire, earthquake and volcano. He destroyed the second by ice, and flooded the third. But each time, my people were saved.'

'How?' Jim was spellbound.

'God put us in holes, in the ground. Then, when it was safe, he told us to come out again. The last emergence was into *this* world. The fourth.'

'How many worlds are there, Ella?'

'Seven. This world, the fourth, will be destroyed too, in time, if people don't learn to respect it better. You should love Your Mother Earth. It's a good way to keep Your Father God happy.' Jimmy was silent. He looked up at the still face of the Hopi Indian. She was watching him without expression. 'White men have no respect. They don't know how the Earth suffers. They pile up rubbish on top of her, they burn her and mine deep into her Body. They poison her and steal from her, and then they wonder why She lets them down! Every time you get up in the morning you should ask her forgiveness just for walking on her.

23

You should thank her when you sit on her, and ask Her blessings when you plant your crops. She's a good Mother, but Her children grow spoilt and proud, thinking they are the ones who bring the rain and the sun and the life in the seed. They're so pleased with their own cleverness, they have no time for Her any more. It's very dangerous. Father God will be angry. And then, what will happen?'

Jimmy was playing with the yellow meal. When Ella had finished speaking, he looked up at her and smiled shyly. 'Why do you stay with us, Ella?' he asked. 'Why don't you go back to your own people, and maybe get married?'

'I was married once, Jimmy,' she said. 'I had a baby too. They died in a motor accident. It was then I came here to help your father. Your mother had died, so I gave you my baby's milk. How could I leave you?' She smiled at him warmly.

Then Jim asked, 'So my mother's dead, is she?' Ella nodded. Jimmy stared at Ella, considering her. 'Do you love my father?' he asked.

'Yes,' Ella answered.

'Then, I wish he'd marry you.'

'But Louis doesn't love me.' Ella smiled apologetically and Jimmy frowned, cradling the meal in his palms, letting the fine powder sift between his fingers and fall to the earth.

'I think he loves Evie,' he said at last.

'Yes,' Ella agreed. 'I think so too.' Jimmy spread the fallen meal over the earth. Suddenly Ella smiled and leaned forward. 'Shall I tell you how it was at the beginning of *this* world?' Jimmy smiled, the pupils of his eyes growing dark and large. 'When the Hopis emerged into the Fourth World, God told them, "This isn't an easy place, like the others were, for here, you'll have to rely on prayer and worship for your food and water, but that'll help you to stay good. And if you keep your souls clean, live harmoniously with one another, and keep the doors on top of your heads open, God will guide you." Then he told them to separate into clans, Snake, Flute, and so on, and go out separately to claim the earth for the Creator, before settling in one place.'

'What door did he mean, Ella?' Jimmy asked.

'The one on top of your head,' she answered. 'The door to heaven.' Jimmy frowned and touched his crown. 'God spoke to

24

the ancient ones through that door. They had the power.' She smiled at the little boy. 'Maybe you have it too!'

'What power? Will I be able to make the sun rise and the rain come?' Ella laughed. 'Will I at least be able to do what Grandpa wants?'

'What's that?'

'Will I be able to save the ranch, Ella?'

'What is this "I"?' she scolded. 'You can't do anything! Only God can do!' Ella was drawing in the cornmeal that covered the floor, where they were sitting. 'When they went out to claim the land, the clans went west, as far as the sea,' she drew a line in the meal. 'Then, north a little way, to make sure they'd reached the edge, then, they retraced their steps back to the centre. That was the first journey. Next, they went north to the ice and snow, and when they couldn't go any further, they turned east, just to make sure, before retracing their steps back to the centre as before. The third journey took them, in the same way, to the east, and the fourth to the south, before they came back to settle at last in the chosen land at Oraibi.'

'Where is . . . ? I can't say it.'

'Oraibi,' Ella repeated. 'Our promised land. It's in Arizona. And now, at last, the government has given it back to us.' She sighed deeply. Jimmy was looking at the shape Ella had drawn in the cornmeal.

'It makes a nice pattern,' he said.

After the fifteenth take, there really were tears in Eve's eyes, and the Indian's horse was plumb tuckered.

'I'm sorry, Mr Polan,' Eve wept. 'I'm really sorry.' The director sighed.

'I guess we've just got to keep in the rattlesnake,' he said.

'I don't know why I couldn't do it,' Eve sobbed. 'It just felt so artificial the second time around.'

'In that case,' the director told her, 'you're not an actress!'

'No. You're right,' Eve agreed. 'I'm a dancer.' Mr Polan groaned loudly.

'Look girl,' he said. 'You better talk to your agent. It does you no good getting in over your head!'

'You've got to start somewhere, Mr Polan,' Eve objected.

'Well, I'm not turning this film into a musical, just to suit you, honey!' Polan sniped. 'There are hundreds, thousands of actresses, probably, who could have done this job a lot better! And here's you, taking the bread out of their mouths! Who the hell do you think you are?' Eve hiccupped. 'Alright. I've bawled you out,' he said. 'Let's call it a day. Blow your nose now. You can go home.'

'I can't,' Eve wailed. 'My lift's gone.'

'What? Oh!' Mr Polan remembered him well. 'The joker with the rattlesnake!' He sighed. 'Come on!' he said, pushing Eve towards a car.

'Where're we going?' she asked anxiously.

'Old Tucson. Got some good film catering there.' Eve slunk into the passenger seat and lurched as the car took off. 'Cheer up,' he told her. 'A nice cup of tea and everything'll seem fine again!'

'Americans've got a really exaggerated idea about the value English people put on tea!' Eve snapped. Polan laughed, and as they drove into Old Tucson, he was in good enough humour to introduce his 'dancer' to Hal Zubermann, who was doing a recce for a new film.

Hal took Eve, and drove her to the airfield at Tucson, where, to her relief, they found John waiting. The two men shook hands and Eve, bubbling with excitement, explained that Mr Zubermann directed musicals.

'Isn't that amazing?' she cried. John smiled patiently.

'Astonishing,' he agreed, as Hal took his leave.

'He said I should go and see him at the studio and he'd arrange a test for me!'

'Sounds friendly!' John laughed, as he started up the plane. 'What sort of test? Dancing, or something a little more friendly still?'

'John Ridley!' Eve was aghast.

'I'm not criticizing, Evie.' John soothed her, as the nose of the plane eased off the ground. 'You want to get to the top? O.K. You better not be too particular how you do it.'

'I do want to get to the top,' Eve said quickly. 'But . . .'

'Hah!' John snorted. 'Miss Prim, eh?!' Eve was silent. 'You better take what comes, Evie. Take that fate of yours by the tail and . . . ' He did a big dipper act, then Eve screamed and laughed and they were friends again.

'John?' Eve asked idly. 'Where did you go?'

'When?'

'When you were thrown off the film set?'

'Scared you did I?' John smiled. 'Thought I'd left you stranded?' Eve wasn't going to admit it.

'Go on! Tell me!' she pressed.

'Went and looked at the cacti.'

'No!' Eve laughed. 'I don't believe you!'

'There's plenty of them! Look!' He nosedived towards them.

'Oh God!' Eve cried. 'We're going to crash!' But he swerved away from the saguaros at the last minute.

'Sure would be a prickly situation if we did,' John observed.

'No, but, where *did* you go, John?' Eve was not going to be put off.

'Went into Tucson,' he told her reluctantly.

'What did you do?'

'Saw a man about a dog.'

'Stop fooling!'

'O.K.,' John admitted. 'I saw an old buddy of mine from Berkeley. He runs a bar in Tucson. Got a few tips from him.'

'What about? Bar keeping?'

'In a manner of speaking.' At last John came clean. 'I'm thinking of opening a night club on the Albuquerque airfield.'

Eve was thrilled. 'Could I dance there? Do the cabaret?'

'Sure,' John said graciously. 'If you're good enough.'

In retaliation, Eve put on her Alabama act, to mock, 'Why, Mr Ridley, I declare you're a real high flyer!' John groaned.

'Who the hell writes your scripts, Miss Lawson?'

Eve lay back, smiling. They'd both scored points. In the love stakes, she was in with a chance. Her eyes went misty and the voice in Eve's head faded in . . .

'John and Eve were two of a kind. Reckless. They took life by the tail. They both knew that, no matter what, they had a great future before them. She looked at the strong, virile profile of her pilot. Only she had the spirit to match his daring. Only she was female enough to control his powerful, masculine nature. They belonged together. She knew it. He knew it. They both knew it.

Together, they'd make it to the top of the tree . . . ' Suddenly, Eve's fantasy, like a twisted spool, juddered and stopped. She looked at John warily.

'John?' she asked. 'Did you fly to Tucson specially for me? Or was it really to meet your friend from Berkeley?' John's laugh roared round the cockpit.

'Honey, you will never know!'

It was dark when they reached the ranch. Switching off the engine, they heard the low hum of the generator, in the shed.

'Better face the music,' John said. He got out first, and made for the light at the gaping kitchen door, closely followed by Eve. The family was sitting round the remnants of a meal. There was a birthday cake at the centre of the table, untouched. They had been waiting for John and Eve, before they cut it. As they made their entrance, all eyes fixed on the door.

'Hey!' John exclaimed. 'You folks shouldn't've waited for us! My, isn't that a beautiful birthday cake? Happy Birthday, Jim!'

'At last! Light the candles, Lou.' June pushed the matches across the table and Lou struck a light. You could've cut the atmosphere with the cake knife. John grinned sheepishly at his sister.

'Hallo, Clara,' he said.

'Hallo, John. Hallo, Eve,' Clara replied formally. Eve sidled out into the light, to acknowledge the greeting.

'Hallo, Clara,' she said. John snapped irritably,

'Hell! Doesn't anybody want to know what sort of a day we had?' He surprised Eve by throwing his arm around her.

'Just why the hell should anybody care about you?' Lou growled. His look took in Eve, who was standing awkwardly, under the weight of John's arm.

'That's more like it,' John grinned. 'Spit it out, brother. Let's get things into the open!'

'There's a few things need airing around here!' Old Jo glared at the company one by one, ending on Ella. 'What's this I hear about white eagles, huh?'

'Not now, Pa,' June warned. She got up and stood behind Jimmy. 'You gotta make a wish, son,' she told him. 'Take a deep breath now . . . ' Jimmy took a deep breath, eyes fixed on the flickering candles of his cake, and the lights went out. 'Hell, don't blow, Jimmy!' June yelled. 'Don't blow!' Everyone moved and talked at once, in the light of the birthday candles.

'That damned generator!'

'Why can't we get it fixed?'

'It's been fixed.'

'Why can't we get a new one?'

'We need a new station wagon.'

'What're we going to use for money?'

'John might think money's for burning up there in the sky . . . '

'I got every right to do what I like with my money.'

Ella had lit the kerosene lamp. It flared livid on ugly, angry faces. Eve saw Jim was in distress and ran to his side.

'What's wrong, Jim?' she asked. His purple cheeks were bulging, eyes popping. 'Lord!' Eve cried. 'He's still waiting to blow! Go on, Jimmy! Blow!' Jimmy blasted air onto the cake. The flames blew across the icing, then died, all at one go. The family clapped, and Jimmy lay back in his chair, exhausted, watching the smoke rise.

'Chip off the old block!' the old man screeched.

'It's my block, then,' Lou reminded him.

'Can we play a game of snakes and ladders now?' Jimmy asked impatiently. June was cutting the cake into sections.

'Not now, honey,' she said.

'But I want to! It's my birthday!' Jim went to get the board and the dice, while June turned on Eve and John.

'So, you two got to Tucson, did you?' she asked.

'Yes, we got to Tucson,' John answered. 'No thanks to that old tin can of a station wagon.' He was deliberately goading on his brother's resentment.

'You got a lot o' cheek, John. I'll say that!' Lou exploded. He rose, hands gripping the table.

'Eve had to get to Tucson . . . ' John explained easily. Eve watched him, suspiciously. 'You couldn't miss your big break now, Evie, could you?' But Eve'd had enough of John's games. She wasn't very good at them. Let him play with someone else. She squeezed onto the seat beside Jimmy and picked up a blue counter before she spoke.

'I'm sorry we inconvenienced you, Louis,' she said humbly. John was stung. This was a sudden change of sides, wasn't it? Then Jim rattled the dice noisily, as Lou rasped,

'I got a ranch to run! Or had you two forgotten?' But, mollified by Eve's apology, he sat down again and watched Jim throw the dice across the table.

'I got a six! I got a six!' the kid yelled. Ella took the dice from him, put her finger to her lips, and went to get some beer for the men. Eve and Jimmy looked at one another and shrugged. But John was glaring at Louis and a new game had started, between the brothers.

'Some ranch,' John observed sarcastically. 'Does you proud, Lou.'

'Oh yeah?' Lou retorted. 'You own ten per cent of it, John. When are you going to put in something beside jibes? It needs investment. New wells. New equipment.' Jim was upset. It was his birthday, and Ella had taken the dice away.

'Why don't you draw something for us, instead, Jimmy?' Eve suggested. She kissed the lad on the head and went to fetch his crayons.

'And what're you going to farm, huh?' John sneered. 'Sheep?' There was silence. Lou had been watching Eve kiss his son.

'What's wrong with sheep?' Ella asked, putting the beer cans on the table. The old man was at the door. They could hear the hum of the generator. He'd been to mend it. Slowly the lights faded up. 'Didn't you used to have sheep, in the old days, Jo?' Jo snarled.

'There's no money in sheep any more! No grazing!'

'Hopis have sheep,' Ella pointed out. 'So do Navajos. Flocks of them.' She was pouring beer for Louis.

'And look how poor *they* are!' John laughed.

'Ella would have us scratching a living off the land, like the Indians!' Jo screeched. Suddenly, he and John were of a mind. 'With their patches of maize and beans, and a couple of lines of squash!' His laugh was vicious. Then he pointed his finger at Ella. '*We* don't get no government subsidy for sitting in barns, grinding corn like primitives!' Eve saw the hurt in the Indian face and was sorry.

'We got some money for killing the pigs,' Louis reminded him. He took his glass from Ella, giving her a courteous nod of the head, then turned his attention right back to Eve. 'That's about all the subsidy we got,' he told her.

'Getting plenty of subsidies in Albuquerque,' June said. 'Place is changing every day. New roads, sidewalks, parks, buildings of all kinds. My, this cake's good, though I says it.' She stuffed more of it into her mouth, then spoke with difficulty. 'I heard talk, they was wanting to build an auditorium there!'

'How're they affording that?' Jo demanded.

'Federal aid, Pa,' John told him. 'Mayor Langley's real pally with the President. And you don't have to be a newsman to know that.' John was sitting opposite Eve, and looking right at her, but Jo demanded his full attention.

'What's he want with sidewalks, parks and auditoriums?'

'Keep the people busy, Pa,' John told him. 'Busy and fed. It's the President's New Deal, Pa. I was talking to Eve about it, on the way here, wasn't I, Eve?' Eve refused to look at him. She wanted Lou to win, to spite him. But the old man'd got the bit between his teeth, and spoke up in her place.

'Why? Ain't there enough people dying of T.B., for him? Albuquerque's full of folk coughing their guts up. Hospitals're bursting at the seams! Town's traditional major industry is that! Ain't there enough of them to keep them busy in this good, dry air?'

'It's the New Deal,' John said.

'What New Deal? Not a new deal for us! What about the farmers?'

'We don't live in Albuquerque, Pa,' John explained dryly. He was staring at Eve, willing her to look at him. But she wouldn't.

'Joshua Ridley made a mistake buying this ranch out here! Darn mistake!' Jo was bitter. At last, Eve looked up, sympathetic.

'They're building a new market for the farmers, Pa,' she consoled him. 'That's something, isn't it? Maybe you *could* farm sheep?'

'A new market? Where?' Clara asked, shooing the crumbs from her lap.

'Fourth Street and Mountain.' June spoke with her mouth full.

'Who the hell're you calling "Pa"?' Eve jumped, like she'd heard gunshot.

'Why, Jo, you're kidding!' she said. 'You know you like it.' Jo fixed her with his steely eye.

'Know what your trouble is, girl? You don't know who your

Pa is! That's *your* trouble!' And then, Jo cackled, pleased with his surprise. Eve stared at the snakes and ladders, a red flush rising up her throat. 'Yup!' The old man was victorious. 'Day you decide to marry one of my lads, then you can call me "Pa", and not before!' He lay back in his chair, grinning like a cheshire cat, to watch the rest of the show. June was too busy choking on her cake to tell him off.

'She's right about the farmers' market, isn't she, Lou?' John was enjoying himself now. Jo'd swung the game his way. But the shocking revelations had put poor Lou right off his stroke, and he was hot around the collar.

'How're we going to get sheep to Albuquerque?' he yelled at his brother. 'In the darned station wagon?'

'You need a new road too. It's real bumpy, ain't it, Eve?' Clara put in. Eve still wouldn't look at John. He would have to try harder still, if he wanted to get the better of Lou.

'What we need's to develop the airport,' he said. 'I've got an idea to start a night club there. Now that *would* be a good investment.' John glanced at Clara, but her eyes slid away. 'If the army base ever gets off the ground, there'll be a lot of money to make in something like that.' Eve refused to take the bait. She was helping Jim draw sheep.

'I don't approve of night clubs, John,' Clara sniffed. 'You know that.' Lou was getting desperate. To hell with the old man. If John and Eve had fallen out, this was his chance to make an impression. But how? He made a bold move.

'If Eve was to dance in your night club, I think even *I* would go,' he said. Surprised, Eve looked up and smiled at Lou. He had scored and won! John had lost. Old Jo whooped and slapped his hand on the table.

Then Ella came out from behind Jim and said, 'Isn't it time you were in bed, Jimmy?'

'Oh no! Not yet!' Jim pleaded. 'Do I have to, Dad?' Lou looked at Ella, who turned away sadly, to sit in the corner by the window. He knew he had hurt her. Feeling guilty, his temper rose up and bit him.

'Clara,' Lou said, 'When Grandpa died, and Pa was too old to take on the Lawe Top . . . leastways he said he was.' Lou gave his father a look. 'As my younger sister, you got left ten per cent of the place same as John. And you got left money, same as him, too. I only got the ranch. What's left after your twenty per cent, that is. Now how about you ploughing some of your cash in here?'

'Ernie and me, we've got plans for that money!' Clara's voice was hoarse. She was choking on a raisin. Jo hit her on the back and it splattered out.

' "Ernie",' the old man mocked. He picked the stray raisin from his beer and held the glass to his daughter's lips. She drank. 'That better?' he asked. Clara nodded and pulled a face. She was teetotal and he knew it. Old Jo'd found a new source of amusement. 'How is Ernie, Clara?' he asked. 'Still playing at cops and robbers?'

'It's not a game, Pa,' Clara objected. 'Ernie's a good cop. It's hard too. San Francisco's not a backwoods town like Grants, is it John? I'll have you know, my Ernie nearly won a medal for that Chinatown raid!' Jo snorted.

'Nearly? Hah!'

'He's sorry he couldn't make it for your birthday, Jimmy.' She smiled at him. 'But he's on duty. And duty always comes first.'

'It's alright, Aunt Clara,' Jim assured her. 'I don't mind.'

'Kids don't give a damn!' Jo mocked.

'*What* plans?' Lou wasn't letting go that easily.

'Just plans,' Clara replied airily. 'Anyway, what about the lumbering round here? Don't tell me it's gone down the pan completely? I bet there's still *some* money in it!'

'Lumber's finished!' Lou bristled.

'It can't be! Not completely!'

'You look out that window in the morning, sister,' Lou threatened. 'If you see a tree, you tell me where, and I'll cut it down.' John was watching Eve. Was that sympathy in her eyes? Sympathy for Lou? Jo's smile twisted like an opened can. And whose side was *he* on? John sighed. That bitch, Eve, was getting him riled. But no woman ever got the better of John Ridley. The game wasn't finished yet. He'd score, if it killed him.

'Hell, I don't know why you don't join the unemployed on Langley's workline, Lou,' he said. 'I hear they're getting thirty cents an hour for digging tennis courts! Suit you down to the ground, would that!' A fight was brewing.

Clara didn't like fights. She tried to distract everybody by changing the subject. 'Oh Eve, you didn't tell us how you got on today.' She sounded like the Queen of England, at a diplomatic luncheon.

'Shut up, Clara!' Jo stamped his foot. 'Things were just getting exciting!'

'Oh!' Eve flushed. 'I got on fine. In fact, I was great!' She shrugged, pretending arrogance. 'What else?'

'She flunked it.' John dropped Eve in it, like a stone in a deep lake.

'I did not!' she shouted at him.

'Yes, you did.'

'If I did, it was your fault!' she retorted. John shrugged. 'It was my best take, and he ruined it!'

'How?' Clara asked. 'What did he do?'

'He played a practical joke. He'd got this rattle, and well, it sounded for all the world, just like a rattlesnake, right in the middle of the filming!'

'No! He didn't!' June whooped.

'He did. I couldn't get it right, after that. Put me off my stroke, the shit! He loused up my lucky break!'

'You mean you thought it was a real snake?' Lou asked. Now he thought he'd found the cause of Eve's coolness towards his brother.

'Yes,' she replied. 'And so did everybody else, except the director. He threw John off the set!'

'It was only a joke,' John shrugged. 'I was bored.'

'He was always the same, Evie, girl.' The old man nodded. 'Since he was a boy. Always playing jokes on folk.' He laughed wickedly.

'I wouldn't put the odd joke past you either, Jo,' Eve grinned at him.

'Snakes make me shiver,' Clara said disgustedly.

'Ain't seen no snakes round here, for some time,' June observed.

'Oh, they're around alright.' The old man nodded sagely. 'Did you hear what happened to Bill Farley?'

'No . . . ' they all said.

'He shot a snake in his own yard, couple of weeks back. Well, he was sitting inside, having a beer, just like we are now . . . ' He looked round the company slowly. 'And he thinks to himself,

"Hell, I should've sliced off the rattle of that snake, kept it for a souvenir." Now it'd come in dark already, and he didn't want to wait till morning, in case some coyote carried it off, so he gets his knife and goes out into the yard. Then he reaches down for the snake, picks it up, slices off its rattle, and comes back inside. Well, he thinks no more about it, till, the next morning, he goes out into the yard, and he sees two snakes, lying there, both as dead as dodos. One'd been shot. The other'd had its tail sliced off.' There was a long pause, then a drawn out hiss from his audience.

'Oh my!' Clara went out the back to be sick. John smiled.

'I think you made that up, old man,' he said. Jo's eyes glinted.

'Maybe I did, and then, maybe I didn't.' Suddenly, Clara was rushing back into the room, handkerchief at her mouth.

'What's the time?' she yelled. Lou looked round for the answer. John showed Clara his watch. 'Oh my! I knew it!' Clara cried. 'I was throwing up, out by the pump, and I was reminded of Evie's serial. I'd sure hate to miss that!' She dashed to the wireless set, to switch it on, and was beating the hell out of it, yelling at it to hurry and warm up.

'You should see your face!' John grinned at Eve. But she scowled and took Jimmy by the hand.

'Come on. Time you were in bed, young man,' she said.

'Oh no! Not yet! It's my birthday!'

'You've got to get your sleep,' she told him gently. 'Otherwise, how are you going to grow into a big boy, riding horses and everything?'

'I don't know,' Jim whined. 'I expect I'll manage somehow.' Eve pulled at his hand. 'Come on now. Put down your crayons, and come to bed.'

'Will you tell me a story?' he asked.

'If I can remember any.' Eve smiled at him, but Jim looked back at Ella, and then at his Dad. Lou, eyes on Eve, had a fond look on his face. Jim sighed. His Pa was soft on her. 'O.K. I'll come,' he said.

' . . . agreement was reached by Great Britain, France, Italy and Germany in Munich today . . .'

'Oh!' Clara complained. 'What's happened to the serial?'

'Leave it alone!' John commanded. 'It's a news flash!' But it was too late. She was already searching the dial for her favourite programme. John hurried over, and took hold of the knob, fiddling, to and fro, trying to get the news back.

' . . . peace in Europe is assured. That is the end of this news bulletin.' John switched off the set.

'Hey! Put it back on!' Clara cried. 'I want to know what's going to happen to Jennifer's baby!'

'Who the hell's Jennifer?' Jo asked.

'Jennifer's the name of my part,' Eve explained. 'She's not in it for two or three weeks, Clara, so I wouldn't worry. I'll catch you up with the story, so far.'

'I hope you do!' Clara pouted.

'Peace in Europe! That must be a relief to you, dear.' June spoke to Eve but Eve'd forgotten all about war and the commotion in Europe. What did any of it have to do with her?

'Pity. I'd like to take a crack at Hitler!' John was like a kid who'd missed out on some action.

'Why? We don't want dragging into anything, do we?' The old man remembered the last war, but John was hot with the news.

'Have you heard what they're doing to the Jews out there in Germany, Pa?'

'Jews? What's Jews got to do with us?' June was slicing another piece of cake onto her plate.

'I heard some pretty hair-raising stories in Gallup last week,' Lou agreed. 'A woman from Farmington said she'd had a letter from her brother and he'd told her they were throwing Jews out of their homes and herding them up like cattle, and beating them up and . . . ' Louis was indignant. 'And I suppose we did swear to defend the rights of people, didn't we, Pa?'

'*American* people. Yeah.' June spoke through a mass of cake and raisins.

'Hell. What's that?' Jo's voice was hushed, shocked.

'What, Pa?' June swallowed hard and looked over his shoulder at the drawing on the table.

'I seen that before.' Jo nodded slowly. John picked up Jimmy's doodling.

'It's a swastika,' he said.

'What's one of them?' June asked.

'It's the Nazi sign.' There was a long silence.

'Where did you learn that, boy?' Lou demanded loudly. All turned to look at Jimmy.

'Ella showed me,' he said. 'Why? What's wrong, Dad?' He ran to his father.

'You never draw that thing in this house again. D'ye hear me?'

'Yes, Pa.'

'Now go to bed. Evie, you better take him. I want to speak to Ella.' Jim was loath to go. Ella was in trouble and it was his fault. But Eve grasped his hand tight and pulled him to the door.

'Say goodnight, Jimmy.'

'Goodnight, everybody.'

'Goodnight, Jimmy. And Happy Birthday!'

One last look, then Eve gave a sharp pull and he went upstairs with her.

'What's wrong, Evie? Was it what I drew?' Jim asked. Eve nodded, helping the boy out of his clothes. 'Why? It's only a pattern. Ella drew it in the cornmeal.'

'It's evil,' Evie said. 'Even I know that.'

'But Ella drew it. She wouldn't draw anything evil.'

'Maybe she didn't know what it was. Come on now. Don't worry your head about it. It's just another storm in a teacup. Go to sleep.' Eve was not now in a bedtime story mood. She stood back from the bed, impatiently.

'O.K.,' Jim sighed, but lay, staring up at her and she found she couldn't go. 'Evie?'

'Mmmm? What?'

'Do you love my Dad?'

'What a question!'

'Do you?' he persisted. Eve laughed and shrugged.

'Come on. I want to get downstairs. See what's going on.'

'You're just trying to get out of telling me,' Jim whined. Eve was angry but tried to cover up.

'Don't you want me to get down there and look after your precious nurse? Your Ella?' she asked.

'She's not precious. Not to you,' Jim objected sulkily.

'What?!!'

'You don't care about Ella. You just think she's an Indian, so she doesn't matter. But she loves my Dad. I won't mind if you love him too. But, if you don't, I sure wish you'd leave him alone

37

and let Ella have him.' There was a long pause. Then, finally, Eve spoke up.

'Who the hell are you to speak to me like that?' she gasped.

'I am his son.' Unblinking, Jim stared at her. 'He loves you. At least I think he does.'

'It's not *my* fault.'

'Do you love Uncle John?'

'That's my business!'

'He's not a patch on my Dad.'

'You're loyal, I'll say that for you,' Evie laughed, uncomfortably. 'Can I go now, please?'

'If you like.'

'Some kid you are!' He waited for her to go. But she still couldn't.

'What are you doing here, Eve?' Jim demanded suddenly. 'Haven't you got a family of your own? I mean everybody's got a mummy and a daddy, haven't they? Who are yours?' Eve didn't know what to say. 'Are they dead?' She had an uncomfortable feeling, like a worm, crawling in the pit of her stomach. 'Don't you know?'

'I came over here to make films,' Eve told him, at last.

'Films aren't real.' Jim shook his head. 'Aren't you going to have babies or anything?' Eve searched desperately for a distraction.

'Hey!' she cried. 'Guess what! I got introduced to a director of Hollywood musicals today!' Jim stared at her across the bleak electric light. 'Isn't that great?' She did a time step at his bedside.

'Yeah. Great,' he answered dully.

'You'll be glad to know me when I'm a star. All the kids at school'll envy you.' Her cheeks hurt. She dropped the smile. 'Alright. Have it your way.' Eve switched off the light and went.

Ella was standing like a cornered animal, back against the range, as Evie entered.

'I don't know what you mean, "Nazi sign". It's an *Indian* sign. Very ancient. You find it in all the old places. Up at Chaco Canyon. You see it there!'

'Chaco Canyon?' John looked round the company. 'What the hell's that?'

38

'Chaco? It's that old ruin over the other side of Cuba Road. Half way between here and Farmington. You know it, June?' Jo asked.

'I ain't never been interested in ruins, Pa!' June wedged herself into the armchair.

'I thought that place was Navajo.' The old man sneered.

'Not Navajo. Hopi!' Ella said proudly.

'I don't know what the hell Indian tribe it is, but they do say, whoever it was lived there, all those thousands of years ago, were the first Americans.' Jo nodded sagely.

'You mean the first Americans were Nazis?' June struggled between the pincer arms of the chair.

'Don't be crazy,' Louis gritted his teeth. 'This isn't getting us anywhere. Ella, what does this thing mean, Indianwise.'

'It's a religious sign,' Ella pleaded.

'Who cares?' June sprang out of the chair like a cork out of a bottle, rubbing her hips.

'It's the sign of the Hopi migrations at the beginning of time,' Ella explained. 'God told us to go out in the four directions, to claim the land . . . ' June interrupted, snapping like an angry coyote,

'Seems to me there's too much time wasted on them Indians. They got no more claim to the land than we have.'

'Hey, be careful, Aunt June.' John wagged his finger at her. 'Indians are a political hot cake. Better not stir things up.' He smiled wryly at his brother, who was uncomfortably aware of Eve's silent presence at the door. He glanced at her, warily, and she took it as an invitation.

'Maybe,' Eve said, 'if it's an ancient religious sign . . . maybe this man Hitler just . . . borrowed it.'

'What do you know about it? Snotty English bitch!' June kicked the armchair and Clara giggled nervously.

'Better not start on religion in this house!' Lou warned.

'June's right,' Jo cackled. 'Hell, what does *Evie* know? Why she even believed that story about the rattlesnakes!' Everyone laughed.

Eve looked at the bared teeth of her American cousins. They were like a pack of hounds, baying at her. She'd been in this country four years now. She liked to think she was at home here, but there were times when the illusion dropped and she knew she was a mere alien, after all. This was one of those times. She sided with the Indian.

'I don't suppose Ella even knows who Hitler is,' she shouted over the din.

'Of course she knows. You've heard of Hitler, haven't you, Ella?'

'I heard you say he hurts Jews. But I don't know any Jews!'

'Neither do I.' June edged John out of his chair and sat, overflowing, on it. 'Hell I gotta start on a diet.'

'My agent's Jewish,' Eve said as though it was a new idea. 'Ida Fischer.'

'It's all crap anyway. All religion.'

'Aunt June,' Clara flushed and bristled. 'I can't just sit and hear you say things like that.'

'Here we go!' The old man slapped the table with his hand.

'How can I, alone, atone for all the sins of this God-forsaken family?' Clara's voice was martyrish.

'*I* never did anything wrong,' June spat. 'Nothing that a Roman Catholic can make up for, anyhow!'

'We're all sinners,' Clara sighed.

'The wages of sin is death,' John mocked.

'Now, John, you should know better than to make light of religion,' Clara scolded. 'And while I'm on the subject, when did you last go to confession?' John put his hands up to ward off further attack. 'The wages of sin *is* death. Sin brings its own reward and that's why there's so much suffering in this world.'

'Crap. What did I ever do except maybe eat too much?' June sulked.

'Yes, Aunt June and that's why you have to go on a diet. And that for you is suffering!' There was no arguing with Clara. June sighed and stared at the remains of the birthday cake.

'One thing I never could hold with in the Catholic hoohah . . . ' Old Jo shook his head over the memory of past rows. 'And that's this business of original sin. Seems to me you just can't win, if you believe that. If you sin you suffer, we're all sinners, because that's how we're made, so I guess we're just born to suffer. Hell. I never could be doing with that idea. I mean, who wants to suffer? Apart from Clara.'

'You broke your mother's heart following your Pa and turning Baptist,' Clara spat at her renegade father.

'My Pa, Josh Ridley, was the founding father of this family, Clara! Pioneer he was, from good old English stock!' Jo nodded proudly in Eve's direction.

'And his wife, Corazón, my sainted grandmother . . .'

'Sainted arse. Pa always called her Cora, anyway!' June spat.

' . . . brought, along with her no doubt, welcome, fortune, her honest to God, Roman Catholic Hispanic traditions! And I, for one, intend to honour them!' Clara rose to new heroic heights.

'There you go. Honour your father, you upset your Ma. Honour your mother, you upset your Pa. Whatever you do, you can't help sinning.' Jo grinned and June grinned back. 'Might as well enjoy doing it! That's what *I* say!'

'Hell, I don't see what any of this has got to do with anything,' Louis said. 'Ella,' he turned to his son's nurse. 'I don't care what this sign used to mean according to the Indians. No disrespect meant . . . but now it means something bad and I won't have you teaching my boy something bad.'

'It's not bad,' Ella insisted doggedly.

'Hell, she doesn't think Hitler's bad!' Jo yelped.

'This Hitler, whoever he is, has no right using our sign!' Ella sobbed and ran out of the kitchen.

'That'll teach you! Using Indians for bringing up your son!' June shook her head at Lou.

'Told you so!' The old man grinned. 'White Eagle, my arse. Now how about a game of snakes and ladders?'

Ella's feet pounded up the wooden stairway. Jimmy heard her, as she closed the door of her room, sobbing her heart out. He got out of bed and switched on the light. Then he walked out onto the landing. He heard a rattle. It came from downstairs.

'I gotta six!' Jo screamed. So, they were playing it after all. He turned the knob on Ella's door. It opened silently, and he went in. Ella was crouched on the floor, head cradled in her arms, like an unborn child.

'Ella,' Jim whispered. She stopped crying and looked at him a long time.

'You're supposed to be asleep,' she said at last.

'I'm not though.' He stared back. 'What did they say?'

Ella sighed and got up, holding out her arms for him. 'Come.

41

Sit by me, on the bed.' They sat and listened to them throwing dice in the kitchen.

'That sign . . . what did they call it?' Jim asked.

'The swastika. It's a good sign. I told you. The white man steals everything and corrupts it. Now this Hitler . . . ' She looked hard at Jimmy. 'That's why Indians are silent about sacred things. And that's why, Jimmy, whatever I tell you, you must learn to keep secret.'

CHAPTER TWO

Eve woke late, hung over from a night of thinking and day dreams. She'd replayed yesterday's scenes over and over, trying out different scenarios for size. Supposing, when Jimmy'd asked, she'd declared her love for Lou? Or, on the other hand, for John? And what if she'd gone back to Hollywood with Hal Zubermann, leaving John high and dry in Tucson? She could just see his face with egg all over it! She tried acting out her radio character too; Jennifer, snotty-nosed English upper crust, who could get away with murder. Maybe she, Eve, could murder old Jo? She day-dreamed her way through the screen test for Zubermann, made several smash hit musicals as a result, and then went on to dance the night away in her own mental blueprint of John's night club, wowing Albuquerque and the entire army base with a variety of brilliant numbers, tap, soft shoe, ballet. She even tried her hand at writing the reviews! So it was no wonder Eve woke up thoroughly exhausted the next morning.

And the next morning, none of these great successes had actually happened. Eve stared out of her window at the brilliant sun of New Mexico. There was no hiding from its reality. At night, it was so pitch dark here, far from the cities, you could see nothing at all, and your imagination could fill the darkness with skyscrapers, lagoons, mountains, tropical forests, even Disneyland, if you liked. But in the day time, you could see everything; miles and miles of it; nothing but blank desert grassland, and the rigid uncompromising form of the pink mesa. And you couldn't pretend. The landscape exposed you, laid bare your insides. And the sun shone right in like a spotlight. Eve didn't like it. She wanted a place to hide.

And there was no hiding from the people either – her 'family', downstairs in the kitchen of The Lawe Top Ranch! June might lull you into feeling cosy, but only to shoot you down in flames! Old Jo played games but somehow managed never to lay a stake. How had he got away with it all these years? He had waived his claim on the ranch, passing it on to his children, for the sake of an easy life. But his humour tore the flesh off of you. (Clara, well, she was a scaredy cat. She didn't really matter.) Now John, he always gave Eve the idea she held all the cards, but he turned out to have the joker every time! Ha ha! Very funny! Joke's on Evie! Jimmy . . . well, she didn't want to think about Jimmy. He saw right through her. The way he looked at her sometimes, gave her the creeps, like that talk of snakes last night!

Eve shivered. And then, to set against them all, there was Louis, dear, sweet Louis. But imagine being stuck here, on this ranch, for the rest of your life, quarrelling with Jo and June, bringing up Jim? It would be like bringing up your own granpa! What was the use? Eve couldn't take that! And then, when all was said and done, why would she want to, when, as that inner voice of hers kept telling her . . .

'Her feet itched to dance. Her whole being ached to be one with the music . . . '? It was true too. Eve couldn't give up dancing, even for everlasting love of dear, sweet Louis . . .

'Her heart ached. The choice was clear, to dance or to lose the man she loved . . . '

Not to forget Ella . . . though she wished she could. Ella was uncanny. She was like a mirror. In her reproachful eyes, Eve saw the reflection of herself. She had to face it. Indian rights or no Indian rights, a woman had the right to get the man she loved. And who was Eve to stand in her way?

'Eve, are you coming down for breakfast or are you going to lie stinking in bed all day?'

'Coming, Aunt June,' Eve shouted. And that was that.

John was shovelling eggs and fries down him like there was no tomorrow. All Eve could manage was strong coffee and toast.

'Me and Clara's taking a trip to Santa Fe today,' he told her. Why did Clara look worried? 'Fancy coming?' John's eyes were frank. It was the clear-eyed look Eve always fell for. And it always meant he was about to try out a new game on her. Well, not today, Johnnie dear!

'No, I don't think so, thanks.' Eve was glad to see he was disappointed. But Lou perked up at once.

'Not thinking of going back, were you?' he checked.

'No. I just don't want to go to Santa Fe, that's all.' Eve smiled at him. 'I get enough of towns. It's nice to be in the country for a change.' Lou swallowed the lie gratefully.

'Maybe you'd like a trip out,' he offered bashfully.

'Maybe I would.'

'Maybe you'd like to use one of the horses,' Eve smiled. Now he was talking. There was no lie to her enthusiasm now.

'Where'll we go, Lou?' she asked eagerly.

'Got to take a look round the ranch. Been some cattle rustling lately,' he prevaricated. 'Got to check up . . .'

'Could we ride over to this Chaco place?' Eve suggested.

'It's a fair distance, but we could, I suppose. I could do the checking on the way . . .'

'Take my word for it, Eve.' John got up from table and stretched lazily. 'Riding and dancing don't mix. Nobody but nobody employs bow-legged dancers. Come on, sis. Time to go.' At last, Clara voiced her anxiety.

'Is that van going to hold out for the whole journey, John?' she inquired tremulously.

'We're not going in the van, Clara,' John reassured her. 'Dropping it off at Grants for Salgado to look at. Ain't that right, Pa?'

'Yup!' the old man answered.

'You going to give me a lift to the restaurant?' June was pulling on her cardigan.

'O.K.,' John agreed.

'Now be sure and be back in time to pick up the boy from school.' June considered the duty beyond question. But John disappointed her.

'Can't guarantee it,' he said. And before June had a chance to get back at him, Clara was butting in again, worried to death about her own hide.

'If we're not going in the van, what *are* we going in, John? I refuse to go all the way to Santa Fe in a horse and buggy.'

'We're renting a car,' John told her. They were going out the door, Clara pulling on her fancy gloves. Satisfied, at last, with her form of transport, she tackled another subject.

'Now, while I'm at the convent, John, seeing Sister Ursula, I thought we might as well pop in on the Father. You know you always used to like him.' John's shoulders sagged, like someone had dropped a bag of flour on them, as they passed out into the yard.

'Poor John.' Louis smiled slowly. 'Looks like he's in for a missionary day.' Jo watched as Lou pulled on his hat, and went out, followed by Eve. She was a study of sultry inducement. What the hell was that young woman playing at?

From the kitchen garden, Ella too was watching. She saw Louis help Eve onto her horse and hold the reins while she settled. Why did he love Eve? she thought. Eve didn't love him. She didn't want his children. If only he could feel Ella's love reaching out to him and turn his face to her, their loves would flare into fire, new life sparking out of them as naturally as laughter out of joy. And she would worship him. Louis was a white man, a Christian, and she dared not speak of her desire to the tribal chiefs. She was afraid they'd scorn her for living with whites and say she'd been polluted by watching too many movies. So, for the time being, only Earth Mother heard Ella's prayers, knowing Louis was good, and that Ella needed Jimmy to replace her lost child.

Now Lou was on his horse, raring to be off. He gave a shout across the yard and waved to Ella, standing in the garden. But Eve didn't wave. She took off, at a canter, laughing, as Lou followed. Then she pulled in the reins to wait for him, only to take off again, teasing him, drawing him on, away from Ella. White games. Snakes and ladders. But the white girl didn't know the power of the snake. In Walpi once, Ella's village on First Mesa, her godmother Myna told her of the Serpent Mound, miles away on the prairies of Ohio. There, she told her, the Snake Clan rested for a while, during the period of the migrations, and made the huge serpent out of clay to protect their village. It had seven curves, a curled tail, and a smaller, egg shaped mound rested between its open jaws. The egg was the symbol of the clan. What if Ella put her loved ones in the serpent's mouth? Would the snake protect them too? Suddenly, she knelt, praying Earth Mother to bless her work, and with bare hands, began to dig.

Unable to free herself from the pull of the woman in the garden, Eve turned her horse at the crest of the hill and pointed back to the ranch.

'What's she doing on her knees?' she asked. 'Praying?' Lou squinted into the sun and shook his head.

'Just gardening.'

'She gives me the creeps.'

'She keeps us in vegetables,' Lou observed gratefully. Eve shrugged off her guilty conscience, and stretched her back.

'Oh boy, I'd forgotten how much I love riding.'

'I'd forgotten how good you were.' Lou laughed. 'You and that horse could be married, you get along so well.'

'Better than that. We don't argue!' Eve retorted. 'You know . . .' They gee-ed up, and started walking side by side over the crest and down toward Ambrosia Lake. 'Sometimes, riding feels almost as good as dancing.'

'Hey! There's hope yet!'

'I said, "almost"!' Eve grinned. Then, Lou dared to ask,

'You'd never give up the dancing, would you?'

'Don't think I could,' she said truthfully. Lou wasn't surprised, but Eve teased him, adding, 'Not yet, anyway.'

Painstaking, Ella ground the earth, pounding it to dust with stones. It was like grinding corn, only harder. But slowly the mound grew. She watched Jo come out of the house, looking for her, looking for his dinner. Head down, she waited, till he gave up, saddled a horse and went down to Grants, to eat at Mrs Perez's restaurant, where June worked. Then Ella got back to work. She wet the earth with water from the well, moulding tenderly the curving body of the snake. More earth had to be ground and the dust wet, to make the head. Then the jaws opened wide, ready at last. A breeze blew, lifting the hair from her face. Ella looked up. There was not a cloud in the sky.

The cattle checked, Lou rested, eating his sandwiches, on horse-back. The sun was high, blasting down; hot for the time of year. He pulled off his kerchief and wiped his face with it. He'd found a steer dead and a couple of head missing. Could be he'd find their carcasses further up still, for what use it'd be. Still, might as well carry on toward Chaco; no point in spoiling Eve's day. His face was bleak.

'What's up?' she asked.

'Hell. It'd take a miracle to save this ranch.' Lou sighed.

'What sort of miracle?'

'I don't know. Pot of gold at the end of the rainbow maybe.'

'A bit of rain would help,' Eve remarked.

'Sure,' Louis sighed. 'I just don't know where to turn, and that's the truth.' They had reached the road and they stopped, looking round them at the monotonous landscape. Only a bare wisp of cloud, moving imperceptibly across blue infinity, broke the sense of being marooned in an eternal purgatory of flat dull brushland; the cloud, and the knowledge, reduced to blind faith, that somewhere, the featureless desert eventually broke into a canyon, a place where human beings used to live. There was no sign of the missing cattle. Eve took a swig from her bottle, passing it on to Lou. His eye travelled the road to Cuba. 'They found oil farther on up there,' he said. 'Round "White Horse".'

'Oil!' Eve gasped, round-eyed.

'Not much. On the reservation. Indians don't believe in ex-ploiting the land.' Lou scratched his head. 'Still . . . '

'Might be worth getting the surveyors in at The Lawe Top!'

'Might. Needs investment, like everything,' Lou grumbled. They rode in silence up the track to the ruins; the only sounds the air banging in their ears and the brush swishing against the horses' legs.

The ride was telling on Eve. She hadn't been in the saddle for some time. She was getting sore, and tired. And this damned country scared her. Its very vastness was like a trap. You could run for hours and still be in sight, or gunshot. She yawned, easing out her neck.

'Not keeping you up, am I?' Lou asked ruefully.

'Had a bad night, that's all,' she explained. 'Couldn't sleep. Couldn't stop thinking.'

'What about?'

'Oh this and that. My brain's never still.'

They'd stopped, overlooking the canyon. The outline of the ruins melted into the barren landscape of a dry riverbed. Staring down at them, Lou murmured, as though trying not to disturb anything, 'These ancient people suffered a drought. Their livelihood was wiped out. That's why the place went to ruins. Either they died or they moved on.' He started down the trail, and Eve followed. 'I guess I'm going to have to oil *my* brain cells just a little bit, else us Ridleys'll go the same way!'

'I don't suppose you'd ever think of selling out?' Eve suggested. Lou turned sharply. 'I only asked. I'm not saying you should, especially if there's money in it. Oil and so on.'

'It's easy for you to talk of "selling out",' Lou objected. 'Land gets to be part of you. Do you know, when they uprooted the Navajo and moved them to Fort Sumner, the people just about grieved to death? They couldn't exist away from their hereditary lands. I can sympathize.'

'Well, I've never owned any land.' Eve shrugged. 'Except maybe the back yard at home. I haven't got any roots.'

'You've got roots alright. You just cut them off, that's all,' Lou told her emphatically. But Eve was irritated with all this talk. She wanted more than a sore rear from her ride. She wanted action. She dug her heels in. The horse kicked up, and quickened its pace.

'Come on, Caesar!' she cried. But Lou reached for the reins.

'Whoa, there!' he shouted. 'Steady down now. Too rocky for racing round here.' Reprimanded, Eve bit back her temper.

Ella's hands were cold as ice. She moulded a clay man, placed him carefully on the ground, then took up more dust and wet it drop by drop, thinking of Jimmy . . .

And now Lou and Eve were in the canyon. The horses picked their way through the stones as they approached the ruins.

'Have you any Indian blood in you, Lou?' Eve asked. Lou laughed and shook his head.

'No. I just love the land. I can understand why the Indians don't want to exploit the mineral rights.'

'Don't they want to get rich?' she protested.

'Some do, I guess. But mostly money doesn't mean much to them, just so long as they've got enough to eat.'

'They're crazy!' Eve was scandalized.

And Lou tried to explain. 'You've got to understand their relationship with nature,' he told her. 'It's almost magical. They think of her as something living. And you have to respect the rights of something that's alive, because if you don't, and you go ahead and hurt it, it might just get up, like your horse, Caesar there, and kick you! Look at Chaco. You can hardly see the houses, can you? The old Americans were self-effacing, humble people, living in harmony with nature; an invisible presence. When they passed on, they left hardly a sign of their existence.' Eve pushed her hair firmly behind her ears.

'That's not my style. I want to make my mark!' she asserted.

'Maybe you'll get rich, then.' Lou smiled mockingly.

'I hope so!' she answered. 'Though it isn't *all* I want.'

Ella placed the clay dolls, man and child between the jaws of the snake . . .

'You know what *I'd* like?' Lou looked almost defiantly at her. 'I'd like to graft you onto my rootstock, Evie.' Eve was shocked at the sudden, clichéd declaration. She'd wanted action, and she'd got it! She jumped into the new role that was on offer . . .

'Lou jumped from his horse and, taking her by the waist, lifted her down, pressing her against his firm man's body. The horse shifted uneasily. He groaned.

"I love you, Evie." His lips searched hers, and they parted for him, allowing his wild yearning to search her out. And her passion stirred, coursing through her, answering his need. This was madness, exhilarating madness, a madness that could drive her to risk her very dreams . . .'

'Schcherrr!'

Sharp, the hiss cut between them. Lou jumped away. Eve's

horse neighed, reared, then galloped off. The other horse was restive. Lou whispered across the space that now divided him from Eve.

'Keep very still.'

'What is it?'

'A snake.'

'Oh my God!' It slithered between them. She felt its weight pass over her feet. She thought she was going to faint. It circled her round, then slithered away into the brush. She moaned, shaking.

'It's O.K.' Lou murmured. 'It was only a warning.' Eve lay back in the shade of the cliff, heart pounding. She closed her eyes. When she opened them again, Lou had disappeared. She turned her head to look for him, and saw, etched onto the canyon walls, the sign of the swastika.

A splash fell on Ella's head. She looked up from the serpent mound. It was raining. She was glad. It was a good omen. She stood slowly, face to the sky, enjoying the heavy drops that tingled her skin, forming ice cold rivulets down her face, as she walked back to the ranch. Faint and watery, a rainbow appeared; uncertain promise, fading over the deserted house like a ghost. She lingered in the kitchen; her kitchen; then went up to Jimmy's room, touching the birthday gifts; the gun from June; the puppet from Eve; the book from Clara; the huge Goofy John had brought. Her own corn dolly lay apart on the window ledge, a feather carefully placed at its feet. She smiled and listened joyfully to the sound the rain made on the iron roof.

Bill Farley came at tea time. He'd brought Jimmy back from school, and he'd brought some mail. There was a letter for Eve, from England.

'Where's the family?' Bill asked. Jo rocked in his chair, drinking his tea peaceably. He'd had a good lunch at Mrs Perez's place.

'John and Clara've gone to Santa Fe,' he answered. 'And Eve's gone with Lou, God knows where.'

'That girl going to settle down one day?'

'Search me.' Jo had a far away look in his eyes, like he was lost in a dream. This was unusual. It worried Bill.

'How's it going, old boy?' he asked cautiously.

'Not so old neither,' Jo complained.

'Nothing wrong with bein' old.'

'Except being old.'

'That's true,' Bill agreed, nodding slowly.

'This darned country's besotted with the idea of youth,' Jo observed. 'Know that?'

'Sure do.'

'No respect for the experience of age.'

'What experience's that, Jo?'

'Life! That's what I'm talkin' about. Experience of life,' Jo intoned. 'These youngsters haven't had time to get their teeth into anything yet!'

'Adam and Eve had good teeth, Jo.'

'Did they now? I ain't got no teeth. Them's been an' gone.'

'That's true.' Bill sighed. The conversation paused for a period of rumination. Then Jo spoke up again,

'That Englishwoman. She wasn't young. Tickled my fancy though.'

'What Englishwoman's that, Jo?' Bill asked.

'Maisie Beattie. Came over with Eve. Couldn't stand it here. Went back again. Tickled my fancy all the same.' Jo chuckled and Bill nodded appreciatively. 'She didn't have no teeth neither.'

'You know, I've been thinking, Jo,' Bill said, 'if Adam and Eve had had no teeth, we'd not be in nearly such a mess as we are now.'

'How's that, Bill?'

'Have you ever tried taking a bite out of an apple with no teeth?' Bill inquired. This last thought called for an extended pause, during which, Jimmy ambled in.

'Grandpa,' Jim pestered, 'what'll I call my foal?'

'Call him what you like,' Jo told him. 'He's your foal.'

'Think I'll call him White Cloud,' Jim said after a while.

'O.K.' Jo agreed. Then the boy turned to go,

'I think I'll go out and take a look at him.' But, Ella called him back.

'It's raining,' she objected.

'O.K.' Jim sighed. 'I'll look at him out of a window.' Then he left the room.

There was a commotion in the yard. John and Clara had come back from Santa Fe. June was with them. Ella put out more mugs, as they steamed in, out of the rain.

'How was your Aunt Cora?' Jo asked warily.

'Sister Ursula, you mean,' Clara corrected primly. 'If you ask me, Pa, the woman's a saint, sacrificing herself for the sake of her heathen family on the altar of love.'

Bill Farley rose to go. 'Silly cow,' he remarked. Jo nodded in agreement. A nun was a black sheep in the family, so far as he was concerned.

'Be seeing you, old boy,' he called after him.

Clara was embarrassed, or maybe she was hurt. She covered up by laying into John. 'I don't know what to make of you, John,' she complained. 'I mean, I'm really disappointed in you.'

'What's he done?' Jo had the feeling it was something he'd approve of.

'He had the chance of making a good confession to the Father and he decided to go for a walk. I ask you.' Clara was obviously upset.

'I'd've done the same!' Jo remarked.

'You're living in mortal sin, John. Know that?' Clara jibed.

'How the hell do you know what sin I'm living in!' John's tone was ugly. Ella watched from the stove as Clara sat, mug to mouth, glasses steaming slowly, too scared to move. 'I'm sorry, Sis. But you asked for it. You know I don't like being pushed!'

'If I push you, it's because I love you, dear. That's all. I couldn't bear it if you weren't saved along o' me!' She was crying.

'What's the good of confessing to something, if you just go on doing it?' John asked.

'It helps you to stop if you confess often enough.'

'Crap.' June pulled on her oilskins. She was going out to feed the hens. 'Come on, Clara, what could John possibly be doing that's so terrible!'

'I don't know.' There was a pause as everyone considered the possibilities.

Old Jo spoke up. 'How're your teeth, John?' Ella laughed. Jo turned slowly and stared at her. Then suddenly, he grinned. 'She's not as daft as she looks, that Indian woman.'

Clara couldn't cope any more and went upstairs with a headache. Jo leaned over the table. 'John, come here, I want to ask you something.' He whispered, so Ella couldn't hear, and John had to lean forward to catch it. 'What do you think? Is young Evie "destined for stardom" like she thinks she is?'

'Hell. How do I know?' John spluttered.

'O.K. Put it another way. Is she really that good?'

'How good?'

'Good enough to make her fortune?' Jo had a shrewd look in his eyes.

'No,' John answered. 'But she might be lucky.'

'Is she the lucky type?' Jo pursued.

'No. At least, I don't think so.'

'Hmm.' Jo sat back again. 'In that case, she might as well marry one of you boys now.' John looked as though he'd been shot.

'You know, Pa, I always got the impression you didn't really like Eve,' he said defensively.

'I like taking a rise out of her.' Jo grinned. 'But she's a darned sight better than that Indian, even if she did get my joke.'

The talk over supper was all about Evie's snake.

'It didn't mean to harm you,' Lou insisted. 'Just warn you off.'

'That's right.' Jo slapped the table. 'You must've disturbed him. It's the cardinal rule with snakes. Never disturb them when they're all coiled up sleeping. It's the only time they're likely to get annoyed.'

'I didn't see it, till it was on top of us,' Eve explained. June gave them an old-fashioned look.

'Why? What were you doing?' she asked.

'Looking at the ruins,' Eve told her. 'We saw your swastika, Ella . . . Ella, are you alright? You're looking very pale!'

'I'm fine, thanks.' Ella's hand was shaking, as she served the steaks. She'd asked for Lou and Jimmy to be protected. So, what were Eve and Lou doing when the snake struck out? Snakes only got angry when there was evil in your mind. Ella looked at Jimmy. He was eating his meat, unaware of the reverberations.

John was busy trying to charm his sister into a good mood, after upsetting her.

'How about coming back to 'Frisco with me?' he coaxed.

'I don't know. I've got my rail ticket,' she sulked.

'Aren't you worried about Ernie's dinners?'

'He certainly does need his dinners. That's true.' Clara was weakening. 'Being a cop in 'Frisco's no picnic,' she said. Evie smirked. John caught her eye and got the joke.

'Well,' he boasted, 'I sweet talked a pal of mine into letting me have seats on the morning plane to Phoenix, and I know I can pick up a connecting flight there, so if you'd *both* like to join me . . . ?'

'Flying's very expensive, John,' Clara whimpered.

'No. It's free,' John persuaded.

'How come?'

'Power of the press!' he grinned. 'I promised them a good write up and competition's growing.'

'I thought you were a crime reporter,' June objected.

'Still got my contacts, Aunt June.'

'What about my rail ticket?' Clara whined.

'You tell me what your plans are for that money of yours, Clara, and I'll tell you what to do with your rail ticket.' John made use of a rare opportunity to tease both sister and brother, at once. But Clara was not to be bested.

'None of your business, John. That's between me and Ernie.'

'I'll buy your train ticket off you, Clara,' Eve put in. John shot her a look. Her face was prissy, like she was getting back at him.

'You're all going off and leaving us!' June sighed. 'What's *your* hurry, Eve?'

'Got an engagement in a club in L.A.' Eve replied sweetly.

'Engagement?' June snorted. 'More like waitressing! You might as well stay here and work for Ma Perez. Keep me company.'

'No. Not waitressing. Dancing,' Eve corrected.

'In a club? You don't mean . . . stripping?' June was horror-struck.

Eve howled with laughter, 'No! What do you take me for? Me and a fellah called Roland Devine've formed a Latin American team. We do the rumba together.'

'Ballroom!'

'At least it's dancing, June! And you never know, I might get talent-spotted.'

'Are you sure this Roland Devine's alright?' Lou asked warily.

Eve simpered. 'If you mean what I think you mean, Louis, I'm

55

in no danger. Roly doesn't like girls.'

'What do you mean, he doesn't like girls?' Jo snarled.

'He's queer!' Eve laughed. There was a total silence.

'My God! And at the dinner table too!' June gasped.

'What's she mean, "queer"?' Clara asked. 'What's queer about him?'

'Jimmy, have you finished eating?' Ella hauled the protesting child from his chair and dragged him upstairs to wash.

'This is what comes of tight trousers,' Jo said, shaking his head. 'One thing about Indians, you don't hear about them having queers.'

'I expect they're just keeping theirs quiet,' June consoled him.

'Hell.' Jo pushed his plate away. 'I lost my appetite for my dinner now.' John flung down his knife. It bounced across the table, and flew off the other side, narrowly missing his sister.

'God, am I sick of these narrow hick attitudes.' He went outside to cool off.

'Get many queers in England?' Jo asked. Eve looked down, embarrassed. She'd really done it now. Jo's eyes scared her. 'That reminds me. There was a letter for you. Bill Farley brought it up specially.' He rummaged in his pocket and brought out a crumpled envelope. 'Real "star treatment"!'

As she opened her letter, a photograph fell out; her mother, taken on the sands at Marsden. Eve was caught off guard. That gentle face; she longed to see it again. Her mother was still pretty. A sort of sweet, old-fashioned softness hung about her like an aura. She had a drawing quality that made Eve want to cry, want to go home, want to be that sort of woman. What sort of woman? The sort who sacrifices her life? The sort who lets people walk all over her? Hell, no! Quickly, before she was thoroughly infected by the germ of traditional femininity, Eve put the picture away in her purse and began to read the letter.

It was newsy. Her mother always wrote newsy letters; not the sentimental stuff you might have expected. It'd been written before Munich, so of course it went on a lot about the possibility of war. Also Ellen, Eve's grandmother, was ill. But Eve wasn't to think of coming home for that. 'Far better stick it out, now you've got this far, pet, and see if you really can make it,' her mother wrote. Aunt Maisie had found a fellah. What?! Eve couldn't help looking at Jo, a grin all over her face. But her smile dropped at once. Jo had picked up his cutlery again, and was stuffing himself, as fast as he could. His anger had apparently subsided. So! 'Taken his appetite away' had she? Had the old reprobate just been bluffing, to take a rise out of her? 'Star treatment'! Damn him. Roly could be a Martian for all she cared, never mind a queer! She decided to put the whole business from her mind; just in time too. Jo was about to ask what was biting her, when she buried herself in her letter again, saving herself from further discussion.

'Afters, Jo?' June asked.

'What is it?'

'Birthday cake.'

'Hell, no!'

'I'll have some, Aunt June.' Louis had a sweet tooth.

Eve read on. Os and his pretty wife had had a baby. Aunt Hester had been let out of the asylum and run amok, so been put back in again. Eve's 'father' was apparently working his fingers to the bone, night and day, to keep the shop alive, and that old dragon, Aunt Harriet, had died, choking on a fishbone. Good riddance! And what about her mother? She didn't say much about herself; just kept pushing this 'father' at her. Working his fingers to the bone? My, but Jack Scott must've turned over a new leaf! She folded the letter, put it back in the envelope and stuffed it in her purse with the photo.

'How's the folks at home?' Jo asked, with a grimace.

'Oh. Fine. Just fine.' Eve smiled and went out into the yard.

Darkness. Thank God for darkness. Just to escape the glare of the electric light! It felt like putting clothes on after a spell in a nudist camp. Eve breathed again, in the cool rain-soaked air. Over by the paddock, she could see the glow of a cigarette end. John. She stood in the shadow of the house watching the red light. It was comforting somehow. Hell she hated coming back to The Lawe. It always unsettled her. But this time . . . She sought refuge in self-dramatization . . .

'She was alone in a world where for a woman to be alone spelt danger, and the lit butt of a cigarette could mean comfort for a

57

while, or . . . ' Eve discarded the scenario. She couldn't be bothered with acting. She was tired. She'd had a bad night, then that snake, and now the letter. She didn't want to be reminded of home, the grey damp streets of Tyneside, the fog horns out in the cold North Sea, pinched faces, skeletons rattling in cupboards, Aunt Hester. Crazy Aunt Hester. There was a story there alright. She didn't know the half of it, and she didn't want to know. It had nothing to do with her. Not any more. Like Lou said, Eve'd cut off her roots and thank God for it. She watched the red light. It rose and fell in the darkness and her mind rested on it. Roots. Did she want to be grafted onto the rootstock of her cousins? 'Day you decide to marry one of my lads, then you can call me "Pa".' Didn't know who her Pa was. That was her trouble. Maybe Jo was right, bastard that he was for betraying her confidence! What kind of a mother got you confused about who your father was? And what kind of a father let another man bring up his child? *If* she was Jack's child. Till she was in her teens, Eve'd believed Davey Lawson was her true father and her mother's lawful husband. And then, the day Davey died, Eve'd caught her mother in bed with Jack Scott and Eve was supposed to start calling *him* 'Father'. And Eve just *couldn't*. Hell! It's funny when your own life's like a film script; not like real life at all. Damn Jo. Why'd she trusted him with the truth? All she'd done was put a weapon in his hands. And damn that letter for reminding her!

Eve walked over to the lighted butt.

'Hi.'

'Hi.'

'I was lonely. Can I join you?'

'You betcha,' he said. She could feel the warmth of his body, without touching him. 'Want a drag?' Eve took the cigarette and inhaled deeply. She reeled, as she gave it back.

'Know what, John? I hate the country,' she confided.

'So do I.'

'Damn snakes everywhere. Damn country hicks. What do they know?'

'You betcha.' He flicked the ash off. 'Know what I hate most?'

'No. What?'

'The silence,' John spoke with disgust.

'Know what you mean,' Eve agreed. 'You get a lot of that in the country.'

'Yeah. You can hear your own heart beating if you listen hard enough. Hear yourself breathing. Thinking; that's the worst.'

'Do you think a lot, John?'

'Yes. Guess I do. Most of it goes by unnoticed, thank God.' Eve tried to think about her thinking, then gave up. 'Why did you turn down flying back with me?' he asked.

'Don't want you to think you own me, John Ridley.'

'That's a pity. I like owning people.'

'Why?' she challenged.

'Safer.'

'For who?'

'Gotcha.' He gave her another drag of his cigarette.

'Can you feel the earth move?' Eve whispered.

'Not yet.' He was joking. She didn't get it.

'Sometimes, when I'm here, I feel as though it's shifting under me,' Eve whispered. 'It's weird. I mean, you do get that in L.A. I mean quakes and so on; and 'Frisco come to that. But not here. But it's here I feel it!'

'They don't get quakes here,' John told her.

'Don't you feel it?' Eve persisted. 'I feel shook up every time I visit this place! It's a different world. It's like God made it yesterday and it's not finished yet. It's still alive! I'm not used to that. Most of Europe's dead. It lay down and died a long time ago. But not here. Lou thinks I'm an insensitive city slicker. The truth is, and I don't like admitting it, even to myself, but I feel things here that don't even register on the Richter scale, but they send my swingometer crazy! I don't know what it is. Maybe you're so used to it you don't even notice. But I do. Some of those rocks, and the Indians . . . ' She shivered. 'This is the real America, isn't it?!'

'Real?' John laughed. 'Hell. I don't know. What's real?'

'I live in Disneyland most of the time, John. I just don't think I can face anything else.' Eve's voice was pleading.

'Disneyland's fun. Enjoy it,' he told her.

'I'm scared,' she whispered. John turned to look at her. Was she fooling? There were real tears running down her cheeks. The tears were black with mascara. No. She wasn't fooling. He took her in his arms. 'Sometimes, I wonder what the hell I'm doing,

59

and whether I'm any good at it anyway.' He nursed her, rocking her gently.

'You and me both,' he murmured.

'What? You? Scared?' Eve was surprised.

'Sure I'm scared. Why d'ye think I make such a big noise?'

'But you go all out for danger. Flying planes, going out on raids with the cops. You didn't have to be a crime reporter.'

'It's not physical danger that frightens me,' John confided. She waited, comforted by the warmth of his arms. 'Know what scares me most?'

'What?' she asked.

'That damned silence. It's like something out there's waiting for me to confess.'

'Yes. That's it,' Eve said at once. 'I get this funny feeling in the pit of my stomach . . . a feeling that maybe I don't like myself very much.'

'Stop worrying. You're nice.' He kissed her on top of her head.

'So're you.' She smiled at him. 'I mean, neither of us has actually done anything wrong, have we?' John shrugged. 'So why should we be scared?' She looked back at the ranch. '*They're* not scared.'

'It's all bluffing.'

'Are you sure?'

'Yeah,' John said. 'And we can bluff with the best of them.' He bent suddenly, and planted his mouth on hers, forcing open her lips, so that his teeth bruised them. She knew she was being kissed alright. Her arms welcomed him. He was real. So was she. And for once, she wasn't scared. It was very reassuring.

The door of the ranch swung open and a stream of light flooded out towards them. It caught them like a spotlight. Louis stood, a silhouette in the doorway, watching.

CHAPTER THREE

A couple of days later, Eve was relieved to be back in L.A., dodging in and out of the built-up streets, camouflaged by the herds of her kind. Trying to capitalize on her meeting with Zubermann, she went to see her agent, Ida Fischer. Ida's offices were at the wrong end of Hollywood Boulevard, but she was a good agent, if she would only keep her mind on the job. She had good days and bad days. This was a bad day.

'Did you hear the President on the radio last night?' she asked.

Eve sighed. Had Ida heard a word she'd said? She decided to indulge her agent now, in the hope of distracting her later.

'No.' Eve asked, dutifully, 'What did he say?'

'He said Wall Street's going up again. I don't believe him, though.' Ida had the air of a seer forecasting disaster.

'Why not?' Eve knew she'd get the answer anyway.

'My uncle left me some shares. It'll keep on going down,' Ida told her triumphantly. Eve had a baleful look in her eyes.

'You know, Ida,' she said, 'some people come to their agents to be cheered up. I come to be depressed.'

'Pessimism is the Jewish strength. How else could we have survived?' Now Ida was onto her favourite topic. Emergency measures had to be taken.

'I was telling you about Hal Zubermann . . . ' Eve butted in. But it was no good.

'Look at what's happening in Germany,' Ida went on. 'And tell me Jews weren't made to suffer.'

'Don't start, Ida.'

'I got relatives over there. I've written to them. "Get out" I told them. Know what they told me? "Read the Book of Job" they said. "Jehovah wants us to suffer. We better learn to take it." '

'Your relatives should visit with my cousin Clara in 'Frisco.' Eve grimaced. 'They'd get on well.'

'Why? Is she Jewish?'

'No. Catholic.' The surprise acted like a spanner dropped in Ida's works. She hesitated, and Eve dove in. 'Ida,' she said, 'Hal Zubermann has offered me a test. I met him in Tucson . . . '

'The musical film is finished.' Ida was willing to write the obituary before the event. Eve gritted her teeth.

'I was feeling great when I walked in here . . . ' she snapped.

'What did I say?' Ida gave her client a smug smile. 'Optimists are always being disappointed. Try being a pessimist, Eve. It's so much better.' But Eve was not so easily put down.

'I don't believe the musical film is finished!' she said emphatically.

'It'll die slowly, of course, but it'll die.'

'How do you know?'

'What was Hal Zubermann doing in Tucson? It's where they make westerns, for God's sake.'

'I know. *I* was there to make a western.'

'So was he!'

'Oh.' Pause. 'Hell.'

'There's not much going for dancers just now. You should be on your knees thanking God for that spot you got at Leno's.'

'So why would Zubermann offer me a test? He knows I'm a dancer!' Eve flung her arrow into the heart of disbelief. And the arrow came flying back.

'You ask that?' Ida nodded wisely and Eve wanted to hit her.

'There must be something for me!' she howled.

'Now if you were a little smaller . . . '

'I could shrink . . . ?' Eve offered.

'Not that much.'

'I could wear low heels . . . ' Ida shook her head. 'How much?'

62

'Midget.' Eve's eyes raised to heaven. 'Yeah. Still looking for Munchkins over at Culver City.' Ida smirked.

'More Munchkins? The place is crawling with them! Aren't there any singing, dancing fairies in *Wizard of Oz* of more or less normal size? Go on, Ida,' Eve pleaded. 'Ring them. I've got this feeling.'

'How does that song go? "Somewhere over the Rainbow, dreams trala" . . . ' Everybody at M.G.M.'s singing it.'

'What're you getting at, Ida?'

'With your starry eyes, kid, you sure could be Dorothy.'

'Yeah. I could, if you'd got me the part!'

'You got cheek. I'll say that.' Ida sighed. She looked very tired. 'O.K. Ring Zubermann. See where it gets you.'

'Don't expect ten per cent when I'm a star!'

'I'll expect thirty per cent.'

'I can't win, can I?' Eve sighed. Ida shook her head.

'Think yourself lucky I don't take commission on your waitressing jobs, honey. Some agents do.'

'If I could be Dorothy, Ida, you could be Toto. Always snapping away at my heels . . . '

'Toto?' Ida frowned.

'Dorothy's dog,' Eve reminded her. 'I saw the script. Somebody'd left it at my dentist's. I read it in the waiting room.'

'Toto. That's good.' Ida nodded, smiling. 'Toto. I like nicknames. They make me feel wanted.' Client and agent smiled bleakly at one another. 'Anyway . . . ' She shuffled through Eve's publicity shots. 'What can I do with these? They don't look like you any more. You look different now. Come to that, you look different every time I see you.'

'I can't get new photographs every time I change my hair, Ida.'

'Know what? You really are like a Dorothy here . . . ' She studied one of the prints. 'Little girl lost.'

'That was when I first came over.' Eve defended herself. 'I've wised up since then.'

'You need new ones. Sorry.'

'Has my pay cheque come in yet, from the radio?'

'You got it a fortnight ago. What happened?'

'I told you. I went to the dentist.'

'New photographs, or I won't represent you any more.' Ida had given her ultimatum. Take it or leave it. Eve had no choice.

'O.K.,' she agreed. Then Ida decided to be nice.

'How d'you get on with Belcher?' she asked. Eve shook her head. 'He's a first-rate teacher. A spell with him and even I might be able to get you work.'

'He's a ballet man. Anyway, he believes in the Cecchetti method. I'm not familiar with the Cecchetti method.' Eve had finally caught Ida's pessimism.

'I'm not familiar with the Maserati.' Ida sighed, chucked the photos aside and began to fiddle with the phone book. She yawned. 'If you'd been on Broadway, it'd help.' Eve rose, and made for the door.

'Bye, Toto!'

'Is that any way to say "goodbye" to your agent?' Ida complained.

'Agent?' Eve retorted. 'You're not an agent, Ida. You're the personification of the "Wailing Wall".'

Leaving the office, Eve stepped onto Hollywood Boulevard, and stood blinking in the sunshine. She was going to ring Hal Zubermann, whatever. But she had something to do first. A few blocks up, she turned in to the single storeyed warehouse where Danny, her tap coach, ran classes.

'Hi, Danny. You asleep?' A black hand slowly pulled the hat from over the face.

'Who's that?' Danny squinted into the darkness at the far end of the hall. 'Oh. You. You woke me.'

'I need to dance.' Eve slung the bag from her shoulder and started putting on her tap shoes.

'It's not class time.'

'I know. I'm not asking you to teach me. Just let me use your floor.' Danny went over to the piano and started vamping.

'Audition?'

'Not yet. Gotta make a call first.' Her feet were tapping out the rhythm and Danny was smiling.

'Be my guest.' He pointed, grandly, to the telephone out the back.

'Gotta work up to it. Just been to see Ida.'

'Gotcha.' Danny smiled wryly. Ida's talent for making you feel good was famous. 'See what you can do with this!' He broke into the lazy melody of 'Paper Doll'. Eve let her feet trail her body, dancing slowly on a limbering beat. Her knees gave to the rhythm, like spring boards, swinging her along, to the easy tune. Her arms loosened, and slowly she began to get that feeling her body loved; the feeling of muscle warming, stretching, like a cat waking from a deep sleep. Her arms explored space, reached into air, questioning the limits of the physical. Danny watched, tuned like a radio, as she grew into the music; not following, but dancing across the surface of the notes, like wind over water. Eve took tap beyond its boundaries into ballet. To hell with time steps. Let's *really* dance!

Danny teased her, reluctant to give. Then suddenly, he broke rhythm. What was coming? Her heart beat faster. 'You like rumba; maybe you'll like this . . . ' he shouted, over the increasing volume of 'South American Way'. This was fun! Now she had cross rhythms and character to play with. She took the tune inside herself, tapping the Latin ballroom steps, till she'd got into the mood. Then she spread the rhythm out, through her hips, and knees, shoulders rolling, head turning with the movement that travelled up her spine. And as her body indulged the tropical luxury, her feet played across the beat, challenging Danny, with fresh spurts of rhythm. Hell, those feet were talking to each other! Danny was relegated to giving background! He broke into 'Deep in the Heart of Texas'. At once, Eve cut the luxury. Her feet stamped, demanding Dan take her deep into counter rhythms, till the tune had gone for a Burton and dancer and pianist were harmonizing in the negro rhythms of primitive Africa. Excitement flushed Eve's face. Nothing could stop her. In this mood, she was master of the world, and she was master, because she was one with it. While she was dancing, Eve was totally, confidently, completely herself. And she was brilliant!

Music and dancer stopped dead. The only sound was Eve panting.

'That was black, sister!' Danny had offered the accolade.

Eve burst out with joyous laughter, then slumped forward, resting, head against her knees, breathing hard. He walked over to her, putting his hand on the sweaty curve of her back. 'I never knew anyone for improvising like you, Eve. Nobody white that is.' He was near to tears. 'Eleanor Powell, eat your heart out!' Eve stood slowly. Her face glowed, and her eyes shone. She had come alive.

'Now I'm ready to make that phone call,' she announced.

'Hell, if it takes all that to get you to make the phone call, what's it going to take for the audition?' Danny laughed. But Eve had walked off, with a determined step in the direction of the office. Danny shook his head and sat at the piano, tinkering. My, those wings of hers had come on something under his tuition!

'Republic 0211, please,' Eve told the answering telephonist. 'Oh hallo, I need to speak to Hal Zubermann's secretary.' Pause. 'Oh I don't think you need to bother Mr Datig. In fact I don't need your casting director, at all. You see, I already met Mr Zubermann in Tucson last week, and he said I should phone and he'd arrange a test for me. I'm a dancer.' Pause. 'Yes, I'll hang on.' Pause. Danny tinkering in the main hall. Paperwork strewn over the desk. Eve looked idly at it. There was a breakdown of current casting. Warner were doing *On Your Toes*. Eve shouted through. 'Danny, what's *On Your Toes*?'

'*On Your Toes* is like what it sounds. The heroine's a ballet dancer. Ballerina, to be exact. Not your scene.' If Eve could only have got herself taken on by Ernest Belcher . . . but he believed in the Cecchetti method. Someone came onto the other end of the line. Eve jumped to respond.

'Oh, hallo, miss. Are you Hal Zubermann's secretary? Have you heard of me? Eve Lawson? No? Oh well, you win some . . . You'd better ask Mr Zubermann. He said he'd get me a test. I'm a dancer.' Pause. She could hear Hal and his secretary shouting in the background. He didn't remember Eve. His secretary was saying how she was fed up with girls calling for tests. She sounded middle-aged and sour. Then the phone went dead. What had happened? Had they rung off? Eve hung on, anxious. Suddenly Zubermann was on the line.

'Hallo, Eve. Nice to hear from you. What can I do?'

'It's about that test you promised me.'

'I'm not casting anything just now . . . '

'A general test. Dancing. You promised,' Eve insisted.

'O.K. Why not?' he sighed. 'Everybody else does them. Come along to the studio next week.'

'When?'

'How about Tuesday?' he suggested. Eve gulped. 'I can't. I've got to be in 'Frisco. I've got this radio part . . . '

'Tough.'

'I could come this week!' she pleaded.

'Hell you could.' This time she knew he'd put the phone down.

* * *

Lou's manhood had shrivelled at the sight of Eve and John kissing. If she'd shouted from the rooftops Lou was nothing of a man, he couldn't have got the message better. Hurt, he retreated within. His vigour failed him and jobs piled up around the ranch. What a fool he'd been. How could he ever have thought he was good enough for Eve? Why, beside his brother, he was a no-no. Yes, John was the American dream. He had everything in this world going for him. Everything Eve wanted anyhow. And why shouldn't she? She was ambitious. She'd never be satisfied with just being a wife. Not Lou's wife, anyway! Ella watched Lou's suffering, helplessly. It hurt her to see him like this. What right had any woman to damage his sense of worth? She longed to comfort him. But, Jimmy put his hand in his Dad's, and loved him. It did the trick. And slowly, Lou gathered strength to face his disappointment.

One day, he rode out till he was alone with the vast sky and the barren land. It was magnetic. It had a force field all its own. And it held him. No. He could never leave the land to forage in the cities. Not even for Eve. He rode back in the sunset, saw a golden eagle soaring in the rosy light, and that night, the house silent, he wrote Eve a letter.

Dear Eve,

I'm not much good at talking. Not much good at writing, either. Don't know what I am good at to tell you the truth. But must be something. God can't have put me on the earth for nothing. Only got to find out why. Don't know why I'm telling you all this. Just wanted to say how much I admire you, for getting out there, doing great things. I haven't got it in me to be like that. You and John are worth ten of me. My life doesn't amount to much, does it? But I know yours will.

Good luck
Yours, Louis Ridley.

67

P.S. Saw a golden eagle today. Hope Jo doesn't shoot it down. They don't steal sheep, whatever the farmers say.

Eve read the letter once then shoved it in her handbag. It gave her the creeps. She couldn't make out what it was, a fan letter, a love letter, a goodbye letter? What? Anyway she hadn't time to mull over Lou, or that dirty rat, Zubermann. She had a job to do. She dashed out to the hire shop for a dress. She had to skip supper to pay for it, but there wasn't time to eat anyway. Then, she had to have her hair done and still get to Leno's in time for the show. But the letter followed her like a cloud, making her feel so uneasy, her nerves started jumping. And by the time she got to Leno's she was in dire need of a drink. The most fashionable club on Sunset, Leno's was packed every night of the week, with the successful of Hollywood. Eve adjusted the straps of her hired dress. It didn't do for your heart to be lower than your decolletage.

'Roly?' she asked her partner, 'Do you think you could palm me a glass of the bubbly, dear? My feet are aching.' He winked and she watched him disappear into the crowd. Roly knew all kinds of people. His was a sort of mafia, a queer mafia. Beyond her. Still, he could be very understanding when he wanted, and she liked him. What he did in his spare time was his business. He came back, a smile of victory on his face and half a bottle of champagne in his hands.

'I hate waste, don't you?' he said. 'Take off your shoe, Cinderella.' She grinned, and responded with the honour of an insult.

'Get lost. There's some cups in the dressing room.'

Eva gave the suspicion of a skip as the band struck up and they walked out into the spotlight. Roly was alarmed.

'Are you drunk, dearie?' he asked in a whisper. Smiling at the audience, she talked back at him through her teeth.

'Just a little light-headed with hunger, that's all.'

'Didn't you have any supper?'

'Couldn't afford it.'

'Silly bitch!' Roly pinched her to show his displeasure.

'I owe on the rent as well,' Eve giggled. 'Isn't it awful?' Roly's grip tightened. He led her across the middle of the floor and swung her round.

'What happened to the last pay cheque?' he muttered, smiling.

'I bought a rail ticket all the way from Albuquerque. And then you know I had toothache.'

'Don't give me the sob story, dearie.' He swung her back, then pushed her round the floor with a virile gusto that fooled no one. 'So ! how're you going to get to 'Frisco for your radio studio?' he reminded her.

'You're going to lend me the money,' she retorted. Roly fluffed. Eve skidded on the tip of her high heel, and the punters were treated to a brilliant manoeuvre, as the dancers slid together from one end of the dance floor to the other. Roly landed on his knees, Eve draped across him. There was applause. Eve grinned. Annoyed, Roly flung her off his knee and onto her feet. It was more like a tango than a rumba, but the audience of professionals loved it. And Eve responded, gingering up her performance with the spice of fantasy . . .

'Eve looked into the smouldering eyes of her Latin lover. His thighs tensed against her, his passion like a tightly coiled spring. And the rhythm coursed through her. Proud, she disdained him, haughty she turned her back, only to be caught in a tight embrace, as, inevitably, his manly arm commanded her. And they moved as one across the floor, hips swinging together, feet sliding, arms entwining, and as she finally, in a gesture of ultimate contempt, kicked out her leg, he fell, a captive, at her feet.'

'I'll get you for that, dearie,' Roly hissed. They bowed to tumultuous applause, the diners rising from their chairs. 'What happened to you?' he muttered. Then, as they stood, smiling and bowing, Roly's eye was caught by a man on the front table. He was looking at Eve. Roly nudged her and she saw Hal Zubermann. He invited her over.

'I never saw a rumba danced like that!' Hal said. 'Who are you?'

'The girl you put the phone down on the other day.' Eve pulled out a chair and sat in it. Zubermann's lady friend wasn't pleased.

'Looks like I've got something to make up. Champagne?' He raised the bottle to pour. But suddenly Eve went cold. She knew this scenario. It led, not to stardom, but to somebody's back bedroom.

69

'No thanks.' She sounded prissy and she hated herself for it. Hal was amused.

'What's wrong? Think I'm going to kidnap you and sell you to the slave trade?'

'You know best, Mr Zubermann.' She sounded like a little girl, the little girl Ida had sneered at in the photographs! When was she going to grow up and take life by the tail . . . Now! Right now! She plunged in, 'If you really want to make it up to me, Mr Zubermann, give me a dance test, like you promised,' she demanded. The lady friend got up to powder her nose.

'O.K.' Hal lit his cigarette and inhaled slowly, watching Eve to see what she would do next. She rose to the bait, the fantasy heroine of the dancing still alive in her . . .

'Eve was the reckless type, especially with a bit of hooch in her. Wasn't everyone? She fixed her eyes on his and reached for his packet of cigarettes. He flipped one out for her, and she took it, sticking it between her bared teeth, daring him to light it . . . '

She was way over the top. Zubermann clicked his fingers. Immediately, a waiter came forward with a lighter and flicked the flame in her face. Eve lay back, sucking nervously. Zubermann was highly amused. She'd given him a second cabaret. O.K. What now? Again the flamboyant character of the dancing came to Eve's rescue.

'Cut the monkey business!' she snapped. 'When can I do a test?'

'Next week.' Zubermann was unimpressed. 'I told you.'

'I can't next week.' This time Eve spoke as herself. He wasn't going to brush her off. She couldn't let him. 'I really do have a radio job,' she explained. 'I'm Jennifer in "The Jones Family". Jennifer's about to have a baby by her English husband and he's trying to make her go home to have it. But she wants it born a citizen of the United States. All America's holding its breath. It's true. We get letters every day to the serials office, and my cousin, Clara Trevor, she lives in 'Frisco, I stay with her when I go up for recordings, well she thinks the whole thing's absolutely true. I mean, she thinks the Jones family's real. Yet she knows I play Jennifer, and I'm not having a baby, am I? Crazy!'

'You said it.' Zubermann's girlfriend was coming back from the bathroom. He had to get rid of Eve, or be in trouble himself. 'Well,' he smiled tolerantly, 'we can hardly interfere with "The

Jones Family" now, can we? O.K. You better come over to the studios Friday morning. I'll see what I can do.'

Friday morning, Eve's face was made up and her tap shoes on her feet. But her heart was thumping so much, she was scared she wouldn't hear the music and fluff the start of her routine. Then she began to shake. Dutch courage was called for. An old movie came to her rescue, offering her a stronger dose of fantasy than any she could think up herself;

' "Sawyer, you listen to me and you listen hard. Two hundred people, two hundred jobs, 200,000 dollars, five weeks of grind and blood and sweat depend upon you. It's the lives of all these people who've worked with you. You've got to go on and you've got to give and give and give! They've got to like you, got to! You understand? You can't fall down, you can't. Because your future's in it, my future, and everything all of us have is staked on you. All right now, I'm through. But you keep your feet on the ground and your head on those shoulders of yours and, Sawyer, you're going out a youngster but you've got to comè back a star!" '
Well it got Ruby Keeler on her feet in *42nd Street*, and it got Eve Lawson on her feet now!

They didn't plan on any fancy camera work. They just pointed the cameras at her and started rolling. The pianist sounded half asleep. Impatient, Eve tapped against him, trying to spur him into life. He was playing 'Amarola' and the speed at which he was playing it was not going to do justice to her dancing. She stopped in the middle of the take.

'Did somebody say "cut"?' A disembodied voice spoke from above. Who was it?

'I'm sorry, Mr Zubermann, if that's you, but the music just isn't right.' Eve called up. The pianist looked even tireder.

'How d'ye want it?' he asked with resignation.

'Faster, for a start, and how about a bit of syncopation?'

'Who's she think she is, Fred Astaire?' the pianist sneered. The camera crew grinned. One of them lit a cigarette. The smoke crossed in front of his lens. Things were only going to get worse if she kicked up. Better make the best of it. The music started again. This time, it wasn't so much faster or livelier, as jerkier. She did her best. She smiled, she played to the cameras, using

71

her body and doing complicated steps that didn't go with the tune. Then, when it finished, there was silence. She stood on the floor, looking up at the gallery. Was Hal Zubermann there, or not? The disembodied voice spoke again.

'Thank you. Have you got an agent?'

'Yes. Ida Fischer. Hollywood Boulevard. Telephone Hillside...'

'Don't bother. She'll be in the book.'

'Is Mr Zubermann there?' Eve called into the silence. The crew had disappeared. Perhaps it was their coffee break. She had one last shot at shouting to the gallery. There was no reply. But the pianist was packing up his music. 'Can you tell me, Mister, do I get expenses?' Eve asked.

'Don't push your luck, sweetheart.'

'It's a forty-mile journey back to Pasadena!'

'What d'ye want to go to Pasadena for?'

'I live there,' Eve told him. 'There's not many buses and I can't afford taxis!'

'You should've thought of that.' He went. The studio was now completely empty. The lights went out.

'Don't I even get offered a cup of coffee?' she whispered. She was going to have to hitch home.

Her lift said he was a script writer. He must've written some pretty sordid thrillers; he had her terrified with his nasty talk and she was sure she'd end up in a ditch. But it got really bad when they hit the freeway. They were going slowly, on account of the smog, which had come down that morning, when his hand slithered off the gear lever onto Eve's leg. She couldn't decide whether to ignore it for fear of something worse, or whack him. She waited till the car was at Hoover and the hand half way up her thigh, then hit him hard. He threw her out. Literally. Beside him, Zubermann was an angel. She laddered her stockings and grazed her knee, as she hit the sidewalk. Then, luckily, she got picked up by a police car and driven home. She was in shock. She slept round the clock. And when she came round, she went straight out into the noise and the bright lights, telling the story of her disasters to her acquaintances, as though it was the biggest joke in town. She was singing for her supper. Roly obliged, and lent her the bus fare up to 'Frisco.

As the bus droned on through the night, Eve sweated. At last, the shock had caught up with her, and the laughter that had greeted the story, told against herself, echoed like madness in her brain, already feverish with the memory of disaster on disaster; flunking the film in Tucson, flunking the test, the lift home, Lou's shadow in the yard . . . His letter had made her feel so bad. Yet she knew that hadn't been his intention. She searched her purse for it, and found her mother's letter instead. They all expected so much of her, all her family. The trouble was they believed in her. What was it Lou'd said? She put her mother's letter back and found his schoolboy writing. 'I admire you for getting out there, doing great things,' she read. What 'great things'? Dancing the rumba? Getting drunk? Messing with shits like Zubermann, Roly, that script writer? (If he was one.) And as for her talent, Eve couldn't act her way out of a paper bag! All she could do was dance. And no one wanted to know. She looked back at Lou's letter. 'My life doesn't amount to much, does it? But I know yours will.' She grimaced. Lou'd seen a golden eagle in the sky. What'd Eve seen? If he only knew how she squirmed with the pain of her humiliation. But he didn't. And she couldn't tell him. There was no one to comfort her, apart from John. Was he really worth ten of Lou? Well, whatever . . . She'd burned her boats. And after all, John was the only one who had seen through her tough cookie act. He understood. And he was in 'Frisco. Eve would see him tomorrow. Thank God. She urgently needed lessons in advanced bluffing.

CHAPTER FOUR

Coming out of Hanno's bar, the air hit John like a blow to the stomach. He leaned back against the wall, breathing like a diver with the bends. Billy Conneelly, sports journalist from a rival paper, was rounding the corner, a young woman at his side. Not wanting to appear drunk and therefore at a disadvantage, John glued his eyes to her legs.

'Ain't you got no manners, punk?' Billy asked. But, Pat Bolan, a comrade from John's own paper, the *Independent*, was just behind. He grabbed Billy by the collar and lifted him up, hurling him against the wall.

'Who're you calling a punk?' Pat hollered.

'John was lookin' funny at Nora. Now Nora happens to be a cousin of mine, and a lady, and I won't have anybody looking at her funny.'

'Hiya, Nora,' Pat said, keeping his hands on Billy's collar.

'Hiya,' Nora said. John's mouth felt like dough.

'Lady shouldn't have nice legs if she doesn't want them looking at,' he said, reasonably enough.

'See?' Pat was pressing Billy against the wall. Then, suddenly, Billy banged him with his head. Pat screamed and pushed the competition into the bar, where a chorus of, 'Hiya, Billy, Hiya, Pat,' greeted the pugilists. Nora teetered gingerly after them. The fight would continue inside, but John had other fish to fry.

He was feeling better now. He pulled his coat back onto his shoulders and walked on up Powell. He had an assignation in Chinatown, en route to the night shift at the Hall of Justice. Maybe he should grab something to eat too. He slid into the oriental streets, collar up, homburg down. He looked like a man who was not to be trifled with. Outside Paul Low's store, he was accosted by a Chinese girl in a short skirt. But John declined her offer.

'No thanks, honey,' he said. She shrugged and watched, as he walked right through the store and out into the back, where they were playing mah-jong.

'Hiya, Johnny. Wanna game?' Paul Low, the manager, asked.

'No thanks, Paul. I've come to collect.' Four Chinese faces stared up at him. 'Your lottery runner got picked up by the police.' Paul shrugged. 'He might talk. And then again, I might get him off.'

'You can if you want.' Low went into the store, to open the till. The girl was in there. She glanced through the door into the gaming room and went in. 'We're moving illegal lottery business out of here soon.' Low spoke quietly. 'Not safe in Chinatown. We getting a nice big marking office tucked away the other end of town where your brother-in-law Ernie won't find us.' John laughed.

'He wouldn't find you anyway. He can barely find his own night stick.' Low counted out the notes and John nodded when he'd been bribed enough. 'So, what's the story I'm supposed to spin about this runner?' he asked. Low handed John a receipt book from his store.

'See what you can do with this,' he said. John looked at the book. It was written in Chinese. He nodded briefly and put the book in his pocket with the money.

'What's these?' He picked up a garish-looking package.

'Fire crackers,' Low told him. 'It's nearly Double Ten Day.' Double Ten Day was the day the Chinese celebrated the revolution against the Manchu dynasty.

'I'll take some.' John pocketed those too and Low returned to his game. At the door, John looked back to wave goodbye and saw the girl, now sitting at the table in the back room, laying bets. The door closed.

It was a short walk to the Hall of Justice, taking John through the lower half of Chinatown. Mostly Chinatown had been cleaned up by Manion's squad, but here and there an old man still stared through watery eyes at an opiate dreamworld, reminder of the bad old days when Tongs ruled and narcotics were big business. You could still find it, if you knew where. John knew. And the traffickers knew him. The old bobcats tracked his markings, uncertain yet what kind of beast he was. John slid down the hill, to Kearney, past crated ducks and melons, watching the drifting lights of steamers crossing the darkened bay. This town got through to him like fog on a winter's day. He loved it. Sentiment sharpened the hunger pangs. He turned in to an Italian bakery at the bottom of the hill and bought a pizza. He was cramming it into his mouth as he walked into the Hall of Justice, where he ran up to the press room on the second floor and walked into a smog of cigarettes and stale beer.

'Hiya, John.'

'Hi, Ricki.'

Ken Houlihan of the *Independent* was twirling his revolver.

'Don't do that, Houlihan. You make me nervous.' Ricki Minchelli's voice called languorously from the couch in the corner. He was feeling tired. He'd been up all day.

'Take it easy, Rick. He's just showing off,' John soothed.

'Hell, I am,' Ken sneered. John looked at him, calmly.

'That thing's not loaded,' he said.

'Want me to show you?' Ken cocked his weapon and pointed it at Rick. A stir passed round the crowded press room. He'd got them scared. Then suddenly, Ken lifted the sash window and blasted his heater up the lightwell.

'Stop fooling, Ken. Put that damn shooter away.' John made towards him. Ken grinned, put the gun in his jacket and lay back on his chair, chewing gum.

'Aren't you bored?' he asked. The cops didn't rush in to investigate the gunshot and the tension relaxed. John checked the notices. There was a message from Ernie about the Oriental. Mostly runners just skipped bail and had their attorneys forfeit the ten dollars or so to pay their fines when they were found guilty. So John looked as unimpressed as he oughta. He sat beside Ken.

'Fancy getting off your arse and coming up to take a picture of an Oriental?' he suggested.

76

'What's happening?' Half the press room was on its feet.

'Nothing. Don't get so excited. Just a runner on a charge.'

'And you want a picture? Must be more to it,' Rick said suspiciously. John shrugged.

'My brother-in-law thinks it's news, the punk. You know how it is. Got to keep him sweet.' Rick was satisfied. Ernie was well-known in the press room.

Ken and John walked up the stair to the cell blocks and hollered to Ernie.

'You still holding that Chinese dude?'

'Sure thing,' Ernie called down.

'Do us a favour. Get him, huh?' John asked.

'Can't it wait till after?'

'Got things to do, Ernie.'

'This is highly irregular, John.'

'Sure.' Ken winked and passed John an official courthouse the Oriental. 'You got an envelope on you, Ken?' John asked, as they waited.

'Sure,' Ken winked and passed John an official courthouse envelope.

'Very appropriate.' John slipped the receipt book inside, along with a twenty-dollar note, as Ernie brought out the runner.

'If anybody asks, I know nothing about this, John,' Ernie said.

'Sure. Who's doing the clerking tonight?' John asked casually.

'Jody Durrell.'

'Thought so.'

'Why?'

'Oh, got a message for him from his missus.' John shrugged. 'Seems he left his cheque book behind.'

'Well . . . ' Ernie was always glad to do a favour, up to a point. 'They should be having a tea break down there, soon, so, if you're lucky you'll catch him.' Ken's camera flashed, catching Ernie with the runner.

'Hold on!' John objected. 'You know I can't go in there, Ernie!'

'O.K.' Ernie gave in. 'Give me the message. I'll see it's delivered.' John passed him the envelope. Ernie stuffed it in his belt.

'Don't I get a thank you?' he snapped, as he pushed the prisoner back inside.

'Thank you, Ernie,' John and Ken chorused. Ernie gave two fingers back.

The Chinese got off. It seemed the book of lottery tickets that had been found on his person was actually a receipt book for groceries. It raised a titter in the press room, but that was all.

'You want to make a story out of that?' Ricki sneered. 'My oh my, John, you're determined to keep the *Independent* a real, cosy, small town newspaper, aren't you? Oh well. You can take the boy out of the country but you can't take the country out of the boy.' John smarted under the insult, biding his time. Then, as the dawn light rose over the bay and crept down the lightwell of the Hall of Justice, just as Ricki, along with most of them, was nodding off, John took his chance. Using the butt of his cigarette to light it, he quietly placed a cracker under Rick's chair. It went off with one hell of a bang. Ricki sat bolt upright, screaming,

'Help! Somebody's shot me! Get me to the hospital!' He was pale, and breathing hard, but everybody was laughing at him. He looked right at John and John just grinned back.

'You can take a joke, can't you?'

'If I get a heart attack and die, I'll sue you,' Rick threatened.

'You wouldn't win,' Ken warned. 'John knows more about the law than anybody! He got a law degree from Berkeley.'

'He may know about law, but he knows nothin' about crime.' And Rick'd got the better of the argument.

As they breakfasted together close by the Ferry Building, Ken was still fuming.

'You gotta do something about Ricki.' John tensed his mouth.

'Let him think I'm a country boy. Suits me,' he said.

'Hah! Coming over to Sausalito tomorrow, country boy?' Tomorrow was Sunday.

'No . . . don't think so,' John replied. 'My young relative's going to be up from L.A. I expect she'll want to go on a trail in the redwoods, or something touristy like that.'

'Is she the girl with stars in her eyes?' Ken asked.

'That's the one.'

'I got a lot of film to develop anyway,' Ken shrugged. What

did he care? John paid the bill from his bribe, and they walked together to the ferry. The fog was lifting.

'I'll be in the lobby of the "Frantic" at 6 p.m.,' John told him. Ken nodded and went.

John put in his copy at the newspaper offices on Mission, dropped into Hanno's for his mid-morning Screwdriver, then, finally, went back to his apartment on Pacific, where he crashed. Meanwhile, Eve had arrived in town. The bus drew up in the depot very early. The light was just coming up on the misty bay. She didn't want to face Clara yet, so she dropped her bag in at the luggage check and wandered the streets, looking for a cup of coffee. She liked San Francisco. The place was pleasantly curvy after the angles and squares of Los Angeles. She stood for a while, watching the cable cars and wondered where John was. The fog horns reminded her unpleasantly of her home town, on the mouth of the River Tyne, host of innumerable, invisible ships slipping down its oily waters into the grey seas north-east of England. She turned in to a small café and ordered coffee and comforting muffins, then went straight on to the scraper on Sutter, taking the lift up to the twenty-second floor where the N.B.C. had its studios. Her voice scraped the lines like sandpaper and the producer was complaining so much, she oiled the wheels with a gargle of port. But, acting was like adrenalin and, as always, Jennifer was in top form. Eve perked up as a consequence, and got the cheek to ask, 'Can I have my expenses, cash in hand, this time, please? My agent takes commission otherwise.'

So Eve got through the work, through the day, and went home to Clara's in the evening, money in her pocket.

She was reading an enthusiastic review of the serial in the *Independent*, when Ernie came home, peeved. Dutifully, Eve put the paper aside and pretended interest in his upset.

'It's a lousy job bein' a cop,' he moaned. 'Low pay, long hours, night work . . . now they're talking about putting me on traffic!'

'You deserve better, dear.' Clara pecked him on the cheek.

'You betcha. I'm going to get it too.' Ernie winked at his wife.

'Why?' Eve asked, interested. 'What're you intending to do?'

'Oh, nothing . . .' He and Clara exchanged furtive looks.

'I don't think Eve'd tell, Erne,' Clara whispered. Ernie nodded. 'Well, Eve,' she said aloud, 'it's not that interesting. But, you know, ever since Ernie dropped out of college, he's been tinkering with cars?'

'Yes,' Eve answered. 'He got John into that flying club because of his engines.'

'Well now,' Clara confided. 'We think that with the money left us by Grandma Cora, Ernie and me might start a little business.'

'What?'

'San Francisco's got a lot of hills, hasn't it?' Eve nodded. 'So, there's a few bucks to be made in car brake linings!' Ernie said triumphantly. Eve laughed.

'Good idea!'

'Now, don't tell, will you? Or I know the family'll try and stop us,' Clara warned.

'Cross my heart and hope to die.' Ernie and Clara smiled at each other. They'd shared their little secret with Eve, and they felt good about it. Eve watched them almost enviously. Clara wasn't so shrill or nervous when Ernie was by. They were well-matched.

But Eve felt lonely. Her mind wandered back to John. 'You expecting John here tonight?' she asked.

'No. Not on a Saturday!' Clara smiled knowingly at Eve, who didn't ask for further information. Clara had, with a mixture of shock and admiration, already confided her older brother's reputation as playboy and man of the world.

John was, at that moment, in the bar of the St Francis Hotel, drinking with Ken. The 'Frantic', as it was called, was a place in which to be seen and John was determined to become a well-known character about town, on the principle that, it was notoriety, and not the lousy column that mattered, in getting you to the top. To increase his reputation, they went on up to Broadway and were also seen frequenting the girlie bars, leering with the best of them.

'He's some joker, is John.' Ernie shook his head, smiling lazily, as he warmed his toes at the fire. 'Oh. I forgot to ask. How was your film test, Evie?'

'Oh fine. Fine. Only thing is, they want some stills now.'

'That sounds promising,' Clara enthused.

'I haven't got the money to pay for them.' Eve looked at Clara hopefully.

'Oh dear,' Clara said. She and Ernie exchanged a look. They weren't going to part with a penny of their nest egg. Brake linings would take all.

'Why don't you ask John?' Ernie said slowly. 'They've got some decent photographers on the *Independent*. What's that guy called that John works with such a lot?' Clara looked up from her mending, to think.

'Irish name. Thin. Oh yes. Houlihan. That's it. Houlihan's the name!'

Clara had gone to the cathedral, and Ernie was on Sunday duty, when the bell rang next morning. Eve opened the door onto the smell of whisky and stale cigarettes. John had had a late night and he looked it. He lunged into the flat.

'I guess I need Ernie's shaving equipment, don't I? I also need to borrow some pants, clean vest, oh, and somebody spilt beer on my shoes. Would you mind finding me some of Ernie's gear, sweetie?' Eve said nothing. She took John's shoes into the kitchen and polished them, then she got him the vest and pants from Ernie's closet, and stood uncertainly outside the bathroom door, holding them. She could hear the water running. Was John having a bath? She knocked timidly on the door.

'Come in!' he shouted. 'You can scrub my back!'

Was he kidding? Seconds passed in dilemma, and Eve did nothing.

'I said, get in here and scrub my back, woman!' John yelled.

'I'm not your woman!' Eve objected. The water swirled and gurgled. He was getting out of the bath! For a second, Eve stood listening, then she dropped the shoes, vest and pants at the door and ran for it. She was hiding in the kitchen, when John emerged.

'Where the hell are you?' he shouted.

'I thought you'd like some breakfast!' Eve called out to him. Frantically she started breaking eggs into the pan.

'What do we want with breakfast? I'm taking you to The Blue Willow.' Eve turned to say she didn't like Chinese food and saw him standing, stark naked, in the doorway. She gasped and

81

looked away. 'What's wrong? Never seen a naked man before?' he jeered. She shook her head. 'How old are you?'

'Twenty-two.'

'And you mean to tell me you're still . . . you know what?'

'I'm a virgin, if that's what you mean,' Eve said, blushing.

'Hell!' He walked away, then came back, shouting angrily. 'Well, you sure don't act like one!'

'O.K. So you're not the only one who's good at bluffing,' she cried.

They stared, blinking at one another. Suddenly John took off for the bathroom and started to dress. Eve looked forlornly at the broken eggs, wishing the floor would open up and swallow her. She felt stupid; like Ida's little girl lost. It wasn't fair. He knew the rules of the game. He knew how vulnerable she was. He shouldn't have called her bluff! Or had he? My God, how far was she expected to take this bluffing business? She was just getting scared, when John's clean, bright face peered round the door.

'Sorry I shocked you. Let me make it up to you.'

'Oh. It's O.K. I'm not shocked,' she lied.

'You were.' His face was tense, the shaved skin stretched across the smiling cheeks. She felt nervous. 'Where do you want to go today?'

'Oh, I don't know. Somewhere fun!' Her voice was bright.

'O.K.,' he said breezily. 'After the Blue Willow, we'll go on to Neptune Beach for a few thrills and spills, huh?'

'Yeah.'

It turned out to be a working lunch. All the journalists on the *Independent* were there and there was no chance of the quiet talk Eve had hoped for. Being a lady, she was expected to order first. She asked for chop suey and was given a dirty look by John and the waiter. So in the end Eve let John choose for her. He chose with easy confidence, and openly held hands with her on the table, claiming her. Encouraged, Eve showed off to John's 'family' as he called them, about her radio, and the dancing and everything. But she could tell by the glassy look in their eyes, they'd all heard better.

'Yeah, but she's headed for the big time, George,' John boasted. 'You had a film test for a musical, didn't you, sweetheart?' he asked her.

'Sure,' Eve answered brightly.

'So, when are we going to see those little feet of yours tapping across the silver screen?' The editor, George, had a fatherly aspect. Eve liked him.

'They want some stills of me before they'll do anything,' Eve told him. 'That's the only thing. As a matter of fact, John's sister suggested I go to one of the photographers on your paper. They said his name was Houlihan.'

'He's a darned good photographer,' George nodded. 'He's had exhibitions over at Sausalito. Arty stuff, but good.'

'Come on, George,' John laughed. 'Houlihan takes pictures of birds, wildlife, that sort of thing. He doesn't do society photos!'

'I don't want society photos,' Eve objected.

'You want somebody to make you look good,' John insisted.

'She looks good anyway!' George injected humour into what was fast becoming an argument.

'Sure she does,' John agreed. 'She's beautiful.' He kissed Eve's hand, and they all clapped and cheered, as though he'd scored a goal. Then, appropriately enough, the conversation turned to the ball game. And George smiled benignly, through a bleary bourbon haze, as John and Eve sloped off to Neptune for the rest of the afternoon.

'Now take care of that little girl, John!' He raised a warning finger. John grinned back.

They were crossing the new Golden Gate bridge, when John dropped his hand onto Eve's knee. She tensed. The act had unpleasant associations; like memories of script writers.

'Know what?' he said, 'I think it's time you gave it a go. Sex, I mean. See, if I'm going to marry you, I've got to know what I'm getting.' Eve didn't know whether to laugh or cry.

'What's got into you, John? You've never been like this before.'

'Must be the thought of getting hitched. It's enough to turn any man's brain.' He gave her his wide smile. She laughed uncertainly. He moved his hand.

'Is this a proposal?' she asked.

'I suppose it must be.'

'Are you joking?' She waited timidly for an answer, but John gave none. 'I mean, if you are, I think it's a poor joke,' she went on.

83

'Who said I was joking?' John sneered. 'Marriage is a very serious business.' Eve was perplexed by his expression.

'Well, it's just you're not very romantic,' she explained. John laughed.

'Sorry, sweetie.' He threw a smile at her. She stared at him, wanting to believe, but not daring to.

'Do you love me?' she asked, at last.

'You want me to say it?'

'Yes.'

'O.K. I love you.' His voice was flat.

'You don't sound as if you do,' she complained. Somehow, she expected him to shout at her, but, instead, a boyish smile was playing round his mouth.

'If you really want to know, I'm scared of love,' he said. And then, of course, she wanted to hug him. 'You love me, don't you, Eve?'

'Yes. I think I do,' she replied softly. John looked almost sad. 'Let's make a pact,' Eve went on. 'However much we bluff with the rest of the world, let's never bluff with each other.' He took her hand and kissed it.

Neptune Beach was not overcrowded. It wasn't the fashionable haunt it used to be, and it was late in the season. Eve was feeling a little emotional and shaky, so she ate a lot of candy, which John enjoyed feeding into her. It was nice holding hands with him. They were like all the other young lovers wandering round the fair, daring one another to ride the Red Devil, have a twirl on the 'Merry Mixup', or a scream on the rollercoaster. John watched the Whip for some time. It was a ride in cars, like planes, that swung you round and jerked you up in the air.

'Want a go?' Eve asked.

'No. What I'd really like's a ride on the Big Wheel. I've not done that since I was in my teens!'

'It looks a *very* big wheel,' Eve laughed.

'Not scared, are you?' She shook her head and scampered after him into one of the cars, lying back, as he swung it, impatient for the ride to start. They rose into the sky, car by car, as passengers got in. There was quite a view over the bay, to San Francisco, and quite a breeze too. It was cold. Eve shivered, and John took off his coat to put round her.

'The age of the gentleman is not yet dead,' she smiled. Suddenly he swung the cab. 'Don't!' she yelled, alarmed. The car was open at the sides. He sighed and lay back beside her.

'Lou's sure let that ranch go,' he grumbled.

'Did he have any choice?'

'Maybe not.'

'He said they'd found oil up on Cuba Road somewhere,' Eve observed. Suddenly, John sat up and the cab swung again. Eve went pale, and gripped the sides.

'He never told me that!' he shouted.

'I don't suppose he thought you'd be interested.'

'I own ten per cent of the place!' The wheel went higher, and stopped again. More passengers got on.

'You don't know there *is* oil there,' Eve reminded him. 'Or even if it's worth getting out!'

'Sure,' John agreed. 'Costs money to find out too.' He sat back again and looked at Eve. 'What's the matter with you? You're looking very pale.'

'It's nothing.' She shook her head, nervously.

'Not scared, are you?'

'No. Course not. I went up in your plane, didn't I?'

'That's different. You've got metal all the way round you, in a plane.' The wheel turned again, and they were one car higher. John was chewing at the inside of his cheek. Suddenly he turned to her and asked, 'Clara said anything to you about what she wants to do with her money?'

'Oh. That.'

'It's alright. You can tell me. After all, if we're going to get married . . . ' Eve looked at him uncertainly. 'No secrets between husband and wife, are there?' He smiled a reassuring smile.

'Sure,' she whispered, pulling his coat tighter round her. Then she told him. 'She said she and Ernie want to go into the brake lining business, so he can leave the cops.'

'Hell they do!' John laughed loudly, scaring a gull that was reeling overhead. They revolved higher. They were now one from the top.

'There's something I want to know, Eve,' he said slowly. Eve sensed threat in his voice. She trembled, as he went on, 'I want to know the real story behind that film test of yours.' He looked at her long enough to see the hurt, then looked away again.

Eve wanted to cry. But he was waiting for her to tell him. She spoke quietly. 'How did you know?'

John shrugged. 'Tell me,' he insisted.

'It was a let-down. I guess all Mr Zubermann wanted was to get me into bed with him. When I wouldn't play ball, he just palmed me off with a dud test . . . I don't think he was even there.' The tears were dropping from Eve's nose. 'I should think my piece of film's in the waste basket by now.'

John snorted in derision. 'Why didn't you sleep with him?' he asked.

'What?'

'You heard.'

'You wouldn't like me to do that! Would you?' Eve was horrified.

John's voice was hard as nails, as he told her, 'Eve, if I'm going to be a great success, and you're going to be my wife, you've got to be a success too.' Eve was silent. The wheel revolved. They were at the top. John swung the car again.

'Please, don't.'

'Why? What's wrong?'

'I'm scared of heights.'

'Hell!' He laughed. 'A scaredy cat's no use to me, sweetheart. You'd weigh me down.' He smiled and began swinging the car again. 'Poor Evie. You're just an ordinary little girl, aren't you? Very sweet, but, just not ruthless enough. You'll never be a star. Nor my wife.' They swung so she could see the ground. Eve closed her eyes, trying not to scream, gripping the sides of the car. The wheel revolved. They went over the top and down the other side, then round and round and round.

Eve arrived back at the flat in a state of shock. She went straight to bed. And next morning, she didn't want to wake up. By lunch time, Clara was getting worried. Doctors cost, but she called one anyway. The doc looked at Eve's eyeballs, sounded her lungs, prodded and poked.

'Know what I think?' he said at last. 'I think this little lady just don't *want* to wake up.' Clara didn't understand.

'Why?' she asked.

'She ain't happy.'

After the doctor had gone, Clara sat on Eve's bed, staring at her.

'Eve, honey,' she said, 'I don't know if you can hear me, and I don't know what's wrong, but, whatever it is, I wish you'd just tell me, so I can help you work it out.' Eve's eyelids moved, very, very slightly. 'I didn't know you were unhappy, dear. In fact, you always struck me as the happy-go-lucky sort.' Tears squeezed through the closed eyelids. Eve was evidently in great distress. With painful slowness, one hand reached out. Clara grasped it. What could be the matter? she thought. Maybe John could cast some light on the situation.

'Tell you what, Eve,' she said, 'I'll get John to call, shall I?' But Eve started shaking.

'No! Please, no!' she breathed. Poor little girl, Clara thought. Why didn't she think of it? Eve'd fallen in love with John! Tears were draining down the sides of Eve's face, into her hair. Clara was shocked. How could John hurt her so? Even if he didn't like the girl, he might at least let her down lightly.

Late that night, at Clara's request, John came round. Eve heard them, murmuring low, through her door. Then suddenly, Clara spoke up, her voice shrill. 'What's wrong with brake linings? Everybody needs them. I just don't see how we can lose out, John.' There was a pause, and John's voice, very low, answering her. Then, she came back at him again, 'No! Oil's far too risky. Anyway, if Grandma Cora'd wanted the money kept in the ranch, she'd have put it into the place herself. It just ain't none of your business what Ernie and me do with the money we was left!'

'And Eve and me "ain't none of *your* business", Sister!'

'She *is* my business,' Clara contradicted him. 'I can't stand by and see you abusing her, John.' Then, John made sweet-talking noises and Clara calmed down. Then, after a while, Eve's door opened and John came in.

'Hi,' he said. 'Hear you've not been too well.' He sat by her, on the bed. There was no response from Eve. 'Aren't you even talking to me now?' he asked. No response. 'Was I *that* bad?' He sighed. 'Well, I guess, maybe I was at that. Clara tells me you're sweet on me.' No response. 'But, see, I told you, Evie, I'm scared of love and all that goes with it; marriage, kids, divorce . . .' He laughed ironically.

87

At last, Eve spoke. 'Doesn't have to end that way.'

'So you *can* talk?' No response. 'See, this love game's always been kind of like a red rag to a bull where I'm concerned. I've always steered clear of any real kind of involvement. But then you come along and . . . ' He sighed and looked at her, shaking his head. 'You're a nice kid. I like you. Hey, let's cut the crap. I guess I'm in a fair way to falling in love with you myself.' No response. 'Well, it scares the hell out of me. And, I suppose, that's why I end up behaving like a heel!' Eve stared at him blankly. Suddenly John leant forward and ruffled her hair. 'Look, just to prove I'm not so bad, I looked up a photographer in L.A. for you. He does all the starlets. Works for R.K.O. most of the time. Not cheap but . . . ' John dug a card out of his pocket, along with a few dollar bills. ' . . . Maybe this'll help. Good luck, sweetheart. Be seeing you.' He went.

Hot tears scalded Eve's cheeks. She'd had the brush-off.

After a while, Clara came in. She stood for some time surveying the patient. At last, she sighed and spoke. 'I suppose you just couldn't refuse John anything, could you? It's my own fault. I should've known better than to trust you with our little secret about the brake linings. I know that to us you feel like one of the family, but . . . Try not to feel too badly, dear. I forgive you. And I'm sure Ernie will too, when he knows the circumstances.' Clara smiled benignly. Eve closed her eyes. 'After all, all's fair in love and war . . . '

'I'm sorry.' Eve was crying again. Like a true Christian, Clara sat right by her, and took her by the hand.

'At least John found you a good photographer, didn't he? And that shows he cares some. He's very kind, you know. He might not be able to keep a secret; I just know he's going to tell the whole family about our brake linings, but he is kind. He'd do anything for you. You know, honey, I think he's actually very fond of you, but you've got to give him time. You see, men like to feel they're the big shots, while deep down, they're just little boys and need their mommas to change their diapers for them. John's more sensitive than most too, and I think it makes it harder for him. He's real scared of his emotional side. Don't tell him I said so, though.' Eve was adrift in a sea of guilt. She was drowning in it. Clara braced herself for the big effort to push her under. 'Do you know, honey, I'd be really glad if you two were to settle down and get married one of these days. Then I'd feel John was in good hands at last. You may not be a Catholic but . . . ' She sighed, amazed at her own capacity for Christian forgiveness. 'I think John needs a good woman to show him he needn't be scared of the gentler side of himself. Show him he can still be a man and love God.' She turned her saintly smile on Eve, who by now was ready to add to the Golden Gate Bridge suicide statistics. 'What you're going through, Eve, is actually a blessing. You'll find, dear, your suffering will bring you nearer to God.' That was it. A spark of anger saved Eve's life.

'Clara, save your sermons for the soup kitchen! I'm sure the unemployed need them more than I do!'

'Well! Really!'

To hell with John Ridley. To hell with Clara, to hell with brake linings and to hell with the Pope! Eve was going back to L.A., and she was going to be a star! If it killed her!

Back in Hollywood, Eve, having missed her spot at Leno's, had lost her job. Two fingers up, Roly told her he'd found himself a new partner. It was her own fault. She'd let him down. She gave him John's money, to pay back his loan, said goodbye, and got herself another waitressing job. It would take a while to save for the photographic session and, till then, she didn't care to show her face at Ida's. But she got back on the casting treadmill, visiting the offices in town, doing the long trek round the studio circuit, showing her face to the powerful, along with all the other familiar, desperate faces. At least Eve had her part in the radio serial to keep her going. Some girls had nothing at all. Thanksgiving came. As they all sat waiting outside some big office, hoping to be seen, a large plate of turkey sandwiches was brought in for the producer. One of the girls, she was called Jenna Spencer, looked up, her eye caught by the food. Suddenly she shot out of her seat and grabbed one of the sandwiches. She ate it, like she was starved. Then she was sick, all over the floor. The secretary sent for a cleaner. The girl, pale and faint, was escorted out of the building. Some time later, hearing of the incident, the producer ordered another plate of sandwiches for the waiting girls. It was a rare and welcome treat.

That afternoon, the atmosphere in the office was like a party. But it was too late for Jenna.

Soon, it was Christmas. Eve couldn't afford to visit the Lawe Top. But she didn't want to be in San Francisco either, so she stayed in Pasadena. There were two other girls in her digs, but competition killed friendship and Eve's thoughts strayed to home, her mother, and to Lou. She sent her mother a Christmas card, and wrote Lou a note.

> Dear Lou,
> Sorry to be so long writing back. It was good to hear from you. But I honestly don't think you should put yourself down so much, or, think so much about me! I'm not that great. It's kind of lonely here. I miss you all. Especially Jimmy. Haven't landed the big part yet, but I expect I will, any day. Then you can all visit with me, in my big house in Beverly Hills, with its swimming pool and deep freeze. Wish them all Happy Christmas from me.
>
> Love, Evie.
>
> P.S. John and I have fallen out.

Lou read Eve's letter over and over. She was lonely. She'd fallen out with John. She was going to be a star and have a swimming pool. It was confusing. What was he to make of it? Ella and Jimmy were silent, staring out of the van windows at the snow-spattered plains. He was driving Ella up to Arizona to see her folks. The child had come along for the ride.

'What's that?' Jim was pointing at Shiprock.

'It's called Eagle Rock,' Ella said. Jim was silent for a while, staring at the huge black rocks. They towered over the plains, like huge wings poised in flight. You could see them for miles around.

'It's a very big eagle. I think God must have ridden on it once,' he observed. Lou looked out at it. 'Are there any more things like that in Arizona, Ella?'

'Yes. Many,' she told him. 'Elephant's Feet, Monument Valley, Rainbow Rock. Many more.' Jim was enthusiastic.

'I think Giant Gods had a big battle here a long time ago,' he said. 'And I want to know which one of them rode on the eagle.

After all, I'm an eagle now!' Ella blushed. Lou said nothing, but pulled up on the side of the road to get a better view of the huge black monolith. How the hell *had* it got there? 'Can I stay with Ella on the reservation, Pa?' Jim asked, wistfully. 'For the Christmas holidays?'

'No, Jimmy,' Ella said quickly. 'Not just now.'

The snow was falling like a gentle mist and the rock seemed to rise out of it, to float over the flattened land. Lou wondered how come he'd taken no notice of the darned thing before. It sure cut you and your problems down to size. That letter from Evie . . . he didn't know what to make of it. O.K. Only thing to do was let it ride. Lou sent her a card, wishing her a Happy Christmas.

Eve spent the holiday doing classes with Danny, and waitressing with an actress, who went by the name of Belinda Malone. Eve thought she and Bel were great pals. Well, she filled a gap, anyway. Then, one day, in early spring, Bel didn't turn up for work. She'd got a part in a Zubermann film and had gone down to Tucson to shoot it. Bitterly, Eve pondered how Bel had landed the part. Had she slept with Zubermann? Was John right? Was it really the only way ahead? 'You've got to take life by the tail!' he'd said. She was reminded of Jo's story of the rattlesnakes. According to him, Bill Farley had just grabbed this snake, by its tail, and cut its rattle right off, walking away with his souvenir, *and* his life. Well, Eve was going to be a star 'if it killed her'. So, taking life by the tail, she went out, hired a dress and showed at Leno's. The doorman knew her and let her in. The barman also knew her and slipped her a drink, then another, and another. She looked round the club, a starling pretending to be a vulture.

The lights faded. Roly and his new partner paraded, aware of her presence in the darkness. Disgusted, Eve looked away and caught the eye of a middle-aged man at the other end of the bar. He'd been eyeing her for some time. Her heart beat faster. Then, mistaking her chance look for an invitation, he came up to say hallo. Flushed with drink, Eve chatted away. But, try as she might, she couldn't get him to say who he was. After a while, he asked her if she'd like to go 'partying' with him. Eve smiled brightly, so, he said he'd see her outside and went. Shaking at her own temerity, Eve asked the barman who her pick-up was. The barman shrugged and said he might be a clapperboy for all he

knew; he'd never seen him before. A clapperboy! The words
struck Eve's consciousness like lightning. Tears of joy fell down
her face. The barman suggested she'd had enough and should go
home. Eve agreed. She had grabbed life by the tail alright and
been glad to drop it again. Well, it might have got away from her,
but she'd got away with more than her life! Hitching back to
Pasadena, Eve discovered how refreshing and lovely was the
balmy air of L.A. And, suddenly, out of the joy burst an over-
powering urge to go back to New Mexico. Why, she couldn't
tell. But the photographs could wait. She was going to buy a
train ticket.

CHAPTER FIVE

'How's stardom?' The old man jabbed the end of his pipe at Eve.

'Oh, I'm not a star,' she said. 'Don't think I ever will be either.'

Louis looked up sharply. He hoped Jo would refrain from rubbing salt in what was plain to see were open wounds. But he might as well hope for a leopard to change its spots.

'Oh? What you going to be, if you're not going to be a star?' Jo persisted. Eve's eyes were down, staring at her empty plate.

'I don't know. And that's the truth,' she murmured.

'Needs feeding up, I know that.' June dolloped some beans on the plate, followed by a hillside of hash. 'Lost some of her nice curves, hasn't she, Lou?' Lou said nothing. He just sat and watched, chewing the cud. Something had happened to Eve. She was a defenceless animal come asking for help. But what kind of help did she want? His kind? Hell! He shifted in his seat, uncomfortably aware of stirring embers and feeling like he was about to make a prize fool of himself.

'She looks tired,' Ella said. 'Been working too hard.'

'Oh?' Jo caught on quick. 'Come for a rest cure have you? Well, there's hospitals aplenty in Albuquerque for that sort of a thing. This ain't no rest home here. You've got to work if you want to stay here.'

'Jo!' June clipped her brother lightly round the ear.

93

'I ain't fooling! With Louis here working on the new airport, we're running short on labour.'

'Least it's got us a new station wagon, Pa.' Louis tried to pacify his father.

'W.P.A. charity. Why the hell this ranch can't be turned into a going concern is beyond me!' Jo banged his fist on the table.

'You was complaining we weren't getting any charity before, Pa! Hell, you're just looking for something to gripe about!'

'Lou's right!' June turned on Jo. 'I don't blame him for getting short with you! You're a mean old cuss!'

'Mean? Me? It's not me that's mean. It's this family!' Jo complained. 'Nobody thinks of ploughing back any money into this ranch, do they? Letting it go to rack and ruin. From the moment Lou here took over this ranch . . . '

'It ain't Louis' fault if Clara's spending her money on brake linings!' June snapped.

'What's she want with brake linings?' the old man sneered. 'She ain't even got a car!'

'I don't mind working.' They all turned to look at Eve. It was as though one of the chairs had taken it into its head to talk. 'Really,' she said. 'I'd like to work.'

Then they looked at one another. Had she gone crazy?

'What could *you* do?' Jimmy asked. It was the first thing he'd said to her.

Cooking was June's province. The garden was Ella's and, of course, mucking out and checking fences were no job for a woman. But Eve could drive, so she agreed to take Jimmy to school in the mornings and fetch him back at night. Jim treated his new lift with caution.

'Are you sure you can drive?' he asked.

'Watch me,' Eve told him. He watched, and Eve felt like she was taking some kind of test, as she drove carefully along to school.

'Are you still doing that radio serial?' Jim said thoughtfully, eyes glued to the road ahead.

'Yeah,' she answered.

'Pa listens in most times, hoping to hear you.' Eve's heart skipped a beat. But she said nothing. Then Jim went on, 'Are you going to marry John?'

'Whatever gave you that idea?' Eve snapped irritably.

'June thinks you will.'

'I don't think so, Jimmy.'

'Oh.' Eve shot him a look. He was crestfallen.

'You sound disappointed,' she told him.

'Does that mean you're going to marry my Dad?' So that was it. If she married John, Lou would be safe from her. It must be nice to be wanted, Eve thought ruefully.

'Do I have to marry anybody?' She spoke brightly, to cover the hurt.

'I don't know.' Jim sighed. 'Why've you come?'

'I needed to get away. Think things out, Jim. Know what I mean?' Her voice was confiding.

'Yeah,' Jim responded. 'I usually go in the corn shed for that. Why're you crying?' Eve shrugged. She dropped Jim off at school and watched the thoughtful little boy drag his steps to the door, then bound inside, shaking off the troubles of the world at a stroke. Apparently, he looked on Eve's coming as a danger, but part of the natural, seasonal course of events, like drought or flood or sunstroke. Inside, he was already taking precautions against her.

Why had she come? Thinking was the last thing she wanted. It was something else. She didn't know what. But whatever it was, it was getting nearer. She paused a while outside the school, feeling the warm spring sunshine and the play of the light breeze through the open window of the van. Her heart hung by a thread, spun out on the silence of the mesa top, buoyed up on unseen currents of air. She was poised, ready to go, like a bird on its first flight. She started the engine, slipped into gear and drove off slowly, feeling the drift of her heart down to the plain, where it rested on the rose-gold earth. Brushed with spring flowers, it held some sort of promise. What, she didn't know. But she held onto that as she drove back, uncertain, to Ridley land.

At the ranch, Lou watched for Eve's return. What the hell! Suppose he *did* make a fool of himself? So what? To him, Eve was the bird of paradise, alighted on his dull and barren ranch. What if John *had* made a play for her, *and* won? He had shot her down afterwards, and she'd come to Lou for help! Would he

95

deny her? No! So, Eve rose in flames from the ashes of his old desire. And here she was, her dancer's body slipping out of the station wagon, into the yard, to stand, trembling like a fledgling fallen, wounded, from its nest. At that moment Lou would have died for Eve and been satisfied only to have held her for a moment, a branch on which she might perch and rest. But she hovered, unsure. And, Lou, knowing his clumsiness, unwilling to alarm her, let her go.

The shed was quiet. Eve slipped the latch and looked in. Ella was there, sorting the corn seed for planting. Eve turned away.

'No. Don't go. Come in,' Ella called. Eve stood, uncertain, in the doorway, but Ella insisted, 'Take off your shoes and come in.' Eve did so, cautiously sitting by the Hopi, on the earth. Ella looked at her for a long time, her eyes peeling off layer after layer, leaving Eve exposed, remembering her mother, years before, tearing strips off her before she left for the States. ' "Do you know what sophisticated means? It means artificial. False. Like you. Just a shell and nothing inside it but a shivering jelly. And you think you'd do well in Hollywood, do you?" ' Then, Ella's hand reached out.

'What's happened to you?' she asked. Eve shrugged, unable to speak. 'Someone's hurt you, haven't they?' Eve nodded. 'But the hurt's only exposed an old wound. My godmother, Myna, told me once that old wounds have to be exposed before they can heal. Otherwise they fester, and make poisons that silently seep into you, to hurt others and destroy you.' Eve fluttered weakly.

'I don't know what you're talking about.'

'I don't mean to interfere . . . ' Sadly, Ella turned back to the corn, and immediately, Eve was sorry.

'It's just . . . I don't understand. Please help me. Don't shut me out.' Ella looked back.

'How can I help you?'

Eve was silent, her thoughts running in confused, aimless currents. After a while, she shook her head. 'I don't know,' she said. 'You can't trust anybody, can you? Not really.' Ella was silent. 'Everybody lets you down.'

'This is the wound talking.'

'How old are you, Ella?' Eve asked.

96

'Twenty-three.' She smiled, seeing Eve's surprise. 'Hopis are born old,' she told her.

'You love Jimmy, don't you?' Eve asked. Ella nodded. 'And Louis?'

'You know I do,' Ella said quietly. Suddenly Eve made up her mind, and spoke out firmly,

'I think, for everybody's sake, you'd better marry him. I'd only make a mess of it. You see if I married Louis, it would just be . . . I don't know . . . ' Eve's strength was fading.

'Running away,' Ella filled in for her.

'Yes. I seem to do nothing but run away and I don't even know what from.' Ella took her in her arms. Eve started crying. 'So, it wouldn't be fair if I married Louis, would it?' she sobbed.

'He loves you,' Ella comforted.

'Does he?'

'Yes.' Ella sighed. 'He loves me too. But in a different way.' Eve closed her eyes. She could feel the sunshine filtering through the window onto her back. Her heart hung by a thread. She opened her eyes onto the earthy face of the Hopi woman and knew what she had to do.

'Take Louis,' she said. 'I'll give him up for you.' She knew at once she'd done the right thing. The earthy face cracked into a smile, brilliant in the rose-gold sunlight.

'Thank you, Eve. I'll always love you like a sister. I promise it. You're a good woman. I'll beg God to watch over you.' Crouching on the earth of the corn shed, Eve and Ella hugged one another. It was as though Eve was setting out on a long and lonely exile. 'You'll find the right man one day. I know you will.'

Eve wiped her eyes, biting back the tears. 'I don't think I could trust a man enough to love him!' she said.

Eve and Lou were watching Bill Farley break in Jimmy's foal. It'd grown to a fair size by now, and Jim was eager to ride it, bareback, if possible!

'That kid's got Indians on the brain,' Lou said, shaking his head. 'Maybe Pa's right. Ella's not the best person to be bringing him up.' He cleared his throat. 'It's high time I married again, Eve.'

'Good idea, Lou,' she said.

'What?'

'I think you should marry her.'

'Who?' Lou asked warily.

'Why, Ella, of course. Who else?' Eve laughed. Lou reeled. Eve was staring right ahead of her at the bucking pony.

'Excuse me,' he said. Lou turned away abruptly. He went into the yard and stuck his head under the pump. Then he shook his brain free of crazy ideas, before walking back to Eve's side. She smiled at him, sympathetically.

'Feeling the heat already?' she asked.

Lou shrugged, then, casual as he could make it, he checked up. 'So, you think I should marry Ella, do you?'

'Sure,' Eve agreed. 'I think you two'd get along just fine. You've got a bit of the poet in you, Louis. Know that? And Ella, well, she's . . . she's poetry. I think you're well matched.'

'Ella's poetry?' Lou stuttered, amazed.

'Yes. Compared with me she is, anyway. I'm just an ordinary backyard girl with ideas above her station. Ella's . . . extra-ordinary. I think you two should have kids together.'

'Hell.' Lou shook his head. But Eve hadn't finished yet.

'Jim needs brothers and sisters, Lou,' she told him. 'I've seen him with other kids. He just blossoms. You know, I've got a brother at home in England; he's called Os. Well, my Mam says he's my brother anyway. But, we weren't brought up together and, I don't know, Lou, but you feel to me much more like a brother than he does!'

Couldn't've made it much clearer, could she? Why that little girl needed mothering more than anything and it was plain as the nose on your face Ella was the best person to do it. The two of them seemed to be getting on just fine, working in the garden together. He couldn't help comparing them as they went about the ranch, linking arms. Eve, slim, and graceful, you had to give her that, but not womanly, not like Ella. Poetry? Ella? Louis looked again. The deep Indian eyes watched, and said little. What was she thinking? It hadn't occurred to Lou before. But now . . . Ella's eyes seemed to have magnets in them. They drew him. And somehow, the more he looked the prettier she got. 'Bloomed' was what you'd call it . . . if you were a poet . . .

Eve watched the drama, indulgently filling the gaps in the romance with fantasy; finding a role for herself . . .

'The tanned face held the mystery of ancient times, the poetry of ancient religions, the glamour of exotic climes, and the white man was powerless under the Indian's spell. What did poor, plain Eve Lawson have to offer? Nothing but her hopes and her dreams, dreams which had been dashed by fate, leaving her with nothing . . . ' Eve decided she didn't like the role, after all. Hell, she thought, better take Jim to see *Wizard of Oz* and get a good dose of somebody else's fantasy.

Eve learned a great deal from the grand 'Kimo' cinema. Hitler had invaded Czechoslovakia, for a start. But, more importantly, according to Dorothy's Aunt Em, you could make anything come true, if you wished for it hard enough. Were the ruby slippers an essential part of the deal? Eve wondered. She came out of the Technicolor world to be dazed by the black and white drabness of Albuquerque, to find Louis waiting for them in the new station wagon, full of news.

'The witch was horrible!' Jimmy told him, wide-eyed.

'Oh yeah?' Lou let in the clutch and drove off. 'We had a visit from General Arnold at the airport, today.'

'Who's he?' Eve asked.

'Something to do with the National Preparedness Program.'

'She had these nasty flying monkeys too!' Jimmy enthused.

'Oh yeah?' Lou replied absently. 'Rumour has it he's goin' to start some air cadet training facilities for the army at the new airfield.'

'What's the nation preparing for?' Eve asked.

'And she had a crystal ball in which she could see everything that was happening everywhere!' Jimmy went on.

'How the hell should I know?' Lou only heard Evie. 'But I do know we're sending a lot of planes over to Great Britain, honey.'

'There's not going to be a war,' Eve said flatly. 'Auntie Maisie, back home, well, she's got "powers", you know, she goes to séances and that sort of thing, well she says all the mediums are absolutely certain there's not going to be any war.'

'Wouldn't you like to live over the rainbow, Eve?' Jimmy asked dreamily. John and Eve looked first at Jim, then at each other. Eve laughed.

'Guess I would, Jim.' The child hugged her, smiling up at her like a long lost friend.

Eve floated back to L.A. still in a daze, no idea where she was headed. She called in on Ida, who was glad to see her, being as business was generally bad.

'No matter if you've not got your pictures,' Ida said. 'Your pal Danny's been on to me. He says I could get you a spot at the Hollywood Bowl.'

'Do you think you could?' Eve clutched at the straw.

'I could try.' Ida warned, 'Don't get too hopeful, though. You've not got there, yet.'

'Ida . . . please, don't! I'm feeling sort of vulnerable,' Eve pleaded.

'Why? What happened? No, don't tell me. There's got to be a man in it somewhere.' Eve nodded sheepishly. 'You should be ashamed of yourself at your age. Haven't you got men out of your system yet?' Ida scolded.

'Ida, I'm still a virgin,' Eve whispered.

'What?!' Ida cried. 'Hell, no wonder you've got your head in the clouds. Better find a man right away and get it out of your system. See, honey, either you put your energy into sex or you put it into your career. Can't do both. Look at Ruby Keeler! And she and Al Jolson are headed for divorce now, so I hear. She should have stuck to her tap shoes. And so should you!'

Eve and Danny worked hours every day, getting a number together. It restored Eve's joie de vivre. Also, she still had to dash up to 'Frisco for her radio part from time to time. Jennifer's younger brother, James, back home in England, had been conscripted, and she was very worried. So was half of America. No one believed there was actually going to be a war in Europe, but it made a good storyline, full of real life drama. And what of real life? John spent half his time up in the High Californian Desert at a flying club, and the other half working on the paper with Houlihan. Eve never saw him. It was just as well. She had a feeling that going to bed with him wouldn't get anything out of her system. It would just make things worse. No. She didn't want John. But what did she want? 'You can make anything come true if you wish for it hard enough.' 'Close your eyes and tap your heels together . . . ' What did Eve want? She stared across San Francisco Bay to Treasure Island. She could see ships, like ghosts sailing through the mist. What did she want? She wanted to be a star. She wanted to be the best dancer in the world. She wanted someone to love her. The fog horns had started up. Eve sighed. Reminder of home. The fog horns were the one thing she hated about San Francisco. Eve closed her eyes, crossed her fingers and wished . . .

'I wish the Hollywood Bowl would give me a break.' Not a husband. No. A career. And now! You had only to look at Ernie in his resignation at the beginning of the year, he could be making his fortune with brake linings, by now, with all the tourists come for the big Exposition on the Island, hiring cars. Yes, Ernie was a great advertisement for how not to make it. Eve smiled, and went back to the studio. She felt better now she knew where she was headed.

But a strange feeling turned her stomach as the lift ascended to the top of the building, where, to her surprise, the publicity machine awaited her.

'Honey, did you know your country's at war?'

'What?' Eve gasped.

'Really. It is. Happened a few hours back. Now this is a great opportunity to publicize the show, dear. So I hope you're not going to let us down.'

'No. Of course I won't let you down.' Eve was a real professional. All the journalists agreed:

' . . . Eve Lawson spoke with the nostalgic longing of the expatriate. Her voice wavered with grief over the plight of her homeland, now in dire need. "Of course my desire is to go home and help out in whatever menial task I'm fitted for, but I know in my heart that Jennifer is an ambassador for my country. Through her I can move the people of the United States to an understanding of what we are going through in England, and how much we are going to need the aid of this great country. Yes, whatever my feelings, I know my job is here." The star was on the edge of tears as she spoke of her mother, and of her brother who would soon hear the call of duty.'

'Crap,' said Aunt June, as she cleaned out the range. 'Put that darned wireless off!' Louis obliged. 'Find yourself something to do!'

'Here, Dad. Play snakes and ladders with me. It'll help pass the time.' Louis sat by his son at the table, and let him lay out the board. The truth was, he was missing Ella more than he'd expected. She didn't ever have much to say for herself, but she was a presence about the place, and a presence he liked. Darned Indian ceremonials! Couldn't they manage without her, but she had to go back up there again? June had cleared the ash from the stove and was gathering it into a pail.

'Do you wish you could have gone with her, Dad? I do.'

'Can't do that, son. Got to be an Indian for that. Close guarded secrets these ceremonies are,' Lou said protectively.

But Jim had it all worked out. 'If you married her, Dad,' he said, I'd be her son. And that would make me an Indian, wouldn't it?'

June gasped and dropped the pail, scattering the ash. 'What's that boy say?' she squawked.

'Didn't say anything, Aunt June,' Lou replied as calmly as he could. June pursed her lips, swept up the ash and took it out into the road. It'd plug a few holes, anyhow. Lou shook the dice and moved his counter up the ladder. June wasn't the only problem. There was Lou himself. How the hell was he going to say anything to Ella? He knew her far too well to find changing the status quo an easy task. It was a frustrating stalemate, which Jimmy also pondered, anxiously wondering how on earth he was ever going to get Ella and his Pa together.

But, in Northern Arizona, deeper forces were at work. Wuwuchim was in progress in the Hopi heartland at Oraibi. On the ninth day, the Two Horn Chief, sustained by fasting and prayer, had looked up at the sky and said, 'If I am in tune with the spirit in the heart, clouds will gather on my head, covering the secret rituals of the night.' Then he had descended through the opening in the Kiva roof, down the ladder into the huge round subterranean temple, where the priests were waiting. As the sun fell in the sky, deep rose rays were caught like fire in the gathering clouds and the night progressed, as forecast, under-cover. Silence, deep and powerful as gravity, held the three mesas, as the cycle of day and night continued to the sixteenth day. Then, when Father Sun was at the high point in the sky, Ella climbed to the rooftop of Myna's house, to watch. Under a sky blue as the turquoise, the Wuchim dancers emerged, tuning their voices to the vibration of Mother Earth. Ella felt the resonance of the deep, powerful sound, that stirred the clay beneath their feet and sang from the walls of the drab adobe houses, as the dancers danced the pattern of the swastika, claiming Earth for the Creator. The Hero Twins, at the axes of the world, watched, were pleased to continue the earth's rotation, and, as the cycle of the day turned to sundown, the Wuchim descended once more into the silent Kiva.

Ella rested in the house. She had surrendered her desire and told the Clan Elder, Chu'ovi, about Louis and Jimmy, and now she would wait for him to receive her answer out of the silence. For he was old and wise, and he knew Ella's heart. Time passed, hours, moments in an eternity of peace. Then, as the highest star in Orion's belt hung over the Kiva opening, to shine on the fire hole of the Kiva Floor, the Fire Ceremony began. And Chu'ovi, Snake Elder, went deep that night, pondering the significance of Ella's petition. Warring factions within the tribes had surely affected the cosmic rhythms, triggering war in the outer world. Harmony must be restored within the clans and between the Indian and the white man too. But harmony was God's blessing. How to merit it? Perhaps Ella had a part to play. So, she wanted to marry a white man? Even in his deepest thought, when the energy of Earth flowed through him, Chu'ovi had never known what was meant, in the old legends, by the door on the roof of the head. So he had never claimed God spoke through him. But he was honest and humble. He tried to consider Ella's request from all sides. No, he decided, he could not risk her unimpeded marriage to Lou Ridley. The other members, and the other clans, would object. He would have to set a test.

As dawn pierced the darkness, Ella stood outside the Kiva, listening to the swelling song beneath her feet. All were now preparing for the public dance. Women, children, tourists and Navajos drawn by the spectacle were crowding in windows, on rooftops and by the roads. The sun had risen high, and the ice had melted on the little pond. Then they heard them; drums, rattling

103

anklets, the soft thudding of feet on the earth, soaring voices. Eve
was a dancer, she thought. Ella desired for herself, but she
desired for Eve too. She closed her eyes. The steady rhythm of
the drum tuned her heart to the pulse of life. And when she
opened them again, her eyes fell on the men, brilliant with paint
and feather, as they slowly danced into the dusty street.

'You can make anything come true if you wish for it hard
enough.' Eve's mother, back home in England, understood that
the Hollywood Bowl was Eve's big chance, and encouraged her
to stay. No point coming home anyway. In England, everyone
had been issued with identity cards, ration books, and shelters,
but nothing had happened. It was a phoney war. Let Eve stay
where she was. Then the phone call came. Eve felt a tremor,
even before it happened. Something, somewhere had moved
mountains. The Hollywood Bowl had finally set Eve a date.

On the day of the audition, Danny got a friend of his in to play
sax. The number began low keyed, with Dan on the piano, and
Eve tapping a lazy sort of solo. Then the sax came in, taking over
the melody, and Dan got up to partner her, his feet forming the
percussion, hers the counter melody, flying between the rhythm
and the soaring tune. It was different. It had heart. It even had
soul. And when they got going, Eve no longer cared what they
thought about her. She just threw herself into the dance, surrendering to the pure joy of the music. Then, exhausted but ex-
hilarated, Eve and Danny stopped, panting, at the centre of the
empty stage. Slowly out of the silence, out of the vastness of the
Hollywood Bowl, they heard the gentle clapping of many hands.
It rose up to the sky and fell like rain on their heads. They had
done it. They had pleased the gods of the theatre, and would be
blessed.

CHAPTER SIX

John strained to see out of the window, through the falling snow of North Dakota. Somewhere down there was the Canadian border. It was marked by a road. But you couldn't hope to see it under its white camouflage. As the B-17 droned on through the silent snowfall, John's mind wandered to the package under the seat. It was Ken who'd organized the deal. They'd both got drunk one night, after being thrown out of the 'Frantic' for gate-crashing. They hadn't paid to go on the dance floor and were mixing with the hoi polloi. The floor walker didn't like it. It had been a humiliating experience and both, drunk as coots, had sworn that one day they'd own this darned town and everybody in it! Then they'd left Hanno's and gone on to Chinatown, where they'd joined in a game of mah-jong, back of Low's shop. They'd lost. Ken'd got angry and pulled out his gun. But Low was pretty cool about it.

He'd just smiled. 'So, you two daredevils want to make money, huh?' Ken's weapon dropped. Low looked at John. 'I been watching you. You want in on the action, huh?' John shrugged. He was pretending he couldn't care less, but his heart was pounding.

'What you got to offer?' he drawled, trying to sound casual.

'Come on up. We'll talk.' They followed Low upstairs, into a

105

sort of office. It was very neat and bare. He poured a couple of bourbons, and watched the boys drink. He didn't drink himself.

'O.K. So spill,' Ken said. He sounded like a gangster.

'I got some merchandise needs getting out of U.S.A. Bound for Germany,' Low said. John frowned. 'Merchandise' covered a lot of things.

'Not guns?' he asked.

'No.' Low shook his head. 'Opium. Very simple. Big shipment came in from Colombia the other day. Now problem is how to get it on its way. If you can help, you'll be well paid.'

Ken shook his head. 'If we can help, we'll want in on the deal,' he told him. There was a long silence.

'I talk to other members of syndicate and let you know,' Low conceded. 'Meanwhile, you better think how to get the substance through U.S. Customs.' And that was how John ended up flying bombers for Lockheed, up to the Canadian border.

Then he saw them, lined up on the ground below, the three or four ships that had already landed. And there were the Canadians on the other side, waiting with their horses and pulleys. John stuck a pink rosette on his window, as signal to his German contact on the other side, and started his descent. He coasted through the snow, bumping on the uneven surface, and came to a stop at the end of the line. Then, he jumped down and started walking away from the plane. A covered truck was waiting in the trees. He went towards it, taking one last look back towards the border. The horses were being led across, the pulleys hitched to the aircraft, and soon the B-17s were being dragged across the border into Canada. The planes were on their way to England, and the package was on its way to Germany. It was a neat arrangement. Not only did Roosevelt circumvent the U.S. Neutrality Act, sending bombers to Britain in spite of Congress, but Mr Low had found his way round U.S. Customs. John tipped his hat in deference to the generosity of the U.S. President.

Eve was thrilled when she heard what John was doing. She didn't know about the drugs, of course. All she knew was, that at least one of her American cousins was helping the war effort back home. Her own impetuous enthusiasm to be a British propagandist had been dampened by attacks from the anti-war lobby. It was a surprise to her to discover that not all Americans loved the British and the publicity people at N.B.C. were doing their best to smother her. In fact, Ida told her, if Eve wanted to keep her job, she'd better keep her mouth shut. But it went across the grain. The flame of patriotism had been lit. For two pins she'd pack her bags and go home to help win the war.

'It's a fight for the freedom of all democracies,' she told the family at Christmas dinner.

'Crap,' said June.

'I second that.' Jo wagged his pipe at his sister. 'Suppose the Japanese invaded Los Angeles, and the Nazis landed in New York, what the hell difference would it make to the people of Albuquerque? They'd still be one hell of a long way off!'

'That's a real hick attitude,' John sneered. 'We've got to support the British effort. Why, they're family!' He smiled at Eve, who thought her heart would burst with gratitude.

'Crap,' said June. 'Eighty-five per cent of Americans is either Italian, or Spanish or German! How the hell're you going to get them to fight a war against their own folks?'

'I second that,' said Jo.

'Bang. Bang. You're dead.' Jimmy was pointing his toy gun at John.

'Shut up, Jim.' June cuffed the boy round the ear, and he ran off wailing, his paper hat fallen to one side.

'It was you who gave him the gun, Aunt June,' Lou protested.

'That boy needs discipline!'

'Ella never feels the need to hit him!' Lou objected.

'When's that Indian coming back?' Jo frowned. 'I miss them muffins she makes.'

'Anyway . . .' Eve wouldn't let the argument drop. 'Roosevelt's all for getting involved!'

'Crap,' said June. 'Why, he thinks, like the rest of us, that the British are just scared of losing their goddam Empire!'

Lou quietly put an end to the rows. 'Election coming up soon. Let's just see how he does, huh?'

John gave him a sideways look, smiled, then said, 'What's this I hear about there maybe being oil on this ranch?'

And another argument, far closer to home, broke like a thunderclap over Ridley land.

Smarting at what Eve saw as a betrayal by her American cousins, she was glad when John suggested they should leave the family to their carols and go clubbing together. But she was nervous, as they drove down the bumpy lane in the van together. She was reminded of the time John had taken her to Tucson.

'You look a lot better than last I saw you,' he said.

'I'm fine,' Eve replied. 'In fact, I'm more than fine. I'm doing very well.'

'Oh?'

'Yes. I've got a spot at the Hollywood Bowl. Dancing.'

'That's great. When?' John was impressed.

'Next May. I'm going to be in the British War Relief programme. And I didn't have to go to bed with anybody, either.'

'That's great too.'

'What?'

'Nobody wants second-hand goods, honey,' John observed.

'You've changed your tune,' Eve gaped.

'Yeah. Well, maybe I was a bit out of line.' John smiled easily. 'You got me scared. Know that?' She saw the whites of his eyes in the darkness, as he turned to her.

'*You* scared?' Eve was amazed. 'Who is this John Ridley? Do I know him?'

'I told you. You shouldn't believe all that drunken bravado, shooting my mouth off. It's mostly bluff, remember? I'm a journalist. I've got an image to keep up. This is the real me. You better believe it.'

'I don't.' Eve wasn't going to be taken in. 'Why're you helping send planes to Britain?' she asked.

'Because the good old British are doing a job for all of us, honey. They're defending the free world. The least we can do is supply them with arms. Do you know, I've delivered more than a dozen aircraft by now?' Eve was silent. 'O.K.' John shrugged. 'If you don't believe I'm sincere, just you look at the paper next week. The article's already written.' His hand reached for her knee, to pat it. She stiffened. 'Don't worry, sweetie. You're in no danger. I've turned over a new leaf. I intend to marry a clean-living, girl-next-door kind of a girl.'

Eve's head reeled. And it wasn't swinging to the big band that did it. It was John, swinging from one big act to another. Sweating after a bout on the floor with him, she sat back, sipping her coke to watch the show. But, out of the corner of her eye, she was watching John too. He knew a lot of people. He kept turning and waving, surrounded by smiling faces, all keen to talk to him.

'Who's the girl, John?'

'Cousin, from England,' he swaggered.

'England? Oh yeah? Have we got a song for her!' The piano player laughed, and went to have a word with the singer.

'You had plans to start a club here at the airport once,' Eve said. 'I was going to dance in it.'

'Yeah.' John smiled at her. 'But on reflection, I thought it wouldn't do too well. Not enough people in Albuquerque to support a night club. Look around you.' The place was half-empty. 'Club's losing money every day. Course it'll be different when they've built the army base. Maybe I'll put in some investment then . . . If the place is still going.'

'Why're they building a new base, if America's not going to war?' The band struck up and the singer was singing for Eve.

> 'Paul Revere took a ride
> Just to look at the countryside.
> All at once the horse got skittish,
> Here come the British. Bang. Bang. (John grinned.)

> Washington at Valley Forge,
> Tried to cross the river, look out George!
> All at once his boat got skittish,
> Here come the British. Bang. Bang. (Eve blushed.)

> Whoa, just look around,
> No matter where
> You'll find the British are there.
> Napoleon at Waterloo

> Writing Josephine a billet doux,
> "Jose I have got to close it.
> Close this epistle,
> There goes the whistle!
> Here come the British. Bang. Bang!" '

And now John was laughing his head off. Eve shook her head. Better believe what?

But in the *Independent*, a week after Christmas, there was an article strongly supporting the pro-British movement. John Ridley had stuck his neck out, in spite of the powerful lobby against involvement in Europe.

'Senator Nye will not countenance Roosevelt's Cash and Carry policy, selling arms to the allies. He says, America cannot stay neutral and yet enjoy the profits from sales of arms for wars engaged in by other nations. He may have a point. But, by not selling arms to the allies, our own factories stand idle and Britain is in danger of losing a war which is going to affect all of us, in the end. Britain is in the front line of freedom. She is fighting our battle. It is in our interests to help her as much as we can, at the same time giving work to American boys. In L.A., this week, Lockheed had to lay off another 700 men. Lay-offs in the industry now total more than 165,000, and all as a direct result of the Neutrality Act. Is Senator Nye so blinkered he cannot see the dangers on every side of his isolationist policy?'

'My!' said Clara, as she put down the paper. 'That's telling them, John!' John shrugged. Eve said nothing. She was watching him warily.

'I thought you were supposed to be a crime reporter,' Ernie sneered. 'Not one of those political boloneyists trying to get our boys killed!'

'I'm flying for Lockheed now, so I'm no longer on the paper's staff,' John explained. 'George gives me free rein to write what I like. Only thing is, he can print it or leave it.'

'Well good for George for printing it then!' Eve spoke at last. 'He's a man of principle.'

'So am I, honey. So am I!' John grinned.

'When're you doin' your next run up to Dakota?' Clara asked him.

'End of the week.'

'Better be careful, dear,' she warned. 'There's a lot of Germans live in Dakota.'

*   *   *

110

At the start of January, Lou finally drove up to Walpi to fetch Ella 'home'. Jim was missing her. In fact, they all were, even Jo. June was hard pressed. And Lou was anxious. Ella had never been away from them so long. Driving through the reservation, Lou saw a number of hogans and caravans belonging to the Navajo. Sheep huddled in pens out of the wind. It was cold and coming in dark. He had better get there soon. There were no lights out in the wilderness and no gas stations either. In the distance, he could see the outline of First Mesa, standing bleak against the reddening sky. He pressed on, passing no one, till, at last, Lou turned wearily up the narrow, steep road that led to the clifftop. Snow lay trapped in the dry grass, like lights along the track. Then the grass gave way to jagged rock, as Lou approached the twinkling lights of the Hopi villages perched precariously on the narrow ledge above. He parked in the village of Sichomovi, fending off the crowding children with bars of candy, then set out along the ridge to Walpi. The ridge was barely ten feet wide and the wind was strong and keen. It bit into him, like an animal, trying to overpower him and throw him down onto the distant rocks below. Lou stopped, regained his balance and struggled on.

'Hold on, Mister. You're nearly there.' Lou strained to see who it was. A hand, pale in the darkness, was reaching out to him. One last effort, and his fingers locked into a young boy's firm grip, pulling him to safety.

'Who you come to see?' he asked.

'Ella.' The boy nodded.

'Come with me. She is in my father's house.' Lou followed his guide past the entrances to underground kivas, and up a sheltered passageway, where cooking smells made him suddenly aware of his hunger. Laughter broke from inside one of the houses. The boy threw back the blanket over the door and Lou bent to enter the home of Chu'Ovi, Snake Chief.

He saw Ella's face at once. In the firelight, she looked flushed with happiness. But, within seconds of his entering the room, an invisible veil had come between them, and a formal stiffness taken the place of warm conviviality. Ella was sitting with Myna on the floor, at the feet of two men. One of them Lou recognized at once: Chu'Ovi, the Chief. But the younger good-looking man, with restless eyes, was a stranger. He got up to offer his seat to the newcomer, and sat on the floor at Ella's side. Lou felt a stab of jealousy. But the Chief was waiting. Lou reached in his pocket and brought out some tobacco. Chu'Ovi grunted, and took it, then indicated to the white man, he might sit on the bench beside him.

'This is Lou,' Ella said. There was a silence. 'Have you not brought Jimmy?' she asked quietly. Lou shook his head.

'We were talking about the Navajo,' Chu'Ovi said, ignoring Ella. 'You saw their hogans, as you drove here?' Lou nodded. 'They drive their sheep onto our land as though by right! The government promised long time ago to protect us from them. But what do they do? They set up a committee! Now they want to reorganize us! My people do not understand committees. Why do we need them? God gave us this land. No one has any right to take it from us. But we cannot make them see this. Perhaps a white man could explain to them better. Yes, we need a white man to speak up for us to these committees!' Chu'Ovi fixed him with a stare. Lou shifted uneasily. What could *he* do?

'I'm no politician, Chu'Ovi. I sympathize with your condition, but you need someone with power behind him to help you. What power have I got?' Ella looked away, disappointed, and Lou was uncomfortably aware that the young man sought her eyes.

'Dan's looking after Ella's stock, which she inherited from her mother,' Chu'Ovi told Lou. 'He wants to marry her. The Eagle Clan to which he belongs are content, and I see nothing against it.' Lou felt his chest tighten.

'It's the woman's right to choose her husband, Chu'Ovi,' Myna reminded him. Lou held his breath. No one moved.

'Ella shall remain at Walpi till she has chosen,' Chu'Ovi decreed.

'I *have* chosen. I'll marry Lou, if he'll have me.' Ella looked at him, and Lou panicked. Where he came from, it was the man who popped the question. But Chu'Ovi had objections of his own.

'So you choose to say goodbye to your people and your religion, Ella?'

'No. I don't.' Ella was near to tears. Dan leaned forward and touched her hand tenderly, but she brushed him away and Chu'Ovi spoke sharply in his native tongue. Chastised, the young man rose abruptly and left the house. Chu'Ovi apologized for him.

'You must forgive Dan,' he said. 'He is very young and he is, by nature, rash. He would do well to learn your forbearance, Lou.'

Lou said nothing. Everyone waited, as though expecting something to happen. Outside, in neighbouring houses, they could hear laughter and singing. The Hopis were a happy race. Lou had never seen Ella in her true setting. And now, he realized he'd never even heard her laugh either; never heard her chattering away nineteen to the dozen like other women. Why did the Hopis veil their true natures from outsiders? He looked at Ella. Her face was sad. But she said nothing. Then, finally, Myna got up, smiled her cracked smile and said,

'You must be tired and hungry, Lou. Come with me. We'll find you a bed for the night and something to eat.' Dogged by an uneasy sense of failure, Lou followed Myna out into the freezing night.

After a supper of corn and meat dumplings, he shook down, on the clay floor of an empty house. He lit a fire in the grate, but didn't sleep. Here in the Hopi stronghold, Lou was feeling like an alien. In common with most Americans, Lou hadn't much time for the British Empire, and had begun to suspect the war was just a cunning ploy to get the people of the United States to defend the British colonies. Gandhi was right: the British should give India back to the Indians. Lou hadn't thought much about the *American* Indians and *their* problems, in spite of having Ella around. He'd been brought up on cowboys and wigwams like most whites, but he was forced to recognize that his ignorance was a kind of arrogance. Weren't his own ancestors colonial exploiters, who took America from her native peoples? Lou had thought that by marrying Ella, he'd be doing her a favour. But now, he cringed with shame as he recognized she had come to work for him, far from her own people, suffering the downright rudeness of his Pa and his Aunt June, and all without complaint. Lou was humbled. What could he offer her in return? His world was upside down. He turned to face the fire, still crackling in the grate, and rested his eyes on the dancing flames, where Ella's face flickered, out of reach.

To the delight of the nation, Jennifer had had her baby, and to crown all, little Daryl had been born a citizen of the United States of America. Jennifer's husband who, according to the scripts, was running the war back home in England, kept telegraphing her to stay put, where she and the boy were safe. His messages were hysterical.

'Disaster approaches. We can't hold out much longer. The Empire and Britain are finished.' Jennifer's reaction was supposed to be pity for her husband and defeated homeland. Of course, it was a marvellous opportunity to act her tiny little head off. But Eve, obstinate as ever, bristled with indignation at the suggestion that her 'homeland' was 'finished'. Meanwhile, in the 'real' world, the presidential election was hotting up. Everyone in America seemed against involvement in Europe. But, encouraged by John's example, Eve stuck her neck out once more. Yet another episode of 'The Jones Family' was under rehearsal. Jennifer was going through her lines with Aunt Meryl.

JENNIFER	The news from home's so awful, Aunt Meryl.
AUNT MERYL	At least you and the baby're safe here with us . . . be thankful for small mercies, dear.
JENNIFER	You know, at first I just wished and wished America would go to Britain's aid. But, if it had . . . Thank God America stayed out of this terrible war. There has to be somewhere safe for children and the old world's finished. (SOBS)
AUNT MERYL	Don't cry, honey . . .

But that was just the rehearsal. The show went out live. Eve had no idea she was going to do what she did. It just sort of happened. The red light was on, the adrenalin was flowing, Aunt Meryl had the usual red dots on her cheeks because of her blood pressure, and the cue light flashed. Eve dutifully began the scene.

| JENNIFER | The news from home's so awful, Aunt Meryl. |
| AUNT MERYL | At least you and the baby're safe here with us. Be thankful for small mercies, dear. |

But the scripted reply stuck in Eve's throat. She paused. Aunt Meryl looked alarmed, the nation heard her heavy breathing, and suddenly Eve's fancy took wings. She launched into unscripted territory.

JENNIFER If the United States had only come to Britain's aid, this would never have happened. But now the demons of Nazism are knocking on the doors of America itself. Soon there'll be no place safe to bring up children. (SOBS) If only it could have been different!

Aunt Meryl didn't know what to say. So, for several seconds, she just kept on muttering, 'Oh dear. Oh dear. Oh dear.' Eve thought she was going to have a heart attack. The producer almost did. After transmission, Eve was given the sack. She fought her dismissal, but it was hopeless.

Even Roosevelt was against her. Two days after Eve's broadcast, he made a speech on the radio too. He said, 'Let no man or woman thoughtlessly or falsely talk of sending American armies to European fields. I hope the United States will keep out of this war. I believe that it will.'

Well, he had to say that, if he wanted re-election, didn't he? But it was Jennifer's death warrant on 'The Jones Family'. They sent her character back to England, to work in a munitions factory in Manchester. Jobless, Eve wondered if she should follow suit. But there was still the Hollywood Bowl for one thing, and for another, life was looking up. John took Eve on as chief companion, showing her off to the people of 'Frisco. Lockheed were, apparently, paying him very well, and he took her out on the town, dancing and dining her at all the best places. She especially liked the 'Frantic', where John tipped the waiters and floorwalkers till their eyes bulged, and they drank exotic potions till her head spun. Eve liked the 'good life'. So, maybe Europe could wait just a little longer. Her mother had written.

Dear Eve,
 Your Grandma is very poorly now, what with her arthritis and her chest. She is wheezing like our old bed. You can

imagine nursing her takes up most of my time, when not spent in the shop. I don't know if we can keep going much longer. Nobody can afford flowers in war time, so what use is a florist's shop? Your Dad is very depressed. But at least Hitler has not dropped any bombs on us yet and Os has not been in the firing line. I hear the Germans have marched into Denmark and Norway. God knows what's going to happen next. The world seems to have gone mad. Well, take care of yourself, pet. We are always thinking of you, and wishing you well. Your Dad and I are very glad you are safe at least.

P.S. Can you send us some tea and sugar?

Eve obliged, though it wasn't easy, on her waitressing pay.

Then, in May, a series of shocks hit the United States. About the time Holland surrendered to the Nazis, Eve was in L.A. preparing her number with Danny. John was down south. He was working on an article for the *Independent* with his old partner, Ken Houlihan. It was to be an exposé of the narcotics trade which, in spite of heavy policing, was increasing day by day. Ken and John had driven, incognito, through the towns and tiny villages of the Mexican border, trailing a scent that went right back through Juarez to Mexico City. There was a variety of drugs for sale, from heroin through to the rough marijuana of Mexico. The latter could be bought cheaply and easily almost anywhere, and was resold in the United States at a fifty per cent mark-up. But it was the heroin that made the really big money, and there was competition within the trade. Mr Low, back in Chinatown, didn't like the way a Mr Siu kept creaming off the best of the market. And this was the *real* reason for the trip. Under the cover of their journalistic activities, Ken and John had been briefed to get enough evidence against the competition's source, to wipe him from the map. The intention was to leave Mr Low king of Chinatown. By a series of bribes and threats, they got a name. With that, they were able to tap the inner circle. And once they'd infiltrated that, they had another name in the inner, inner circle, and once they had that . . . they had *the* name. The source of the competition turned out to be Hispanic. He shipped most of the stuff in small craft, landing much of it at

116

Sausalito, Ken's hunting ground. From there it passed through the Chinatown laundry of Mr Siu, who was thus able to compete with Low for trading rights in the home and European markets. Ken and John didn't wait to meet the Hispanic. They did their deal, stowed the merchandise, by soldering tins of the stuff onto the petrol tank, and took off for the border. There, they simply declared what they were carrying and gave the police all the information they required. Mr Siu's days as a big noise were over. He would be left with no merchandise to market. Pleased at this unexpected coup, the police hardly bothered to search John and Ken's car. And in any case, the smell of the spilled coke all over the interior, put off the sniffer dog. So it was with some feeling of exuberance that John and Ken drove into Yuma that night. They were in a mood to celebrate.

They checked into a small hotel close by the town square. Yuma hadn't much to offer by way of hot spots. The best was a poor flamenco club where Mexicans, pretending to be Hispanics, paraded to the clatter of castanets. Ken was bored. The inept rattling was getting on his nerves. He went to the lavatory, to pep himself up with something and then, a glint in his eye, took off, prowling the town in search of adventure. John went back to the hotel, rolled himself a cigarette and lay back on the bed to dream a while. Over at the club, they'd started to play records. He could hear the strains of Lester Young on the balmy air. John breathed deeply. The bed started to float. It was a pleasant sensation, like being just a little bit drunk. The music sounded like they were playing sax through feather pillows. Nice.

At the Hollywood Bowl, Eve was tapping gently over the stage to the echoing notes of Danny's piano. Then Carillo's sax came in, low and plaintive, like a voice crying in the dark. The huge audience held its breath. Danny had stopped playing. The spot was on him, as he tap-toed to Eve's side where, suddenly, he stopped dead. The spot shifted. Eve replied, sharp as gunshot. Danny interrupted with a wry comment of his own, and the sax held them together, teasing, improvising against them, challenging them for mastery. The sound floated gently from the earth up to the starry sky, and held eighteen thousand people suspended. Magic had taken place. When they stopped dancing, there was a long silence. All you could hear were three people

117

panting hard. Then the audience rose to its feet and they could hear the stamping and the cheering over in Pasadena. Eve, Danny and Carillo had taken Hollywood by storm.

John was still floating when the door of the hotel room opened and Ken came in. He was covered in blood. John couldn't help laughing, making Ken even more angry.

'Stop it. Do you hear me? Stop laughing!' he commanded. But John couldn't stop. He was high as a kite and Ken couldn't do a thing about it. In the end he got out his gun and the trip turned nasty. John was reeling. He felt sick. The gun dropped on the bed. 'For Chrissake, stop laughing!' Ken screamed. 'I just killed someone!'

'What?'

'You deaf, or something?' he yelled. 'I killed someone.'

'Sh! Who?'

'A girl. We've got to get out of here.' Ken started throwing things into his bag. John was sick over the bed.

'Was she white?'

'Mex.'

'Even so, we can't just go,' John said.

'The hell we can't!' Ken hit John and he fell back against the wall. His cheek was bruised and he was bleeding under one eye.

'Look, Ken,' John reasoned, 'don't tell me what happened. Or why. I don't want to know. All I'm saying is, if we're smart, we'll go to the police.' Ken screamed abuse. John tried to calm him. 'Come on! All we've got to do is spin a story about how this girl was spying for the Hispanic.' Ken stopped throwing things. He shrugged. Then he smiled.

'Yeah,' he said. 'We got into a brawl with a few of them drug-smuggling dagos and, unfortunately, it was the dame that got it.'

'Sure.'

'No-good whore shouldn't've been consorting with types like that anyway,' Ken giggled.

'Yeah. It was her own look-out,' John agreed.

A couple of days later, reluctantly freed by the Arizona State Police, John and Ken were on the highway, heading away from Yuma. Ken was singing at the top of his voice. John was smoking, to steady his nerves. And then another shock hit

America. This one was 7.1 on the Richter Scale, and the epicentre was Imperial Valley. The car wheels left the road. John stalled. They fell out of the car. Ken was scared and started screaming so John gave him a smoke.

'It's only a quake,' he reassured him. 'It'll pass! Hell! I haven't switched off the ignition!' John struggled back to the car, falling at every step. The car was dancing. How the hell was he going to get hold of it? He started to laugh. But he had to get his copy. His article for the *Independent* was in the glove compartment. He made it to the car door. It slammed back against him, knocking him senseless. Then, Ken tried to get it. It was weird! Like walking over an ice float that was breaking up under the impact of a tidal wave. The arms of giant saguaros were moving, like policemen directing the traffic. Then they too started to dance. The cacti were dancing in formation, and heading his way. Hell! Were the goddam saguaros playing castanets too? No. That was the keys. The keys in the ignition. He had to stop them rattling. He couldn't stand that. It was driving him crazy. He crawled onto the driving seat, and grasped them. The rattling stopped. But the car was still dancing. He reached into the glove compartment, pulled out the marijuana first, then his camera, and only afterwards, rescued John's copy. Then, he sprang out of the car, back into the brush. He expected to land on John. But John seemed to have gone. Had he fallen down some gaping hole in the ground? Then he saw him, reeling crazily across the drunken landscape. There was something fiery just ahead. Ken started shooting pictures. Some distance from the fire, John fell on his knees. His body seemed to melt, and wave in a haze of heat. Was he going to disappear? Ken fell, still clutching his camera. He clung to the heaving earth, still trying to get his picture. But there was too much movement. He put his head down. Then slowly, the ground stilled. After a few seconds, he looked up again. John was still there, on his knees. Ken heard him cry out, and he ran towards him. He was close to a huge gash in the earth's crust. Debris, thrown up by the black smoke, was falling all around him. His eyes were white and wild.

'I saw him,' John said hoarsely.

'What? Who? Who the hell did you see?' Ken shouted at him.

'Don't know. But I think he came for me.'

'Who?'

'Don't know,' John repeated. 'Death. Maybe.'

'What?'

'I saw him. He rose up out of there . . . ' John pointed to the fiery, smoking chasm. 'A huge man, dressed like, I don't know. He was on a great black horse that breathed molten steel from its nostrils, and flames from its mouth. He looked all around him, then he just rode off, disappearing into the smoke.'

'Some trip.'

'Wasn't a trip,' John insisted. 'I saw him. Whoever the hell it was!'

'Sure you saw him,' Ken soothed. 'Why not? You see all sorts of things when you trip. Maybe they're there, maybe they're not. Who's to say?'

'Who was he?' John whispered. 'I got the feeling that my caballero's going to send this country of ours crashing into the Pacific never to be seen again, one of these days.' Ken stared at him.

'Might as well enjoy ourselves while we can, huh?' Ken was smiling. John started to laugh.

'Hell, that stuff's good!'

'C'mon! Let's get back to the car.' The car was on its side, its windows smashed. They would have to walk to the nearest town. What a story this was going to be!

Eve's success at the Bowl was overshadowed by John's. He and Ken drove back into 'Frisco, the toast of the town. A press reception, given jointly by the city and the *Independent*, was held in their honour at the Frantic. Anybody who was anybody was there. John lapped it up. Eve had come, by invitation, to be at his side. By now, she was something in her own right. Now her photograph was sought by every newspaper, even the exclusive Beverly Hills local, which had dubbed her 'Miss Magic Toes of 1940'. Best of all, M.G.M. had expressed an interest. She didn't know what, but something was definitely on the cards. Yes, the hero and the starlet made a glamorous duo in the Mural Room of the Frantic, where champagne glasses clinked and the genteel voices of the rich were punctuated by the brash babble of reporters. Dressed in pink satin and feathers, Eve glowed. Men were drawn to her like moths round a naked bulb; all the men but her escort, John. Irritated, she watched him from the corner of her eye. He was with Ken Houlihan. Houlihan was wearing a navy shirt and a white tie, which he'd pulled away from his neck. He was obviously the worse for wear, and was boasting loudly.

'My friend here . . . ' he was pointing at John, 'he saw the devil himself, coming up out of the chasm . . . ' John grasped his arm, and squeezed it tight.

'Mr Houlihan's right . . . in a manner of speaking. We did see the devil. We saw the devil of an earthquake!' Everyone but Eve laughed.

'Mutt's assholed!' The N.B.C. shut off their microphones as John strove to calm his companion. Ken Houlihan didn't like people laughing at him. His temples were working, and his jaw was taut. He looked like he could spit daggers. He generated such fear, in fact, that people vacated the space around them, and it was then that Eve saw quite clearly that Ken Houlihan was dangerous. Here was the source of John's cruelty, that day at Neptune Beach. She had never quite forgiven, nor forgotten that. But it wasn't his fault. John was a hero, fast developing a reputation as supporter of justice and good causes, with his article on the drug ring. The police had cleaned up a whole operation because of him. No. Houlihan was the one to blame. He was a bad influence, an incubus. No doubt about it, he had to be kept out the way.

Houlihan was trying to shake John off. He was getting out of hand. But George, editor of the *Independent*, saw the danger and sought to split the pair by bringing in Eve. He grabbed her arm and dragged her over, drawing behind them a few more reporters, including the man from N.B.C. Grinning hugely, George thrust Eve at John.

'Why don't you take this little lady for a turn round the floor, John?' he suggested pointedly. Houlihan hung back, sulkily, leaning against the wall. But the N.B.C. microphone was thrust in their midst.

'Is this a romantic attachment?' the journalist asked the hero and the starlet. Eve didn't know where to put herself. 'Can you tell our listeners, are you two considering marriage?'

'I think you can safely leave that question to Miss Lawson and myself.' John spoke as the practised interviewee. And the cameras flashed as he put his arm round her waist and whisked her onto the floor.

'Adios, muchacho!' Ken called as he lurched from the room. John looked anxiously after him, then he heard Eve's voice.

'That man's going to hold you back, John.' He turned back to look at her. 'You should give him up. He can't be that good a photographer!'

'He's the best there is, honey,' John smiled.

Eve returned to L.A., and her waitressing job, in a dangerous condition for a woman. She was beginning to see John as a dog who had to be rescued from a bad owner; Ken Houlihan. In fact her mind was more on that than on her career. The script came in for her test at M.G.M. They didn't want her to dance. They wanted her to play an English girl in a film about the Nazis. Her heart sank.

'But, Ida, I can't act,' she complained.

'You managed fine in "The Jones Family" till you started shooting your mouth off!' Ida snapped.

'I know. But film's different. I pull faces . . . overact. I know I do.'

'Well stop,' Ida told her.

'It's easier said than done. Why can't I get a dancing part?' Eve bleated.

'Nobody's making . . .'

'Musicals any more. I know! What am I going to do?'

'Take a few acting classes,' Ida suggested.

'O.K.' Eve sighed. 'Never say "die"!'

'That's about it.' Ida looked sad.

'What's up?'

'Nothing much.' But Eve sensed distress.

'How's your family?' she asked sympathetically.

'Not heard anything in ages. God knows what's happened to them. They should've got out of Berlin when they had the chance. The Jews are destined for suffering. And nobody cares a jot.'

'Rubbish!' Eve contradicted. 'Look at the films coming out of Hollywood now! They're all anti-Nazi.'

'Yeah, but nobody takes them seriously, honey.'

Then came the third shock. A plump little man called Churchill who'd taken over in England was pumping out propaganda

122

about the evil Nazis now that the Blitzkrieg had started. Mr Roosevelt had been re-elected, on the basis he was going to keep America out of the war. Everybody was feeling just cosy. It was nice sympathizing with the British, as long as they fought their own wars. And as for what this Churchill was saying, surely the Nazis weren't as bad as all that? Why, Charlie Chaplin had Hitler to a 'T' with his little moustache and his toy soldiers. He was just a figure of fun. So, the nation was unprepared, when it turned on its radios and heard Roosevelt say, 'My friends, this is not a fireside chat on war. It is a chat on National Security. If Great Britain goes down, the axis powers will control the continents of Europe, Asia, Africa, Australasia and the high seas. It is no exaggeration to say that all of us, in all the Americas, would be living at the point of a gun. There are American citizens, many of them in high places, unwittingly in many cases . . . aiding and abetting the work of the Nazis. I do not charge these American citizens with being foreign agents, but I do charge them with doing exactly the kind of work that the dictators want doing in the United States.'

The tide of war was turning towards America.

CHAPTER SEVEN

Lou and Jimmy were at the cinema in Gallup. The 'Navajo' wasn't as smart as the Albuquerque 'Kimo', but it got the new Walt Disney first. Jimmy was pining for Ella and Lou'd heard nothing from her, since he was up at Walpi, some eight months before. He'd had a lot of time to think in those months. He kept on seeing her face, as he'd come on her that night, glowing in the firelight. It was a different Ella from the one he knew and he'd love to get to know her. But it seemed he had to be an Indian to qualify, and what could Lou do about that? He was helpless. The newsreel was on. They were showing the skyline of London. You heard the drone of the engines first. Quentin Reynolds sounded choked.

'Here they come.' Then, on the screen, you saw the dark outline of the planes, like birds of prey. 'The night is long. But sooner or later the dawn will come. The German bombers are creatures of the night. They melt away before the dawn and scurry back to their own aerodrome.' A close-up of a German plane, a swastika on its tail. Then a flash; an explosion; the first bomb. The skyline was lit up. Flames started. Lou had forgotten Ella for the moment, moved by the tragedy of the Battle of Britain, translated to the silver screen.

'Hell, the Brits are goin' to lose this war!' Lou turned to the man on his left. 'Charlie Lindbergh's right!' his neighbour went on. 'If we start fighting for democracy abroad, we'll end up losing it at home!' Jimmy was holding on to his Pa's hand. The bombs scared him. This wasn't what he'd come to see. Lou put his arm round him.

'Is America going to join the war, Pa?' Jimmy whispered.

'Doesn't look like it,' Lou reassured him. But what if they did? Lou was a farmer, of sorts, and could probably avoid conscription. But was that shying away from the problem? He'd said, at first, he wanted to fight. But it was men like Gandhi Lou had most time for. He'd seen him on Movietone with his passive resistance. And if Germany was doing in Europe, same as England was doing in India, dominating other peoples, then Gandhi surely had the right idea, and fighting was out! But were they? Ella'd said the Nazis had stolen the swastika and perverted it. Well, the swastika was a religious sign, so doing that was like turning the cross upside down! Maybe that Churchill fellah wasn't exaggerating, after all, when he'd said the Nazis were evil! In that case, Lou should fight! But how do you fight evil? Sword with sword? Fire with fire? Maybe. Lou just didn't know. He wished he could talk it through with Ella. He had a feeling she'd have something to say about it. Jimmy was huddling in to Lou's side. Poor kid. He was missing her just as much as he was! Then, at last, the drab black and white of England was transformed into the technicolor land of Disney. It was time for the big picture, *Fantasia*.

Eve's test was a flop. They said she didn't sound English enough. She cried on Danny's shoulder and, trying to help, he encouraged her to teach tap, like him. At least it was better than waitressing. So Eve started a class in Bay City, advertising for pupils in the papers and libraries. Soon she'd got a small group together, mostly women, and mostly rich. Thanks to her success at the Bowl, she was able to charge them exorbitant fees. So it wasn't so bad. Amongst her pupils were budding starlets, who couldn't dance a step, but the studios wanted them to learn; so out they came to Bay City, and Eve bit back her resentment, resolved to teach them as well as she could. And she found she had a talent for the job. In fact, Eve could teach a bat to do double pendulum wings if she wanted to. In other words if you had legs, Eve could teach you to dance. And soon she was running four classes, some private sessions, and had a waiting list of eager pupils. Besides this, she was often called on by charitable organizations to perform for them. It didn't earn anything but at least she was seen. She was on the map.

And Eve enjoyed Bay City. Now she was earning better, she decided to move out there. What did she care if half the population was old? At least it was peaceful. She leased a small apartment in the least fashionable area, away from the sea, and settled down to a new life. She was still sending food parcels home. And she was wondering why she hadn't seen John in a long, long time.

It was a humid afternoon in late fall. Eve was teaching a class of heavyweights, and the floor of the hall was giving in the middle. Her legs were aching, and she was longing for a dip in the sea, when the door to the hall opened, and John walked in. He smiled at her, and pulled out one of the chairs, stacked against the wall. The women in the class grinned at one another. So, Miss Frigidaire from England had a beau! But Eve's heart was jumping. When she finished the class early, no one was surprised. They took their time getting changed, and Eve had gone, by the time they emerged from the ladies' room. Hurrying out onto the street, Eve's pupils saw her disappear in the direction of the beach. She and her beau were holding hands.

Eve'd never seen John like this before. He was dazed, the veneer of confidence cracked. She took his hand, as a woman might take the hand of a child who was crying because it couldn't find its mother. And for a moment, her head reeled under the potent stimulus of 'doing poor John good'.

It was the answer to her dreams . . .

'Eve received the prodigal back into her arms. It wasn't his fault. He'd been led astray, and now, badly frightened, had come home. Who was she to turn him away? Her loins moved with compassion . . . ' Her loins!? Eve shuddered. For God's sake, she told herself, cut the crap! It was no use dressing up her feelings of animal attraction with dignified phrases. Eve was a modern woman, living in 1940, not the dark ages. Times'd changed. Now, if you wanted a man, you had to go get him. Never mind wrapping him up in cellophane and pink ribbon first! And before

126

you dove in there, you'd far better find out what was on offer! So, before getting *completely* carried away, Eve sat John down under the shade of an umbrella, at a café on the waterfront where they could watch the boats toing and froing; a nice distraction for what she suspected was going to be a sticky conversation. The waiter came to take their order. John didn't seem to notice. Perhaps the boats were *too* distracting.

'What do you want, John?' she asked. He didn't hear her. So, Eve ordered a couple of cokes with a lot of ice, then lay back in her chair, waiting. After a while, John, with what seemed a great effort, turned to look at her.

'The fat's hit the fan,' he said. Eve frowned, indicating she needed more. 'Ken Houlihan's been arrested for murder,' he told her. She didn't say a word. She couldn't. 'Seems, the night of the party at the Frantic, Ken went up to Chinatown. You remember, he was pretty drunk? And . . . well God knows what else he was on . . . but, anyway, he knifed a prostitute.'

'What do you mean, "what else he was on"?' Eve asked.

'What do you think I mean?' he snapped. Eve bit back a defensive response. 'I mean he must've taken something.' John spelled it out.

'Drugs?' Eve was horrified.

'What the hell else would I mean?'

'I'm sorry,' she said. The waiter brought the coke, but John only picked up his glass and smashed it to the ground. 'I'll pay for the glass,' Eve pacified the waiter, who scurried back into the café. 'John,' she went on, 'are you involved in this murder in any way?'

He gave her the look of a hunted animal and replied in a hoarse voice, 'Police tried to make out I was an accessory. You see, there was another little incident, in Yuma, before the quake. A Mexican girl.'

'He killed her too?' Eve asked. John nodded. 'Why? Why would he kill anybody? Is he crazy?'

'He is when he gets dope in him,' John sobbed. Eve was shocked. John seemed to have disintegrated completely. 'He's crazy now,' he cried. 'Going out of his head. They won't give him any, see. So, he's suffering. I've seen him.'

'But you're here. So . . . ?' Gently, Eve probed.

'They had to let me go, eventually.' John spoke in a tight voice.

'They've got no proof. And Ken won't implicate me.' Eve thought for a long time before she spoke again.

'John, *were* you implicated?' She had to know. 'Please. Tell me the truth.'

'No,' he told her. 'Ken did it all on his ownsome.' Eve felt weak. She thought she was going to faint. She took a sip of the coke. Then, John spoke again. Now his voice was different, it had a confident ring to it. 'Ken says the crooks running the drugs outfit in Mexico must've set him up. He says they want him out of the way. He took photographs of some of them. So they set their thugs on him . . . '

'He's saying there's women thugs?'

'They're not all Shirley Temples like you!' John retorted angrily. Eve flushed. 'Sorry.' He sighed. 'Anyway, the men get away, and the woman's left behind, so, well, maybe she's some sort of a decoy.'

'They wouldn't use a woman like that, would they?' Eve didn't want to believe it. John shrugged.

'We're dealing with desperate people, Eve!' he said. For a second, she doubted him. It was too pat, like a bad script. Seeing her doubt, John shook off responsibility for his story. 'Anyhow,' he said, 'that's what Ken says. Could be true. They picked up the big fish, and now the little ones are causing trouble! Figures!'

'Did they ever find the contact in Chinatown?' Eve asked thoughtfully.

'No,' John sighed. 'Never showed up.'

'And you don't know who he is?' Eve was angry. John shook his head. 'So, all he's got to do is bide his time, then start another racket like the last one, and all your work'll have been wasted!'

'No!' John snarled. 'We've loused him up good and proper. It'll be a long time before he causes anybody any trouble. You betcha!' Eve felt better. But something was still bothering her.

'You said Ken uses drugs . . . ' she said slowly.

'Yeah. He started for kicks, then got hooked. He's getting his chance to dry out now, anyway. Poor bastard.' John looked Eve straight in the eye, like he was coming clean. 'I don't use them, if that's what you're thinking.' It was what she wanted to hear.

'Is Ken going to get off this murder charge?' she asked more easily.

'Doubt it.' He laughed. 'But they won't keep him in the slammer for too long. He's a hero. He broke a drugs ring, didn't he?' Eve's smile faltered. As far as she was concerned, the longer Houlihan was behind bars, the better.

It felt like moments snatched out of time; moonlight over the bay, feet on the cooling sand, holding hands, a night to remember. The old folks, and there were a lot of them in Bay City, turned to smile, as John and Eve passed, a pair of innocents, in love. But, inside, John was running from the pressure to live up to the image. Eve was so nice, he just might be tempted to give in to it and conform. It was what *she* wanted, wasn't it? His hand slipped round her waist, and she, not a bit surprised, just turned and smiled at him, before sliding her arm round him too. It was friendly. Nice. John liked it.

'Did you come down just to see me, John, or was it business?' she murmured.

'Not business. No. Well, you don't get up to San Francisco these days, do you?' John smiled. 'So, the mountain had to come to Muhammad. I've missed you, Eve. Know that?'

'I missed you too,' she whispered. They were standing on the shore, almost on the waterline. Eve slipped off her sandals, and freeing herself from John's arms, ventured into the shallows. The ocean rippled over her feet, warm and welcoming. It wasn't like the sea back home, its coldness punishing, stinging your feet. The Pacific embraced her, like a long lost father. Eve's heart opened and tears ran down her cheeks, as a confusion of images rushed out of memory into painful consciousness. Jack Scott, in bed with her mother. Davey Lawson, dead from drink, trying to forget Remembrance Sunday. The poppies. The service. 'Our Father . . . Forgive us our trespasses, as we forgive . . . ' How *could* she forgive? Silently, John came up from behind and wrapped her in his arms.

'Sh! It's alright,' he whispered. 'You and me, we've got to look after each other, Eve. We're two of a kind.' She nodded dumbly, face wet, mouth filled with salt tears. Then suddenly, she turned and threw herself on him, holding him tight, as though trying to squeeze the love out of him. And he gave in, comforting her, swaying, his body against hers, to the sound of the incoming waves.

She sighed, and said softly, 'I can't forgive him.'

Silently the sea receded from their feet. The tide was going out. John had stopped swaying.

'Who're you talking about, honey?' he asked.

'My so-called father, Jack Scott,' Eve sobbed.

'Your father?! Why the hell do you need to forgive him?' John shouted. 'What's the poor bastard ever done?' Eve looked at him with accusing eyes. 'From what I hear, all he ever did was to go to bed with your mother! Are you jealous, or what?' Eve fluttered in panic.

'Jealous? Who of?' she stuttered.

'Your father!' John pushed her from him. 'You don't want to share him with anybody. And you don't want to share your body with anyone either, you frigid little bitch!' Eve's hand flashed across his face.

'Get away from me, John Ridley. I don't ever want to see you again!' she cried. His hand touched his stinging cheek.

'Can't face the truth, huh?' He gave her his wide smile.

'It's *not* the truth!' Eve bawled. 'You're talking bullshit! And you know it!'

'Please yourself.' John walked away from her.

She watched him disappear into the darkness. The sea whispered behind her. She turned back to it, heart aching. 'How can I forgive my father?' she murmured to the receding waves, 'when I don't even know who the bastard is!' A light breeze lifted her skirt, and the stray hairs round her face brushed her skin. She shivered. What was she doing here, on the edge of the Pacific, thinking about home, when there was a war on? Better go back. Do something useful. A moment of panic. Would she ever see California again, or the pink mesas of Arizona? She'd barely tapped the depths and resources of this great country. She'd been too scared, hadn't she? Still was. She'd messed about in a sort of Disneyland, while all the time, the power of the landscape was there, beneath her feet. She and John were two of a kind. Just like he'd said, always running away, always bluffing. She had better go back to England and do her bit. If only Eve'd been born a man! She'd have liked to join up!

It was early in '41 that Lou joined the labour force extending the airport runway. The army air base had risen overnight on East

130

Mesa and the construction work had provided valuable jobs for the citizens of Albuquerque and the beleaguered New Mexican farmers. But things were extra tough on the Ridley ranch. Jo was having to work! Aunt June couldn't afford to give up the café, because, if they needed help on the farm, they needed June's wages more. Lou was out all day, every day, working his butt off. And what about the oil? Who could afford to try drilling for it? It was a chancy game. A loan might become a debt, and if they sold shares in advance, they'd lose out on the stuff even if it did come up like a fountain out of the ground! Either way they were likely to lose. And, according to the books Lou'd got out of the library, the rocks round about just weren't favourable anyway! Jo viewed Lou's newfound enthusiasm for books with suspicion. He'd never seen him as an egghead. So what was he doing thinking? And he *was* thinking. You could tell, by the way Lou kept staring out at the mesa, as though expecting God to come down on one of them clouds and give him the whole story. Well, just so long as Lou wasn't thinking about that 'darned Indian'! There was a distant buzzing. Jo sighed and looked up at the blue sky. Them goddam planes were homing in on them again. There they came, like flies in a heat haze, over the top of red mesa, sending the hens squawking to the sheds. They knew what was coming. Damn B-17s, 18s, 19s, 20s, what the hell did Jo care what 'B' numbers they were, scaring the daylights out of the cattle? And the hens weren't laying neither! Why the hell'd they have to practise for a war that wasn't going to happen? And why the hell did they have to use the Lawe Top for their target practice? Jo dragged on his pipe, then knocked it out on the stockade. White Cloud knew what was coming too! He was bucking that boy in there!

'Hang on, Jim! You'll be O.K.' Jo hoped so, anyway. 'Show him who's master!' Frantic, the boy's eyes searched for help. But there was none; only a shady-looking character walking up the lane, with a knapsack on his back. He strained to see who it was, and the horse threw him. 'Told you to hang on, didn't I?' Jo said wearily.

'Hi, Pa.'

'Hi, son.' It was John. Jo greeted him like he'd seen him only yesterday. 'Want some coffee?'

'Sure.' John saluted Jimmy and went inside. Sitting on the

hard earth of the corral, Jimmy watched after him. What was Uncle John doing in uniform? Then the mock attack began and Jimmy ran into the barn for shelter.

John was looking at a newspaper clipping stuck in the corner of the kitchen dresser. It was yellow with age. Eve and himself grinned out of the past at him. 'Starlet and hero-ace contemplate marriage.' Jo banged a mug of coffee down on the table.

'Ain't going to be a war. People of America won't have it!'

'Sure, Pa.' John sat and amicably drank the thick coffee. He pulled a face.

'What's wrong? Tastes too sophisticated now?' John shook his head. 'Where you been all this while? Clara says she's not seen you in months.'

'Went away for a spell,' John said.

Jo eyed him. 'Where d'ye go?'

John spilled his coffee into the sink and took a mouthful of water. 'I've been doing a lot of flying, Pa. Made a few bucks.' He eyed his father laconically. 'Now, I've come to stay,' he said.

'Stay?' Jo was shocked. 'What the hell for?'

'It's O.K. I'm not staying here.' John grinned. He'd got his rise out of the old man. 'I'll be on the new base. I'm with T.W.A. now. I'm going to train bomber pilots!'

'Well I'll be . . .' Jo slapped the table and John reached into his inside pocket.

'By the by, Bill Farley . . . he gave me a lift to the end of the lane . . . he asked me to drop this in,' he said. It was a letter from England. It was addressed to Lou, and the handwriting was Eve's.

Lou looked uncomfortably at John's uniform. June had pressed it and it was hanging in the porch to air.

'Thought I saw you down at the base today, John,' he ventured. 'I was working on the barracks building.'

'Thought they was using all Indian labour for the construction work, Lou,' John replied.

'Not all Indian. One or two Mexicans. And me.' Lou sat and picked up the letter that was lying on the table. 'And most of white Albuquerque,' he added, as though it was an after-thought.

132

'Postmark London,' Jo told him. They were all eyeing Lou, waiting for him to open it.

'From Eve,' Lou said. 'Not heard from her in ages.' He looked at John. 'You heard from her?' John shook his head. Lou put the letter in his pocket. To their disappointment, he was going to keep it for later.

'Supper's ready,' June screeched from the kitchen. Lou sighed. The hens were still scratching in the yard. Someone should get them inside before dark.

'I'll be with you in a minute,' he called back. Jo and John left Lou to chase the hens into the sheds. The sun was getting low in the sky and the hens looked like pink puffballs on legs, darting hither and thither. It was peaceful. Too peaceful. It made Lou uneasy.

'Pa!' It was Jimmy. He'd come out of the barn, and was standing like a lost soul in the late sunlight.

'Where've you been?' Lou asked, surprised.

In the barn. There was a mock attack. I was scared.'

'Won't have my boy a coward!' Lou frowned at him. 'Nothing to be scared of, anyway. Just a lot of noise.'

'Has Uncle John joined up?' Jim asked tentatively.

'No. He's working for T.W.A. He's going to be one of them darned pilots before long, up there in the sky, disturbing the peace.'

'I don't like Uncle John,' Jim muttered. Lou said nothing, then father and son chased the last of the hens into the sheds. When they'd finished, they lay back against the warm wood of the walls for a breather.

'Pa, you won't join up, will you?'

'I might have to, son, if we get involved in this war. Don't want to, though.'

'Don't then.'

'C'mon,' Lou objected. 'You can't just say no.'

'Ella wouldn't like it.' Lou looked at his son. He was staring at the empty sky. 'Is she ever going to come back, Pa?' Lou sighed.

'I don't know, son. But I sure wish she would.'

'Ella told me that the Great Spirit doesn't like war. It only likes peace.'

'Supper's getting cold!' June was in the doorway, hands on

hips. Hell, *she'd* scare the life out of any Nazi that came prowling!

After supper, when Jimmy was in bed, Lou took himself up to his room, lay back on the bed and took Eve's letter out of his pocket. He stared at the postmark. So, she was in London now? Lord, but that girl sure knew how to walk into danger, one way or another. He opened the envelope and started to read.

> Royal Naval College,
> Greenwich,
> London.
> 23rd December 1940

Dear Lou,

Hope you're impressed with the address! Only trouble is, they say I'm too old for entry to the WRNS. *And* they never go to sea, anyway! Still, I've got to do something, and I don't fancy either being a land girl, or a munitions worker. So I'm crossing my fingers that after all the humming and hahing they'll take me on here, after all. (Maybe they'll have to make me an officer, because of my great age!) I did a spell of fire-watching last night. The worst is over, though. Hitler seems to have given up bombing London. But you've never seen such a mess. Liverpool's even worse. And the smell's funny. It hits you as soon as you land. Smoke, death, damp rubble, everywhere. After a while you get used to it, though, and stop noticing. I've palled up with a nice girl from Stoke. She wants to decode secret messages. I don't mind what I do, as long as they'll have me and train me to do *something* useful! I lied about my family and put on a posh accent, so the Chief Wren here thinks I come from a 'naval tradition'. (Well, my ancestors were river pilots or something, so it's not a complete lie, is it?) I'm kind of homesick for the States. Everybody here thinks you Americans should be in the war. They think you're all selfish cowards. I do my best to defend you. Oh well, better close now, before I make the page soggy with my sloshy tears. Everybody's really sentimental here. It's catching. Only they manage to hide it under stiff upper lips. My lip's really wobbly and useless. Hope this reaches you, eventually. By the way, before I forget, Happy Christmas.

Love, Evie.XXXXXXX

P.S. Special love to Jimmy and Ella, wherever she may be. (If you're not married next time I hear from you, I shall want to know the reason why!)

'23rd December 1940.' She'd written that letter five months before. Lou stared at the ceiling. The sun had gone down some time back, and now shadows flitted across the beams overhead, cast by the flickering lamp. They still needed that new generator. He sighed. What the hell was it all about? War, Peace, Love, the whole goddam drama. And where the hell did he fit into it? Suddenly, Lou frowned, and looked at the letter again. She'd said nothing about her folks, except that she'd lied about them ...

*　　*　　*

Eve had arrived in November. She'd come straight from the devastation of Liverpool, travelling for three days, through a misery of dry sandwiches, Camp Coffee, cancelled trains and blackouts, to reach her home town of South Shields, early in the afternoon. The first thing that struck her had been the feeling of cramped meanness in the faces of the people she met; so many of them, on such a small island, suffering together. No wonder that upper lip had stiffened. It was a form of defence, typical of the stoic resisting spirit that was the bane and the saving of this island race. Because, if it made them strong in adversity, it also made them insular. Eve's American accent meant even she was classed as an outsider, till she dropped it. And then suddenly, taking on the local colour, she was accepted. She belonged. But Eve wasn't grateful. To her, coming back felt like being sucked out of the fresh air of the open country into a tiny, dingy room. She hated it and the nearer she got to Shields, the worst it got. The flower shop where her family had lived and worked for generations felt like a prison, opening its gates to take her. Such was Eve's frame of mind, as her train pulled into Newcastle Central Station, and she changed to the local line, the last leg of her journey home. It wasn't so much England that was getting her down, it was the prospect of seeing her own family. Stiff upper lip. She braced herself for the shock.

Taxiing through terrace after terrace of grimy houses, with smoking chimneys, pubs and little corner shops, Eve finally arrived in Fowler Street. It was a main thoroughfare, wider than most, accommodating the heavy portico of the Queen's Hall. Gathering her bags, Eve turned her back on the imposing columns, to face the familiar front of the humbler florist's opposite. This was it. The bell clanged on the shop door, as she entered, and the girl behind the counter looked up. Eve's sister-in-law, Mary Jean. An ordinary local lass, Mary'd come as shop girl when they were short-handed, only to marry Eve's brother Os, and stay on. Her face used to be rosy, but it was pale and thin now. Beside her, a child was crying. He was Eve's nephew, George.

'Shurrup, Georgie,' Mary Jean commanded. Then she looked straight at Eve. 'Can I help you, madam,' she said, eyeing Eve's bags.

'Hi, Mary Jean,' Eve said. 'It's me. I've come back to help you win the war.' A confusion of feelings jostled in Mary's breast.

Finally, she said. 'Well!' Then after a bit, she added, 'Are you a film star now?' Eve's face forbade further enquiry and Mary took refuge in family matters. 'Your Mam's out. But I can get your Dad for you.' She made for the stair at the back of the shop and ran up, followed by George, to knock on the office door. Suddenly, remembering her manners, Mary turned, leaned over the balcony, and shyly shouted down, 'Oh, welcome home, by the way.'

Then Mary disappeared inside with George. Eve heard her father's voice. He was on the office telephone. Alone in the shop, Eve looked round. The place was filled with artificial flowers, and home-produced pot plants, mostly geraniums. None of them were in flower. It made the shop feel dead. Yet, to her surprise, something moved and attracted her. Was it in the dark wooden drawers and shelves, the smell of cabbage cooking in the kitchen, or something less tangible, living and breathing in the atmosphere of the house? At the back of the shop, under the stair, was a huge statue made of darkened wood. She was facing

136

it, as she stood, back to the door, waiting for her 'father' to emerge. She edged forward, closer, to look at it. It was some sort of elephant. At its feet, like an offering, were the only live flowers in the shop; a bucket of red roses.

'You're looking at Ganesha.' Eve looked up suddenly to see her father leaning over the balustrade. 'Fine piece of work. I thought it deserved better than the cellar!'

'The cellar?'

'That's where I found it.' Jack smiled down at her.

'Where'd it come from? Originally?'

'India, so I'm told.' Jack hadn't budged from his superior position on the balcony, and feeling awkward in his presence, Eve asked,

'Where's Mam?'

'Out with your Auntie Maisie,' Jack told her. 'They're looking for a cheap headstone for your grandma's grave. They cost a fortune these days. I told your Mam she should've had her cremated.'

'I never knew she'd died!' The surprise threw Eve back into her native accent.

'Couple of months ago.' Jack eyed his daughter carefully. She didn't care. But why should she? She'd hardly known her grandma, hadn't even been brought up as one of the family. 'Why didn't you tell us you were coming?' he asked.

'If I'd known you were comin' I'd've baked a cake, baked a cake, baked a cake . . . ' Joking her way out of her unease, Eve tapped across the floor to the foot of the stairs, singing.

'You'd be lucky,' Mary told her, as she swung back down into the shop. 'We've not got any sugar, or any eggs, either.' Then she darted a look at Eve's bags. 'I don't suppose you brought some with you?'

'I brought some chocolate, and some nylons . . . '

'Whoopeeee!' Mary Jean now welcomed her sister-in-law with open arms.

Eve was bubbling with chatter about her experiences, but nobody seemed to want to hear.

'I expect you're tired,' Mary Jean said, and plonking a cup of strong tea in her hand, sent her up to the 'spare room' to rest. The 'spare room' was at the top of the house. It was damp and cold. Eve drank the tea, bittersweet with saccharine, put on a couple of jumpers, and crawled under the coverlet for warmth. 'If I'd know you were comin' I'd have aired the room,' she thought. That damned song! She couldn't get it off her mind. Her head fell back on the cool pillow. She closed her eyes, then opened them again, brain buzzing. She was all churned up. A cobweb hung from the ceiling. It was swaying in the draught. Eve turned her head to see a broken pane in the dormer window and a cool breeze fell on her face. It was soothing. She closed her eyes, enjoying the refreshing shower of air on the burning lids. For inside, she was on fire. Heat rose up her spine, blasting onto her throat and face. Was she ill? Feverish? She felt her forehead. It was hot. She'd been overdoing it. That was it. Mary Jean was right.

Eve slept. When she woke, it was dark and her head was aching. There was a row going on downstairs. Her Mam was back. She could hear Maisie too, and Jack. She couldn't bring herself to call him 'Dad'. She shivered and sat up, on the edge of the bed, rubbing herself for warmth. She'd love a hot tub right now. It'd been four days since the last one and her clothes were crumpled from the bed. She sat there for a while, watching the moonlight playing on the walls of the room. The cobweb was still wafting about in the breeze. Time didn't seem to matter. It stood still for you, here in England. But inside, Eve was speeding. Her stomach rumbled. Was it supper time? She got up and tried the light switch. Nothing happened. In the moonlight, she could see there was no lamp in the holder. In any case, a light would have contravened the blackout regulations. It was strangely quiet. Out of the window, you could see ghostly roofs shining, but the houses all looked dead, empty. Suddenly the door opened and her mother stood in the light from the passage. She shut the door quickly, and came straight towards Eve.

'Hallo, pet. Welcome back.' She took Eve in her arms. Suddenly Eve sobbed. Her mother rubbed her back, as though she was winding a baby. 'I thought I heard you moving about,' she said. 'Why didn't you come down? You must be starving.' In the darkness they found it necessary to whisper.

'I'm sorry about grandma,' Eve muttered.

'It was a blessed relief, really,' her mother answered. 'Blessed

138

relief'. It sounded quaint to Eve's American ears now. 'She was very bad with the bronchitis. Well it developed into pneumonia and that was that.' They hugged for a few moments more. It was warm and cosy.

Eve took a deep breath, before asking, 'How is everybody?'

'See for yourself. Come on down and have some supper.'

Descending to the kitchen, Eve blinked in the glare of the naked light bulb. The darkness had hidden the changes in her mother, whose eyes were sadder, the red hair greyer and duller, and the old familiar clothes, now shabby and old-fashioned. Looking at her made Eve want to cry. An anchor had slipped away while she wasn't looking. She turned to Maisie, her mother's old aunt, Eve's chaperon when she'd first gone to the States. To her relief she saw the pale damp eyes, the sunken mouth, and heard the badly-fitting false teeth, clicking just as before. At least Maisie hadn't changed. And she'd been to America, even if she *had* hated it!

Bubbling, Eve distributed the presents, concealing awkwardness under a pretended gaiety. But her mother barely smiled. She was preparing the supper and soon had them sitting at the kitchen table. Disoriented and unable to take on the old persona that the family remembered, Eve struggled to fend off the bits of her American life which kept shooting to the surface, like flying debris. As usual, she fell back on fantasy . . .

'Eve had crashed into their lives like a falling star. Her brightness dazzled them. She was the forerunner of what was to come. In her wake surely America would follow. Hitler would not prevail!' she told herself. But, looking at her plate brought Eve down to earth with a heavy thud. It was supposed to be mutton dumplings. Only you'd be hard pushed to find the mutton. What meat there was was dry and black . . .

'In the States, she was used to steaks, huge ones. Why, even at the ranch, where times were hard, they always had good meat on the table. Her heart melted with compassion for the poor, undernourished Brits.' But her mother had a light hand and the dumpling was soft and fluffy, slipping down a treat with the Marmite gravy and the mashed spuds. Eve was very hungry. They all watched her eat, fascinated by her appetite.

'You'll get indigestion if you don't slow down,' her mother warned. 'You haven't told us about your big success, yet, at the

139

Hollywood Bowl! I thought you'd be full of it.' Eve was. She jumped at the invitation . . .

'She was like a falling star. They listened open mouthed to her tales of glamour and success,' reviving wilting dreams.

'Oh, Jack, you should've been there,' Eve enthused. 'The Bowl was packed. It seats eighteen thousand people, you know.' Jack looked suitably impressed. 'And they all rose to their feet every one of them. It was marvellous!' Jack's eyes misted. Eve brought back memories of his own days on the halls, when he and Frances had been young. 'I'd like to show you how I've come on,' Eve went on. 'My pendulum wings are the best in Hollywood. They said so in the papers.'

'Fancy,' her mother commented dryly.

'You're only jealous, Mam,' Eve laughed. Frances bit her lip, but said nothing. She'd been watching her daughter, ever since she came down. She had an ego the size of a football. 'I'll give you a demonstration, shall I?' Eve rose to perform. Mary, Jack and Maisie were enthusiastic, but not so Frances.

'Shurrup and eat your supper, our Eve,' she snapped. Eve was hurt. She shrugged and ate a little more, but her appetite had gone.

'I don't suppose you've got such a thing as a bathroom yet, have you, Mam?' she asked. 'I must stink to high heaven by now.'

'Don't speak to me in that superior voice about bathrooms, Eve,' her mother warned. 'There's nothing to be proud of in being smelly. And no we haven't got a bathroom. We've not got a swimming pool, either. So just eat your dumplings before they get cold. We're on rationing here. There's a war on, you know.' Eve picked up her fork again. 'What's the matter with your knife? You're not in America now.' Eve picked up her knife. Jack and Mary were embarrassed and looked away, but Maisie still had stars in her eyes.

'I kept a scrap book of all them cuttings you sent home, pet,' she said. Eve perked up at once. 'I'll get it out and show you!' It was in the dresser drawer. Maisie laid it down on the table beside Eve, and opened it proudly. 'Starlet and hero-ace contemplate marriage.' Frances looked at the picture of her grinning daughter and her companion.

'And who's he when he's at home?' she asked.

'Oh, that's John Ridley, Mam,' Eve explained. 'One of the cousins. You know.'

'No I don't know.' Frances eyed the cooling dumplings, then the photograph. 'What all this about marriage, then?'

'Oh newspaper gossip, that's all.' Eve shrugged it off. 'They're always doing it. Anything for a story. You know.'

'I see. Well I only hope you've been as good as you ought to have been,' Frances sniffed. Eve blushed deeply, and seeing it, her mother was relieved. She'd found out what she wanted to know. Her tone softened. 'Alright. Finish your dumplings, pet,' she said. Then the sirens sounded. Immediately, the family jumped up, gathering things together, and made for the door. 'Come on, Eve. Out to the shelter,' Frances shouted. Hell! They were going to be bombed!

You could hear them in the sky, like a swarm of flies buzzing toward you. But this was not the movies. This was real. This was happening. It sounded like there were hundreds of them. Eve quaked with fear, clutching the blanket that had been thrust into her hand, blindly following her mother, Maisie and Mary Jean with little George in her arms into the tiny corrugated shelter out in the yard. The siren had stopped. The attack was about to begin. There was a note of panic.

'Jack, did you turn off the gas?' Frances whispered urgently.

Jack nodded, his torch waving this way and that, in the darkness.

'Save your batteries, man!' Maisie hissed. George had an orange box, complete with bedding, ready and waiting. He hardly woke. He fell asleep in his bed, and woke up in the shelter, most nights. So he was used to it. The rest of them sat on benches, huddling together under the blankets. The planes were overhead now. Sinister shapes in the darkness, the wings tipped with silver moonlight.

'They'll be making for the docks as usual,' Jack said. He put an arm round Eve but she shrugged him off. A stray bomb fell. They felt the tremor. The walls of the shelter rattled. 'That was close.'

'They get earthquakes in California, you know. John was in one,' Eve volunteered. Talking was a reflex. Automatic.

'Fancy,' said her mother.

'Did anybody remember to bring the cards?' Maisie asked. 'We've got enough people for a good hand of gin rummy.'

'Sorry, Maisie.' Jack shook his head.

'That's a pity. I brought a candle out,' she pouted.

'Have you got any matches?' Frances asked.

'Oh. No. I forgot about them,' Maisie admitted. There was a long silence. They all listened to the planes droning on toward the docks. Then it started. Eve gritted her teeth as the barrage of bombs fell, shock after shock. She thought it would never end. For a moment, she wished she hadn't shrugged off her father's comfort.

'You'll have to register for your identity card in the morning,' Frances told her daughter in a practical voice. 'Then you can get your ration book as well.' Eve gasped. 'What's wrong, pet?' She waited, anxiously, as Eve tried to speak.

'I don't know. I can't breathe. I feel as if my lungs are full of water.' Her mother rubbed her back. It felt warm and nice, but it didn't help much. Eve began to panic. Her breathing sounded like bed springs, twanging. Maisie laughed.

'Hark at her!'

'Sh, Maisie,' Frances reprimanded. 'It's not funny.' And it wasn't. Eve was dying! Nothing like this had ever happened to her before. She got up and dashed out into the fresh air, gasping.

'Stop her, man!'

'She'll be better outside, Fran. I'll make sure she's alright,' Jack hissed back into the shelter. Then the door closed behind him.

Eve's head reeled. Lights flashed in the sky, like a grand firework display. Bombs crashed in her ears. She could hear a fire engine, its bell ringing in the distance. She had to breathe. Had to. But she couldn't bear the confusion in the yard. She ran into the house, straight through the kitchen, and out into the shop. The moon shone in through the lattice pattern taped onto the shop window. Criss-cross. So the glass wouldn't fly when the bombs fell. It made a pattern on the floor. Exhausted she fell on her knees. Then Jack was with her. He picked her up, and flung her over his arm, holding her head.

'Come on. Breathe. Just keep calm. You can do it. There's a good girl. It'll be alright. Breathe slowly.' She tried. Oh God, she tried. The bombs stopped. They could hear the planes again,

142

droning overhead. Jack held onto her, alert, ready at any moment to fling himself and his daughter to safety behind the shop counter. But they passed on, towards the North Sea and home. Eve was breathing more freely. She lay, wet with sweat, in her father's arms. He wiped her forehead with his handkerchief.

'All over now,' he said.

She opened her eyes. Alarm bells were ringing all over Shields but the all clear still hadn't sounded. The huge wooden statue loomed under the stair. The roses looked dark in the moonlight, the colour of blood; but their fragrance was sweet.

'What did you say that statue was?' Eve asked.

'Ganesha, the elephant-headed God of the Hindus.'

'Why's He got an animal's head?'

'His Father cut off the first one!' Jack smiled at her, glad that at least she was talking.

'Whatever for?' She was quite shocked.

'He didn't realize Ganesha was His Son. It's not so unusual,' Jack explained. 'It's a sacrifice, like Jesus was. In all the myths, God always seems to sacrifice His Son, the innocent lamb, then, somehow or other, He's resurrected.'

'With an elephant's head . . . ?'

'Yes. In this case.' Jack laughed.

'He looks quite happy about it anyway,' Eve observed, 'dancing away . . .'

'Yes . . .' Jack was listening to the bells. 'It's a war dance, though. He's fighting evil.' There was an almighty bang. 'I wondered why they hadn't sounded the all clear.' They waited, listening for another bang. None came. A lone plane was heard put-putting across the sky. 'It's been hit. Watch out. It might off-load what's left of its cargo on us!' Jack pulled his daughter behind the counter. The plane was wheeling crazily over the town. Was it going to crash on top of them? Would the pilot bale out, and come parachuting down into their midst? If so, what would they do with him? 'I think Hitler must be trying to use the power of Ganesha,' Jack said. Eve turned to look at him in the half-light.

'What do you mean?' she asked.

'Well, I've heard say he's interested in the occult, and he's used Ganesha's swastika.'

'But the swastika's a Red Indian sign,' Eve told him. 'I've seen it, in their old ruins. It's an ancient religious symbol.'

'Well, well,' Jack shook his head, smiling in wonder. 'It's a small world, isn't it?'

'Jack,' Eve said suddenly, 'are you saying Hitler's using black magic against us?'

'Maybe he thinks it'll make him more powerful,' he answered. Eve went cold. 'But, don't worry,' he consoled her. 'Power maniacs always lose out in the end. Look what happened to Lucifer!' Eve smiled bleakly.

'You're not as daft as you look, our Jack, are you?' she said. Jack laughed then said, more seriously,

'I'm glad you came back, Eve. You're part of this family. We need you. And you need us. We're on the same side. And you know, a soldier that runs away, runs into the hands of the enemy.'

'You're forgetting no-man's-land, Jack,' Eve reminded him. 'There's always no-man's-land.'

But Jack shook his head. 'There's nothing there,' he told her. 'Only death.' He was looking at her, intently. It made Eve shiver.

'You're not just talking about this war, are you, Jack?' she said sharply.

Jack sighed. 'Eve, love, I know once upon a time I said you could call me Jack, but I wish you could bring yourself to call me Dad instead.' Eve shook her head. 'Please. Let's let bygones be bygones.'

'I can't!' she cried. 'I can't ever forgive, or forget what you did to me!' In panic, Eve stood, wanting only to get away from the man who had turned her world upside down, till she didn't know even who she was, or what she was. And then a second blast, rocked the house. The stray plane had come down. The shop window cracked from top to bottom. Eve screamed and in a welter of flying glass, pulled away from Jack, who was trying to hold onto her and bring her back to safety behind the counter. She ran upstairs and shut herself in her room. Then, at last, the all clear sounded.

Half an hour later, Eve's Mam came up with a cup of hot milk.

'It's only powdered, but it's the best I can do,' she said. 'I'm sorry there's no light. We've not got any spare bulbs.'

'Doesn't matter.' Eve sipped the milk. It was comforting. 'Mam, why've you got a down on me? Are you not glad to see me?'

'Course I am pet,' Frances comforted. 'It's just, well, you have turned into a bit of a show-off, haven't you?' Eve spluttered milk onto her jumper. 'Never mind. It'll come out in the wash.'

'Literally!' Eve laughed. 'What's Jack going to do about the shop window?'

'Oh, I expect he'll board it up in the morning. It's the first time we've been hit. We're lucky.' Frances sat on the bed, holding Eve's hand. 'You know they're talking about compulsory war service for women. If you're staying, pet . . . and I hope you are . . .'

'It's alright,' Eve told her. 'I've already decided what I want to do. I'm goin' to be a Wren.'

'Trust you to go in for something glamorous,' her mother jeered.

'Stop it, Mam.'

'Aye, well,' Frances sighed. 'I'm supposed to be going up to the hospital tomorrow to see your Great-Aunt Hester. I don't suppose you'd go with me?' Eve frowned. Was that the sound of rattling skeletons she could hear?

'Yes. Glad to,' she answered, and there was a smile in her voice. Frances was pleased. She hated the lonely bus journey out into the wilds to the asylum. 'How is she?' Eve asked politely.

'Oh she comes and goes. Sometimes she sounds quite lucid.'

'What's wrong with her?'

'Religious mania.' Frances sighed. 'Well, it's one name for it, I suppose.'

Eve just couldn't help it. In spite of herself, in spite of knowing her mother's touchiness on a delicate subject, she asked outright, 'Mam, why wouldn't you let our Os marry Hester's daughter? He wanted to once, didn't he?'

'Your Great-Aunt Hester killed your great-grandfather; isn't that enough for you?' Frances was bristling.

'It wasn't Anna's fault,' Eve objected.

'No. Well. There is something else. Hester's not normal. It could be inherited.'

'You mean Anna could go mad as well?' Frances nodded. 'But why?'

'Ask me no questions, I'll tell you no lies.'

'Oh, Mam!'

'You don't need worry. You're not descended from that line of the family.'

'Thank God for that.' Eve sighed with relief. It was easier to talk in the darkness. The moon had gone down. But the glow of fire lightened the window. 'Are the Americans cousins?'

'No. They're a different branch altogether. They go way back, to long before . . . '

'Before what?' Frances pursed her lips.

'In any case . . . ' she said, 'it's all guesswork.'

'How is Anna?' Eve asked. 'I've not heard anything about her for ages.'

'She's gone and got herself married,' Frances said bitterly.

CHAPTER EIGHT

Unable to sleep, Eve rested her eyes on the darkness. From time to time she heard the clanging of fire engines, or the ominous sound of falling rubble. It was coming from somewhere near Market Square. The dull glow of fire still lit the sky and, by its lugubrious light, she could just make out the Spartan outlines of the room. It was a monotone world. But when she closed her eyes, she saw in brilliant technicolor, a film retrospect of herself, as starlet, woman in love, career girl and dancer. It had seemed real at the time, but now she was in England, she began to wonder if she'd only dreamt it. Eve was battling with an army of exhumed feelings. She wanted to scream and run. She squirmed at the memory of Jack's embrace. How dare he expect love from her? Some father he was! Love him? She hated him! And as for the rest of them! Yet, they were nice people, her family. Ashamed, she comforted herself with the knowledge that she had, at least, been nice to her Mam, promising to go with her to see Auntie Hester. After all, she'd never seen the old dragon in her life, and there was no reason why she should now! Except, of course, Eve loved her Mam. She just didn't understand why she'd led her on to think Davey Lawson was her father, while secretly conducting an affair with Jack. Her mother had betrayed her.

The comfort evaporated. Tears bulged at her eyes. If only she could sleep. Perhaps, if she imagined herself back on the ship, the sea swaying under her, rocking her . . . Eve closed her eyes, but immediately the technicolor world sprang back to life. She gritted her teeth and banished the vision, conjuring in its place the cool sea, the moonlight, and the days before they'd docked in Liverpool, peacefully adrift in the Atlantic never-land between the two worlds. And at last, she slept.

Next morning, the sky was like ash. As a treat, Frances gave her daughter bread and dripping for breakfast. Eve spread the meaty fat onto her slice with satisfaction. There was a little cut on her forehead, just above her left eye. It had bled in the night.

'Eeh, let me put some plaster on that,' her mother said, rummaging in the dresser drawer. 'I never knew you'd been hurt!'

'It's alright. Neither did I!' Eve laughed. The laughter broke the greyness that clouded her head. 'Will it leave a scar do you think?' she asked, as the plaster was checked for size, cut, and put in place.

'It might. But it'll fade in time, I expect. Don't worry.' Frances looked at Eve critically. 'You can always cut a fringe to hide it. You'd suit a fringe.' She was snipping the air with her scissors. But Eve wouldn't let her do it. It was far too drastic. So, while Eve finished her breakfast, Frances started packing a basket of food for the hospital, slipping in a pair of Eve's nylons. Little George watched suspiciously.

'Where're you going, Grandma?' he asked.

'Never you mind, pet,' Frances told him. But George *did* mind.

'I don't want you to go out,' he said.

'Mind!' Frances objected. 'Hark at him!'

'George!' Mary reprimanded her son, but he just began blubbering on about how he didn't want his grandma to go out, till Mary Jean asked him, 'Why ever not?'

'I just don't that's all,' he cried. There was going to be a tantrum.

'Haway, Eve. Better get out quick,' Frances said quietly. Eve pulled on her coat, picked up her bag and they left, via the shop.

'Give her my love!' Maisie shouted after them. At the kitchen door, George stood, howling his head off.

'What got into him?' Eve asked, as they swung along Fowler Street. Frances shrugged and sighed.

'Bairns. You'd think they knew, wouldn't you?'

'Knew what?'

'Nothing.'

'Ooh, Mam!' Eve groaned. 'I hate it when you act mysterious!'

It had begun to drizzle. Frances put up her umbrella and linked arms with Eve, to bring her under its protection. A yellow double-decker trolleybus was coming down the hill towards them, and Frances hurried Eve to the bus stop.

'What happened to the trams?' Eve asked.

'Damn. It's going down Ocean Road.' Frances let the bus go. 'Come on. It'll be quicker to walk.' So they walked on, in the spitting rain, round the corner into King Street, where they were faced with devastation. There was water everywhere. A trolleybus was scrunched up against the side of a half-demolished building, and a hill of bricks lay between them and the bus depot on the other side of the Old Town Hall. They stood for some seconds, stunned. Undefeated, Frances said, 'We'd better see if there's any trains.'

They had to walk miles, through back streets to reach the station. But the train came, which was a relief, because it might not have done. Then, at Newcastle, they had to walk again, to the bus station, and by the time they'd got on the bus to Durham, their feet were wet, their stockings were black and both women were thoroughly exhausted. They scrambled up the stair to the upper deck, and claimed the front seats. They were all alone up there. The engine started. The bus moved off. Frances rummaged in her basket. 'I put some chocolate in for Hester. Do you think she'd mind if *we* ate it?'

'Mam,' Eve said emphatically, 'what the head doesn't know, the heart doesn't grieve for. Give's a bit.' And they ate in satisfied silence.

'Eeh, I'd forgotten how good chocolate was!' Frances moaned with delight. It was good to have a treat when you knew you deserved it.

They enjoyed the ride, out of the town, beyond the trolley lines and the buzzing wires, into the country.

'There's times you can forget all about the war,' Frances said, as she looked at the cows and the green grass. 'In fact, if it wasn't for having to see our Hester, I'd really like these trips out to the hospital.' Eve laughed and put her arm through her Mam's. They were the best of friends, just like old times. 'You're not a bad lass,' Frances said. There were tears in her eyes and Eve was beginning to be glad she'd come. Then her mother went and spoiled it, by adding, 'If only you'd be nicer to your Dad.' Eve sighed. 'It wasn't all his fault, you know. I played my part. And if you can forgive me, surely . . . '

'Mam,' Eve said, 'you told me once Jack cheated you into coming back to the flower shop, when you'd just carved out a nice career for yourself on the stage. Now he did that so he could get his hands on the shop. Didn't he? Eh? Admit it, now!' Frances nodded.

'That's true. He did. But, you know, pet, I *was* pregnant, with our Os. I had responsibilities. My trouble was, I didn't want to face up to them. And then, out of spite maybe, I went with Davey Lawson, while your Dad was away at the war. The First War. One daft moment, and I've been paying for it ever since.'

'Are you sure I'm not Davey's?'

'I thought you were, till the day you were born. And then, when you came earlier than expected, the penny dropped. You weren't early at all. It was me. I'd got the dates wrong. You were my husband's child. But it was too late. I'd let the cat out of the bag. Eeh, what a mess!'

'But Jack pushed you into Davey's arms, in a way . . . !'

'Don't be so bloody melodramatic, our Eve. Eeh, what *has* Hollywood done to you!' Frances tut-tutted, till she remembered what she was going to say. Then she went on, choosing her words, carefully. 'There were other things bothering me, besides Jack. Family problems. I was running away. Just like you, pet. Only I ran into a man's arms. You ran all the way to America.'

'What were you running from?' Eve pressed angrily, feeling her mother was hiding something from her.

'Every family's got its skeletons,' Frances said, tight lipped. 'Ours is no exception. But, I'll tell you what, it's rattling ever more loudly, now your grandma's dead!'

'Why?' Eve asked. Frances took a deep breath, before she

spoke. It was as though she was weighing how much to tell her daughter.

'Your Auntie Hester has a half share in the shop,' she said. 'How she got that's a long story. Anyway, when she was committed to the asylum after killing her father, your grandma was made trustee. Well, pet, your grandma's dead, isn't she? So now what's going to happen?'

Who needed Hollywood? Drama. Suspense. You could get it all at home!

At Durham they changed again, to the Sedgefield bus. And at Sedgefield they changed to Shanks's pony for the long trek out to the hospital. At lunch time, gasping for a cup of tea, they finally walked through the grounds and in through the doors of the forbidding Victorian Institution.

Hester Fairbairn (Mrs) had a cell to herself. She was classed as a dangerous patient, and spent most of her time drugged up to the eyeballs. Eve knew this. But nothing prepared her for the woman she now saw escorted into the interview room. She was painfully thin. She kept rubbing her hips, knees, and elbows, as though they hurt. But it was her eyes which dominated you. They were huge and black, and the pupils slid about, drunkenly.

'She must be dosed,' Frances whispered in Eve's ear.

'Now, Hester, try and be nice. Your relations have come a long way to see you,' the nurse said loudly. Hester slouched to the chair, at the other side of the table. 'Would you like a cup of tea, Mrs Scott?'

'Yes, Mrs Stringer,' Frances said. 'Thanks very much. I would.'

'I'll get you a pot,' the nurse replied kindly.

'What about me, Mrs Stringer?' The words were drawled. Was Hester drunk?

'You've had your dinner, never mind tea!' Mrs Stringer snapped. 'I'll leave the door open. But you won't have any trouble,' she said softly to Frances and Eve. Then she went, leaving them alone together. Immediately, Hester reached for Frances' bag and started searching through it. But the nurses had already removed the nail file and the safety pin.

'How are you, Hester?' Frances asked nervously.

'Who's this?' Hester was now staring at Eve.

151

'It's our Evie, Hester. She's come back from America.'

'Who?' Then she reached for Eve's bag and searched that. The pen had been removed.

Frances whispered, 'She doesn't remember you, pet.'

'I'm not deaf, you know!' Hester screamed.

From somewhere down the corridor, Mrs Stringer called out sharply, 'Now then, Hester! Mind your manners!'

Hester swore, 'Filthy cow.'

'Who?' For a moment, Eve thought her aunt meant her.

'That Mrs Stringer,' Hester confided, 'she's a whore. I've seen her doing things to herself under her apron.'

'I'm sure she doesn't!' Frances was embarrassed at such talk in front of her daughter.

'They're all whores,' Hester announced. 'God has thrust His Handmaiden into a den of iniquity! And none of you buggers cares!' She was crying wildly, ripping at her blouse, till the buttons flew from the cloth, and her bosom was laid bare.

'Eeh, I'm sorry, pet.' Frances took her daughter's hand. 'The drugs must've worn off.' And then Eve saw the slashes on the bared breasts of the madwoman.

'My father did this to me!' Hester was dribbling from the corner of her mouth. Frances shook her head slightly, to reassure Eve. 'He was the devil incarnate. I, Hester, am God's avenging angel.' They heard footsteps coming back along the corridor. A cunning look crossed Hester's face. Suddenly, as though someone had thrown a switch, she changed. She tucked her blouse into her skirt, and neatened her hair, pulling it behind her ears, as Mrs Stringer walked in. 'Ah, tea. Thank you, dear,' she said to the nurse. 'Shall I be mother?' Then Hester began to pour. Mrs Stringer nodded and left them again.

'I've got bad news, I'm afraid, Hester.' Frances dared broach the difficult topic, now Hester was calm.

'Oh yes?' Hester said absently.

'Mam's dead.'

'Who?'

'Your sister. My mother. Ellen. She's dead. Two months back. She had pneumonia.'

'Serve her right. Good riddance.' Then sharp as a needle, Hester asked, 'Who's got my share in the shop now?' Her eyes darted to Eve, who shook her head, disclaiming any rights she

152

may or may not have had. 'You'll have sent for Anna, then?' Frances looked uncomfortable. She shook her head. 'Well, you'd better! She's my daughter, and she'll inherit my share!'

'I suppose she wrote and told you she got married?' Frances ventured.

'Anna? Oh yes. She did. Little harlot. Is she pregnant?'

'Not that I know of.' Frances coughed and stirred the sugar in her tea. At once, Hester grasped the spoon and stowed it up her skirt. Suddenly Eve wanted to laugh. Trying to stop herself, she choked, and had to go out of the room to recover herself.

'Is she a virgin?' Hester enquired of her mother.

'That's none of your business,' Frances rebuked.

'Like mother, like daughter!' Hester shouted triumphantly, clapping her hands and gurgling with laughter. Then she hissed, as Eve re-entered the room. 'Fornicator!' Eve faltered, and stood in the doorway. 'Been to America, eh?' Eve nodded. 'Where?'

'Hollywood.'

'Babylon!' Hester screamed. 'God will avenge Himself on the iniquities of the city, fallen unto evil ways. It shall be cast down into the sea and shall be found no more at all. And the voice of harpers and minstrels shall be found no more in thee. For with thy sorcery were all the nations deceived. And in her was found the blood of prophets and of saints.'

Frances sighed, 'She's off.'

'And I saw an angel coming down out of heaven, with a sword in his mouth . . . '

'Alright, Mrs Fairbairn!' Mrs Stringer was back. 'That's enough of that.'

For a second, Hester looked as though she was going to murder Mrs Stringer. Then suddenly she broke down and cried like a child. 'Why doesn't God love me any more?' she whimpered. Eve thought her heart would burst. Hester's grief and loneliness pierced her like a knife. 'I am not worthy to live on His Earth. I am tainted with the filth of the fornicator.'

'There, there,' said Mrs Stringer, smiling, and patting her hand.

'He casts me from Him, for my mother is guilty of the sin of my conception and my birth is a blasphemy upon the earth.'

'That's right, pet.' Mrs Stringer was helping Hester out of her chair, her eyes scanning the room. 'Where's the teaspoon?' she asked. Frances' face told the tale. 'I thought as much.' She started feeling Hester's body.

'Get off me! Whore!' Hester screamed.

'Where is it? I know you've got it!' Mrs Stringer said sharply. There was a struggle, during which, the nurse's hat slipped to one side. But she found the spoon, tucked up Hester's knicker leg. She held the implement up, a victorious smile on her face. Now Hester was whimpering.

'I brought her a basket of stuff,' Frances said. 'And there's some nylons for you, Mrs Stringer. Eve, my daughter, brought them back from America.'

'Nylons!' Mrs Stringer beamed and hugged them to her. 'Well, that *is* nice! Don't worry now, Mrs Scott. I'll take care of your old auntie.' She encouraged Hester out of the room, looking in the basket as she went. Hester was crying. 'There, there,' Mrs Stringer comforted her. 'You've got tinned peaches for your tea, pet, so things can't be all that bad, can they, now?'

Eve and her mother walked back into Sedgefield in silence. A light rain washed their heads and Eve was glad of it.

'Thanks for coming, pet.' Frances took Eve's hand as they walked to the bus stop.

'Poor Mam,' Eve said. 'You've got a lot to put up with.'

'Not as much as that poor woman in there,' Frances said quietly. As they sat on the bus in the darkening afternoon, Eve began to cry.

'Why?' she asked, as the tears dripped onto her hands. 'Why did Auntie Hester have to end up like that?'

'Who knows, pet,' Frances said.

'You know!' Eve snapped. Frances shook her head.

'If I tell you, you'll only start blaming others for your own problems. First make your peace with your Dad. Then with yourself. Then, maybe there'll be some point in telling you.' Frances was gripping her hand so hard, it hurt. Eve couldn't bear the pressure. She tried to change the subject.

'What were you all rowing about yesterday?' she asked.

Frances hesitated. 'Hester's daughter. Anna Fairbairn, as was. Your Dad agreed to go down to London to see her father, after a bit of persuasion, like.' Eve laughed at her wry smile. 'We had an agreement, you see. Anna wasn't to get married without consultation with us first.'

'But why?' Frances sighed.

'Alright.' She gave in. 'I'll tell you.' Then her voice dropped so low, Eve had to lean towards her, to hear. 'Your Great-Aunt Hester lives under the shadow of her own birth. Or at least, that's what your father and I suspect. You see, your great-grandma, Jane Beattie, had a brother, Robert. He ran away, disgraced, just before . . .'

'Don't tell me.' And Eve turned away.

Frances and Eve arrived home, cold and weary in body and spirit. But Maisie had talked her 'boyfriend', a butcher down Harton way, into delivering some sausages, in return for a few potted plants, so the traditional Geordie dish of Pan Haggerty was waiting for them when they got in; layers of sausage, onion and potato, roasted in the oven. It warmed the cockles of your heart. Good old Maisie!

'Jo Ridley's still got a soft spot for you, Maisie,' Eve teased her great-aunt, as she shovelled her supper down.

'Huh!' was all Maisie said, but she was pleased. You could tell by the way she had trouble keeping down the corners of her mouth. It was nice to be 'nearing sixty' as she put it, and still have somebody hankering after you! And it was just as well she *was* buoyant, because Frances and Eve were feeling very low. Mary Jean had given up on the day long since, and gone to bed, muttering about flu, and Jack had been out for hours on Home Guard duty. So, stomach full and a hot water bottle under her arm, Eve went up to bed just as soon as she could. Somebody had put up a black-out curtain in her room, and there was a naked bulb in the ceiling light. Maisie again, Eve supposed. She undressed quickly, switched off the light, and slipped under the sheets, curled like a baby, round the hot bottle. She fell asleep at once.

It was one in the morning. Somebody was screaming blue murder. Eve woke, heart pounding. For a second she didn't know where she was. Everything was black. She wasn't at the ranch, or in Santa Monica. Was this Clara's? The screaming pierced her consciousness. Who was it? Not Jimmy. No,

Georgie. Of course. She was at home. Eve got out of bed and dragged her jumper on over her nightie. She could hear another voice. Maisie's. Eve opened the door. Downstairs there was commotion.

'You stay there, Mary Jean,' Maisie was calling. 'I'll see to him. Come on now, me little laddie. Have you been havin' nightmares again?' Doors closed. Eve could go back to bed. But she was wide awake. Her throat was dry, parched. She could die for a cup of tea. She went down to the next landing. She could hear Maisie soothing George. She opened the door to Maisie's room, and surprised the pair of them cuddling in Maisie's bed.

'I thought I'd make a cup of tea, Maisie. Would you like one?' she offered.

'Oh, smashin'!' Maisie enthused. 'And how about a nice warm drink of milk for you, eh?' George moaned. 'Aye. Get him one, Eve, there's a pet.' Eve went down to the kitchen. She could hear George, sobbing intermittently upstairs. She put on the kettle and stood staring at the black cloth over the kitchen window. There was a draught coming from behind. The door to the cellar had opened an inch, and a damp gust was blowing up the stair from the darkness below. Eve shivered and jammed the door shut. Watched kettles never boil, she thought. So she wandered into the shop, and stood in the light streaming from the kitchen. Perfume hung on the air like the memory of flowers; lilies, roses, freesias, narcissi, peonies, chrysanthemums. Once, when her great-grandfather was mayor of Shields, this shop was a thriving business. Her great-grandma's family were river people, seamen and pilots. Jane Beattie. Eve shut the door on the thought. Back in those days, there was prosperity. What had happened to this family? Eve turned to go back into the kitchen, but stopped, rooted to the spot, as she came face to face with the dancing figure of Ganesha. 'He died for us, that our sins be forgiven'. 'Forgive us our trespasses as we forgive those . . . ' 'Make your peace with your Dad, then with yourself.' No. Please. There must be another way. The elephant-headed God was silent. Stubborn, Eve went back into the kitchen, made the tea, mixed the dried milk, and took the tray up to Maisie's room.

George had stopped crying, but he had an anxious look on his face, as though he didn't feel quite safe.

'I don't know,' Maisie sighed. 'He doesn't seem to mind bombs going off, but whenever your Mam goes to see our Hester, he gets nightmares.'

'She didn't ever take him with her, did she . . . ?'

'Why no, man!' Maisie scorned the very idea. 'D'ye think she's crackers?' Eve shook her head and drank the tea. 'Crackers' was the last thing she'd have called her Mam. 'Come on, Georgie,' Maisie encouraged. 'Settle down now. Go to sleep, eh?' But George was restless.

'Can I have a 'tory?' he begged.

'Oh alright, then,' Maisie said unwillingly. 'What do you want?'

'Don't want fairy story. No horrible witches, Auntie.'

'Well, that narrows the field down a bit, doesn't it?' Maisie grimaced at Eve. 'I know. I'll tell you a story that's so old, I don't even know where it came from.' George stared at his auntie. 'It's a story that my Mam, your great-great-grandma told me when *I* was little.'

'Great-great-grandma? How big was she?' George gaped. Maisie laughed.

'Not that sort of "great", pet. I mean she was your dad's mother's mother's mother.'

'I don't understand.' Eve laughed indulgently at the little boy's confusion.

'Never mind.' Maisie gave up. 'Just listen. Once upon a time, there was a little baby elephant, and it lived with its Mam and its Dad and all its brothers and sisters and uncles and aunts, just like we do, in a far away country, where there were rivers and lakes and forests, and it was very happy. Now, in one of them rivers, there lived a big bad crocodile. Now this crocodile liked elephant, as much as you like sausages, our George.' George giggled. 'But the little baby elephant was quite safe, because it never strayed from the herd and the crocodile didn't stand a chance against the lot of them, now, did it?' George shook his head, eyes round with interest. 'But, this little baby elephant was cheeky. It was determined to go its own way, no matter what anybody said. And one day, it got a bit above itself. It was playing hide and seek with its brothers and sisters and it strayed away from the herd, and soon found itself down by the river-bank. Now it was a hot day, and the baby elephant was very thirsty and it couldn't see anybody about, so it thought no harm to goin' down to the water, and dipping its trunk in for a nice long drink. When suddenly, the crocodile, jaws open wide, jumped up from under the water, and its jaws snapped round the leg of the little elephant. Now the elephant trumpeted away, hoping his brother and sisters and his Mam and Dad would hear him. But they were a long way off, and by the time they reached the river bank, our little elephant was quite dead . . . ' George started blubbering. Alarmed, Eve took over the story, improvising.

' . . . well the Mam stood there, tears falling from her big sad eyes, like raindrops, onto the body of her little baby. And her tears had magic in them. Because, you see, the mother loved her child very much, even though it'd been naughty and strayed, and her tears had so much love in them that when they fell into its wounds, and mixed with the baby's blood, a miracle happened. The baby's heart began to beat. And its body healed. Then it opened its eyes and it stood before its mother, and said, "Mam, I'm sorry I was naughty. I'll be good now. I promise." And the mother elephant raised her trunk high into the air, trumpeting with joy, because her baby was saved. And never again did that little baby elephant stray from the herd, and it lived with the rest of the elephants happy ever after.' George's tears dried on his cheeks. He sniffed a bit, then slowly his eyelids drooped and he was asleep. For a while, Maisie and Eve sat, watching his little face, puffed and rosy, as he sank deeper and deeper into peaceful rest. Then, very gently, Maisie picked him up and carried him to his cot in his Mam's room.

Hitler must have given his lads the night off that night, because there were no bombs dropped on Shields, anyway. So the family woke, rested after a long sleep. They were late opening, not that customers were actually banging on the door, but Eve was dissuaded from helping in the shop.

'Jack,' Frances said, 'take our Eve down to get her identity card and that sorted out, and then, why don't you two go for a walk, eh? It's a nice day for the time of year.' It was a conspiracy to bring her closer to her father, and she knew it, but Eve was too tired to resist. The day at the 'loony bin', as Maisie called it, had taken it out of her. So she let Jack manoeuvre her through the

158

red tape at the register office. After checking her passport, they asked to see her birth certificate.

The clerk looked at it, glanced at Jack, and asked, 'Is this your father?' Eve shook her head.

'No. My father's dead,' she told him. Father and daughter were too embarrassed to look at one another. But the name on the birth certificate was 'Davey Lawson', not 'Jack Scott'. So what else could she say? Finally, they told her her ration book would follow 'in due course', and meanwhile issued her with emergency coupons. Formalities over, Jack and Eve took themselves off to the pier for a walk and a bit of fresh air.

There was a man down there, hiring out fishing rods. Jack paid for one, then set out with Eve, for the end of the pier. There were a lot of fishermen already trying their luck. A bit of fish eked out the rations a treat. Choosing his spot, Jack swung his hook and Eve watched as it skimmed across the blustery waves and sank, clear of the seaweed. The wind was fit to cut off your ears. Eve pulled her mother's woolly hat down, and held her collar tight. An old trawler was coming in between the north and south piers.

'Minesweeper,' Jack said. 'I fancied doing that.'

'How could you? You've never been to sea,' Eve said curtly. 'You were a comedian on the halls.'

'True,' Jack sighed. 'But you can't live here long, without fancying a life on the ocean waves. He burst into song, ' "A life on the ocean wave . . . " ' Eve laughed. 'It's in *your* blood anyway,' he pointed out.

'I was thinking of joining the Wrens,' Eve said.

'Good idea, love!'

'Only they don't let women go to sea.'

'You've got to do something,' Jack told her. 'Unless you get married and have a bairn, of course . . . ' He gave her a sly glance, then looked back at his line. The fish were being shy. 'This John Ridley chap . . . is it serious?' Eve flushed.

'To be honest, I don't think I want to get married at all,' she snapped.

'Why ever not?' Jack was shocked. He forgot all about the fish and looked directly at Eve.

'Men aren't all they're cracked up to be, are they? Look at you!' Eve's voice stung him.

159

'Don't go by me,' Jack said softly. 'I know I'm not up to much, but there's others that are.'

'Who? Come on, Jack. Women always end up holding the wrong end of the stick. Look at what happened to me Mam!' Jack sighed. He knew he'd done Frances wrong. He was in no position to put his daughter straight about men.

'Well, love,' he said at last, turning back to the bobbing line, 'it's a good job not all women think like you, or the human race would soon die out.'

'And a good thing too!' Eve hit back. 'I mean who'd want to bring a child into a world like this! It's criminal, if you ask me!'

'You've got a point, at that,' Jack admitted. 'Well, you pays your money and you takes your choice. You've chosen a career. I wish you well in it.' Eve knew he meant it. Poor Jack. Perhaps it *hadn't* been all his fault.

'I gather you had a rough ride at the institution yesterday?' Jack said, changing the subject.

'You could say that,' Eve said dryly. The waves bucked over the rocks, foaming and leaping like maddened horses. 'I hear you're going down to London to see Anna's father?' she hinted. Jack nodded cautiously. 'Can I come with you?' she begged, adding hastily, 'not that I want to see Anna's father, or Anna, come to that. But I do want to go to London.'

'Yes, Eve. I expect you do,' Jack sighed. They sat silently, for some time, staring at the choppy water. Then Jack looked up, scanning the mist that was billowing in from the sea.

'You remind me of a story I read, some time back,' he said. 'I'll look it out for you.' Eve was intrigued. On the quiet, Jack was a bit of a scholar. He knew things they didn't teach you at school, and the funniest thing was, he didn't boast about it. Eve said nothing. It was, in a way, her mark of respect. Jack flexed his chilled hand. It was stiff, a result of injury in the first war. He rubbed it.

'Too rough for fish today,' he observed. 'Pity. I could just fancy a bit of mackerel.' Jack sighed. 'Let's go home and have a nice hot cup of tea.'

Gods and Myths of India. He had put a marker where she was to read. Eve took it to her room, and lay on her bed. She was feeling tired, but, her interest grew, as she opened the book, and

160

started looking at the pictures. They were mostly of statues, and sacred stones. 'Swayambhus' they were called. Some of them were huge rocks, some had formed out of ice, but most were simply statues like the one downstairs, in the shop. There was Ganesha, with the four arms, dancing, weapons flailing. And there were other pictures too, of Shiva and Parvati, His Mother and Father. And there was His brother, Karttikeya, who had six heads, all of them human! Shiva had a snake hanging round His neck. And every chapter was headed by the sign of the swastika. Snakes . . . Swastikas . . . Eve shivered, and began to read.

'Parvati and Shiva thought that their two sons had attained to marriageable age, but how best should their marriage be celebrated? The six-faced Lord Karttikeya was their great, beloved son. Ganesha likewise. But a wonderful expedient was devised. They called their sons to them and spoke as follows:

"Both of you are good sons, equal in our eyes. Hence a condition that is beneficial to both of you has been made. The auspicious marriage will be celebrated of that boy who comes back first after going round the entire world." On hearing their words, the powerful Karttikeya started out immediately. But, Ganesha, of excellent intellect, stood where He was, pondering in his mind. "What shall be done? Where am I to go? I cannot cross the earth." So he performed the ceremonial ablution and returned home. He then spoke to His Mother and Father.

"For your worship, two seats have I placed here. Please be seated, dear parents." Parvati and Shiva sat on the seats, for receiving worship. They were circumambulated seven times and bowed to seven times. Then, joining his palms in reverence and eulogizing his Parents with love and affection, Ganesha, the ocean of intelligence, spoke thus,

"O, Mother, O, Father, my auspicious marriage shall be celebrated quickly." On hearing these words the Parents spoke to Ganesha.

"You shall circumambulate the earth with all its forests. Karttikeya has already gone. You too start and return first." On hearing the words of his parents, Ganesha said, "O, Mother, O, Father, the earth has been circumambulated by me seven times! So why should you say this?"

161

"O son, when was the great earth circumambulated by you?'
"By worshipping you, Parvati and Shiva, I have intelligently circumambulated the earth extending to the oceans. Is it not the verdict of the Vedas that 'He who worships his parents and circumambulates them, will certainly derive the fruit and merit of circumambulating the earth. He who leaves his parents at home and goes on a pilgrimage incurs the sin of their murder'." '

Eve re-read the last line, cried out and threw the book across the room. Jack Scott! How dare he?!

Eve couldn't leave at once. She was forced to wait for her ration book. So she stayed at home till the end of the following week, taking Mary Jean's place, working in the shop, cleaning and cooking, while Mary Jean enjoyed a change, devoting herself entirely to George. Then, Eve's ration book arrived and, without waiting for Jack, Eve packed her bag, kissed Maisie goodbye and left for Newcastle and the train south. Her Mam accompanied her as far as Central Station.

'Well, you did come with me to see our Hester,' she said. There were tears in her eyes. 'I'll miss you, pet. Honestly, it feels worse than when you went off to America!' Eve swallowed hard. In spite of herself, her chest was aching with the pain of leaving home. 'I love you, Eve,' Frances said. She was holding onto the train window, and the train was moving . . . That did it. Eve howled like a baby.

'I love you an' all!' she yelled. Then the engine got up speed and the two women waved and waved till lost to sight. Forlorn, they had gone their separate ways. That night, in a Y.W.C.A. in London, Eve was cleaning her teeth. She froze, the brush poised in mid air. The woman she saw in the mirror was a stranger.

CHAPTER NINE

Royal Naval College,
Greenwich.
May 31st 1941

Dear Clara,

So now we Wrens are officially part of the armed services! (And they *still* won't let us go to sea!) But at least I've got a decent uniform. You wouldn't believe how much clothes cost here, and they're going to ration *them* soon. Your food parcel was appreciated by everybody on board! I am very popular. But not so popular with the Chief Wren. I made a fool of myself during the semaphore test. Well they had us on opposite roofs, waving flags at one another, and you know I don't like heights. I got mixed up and told the girl opposite, 'Send green packets to camouflage your men.' It should have been 'jackets'. Fire watch was even worse. Once I got dizzy and passed out. I can't type and apparently I haven't got a 'crossword mind', so I'm not the right material to be a code cracker (or, come to that, a pay writer. Naval accounts are enough to bamboozle a Wall Street whizz kid!) (By the way, that was a mean deal you folks made on Lend Lease! Don't you know we're fighting a war for you?) Oh well, I'm so dim, I'll probably end up packing parachutes! Also, I'll be lucky to be ranked as high as Petty Officer, in spite of my great age, and all them lies about my family's naval background. Never mind, I'm having a marvellous time. So, *che sara sara.* I miss the dancing and the sunshine and I seem to suffer from permanent heartache. No. It's not what you think. I don't give a damn about John Ridley! You can tell him, I've got the guys buzzing round me here like flies round a honey pot. I've never been so happy. In war time, anything goes. Suits me! Last week I went out with a naval rating. This week it's the very posh brother of a shipmate. (Army Captain, my dear.) He took me to the Waldorf for tea. *They* didn't have any sugar, either. Write me all the news, soon as you can. And if you're thinking of sending another food parcel, please put in a few bars of soap, perfumed, if possible. I'm sick of smelling of carbolic. Good luck!

Love, Eve

P.S. I've just re-read my letter. Don't worry. The heartache's probably heartburn. Do you *know* what mock fish is made of?

Lawe Top Ranch
Ambrosia Lake,
Grants,
New Mexico
August 28th 1941

Dear Eve,

We are so glad the food parcel arrived without any trouble. We'll do our best to get another one to you just as soon as we can. Unfortunately, things are not that easy with us. Ernie had to resign from the police service. Know why? Well, it was because of that no good friend of John's, Ken Houlihan. Houlihan tried everything he could to get the judge to moderate his sentence. Even accused the police of corruption. He said my poor Ernie had taken bribes off of him and John. He couldn't prove it, of course, but mud sticks. And, after all, there was a family connection. I only hope and pray that our sacrifice will not have been in vain, and that this will be a lesson to John not to mix in bad company. Anyway, you'll be glad to hear John's doing well at the new base at Albuquerque. He's working for T.W.A. as one of their top instructors. Apparently his boys have a high success rate. Well, I guess it keeps him out of harm's way.

I'm on a visit here just now, while Ernie's trying to get work back in San Francisco. We're worried if we start the brake lining business at this moment in time, it'll fail. Suppose America was fool enough to go into this war? Then what would happen? Roosevelt's capable of anything if you ask me, never mind what most of us Americans actually want. 'Defend America First'. That's what I say. (I'm sorry, dear, but you know I always say just what I think.) Jo's been poorly. Overwork, he says. I say it's too much beer and cigarettes. June's worn out. She's got the café and Jimmy on her hands most of the time. He's a good boy, but, well, you know what children are. He broke his arm, falling off that horse of his a month ago. Took it into his head to ride it bareback! That Indian woman's got a lot to answer for. At least I can help out there, patching up some of the damage she's done. Do you know that boy has never even learned to say his catechism? I suppose you can't blame Louis. He's only a man. By the way, Lou's still doing construction work on the base. It's good money. He sends his kind regards.

Yours truly, Clara Trevor (and family)

H.M.S. Excellent
Portsmouth
November 18 1941

Dear Clara,

Forget the soap, I like smelling of carbolic. It's patriotic. You can forget the food parcel too, now you and Ernie are so poor. After all, I do get one ounce of cheese a week, and I'm only the size of a mouse, so I shouldn't complain, should I? I'm being moved on to a top secret establishment soon, so I can't give you my new postal address, which is just as well, because I don't much want to hear from you, anyway. I think Americans are selfish money-grubbers. By the way, I never learnt my catechism, either!

Love, Eve Lawson

'My!' Clara gasped as she read Eve's letter for the third time. 'For a beggar, she's mighty proud, don't you think, Ernie?'

'You said that before, Clara,' Ernie grunted.

'But that's just typical of the British. They hold out their begging bowls, then put on that superior look they've got.' They were sitting in Victoria Park, where they'd gone for a breath of air, following Sunday service. Ernie pulled on a piece of grass and chewed the end of it thoughtfully.

'Clara, you know I really think that garage we saw today was in a good spot.'

'Ernie, dear, you don't need me to tell you to exercise caution. Not after what we've been through.'

'Clara, we'll not get a better place than this. Believe me.'

'I don't know, honey . . . it's an awful lot of money . . .'

'Yeah. And it should be earning.' Ernie gave his wife a hard look. 'Just think about it, honey. But don't take too long. I mean, hell, no place is good enough for you, and my patience is just about running out!' He got up abruptly, brushed the grass off his trousers and started walking. Clara followed in a flurry. But he was going too fast and he was on Fisherman's Wharf before she caught up with him. Panting, she made a grab for his arm.

'I'm sorry, Ernie. I didn't mean to nag! It's just that I'm so anxious, dear. Once that money's gone, you know, it's gone!'

'Shut up!' Ernie stopped walking and yelled at his wife. You could have heard him in Sausalito. 'You were keen enough on the idea before I got fired from the cops.'

'Sh!' Clara looked round anxiously. 'You didn't get fired, Ernie. You resigned, on health grounds.'

'I liked being a cop, Clara. I even liked moaning about it. Now I'm nothing. Please, let me do the one thing I know I *can*! I've got to have this garage!'

There was a commotion over the road. People were coming out of the restaurant, shouting and waving their arms about. Then they came out of the warehouses on the quay too, wandering, sort of dazed, onto the street. A ship's hooter started up and then there was a long, low wailing noise, somewhere round the other side of the Bay.

'What' the hell's that?' Ernie asked. He grabbed at a passer-by. 'What's happened?'

'Japanese just bombed Pearl Harbor,' the stranger told him. 'It's on the news.'

'What?'

'Surely not?' Clara protested. 'Why, it must be a hoax.'

166

'Some hoax!' Ernie snorted.

'They've tried it before,' Clara informed him. 'The British just want to get us all riled up so we enter into this war of theirs. No. I don't believe the Japanese would dare to bomb us!'

The Albuquerque Army Base was almost empty. The 32nd BS and the 38th RS had already gone, some to Australia and some to the Philippines. So work was pretty slack, and John was having a cup of coffee, listening to the radio. 'The stupid bastards!' he thought. 'Why'd they do a dumb thing like that? They might just as well bomb the White House!' He walked out onto the field and looked around. Hell, there were going to be some changes around here. He threw his hat into the air and hollered fit to scare the crows. Within a week, the bombardier school started arriving in Albuquerque. The 56th and 88th squadrons reached there on December 18th, and on Christmas Eve the base was designated 'The Air Forces Advanced Flying School, Albuquerque'. John was in his element.

News of the Japanese attack took a little longer to reach the Indian strongholds of Northern Arizona. There, far from the sea, the pearl was understood to have a special significance. Moon-like, it was a symbol of chaste womanhood, transforming impurity into beauty through her natural grace; transforming the seed, nurturing the life, no matter what the cost in suffering. Womb of the world, sanctuary of man, could Goddess Woman be destroyed and man remain unpunished? This act of sacrilege would surely bring disaster on all their heads. Perhaps God, seeing how far man had gone, would destroy this world as He had the others. The Hopis waited for an indication, neither hearing, nor seeing nor speaking any evil.

It was Christmas, cold and bleak. But the pull of the reservation was too strong for Lou. No matter what the season, he knew he had to go north to see Ella. So he got in the van and started driving. No one knew he'd gone. He hadn't packed any bags. He hadn't planned the route. But he drove right through Grants, on to Gallup, then north-west, by Window Rock, to Indian land. The great mesas reared like rock fortresses, and a lone Navajo on horseback stood watching him pass. The place felt like a town preparing for a siege. Lou saw the car of the Indian agent driving fast towards him. Lou pulled in to let him pass, then watched the car speed off into the distance. Then, with a sudden sense of urgency, Lou screeched back onto the road, and drove hell for leather up the steep erratic slopes to Sichomovi. There was fear in the eyes of the women, as they saw the white man's car in their midst. But there wasn't time for pleasantries, so Lou started across the bucking ridge, alone and unassisted. Once in Walpi, he discovered Chu'Ovi was in the Kiva with the elders. What was going on? And where was Ella? A child gave him brief directions to the sheep corral, and Lou set off, recrossing the ridge, to drive back down the steep slope and on out to Sweet Spring.

He saw Ella from far off, astride a horse. She was herding the sheep. Her head lifted, and he saw the horse rear, as he stopped on the road. She was shading her eyes, straining to see who it was. Then she dismounted, and tethered her horse to the stockade, waiting for him, as he walked, on and on, over cracked clay and vermilion rock, shading his eyes against the lowering sun, until, at last, they stood face to face in the blank wilderness.

'What's happening, Ella?'

'India agent's been. He's gone for the sheriff.'

'Why?'

'Dan and a few of the other men won't register for selective service,' Ella told him calmly. They were alone in the vast landscape. Specks on eternity. At any moment, the hand of God might wipe them away. The wind blew the hair across her face. She blinked and brushed it aside. Lou felt paralysed by the immensity of the place and the time. But the sheep were scattering so he sprang into action, untying the horse, and leaping on its back.

'You stay here. I'll round up the flock,' he commanded. Still calm, Ella watched as he wheeled the straying sheep, bleating and scampering, into the corral. Then she shut the gate behind them and tied the rope tight round the posts. When he got down from the horse, she surprised him by crying fiercely.

'Why did you come? Why?' Lou leaned on the palisade, staring up at the sky. 'Have you come to talk our men into fighting in the white man's war?' He shook his head.

'I don't know that *I* want to go to war, come to that,' he said.

Ella looked at him, surprised. 'What do *you* think I should do?' he asked. 'I'm white. Should I join up?' She stared. 'Anyway, what's Dan got against fighting?'

'The Hopi people are not attached to this world,' she answered slowly. 'We're attached only to God. And when this world ends, God will save us for the next. That's why we don't care for worldly things. They come and they go. That's why we're a people of peace.' Lou nodded.

'I know. But the Japs and the Germans and the Italians, they aren't peaceful, Ella. This Hitler . . . he's evil. We've got to fight him!'

Ella shook her head. 'You don't understand. Any action of ours is not only dangerous, but unnecessary. Evil brings evil on itself. It's the law.'

'And meanwhile how many people are going to be killed?'

'Lou, try and see that action only brings reaction. It's the story of mankind. Back and forth, back and forth. We have to be outside history.'

'Sounds pretty uncaring,' Lou sighed.

'It doesn't mean we don't care.' Ella looked across the desert waste, eyes glowing in the gold of the evening sun. 'We're not cold-blooded, Lou!' As they looked, a huge bird fell out of the sky, diving onto the rosy clay, to catch its prey up in its beak and carry it, writhing, high over the mesa top. 'America! We love this beautiful land.' Her smile faded as she looked back at Lou. 'But I'll never marry you, Lou, if you fight in this war.' Her hand reached up to touch his face. Her fingers were light and cool. It was like being bathed with soft, sweet water.

He closed his eyes and murmured, 'I won't fight, Ella, if that's what you want.' Lou opened his eyes. Ella's eyes were full of love. His arms circled her round, holding her, claiming her. Still as rock, they stood, whether for seconds or hours, neither knew. Their embrace made a mark on the page of eternity. Then, Lou bent to kiss the top of her head.

'Come on,' she whispered. 'We'd better get back to the village before the sheriff comes.' As they turned to walk back to the road, they saw that though they stood in sunshine, the sky had gone dark ahead. And bright, against the backdrop of purple black, the sheriff's wagon was hurtling up the road towards First Mesa. Reluctantly, they dropped hands. Ella swung onto the horse's back, Lou ran to his truck, and both hurtled down the road to Walpi.

Sheriff Wilkins was O.K. He talked to the men for a while, trying to persuade them, nicely, that, if they were real men, they'd surely not just stand by and see their wives and sisters raped by Nazis and Japs! Or maybe they weren't men? Huh? The Indians all stood stone-faced. And in the end, Wilkins had no choice. He had to arrest them. Most of the village was out there, watching the proceedings, including the Chiefs of the Eagle, the Snake and the Antelope Clans. The sheriff made a last appeal to them.

'They're only refusing to register because of your say-so,' he said. All three Chiefs shook their heads.

Then Dan spoke up. 'This is our own decision. We won't fight. It's a principle. You understand?'

The sheriff shrugged. He didn't understand at all. Then this white man drove up and elbowed his way to the front. Wilkins greeted him like a long lost friend.

'Hi, stranger. Am I glad to see you.'

'What's going on?' Lou asked.

'Well, I'm going to have to arrest these young men here, for not electing to do their service for the nation.' The sheriff appealed to him. 'Can you help me?'

Lou shook his head. 'You can't arrest them. They're conscientious objectors. It's against their religion to fight.'

'What religion?' The sheriff laughed. 'Hopis don't have no religion.'

'Hell, they do!' Lou retorted.

'What? They're not Catholics, they're not Baptists, they're not Quakers, they're not even Jehovah's goddam Witnesses! So what the hell are they?' the sheriff bawled.

'They're Hopis,' Lou told him quietly. 'Their life is their religion.'

'I never heard such goddam crap. Who are you, huh?'

'My name's Lou Ridley.'

'So?'

'So, I'm saying you can't arrest these men. That's all.'

Excitement stirred in the people, like a breeze rustling the leaves of a tree. They looked from the sheriff, to Lou, to the

Chiefs. Dan started laughing. Then, suddenly, he saw Ella, threading her way through the crowd to Lou's side. His voice froze in his throat. He knew, in that second, he'd lost the woman he loved. But there was no time to grieve. The sheriff ordered the objectors into the wagon, then started the engine.

'You've forgotten someone,' Lou said. The sheriff gaped. The prisoners watched. Lou undid the chain and jumped on board, where he settled, cross-legged, among the Indians. Ella didn't know whether to laugh or cry. They all waved, as though the men were going off on some holiday, and they waved back. But when the truck was way down the road, out of sight, Wilkins stopped. He got out, went round the back and loosed the chain.

'Come on,' he said to Lou. 'This is where you get off.' But Lou didn't budge. He just smiled at the sheriff. 'Are you deaf, or what?' Lou shook his head. The Indians all started grinning, which made Wilkins wild. 'Are you some kind of a nut?' he asked.

Lou sighed. 'I think I'll just come along for the ride, sir.' He nodded at Wilkins amiably. The sheriff slammed the chain back and, as he took off again, the engine stalled. 'Don't think I'm too popular with Mr Wilkins,' Lou observed. The Indians grinned and slapped him on the back.

It was a long ride. First they were driven to the jail at Keams Canyon. Then, discovering Lou hadn't signed up for selective service, either, and on top of that refused to put in a special plea, like being a farmer and therefore exempt, he too was formally arrested and went with the Indians to Prescott. There they endured their imprisonment for three months, hoping that at Phoenix, where they were to stand trial, the misery would end. Lou endured it with them, little by little coming to know the Hopis, and in particular Dan Kokostawis. Dan had been named 'Kokostawis' because it meant 'carrying coals to build a fire', and the name was true enough. Dan would flare up whenever the guards came near. But, afterwards, he would look at Lou, a kindly expression in his eyes.

'Chu'Ovi was right,' he'd say. 'I've got a lot to learn from you, Lou.' And he wondered what formed the basis of Lou's peaceful nature. Finally, he asked him, 'Are you what you call a "conscientious objector", Lou? Is that why you don't register?'

'Not exactly. I just promised Ella I wouldn't fight,' Lou told him. 'Anyway, with me here, maybe you guys won't get such a raw deal. Huh?'

'Maybe.' Dan nodded and gave him a hard look. 'I forgive you for taking my woman from me,' he said. 'Forgive me for having wanted to kill you for it.' He held out his hand. 'Now we are brothers.' Lou shook the hand uncertainly.

'Aren't we supposed to mix our blood?' Lou asked. He remembered having done something of the kind, when he was a kid. He'd used a penknife, and made a Mexican boy his blood brother, just like they did on the movies. Dan shook his head.

'Not necessary.' He laughed, and slapped Lou on the back. 'You mean to do us some good, we make you honorary member of the Eagle Clan! What you going to call yourself?'

'I don't know,' Lou pondered. 'What do you think?'

'White something. Got to be. White Hawk. Huh?'

'O.K. Sounds good to me. White Hawk it is.'

As the white among them, brother or no brother, Lou had responsibilities. He was expected to do 'some good'. So he wrote to his real brother at the base. 'John, you've got a reputation for sticking up for the underdog. How about sticking up for a bunch of harmless Indians, not to mention me?' The press was a power in the land, and if the Indians needed power, it was all Lou could tap.

Chained together, two by two, they were led from the jail to the courthouse. Lou insisted on being treated the same way. And so it was, yoked to Dan, that John Ridley saw his brother enter the dock. In response to Lou's letter, John had taken leave to attend the trial. He was still working for T.W.A., while writing freelance for any paper that would pay him. So, as his brother emerged into the courtroom, John took up his pen and notepad. He was on the scent of a good story, which, when it was printed, merited a centre page spread.

'It was with some disappointment that I saw Louis Ridley, chained to an Indian, walk into the courtroom in Phoenix today. I had half-expected to see a feather in his hair, or a tomahawk hanging from his belt. But no such thing. He was dressed soberly in a shirt and trousers, much like you or I.

172

He was clean shaven, and if his hair was a little long, it was well combed. No, this was not the wild man I had expected to see. But that he was an Indian lover, no one could doubt. Louis Ridley is a white New Mexican, born and bred on a ranch, which he now manages, close to Albuquerque. He was baptized a Christian, and yet, when questioned in court, he gave his address as 'Walpi Village, Hopi Reservation, Arizona', and his religion as 'Hopi'. (Whatever that means.) Why? Louis Ridley has allied himself with the cause of a band of Hopi Indians, who are accused of unlawfully refusing to fight for their country. They say it's against their religion to take up arms against any man, and especially against the white man. (I think maybe, in view of what the Apaches did, we should be grateful for that.) It seems, a long time ago, that the Guardian Spirit of the Hopi people told them a white brother would come, bringing an age of brotherhood into the world. Lou Ridley has strongly denied that he's this long-awaited messiah, though the Indians don't seem quite so sure. Anyway, what is certain is that Lou has become champion and spokesman of these peace-loving Hopis, sharing their suffering and their fate, whatever that might turn out to be. I, for one, hope they get off at this trial but there's a problem. This 'Hopi Religion' is not recognized in white law. I mean, it's not Christian so how can it be a religion? (My tongue is in my cheek, in case you didn't realize it.) So, in law, they cannot be exempted as conscientious objectors. Maybe it's time the law was changed to include the religion of the indigenous population. Maybe it's time the Indians (and the word Indian, you know, does mean 'native to the land'), told us incoming whites what sort of law they want, instead of us telling them. After all, they were here before us! Let's see what the judge decides. I say that the American Constitution is on trial here, and not just a band of Hopis. Meanwhile, the presence of a white man in their midst does at least draw the attention of the white majority to this extraordinary case, the outcome of which could be a turning point in Indian history.'

But it was not a turning point. The verdict was guilty. Lou and the Hopis were sentenced to three years' hard labour, and taken to a prison camp at Tucson to work in a gang building a road up

Mount Lemon. They were a mixed group of whites, Negroes, Mexicans, and some Quakers, all deeply opposed to killing, and all brothers of a kind. But the Hopis were small-built and found the work extra hard. At night, exhausted and demoralized, they gathered round Dan, complaining.

'We aren't alone here,' Dan comforted them. 'Our Mother is with us. She breathes on us, when the wind blows. She wets our lips when we drink water. She is the corn in the food we eat. Would a Mother have us kill our brother? Would She, who is the Earth, have us shed blood on Her? Take heart. We know we're doing right.' Then, murmuring, and anxious, the men turned in for the night. But Lou lay awake, watching, as Dan went out into the moonlight to pray. Silently, Lou threw back the rug and followed him into the yard. Dan had his back to him. He was sitting on the earth, spreading cornmeal on the ground. He jumped as he heard Lou's footfall.

'It's O.K. It's only me,' Lou whispered. Dan nodded and Lou sat, watching the deft movement of Dan's hands. 'I hope Corn Mother gets us out of here soon!' Lou muttered.

'That's not what I'm praying for.'

'What then?'

'I'm praying for a sign, to show we're right, refusing to fight,' Dan explained. In his heart Lou almost wished God would oblige, just this once. But night after night the performance was repeated. And night after night, Lou sat beside Dan, praying in his way. Then, one night, when Lou and Dan were sitting in the compound, as usual, Lou looked round, on the watch for guards. It was very dark, but, in the north, there was a distant light. It flickered and glowed like a bonfire in the sky. What was more, it was moving towards them! He nudged Dan, who looked up and saw it too.

'Go wake the others!' he whispered urgently. 'Tell them Masaw has come!' Lou hurried back inside, shaking the weary Hopis out of deep sleep, repeating Dan's words. Awestruck, they scurried out into the night, to stand watching. It was a huge fireball. It seemed to pass through the forest, without burning, through the gap in the mountain, and then south to the mountains east of Tucson. Then it turned and went back the same way.

In the cold light of day, they wondered if it had only been a

174

dream. But the next night the vision returned, and it returned again, four times. And then all, including Lou, believed and were reassured. Masaw had told the leader of the Fire Clan, at the beginning of the fourth world, that after the migrations had been done according to the plan, they would find their permanent home and settle there. But they would be overcome by a strange people and forced to live according to their laws, or else be treated as criminals and punished. They were not to resist. They were to wait for the white brother who would deliver them.

Then John wrote another article.

'It seems ironic, that as America goes to fight a dictator abroad, she should behave like a dictator at home. We complained that Britain was an empire builder. Give up your empire, we said, and we'll come to your aid fighting Hitler. But here we are, suppressing the race which is indigenous to this land. The Indians have more right to be here than any white man. They were here before us. If Roosevelt is going to say to Churchill, give India its independence, if we Americans are going to say to Hitler, hands off France, Holland, Belgium and Africa, ought we not to clean up our own back yard first? Ought we not to give the native peoples of America their independence? Or, if we cannot manage that, ought we not to give them equal rights? What are we doing, not recognizing their ancient religion? What are we doing, imprisoning them for not fighting in our war? What are we doing? Are we hypocrites, or did we swear to defend the freedom and the rights of other races? I say that those Hopis condemned to hard labour, for not wanting to fight, are genuine conscientious objectors and should be given their liberty as of now.'

It had its effect. The Indians were taken off the road gang, and sent to work on farms. And Lou was free to return to the Lawe Top. In spite of protests, both John and Lou were made honorary members of the Eagle Clan. Jim was overjoyed: the way was clear for his Pa to marry Ella. So in the face of hostility from his family, Lou finally took her as his wife, in a civil ceremony in Flagstaff. Jim had a real Mom, now. He was her papoose. And he loved every minute in Walpi, away from Clara's tight control. Instead of going to school, he played truant with the Hopi kids on the ridge, joined in the games of hide and seek among the tiny adobe houses on the top, and rode bareback, as he'd always wanted. It was great being an Indian! But he had to have his initiation ceremony first.

Dan put a white feather in Jim's hair.

'This is a prayer feather,' he told him. 'An eagle feather, because, when we came into the fourth world, the eagle was the first creature we saw, and he promised he would carry our prayers up to the Sun Father. So, you see, the eagle is the loftiness of the spirit. Now think what a great name you have, Jimmy, "Little White Eagle".' Ella smiled. But Jim was suddenly scared. This was only the beginning. And it wasn't play. What was he letting himself in for? Aunt Clara said Indians weren't Christians and they practised voodoo. That wasn't true of Hopis, because Ella said evil brought evil on itself. All the same, the Hopi God was far more terrifying than the Pope. Jim looked at Ella, eyes round and black.

'No need to be afraid, with Dan as your godparent.' Ella's voice was gentle. 'He'll look after you.' Her eyes were kind. He trusted her, because she was his Mom and his Pa loved her. So, he would make her proud and grow up to be a brave son. Jimmy swallowed his fear and let Dan take his hand, leading him firmly away from his parents, down the street to the Kiva, where they descended the ladder into the sunken chamber below.

'I love you, Lou,' Ella said softly, when they were alone. Lou gathered her up into his arms, and held her still. Already, they could hear the chanting. The earth beneath their feet vibrated with the sound. The dancing had begun. Squatting on the floor of the Kiva, Jimmy watched, with the other boys, bemused by symbols, strange words and music. And the power beneath the earth trembled, holding him, deep in the knowledge of eternal potency, out of time, beyond his understanding, beyond even the Hopis and the fourth world.

CHAPTER TEN

John was singing as he crossed the Atlantic and the indicator lights on the automatic controls flashed the lazy rhythm, while the boys in the back dozed away the subarctic night. Then, pale, the sun rose over Europe.

The navigator popped his head in to report, 'In half an hour we'll see the coast of Ireland.'

'We will if the damned clouds clear,' John remarked, then resumed his singing. The navigator's fingers were beating out the rhythm, on the side of the ship. 'You like Woody Herman, Paul?' John asked.

'Sure.' Paul smiled. There was a break in the cloud ahead. They looked down, and through the hole saw the cold green ocean. There was more cloud, banks of it, for what seemed hours, then suddenly it cleared, and below they saw the Emerald Isle. Paul squeaked with excitement. 'Hell! Look at that! Know what it reminds me of? Oz! You know, the Emerald City . . . ?' John nodded.

'Yup,' he said. 'And here we come, the flying monkeys, to fight that wicked old witch of the west! Hitler!' The boys had woken up. The joke was passed down and slowly the laughter rippled round the ship, taking the sting out of the fact they had come to do war.

'Hey! Aren't the fields just tiny!?' Paul shook his head in amazement.

'Yeah,' John agreed laconically. 'Everywhere looks the same. How the hell do people find their way around here?' He adjusted his head set and before they knew it, they were homing in on East Anglia. Norwich announced its presence beneath a flock of barrage balloons. Each one had a transmitter that made the phones squeak. Then Paul called the tower and a very English voice answered him.

'Not reading you, old chap. Afraid I don't speak the lingo. How about a slower delivery, hah!' Paul stared at John, bewildered.

'What the hell does he mean?' he asked. It was like they were speaking a foreign language. But, finally, the Englishman and the American reached an understanding. The plane came down, rolled to a stop, and taxied over to the park where their Captain, sitting in a jeep, was waiting for them.

'Hi, welcome to the war,' he said. 'Now I want you to just settle in and relax a bit. We'll be operational in a couple of days!'

John slung his bag down on his bed, and strode out. He was tired, but he had an itch to explore. Maybe a bicycle would be a good idea. He winkled out the Supply Office, a largish wooden shed at the far side of the field, and walked in. There was a girl, in uniform, behind the counter. She had short wavy hair, and she was going through some figures. She didn't look up. He went and stood right in front of her. Then he coughed.

'You British sure could learn some manners!' he said loudly. Startled, the girl glanced up.

'I beg your . . . ?' Petty Officer Eve Lawson gaped in amazement. For an irrational second, she thought she was looking in the mirror.

'What've you done to your hair?' John complained. 'I didn't recognize you!'

'Waves are all the fashion, in case you didn't know!' Eve's hand was touching up the stray curls. 'Anyway, what are you doing here?' she objected.

'Just part of the cavalry sent over to save you British.'

'Huh!' She stared at him, the full horror dawning. 'You mean you're posted here?'

178

'Aha.' Suddenly she became very business-like.

'Well, what can I do for you . . .' she searched for his rank.

'Lieutenant would do,' he informed her. 'And I want a bicycle if you've got such a thing.' Eve went out to the store. There was a lot of bumping and shoving behind the door, then finally she shouted through,

'I'll wheel it out the back. Sign the paper on the counter.' John signed and strolled round the back of the shed, where Eve was waiting with a squeaky old bike. 'It needs a spot of oil and you'd better test the brakes before you take it out, Lieutenant,' Eve warned.

'Yes, ma'am.' John saluted her, then smiled. 'Care for a spin?' She shook her head.

'I'm on duty.'

'I'll take a rain check on that. And by the way, I like the hat! Very jaunty.' He winked. Eve watched him wheel crazily out of the compound. Obviously, he'd never ridden a bike before.

Eve didn't see him for the rest of the day. Of course, he was just another Yank, just another airman. They came and they went, and one looked much like another. They chewed gum and they wrote graffiti on the sides of their planes. Her mind wandered from the stock figures. There were three petty officers on supplies at Norwich; Eve, Betty Treacher and Geraldine Hewitt. Betty was out the back right now, checking stock. She was yelling out the information. Eve was supposed to be cross-checking it in the records and writing down the discrepancies.

'Fifteen pairs goggles,' Betty yelled. 'Oxygen equipment. Hell! One hundred and twenty-two! That can't be right. Can it?' Eve was chewing the end of her pencil, wondering what John would call his plane, when the door opened and a man came in. Eve jumped. Had John come back? No. It was the commander. Eve shook herself, took his order, and passed it through to Betty.

'Well?' Betty said.

'Well what?'

'What have you got in the book?'

'Eh?'

'Oxygen equipment! What's the matter with you?'

What *was* the matter with her? Why, the bastard had rolled in like nothing had happened, and she'd fallen at his feet like a ripe apple! She'd better pull herself together and no two ways about it!

That night there was a dance in the village. Eve dolled herself up, and went out with the girls. The village hall was jumping. She smiled, grabbed hold of Betty Treacher's hand and jived. It was great! the antidote to all life's ills! The hall cleared for them, and the uniformed men stood, clapping, cheering them on, as they danced ever more wildly. At last, the music ended and Eve flung herself onto a chair. She accepted a lemonade from the hands of a doting local youth and drank it gratefully. She was flushed and sweaty. As the band struck up again, couples slowly eased back onto the floor. But no one asked Eve to dance. She was far too good.

'That's what you get for showing off, Eve Lawson!' Geraldine Hewitt threw the words over her shoulder as she was whisked into a fast number by a handsome young Captain.

Bitch!' Eve muttered. Betty giggled.

'You don't want to take no notice of her, Eve. She's only jealous.' Eve drank her lemonade.

'Stuck-up tart,' she commented.

'Yeah.' They were in total agreement. Cockney Betty and Geordie Eve. They had struck up a seemingly inseparable friendship, based on the fact they were both good dancers and virgins too. The alliance helped to bolster weakening defences, in the face of Geraldine's sneers and the continuous Yankee come on. After a while, the two girls threw on their coats, linked arms and walked out for some fresh air. It was late. Almost eleven. There was a low throb of engines in the sky. They looked up.

'R.A.F.'s out again!'

On the base, John was waking from a long sleep. He peered out of the window and saw the black planes, outlined against the sky. They were heading for Germany. His skin tingled like he'd been bitten by a million mosquitoes. He shook the sleep out of his hair, slung on some clothes, and wandered out. There were no facilities at this time of night, but he badly needed a coffee. A damp chill penetrated, as the night air of the English summer hit him. Hell! Summer? He buttoned up his jacket, meaning to walk to the mess. But there was a commotion at the Main Gates; jeeps blaring their horns; returning revellers shouting and singing at the tops of their voices, drunk, or maybe just happy. He stopped to watch, as they dropped down from the jeeps and made for their quarters. Eve was with them, linking arms with another girl, as though for safety. They were being harassed by a pair of airmen. The girls were giggling but they fended off their assailants firmly. So, still an ice maiden, huh? John smiled. He felt better now. The air and the sound of laughter had refreshed him. No need for coffee. Turning back to his quarters, he swallowed some cold water, and hit the sack for another few hours.

John avoided the Supply Office for some days. Part of the idea was to keep Eve dangling but he was fully occupied anyway. John was attending lectures from seasoned pilots, who had got their experience flying in Ted's Flying Circus in the Battle of Africa. For now, at last, the Eighth Army was going to cross the borders into the Reich. The nearness of danger was exciting. After all those months training others, back in Albuquerque, John himself was finally going to get his feet wet. And he'd need all the tips he could get! John'd never killed a man. He didn't even have a revolver of his own, and somehow or other, he'd always avoided confrontations; unlike Houlihan, who loved a fight, blasting his heater, his face transfigured by joy. He really got a kick out of killing. Well, those Nazi bastards over there seemed to enjoy it, too. And if you can't beat 'em, far better join 'em! Who knows, John thought, he might even get to like it. Certainly the experience was going to be interesting. He couldn't wait to see what it would be like. And he didn't have to wait too long.

Just before dawn, in late August 1943, John was called to the briefing room. He was going on a mission. The layout had been planned the day before. The Lieutenant Colonel was to lead in number one plane and John was to fly on his right wing. Their target was north-west of Bremen, a big factory. They would not have friendly fighter support. Silence, thick as the clouds over England, greeted this news. Three groups of B-24s were assigned to the mission. Fully equipped, John and Paul walked out to their plane. John glanced at the graffiti painted on the side. 'The Tin Man', it said. Paul's work. He managed a smile. Then, together, they climbed in past the bomb bay, where, destined for the enemy, the bombs lay stacked, like eggs, all fused and ready to go.

Sergeant Stone bawled, 'Clear!' as John turned on the switches.

One by one the big props turned over, and one by one the engines gasped, choked then roared into life. The Colonel was taxiing to the runway already. John rolled after him, to wait in line, for takeoff.

Paul filled the nervy silence by cracking jokes. They were bad jokes, but the guys laughed all the same. It was more virile than crying. John kept seeing pictures in his head, snapshots of the past; Houlihan, blood all over him, walking into the hotel room, pointing his gun; the ground gaping; the caballero on the fiery crater's edge; black smoke. He was terrified. His lips were white. Then, at last, the signal was given. There was a brief second's pause before John responded. Then suddenly they were airborne, rising up at the end of the runway, to join their group, before heading out together over the North Sea. The heavy drone of the engines steadied John's nerves. One of the groups lost its leader in the clouds, but John's went on. Paul was on the ball with his navigation and very soon, too soon, they were over Germany, and heading for the target. The first group could be seen clearly ahead, already on their bomb run. The little town, where the factory lay, was covered by a smoke screen. But the wind blew it hither and thither so that now and then the bombardier got a view below. Finally, he called,

'I've got a target in sight . . . don't know if it's the right one, but it's all I can see.' John held the course for what seemed an age, then the indicator lights flashed the message that the bombs had dropped.

'Bombs away!' called Harrison.

They had entered the town's defences, and were getting a lot of flak. Bursts were rocking the ship, so John turned. But the plane behind had been hit. Black smoke was coming from one of the wings.

The pilot called over the radio, 'I'm hit bad. Lost number two. I'm letting down.'

'Good luck! Don't let the bastards get you!' John called back.

'No friendly fighter support'. That meant they had to say goodbye to the crippled plane. John watched it drop. Suddenly, there was a call,

'Fighters at eight o'clock!' They were coming in from the rear, five German twin engines. He could see the swastikas clear on their tails. They went for the crippled plane. It exploded in a ball of fire. Then another American got into trouble. The Nazis homed in. It was a dog fight, all guns going, rat tat rattling, spitting venomous blasts into the eyes of the attackers. John's blood was racing with a kind of terrified excitement that made the sky bluer and the clouds whip across the sky. It was like he'd taken a shot and been yanked into a different level of awareness. Let the flak fly! He'd outwit the bastards! He'd get them! He aimed his guns, took a dive and, just as the man inside came into view, let them go. He saw the shocked expression, seconds before, blinded by the exploding flare, the human enemy went screaming down. John yelped with glee and took some persuading not to go on, picking out fresh targets, off course. But finally he obeyed his leader's crackling voice and brought his ship into formation. It was John's first trip behind enemy lines, but when they landed back at base, unlike most others, he was raring to get out there again.

Eve had watched the sky, heart in her mouth. She knew they were late coming back and had begun to fear the worst. Then, when the first planes appeared through the clouds, she looked for John's. There were some gaps in the formation; maybe stragglers; maybe gone down. Then she saw 'The Tin Man' as he'd called it, and she knew he was safe. There were tears on her cheeks. She brushed them away. But Betty had seen. She raised her eyebrows, but didn't comment.

'You coming down to the club tonight?' she asked. Eve shook her head.

'No. I think I'll wash my hair,' she said. Betty closed the office, and walked Eve over for a cup of tea. John would have gone straight to his debriefing. Eve knew that. But still, she was watching for him. She jumped as each new man came into the canteen. In her turn, Betty was watching Eve, and with growing suspicion.

'Who is he?' she asked at last.

'Who?'

'The man you're soppy about,' Betty snapped.

'O.K.' Eve admitted. 'There is someone. But he's a bastard, so . . .'

'So . . . you're in love with him. It follows,' Betty drawled. Eve gaped. Her friend was either very wise or psychic. 'I always fall for bastards too,' Betty explained. 'That's why I'm steering clear of the Yanks. I know my weaknesses. Do you?' With that, she got up and went, leaving Eve to wash her hair . . . if she could find any shampoo!

The mess was full that night. John got drunk and had to be helped into the sack. But Eve had stayed in, like a cloistered nun, with itchy feet. And next day, in the Supply Office, she found Betty cool. Time dragged. There was no sign of John. Then she heard a bicycle pull up and a bell ring. The door opened. It was John. Betty clocked the flush that spread over Eve's cheeks, when she saw the stranger. So, that was him! She eyed him critically, as he strolled over to the counter and spoke to Eve.

'When's your free day, honey?' he asked casually.

'Thursday.' Eve's reply was unnaturally curt.

'Why don't you requisition yourself a bike so we can go out together, huh?' Eve said nothing. She just looked at him, her jaw set hard. Then, from behind his back, John produced a red rose. Eve was startled, pleased, and confused, all at once. She took the rose, simpering like a girl of fifteen. 'Be at the gate at eight sharp!' John commanded. Eve saluted awkwardly.

'Yes, Sir!' Her hand drooped awkwardly, as he turned and left the office. Eve felt a fool. She could feel Betty's mocking eyes on her back. Suddenly she threw the rose down on the counter.

'I know!' she shouted at Betty. 'I could kick myself!' But Betty only laughed.

'Have a nice time, dearie,' she said compassionately. Then Eve started crying.

'I'm sorry,' she wailed, shaking her head at her own stupidity. 'But what can I do?'

'He's good-looking, I'll say that.'

'He's a bastard!'

'They all are, my dear.'

The rose was taken back to Eve's quarters and ceremonially placed in a milk bottle on the window sill. No one had ever given her a rose before. It was romantic. In spite of herself, Eve liked it. And when, after a couple of days, it started wilting, she placed it in a book, under her mattress. Betty would laugh if she knew what she'd done, so sentimental dreaming was relegated to the ranks of shameful and secret pastimes and Eve began to lead a double life, assuming the air of the independent woman in the company of her friends, while secretly indulging the dreams of a lady in love, when alone. Then the morning of the date arrived and dreams threatened to become reality. Eve put on her best cotton dress, dabbed on some old perfume, and telling Betty she was going shopping, rode her bike out to the gate.

He was late. The bastard was late. The guards on the gate were all watching her, knowing some man had stood her up. How could John do it to her? How could he humiliate her like this? Well, he'd had his chance, and he'd blown it! She was going shopping, like she'd said! Eve wheeled her bicycle through the gate, waved cheerily to the guards, and swung out onto the road. Then, she wobbled, put her feet down and looked up into the sky where the American planes were wheeling into formation. Suddenly she realized what had happened. John had gone on another mission. How awful, to think such dreadful things about him, when all the time he was risking his life for *her* country! Oh God! She felt terrible! And now, there was the long wait to know whether or not he would come back. It was a fitting punishment, she decided. But, supposing he didn't come back? Supposing she never got the chance to make it up to him? It didn't bear thinking of. Cycling as though in a race, Eve rode into the village. Some of the trees were just beginning to turn. Autumn was sad, even in sunshine. Her nose ran with unshed tears. She'd get John a present. Yes. But what? The Americans had access to things she didn't. Everything English was scarce; food, fuel, blankets . . . She wheeled into a country lane. Some early birds were gathering blackberries. She stopped, picked a few and ate them. They were sweet. But they stained her fingers. She frowned, took out a mirror, and carefully applied the juice to her lips. They went a bluey red. Quite nice really. It would go nicely with her pink and blue dress. Perhaps John would like some berries. She made a

185

packet out of some paper she had in her pocket, and filled it. Then she went back to the base, to wait.

They had been to Norway; target, power stations. They'd missed them. John was furious. Next time, he said, he'd ask to lead the mission, see if he wouldn't. As usual, after a raid, he drank heavily. Disappointed, Eve left him the blackberries and turned in early. Twice more, Eve and John arranged a day together, and twice more, it was cancelled at the last minute. Then, one sunny day in early September, the pair cycled out of those gates together into the English countryside.

The leaves fluttered dark red and golden yellow onto the road. They caught in the spokes of the wheels, whirring round, then flying out again, and away, to hurtle down the street. It was warm for the time of year but a light breeze freshened the atmosphere and settled, cool in shady places. They entered one of the many woods around the drome. Small lanes cut through to pockets of habitation. Crows and game birds scattered through the trees to disappear in the undergrowth. This was the England Eve loved, gentle, mellow, with winding lanes, leading to golden haystacks and ancient villages. John watched how she changed and softened in this new environment. It suited her. Her face took on a fragile femininity which invited kissing. She darted him a look and a smile, which spurred him. And by the time they stopped to picnic, his heart was pumping like he was going out on a mission. They had chosen a gap in the woods, a spot where a fallen tree gave sheltered privacy. John spread a rug under the protective branches. Then, having eaten the luxurious American rations, they both lay back to watch the squirrels jump from branch to branch above their heads. From time to time a twig cracked and the squirrel fell, hung on a branch beneath, then swung out like a monkey and down, down to the forest floor, gathering nuts. The sunlight split into rays, glancing through the trees. Eve closed her eyes. The war seemed a million miles away. Her mind drifted. But, from far off, she felt John's hand, warm, holding her own. She turned towards him, asking to be cradled in his arms and he started kissing her hair, then her cheeks. She opened her eyes, sleepily. His face was red, looking down on her. He kissed her full on the mouth. She fell back on

186

the hard earth, and he fell on top of her. She couldn't stop him, even if she'd wanted to. And she didn't want to. John Ridley, hero of the skies, playboy of San Francisco, defender of the underdog, unpredictable bastard, was her own dear love. Eve wanted him, and was glad, at last, to take him into herself. In accepting his manhood, she became, herself, a woman.

The breeze flurried in their clothes, chill, as the afternoon darkened. They hurried to gather their things. Eve had slept peacefully in John's arms and, suddenly wakened, found the weather changed. Cold and disorientated, she wheeled her bike back onto the lane, behind John. A huge American army truck passed them by, smashing twigs on the roadside. The boys inside waved and leered. Eve blushed. But John was laughing. He patted her on the rear, in full view of them, which annoyed Eve a lot. Then he swung onto the saddle. He'd got the hang of the bike now, and he took off, victoriously careering down the road ahead of her. Why couldn't he have waited? It wasn't very gentlemanly to take off like that, leaving her behind! Oh God, would he boast to the other men that Miss Frigidaire'd been defrosted? If he did, she wouldn't be able to hold her head up again. Sometimes men did that, Eve knew. Panicked, she followed him, pedalling hard. Looking back, he slowed for her and gave her a friendly smile. That boyish look again. She smiled back, reassured. After all, what had she to worry about? John was O.K. when he was clear of Ken Houlihan's evil genius, and that had long since been bottled and corked by the American judicial system.

After a bit of manoeuvring, Eve and John managed a whole weekend off together. It was early October, and the evenings were drawing in. The journey was long and tedious and they arrived at the flower shop in Fowler Street late on the Saturday afternoon. Jack wasn't back from Home Guard duties, and Maisie and Mary Jean were in the shop.

'Eeh, we thought you weren't coming!' Auntie Maisie could hardly contain her enthusiasm, while Mary Jean put out a shy hand for John to shake and her cheeks dimpled softly.

'Eve's Mam's round the back. You'll find my husband there too,' she said, pointing the way into the kitchen. John skirted the great wooden statue, eyeing it with some suspicion, then followed Eve into the kitchen.

Os, still in uniform, was sitting at the table, with little George on his knee. They were having tea. Frances was cutting sandwiches. She looked up startled as John and Eve walked in.

'We thought you weren't coming,' she commented. Eve smiled bravely and introduced a reluctant John. Os gave him a brief nod. Then Frances went on, 'You're very welcome, John, I'm sure. But I'm afraid the rations don't extend to Yankee hospitality. You'll have to excuse us.' Eve grew tense, as her mother's welcoming address continued, over the pouring of the tea. 'You're a journalist, I believe.'

'Yeah. That's right, ma'am.' John grinned. Frances gave him an old-fashioned look.

'I've put you in the room next to us, John,' she said. Eve felt a warm flush rising up her throat. 'You're in the usual place, our Eve.' Upstairs, in the attic. The room with the broken pane. 'Well, I expect you'd both like to rest. You must have had a tiring journey.' She handed them their cups of tea, and sent them to their respective beds. Obviously they weren't wanted. As they walked upstairs, they heard Frances and Os, chatting away nineteen to the dozen. Frances had her son home on leave and there was a lot of news to catch up with. Eve felt shut out. Well, it worked both ways, did that. She left John at the first floor, and went on up to the attics. A strange smell hung about the landing; a smell of damp and lilies . . . or was it chrysanthemums? She opened the door of her room and went in.

It was dark. The blackout curtain was still up at the window. Eve went across and took it down, allowing the last rays of daylight to cut through the dusty air. Nothing had changed. Jack's book lay on the chest of drawers. Beside it was a dried rose. Eve frowned. Was it hers? No of course not. That was back in Norfolk! She shivered. It gave her a funny feeling, a feeling of déjà vu. She put the rose inside the empty drawer and slipped the book in to keep it company. She looked at it for a second, lying there. Ganesha had said that the one who went away from his parents murdered them, while the ones who stayed behind derived the fruit . . . or something like that. Well, Os had stayed. She had left. She shut the drawer on the book and flung herself on the bed, to indulge her feverish thoughts.

188

So, her mother didn't like John. She'd taken against him at first glance. Eve's heart sank. She was twenty-six years old. For the first time, she'd found a man to love, and her mother was putting spokes in the wheels. It made her feel tired. Eve closed her eyes, half-dozing. Her period was due. She always needed rest before it came. She had better sleep. What with the journey and . . . Suddenly, her eyes sprang open. She was two days late. She smiled. She hoped. Was it possible she was carrying John's baby? Bubbling with happiness, Eve's mind raced ahead. Would he be pleased? Imagine him, a father! Imagine her, married. But she might be wrong. Two days was nothing. And she did feel tired. No. Probably not. She sighed, and dismissing the whole idea from her mind, fell asleep.

Jack came back at half past six, weary after his spell of duty on the Home Guard, to find John, sitting in his chair, smoking. He greeted him warmly and sat at the table for his tea.

'John here seems to think the Yanks won the war in Africa,' Os said bitterly.

'That a fact?' Jack took in the situation at once. 'I suppose you won the Battle of Britain as well?' John shrugged.

'I was in the desert,' Os said, pointing his finger at John. 'And I never saw sight nor sign of you lot. But I tell you what, we're seeing a damn sight too much of you now.'

'Now then.' Jack tried to pour oil on troubled waters. 'John here's risking life and limb, fighting alongside our lads in the sky. Give him credit now.'

'Alright. Alright.' Os sighed, and lay back in his chair. John was blowing smoke rings. George watched, fascinated, and Os couldn't take his eyes off the fiery tip and the growing length of ash.

'I'm sorry. Do you smoke?' John offered his cigarettes. Os took one at once and John, smiling, lit it for him. But Os was not to be bribed into comradeship. The shop doorbell clanged. Maisie would answer it. But Jack got up to see who it was.

'It's David Jackson!' Maisie shouted through. David, Os's friend. They were in the same regiment. But Os didn't look up. He was staring at John.

'Have you asked our Eve to marry you?' he asked abruptly.

John was taken off guard. He changed colour, cleared his throat, and looked all round the room, before murmuring, 'Not yet. Give a fellah a chance!' He smiled. But it wasn't enough.

Os pursued the question. 'I know girls in uniform've got a bit of a reputation, but our Eve's a good girl. And if you've been up to anything you shouldn't, you'll have me to answer to.'

'Sh, our Os!' Frances warned. David was standing in the door. She smiled, welcoming him. 'Hallo, David. Will you have a cup of tea?' David was more welcome than John. John put his cigarette packet back in his pocket. He didn't say what he was thinking, but his face betrayed him.

That night, the men went out to the local pub, while the women stayed, sewing, mending and making jam. Mary Jean and George had been out blackberrying on Cleadon Hills, and Frances had gathered apples from the old allotment garden across the way. It was cosy. Eve enjoyed the warm domesticity, and it made her hanker for a family of her own. She said nothing, knowing she was probably living with false hopes. Still, she thought, the fact she wanted John's child at all told her she felt the right way about him. He was the man for her alright!

Frances mellowed too. She was laughing, because the jam wouldn't set. They'd had to use half honey because they were down on sugar.

'Put some tapioca in it, man,' Maisie instructed. 'It'll thicken it up a bit, anyway.' For a moment, Eve was on the verge of telling her mother how she felt about John. She wanted her to share her joy. But Frances avoided any private discussion, and Eve went to bed with an aching heart.

Next morning, John slept in. Os was in a funny mood. He and Mary Jean went off to church. Then, after a look from his wife, Jack suggested he take Eve down to the sea front for a walk. Eve smelt a rat at once. Jack had been set up to have a talk with her. They walked down Bents Lane to the sea, and stood on the dune tops, watching the wind blowing spray from the waves.

'I gather you're rather sweet on that young man, Eve,' Jack said at last. Eve wouldn't look at him. She set her mouth tight. Jack cleared his throat and started walking. Reluctantly, Eve followed him, slithering down the dunes, to the hard sand below. His footprints spread and filled with water, as she trailed after him. It was cold, misty. She stopped and looked out to sea. A few yards ahead of her, Jack stopped too. 'I'm afraid John got into a bit of an argument with Os and David last night,' he said.

'Trust our Os!' Eve snapped. 'He's a bad-tempered little . . .'

'He was defending you.' Eve's heart jumped. She wouldn't look at Jack. Instead, she steadied herself, staring out to sea. A fog horn blew. How she hated fog horns. Defending her? Who or what from? John? Why? What had he said?

'He had no right to!' she blurted out.

'You're his sister,' Jack retorted. 'It's his duty.'

'He hardly knows me. And as for that David, he doesn't know me at all! I mean, who's David Jackson when he's at home?'

'He's a nice fellah. He's an electrical engineer.'

'Big deal. Anyway, I don't need defending!' Eve's mouth snapped shut. Jack sighed. He had to choose his words carefully.

'Has John actually asked you to marry him?' he asked. Eve swallowed hard.

'No. Not yet.'

'Well, if I was you, I'd not rush into anything. If you take my meaning.' Eve flushed. The salt stung her cheeks.

'What've you all got against him? Eh? No. Don't tell me! He's a Yank. That's it, isn't it? Him being here upsets your national pride. Isn't that what's bothering you? Eh?'

'I don't like him, Eve. And not just because he's American. I don't like him because I think he's a . . . a . . . ladies' man.' Jack's look went straight through her. Eve went cold. She was shaking, as she defended her lover.

'In all the years I've known John Ridley, he's never gone steady with anybody. He's played around a bit, I admit. He's got a reputation for it. But he's settled down now. He loves me. I know he does.' Her voice was desperate. The Souter lighthouse blew its warning and Eve shouted hoarsely into the wind, 'God I hate fog horns! Shut up damn you!' Jack was watching her. He would have liked to take his daughter in his arms but she was too far away. So, he just stood, helplessly, unable to comfort her. And his failure pained him. 'I love him, Jack,' Eve pleaded. 'Don't spoil it for me. Please!' Jack couldn't take it. He turned back to the road, and Eve trailed after him, sobbing, as the mist rolled in, enveloping the town in a chill, damp greyness. 'I hate Shields,' she said bitterly. 'I can't wait to get back to California.' Silently, father and daughter walked back to the shop and a Sunday lunch of baked lentils and cold comfort. John had a black eye. It was funny in its way. No one dared speak or look at him. Then, unable to take it any more, Maisie started giggling. It was the last straw. John went up to his room and packed his bag.

John put the whole thing down to the 'Yankee Go Home' syndrome. 'Hell they might be a little more grateful,' he complained.

Eve was ashamed of her family. As she told John, she hadn't been brought up with Os, and neither he nor Jack Scott had any right to speak to John the way they had. And as for punching him in the eye! Well, she just wished they were at the base when John received his Air Medal. Eve clapped till her hands were stinging. It was a happy moment in a period of darkness. For, during October, the losses on missions from Norwich were particularly heavy. It was an anxious time for Eve. She had found she was, after all, pregnant but somehow she hadn't been able to tell John. He had enough on his mind, she told herself. She hated to pressure him. And yet, supposing one day he didn't come back? How would she feel then? For his part, John was concerned about his Christmas presents. The folks back home had been told to mail their presents early, and they'd arrived in early November. The question was should he open them now, and ruin Christmas, or leave them, with the strong chance that they would be 'returned to sender', when he failed to come back from a mission. Eve told him to keep them till Christmas. He was bound to come back, she said. He wanted to believe her, so he left his presents unopened. And, at last, John's chance to prove himself as a leader came.

The target was a German repair and maintenance depot in Norway. 'The Tin Man' led the group. They took off in heavy cloud, so heavy they could barely see one another. Only three planes made the formation and took off from the friendly coast. But by the time they reached Norway, another two Liberators had found their way and joined the group. They were now five. The sea beneath was icy cold. A man couldn't survive in it for more than fifteen minutes. Ahead, were four German fighters.

John called up the rest of the group, 'Fighters coming in at two o'clock high.' They were peeling off. The first opened fire at short range; long bursts. Then the other three. The gunner called in.

'Number four's losing oil.' They'd been hit. The fighters turned away and re-formed for another attack. The plane behind was ripped apart. It fell, burning flotsam, towards the sea. And another of the group was badly crippled, while 'The Tin Man's right wing was black with oil.

'If we get hit again, we've had it,' John said. The enemy fighters concentrated on the cripple and John was free to fly on. They were approaching the target, when the oil gauge started zooming down. 'Feathering the prop,' John said. He pushed the button, cutting off the gas to the engine. There were three engines left. Three engines, and three ships. The group formed over the target and let the bombs away. Now, there was the problem of where to bail out. The engines were doing fine; no sign of burning. Should John bail out over Sweden or, risking the North Sea, try for home? He chose the latter. They were doing well, when the German fighters showed up again, swastikas glaring in the bright light. John sent up fire, and smoke issued from one of the attackers. And then John saw they were launching rockets. The group dived and turned, evading the rockets which exploded short of their targets. Time and again, they outwitted the enemy in the same way. Ahead was a bank of thick cloud. If they could reach that, they would be safe. But, as they entered the clouds, the left gunner reported smoke coming from number three. They had lost another engine. John alerted Air Sea Rescue, and supported by the remaining two Liberators, 'The Tin Man' limped towards home. In spite of precautions, the fire was spreading. But they were nearing East Anglia.

'Check the tyres,' John called. The tyres were O.K. 'I'm going to try to land.'

He set a nice glide, and touched down. Then the ship began to wobble. It was pulling to the right. John jammed on the left brake. Obviously his information was wrong. The right was flat. He heard it grinding, then tearing off. John steered the ship off the runway, so as not to block it. He spun the tail and the ship turned, tilting badly. Then it dropped. They were moving very slowly, dragging along the ground. 'Bail out!' John ordered. The crew did as they were told. John cut the engines, and followed suit. The plane blew as he jumped.

Eve and Geraldine were on duty in the Supply Office when it happened. They heard the planes coming in and, as usual, went out to watch. The clouds were swollen purple with rain. But they could hear the engines and knew that one of them was crippled. It was John's. Eve's certainty was irrational, but beyond question. Faint, she leant back against the shed. Geraldine was very excited. She gave a running commentary, when the planes appeared, as if out of nowhere, and started circling ready for landing. Eve closed her eyes, listening. Geraldine knew, not that Eve was pregnant, but that she was deeply involved with John. And yet she rubbed in every terrifying second.

'He's going to crash. No, he's spun round. Oh, but the wing's dipping . . . Oh God. It's gone. It's smashed, the crew are all bailing out.' Eve closed her eyes. Where was John? Then, she saw him, jumping, as the ship exploded, like a fireball, and John rolled away. 'The idiot. Can't have switched off his engines,' Geraldine snapped.

'Cold-hearted little bitch!' Eve slapped Geraldine across the face and started running across the field. An ambulance was already on its way. John was dragged clear of the flames and taken off. Eve ran harder, as though she might catch up with it. But the ambulance was speeding towards the tower. Her feet were dragging in the tufts of grass, slipping on the frost. Her legs gave out. And she fell, chest paining, gasping for breath onto the frosty grass, as darkness closed her eyes. She came round in minutes and looked up, trying to focus on the area by the tower. The ambulance had gone. She was very cold and soaked in sweat. Her head pounded. A couple of Wren engineers, who had been working on a plane nearby, were running towards her. Between them, they chair-lifted Eve to her quarters, where she lay, dazed and crying, till the doctor came and administered a sedative.

They told her John had fractured his hip. But they wouldn't let her go and see him. She was pregnant. She'd had a fright. She should rest. The news of her pregnancy had come as a surprise to her Chief, but it was confidential information. No decision had been made on Eve's future, though she knew only too well what it would be. After three days of resting, Eve felt she was well enough to go and see John. But then she was told he'd been shipped out. He needed a special operation, not available in England, so they'd sent him home. Had he left her a letter? A message? No. Deeply shocked, Eve was given compassionate leave. She went up to Shields. There was nowhere else she could go.

Eve arrived to find Hester's daughter, Anna, already in residence. Anna had brought her eight-week-old little girl, Elizabeth, with her. Her husband, Henry Strachan, was, apparently, doing heroic work in the London Fire Brigade but, supporting Anna's need for a safe billet, he had encouraged her to leave him behind and stay in Shields for as long as she liked.

'I'd've come earlier,' Anna explained, 'but carrying a baby makes it that hard to get about. I was the size of a house, and my legs're like a map of the Mississippi Delta as it is, I've got that many varicose veins! Anyway, I came as soon as I could. After all, there is my inheritance to sort out. And by the looks of this place, you could do with some fresh blood to give the business a new lease of life.' Anna was looking askance round the old shop. 'Have you thought about getting modern units installed and changing to a more lucrative line? I was thinking of something more like a hobby shop. There's a lot of people suffering from nerves, you know, because of all the bombing and bad news and that. And my doctor recommends hobbies. I paint myself. As a matter of fact, I brought you up one of my paintings as a present.' Frances cringed but accepted the tiny parcel, graciously.

'Thank you very much, pet,' she said. 'But you shouldn't've bothered!' Anna smiled encouragingly. There was nothing for it. Frances had to open it. Mary Jean, Maisie, George and Jack stood expectantly by. Os, fortunately for him, had gone back to his regiment. The last piece of newspaper was removed. Frances frowned. It was funny. She couldn't make it out. Then she realized she had it the wrong way up. She turned it, and her face showed pleasant surprise. It was a still life, done in oils, and it was so tiny, so delicately done, in spite of herself, she gasped with admiration.

'Well, Anna! I never knew you had it in you. It's really nice, pet.' Anna beamed. In amazement, the family inspected the little painting. 'Eeh. Where do you get it from? That's what I don't understand.' Frances shook her head in wonder.

'There's nobody on our side can paint like that,' Maisie agreed. Jack studied the picture at some length. He had his own ideas. He gave his wife a look. She frowned, not understanding, then took the picture into the upstairs parlour and put it in pride of place.

Anna was given the front attic and, when Eve came, she found herself, back where she was, in the room with the broken pane, across the landing. Anna's presence dominated the house. For one thing, she never stopped talking. She cried at the drop of a hat, and she insisted on working, scrubbing the cellar stairs, cleaning the shop windows, brushing out the yard, scouring the grate, till she was thoroughly exhausted. Then, having overworked, she became overtired. This made her irritable, so she had to paint to calm her nerves. But nothing suited her in the house. The light wasn't right. She tried every room in succession, then gave up, screaming, throwing her paints across the room. Her temper set off the baby, who wouldn't sleep. Worn out, Eve lay listening to her howling in the room across the way. Then George started having nightmares. A bombing raid would have counted as a welcome relief in the general cacophony. Everyone was tired. But Eve was growing desperate. She hadn't told her family she was pregnant. All they knew was that John had been injured in a crash and had gone back to the States. Eve was obviously cut up about it but, compared to the advent of Anna, her problems seemed small. She looked pale, yes. But who wasn't run down in war time?

So, if Eve had expected sympathy from her family, she was sorely disappointed. Part of the problem was that, not liking John themselves, they simply couldn't believe Eve might feel deeply about him. They were all sorry for her, of course, but, in their hearts, they were glad he'd gone before he'd had a chance to do her any real damage. She'd get over him, settle down and find some nice lad she could have bairns with, just as soon as the war was over. So, Eve was treated with silent tolerance by her preoccupied family, and her hurt, uncomforted, was buried in her heart where it burrowed deep and made its home.

By the Sunday, Eve had had enough of Anna and her offspring. That morning, Anna had announced that she wanted to go down to the sea, to try her hand at seascapes, so would Eve keep an eye on the baby, while she was gone? Eve was suffering from sleepless nights, morning sickness and backache and had had enough of the lot of them. So she declined, using the service at the Cenotaph as her excuse. It was the first Sunday in November. Remembrance Sunday. Walking with Jack, Frances and Auntie Maisie, up Fowler Street and Westoe Road, to the sound of marching bands, Eve fought to suppress bitter memories of Davey Lawson's death, drowned in his own drunken vomit. She remembered the sour smell of whisky and sick, and the doctor's disgust, as the drums rolled down at the Cenotaph. No wonder Davey'd got drunk. The First War destroyed his faith in life. Here today and gone tomorrow. Just like Oz. Eve knew how he felt. 'My, people come and go quickly round here!' Look at John! And who to turn to? Eve's mother had been Davey's only comfort. Poor Davey. Eve'd gone looking for her mother at Auntie Maisie's to tell her Davey was dead and had found her in bed with Jack! It was farcical. The whole thing. Love, marriage, children. Just a wicked farce. A plot to trap the unwary. And Eve had nearly been taken in; she'd seen the writing in the sky, black smoke from the crippled 'Tin Man' writing her sentence; 'surrender Eve'; yes, and she'd nearly surrendered, nearly got sucked in, just as America had got sucked into this war. 'Here come the British, bang bang!' But she would escape. 'You can make anything come true if you wish for it hard enough'. The priest was giving his sermon, a rally cry. 'We shall fight them on the beaches . . .' Lionhearted England, roaring for help, for fresh blood. The blood of the martyred innocents, shed for what? The mayor was laying the wreath of poppies. Poppies from the fields of Flanders. Fields of poppies. 'And now my beauties, something with poison, with poison, but attactive to the eye . . .' The band was playing 'The Last Post'. 'Now they'll sleep'. But not her. Not Eve. She would not be sacrificed, as her mother was, brought home, pregnant, condemned to a life of servitude. Who had the right to demand that of her? 'We hold these truths to be self evident, that all men are created equal, that they are endowed by their Creator with certain inalienable Rights, that among these are Life, Liberty and the pursuit of Happiness.' There was a distant rumble of thunder. 'Here come the British . . . ' The crowd was agitated, looking up at the sky. The band struck up a rousing march. Order in the ranks! What Life or Liberty was there in England? Look at her family! The bonds that tied them crushed the life out of them. And as for happiness . . . ? 'Bang, bang.' But Eve was not going to give up. She would escape, pursue her own dreams in the one place they let you, America! Click your heels together three times, and wish. She would take life by the tail! A crackle of forked lightning singed the roofs of the town. The crowd was beginning to disperse, and the notes of the blaring march scurried along behind the departing mourners. As the first drops fell, poppies scattered on the street, trodden down by the feet of the fleeing.

'Hurry up, our Eve. We'll get soaked!' Frances called. But Eve couldn't hurry. Her back was breaking and a pain ground in her womb. She stopped, clutching her belly.

'What's wrong?' Jack put his arm round his daughter. But Frances was staring at Eve's leg. There was blood running down it.

'Oh God,' Frances said. 'Maisie, run for help.'

Eve was hanging in her father's arms, unable to move. Frances hurried close, to help support her. The blood had reached her shoes, coating them ruby red.

'Eeh, love. I had no idea . . . ' Eve's eyes pleaded like an animal in pain. 'I had no idea,' Frances repeated. 'I'm sorry, pet. I'm really sorry . . . ' And as Maisie ran to a nearby policeman, the rain started to fall, huge drops pelting their heads, splattering the poppies on the Cenotaph, washing the blood that oozed down Eve's leg, over her shoes, onto the street, where it ran thinner and thinner in the pouring rain.

CHAPTER ELEVEN

'The Russians are closing on Berlin, mein Führer.'

The swastika, black on white, fluttered like a flag from the ceiling of the room. The Führer gazed at it for a second, digesting Hilpert's news. Then he lay back in his chair, and said,

'If the German people lose this war, they have shown themselves to be unworthy of me!' He was invincible. He had powers unknown to other men. But other men were cowards and had no faith or sense of loyalty, even his own Generals. He reached for the drugs. His face was yellow. He was twitching. He would not leave Berlin, he would move into the bunker, his last refuge. There, he would celebrate his birthday.

It was the 20th of April. Eva had come to join him, in spite of the danger. For two hours the Americans and British had been bombing the city, which was without gas, sanitation, or electricity. And now the Red Army had finally reached the beleaguered capital and opened fire. Things might still have worked out. But the Führer's commands were no longer obeyed, and all his plans backfired. In the beginning, nothing could go wrong and now, nothing would go right. Like a boomerang, the swastika had been hurled out against mankind, only to return to the thrower, its might redoubled. Defeat was inevitable;

surrender impossible. At the end of the birthday celebrations, the leaders parted. Only Goebbels remained. And Eva. She wanted to share his fate, his 'Angel of Death'. He would do her the honour of marrying her. She had proved herself worthy.

On April 27th, when the screaming whine of approaching destruction could be heard from the bunker itself, Magda Goebbels sought help to kill her children. Hitler's personal physician gave her poison to put in their mouths. Then, on April 30th, Hitler, with his new bride Eva Braun, followed suit, taking cyanide capsules. Their bodies were later found near the bunker's emergency exit, charred beyond all recognition, but for the expertise of dental specialists.

The news of Hitler's death broke on May 1st. The ten most popular American tunes of the week were faded out for the news flash. In South Shields, Frances switched off 'Music While You Work'. The war wasn't over yet, but the devil who had started it was finished.

'Hey ho, the witch is dead, the witch is dead, the witch is dead. Hey ho, the wicked witch is dead.' That's what they sang in Norwich at the air base. But in Germany, strains of Wagner heralded the news that the hero had passed on, his dreams of Nordic expansion unfulfilled.

On May 5th 1945, Ernie Trevor, engineer attached to the American 11th Armored Division was crossing the border into Austria. They were still meeting with Nazi resistance. The commander ordered artillery fire to put a stop to the snipers. The fire power blew the doors off a freight car. Immediately, a stench that turned Ernie's stomach was released. He didn't want to look. Yet he knew, if he didn't, what he'd missed would haunt his imagination. He glanced at the gaping car. Inside were stacked the skeletal bodies of prisoners, abandoned by their German guards and locked in, days before, when an air strike had destroyed the line. Some were still alive. Just. A few found the strength to wriggle free and wander dazed onto the line. Their heads and faces loomed large from their shrunken frames. The living dead. Slave labourers on their way to camp. The G.I.s shrank from them in horror. Were they human beings? Were they contagious? Did they feel any pain? The tanks rolled on. What in God's name was in store for them at Mauthausen?

And at Mauthausen, they walked into a compound littered with bodies, naked, covered in lice and vermin. Their feet sank into a putty of excreta and clay. And the smell: burning, death, urine, God knew what else, hung like fog in the foetid air. Some of the skeletons got up and walked or crawled towards their liberators, trying to kiss them. Ernie cowered back to the centre of his group as they milled around them, ghosts, insane with hunger. Ernie felt in his pocket for candy. The bar was passed through to the nearest creature. It took it and ran, bestial, choking on it, rather than share. Why had Ernie's Division come here? What could they do? How could they liberate these . . . sub-humans. And yet, the huge eyeballs expressed joy, even gratitude. A G.I. started laughing. His lone voice sounded crazy and macabre. Then, desperate to restore some sense of normality, the commander started giving out orders. His voice was unnaturally high and pinched.

Ernie was attached to a group of men checking the stacks of bodies. As he walked over to a stack behind the barracks, a German soldier appeared from hiding and tried to surrender to them. But one of the skeletons saw and, picking up a rock, battered him to death. They stood numb, watching, then passed on to the stack. It was about twenty feet long, and as high as Ernie could reach, a pile of yellowing skeletons, covered in skin, like parchment. Impossible to recognize as individuals, they would, if at all, be identified by their teeth. They hauled the first ones from the top, and threw them into a truck for burial. Then, as he went back for more, Ernie glanced at a head sticking out from between a pair of knees. The eyes stared. He gritted his teeth, went forward, to take the next body from the top. The eyes blinked. Screaming, Ernie ran back to the gate, where he retched his guts up.

As he stood, gasping, a prisoner reeled up to him, and grinned. 'Cheer up, soldier,' he said. 'It's V.E. Day.' He had a swastika cut into his face. Ernie stared at it, with hatred.

In Norwich, they were celebrating. Rehabilitated into her old job, Eve was drinking with Betty Treacher. Couples were smooching on the floor. Rather than see them, the chaplain

201

approached the girls. The girls exchanged looks of impending doom.

'Hallo there, Eve, Betty.' He smiled benignly..

'Hallo.' They answered without enthusiasm.

'Good turn-out.'

'Yes.'

'It does one good to let one's hair down. Necessary part of our recovery from the shocks of war,' he said.

'What about you, sir?' Eve asked. 'I've not seen you let your hair down yet.' The chaplain laughed uncomfortably.

'Hope the turn-out will be as good at the thanksgiving service tomorrow.'

'Who do you want to thank?' Eve asked belligerently. The chaplain tried not to look shocked.

'Now, Eve. I know you're not Godless. God didn't organize this was, you know, or any of the things you've gone through personally.'

'If He didn't, then who did?' she snapped.

'We do it to ourselves,' he sighed. 'All our miseries, we bring down on our own heads.'

'I don't believe that! What have I ever done to deserve what happened to me?'

'Don't be angry against God, Eve. It's yourself you should be angry with,' Eve blustered with fury.

'I never heard such pompous rubbish in all my life!' she shouted.

'Or against His representative,' the chaplain reproached gently. 'I'm only trying to help.'

'Go and help somebody else!' Eve folded her arms defiantly. Under her anger, she was close to tears. The chaplain sighed, nodded to Betty, and, as he left, bumped into a woman, who spilled her beer all over him. Eve laughed. 'Serves him right,' she said.

They danced the conga all the way round the village, yelling and singing their heads off. Then, dizzy with protest, Eve and Betty wheeled back to base and bed. Betty conked out at once. But Eve couldn't sleep. She was crying. Why had God deserted her? God the Father. Men always let you down, didn't they? It was plain to be seen God was a man. Look what a mess He'd made of the world! Smiling, pleased with her turn of phrase, Eve lay staring at the ceiling. She was making plans; plans for her future, after the war. She would go back to Hollywood, pick up her career from where she'd left off and to hell with men for ever. In the bunk beside her, Betty snored. Eve turned her head to look at her. Outlined black against the darkness, Eve could see Betty's chest rise and fall in time with her snores. Dear old Betty. You could depend on women. Men came and went. Friends you kept forever. Yes. Eve was older and wiser. Things would be different, after the war . . . But the war wasn't over. Not yet. The Japanese considered surrender dishonourable. For them as for the Americans and the British, the Pacific war was a fight to the death.

On July 16th, John's train was near to Mountainair. He'd been travelling all night, working on an article for the *Albuquerque Guardian.* He'd bought his way into the paper, while convalescing at the nursing home. He'd been trying to get information about Los Alamos from an old military pal in Texas. Something interesting was going on up there in the Santa Fe mountains, but he was damned if he could get to the bottom of it. Everybody was keeping stumm. Even his old pal. They'd built a whole village, self-supporting, with labs and God knew what, on the edge of the Valle Grande, a volcanic crater north-west of Santa Fe. The volcano was dormant, and the crater vast. They were banking on it not blowing. Well, it hadn't, not for a long time. There used to be a school there once; an open-air school for ailing boys. But not now. Place was closed to newsmen too, which was precisely why John was interested. When the embargo on reporting broke, he wanted to be first with the full story, whatever it was. It was something to do with bombs and boffins . . .

Had he known it, John, on the train, was at that moment in a good position to observe the culmination of the shady work of those boffins. It was half-past five in the morning. The carriage suddenly started shaking. Looking up from his notes, John saw an explosion over the air base reservation of Alamogordo. The flash lit up the whole sky. It was like the sun. It lasted several moments and then, towards the south-east, a crimson light appeared. It was only after that he heard the explosion. Everyone on the train was talking about it.

'It was a bomber exploding!' one man said.

'No. It was surely a meteor. I saw it burning up!'

'Could be an earthquake. I think this train oughta stop, here and now, before we disappear down some crevasse!' On and on they speculated. But John said nothing. Instead of going on to Santa Fe, he went straight into the paper's offices in Albuquerque. The telephone lines were hot. Reports were coming in from everywhere. Windows had rattled in Gallup, over two hundred miles from the blast. What the hell was it? He had to write something.

'A considerable display of pyrotechnics and high explosives took place today in the White Sands area, south of this city . . . ' It might beat the story of the Kirtland air crash the Saturday before, but it wasn't the story John wanted. He tapped his sources at the base, feeling certain that somehow they must have had a hand in the operation. He was right. They'd been testing a new bomb. So what? But there was something different about this bomb, something exciting, dangerous. It was bigger than anything in the history of the world. Not that John could report it, not yet. Which was just as well, because it smacked of politics. And that meant it was important John should know what slant to take when the wrappers were taken off. John had a carefully nurtured reputation in the department of worthy causes and his whole future as businessman and politician depended on keeping it. Was the Alamogordo blast a worthy cause or not? Only the tide of public opinion would be able to tell him.

As a local man whose family lived at the poor but respectable Lawe Top Ranch, west of town, John was in a good position to rise to power in the up and coming city of Albuquerque. Certainly it would be easier there than in 'Frisco. So John fostered relations with his kin, even to taking his little nephew, twelve-year-old Jimmy Ridley, to football games. In public opinion, a second-hand family was better than none at all. And so John, one leg shorter than the other, limped into the Lawe kitchen, to test the water. He sat, allowing Aunt June to pamper him, putting cushions in his back, plying him with coffee, tut tutting away.

'Why, them Brits've got a lot to answer for,' she said, shaking her head.

'It wasn't Brits shot Uncle John down,' Jimmy corrected her. 'It was the Nazis.'

'Hell, comes to something when a kid starts answering you back!' June glared at Jim. 'I blame them Indians he mixes with up on the reservation. Kids're all cheeky bastards up there!'

'They are not!' Jimmy's cheeks were growing red.

'Hear the blast couple of days ago?' John asked mildly.

'Hear it? Why, I lost twenty-seven plates, down at the café. Came crashing down off the goddam shelf! What the hell was it?'

John smiled, 'Oh, just the military testing something.'

Lou and Jo had been to Gallup, selling stock. They wandered in now with Bill Farley and sat, hands on the table, waiting for food.

'Well, I sure as hell hope whatever they're testing is mighty powerful!' Jo said.

'I second that.' Bill nodded and sighed.

'Japs don't fight fair! We need to teach them a lesson.'

'I second that.' Bill nodded.

'You can't fight fire with fire,' Lou objected.

'Crap.' June banged his coffee down on the table, so it splashed over him. 'Conchy Indian crap!' Jo leered his approval and Bill nodded.

'It's not!' Jimmy shouted and ran out into the yard. There was a long silence. Finally, Bill Farley looked out the window and said,

'Think this drought's ever going to end?'

The stillness took him. The air was heavy with summer, the light red from the late sun. Jimmy wandered past the corral, shaking his head at White Cloud.

'Ain't got nothing for you today, old son,' he said, and passed on to the old stockade. They didn't use it much these days. Stock was almost finished. Lou hadn't even bothered to hammer back the gaping timber, where a young bull had forced his escape the year before. So Jim had taken it over. It was his target range now. He had painted a white circle with a red centre onto the wood. He stared at it. The red bull drew him, like a magnet. His hands flexed and he reached for his weapons, hidden behind the fence. Reverently, he picked an arrow from the sling, and placed it against the bow. He loved to feel its slide between his fingers, smooth and cool. He took a deep breath. His shoulders eased and spread, and he pulled back the bow, tensing his muscles, till the bow was taut, ready to spring. But he didn't release the arrow. Not yet. His eyes were focused on the bull. This time, he would get it. But he had to be sure. The strain of holding the bow was almost too much. His arm began to shake. At last, he let go. The arrow spat, and arched into the air, whirring towards the target. Then, with a dull thud, it landed just short of the red circle.

A slow hand-clap made Jimmy turn sharply to see his Uncle John standing behind.

'Where the hell d'ye learn to do that?' he asked. 'No. Don't tell me. I know.' Jimmy hung his head, his feet making a pattern on the dry earth. He hated talking about his Indian life. It was separate. And John was trespassing. 'Hell you've got the look of your Mom, standing there, sulking,' John observed.

'I'm not sulking.'

'Hell, you ain't.' John smiled, and sat on a rock.

'What d'ye want?' Jim asked sourly.

'Wondered if you'd like to come to a game this Saturday?'

Suddenly, Jimmy smiled, his eyes sparkling. But he confined his answer to a curt nod of the head. It was enough.

'Great,' John said. 'I'll fix it up,' He was staring at the bow. It made Jimmy uncomfortable. 'Handsome weapon, that, boy. Not a toy.'

Jimmy shook his head. John rose and came towards him. Instinctively, Jimmy clutched the bow closer to him.

'Hell, I only want to look at it.'

Jimmy was forced to let John take it, his big man's hand stroking the wood, flexing it gently. Then he looked at Jim. The boy's eyes were black and anxious.

'Guess it's kinda special to you, huh?' Jimmy nodded. 'Bit young for a weapon like this, though.'

'No, I'm not,' Jimmy retorted defiantly. 'I was given it by my godfather. He said I was old enough now to know right from wrong. *And* to know when to use it.'

'Oh? And when's that going to be, huh?' John sneered.

Jimmy's confidence suddenly left him.

'I don't know,' he murmured. John laughed and Jimmy got angry, shouting, 'But he did say I had to choose my own way to make the world better.'

'Oh? And how are you going to do that with a bow and arrow, son?'

'I don't know.' John laughed again.

'Better come into politics, like me, huh?' Jimmy shook his head. 'Get more done that way than sitting around in holes in the ground spouting mumbo-jumbo!'

'We don't spout mumbo-jumbo!' Jim cried, outraged.

'Hell you don't!' John was laughing. Jim stared at his open mouth, teeth grinning like an angry coyote. 'Son, if you knew what I know . . . your bow and arrow ain't going to protect you one jot against the weapons we got now.'

'It's not meant to. It's a weapon of the spirit! Oh, you wouldn't understand!' Jim grabbed at his bow, taking it back.

'Guess not. I'm just an ignorant fool,' John mocked. Then he seemed to grow serious. 'But I'd like to learn,' he said humbly.

Jimmy frowned. Uncle John had helped the Indians get out of jail. He was even an honorary member of the Eagle Clan. Surely it was alright to let him in on it?

'I was given the bow and arrow this year, at Niman Kachina. I'm going back with Ella in a few days, to show Dan how much I've learnt.' Suddenly his face fell. He realized he wouldn't be able to go to the ball game, after all.

'Niman Kachina?'

'Yes. It's a very important ceremony. It takes place at the summer solstice, when the eagles are sacrificed.'

'The eagles are what?!'

Jimmy jumped. In the corner of his eye, he saw Ella. She was standing watching them, darkly silhouetted against the rosy rocks. Following Jim's eye-line, John too saw her. 'Hell. How long's she been there?' he whispered, as though to himself. Suddenly Jimmy was afraid. Had he said too much?

'And it was just getting interesting.' John grinned. 'Better run to Momma, boy.'

Jim backed off, his bow hanging by his side. He looked at the dark figure of his Mom, then at John, face spotlit by the low rays of the setting sun. 'What are you waiting for?'

Suddenly Jimmy turned and ran for the corral. White Cloud whinnied, frisking, as Jim jumped onto his bare back, and took off for the darkening hills.

John's mind was now clear. The American people were right behind the bomb. And on August 6th, when at last the embargo on reporting was lifted, John was able to write his article. For the Americans had dropped the first atomic bomb on Hiroshima.

'At last, America has put the Jap warlords in their place! This was the overall opinion expressed by Mr and Mrs Albuquerque today. "We are rightly proud to be the nation to harness this great discovery for the use of mankind." Albuquerque's Mayor joined in the general acclamation, adding, "I wish that President Roosevelt were alive to see one of his dreams to end all wars become a reality." But what of the men at the centre of this historical event? The men who dropped the bomb that wiped out Hiroshima and its 340,000 residents? That honour fell to weaponeer Naval Capt. William Parsons. His wife declared today, she was the proudest woman in the State. Even the Police Chief had his say. "The good thing about the atomic bomb is that it not only kills the little devils but it buries them too!" '

So that's what they were doing up at Los Alamos! The only note of public dissent came from a physicist who had worked on the bomb. He had phoned John, telling him scare stories.

'My readers don't want to hear things like that,' John told him. 'This bomb's a victory for this nation. Don't spoil the celebrations!' Then he'd hung up, without giving the good doctor time to say more. But the rival paper had taken up the story. An article by Dr Jacobsen appeared on the bottom of their front page, 'Blast Leaves Rays Behind Which Destroy Blood'. John laughed about it in the bar with a County Commissioner. What a scare-monger! Why, the doctor said anyone going into the blast area within seventy years would risk death. He warned of rain taking lethal rays into rivers and seas, killing all animal life. He said secondary radiation breaks up the red corpuscles in the blood, causing death, in a manner similar to leukaemia. Somebody sure ought to silence him, before he killed off a major local industry! The conversation moved on to the change in the weather.

'Did you hear what happened to Barney Pereira?'

'No.'

'Struck by lightning!'

'You don't say.'

'Leaves a gap on the Commission. Don't suppose *you'd* care to stand for election, would you, John?' Within days, Dr Jacobsen had been sat on. He retracted almost every word of his article. And John was standing for election.

On 14th August, Japan surrendered. The war was over. Following the news, June, Jo, Ella and Jimmy stood silently round the radio. Then June turned to get on with the ironing and Ella went to feed the hens. It was unreal. Or was it? Jim went out to find his Pa. He was in town, working on the new theatre building. Jim hitched a lift in, hoping to meet him after work. But the traffic was slow. Albuquerque was coming out of its stunned silence. Somewhere a siren sounded, then some church bells started up and a whistle blew.

'Hell! Just you listen to that!' Jim's lift threw back his hat and chortled. 'Well I never did. I never did.' And he leaned on his horn, adding to the growing cacophony. 'I guess we must have won this darned war!' Jimmy grinned at his lift. 'And it's all thanks to those folks at Los Alamos. God bless 'em.' Jim looked away. The car had stopped. They were stuck in a jam close by Fourth and Central.

'Wonder what the hold-up is?' he asked. Then they heard them, singing, as they snaked through the cars, a long line of High School kids, doing the conga. Jim put his hand on the door handle.

'Go on, son. You get out there and give the Japs hell!' The lift was laughing, tears streaming down his wrinkled cheeks. Jim sprang into the writhing line of youths, yelling and cheering.

'Here comes Indian Jim!' a girl called out. Jim looked round to see who it was. A fair-haired girl with plump cheeks was grinning at him. He grinned back, shrugging off the insult. Suddenly, tiny bits of coloured paper were whirling about their heads. They looked up. Office workers were throwing confetti out of the windows.

'Isn't this just great?' The girl whooped, as she fought her way through to him. Before Jim had time to agree, they were dragged off further down the street, dancing and singing through the crowds and the traffic and the hysterical din.

Ella was angry when Jim finally arrived home at three in the morning. She'd been crying.

'Your Mom's been worried to death about you!' Lou reprimanded.

'I'm sorry.' Jim shrugged. 'I went to find you, Pa, but you'd
gone, and then I got caught up in the crowd, and . . . ' His voice
was slurred.

'You been drinking?' Jim shrugged again. 'Hell, boy, you're
only twelve!'

'I'm thirteen in September!'

'God save us!'

Ella started crying again. June was coming down the stairs,
wakened by the din.

'What's going on down here?'

'Nothing that need worry you, Aunt June,' Lou said. June took
one look at Jim's hang-dog expression and said,

'Crap.'

'I wish you wouldn't say that word.' Ella, fired by general
indignation and distress, snapped the words out. She'd been
wanting to say them for a long time.

'What did you say?' June voice was dangerous.

'I said . . . '

'She didn't say nothing. Go back to bed, Aunt June,' Lou
pleaded.

'Hell I will,' June snarled back. And then they heard Jo
stirring. 'I want to know what that Indian woman said.' Jim
hiccupped and dropped his head into his hands.

'I said I wish you wouldn't use that word,' Ella spoke up
bravely.

'What word's that, honey?' June oozed with artificial
sweetener.

'I won't say it. I won't be dragged down to your level.'

'Ella. Shut up,' Lou warned.

'Say it.' Jo was at the kitchen door, pulling a blanket round his
shoulders.

'I will not!'

'This is crazy!' Jim sighed. He was pulling his eyes down with
his hands. They looked bloodshot.

'What's the matter with him?' Jo peered at him in the semi-
darkness.

'He's drunk.'

'I am not. I only had a couple . . . '

210

'Kid got caught up in the victory celebrations in town. That's all.' Lou decided to make light of it. 'Now can we all get back to bed?'

'I want to know what word that Indian woman's talking about,' June said flatly.

'Crap,' said Jimmy. There was a stunned silence.

'Ain't heard the kid use a word like that before,' June said at last.

'I wonder where he gets it from!' Ella retorted. June glared at her, teeth bared. Both Lou and Jo stood poised, ready to part the female combatants, if necessary.

'Come on, honey,' Lou tried to smile. 'I thought you Hopis were a peaceful people.'

Ella hung her head. 'Sorry, June,' she said.

'Bull-shit!' June had excelled herself. Jo let out a whoop and, the party over, the family turned in for the remainder of the night.

The incident had its repercussions. On the surface, nothing in the Ridley family had changed; the status quo remained the same, June and Jo in the ascendant. But another war was being waged on a subtler level and Uncle John was in the thick of it. Hearing about Jim's 'drunken orgy', John decided to pay his new sister-in-law a brotherly visit. She was beside herself with worry about her boy. Well, every Mom found it difficult to come to terms with her boy's growing up! But Ella had a point.

'Ella,' John said gently, 'I know what you're saying. We've gotta protect our young boys from vice. And I want you to know that I am running my campaign on a clean-up ticket.' Ella nodded slowly, trying to understand. 'This gambling that's taken hold of young and old alike, has got to stop. Bootlegging on Sundays too! And I know, for a fact, joints have been selling liquor to minors like our Jim here. Well, if I'm elected, I'm going to put a stop to all that!'

Ella let out a little cheer and slapped him on the back. 'You've got my vote.' She beamed. Then her smile fell. 'Have I got a vote?' she asked.

'Sure you gotta vote, honey. Now you make sure you use it.'

In need of allies, Ella warmed to John's reassurance and smiled

211

on Jim's outings to the football. She decided John had matured. Probably the war had matured him. He wasn't as bad as she'd thought. So, that fall, the University of New Mexico having a championship football team, Jim went with his uncle to a great many games, with his Mom's blessing, and relieved his inner tensions by melting into the mass identity of the Lobo fans. John proved a good chaperon too. Not a drop of liquor passed either of their lips. It would have looked bad to the voters. In this way, John bolstered up his image as a family man, Jim enjoyed basking in his uncle's reflected glory, and both were happy. Soon, Jim had attracted a bunch of pals, every one of them positively keen to be seen hanging around with him. One of the bunch was a girl called Louise; she was the fair-haired one with plump cheeks he'd danced the conga with. She was a cheer-leader for the Lobos, and Jim was in a fair way to getting smitten, as he watched her jumping up and down, waving her arms about before the game. She even had breasts. Little ones. Jim thought about them a lot. He even wondered if he'd ever be able to date her.

Then Christmas came, and Ella assumed Jim would be going with her to the reservation. Jim's heart sank. The Lobos were down to play Denver at the Sun Bowl in January. It was going to be a great game. He'd hate to miss it.

'Do I have to, Mom?'

Ella was shocked. Soyal would be celebrated at the winter solstice and Jim was to be initiated in a year's time. He should be there, sucking in the deep knowledge of the Hopi people at this important time, or how would he be mature enough to take on the responsibility of a Society member? But Jim didn't want to know about responsibility.

'Oh, Mom, don't say I have to save the Indians as well.'

'What do you mean, "as well"?'

'Granpa said I had to be the saving of the ranch. I don't want to have to save everything.'

'Who is this "I"?' Ella reprimanded. 'I told you. Only God can do, and only God can save.'

'Yes, Mom.'

Ella thought she'd won. But she'd reckoned without John and Lou. For one thing, Lou fancied a traditional sort of Christmas at home, for a change, and he wanted his son home with him.

And then, John spoke up. 'All work and no play makes Jim a dull boy. Ain't that right, son?' he asked, brushing the back of Jim's head with his hand.

'Suppose so,' Jim answered, not looking at his Mom. In his mind, he kept seeing those tiny little breasts and he was rosy pink at the thought of them. Ella said nothing. She packed her bag and let Lou drive her up to the reservation alone, in good time for the solstice, neatly missing Clara's arrival from 'Frisco for Christmas.

She had brought Jim a razor for his Christmas present. Jo was tickled pink. He peered at Jim's chin over his dinner, chortling and yelping, when he discovered a few stubbly bits of hair.

'Boy's growing up! Be chasing after women before long, I expect!' he said gleefully. Jim squirmed with embarrassment but he was pleased inside. He hoped Louise would notice the little cut he'd got from his first shave. He'd done it on purpose. 'He'll be dressing up like them zoot-suiters, before we know where we are!'

'Don't encourage him, Pa,' Lou objected. But Jo only nodded and smiled, chuckling intermittently throughout the meal, and Jim tried hard to imagine himself in the flamboyant dress of the Albuquerque gangs. He had every right to wear it. He did have Hispanic blood in him, after all. Then, earlier than expected, Ernie Trevor arrived in their midst.

He got a hero's welcome. But he didn't seem to care two hoots about it. He wouldn't even let John write an article about his heroic exploits relieving the prison camps of Europe.

'It's all your fault I ever went to Europe in the first place!' he said bitterly. 'I'll never forgive you for that, Mr Goddam County Commissioner Almighty!'

'How's it *my* fault?' John appealed to his sister, who was stunned by the change in her husband. She said nothing.

'You and that goddam Houlihan!' Ernie growled.

'Come along, Ernie,' Clara said at last. 'It's Christmas. Can't we let bygones be bygones?' Ernie shook his head and reached into his jacket pocket. Everyone was watching. He fetched out a bundle of photographs and started passing them round the table.

'What the hell's this?' John asked.

213

'I took them at Mauthausen. One of the Nazi camps. Take a good look.'

'What for?' June asked. She was white, her strong stomach heaving at the ghoulish sights.

'I want you all to know what it was really like. What them fascist bastards really did. Churchill was right, you know. Hitler was evil. All Fascism is evil. Look!' He pushed more pictures onto them. 'I dream about them faces. I do. Night after night.' A sob caught in Ernie's throat. He paused, coughing.

'Why, these are faked!' Clara started laughing. Ernie stared at her. 'They are, aren't they, Ernie? You had these made up for a joke. Just to see how we'd react!' She looked round the table for approval. Lips quivered on white faces. Were they dying to laugh as she was?

'They are not faked!' Ernie yelled so loud, Clara jumped. She looked back at the pictures and began to moan.

'Please, Ernie, tell me they're not true!'

'They are true, honey.' He put his hand on her back to comfort her, and she turned to howl in his arms. 'I promise you. Every single one of them. And that wasn't the worst of it. I could tell you stories . . . '

'Don't!' June yelled. She began tearing up the pictures. Ernie stumbled out of his chair and made a grab for them, but she reached away, throwing them into the fire, where they peeled, and burned in tiny rolls.

'Best place for them,' John said, coughing.

'You would think that,' Ernie spat. 'Why, you and the Nazis, you're two of a kind!'

'Hell, Ernie. That's going a bit far!' Lou put in. Jo was beating a rhythm on the table top with his fingers. They all turned to look at him.

'What do you think of the bomb, then, Erne?' he asked, grinning like a Cheshire cat. Ernie sat down suddenly, floored. 'Atom bomb. Ain't it the greatest invention?'

'Wiped out more people in one go than Hitler could do away with in six years!' John agreed.

'Well, as extermination goes, I daresay it's slightly more humane than the camps.' Ernie left them and went up to bed.

But he didn't sleep. His brain seethed with hatred, not so much for the Nazis as for John. If it hadn't been for John, Ernie would have stayed on the 'Frisco police force. He might never have been drafted, might never have seen what he had seen. But then, again, he needed to see it, needed to empathize with the creatures he'd liberated. In his dreams he saw himself as a prisoner, and groaned with the agonies of torture endured in sympathy.

Clara was beside herself. She didn't know what to do with him. Her Ernie had changed. He was not the man she'd married. And yet, having seen those pictures, she almost understood his torment. Nursing him in her arms, wiping sweat from his forehead, she let him talk and talk far into the night.

'How could God let things like this happen, Clara?' he asked. And Clara sighed, shaking her head.

'Jews never recognized Christ,' she said. 'Maybe that's why God punished them.'

'Wasn't only Jews in the camps. Maybe mainly Jews. But not only. There were gypsies, resistance fighters, queers . . . anyone the Nazis took a dislike to. No logic in it. You just can't understand.'

'Best not to try, honey,' Clara encouraged.

'I've got to. I can't live with myself if I don't.' Ernie rocked to and fro, moaning, as though in pain. 'And God didn't do it. Man did. God only looked on.'

'You know, Ernie,' Clara sighed, 'I sometimes think God would rather we suffered now, in the body, than suffer the torments of eternal hell. After all, not one of us is perfect, dear. We all deserve to suffer one way or another. Yes,' she sighed, 'having us suffer on earth could just be God's way of being kind.'

'No. No.'

'Yes, Erne. It's what the Father said. He said we should follow the example of Christ's suffering. Those people in the concentration camps should be glad to be martyrs. It's their ticket to heaven.'

'But most of them were Jews . . . '

'Oh yes. That's true.' Clara was silent. The Father hadn't explained that but she was sure he *had* an explanation. She'd put it to him, once they were back in 'Frisco. He would set Ernie's mind at rest. Then he'd sleep. And so would she.

Jim heard them talking in the darkness. Guilt oozed from their room, along the passage and under Jim's door, seeping into his unconscious and taking root. And all Jim knew was, he felt uncomfortable. Even the Lobo game failed to relieve his trapped spirit. And it was a good game; it kept them on the edge of their seats the entire time. Denver was a great side. Right until the fourth quarter they were winning, and then, spurred on by the fans, three blazing touchdowns brought final victory. Swept along by the tide of elation, Jimmy whooped and cheered the heroes of the hour. But, inside, he was cast down. It was like there were two Jimmys. One of them was here, at his uncle's side, letting his hair down with the best of them, and the other was up at Walpi with his Mom. In amongst the images of waving flags, flying ticker tape, grinning mouths and girls, pretty girls, Jim kept seeing Ella's hurt expression as she silently left the ranch. He was sorry he'd hurt her. He'd make it up to her somehow. He'd make her see he wasn't a bad boy. She'd be proud of him one day when, as White Eagle, he was admitted to the society. He'd be strong, silent, wise, as a brave should be. A real man. He touched his cheek. It was rough. He wished he could kiss Louise so she'd feel it.

When Ella returned, she said nothing to Jimmy about the ceremonies and dances he'd missed on the Reservation, and he felt somehow left out. In retaliation, he went out with his friends from High School even more.

'It's in your own interests, Ella,' June said. 'No use thinking you can keep that boy imprisoned on the ranch. If there's bad influences about, you gotta let him learn to deal with them his own way. Yes! You've got to give him away if you want to keep him.' Ella recognized the wisdom of this advice, even if she didn't like it. So she watched and waited with a gentle patience that increased Jim's feelings of guilt still further.

There was a volcanic atmosphere about the towns and villages of New Mexico since the war. It set the nerves twitching and Jimmy, like most adolescents, responded to its excitement. Maybe the young men missed the fighting. Maybe they chafed at lost opportunities to prove themselves. Maybe they were just bored. Anyway, they organized themselves into gangs, sporadic

216

skirmishes breaking out all over, in dance halls, outside cinemas and liquor stores, anywhere. And they weren't just poor folk. All sorts, even middle-class students from the University rubbed shoulder to shoulder with the Chicos, Hispanics, Anglos and Blacks in the melting pot of Albuquerque youth. Jimmy drifted towards the roaming gangs, and away from his 'law and order' Uncle John. Now he had his weekend job in the grocery store, Jimmy had money of his own to burn, and who needed a County Commissioner on his back?

One day, in early spring, when the Rio Grande was flowing with water, Jimmy left his grocery store and, instead of going straight on home, he went up to the old town, where he'd arranged to meet with Louise. She was sitting there, in the café, sipping orange juice, her fair hair gleaming in the sunshine that filtered through the tiny window. Jim looked for a moment, staring, chest swelling fit to burst. Then, she looked round and smiled at him, and he knew he was 'in love'. Jim touched the well-preserved stubble on his chin, and sauntered in.

'What you want to do tonight?' he asked. Louise shrugged.

'Dunno.' She put her head on one side, and her eyes slid to look at him. 'I did hear there was something going on at the University, though.'

'Oh? What?'

'You know the "Engineer Queen"? Engineering students're real proud of the girl they crowned this year. And she makes quite a pretty little mascot, I've got to admit.'

'Yeah.' Jim tried to sound interested without being too enthusiastic. He didn't want to cause any jealousy. He succeeded. Louise's voice dropped to a whisper.

'Well,' she went on, 'the guys from the Arts faculty are planning on kidnapping her!'

'No!'

'Yeah. Isn't it great?' she squealed. Jim smiled, then frowned.

'So, where do we come in?'

'Let's help them!'

'But we're not students,' Jim objected. 'They wouldn't want us around. They think we're just . . .'

'What?' she challenged. Jim blushed. Louise was a year older than him. He had to work hard if she wasn't going to think of him as 'just a kid'.

'O.K.' he said smartly. 'Let's go.'

Louise had borrowed her father's Packard for the night. They parked it just off the campus. The 'Engineer Queen' lived a couple of blocks away, and from their vantage point, they could see everything. They sat, waiting for the big moment, eating fries.

'Isn't this just great?' Louise asked. Jim nodded.

'Great.'

'I like your shirt.'

'Thanks.' Her fingers fluttered the fringe on the yoke.

'Is it Indian?' Louise's jaw revolved into a sort of leer, and her voice had the timbre of excitement. Picking it up, Jim swallowed hard.

'Sorta.' He looked straight ahead, stern-faced, at the kidnap house.

'Are you really half-Indian?' she breathed.

Without batting an eyelid, Jim said, 'Uhuh!'

'I heard you were brought up on a reservation?' Jim said nothing. 'Hunting and shooting and fishing like a primitive?'

'Uhuh.' Louise shivered with delight. She touched the dark hair curling on his temple.

'You got your Indian Momma's hair alright. Jet.' Jim's skin tingled at her touch. He began to shake with fear.

'Get off. You're tickling me.' He laughed with embarrassment. Louise giggled, and her hand dropped into her fries. 'Dames!' Jim said, shaking his head. 'A man sure has a job keeping you in order!'

At that moment, a green Buick swung round the corner and into the street. It pulled up a couple of doors away from the kidnap house. There were five guys inside. They all got out, three hung around the car and the other two went right on up to the door of the 'Engineer Queen'.

'Come on,' Louise shouted, 'let's get nearer.'

Heart pounding, Jim slowly cruised down the street, and parked beyond the house. Now they could watch the proceedings in their mirror. The door opened. A man stood there talking. There was some movement, a scuffle. One of the boys beckoned the ones waiting by the car, and they barged their way into the house. There was a loud scream. After a few minutes, the girl

218

was dragged out, kicking and screaming, in the middle of an almighty dust-up. The Arts students got her to their Buick and shoved her inside, piling in after her. Then the Buick took off.

'After them!' Louise yelled.

Scared out of his mind, Jim started the engine and slowly eased into the road. An engineering student, sprawling on the pavement, saw him and made a rush for the car door. He got in.

'Follow that car,' the engineer commanded.

This was more like it. Jim put his foot down. Louise was gripping the edge of her seat. They were closing in. Then, the roadside door of the Buick swung open, and a pair of hands emptied an oil can onto the road. Jim yelled. The Packard swung, slid, and toppled right over and back onto its wheels. Dazed, the three inside moaned, moving bruised bodies gently, but gently. Then they heard the police sirens. The student got out and ran. The fun had turned nasty.

'We've got to make a getaway,' Louise breathed.

'Oh shut up!' Jim said, and lay back, eyes closed, waiting.

John was at a Democratic dinner that night and wasn't best pleased to be hauled out to bail his nephew from jail.

'How the hell am I supposed to keep my image as a law and order man, with you doing your best to scupper me?' he sighed. 'And who the hell's the Packard belong to?'

'Louise's father.'

'O.K. I'll pay for the Packard.' John turned to the cop. 'Can you get him home?' The cop nodded slowly. 'Thanks.' Suddenly, John launched his fist at Jim's mouth. The boy yelled, tasting blood. And John went back to his dinner.

Chastened, Jim gave himself up to Ella's rule. After discussion with Chu'Ovi, she came to the conclusion that the sooner Jim went through the final stages of initiation the better. For he was in mortal danger from the influences of white corruption. So, the following November, Jim went with his Mom up to Walpi, and prepared for the great ceremony of Astotokya. Lou was not to be present. It was too secret, too solemn an occasion. Even Ella was excluded. The village roads were closed and sealed, isolating the initiates from all but the priests and the incoming spirits. And, on the appointed night, purified by the Great Fire Ceremony,

Dan took his godson down into the Kiva. There was no way out till morning. If any evil being broke through bringing corruption to the ceremony, not one of them, priest or boy, would come out alive. A deep silence descended on the youths, seated round the subterranean walls, in the glow of the fire. While outside, in the village, the periodic rattling of turtle shells announced the patrols of Two Horns and One Horns. Daggers poised to strike at any intruder, their job was to guard the roads and God help any man fool enough to dare his fate.

Even from Myna's house Ella heard, just before the dawn, the eerie humming of the spirits, growing louder and higher, till they swept through the village, like the winds of another world. Then howling and yelling, the initiates, stark naked, spilled in confusion up the Kiva ladder and into the light of day. Hot, streaked with sweat, Jim felt the shock of cold water as it was poured over him and shivered. Naked, wet, like a newborn babe, Dan took him home. But, his initiation wasn't over. Not yet. White Eagle still had to prove the strength of his spiritual wings.

The following spring, bow and arrows on his back, Jim Ridley made his way, barefoot, to the Grand Canyon. Alone, guided by the stars and the sun, for days on end he wandered across the Painted Desert, sleeping rough and finding food and water where he could. His skill with bow and arrow had suddenly become a matter of life and death. His aim sharpened with hunger, until, after the initial failures, he made his first kill. Then, skinning the mule deer, he made a fire, and roasted it, gorging on the meat till at last his hunger was sated and he lay down to sleep off the feast. Next day, he slung the carcass on his back, and walked on, till at last he came to a tributary gushing down the gorge into the canyon, where it merged with the great Colorado River.

Dazed by exposure and silence, Jim found his way down and down and down, layer upon layer of rock, descending through aeons of time, till, hours later, he reached the bottom of the Canyon. There, near the confluence of the two rivers, the sacred hole in the earth could be found, through which the Hopis had emerged into the fourth world. Like a man in a trance, Jim observed the ritual prayers, then throwing off his clothes, he ran into the river. Washed in the merging currents, he lay, floating on the surface of the water, looking up the steep canyon sides to Cape Solitude. The river bubbled in his ears, cold, numbing, the sound breaking the lonely silence. Then he stood in the rays of the noonday sun to dry, before pulling on his clothes. At last, he was ready to make for the East Tonto Trail.

In the depths of the Canyon, the silence grew more profound, his presence more real. Every footfall echoed like a friend. He found himself singing, then talking to himself, checking the map, pointing out, as if to someone else, the towering rock temples of Vishnu, Brahma, Zoroaster and other Gods of other worlds, gathering in this Great Natural Temple of the Earth Mother. And everything was pink, varying shades of pink, from red, to mauve everchanging in the changing light, deepening in the sunset. Before dark came, he set up camp, gathering twigs and brittle herbs that burned like incense, as he drifted off into a half-sleep, where dream and reality fused. He woke, cold, coughing. The pink rattler that had settled on his legs uncoiled and slithered into the brush. Jim watched it, unbelieving, then got up, splashed his face with water, and walked on, down the trail, through the Granite Gorge. Days merged into nights, food scarce, till, a night spent at Phantom Ranch, and a meal purchased from a stranger, White Eagle had passed Bright Angel, and was travelling west to the creek, where he would find the salt he was to take back as offering to the Hopi priests, proof of his completed task.

It was mid-afternoon as Jim reached the point below Hopi Fire Tower. He looked up at the South Rim. The canyon walls were striped with angry vermilion, purple and livid gold. The Inferno. At the base of these rocks, he would find the salt. Foraging with bare hands, he dug the crystals, prising them from stone. He held them up in the sunlight. They shone, now white, now grey like ash, now a rainbow of colours against the purple sky. He had done it. His eagle wings had soared, carrying him to the beginnings of the world, to the source of life, carrying him to the carry him back again, taking the precious crystals with him. A drop of water fell on the crown of his head. A breeze swept down the gorge. Jim slipped the salt into a piece of cloth and tied it tightly, binding it to his belt, then, as the breeze whipped into

221

a howling gale, he hurried on to find shelter from the coming storm.

Overhead, Sky Father's anger rumbled dangerously. It rode into the gorge, on the back of the shrieking wind, bouncing back and forth from the canyon walls growing louder and louder in a deafening rodeo of sound. Pinned down by the roaring terror, intensified by the overheating of his mind, surrendered to Hopi perceptions, starved of the 'normal', Jim clung to the rocks, screaming. Lightning crackled deep into the inner canyon, shooting out webs of electricity, scorching the rocks. Then, before the first clap of thunder had rolled away, another crashed against him, and a sheet of light displayed the Shiva Temple Rock, setting the North Rim at the canyon top afire. Quenched, darkened into dull red of rock and sky, the mountain disappeared as suddenly as it had shown. Splayed against the rock, Jim suffered the torments of wind and fire, deafened by the crashing anarchy of sound, lashed by the rain. And when it ended, he fell exhausted to the ground, and wept.

He woke, in mist. The trail disappeared like a ghost in the early morning. Light-headed with fever, he followed it back to Bright Angel and there he stopped. He had a choice, either to go back the misty way, on foot, through the Granite Gorge, across the desert to Walpi, where he was to make his offering; or to climb the Bright Angel Trail to the hotel at the top. Shivering, he stood for minutes, afraid of either choice, then, resolutely, his feet turned up the trail that led to the Rim. Slowly, he climbed, the cloud lifting with him, up and up, out of infernal chaos into daylight, to see tourists hanging over the rails, gaping, as though they hung over the sharp edge of the world. They made way, as he approached, out of respect or fear, or God knew what, and he stood, as they did, looking down through the layers of gemlike colours to the invisible bottom, then up and across to the opposite edge of the chasm, to the other world on the other side. Who was he to think he could span the gap, the split between old America and new? Ella wasn't his Momma, and he was no Indian. Jim was a white man. An Anglo. Better stop pretending now. He untied the bag of salt from round his waist, and opened it. This salt was not to be an offering to a priest. If God existed, Jim had met him at the canyon bottom, alone, without the benefit of priestly rituals, as himself. And that self had nothing to do with Ridleys, with Catholics or Buddhists, or Hopis or anything else! That self was something deep within, sacred, too sacred to be given away to just anyone, just because he wanted to belong. Jim had stood alone in the Canyon. He would stand alone in his life. He was his own master. Raising his arm, he hurled the bag of salt over the edge, and watched it falling down and down and down to Mother Earth.

PART TWO

April 1952

'The force from which the sun draws its power has been loosed . . .'

Truman

CHAPTER TWELVE

Stomp beat step slide spring land heel heel double wing spring right swivel drop. Eve splayed her arms triumphantly on the last chord. There was a brief smattering of applause. Tap was definitely on the way out. She made her exit quickly, before the clapping stopped altogether, and slipped into the refuge of her dressing room. Victor Flamm's club was the last stronghold. But fashion was catching up even with Las Vegas. Eve would have to change, go on to musical comedy, soft shoe. And at her age too! She was wondering whether Danny, back in L.A., had any ideas on the situation, when there was a knock on her door.

'Come!' she called out. In her mirror, she saw the door open, and a hand, holding a glass appeared. She stared at it for a moment. 'Come on in! I won't bite you!' she yelled. And Victor Flamm walked into the room. He shrugged, and handed her the glass. 'Cheers,' she said, drinking it down. 'Come to give me my cards, Victor?' she asked.

'Honey, you've been around too long.' Vic's words sent memories ricocheting through Eve's brain; too long in England after the war, sharing the miseries and the hunger; too long in New York, trying to get onto Broadway, and ending up on tour in the outback; too long fighting a lonely, losing battle for recogniton. And of what?

'Yeah. I know,' Eve sighed, and turned back to the mirror. A

227

fuzzy reflection stared back at her. Were her eyes going, or had her face lost its definition? She was thirty-five years old; past her best.

'I'll give you till the end of the week. O.K?'

'O.K.'

But Victor was still standing uncertainly, near the door. 'Unless of course, you want to change your mind about the stripping?'

'No!' Eve turned on him furiously. 'I've got some self-respect left, Victor. I'd rather teach.'

'Just a thought.' He sighed. 'Pity though. You're still a very attractive woman . . . ' Eve laughed, her anger dissipated. Those were words she liked to hear. 'Matter of fact . . . ' Vic knew he shouldn't, but went ahead anyway, just as he usually did, 'I wouldn't at all mind making an honest woman out of you.'

'I'm honest already, thanks!' Eve flashed. Victor's face fell, and immediately, Eve was sorry. He was a nice man; his hard exterior hid a soft inside. But his face was sad. Business wasn't doing so well. Eve couldn't blame him for sliding down the pan morally. It was either that or slide down it financially. Something had to give. Folks just didn't want good clean entertainment any more.

'What we need is bigger bangs,' Victor said reflectively. 'The American people need their kicks.'

'Bigger bangs?' Eve repeated. 'You mean, bigger bombs?'

'Yeah. When they first started testing them bombs in the Nevada, business really picked up. Folk came from miles around in the hopes of seeing one of them mushroom clouds.'

'That's gruesome.'

'Don't see why. Nobody ever gets hurt, do they? And we've got to keep ahead of the Commies!'

'That's fightin' talk, Victor.' Eve smiled at him from the mirror. He smiled back. She was wiping the make up from her face.

'Why don't you come out front and have a dance with some of the punters,' Victor encouraged. He thought it would cheer her up.

'I'm not one of your floor girls, Vic,' Eve said.

'I know but . . . hell . . . come and have a dance with me!' Eve laughed.

'That's more like it. Now get the hell out of here and let me get undressed.'

228

Victor ambled out into the corridor, where he leaned against a wall. It hadn't been as bad as he'd feared. But then, Eve was a sensible girl, not given to melodrama. A real trooper. Yeah. She'd make somebody a fine wife one day, he thought wistfully.

Suddenly Eve's door opened and her head popped out.

'Vic . . . !' she said urgently in a hushed voice. 'Vic, can you lend me some dough?'

'Honey! Anything! How much do you want?'

'I don't know . . . ' She was unwilling to name the sum, but Victor already had his wallet out. 'Five hundred?' she asked.

'Make it a grand. Pay me back, when you're flush.' Eve took the money, grasping it in her fist.

'Don't bank on it,' she said.

'What the hell. I can spare it. I'll get a few strippers in. I'll soon be back on top.' Was Eve crying? She was wiping her cheeks with the back of her moneyed fist.

'Hell, Vic, what's going to become of me?' she asked. He took her in his arms, comforting her.

'Know what I think, honey?'

'What?'

'I think that talent of yours was the greatest curse God could ever have given you.' Eve looked up surprised. Was he joking? But Vic's face was serious.

'Why?' Her voice croaked with emotion.

'Because, if it hadn't been for that, you would probably have gotten married, settled down and you'd have a couple of kids by now. You'd be contented, Evie.'

'No, I wouldn't. I'd never've known whether I'd have made it to the top or not.'

'You didn't make it to the top, Eve.'

'I know. But I nearly did.' There was a note of desperation in Eve's voice. 'If it hadn't been for the war and . . . '

Vic said nothing. There was a gap in his knowledge of this bright, nice woman, this attractive, witty, warm, person that he liked so much. The war and . . . what? That was the gap. He didn't know what. He couldn't guess what made her turn down man after man (not that any of them was anything like good enough for her), and yet, he knew, you could see it in every second of her life, even out there on the stage, she was desperately looking for love. She had dropped her head to hide

229

her face in Vic's shirt. For a moment, he almost asked her, 'The war and what?' But the moment passed. He wasn't that brave. Did he really want to know, after all?

'You'll never make it now,' he said.

'Don't say that!' Eve's words were muffled in the cloth of his shirt.

'You've got to start facing facts, honey.'

'Why? I never have up to now!' She was laughing.

'You're a nice woman. It's a waste.' He sighed, sadly admitting his defeat. You couldn't talk sense to Eve Lawson. But she put her hand on Vic's chest, and pushed herself away from him with some determination.

'Don't start, Vic,' she warned.

'I wasn't starting. But, all the same, it *is* a waste,' he repeated. He meant it. Eve couldn't brush it off. He wouldn't let her. Did the gap in his knowledge of her really matter? Hell, did anyone ever really know anybody else? Let it pass. It was the future that mattered. And he wasn't getting any younger . . . 'Look, honey . . . ' One of the musicians, George Vernon, came off the stage to go to the john. Vic waited for him to disappear behind the door, and went on, whispering urgently. 'I'm in my prime, Eve. O.K. you're a lot younger than I am, but lots of folk wed, in spite of age differences, these days. It can be a good thing. My experience of life would be a great help to you, you know that?' Eve was embarrassed. Poor Vic. She couldn't bear for him to make a fool of himself. How could she put him off without putting him down?

'Vic,' she said softly. 'How would you feel, I mean, really feel about having kids?' Vic paused. 'Just think about it now.'

Vic shook his head slowly. He just couldn't stretch himself that far. 'You see, honey . . . I got kids already; grown up. Jean and me we . . . well, we went through all that.'

'I know, Vic. And I don't blame you for not wanting to go through it all again with me. But, you see, I've never had any of that. And if I got married, I'd want it alright. You know, I really want to have a baby.' Vic nodded. 'Come on, Vic.' Eve put her arms round him, hugging him tight. 'You're the best father figure I ever had. I'm not going to mess that up by marrying you.'

'Father figure, am I?' Vic said bitterly. Then he sighed, as Eve looked up at him, her big eyes wet with tears. Slowly he reached his hand to her head and stroked it. 'Well, I guess I just gotta make do with that, I suppose.'

'Thanks, Vic. And I'm sorry about the stripping. I just couldn't . . .'

'Hell. Forget it. I don't want no daughter of mine exposing herself!' He managed a smile. The musician came out of the john. He had lit a cigarette and the smoke billowed out into the corridor. He eyed them curiously before disappearing back on stage. Eve was holding up her fistful of notes like a threat.

'I'll pay you back,' she said.

'Hell, you will.' He slapped her on the behind, and walked off.

Eve leaned against the closed door of her dressing room, listening to the music as it filtered through from the stage. They were playing jive. The very sound of so much energy made her feel tired. She held up the fistful of money and looked at it. Dear old Vic. Pity she couldn't marry him, really. She levered herself from the door and sat again in front of her mirror. Her face looked small and blank without the make-up, the skin mottled and shiny. She touched it curiously with one finger. Skin. Fragile, thinning, translucent. She'd lived on the edge so long, she was beginning to fade away. It wouldn't do. She snorted, and her reflection snorted back. Maybe she should have accepted Vic's proposal. It'd be an easy life. But Eve had never settled for the easy life, had she? She'd never sold out and she wasn't going to start now! She flung down the money, and put on some street make-up. Vic was right. She'd better start facing facts. What were the facts? Eve was thirty-five year old; unmarried; childless. Her career had never taken off since she came back to the States in '49. But what else could she do? Teach? Not tap. Tap was out. O.K., ballroom dancing. Yes, that was a possibility. But her heart sank at the prospect. Teaching old men and old ladies how to do the rumba was not what she'd had in mind when she'd left home, stars in her eyes, more than ten years before. And as for marriage . . . She wanted it alright. She still carried a torch for connubial bliss. And she'd gotten over John Ridley long ago. The bastard! It's just that good old Mr Right had never come along. Eve sighed and her breath clouded the mirror. Well . . . time was running out. Yes. Maybe she should accept Vic . . .

Except she didn't love him; not in that way; and she couldn't fake. Faking wasn't in her nature.

Eve was standing at the bar, watching the punters jive. Those musicians were hot stuff. Vic'd got himself a good band in. She started nodding in rhythm to the music. George Vernon, looking up from the sax, saw her looking back, and he winked. It was a 'see you later' sort of a wink. Eve turned her back, and ordered another drink from the bar. Damn George Vernon. Just another guy thinking she was fair game, easy stuff, whatever else they liked to call it. Well, he'd learn, like the rest of them. She paid for her drink, and downed it quickly. Was it the shock of the liquor or had the music stopped? She shook her head, to clear her ears.

'You want to take a little bit of tomato juice with your vodka, Evie,' the barman told her. She grinned at him.

'Ruins the taste,' she said.

'Vodka hasn't got any taste,' he replied.

'That's funny. I thought it had. You'd better let me try it again.' She pushed her glass forward for him to fill. He pulled a disapproving face. A feeling of prickly heat rose up Eve's spine. The barman wasn't going to fill her glass. And he was serious. The inference was that she, Eve Lawson, was turning into a lush. Was this really happening to her? But a hand touched her shoulder. It was George Vernon. The comic was on.

'Beer, Bernie. And fill the lady's glass for her, will you?' The barman obliged.

'Thanks,' Eve said, as she took her brimming tumbler. This time she was going to sip it slowly. He clinked glasses with her. She smiled at him, but she still didn't like him.

'Don't spend it all at once,' he said. Eve looked blank, then her eyes followed his to her purse.

'You don't miss much, do you?' Eve objected.

'Must've done the old man quite a favour, huh?' he remarked smugly. Eve gritted her teeth. It was just the smarmy sort of remark she would have expected of him. Then he leaned forward and whispered lasciviously in her ear. 'Wish you'd do *me* a favour.' Eve pulled away from him.

'If you really want to know, George,' she said, 'that money's my pay-off. I got my cards tonight.'

'You want to throw that line to the comic. He isn't getting many laughs tonight,' George sneered.

'Ha ha.'

'O.K. If Vic thinks you're worth that much, why didn't he keep you on?' George asked. Eve said nothing. 'Well, don't blow it at the tables, will you? You don't know how long it may have to last!' Eve threw him a smirk. She wouldn't *jive* with a jerk like him, let alone . . .

'I'll try, George. I'll try,' she said wearily, turning her back on him. George took it in his stride. He sauntered off backstage, and made a phone call.

From the other side of the room, Vic watched Eve sip her drink. He'd seen the whole show. He was glad she'd given Vernon the bum's rush; made it easier to accept his own rejection. But he was fond of that girl; really fond. Her back was bowed, her head low. She was turning her back on the world, not just the men in it; and that wouldn't do. She had too much to give for her to, well, give up! Hell, 'the war and . . . ' what? Perched on a bar stool, sipping her drink, Eve knew someone was watching her. Her back had that queer creeping sensation she always got. She tried to shrug the feeling off. But she couldn't. It must be that bastard George Vernon, sizing her up for his bed, no doubt! Yes. She was right. Out of the corner of her eye, she saw a shadow creeping towards her. The stinking, disgusting, little worm! She could feel him getting nearer, closing in on her. Then she felt his breath hot on her bare back. Any minute and he'd have his arm round her.

She turned, spitting fire, 'Why don't you just take no for an answer, like everyone else, you pimply, lousy, little creep!' Then, she gasped.

The man standing beside her was John Ridley.

For a moment, Eve thought she was going to pass out. She reeled on her bar stool. John caught her by the arm, to steady her, but she pulled away from him. Then, Vic was there.

'This gentleman causing you trouble, Miss Lawson?' he asked. Eve was speechless. She shook her head, then nodded, then shook her head again.

'Seems the lady can't make her mind up,' John remarked good-humouredly. Vic looked at him for a moment, then stepped forward. He was about to put his hands on the intruder's collar and haul him up off of his bar stool. Then Eve found her voice.

'It's O.K., Vic. We're er . . . related,' she said.

Vic hesitated. He didn't like this. He didn't like it at all. But he backed away, to watch from a safe distance.

'Sorry I surprised you like that,' John said. His smile was gentle, disarming as ever.

'Snakes creep up on people, John,' Eve remarked. Her face was pale.

'O.K. I accept I deserve all the mud you can sling at me.' Eve looked away. He had a way of pulling down her defences, leaving her with no ammunition to use against him, except, perhaps, bitterness, and hatred.

'Don't think you can slink back into my life just like that, John Ridley!' she spat. 'How did you find me, anyway?'

'I wasn't looking for you, honest!' John held his hands in the air, as if to show he had no weapons up his sleeve. 'I came up here on bona fide newspaper business. Honest Injun.' Eve stared at him. She knew it was true. He'd come on her by chance. He hadn't been looking for her at all. The realization was humiliating.

'I didn't suppose you were!' she lied. But she knew too that John had seen through the lie. It made her humiliation more complete. She took another sip of her drink, before she spoke again. 'So, what business are you talking about?' she asked acidly.

'Newspaper business. You know. The usual.' Memories flashed across Eve's inner screen; the reception at the 'Frantic', Ken Houlihan, exuding danger from every pore; herself, the romantic starlet pictured with the hero drugs smasher. Those days would never come again. Thank God. She tried to fend the memories off. 'Don't suppose you've heard anything, have you?'

'What about?' Eve asked.

'The tests.' John spoke as though she should know all about it. 'I suppose you have heard they're testing nuclear stuff out there in the Nevada Desert, have you?' Eve nodded. 'Well, there's stories about sheep with burns, and high radiation counts sweeping across the nation in rain clouds. Know anything about it?'

234

'No. I suppose the sheep got burned from the blast, poor things,' she said.

'I expect so,' John agreed cynically.

'You still digging up trouble, fighting for the underdog?' Eve asked. She was melting. She'd remembered the good things he'd done. He'd broken a drugs ring, hadn't he? He'd flown against the Nazis and risked his life, hadn't he?

'I've got a reputation to keep up,' John said, smiling. 'I'm going into politics.' Eve was astonished. She laughed.

'You sure are a go-getter, John,' she said.

'Always was, honey. Just like you.'

Eve shook her head. 'Not any more, John,' she said.

'What's wrong?'

'I just got the sack, that's all.'

'From this godforsaken club? So what? You'll find another job. A better one.'

'It isn't so easy these days,' Eve snapped. 'Anyway, it's not so much a new job I want. It's a new start. A new life.'

'You can do it. Off with the old, on with the new!' John raised his glass to her. 'I give you the butterfly about to emerge from the chrysalis.' Eve shook her head.

'I've made too many new starts,' she said. 'Since the war, I'm running out of species to turn into.' John said nothing for a moment. Then he reached out to touch her hand. Eve jumped, as though she'd been singed. 'Don't,' she said. John studied her thoughtfully. She wasn't looking at him. She was looking into her tumbler, and she was obviously deeply distressed.

'Look, Eve,' he said quietly. 'The war did a lot of things to a lot of people.' She just kept staring down at the empty glass. He went on. 'When I got back home, I guess I just didn't want to know about England or the goddam English any more. I'd had them up to my ears. And more. I wanted to forget.'

'You wanted to forget me,' Eve said bitterly.

'Not exactly,' John sighed. 'But you were part of it.'

'Thanks.'

'I'm sorry. But look, we had a good time, didn't we?' Eve darted him a fierce look.

'And now the party's over, huh?' she said.

'No!' John laughed. 'In fact, it's only just beginning!' Eve frowned. She felt strange; a little dizzy. Bernie was right. She shouldn't have had that extra drink. She had a weird feeling, like she was on a Big Wheel, going round and round, passing the same point again and again. 'Why don't you come along? As my guest?' His arms were an open invitation. Eve started laughing.

'You make it all sound so easy,' she said.

'Why not? It is, isn't it?' He believed himself. 'Your trouble is, you take life too seriously. Typical of the Brits.' Eve flared.

'Don't start knocking us! You bastards reneged on the Lend Lease! You dropped us right in it! Do you know, after the war, people starved, back home? I mean, really starved!'

'Still the same old do-gooding Evie,' John mocked.

'What's wrong with that?' Eve challenged him. 'What about *your* reputation as a do-gooder? Huh?'

'Sure.' John gave in. 'I'm just like you.' His voice was reassuring. 'Now come on, Evie. I'm all alone in this town. You know all the clubs. Show me a good time, eh?' The music started. The big wheel turned. What the hell! What was there to lose? Victor Flamm watched Eve go backstage for her coat, followed by the 'relative'. He'd not see her again, that night.

Eve's energy had the twin boosters of alcohol and admiration, and she went like a rocket on the dance floor, spinning round her disabled partner like a catherine wheel. But when the music stopped, and she reeled back to her seat, amidst applause, she was sweaty and not too sweet to the touch.

'You're not getting paid for this, you know,' John reminded her.

'I can still dance just for the sheer pleasure of it,' she replied, lighting up a cigarette. She felt reckless. She blew a smoke ring in his face, and her eyes gave him the 'come on'. Live now. Tomorrow might never come! She drank down another vodka, to silence the warning memories of pain, laughing, as she asked the waiter for a refill. And John was laughing too. His teeth glinted in the refracted lights of the crystal ball revolving over the dance floor. Pretty lights, like moths or butterflies, they danced, round and round the room, over the faces of the clientèle, up the walls across the ceiling, to fall through the musicians in the band, and scatter at the feet of the dancers. Eve's smile was gentle as she watched them. And John watched her. And she knew he was watching her. And she played up to it, knowing she looked like a little girl lost in the big city. It was appealing. Men liked it. And John liked it. He sat back, taking in the little display. And then, as though taken by surprise, she turned, eyes huge, and caught his smile.

'Sorry. I was miles away,' she said. John wasn't taken in. He knew she'd been playing up to him. That was O.K. It was all part of the game. But there was amusement in his smile. Eve saw it, and her confidence faltered. She began to doubt herself. She felt suddenly cheap. Eve Lawson wasn't a faker? Was that really true? She could fake with the best of them! 'I need another drink,' she said.

'Your word is my command,' John answered, and he laughed as the waiter put Eve's drink on the table. It was red. Eve frowned, staring at it. Why was her drink red? Was it a warning, like a red light? 'That sure was good timing,' John was saying to the departing waiter. But why was her drink red? John, realizing the mistake, tried to call the waiter back. 'Hey! You brought the wrong drink!' he shouted. 'The lady wanted a straight vodka, not a Bloody Mary!' But it was too late. He'd disappeared. Eve's fingers curled round the stem of the glass. The red liquid swirled as she picked it up and put it to her lips. Blood. She tasted it. She spilled it over the table, crying. John was alarmed. 'Hey! Hey, what's wrong?' he asked. Eve looked at him, face streaked with tears, dress dark with the shadows of cooling sweat.

'I want a baby,' she said quietly.

John felt the tremor of shock as the reality of Eve's remark touched him. He tried to smile, but couldn't. There was no way he could shake this one off. He was caught in some sort of trap.

'I want a baby, John.'

She was pleading with him. The ache in her womb made her voice curve with desire. And it was compelling. But he didn't know what to say. He didn't know how he wanted to react. This was an entirely new situation. Eve seemed to have sobered. She felt cold and her lips quivered as she spoke in an urgent voice.

'I wrote to you. Did you get my letter?' John stared at her blankly. 'I wrote you about the baby.'

He said nothing. How could he just sit there saying nothing? Eve's insides cried out against him. And she heard her voice, like the voice of another woman, high pitched, shrewish, echoing on the stifling air of the club.

'I was pregnant by you, John. You bastard.'

John was embarrassed. 'I didn't get any letter,' he said quietly. Then he touched her hand across the table, by a gesture, reminding her they were in a public place, and people were looking. Eve remembered where she was. She lowered her eyes and her voice.

'I lost my baby.' She was crying, tears streaking her make up. 'I want another one. I want you to give me another one.' John cleared his throat.

'Come on, honey,' he said. 'Let's get you home . . .'

'Home!' She hurled the word at him, like it was an insult.

'O.K. Let's get you back to the hotel, huh?' She let him prise her from her seat. Her skirt flapped limply against her legs. It felt wet and cold and the sequins scratched. Then he held her arm, to escort her from the club. There was red juice on her thighs. It made him want to retch. But he suppressed the impulse, wrapping her in his jacket, and holding her close, as the taxi drove them back to the hotel.

Light was dawning, pale, in the charcoal grey of the sky, as Eve and John, huddled together, made their way up in the lift, scurrying into Eve's room, closing the curtains against the sun, like vampires, afraid of turning into ash. He stripped her, and helped her into bed. Then he got in after her, curling round her, holding her, as she passed into a dreamless sleep.

At midday, they made love. Sleep had bonded them. They felt warm and close: it seemed as natural as orange juice for breakfast. And afterwards, Eve held him close in her arms, like she didn't want to let him go.

'You going to make an honest woman of me now, John?' Eve asked wistfully. John half-laughed and said nothing. She shook him with her hand, insisting, 'Are you?'

'If you like.' Was that a shrug? Surely it meant more to him, to anybody than just 'If you like.'

'Stop it!' She shook him again. He peered down his nose at her, over the fold of his chin. Suddenly, he laughed.

'You look like a demented panda,' he said. Eve pouted. 'Don't be angry. It's kind of sweet. Your eye make-up's everywhere!' Eve started laughing gently.

'Still love me, though?' she asked.

238

'Uhuh,' he answered.

'So will you?'

'What?'

'Marry me, you clot!'

'Clot? What's a clot?'

'It's English. It means . . . twerp.'

'Thanks.'

'No, but will you?'

Looking up at the ceiling, John smiled to himself. Eve was still a good-looking woman. She still had kudos. Supposing they did marry, and have children too! Would that be such a bad thing? Especially now he was going into politics . . . ? And the poor thing seemed so keen, it was a pity to disappoint her.

'O.K.,' he said easily.

Eve's breath stopped. Had she heard right? Her head reeled. She'd like to check with him, but didn't dare, in case he changed his mind. She loved him. She adored him. She longed for his children. Oh, she would be such a good wife to him! She'd pull herself together, stop drinking . . . !

'Think you could deal with being a political wife?' John asked. It was as though he'd been reading her mind. She pushed herself up onto her elbow and looked down at him seriously.

'I'll stop the drinking,' she said.

'I believe you.'

'I'm not addicted. At least I don't think so. I only drink because I'm miserable. And I won't be miserable, married to you, will I?'

'Sure hope not.' He was smiling up at her. He flicked her nose with his finger. 'I wonder if you caught fire last night,' he said idly.

'Sure felt like it,' she answered, and bit his finger lightly.

'I want a son,' he said.

'You'll take what you get,' she answered. He slapped her on the behind, half-joking.

'I want a wife who knows her place,' he warned.

'And what's that?' Eve asked.

'In bed, in the kitchen, or looking after my kids.' Eve snorted good-humouredly.

'And what about my dancing?'

'You'll have to give that up.'

'O.K.' She rolled onto her back, and sighed contentedly. After all, what was there to give up? It sounded good to her. She'd be a real wife, at last. John and Eve lay side by side, staring up at the ceiling. From time to time, John snorted, as though amused. 'What's funny?' Eve asked.

'Won't the family be surprised!' he laughed. The family? Which family? Eve's mind lurched home to Britain, to her Mam, and Jack and Os and Maisie, then it lurched back again, to New Mexico, to June and Ella, Lou and Jimmy. She'd shut them out of her life; because of John. When she'd come back to the States, she hadn't wanted to look them up, or even know them, because her bitterness over John had extended to them. Somehow she'd blamed them too.

'How are they?' she asked. Her voice sounded cool, even to her own ears.

'Funny . . . you've not asked up till now, have you?' John said. His head turned and he looked at her, searching her face. But it was closed. She shook her head. 'Well, you know Ella's had a son . . . ?' Suddenly a smile broke through, and Eve was beaming with delight.

'No! Why that's marvellous. I'm glad for them!' She laughed. 'How did June take it?'

'She grunts on about it, "mixed litters" and all that, but she kind of dotes on the little thing, all the same. Now Jimmy's grown up, a kid makes a difference about the old place.'

Jimmy, Eve remembered Jimmy. She remembered that night she'd read to him in bed, and he'd asked her if she was going to marry his father. He'd been angry at her for playing Lou around. And he'd been right. She was, at the time. He'd made her look at herself, and he'd helped her turn Lou down, in the end. He was a powerful little boy in those days.

'How is Jimmy?' she asked.

'In Korea.'

Eve was shocked. Of course. He would be. He must be going on twenty by now! Korea!

'How long's he been out there?'

'Quite a while. Since before the stalemate,' John said. 'My leg kept me out, thank the Lord.' Eve was silent, thinking about the little boy she'd once known, now fighting in the rice fields and the hills of Korea.

240

'Is he O.K.?' she asked.

'Got a little nick, last year,' John said. 'Nothing much. They send 'em right back these days. No easy discharges in this war. Need all the men we can get to fight the Commies!' Eve stiffened. 'The Commies.' Her throat was dry.

'I suppose you'll be checking out your newspaper story today?' she asked tentatively. John groaned and sighed.

'I don't know,' he said, settling further under the bedcover. 'Probably just a lot of scaremongering.'

'What is?'

'All these reports of burns, radiation and so on . . . I mean, who cares about a few sheep, anyway?'

'I guess the sheep care!' Eve objected.

'Honey, the bomb's a big issue. Know that? Know what it's really about? It's about defending democracy! The freedom of millions depends on it. You can't go round worrying about the odd sheep.'

'What about the farmers?'

'Or the odd individual, come to that! The State's more important than anybody! Honey, it's what Jim's fighting for in Korea.'

'But I thought, I thought Freedom meant the freedom of the individual!' Eve was genuinely confused. But she'd made John angry.

'What was that I said about a wife? I don't want you getting involved! I don't want you arguing. You leave the politics to me. O.K.?' Eve said nothing. She was anxiously thinking about Danny. He'd been blacklisted for taking part in a May Day rally, and nobody in show business would employ him any more. That was why she'd needed Vic's money. Well partly why. She was helping him. But she didn't dare say so. Not to John. Not just now, anyway. He was shifting restlessly in the bed beside her, obviously annoyed.

'Hell, I should think these scare stories have been put about by the Commies in the first place! They don't want America to be strong! Stands to reason!' Eve hadn't thought of that. Maybe John was right. 'Like you said, the sheep are probably just suffering from blast.' He turned on his elbow and looked at her, smiling now. 'They're planning a few bright lights in the desert, end of this week. Know that?' Eve shook her head, looking up at him.

'How do *you* know?'

'I got my contacts at Sandia.'

A sudden thought came to Eve. 'Would it be O.K. to tell Victor?'

'Victor?'

'Victor Flamm. He owns the club I've been working. He's having a tough time. If he knew there was going to be a few bombs, he could set up a book.'

'Betting?'

'Yes. He gives odds on whether there'll be an explosion on a given night. It's good business.' John laughed and thought for a minute.

'O.K. You tell him that a friend of yours in the airline's had advance warning. There's to be no flights to Rio on Thursday.' Eve nodded. 'And you might tell him, your friend want's in on the action.' It was fair enough, Eve supposed. Why shouldn't John make a killing? He was selling information, after all. People did it all the time. And it was worth it, for Victor. He stood to make a fair bit over the coming weekend.

Victor listened to the news gravely.

'So, you're getting married, huh?' Eve nodded slowly. She hadn't been looking forward to telling him. His face looked grey and tired. 'Oh well . . . ' He sighed and managed a smile. 'I guess it's time I started acting my age. So, who is this schmuck?' He looked at her, hoping against hope. 'Not the "relative", huh?'

Eve nodded. 'He's just a distant relative, you know.'

'From what I saw, you and him didn't exactly see eye to eye.'

'It's a long story, Vic.' Eve looked down. Obviously, she didn't want to tell him. 'The war and . . . what?' 'The war and . . . the schmuck.' The answer had appeared before him in the flesh. 'He hurt you, didn't he?' he asked gently.

'Yes. It was during the war . . . '

'So. This is the guy you've been waiting for all this time, huh?' Eve sighed. 'You must really love him a lot.'

'Yes. I must, mustn't I?' She laughed a short brittle sort of laugh. 'I didn't realize . . . I thought I'd got over him.' She shook her head. 'And time's running out for me, Vic. I want a baby.

I'm going to grab this chance now, before it's too late. Don't try to put me off. Please.'

'You don't have to get married to have a baby,' Vic said.

Eve was shocked. She looked at him in surprise.

'Vic! You're very modern!'

'I care about you. I don't want you to make a mistake.'

'It's not a mistake!' Eve was getting angry and upset. 'I'm going to be the wife of a great political figure! You'll see! It's going to be a wonderful life!'

'Don't believe all you read in the papers, honey,' Vic warned.

'You're only jealous!' As soon as she said it, Eve wished she hadn't. She put her arms round the crumpled old man and hugged him close. 'I'm sorry. Oh, Vic. I'm sorry. Please forgive me.' She felt his hand on her back, soothing her.

'Maybe you're right, hon,' he said brokenly.

'No! No, I'm not! That was a stupid, ugly thing I said. Vic, Vic, I'm so fond of you. Please promise me, you'll always be there. You will, won't you?'

'Sure I will.' He held her from him and looked her straight in the eye. 'I'm kind of fond of you too, Evie. I'm going to miss you.'

Eve felt the tears gathering in her throat. 'Don't, Vic! You'll make me cry. And I'm supposed to be happy. I just got engaged!' Vic nodded and smiled.

'When's the big day?' he asked.

'Wednesday.' Eve looked at him seriously. 'Vic, I want you to do something for me.'

'Anything. You know that.'

'Please, Vic, will you give me away?' Vic's face creased into a big grin and he held Eve close.

'Sure I will. It'll be an honour. Believe me.' Eve's face beamed with pleasure. He liked to see it. He liked to see her happy. 'So!' he said expansively. 'What do you want for a wedding present?'

'Oh Vic . . . no . . . Anyway, I already got it.'

'What? Oh, the money! Forget the money!' he said generously.

'Oh! I nearly forgot!' Eve laughed. 'Actually, I know a way of paying you back, Vic.' Vic tried to put her off, but she wouldn't let him. 'No, seriously, I do. I've got news for you, news that's going to please you. There's going to be a big bang.' Vic was puzzled for a moment, then he understood.

'A bomb?'

'Sh! not so loud!' She went to the door of Vic's office and looked out. There was no one there. Then she tip-toed back, and whispered, 'Let's just say I got a tip from a pal in the airlines. Looks like there's going to be fireworks early Thursday a.m.'

'Thanks, hon!' Vic kissed her a smacker on her forehead. 'I'll have to get moving, you understand, don't you?' Eve nodded.

Vic wanted her out of the way so he could make his phone calls, setting the publicity machine in motion.

'Only, Vic . . .' Eve stopped him for a moment. Vic looked up sharply. 'My friend, he wants in on the action.'

Vic smiled slowly and nodded. 'Can't blame him for that. Tell him to come and see me. We'll sort something out.'

Vic was already dialling, when Eve reached the door. She turned, and he looked up to wave goodbye.

'I'm glad you two are getting to know one another,' she said. And then she went.

There was a lot to do. Eve was glad John was fully occupied, setting up the tote with Vic. Of course it was in his own interests. He was getting a percentage. It was funny, like your father getting to know his prospective son-in-law. Eve liked it, though. It was all part of the fun; part of the business of getting married; and she was feeling the proverbial song in the heart as she went shopping for her dress. She wanted something special, something in silk, and she wanted flowers. Sentimentally, she longed for lily of the valley, but she knew she wouldn't find it and had to make do with an order of hothouse gardenias. Then there was the reception. They ought to have something. Except, who to invite? She'd have liked Ida and Danny and . . . she sighed. Well, why not? John didn't know Danny was blacklisted. And it was her wedding. She was entitled to have a friend present, wasn't she? She wanted the works, a full white wedding, the cake, the silver horseshoe, everything. She couldn't have them. She knew that. But she could have Danny. So, Eve called in on the telegraph office and wired him the money to come. He could make it, if he hurried. Oh how she longed to see his black face again! How long was it since she'd seen him? Bubbling with excitement, Eve made her purchases, ordered button-holes for

John and Vic, and tried on hats. Then, tired but happy, she arrived back at the club, in good time for her spot.

Vic and John were eating sandwiches in the office. Both looked up as Eve walked in. She sensed a strain in the atmosphere which both men were quick to dispel, greeting her effusively, dying to know her news, what she'd bought and so on.

'I invited a friend to the ceremony. Hope that's O.K.?' she asked.

'Sure,' John said easily. 'Why not?'

'He's a dancer. He's the one I danced with at the Hollywood Bowl.'

'Fine!' John smiled. 'Well, you'll be glad to know Mr Flamm and I have set up quite a party for the night of our wedding.'

'Really!' Eve squeaked with excitement.

'Yes, honey. Quite a party.'

Danny arrived in good time and came straight to Eve's dressing room, where she was getting ready for the wedding. He looked neat and dapper for the occasion, and what is more, he'd brought his tap shoes with him. Immediately she saw them, Eve knew what was on his mind. She grinned at him. He grinned back.

'For old time's sake, honey?' he asked.

'It'd be great,' Eve agreed. 'But I've got to ask John and Vic first.'

'Sure.' Danny tried to look easy about it, but an awkward note had crept in. The blacklist. Eve found herself torn between two loyalties, between her loyalty to Danny and her loyalty to Vic. She smiled, covering up her confusion, and they stood, just looking at one another like a pair of lemons.

'You've got a few grey hairs, Danny,' Eve remarked.

'Don't tell me.'

'They suit you. You look distinguished. No. Really.'

'No kidding?' Danny preened in front of the mirror. Then looked back at Eve. Her face was taut. 'You O.K.?' he asked.

'Yes. I'm fine. Nervous though. Tell you what, Dan. Could you get me a drink?'

'Sure.' Eve was fishing in her sateen bag for the money. 'It's O.K. You sent me plenty.' He paused, looking at his boots. 'I'm going to pay you back one day.'

245

'You don't have to, Dan.'

'I'm going to, all the same.' Then he went.

Eve sat in front of her mirror, smoothing her make-up. Her hat lay beside her on the table. It was cream with blowsy pink roses strewn across the brim, and a net veil draped across the front. She tried it on and looked at herself. She looked better since John'd come. Love obviously suited her. She definitely had that traditional bridal bloom on the cheek. She giggled at her reflection. How long had she hoped for this day? She was going to be so happy. No one would stop her. No one could. She'd not told her folks at home. She'd write them a letter, when it was all over. Her Mam wouldn't approve. Oh well. Her Mam was on the other side of the Atlantic. The sadness in Eve's face lifted, and her eyes sparkled as she sat in her seat, her feet tapping out the remembered steps of her number with Danny. It would be great to dance with him again. It would be her last fling. She'd go and ask Victor now.

Throwing her hat aside, Eve ran up to the office and caught Vic doing up his necktie. He smiled and opened his arms out for her. She fell into them, and they hugged close.

'Happy?' he asked.

She nodded. Her eyes were filled with tears. 'Only Vic, there's one last thing, I want to ask of you . . . a big favour.'

'Try me,' he said, resuming the struggle with the tie.

'It's Danny. You know, my old tap coach. Well, he's arrived. And he's brought his tap shoes, and . . .'

'He wants to do a number with you?' Eve nodded. 'Why not? This is something I've got to see.'

'Yes but . . .' Eve's gentle voice sounded urgent; there was more to come. Vic looked at her, waiting. 'He's on the blacklist.' Vic took a step back, looking at himself in the mirror, rather than look at her.

'Hell, honey, I'm not employing Commies.'

'You wouldn't have to employ him. He's willing to dance for free. For old time's sake.'

'Even so . . . a red! In my club!'

'He's not red, Vic! Only maybe a little bit pink!' Vic laughed, shaking his head. 'Please, Vic. For me. Let me go out with a bang!' Vic snorted, sighed, then nodded.

'I must be crazy, but . . . O.K. I don't know he's blacklisted. Right?'

'Right.'

'And I'm not going to tell your John, either.' Eve's heart missed a beat.

'Why not? Do you think he'd disapprove?' She knew he would.

'He may never find out.'

'It's not a good way to start a marriage, is it?'

'So, tell him!' Vic said lightly.

'After we're married, I'll tell him everything,' Eve said. 'Up till then, I'm my own boss. Last fling, Victor!'

'Make sure you enjoy it, honey!' He was about to ruffle her hair, but she stopped him just in time.

'Hey! I just paid for a fortune for this hair-do!'

Then she was off like a girl, flying out the door, down the stair and back to the dressing room, where a drink and Danny awaited her.

The Chapel of Marriage was very pretty. It was garlanded with flowers, most of them real. And they played piped music for you. Most of the band was there, however, and Eve's entrance, on the proud arm of Victor Flamm, was heralded by a trumpet voluntary. She burst out laughing before she could stop herself. This really was great fun! There, at the front, John was grinning back at her. But, for a second, she faltered. There was someone at his side. Who was it? Not Ken Houlihan? No. No. It was . . . could it be? As she walked towards the altar, Eve's eyes were on the best man. It was. It was Jimmy Ridley, in full uniform! He made a slight bow, and she smiled at him, then turned her gaze back to the bridegroom. She was relieved. The ghost of Ken Houlihan was surely dead.

Afterwards, leaning on the arm of her husband, Mrs John Ridley levitated out of the Chapel of Marriage and threw her bouquet straight into Danny's arms. Then, the celebrations really began. Vic, over the moon to have a wedding in the family, made quite a spectacle of the club. There were flowers everywhere, and the place was packed, buzzing with excitement. Bets were being laid right left and centre. Would they see a mushroom cloud at dawn, or would the weather deter the operation? And where exactly was the site of the blast to be? Would they be able to see the show from the hills around Vegas? How powerful would it be? How big a bang?

At that moment Eve didn't care. She was too busy trying to remember her number with Danny. He was in her dressing room now, going through it with her, and she was sweating.

'It's O.K. You can do it.'

'I'm not as fast on my pins as I used to be,' Eve panted.

'You're O.K. Now just relax.' Danny put his hands on her arms and held her still. She took in a deep breath. There was a knock on the door.

'You're on, Miss Lawson.'

'O.K. We're on our way,' Danny shouted back. Then he took Eve's hand and led her out onto the stage.

Of course, they didn't have Carillo on the sax, but Vernon was alright, once he got in the mood. And Eve, sensing the warmth of the audience, gained confidence quickly. Her feet flashed across the tiny stage, always in danger of ending up in the audience, but they lapped it up, feeling the dancers were really giving it their best. For Eve, it was her last fling. For Danny, it was a chance to perform. However you looked at it, it was special. And at the end, panting and glowing, Danny and Eve bowed to tumultuous applause. Then Vic came on, leading John by the hand, and all four of them stood in line, as the band struck up 'Here Comes the Bride'. There was more applause, almost drowning Vic's announcement, and clouds of confetti, suddenly released, fell from the ceiling like a snowstorm. It was wonderful. Eve had never felt so happy. She smiled as the cameras flashed, and wondered why Danny, modestly, pulled back, and disappeared backstage. Then Vic too, stood aside, and in the end, it was John and Eve together, hand in hand, bowing and waving to the generous-hearted audience. Amongst them, Jimmy Ridley, clapping till his hands were sore, stood in honour of his aunt. He was glad he'd seen her dance before she gave it up for good. She was, he had to admit it, fantastic. He took his soldier's hat off to her.

The revelry went on all night. But Eve dropped out for a while, to shower and change. This was her wedding night. She wanted to look every inch the bride. John was going to drive her out into the hills before dawn. She sprayed on her perfume, hugged Vic, hugged Dan, and Jimmy, then wrapped in a rug, left with John in the hire care, to join the pied piper's procession out of the city, and into the darkness.

As the light paled the sky, Eve huddled close to her new husband. She looked shyly up at him. His face was relaxed, smooth, happy. It was reassuring. She wanted him to be happy too. She wanted them both to be happy. And they were. They surely were. They looked out over the plain. The sun was coming up. Then it began.

There was an almighty blast, and suddenly Eve felt herself to be in an ocean of light, beyond seeing. And then the light was drawn back, as if by a magnet, into a devouring globe of bubbling bluish white and oily black cloud, going up and up, and the blue light was filled with poisonous, purple shadows . . .

CHAPTER THIRTEEN

Being whisked off into another life, was, if exhilarating, also disconcerting. And the most disconcerting thing of all was the way in which the most familiar landmarks seemed to have remained the same, while she, Eve, now become Mrs John Ridley had, as it were, entered a different skin, and now viewed those same familiar landmarks with different eyes, from a different time, almost from a different dimension. This was the weird sensation Eve felt, as John turned the car up towards Ambrosia Lake and the Lawe Top Ranch.

'Have they done anything about the oil at The Lawe Top?' Eve asked. Oil was sure changing the landscape all around.

'Do they do anything about anything at The Lawe Top?' John said acidly. Eve thought better than to pursue the subject. It was obviously one she was going to hear more about. Silently, she stared across the familiar terrain, now blemished with strange shapes, drilling platforms, huts, some ramshackle, some not, the roadway littered with a motley selection of vehicles, which John had to manoeuvre around as he turned, bumping up the lane to the Lawe Top Ranch.

A little boy ran out to greet them; a darker, jollier, curlier version of Jimmy Ridley, when *he* was young. His huge black eyes laughed, as he came towards them, dragging a banner on the dusty ground.

'Hi!' Eve grinned at him. 'Who are you?'

Suddenly the little lad grew shy, and gurgling, dropped the banner, to hide behind his mother's skirts.

'Sam! What're you doing? You're supposed to hold your banner high, so's they can read it!' Ella laughed, fondling her son's head.

'Hi, Ella,' Eve smiled. She was really glad to see the warm, friendly face of the Indian woman again. 'Where'd he get those curls? Not you, Lou . . .' Lou was just emerging from the house. He nodded in greeting.

'And not me!' Ella laughed, pulling out Sam's tight curls, delighted with everything about him. Sam pulled away from her. He didn't like his curls. After all, he wasn't a girl, was he?

'You're looking well, Ella,' Eve remarked.

'I've put on weight! It must be contentment,' she said. 'Come on in.' John, picking up the banner, saw that it read, 'Welcome home to the Newly Weds'. He nodded, smiling at the little attention, and followed them in.

The table was spread for a celebration. There was a huge cake at the centre, with silver bells round the side, and a garish matrimonial couple stood stiffly in the icing on the top. June, Old Jo, Bill Farley and Jimmy were all sitting in their places round the table, waiting for them. A flash of memory; Jimmy's birthday party, the day Eve'd gone to Tucson. She shook it off. Another time, another occasion. Then she smiled and sat in her place, next to her husband, at the head of the table.

'We weren't going to let you cheat us of a reception, Eve!' June said, thrusting cookies on her. 'And I sure hope you've brought us some photographs, so we can see what your ensemble was like. Did you get married in white?' Eve blushed.

'Er . . . not exactly white . . .'

'Off white!' Old Jo guffawed. He hadn't changed.

'I was going to say creamy white,' Eve corrected him. 'It's softer. After all I'm not a spring chicken any more,' she offered by way of explanation to the women. June acquiesced.

'I'm sure you looked very nice, dear.'

Then Eve got out the snaps, and they were passed round the table, one by one, each accompanied by a full explanation from Eve, supported by John and Jimmy. The pictures were a godsend. Every person on them had to be introduced and talked about and that took them through right up to cutting the cake. Then, finally, as the knife plunged into the sugar, like a signal for the resumption of warfare, John began,

'Had a new survey done yet, Lou?'

'What survey?' Lou was already surly and defensive.

'You know!' June nudged Lou in the ribs.

Old Jo and Bill Farley rubbed their hands together in glee. They liked a good cabaret after a meal. It aided digestion.

'Surveys cost,' Lou said.

'They're an investment.' John's fist hit the table.

'O.K. You do the investin'!' Lou told him.

'O.K.' John agreed, sitting back in his chair. Lou had not expected this. It took the wind out of his sails.

'And what if they do find oil on Ridley land, Lou?' Ella asked. 'What are you going to do then?'

'I don't know. I'll deal with that if and when it happens.' Ella's jaw tightened.

'It's an offence to Mother Earth to pillage her, Lou!' Ella said, defying the amused faces of her in-laws.

'Mother Nature won't mind,' John said easily.

'Shows what little you know!' Ella retorted.

'Any road,' Jo put in, hoping to pep things up a bit now that the old rows were getting boring. 'Never mind oil. That's chicken feed. What about the uranium!'

'What?' Eve gasped. John nodded.

'Yes. They've found uranium round about these parts,' he told her.

'And now they want to use the body of Mother Earth to make bombs! It's wicked! No Indian would allow that!'

'Hell. That's funny.' Jo scratched his head thoughtfully, 'I thought it was an Injun discovered uranium in the first place.' He grinned at Bill, who added his own point.

'Sure was. Paddy Martinez. He found the ore in Poison Canyon.'

'He was Navajo!' Ella spat.

'Come on,' Jimmy sighed, rocking on his chair. 'If you ask me, this is just a big fuss about nothing! We already know the oil's too far down for us to reach and it won't have changed its position. So what's the point of arguing about it?'

'But what if we got uranium round here instead!' John flung the idea across the table, like a challenge. But Jimmy's voice cut firmly across the ensuing uproar.

'If you ask me, we're all arguing about something which really doesn't apply!' he said. Everyone turned curiously, to look at him. Jimmy'd changed. There was a quiet confidence about him these days. He didn't say much, but when he did, it was to the point, and in the Ridley family, this was something new. The novelty attracted respect. 'As it happens,' he said, 'I've been taking a look at a lot of old maps. And a lot of new ones too. And . . .' He reached for some paper and dragged a pencil from his pocket. 'This is what the current state of survey has revealed.' He began drawing wavy lines, then put more lines through them. 'See, here's Poison Canyon . . . Now we know they've found uranium there . . .'

'Is it called that because this uranium stuff's poisonous, or what?' Eve asked, remembering the burnt sheep of Nevada.

'No,' Jo laughed. 'Been called "Poison Canyon" for as long as I can remember, anyway.'

'But why?' Eve persisted.

'It's the loco weed,' Lou informed her. Eve looked blank, and Bill Farley butted in to enlighten her.

'See, dear, it's a weed grows round there. And any beast that strays into that Canyon and eats the stuff, ends up dead.'

'Presence of that weed could be a sure sign of the ore!' John remarked. 'Have we had any trouble like that lately? Sheep, cattle dying, for no apparent reason?' Lou shook his head.

'Ain't got none of that weed round here,' he said.

'Pity,' John sighed.

'I think we should let Jim go on,' June said, watching the boy drawing his wavy lines on his paper, filling in interesting dark blobs. 'See, he's drawing a real scientific diagram to show you.'

'He's doodling!' Jo snarled.

'No, Grandad. I'm drawing a sort of map,' Jim exlained. 'Now, here's Blue Peak and here's Poison Canyon. Also, they've started looking round Laguna . . .' Jim filled in some more dark blobs.

'Place is riddled with the stuff. I reckon we should start digging!' John said snappily. But Jim went on, as though there'd been no interruption.

'So far, there's no proof of anything at all round Westwater, or

253

Ambrosia itself. Now it seems to me, that till somebody finds that proof, we should all just stay here, sitting pretty. Let someone else do the work, spend the money, and check it out, before we waste our time, energy and resources looking for what may just turn out to be a pot of gold at the end of a rainbow. Pure fiction.' There was an awkward silence. The advice was good but somehow disappointing. And within seconds mayhem had broken out again.

'O.K. But we gotta argue out among ourselves how we stand, *before* the ore's found,' John insisted.

'Why?' Jim asked.

'So's we're all of a like mind, and can act on it straight away,' John explained. 'Hell, you should take an interest, Jim. You do stand to take the ranch on, after Lou . . . '

But Lou put in, 'Who says we're going to act on it, even if they do find goddam uranium!'

'Look!' Jim sighed. 'Here we all go again. What's the point of arguing about something that may never happen!'

'You're copping out, Jimmy Ridley. That's what you're doing.' The voice was Ella's. She was cold and angry. 'It's just typical of you!'

'Fighting in Korea's hardly what I'd call "copping out", ma'am,' Jim pointed out.

'Do you hear yourself? You're talking like a white man. Fighting a white man's war!'

'I *am* white,' Jim said quietly.

Jo clapped his hands together and hooted with joy. Ella left the room. Jim looked at his father.

'I'm sorry, Dad,' he said.

Lou shrugged and just watched while his son eased himself out of his chair, and ambled out into the yard for some fresh air.

After a few minutes, Eve followed Jim outside. She found him by the corral, fondling the nose of his old horse.

'*Plus ça change* . . . ' Eve said quietly as she came up behind him. Jim turned and smiled gently at her.

'Why've you come out?' he asked. 'It's *your* celebration!' Eve laughed.

'I don't know, Jim,' she said. 'I don't really belong here. Never did. Once an outsider, always an outsider, isn't that so?'

'I'm an outsider too,' he said quietly.

'You?' Eve raised her voice in surprise. 'How can you be an outsider? You're Lou's son. You stand to inherit the ranch. You're responsible for whatever decision the family comes to, in the end.' Jim kissed the horse's nose. It whinnied, tossed its head, and scampered off.

'I'm twenty-one next year,' he said.

'Exactly!' Eve nodded firmly. 'So you'd better make up your mind where you stand, hadn't you?'

'I've got my plans.'

'What plans?' Eve coaxed. 'Come on. You can tell me.' Jim, looking straight at her, hesitated.

'Wait and see,' he said at last. Eve felt a pang of hurt. Evidently Jim didn't trust her. But why? As he turned to leave her and go back indoors, Eve stared after him. He was a stark figure in the rosy glare of the late afternoon sun, a figure set on its own course, alone. He had set himself outside the family. While she . . . where was she? She was pretending to be part of it.

The next day, Eve and John left for their smart new home in the expanding suburbs of Albuquerque, while Jim prepared to go back to his unit. Quietly, so no one else would hear, he asked June if she was still running the little charity store in Grants. She looked at him strangely.

'I need some clothing for a kid,' he said. 'A little girl.' He fished a snapshot from out of his inside pocket. It was bent and crumpled. June took it and stared at the naked little figure for a long time.

'She don't look much like you,' she said at last. Jim laughed.

'Aunt June, this kid is five years old. How long have I been out in Korea?'

'Oh,' said June, handing back the snapshot. 'So who is she then?' Her voice had sharpened, already rejecting the child, as not of her blood.

'Just an orphan. She's at an orphanage in Seoul. I'd like to take her some clothes back.' June sighed.

'I'll see what I can find for you,' she said. 'But it won't be a kimono!'

'Whatever it is,' Jim replied, 'make it colourful and bright!'

So who was this child anyway? June thought better of asking. If she did, she might get to know its name, and get involved. And she didn't want that. There were enough problems here at home, without taking on any more. So she just wrapped up a bundle for him, and took it to Jim's room.

'Don't do anything soft, now, will you?' she said brusquely.

'Like what?'

'Like bringing this kid home with you.' June was tight-lipped. 'We already got enough dark blood here.'

'Come off it, Aunt June. You just adore little Sammy. You know you do.'

'All the same . . . ' she said, and thrust the bundle at him. It was as though she'd washed her hands of his burden. He didn't show the picture to Ella, or anyone else, come to that. It was June and Jim's secret. To Jim, it was a precious secret; to June it was somehow too dangerous to mention. And so, Jim left his bundle unremarked, his inner life unknown to those who believed they were his nearest and dearest.

Jim felt a little sad at going, but leaving home was hardly the wrench it had been once. His presence was now a thorn in his stepmother's flesh. If she could no longer possess him, in her Hopi ways, she would reject him. But, after all, he was not a puppet to dance to her or anybody else's tune. He was an independent man, slowly but surely forming his own ideas about things, taking what suited him from here and there, letting what he liked attach to him, but never letting himself become attached; except perhaps to Kim, the little girl in Seoul. Jim had come across her one day in the early summer, when his unit, following a bombing raid, had crossed the line into a small village in North Korea. This little thing, no clothes on, blood running from its back, pursued him, hanging on to his sleeve, demanding he help her Mum. In the end, Jim gave in, and let the child lead him back to its hut, where a woman lay, sprawled awkwardly on the ground. The child blubbered pitifully beside her.

'Save my Mummy. Please. You must save my Mummy.' Jim leant over the woman, and pulled her up by the shoulder. The mother was dead. There was nothing he could do. But how could he explain death to this little kid? He'd dealt out death himself. He'd almost been killed. But this child didn't understand what it meant. What to do? He couldn't desert her. Not entirely. He was all she'd got and she was going to hang on to him. She was hanging on to his sleeve, as he went back to his commanding officer. Jim's situation was clear. The child was stuck to him like a limpet. They had to do something. Finally transport was arranged, and the kid was taken away to Seoul, bawling and crying. Jim couldn't bear it. He had to know where they'd taken her. He made it his business to find out, and from that time on, he felt Kim was his responsibility.

As Jim's ship approached Korea, the stench of the land greeted him. Human fertilizer. The Koreans had used it for centuries. It was familiar now, like the smell of home. Not that Jim acknowledged anyone as owning him. But in Korea, where his survival depended on self-reliance, he felt more comfortable than he felt back in the States, either on Hopi or on Ridley land. Because here, in Korea, he was free to be himself. And what was he fighting for? He didn't kid himself it was for the freedom of the western world. For him, it was just a platform on which he could fight his inner battle, for his own personal freedom; his battle against all the conditionings and ideas that had been imposed on him since his birth, and even since before that. For a story was also written in his genes. But he was none of those things. And he had an idea, that if he could only free himself from all that history, he'd find out who he really was; a free spirit, he was sure. As for the carnage and the suffering and the destruction that was going on all around him, Jim watched it, compassionately, but without any feeling of responsibility. What was, was a result of history and indoctrination. It was up to each one of them whether they got sucked into it, or not. Only the children could be said not to be responsible. Someone had to take them on board, had to take responsibility for them.

There were a couple of days before Jim was due back at the front, so he went up to Seoul, to the orphanage, his bundle in hand. Kim ran out to greet him, arms open wide. Jim grinned with delight, taking her in his arms and holding her high up in the air. Then he held her close to his chest, feeling love for her, wanting to cry for her palpable innocence, glad to be loved in return. Then, swanning around in a multicoloured pair of seersucker pyjamas, Kim showed herself off in the orphanage compound.

She looked ridiculous but she was very pleased with herself and that was all that mattered. Jim stayed to play with her and some of the other kids, handing out candy, a couple of old books he'd brought from home, feeling as welcome as he'd ever felt in his life. But when the time came to go, Kim held onto him again. She had him by the sleeve. He couldn't shake her off.

'I have to go, Kim. I have to go and fight.'

'You get killed,' she wept.

Jim shook his head. 'No. No. I won't, I promise.'

'You get killed like my Mummy.'

'No. I won't. Truly.'

'You get killed,' she repeated. Helplessly, Jim looked for the matron. A nun came flapping out to his assistance.

'She won't let go. She thinks I'm going to get killed,' Jim explained. The nun looked at him. It was a funny wry look. Then she turned to the child.

'Jim not get killed,' she said firmly. 'Repeat after me. "Jim not get killed".'

'Jim not get killed,' Kim repeated obediently.

'That's better!' said the nun, smiling. 'And when the war's over, who knows, but he might take you back to America with him.'

Jim pulled a face, and the nun laughed at him. But Kim was jumping up and down with joy. She'd forgotten Jim was going to fight. All she could think of was an endless supply of Coca Cola and seersucker pyjamas, a fairytale come true in the good old U.S. of A. Jim shook his head, and made his escape before Kim remembered, working his way back through the ruins, where other children scavenged for food, uncared for, to the depot and his lift north.

Within three days, Jim was back at the front, at a place called Pan Mun Jom, just beyond the 38th. He returned to the same trench he'd left a couple of weeks earlier, and settled down to the routine of the stalemate. Through the daylight hours, American planes flew north, over their heads, to bomb the towns and villages of North Korea. At night, vicious attacks were made, by both sides, feeling out the weakness of the opposition, killing, and taking prisoners wherever possible. But once in a while, a daytime attack was launched and then Jim went out with a party, charging through the countryside, with flamethrowers gushing fire before them, till the enemy, temporarily dropping back, let them through. And then, before there was time to dig new trenches, the situation was reversed, the Communists reclaiming the lost land, and the forces of the U.N. retiring to their original positions. Before each sortie, Jim would kiss his picture of Kim.

'Jim not get killed.' He heard her voice repeating the words over and over in his head, like a mantra.

'Most men've got pictures of their sweethearts or their Mommas in their pockets,' one G.I. remarked laconically. 'What you doing with that kid there? I mean it's not as if it was yours, is it?'

'That kid's the future of Korea,' Jim said, smiling. Well it was something to say. And anyway, it was true, wasn't it? The kids were the future of the entire world! Anyway, the G.I. accepted it as reason enough and didn't pursue the interesting subject of Jim's love life. And Jim's love life was something Jim kept very close to himself. For Jim was not sentimental, but neither was he the bestial type, given to using women and dropping them. His few involvements had been short and sweet but they'd left him unsatisfied. The women, or rather girls, had been shallow, and once he'd got to know them, he'd lost interest. One day, he'd meet the 'right girl', like the magazines said. Jim grimaced as he considered the possibility. If she ever did turn up, he had a feeling she wouldn't be anything like he'd ever met before! Meanwhile, there was Kim.

One night, Jim had kissed his picture and crawled out of the trench, his tin hat a silhouette against the sunset. He was on active patrol. He carried his gun in his hands, and his heart in his mouth. The Commies were wily bastards. They crept up on you without your getting a chance to hear them. But Jim was wide awake and his reflexes were fast. The scorched twigs crackled under his feet as he crept on towards the enemy line. He stopped for a moment, to listen. A trickle of sweat fell down his brow and nestled over his eye. He waited for it to slide and drop, then went on, step by step. If there was a bunch of them out there, he couldn't hear them. But he sensed something, all the same. He stopped again. He was now some distance from his own line. He hid behind the blasted stump of a tree and watched the skyline. It stood out, luminous above the darkening earth. After a while, he saw some shapes moving across the bleak landscape. He whispered the news back to his patrol, pointing out the direction of the enemy. The other men moved closer, finding what cover they could. But the twigs crackled, sharp as gunshot, on the night air. The Commies heard, and stopped, orientating to the sound. Then they started moving towards them. The officer in charge told his patrol to stay put and get out their grenades. When the enemy was within hurling distance, Jim took the pin out, and threw the first shot. It landed at the feet of the first comers. Screams curdled in the smoke of the blast. Then, from behind, Jim heard a G.I. yell as he threw a second grenade. But this one didn't reach the target. It bounced off a tree stump, landing back amongst themselves. The patrol split. Men were screaming and running in all directions, pursued by the Commies. It was mayhem. Then the grenade, which had been lying dead, suddenly exploded, and Jim, thrown by the blast, landed hard, hitting his head on a stone. He was out for the count. No one knew where anyone else was. When the sun came up the next morning, and a search party went out looking, Jim was nowhere to be found.

Head buzzing, Mrs John Ridley was flung into the socio-political life of Albuquerque, meeting new face after new face, in the ever expanding city. John had friends at Kirtland Air Base. John had friends at Sandia Secret Weapons Lab. John had friends at the University of New Mexico. Most of all, John had friends in power. There was to be an election in '54 and he intended to run for the City Government. Already chief editor of the town's main newspaper, he was in a prime position. And he took a strong American line which was proving very popular. When reports came in of four pilots captured by the Commies, confessing to having dropped germ bombs on North Korea, John was hot in defence of American honour. He wrote the leading article himself.

This is entirely propaganda, he said. It is well known that the Communists use a technique of brainwashing second to none, supported by the most cruel methods of torture, to extract confessions such as these from their captives. Maybe by now those four pilots really believe what they've said. Who are we to blame them? This is but one more proof of the ruthless tactics employed by the Communist enemy to undermine our own social system. Americans would never stoop to germ warfare. What the Communists would do, is another matter.

It was good rhetoric. The newspaper sales soared, as did John's standing in the community.

Pregnant, and feeling the heat of the summer, Eve didn't want to think about it. The city services were vastly overstretched. It was one of the issues John was hot on. And she didn't blame him. She longed for cool air and swimming pools, when she had to suffer water shortages and desert heat. Her back ached, her head swam, she felt sick. What was more, she was lonely. She'd tried to keep up with John's social engagements. She'd tried to find friends among his, and found they weren't really friends at all; merely contacts. There was no one she could talk to, not for longer than a few minutes anyway. Life was like that. It was like a cocktail party, or a roller coaster, in a perpetual state of motion. Eve felt she was always about to scream, enjoying the thrill, but wishing, just wishing the trip would stop.

'What you need is a good shoulder massage,' John said, digging his thumbs into the back of Eve's neck.

'What I need is inner peace,' she replied tersely, adding as an afterthought to herself, 'or a drink.' But she didn't give in to the temptation. She was better on the wagon. She looked better for it too. Her skin had cleared, and her perception of things had become sharper. How long had it been? Three months. That was all. That was all the time that had passed since her wedding to John. And it felt like a century to both of them. For when John had considered the possibility of a baby, he hadn't bargained on Eve's being indisposed. That side of things irritated him. What was the point of a wife, if she couldn't be by his side the whole time, attending rallies, receptions and acting the hostess for him?

'Why don't you go away?' he suggested. 'Maybe pay a visit to Clara and Ernest in 'Frisco? The cooler air might do you good. Later on, when you're really big, you know you won't be able to move.' Eve jumped at the chance. Already she could feel the refreshing breeze over the Bay, and the tingling San Francisco atmosphere. But, as she waited at the airport for the plane to Phoenix, her nerve failed her.

'Will you be alright?' she asked John.

261

'Sure. While the cat's away . . . ' He laughed, teasing her, giving her a reassuring squeeze of the arm.

'Maria'll make sure you're fed properly,' she said. John nodded. Their daily help was a very motherly little person. Eve need have no fear of John's welfare in her absence. But perhaps, that's what scared her. 'Are you sure you'll miss me?' she asked.

'Of course I'll miss you.' John was patient. Pregnant women were known to get funny ideas in their heads. You had to pander to them.

'I might pop down to L.A.,' Eve said slowly. 'I'd like to see Ida again . . . and maybe Danny.'

'Why not?' John smiled. He was in a generous mood. 'If you run out of money, you just let me know.' Eve laughed. He was very kind to her in that way.

'John, you've already given me a fortune in spending money. I surely won't need any more!'

'All the same . . . ' She nodded. Yes, she'd let him know, if she ran out of funds. Then, at last, her flight was called, and Eve waved goodbye to her indulgent husband.

And how indulgent he'd been was revealed to her when it came to changing planes at Phoenix. John'd made good use of his contacts. There was someone designated to meet her, see to her luggage, buy her coffee and escort her to the ongoing flight. She lay back in her seat, shaking her head in wonder. My, she was lucky! There weren't many husbands who'd bother so much! Why John was even considerate in their intimate life. Now she was pregnant, he left her entirely alone. 'Don't want to risk my baby!' he'd said, as he turned over to sleep at her side. And she just put her arms round him, nestling close, to fall asleep herself. It was cosy, warm, safe. Yes, if it wasn't for the boredom, Eve'd be very happy in her life with John. She opened her purse, and inspected the wad of notes he'd thrust into her hand before leaving. She'd never need so much. There'd be plenty to spare for Danny, and she had permission to go and see him, hadn't she? Smiling with satisfaction, she closed her eyes for the trip west.

Ernie met her at the airport. He seemed really glad to see her. Eve asked him how the brake linings business was doing, and he said,

'Great! Just great!' But there were dark shadows under his eyes, and he looked strained, as though under some sort of pressure.

'And how's Clara?' she pursued.

'Fine. Just fine.' He was sounding like a china doll with a loose nut.

'Family was asking after you,' she lied.

'No kidding?' Ernest was genuinely surprised. But he answered the mystery for himself. 'Scared I'd turn up on a visit, I suppose. Otherwise, I doubt if they'd give a damn.' Eve wanted to change the subject, but she'd touched a nerve somewhere. It was like a start button and now Ernest couldn't be stopped, as he drove her along towards the city in his smart new car. 'Matter of fact, I doubt if this entire nation gives a damn about anything!'

'How can you say such a thing?' Eve was really shocked. 'We're fighting the spread of Communism for the rest of the western world, aren't we?'

'That's what the Brits said about the last war. "Fighting the Nazis for the rest of the Western World." Nazism, Stalinism, what's the difference? Folk here really don't give a damn. Don't even want to know.' Eve couldn't make sense of him.

'Want to know what?' she asked.

'What those bastards did!' Ernest was crying. His face was all screwed up and his eyes were wet. He rubbed them with his fist. 'Nobody listens. Nobody. But I got to live with it. What I saw. I got to live with that for the rest of my life!' He was howling by now. Eve was afraid he'd crash the car, he was pulling at the wheel so. But she tried to keep calm, putting an arm on his shoulder, soothing him;

'What we've got to do, Ernie,' she said, 'is to think about the future. Forget the past.'

'I can't!' he wailed. 'The past is all . . . all . . . locked up inside me!'

'Stop the car, Ernest,' Eve said quietly. Like an obedient child, Ernest drew up by the side of the road, and fell into Eve's comforting arms.

Clara was beside herself. She'd taken about as much as she could. Night after night Ernest had wakened her with his screams, and his moaning, till, exhausted from lack of sleep, she'd made him

263

up a bed in the spare room, and now they slept separately, but at least, they slept. Or at least, Clara did. It was a surprise to Eve to learn that the business really was in great shape. They were making money hand over fist.

'Business takes my mind off things,' Ernest explained.

And Clara sighed, with the relief she felt when he was out of the house.

'It's as though he blames me,' she said, when he was.

'What for?' Eve asked.

'For what the Nazis did. For the concentration camps. It's as though he wants to punish me, and himself too. I mean, we're not to blame, are we?' Eve was perplexed. Poor old Ernest. He was a haunted man. Eve did her best to help. When he came in again, Eve told Ernest the Nazis were part of the past, and the past had to be put behind you if you were to go on living. But he said,

'I dream about those people. I see them, skeletons drifting through the camps, and I run after them, to help. But, when they turn, they've got my face. They've made me a prisoner too. I'm one of them.'

What could Eve say? What was the point of caring so much about something that had already happened. You couldn't *stop* it happening, could you?

'If you care, Evie,' Ernest pleaded, holding onto her hand, 'just make sure nothing like it ever happens again.'.

Deeply moved, feeling the responsibility he'd thrust on her, Eve came up with the only hope; 'John'll do something. You'll see. He's going into politics. He's going to be a really powerful man in this country. And you know what he's like. He's a freedom fighter, if ever there was one! He'll make darned sure nobody, but nobody, ever gets in the position Hitler got into, ever again. He'll make sure nobody gets the chance to cruelly dominate the free spirit of the west!'

'My Lord,' Clara remarked. 'That was quite a speech. I can see you're going to be a great asset to your husband.' Eve was glowing with pride. Clara had meant what she'd said. It was a revelation, and Eve was filled with the pleasure of knowing, at last, what her role really was! She would be a good wife. She would be a real support to John in his political career, a real woman behind the throne. Because John was going to do so much good for the world. If only she hadn't been such a drag these last weeks, pulling him down with her moaning and groaning, deserting him to go on holiday! Well, now she'd better make the most of her rest, and gather her strength to continue her life at John's side. She would attend functions, hold dinner parties, pamphleteer; whatever John needed her to do, she'd do, and not complain, either. She was going to turn over a new leaf; no regrets about her past selfishness, just come up to her job in the future! And my she was lucky! What an exciting job it was going to be!

Then, while Eve was still with Clara and Ernest in 'Frisco, news came that young Jimmy had been taken prisoner by the Communists. Ernest was beside himself. Now he saw Jimmy, in place of himself, in the striped pyjamas, his face gaunt, tortured, humiliated, starved.

'They don't treat prisoners like that now.' Eve tried to reassure him. 'Do they?' She wasn't so sure. Thousands upon thousands of Americans were being held as P.O.W.s by the Chinese and the rumours about their treatment were ugly. Well, John was anti-Communist, and a staunch supporter of the American war effort. The best way to help Jimmy was, therefore, to help John. Through his efforts, and the efforts of people like him, the war would surely be brought to a speedier end and Jim would be freed. Yes, if Britain had led the fight against the domination of the Nazis, now America was leading the fight for freedom and Eve was glad to be American.

Eve's heart was heavy as she boarded the train to L.A. But she was glad to have found her direction in life. This trip back to the old Hollywood haunts would be her last. She'd come to say good-bye. She called in on Ida, first of all. Nothing changes. Ida went on and on about the Jewish fate, making jokes about her own pessimism and suffering, cashing in on it, as it were. Eve smiled and nodded as Ida rattled on, waiting for a pause in the flow to ask about Danny. At last, it came.

'And how's Danny doing, Ida? Have you seen him lately?' Ida acted like she'd been stung.

'Are you kidding? I want to stay in business, honey. Don't even mention his name in here.' Her eyes darted round the room, as if looking for bugs. 'Walls have ears,' she whispered.

'You're joking!' Eve laughed.

Ida shook her head. She wasn't joking. Her eyes sharpened like a ferret's. 'Have you been in contact with him?'

'He came to my wedding!'

'You better get out of here.' Ida rose and showed Eve the door. Her face was pale. Her bottom lip was quivering.

'Ida!' Eve was shocked. 'You can't just turn your back on friends! I mean, Communism isn't catching, like the plague.'

'Dorothy. Still living over the rainbow, huh?' Eve got out of her chair, slowly. Her head was spinning. Either Ida'd flipped, or Eve had been very naive indeed.

'I'm sorry if my coming here's embarrassed you.' She sighed, as she stood at the open door.

'Good job you're married now,' Ida remarked tersely. 'You'd not get any work, anyway.' Eve passed sadly through Ida's door, out into the corridor. Then she turned, hoping to see a friendly goodbye in her agent's eyes. But she was disappointed. 'And don't expect any wedding presents from me, either.' Ida slammed the door, and somehow, Eve knew, as she walked down the boulevard, that Ida was sitting at her desk, chewing her nails compulsively, and staring at the phone. God had spared her Auschwitz, but who was she to escape suffering? He'd sent her McCarthy instead. *Oy veh!* That was life!

Eve too was glad she was married now. Someone, somewhere was surely looking after her. Otherwise, God knew what trouble she'd have got herself into. Who knows but she might be like Danny, forced to sponge off other people for a living. Poor Danny. She was really fond of him. He was the one true friend she had, apart from dear old Vic. She had to look after him. But fear was catching. She looked this way, then that, before entering the little café where she'd arranged to meet him, every inch the subversive. He smiled with relief as she came in the door, waving a greeting.

'Hi, Danny,' she said, sitting opposite him. 'How are you?' He shrugged for answer. He looked older, and thin. She put her hand on his. 'Are you looking after yourself?' she asked.

'How do I do that? I owe on the rent. I can't get credit any more. Grocery stores won't serve me.' Eve frowned and looked at the man behind the café counter. Dan read her thoughts. 'He's alright. He lets us sit here, drink free coffee . . . '

'Us?'

'Yeah. Us. We form a sort of underworld. It used to be the blacks. Now it's the blacklisted.' He laughed at his own bitter joke. 'We're the new bums.'

'Eat something.' Eve thrust the menu at him. 'Go on. Make an order.' She called the waiter over. Danny hesitated, feeling somehow guilty, so she ordered for him, a huge plate of steak, fries, salads, the works. Then she got out her wad of notes. He eyed it warily.

'Where d'ye get that?' he asked.

'It's O.K. It's pocket money. John gave it me before I left home. He doesn't know I'm giving it to you, and he doesn't have to know either.' She held it out to him. He took it in his hand and looked at it suspiciously.

'Where'd he get this much money? Huh? They must be paying city editors more than they used to.' Eve bristled slightly. The ungrateful little . . . She swallowed her resentment and replied lightly.

'Oh, he's got business interests too. Most men have, haven't they? After all, he's been around a lot, you know.'

'He must have been,' Danny remarked, stuffing the notes in his pocket.

'What do you mean by that?' Eve asked sharply.

'Nothing.' Danny shook his head and sighed. What was he doing, biting the hand that fed him? He was getting bitter in his old age. But Eve wasn't prepared to let it go.

'You can't just say things like that and get away with it, Dan,' she told him. Dan said nothing. She wanted him to smooth things over, repair the tear in their friendship and she got upset when he didn't. 'I mean, I don't know I'm doing the right thing here, helping you at all,' she went on. Dan looked up sharply, watching her. 'I mean, you've never talked about politics . . . not to me, anyway. And I thought . . . well, maybe I'm naive . . . but I thought you were just the victim of an overzealous purge. I mean, I do know what's going on. I mean, stars, writers, producers, all getting blacklisted because they say there's a Communist conspiracy in the entertainment industry. They can't all be Communists, can they?'

'There ain't no conspiracy.' Dan laughed bitterly.

'You swear that?' Eve, in her new role of political wife, pushed hard. Now it was Dan's turn to bristle.

'If this is the effect that husband of yours has on you,' he said, 'I don't think I'm going to like him.'

'You may never get the chance to know him!' Eve retorted. 'I mean, if you're not Communist, why don't you go out to Korea and fight them, huh?'

'Because, honey, I don't believe in war,' Dan said quietly.

'You mean, you don't believe in fighting the Commies,' she said. 'And why? Is it perhaps because you are one?' Dan sighed. He wanted to explain it to her. He could see there was a brick wall in the way, but he was willing to try.

'Evie, look at the way you were treated in Hollywood. You got a raw deal from all them powerful people with vested interests. It's the old capitalist network. It kept you out. Kept me out too. And why? Not because you didn't have the talent, but because you weren't useful. That's what they do. They use people. Now you've never let yourself be used, have you?' Eve shook her head. 'Neither have I. I've never sold out.'

'Dan, you're absolutely right. Selling out just isn't in my nature,' Eve said. 'But that doesn't make me Communist!'

'Doesn't make me one either. But I'm for the workers!'

'O.K.!' Eve challenged him. 'If you're not a Communist, if you're a good American, why don't you volunteer for Korea?'

'Apart from being too old, you mean?' Dan smiled.

'It'd prove to the Freedom of Information Bureau that you weren't a Communist. Then you'd get work.'

'If I ever got back from Korea, that is!'

'They wouldn't take you up on it. Like you said, you're too old to fight.'

'It's a matter of principle, Eve. I don't believe in war. How can I volunteer to join the army?'

'You're a Communist,' Eve said slowly. Dan looked at her for a long time, then he sighed.

'O.K. Yes. I am a Communist,' he said. The schism between them had widened into a chasm. There was nothing more to say. But that wad of money in Danny's pocket hung on the silence, suspended by Danny's need to eat and Eve's compassion, on the one hand, and opposing principles, on the other. The steak arrived.

'Enjoy,' the waiter said. Danny looked at his plate. He was very hungry. Eve hadn't the heart to ask for the money back. Danny, feeling like shit, couldn't bring himself to offer. He picked up his knife and fork, and Eve left.

She'd wanted to go up to Vegas and see Vic Flamm. But she was feeling tired and, to her surprise, Eve was homesick. She was missing John. He seemed like an anchor of certainty in a sea of change. She had to get back to him, to stand at his side, and the sooner the better. My, she'd had her eyes opened this trip! And she was glad! She cringed inwardly at her disloyalty, using John's money, without his knowledge, to aid and abet the Communist conspiracy! How could she ever have been so stupid? How could she make it up to him? And what would Jim say if he knew? There he was, a prisoner of the Commies, and there she was ... Dear God! It didn't bear thinking of! And how could she put her own marriage in jeopardy ... ? Her marriage and her coming child! She had responsibilities now. It was time she faced them. She hadn't known it, but her marriage had been on the road to failure. Eve'd had too many failures in her life. At her age, she couldn't afford any more. It was with a determined step that Mrs John Ridley got off the plane at Albuquerque, prepared to meet her husband, and make a go of things.

But he wasn't there. John'd sent one of the office boys to meet her.

'Why? Where is he?' Eve asked. 'He's usually so considerate of me. It's not like him.' The office boy shrugged, and helped her into the house with her bags.

'Don't ask me, Mrs Ridley,' he said, saluting her. Then he went. The house was like a new pin. Maria had done her proud. In the silence of the empty house, Eve watched the rays of light fracture in the dusty air, and fall on the highly polished surfaces of her furniture. They lit on a white envelope on the sideboard. She went towards it and picked it up. It was from John and it was addressed to her. She tore it open. Was Jo ill? Was there fresh news of Jimmy? She read the note quickly. It said, 'Have gone to Washington, summoned by the Committee for Un-American Activities. Will phone.'

Eve's head reeled. She dropped the note. It fluttered like a leaf

269

to the floor. Oh God. What had she done? Then she sat, waiting for the phone call.

Hours later, in the cooling evening, Eve was still sitting waiting, still in her hat and gloves, her bags on the floor beside her. No one had called. No one at all. She had never felt so alone. Then, when the phone did finally ring, Eve jumped, and her throat went dry, so she could hardly speak.

'Hallo,' she croaked. John's voice was wary.

'Is that you, Eve?'

'Yes. It's me. What's going on?'

'Can't tell you that now. But I'm alright.'

'Thank God. When am I going to see you?'

'They want to interview you, honey,' he said. The words were sweet, but the tone was harsh.

'Me? Why?' Eve felt faint. This was Danny's doing. It was all because of Danny.

'You'll come, won't you? You'll tell them whatever they want to know?'

Eve nodded, then realized he couldn't see her. So she said, 'Yes, dear. When shall I come?'

'Right away. They've made a booking for you on the T.W.A. 10 o'clock flight. All you've got to do is get yourself to the airport.'

There was no one to help her. Eve counted what money she had left, and called a taxi. She could manage to pay for it, if she didn't buy any supper. Anyway, she thought, they'd give them something on the plane. But when they did, she couldn't eat it. Her insides had twisted into too many knots. This was something big. Otherwise, why call John to Washington? Surely they had people out west? But of course, John was editor in chief of a big newspaper. He was in politics. They had to be sure he was O.K., didn't they? Her fear fermented into poison inside her. This was all Danny's fault. All Danny's fault. Grey with worry and exhaustion, Eve arrived at Washington, to be met by a man in a black limousine. He didn't say anything, just checked who she was, picked up her bag, and expected her to follow. Feeling like a sheep, she did so. By the time she finally arrived at the building where John was being interrogated, Eve was feeling sick. She followed the man into the building, and up the stairs.

She stopped half way. Ahead of her, the man waited, impatiently.

'You alright, lady?' he asked.

'Yes. Sure. I just feel . . my but the humidity is certainly something in this city!'

'Don't worry. They've got air-conditioning upstairs,' he said, and went on. Eve followed, her knees quaking, feeling guilty as hell.

John was in the room. He smiled a tight little smile when she entered, and she sat in a seat next to him.

'Now there's nothing to worry about, here, Mrs Ridley.' An affable, middle-aged man was now speaking. 'All you have to do is tell us the truth.' Eve nodded, then looked sideways at John for encouragement. He took her hand in his and squeezed it. Eve would be forever grateful for that squeeze. The middle-aged man was holding up a photograph in his hand. The chauffeur took it from him and handed it to her. It was a wedding photo. It was one of those that'd been taken at Vic's club. There she was, on the stage with John, at the centre of the picture. There was Vic, holding her other hand. And, among the falling confetti, she saw Danny, turning away. 'Do you recognize any of those people, Mrs Ridley?' the man asked. Was he stupid? Eve thought. She looked at the name on the plaque in front of him. 'Barrie Northam', it said.

'Yes, Mr Northam,' she replied as politely as she could. 'I recognize myself, my husband here, Mr Victor Flamm, and Danny Collins.'

'Good,' Mr Northam said, smiling at her. 'We're getting somewhere, I think. You're obviously a very cooperative person, Mrs Ridley.' Eve bristled. It sounded like an insult. She thought maybe he was going to give her a lollipop as a reward. But he just went on,

'Are you, or have you ever been a member of the Communist Party?'

'Don't be daft!' In surprise, Eve reverted to her native Geordie accent. 'I'm sorry, Mr Northam, but I've never been interested in politics.'

'Really?' he said. 'You surprise me. I thought you'd made an impromptu propaganda broadcast for Britain on the radio, at one time?' Eve flushed.

'Yes. I suppose I did, in a way. I wanted America to help the war effort. Britain was in danger of losing and, after all, we were fighting for the freedom of the Western Hemisphere.'

Eve felt she had scored. Mr Northam changed tack.

'Yes,' he said. 'Of course, the Soviets also fought against Hitler.' His clear pale eyes looked straight at her. She felt she was staring at an empty sky into clear space. She said nothing. John coughed, clearing his throat, for permission to speak. Mr Northam looked at him.

'My wife is not what you'd call a political animal at all,' John said. 'She's just patriotic. And patriotism is surely a sentiment we can all relate to?' Mr Northam nodded assent. 'Because she accepted the Soviets as an ally against Hitler, doesn't mean she accepted their politics. Why, Mr Churchill himself fought alongside with Stalin, but after the war was won, he came here to America and he warned us against the Soviet threat.' It was a good argument. Mr Northam had to give him that. 'So, I think Eve here's in good company,' John finished.

'Yes,' Mr Northam agreed. 'But what I want to know, Mrs Ridley,' he turned, smiling to Eve, 'is what you were doing consorting with a man known to be blacklisted for his Communist activities.'

'I . . .' Eve faltered. 'I didn't know he was blacklisted when I invited him to the wedding.'

'But you'd been sending him money, hadn't you?' Eve swallowed hard. She felt John tense beside her.

'Yes. I knew he was out of work. I knew he needed money. He was an old friend. Not that I'd had much to do with him lately but . . .'

'Why did you not tell your husband you were giving him money?' Eve could hardly speak. She wanted to look at John, but didn't dare. She hung her head and said nothing. 'You recently went to Los Angeles, didn't you?' Eve nodded. 'And you sought this man out, and you gave him more money.'

Eve nodded. Then she burst out, turning to John, 'I'm sorry, John. I've been so stupid. Please forgive me. I didn't believe Dan was a Communist.' Then she turned to her interrogator. 'I didn't. Really I didn't. I thought . . . I thought it was all just a big mistake.'

'I see,' Mr Northam drawled. 'And do you still think it was

just a big mistake?' Eve shook her head, tears dribbling down her face.

'No. I don't know whether there's a Communist conspiracy or not, but . . . ' she cried, and John handed her his handkerchief. She blew her nose, before she spoke again. 'But I'm afraid Danny's a Communist.'

'You're afraid. You mean you don't sympathize with their opinions?' Eve shook her head. 'What about your friend, Mr Flamm?' he asked. 'Does he sympathize with them?' Eve's heart lurched. This was something different, unexpected, and yet, she should have seen it. She couldn't hurt Danny by exposing him, he was already blacklisted, but Vic . . .

'Good God! You don't think he's a Communist, do you?' she asked. She felt like laughing. It was all so ridiculous.

'He employed your Mr Collins to do a number in his club, I believe,' Mr Northam said.

'He didn't know Danny had been blacklisted,' she lied.

'And you didn't think to tell him?' Eve shook her head.

'No,' she said. 'Like I told you. At the time, I thought that was all a mistake, anyway.'

'I see.' Mr Northam nodded and looked down at his notes, as though considering some deep problem. Then, slowly, he picked up another photograph, gave it to the chauffeur, and the chauffeur gave it to Eve. It was one taken in the Chapel of Marriages. It showed Vic and Danny sharing a joke together. 'Mr Flamm gave you away at your wedding, I believe,' Mr Northam said.

'That's right, sir. He did,' Eve agreed.

'Looks like he and Mr Collins got on pretty well, wouldn't you agree?'

'They didn't talk politics,' Eve said. Then she started getting rattled. 'Look, Victor Flamm is no more a Communist than I am. Why, he thinks the weapons programme is vital to our defence from the Communist threat. I've heard him say so.'

'He's talked about the American Weapons Programme?' Mr Northam sounded like he'd hit on something.

'Only in passing,' Eve said.

'Only in passing!' Mr Northam laughed.

'I swear to you, he's not a Communist.'

'Mrs Ridley,' the interrogator leaned across his desk, assuming

273

an intimate tone, 'it does not behove you to protect the enemy.'

'Vic's not the enemy!' Eve cried. John gripped her hand hard, so hard, she winced, and shut up.

'I told you, my wife doesn't understand politics,' John said. 'She's an innocent at large. I haven't told her anything . . . '

'I understand,' Mr Northam said compassionately. Suddenly Eve was sick all over the floor. The men looked down in dusgust at the pool. 'Also, she's pregnant,' John explained.

'Ah,' Mr Northam said. 'Yes. I forgot. You did tell me, Mr Ridley. Well, I don't think we need detain Mrs Ridley any further. I'm sure she's learned her lesson by now, and I know we can get on without her.' John took Eve by the elbow and levered her from her seat. He wanted to get her out of there, before she did any damage. But Eve wasn't going to leave before she'd made it clear about Victor.

Wiping her mouth clean of sick, she spluttered at the door, 'Victor Flamm is innocent.'

'If he's innocent, then he's got nothing to worry about, has he?' Mr Northam smiled. 'Now why don't you two newly-weds just go and enjoy this lovely city.' The chauffeur escorted them out, with their bags, to a taxi. 'Have a nice day,' he said, as he slammed the door on them.

'Where to?' the driver yelled.

'The airport,' John told him.

Eve's head was spinning. She kept on apologizing to John, as they crossed the city in the taxi. She went on and on until he'd had enough.

'Eve,' he said, 'will you shut up?' His arm was round her, but his tone was cold. For a minute, she thought he was going to hit her. She would have deserved it, and John did have, used to have, a cruel streak. Was it still lurking there underneath his bland exterior? If it was, it would surely come out now. Her fear made her hiccup. The hiccup annoyed him.

'Will you just shut up and wipe your face?' he repeated. The hanky was covered in sick and she didn't have another, so she wiped her cheeks on her sleeve, like a child.

'I'm sorry, dear. I'm very tired,' she explained. 'I've been travelling for what seems like days. Maybe it is days. I don't know. I've hardly eaten anything, I'm sick with worry, about you, about Victor . . . I'm angry at myself, at that damned Danny . . . !'

'It's going to be alright,' John told her.

'What about Vic?'

'They'll investigate him, of course.'

'But why? He's not done anything!'

'Better him than me, honey,' John smiled. Eve looked at him, a puzzled expression in her eyes. He was smiling at her, a gentle warm smile. He had forgiven her for all her disloyalty. She had put his career, all his good work, on the line, and he had forgiven her. 'They'd have looked into my background sooner or later, honey,' he said. 'Well, I've got it over with now. I'm cleared. You could say, you've done me a favour!' He was relieved. Why? Eve remembered what he'd said, in the interrogation, just before she was sick.

'John, what did you mean, when you said to Mr Northam, you hadn't told me anything?' she asked.

'Honey, you've got to realize, these days, I'm in a position where I'm likely to get to know things; things that are vital to this nation's interests. Now, Mr Northam wanted to be sure I didn't blab! Even to you! Huh?' He kissed her on the forehead, then pulled back sharply. 'Honey, you stink!' he said.

'Sorry. It's because I was sick. I need a bath, John. I need a bath more than anything in the world.'

CHAPTER FOURTEEN

Eve was bleeding before they got home. John called Dr Morrison from the airport, and he was waiting for them on the doorstep, when they reached the house. They helped Eve out of the taxi and into the bedroom where she stood, confused, before the twin beds.

'Thought this would be kinder on you, dear,' John explained. 'You'll be getting very big soon, you know, and you won't want me taking up more than my share.' Eve smiled weakly, stepped out of her shoes, and allowed herself to be put to bed.

'What started it off?' The doc had begun his examination.

'Hiccups,' John said. 'She had a fit of hiccups. Lasted most of the way over.'

'Stopped now anyway,' the doc observed. 'Nasty things hiccups. Can be, anyway.'

John shook his head. 'I'm not ever going to laugh at hiccups again.'

'Please, Dr Morrison, I don't want to lose my baby,' Eve whimpered. 'I'm not going to, am I?'

'No,' Morrison said firmly. 'You won't lose that baby, just as long as you stay where you are till further notice.' Eve looked at him from dark rimmed eyes. Stay in bed? How long for, she wondered? 'You need rest, Mrs Ridley. No more travelling for you. You've got to take good care of yourself now.'

'Don't worry,' John reassured him. 'I'll make sure she does.'

'Will the bleeding stop soon?' Eve asked.

'Stop worrying, Mrs Ridley. And that's an order.' Dr Morrison smiled and John left with him, to show him out.

When John returned, Eve was fast asleep. She looked very, very tired. He called Maria, and when she came, he went back to the newspaper offices, and to work. He had an article to write. When Eve woke, it was getting dark. Maria was sitting by her bed, knitting. Her gentle smile was like sunshine in the room, Eve thought as she opened her eyes and saw her.

'Hallo, Meesees Reeedlee,' she said, in her thick Mexican accent. 'How are you feeling?'

'O.K.' Eve raised her head, then put her hand to it, wincing painfully. 'Did somebody hit me?' she asked.

'Why? You got a headache?' Eve nodded warily. 'I get you some tea.'

'Yes. Thanks. That would be nice.'

'You hungry?'

'No. Well, yes. Maybe I am. I should eat, shouldn't I? For the baby's sake?' Maria nodded. Yes, Meesees Reeedlee definitely should eat. In the twilight gloom, Eve stared into nothing. She was very anxious about Victor. She hoped she hadn't got him into hot water. 'Better him than me,' John had said. What did he mean by that? Her brain began to race through all that had been said, all the questions and answers, 'I haven't told her anything.' 'They'd have looked into my background sooner or later.' All these secrets, conspiracies, she hated them. Just to think, somebody had been watching her while she was in L.A. She'd laughed at Ida for being paranoid, but . . . Suddenly, Eve sat up in bed, heart thumping. What if the house was bugged? What if the telephone was tapped? She was scared, really scared. She jumped when Maria came in and switched on the light.

'Hey, you gave me a fright!' Eve said, as she took her tea.

'You're all jumpy, Mrs Ridley,' Maria scolded. 'You want to take something for your nerves. My mother, she knows a good herb tea. I'll make some for you, later.' Eve smiled her thanks, and Maria left her again, saying, 'Excuse me now. I get you some food.'

As she drank the tea, Eve slipped back into her thoughts. John'd been so nice to her about everything. Eve could hardly believe her luck. Or was he saving his anger for later? Was she in for one hell of a pasting, some other time? No. She was pregnant. He wouldn't. And anyway, for some reason or another, he seemed grateful to her because she'd brought things to a head. It was funny that. He seemed almost as scared of the F.B.I. as she'd been; as Danny was. Danny! She could hate him for all the trouble he'd brought. At least John was out of the woods now. But what about Vic? 'If he's innocent he'll have nothing to worry about.' That was surely true. This was the United States, where justice and freedom were the sacred trusts of government. The F.B.I. was thorough, but only doing its job, when all was said and done, protecting their freedom. She had to hold on to that. She had to. Because she mustn't worry. The doctor'd said so! Hiccups indeed! It was worry'd brought on the bleeding, and nothing else.

Maria's herb tea tasted foul, but it had a pleasant effect. After drinking it, Eve felt her heightened senses soothed, dulled, and she swooned into a deep sleep, not waking when John came in, late, not noticing him get up again the next morning. When she finally did wake, it was to a tray of breakfast, brought in by Maria at 11 a.m.

'You feel better, Meesees Reeedlee?' Eve groaned her yes. Stretching luxuriously, she opened her eyes and saw the flowers. The room was filled with them. Maria'd run out of vases and stuffed them into buckets. Eve gasped.

'Who? Why?' she asked. Only then, noticing the paper tucked under Maria's arm, did Eve remember the F.B.I., the bleeding. The ache in the pit of her womb had dulled. She sat up carefully. 'I didn't know so many people knew I was pregnant!' she said, 'let alone cared!' She took her tray and asked to see the paper. Maria gave her an old-fashioned look.

'As long as you don't worry, huh?' Immediately, Eve was anxious. 'Why? What does it say?'

'Nothing! It's an article by your husband. That's all. Everything O.K.' Eve sighed, took the paper, and started reading. The headline made her stomach lurch.

'CITY EDITOR INTERVIEWED BY F.B.I.'

'Don't forget to eat!' Maria said, as she ambled back to the kitchen. Eve didn't hear her. She was reading.

I would like the good people of Albuquerque to know that I, John Ridley, and my wife Eve, have recently been interviewed by the Federal Bureau of Investigation, which, as we all know, investigates Un-American Activities. Now I want to say something categorical here. I applaud the F.B.I. and all its works. I know a lot of woolly-minded individuals in the community would like to throw a spanner in the works of this diligent committee, wailing on about civil liberties and so on. But I say to them, what are you afraid of? Are you not, yourselves, afraid of being found out? Are you not, in fact, by attacking the F.B.I., part of the Communist conspiracy yourself? For the F.B.I. is there to *defend* those civil liberties, which the Communists have a mind to take away! If you are innocent, submit, like I did, to their questioning. Now my record is well known. I have fought for my country, and received honours for it. I have defended the underdog, and I have attacked the criminal. And I have done this because I am a believer in the truth, and more important still, I am a believer in the American people knowing the truth!

Now the truth is that there is a Communist conspiracy. But the Communists are not innocents as we are. They are subtle, clever, insidious. They'll use anyone in pursuance of their aim to spread worldwide Communism. And that means we all have to be very very careful of the company we keep. This is something I have learnt the hard way. You see, good people of Albuquerque, the F.B.I. do not summon you for interview for nothing! So why did they send for me? Well, I am ashamed to say that I, without knowing it, have mixed with Communists! It's true! I can only console myself by thinking that they must believe I'm something, if they bother about me so much. They must think I'm going to be a powerful man in this country, that they must sully my reputation, attempting to prevent my rise in the political life of this great nation! Why, one of them even dared to turn up at the very private celebration of my recent marriage, and tried sponging off my poor, soft-hearted wife, who is always good for a sob story from someone from the old days in Hollywood! (As many of you know, my wife was something of a star.) But, even as I write, she is lying sick in bed, in danger of losing our first child. The shock of knowing how nearly she was used brought her to this! So I say to you, good people of Albuquerque, be on the watch, trust no one, even those of us in positions of power! For you never know who might be working on the side of the enemy. And remember, if the Communists succeed in infiltrating our society, by secret means, our boys will have died in vain on the battle-field; our boys will have suffered torture in the prison camps of North Korea, only to come home to what? My nephew, Jim Ridley, was taken prisoner by the Communist forces a few short weeks ago. Am I going to let him come home to an America which has become another satellite of the Soviet system? No, sir! Good people of Albuquerque, I will not run for office in the coming election year. For, though my wife and I have been cleared by the F.B.I., that is not enough for me. It is you, and you alone, who can truly judge me. So, I leave it to you to say whether I am innocent or no. Public service demands the confidence of the people we serve. Have I forfeited that confidence?

John Ridley

Eve looked up from the paper. All those flowers! They weren't for her at all. They were for John. He'd pulled off the boldest stunt of his life.

*   *   *

Jim Ridley had fallen into the hands of the Chinese. He was sitting in line. He'd been sitting in line for two hours now; the second two hours of another day of indoctrination. The voice of the camp commandant seemed distanced, deadened perhaps by the awning over their heads, to keep out the afternoon sun. Jim's head felt heavy. His eyes closed momentarily then, sharp as a whip, the stick caught him on the back, and stung him like a burn. But he managed not to cry out. He was awake now, and the commandant was looking at him.

'Prisoner Ridley!' he called out. 'Perhaps you would come here and give the other prisoners a résumé of my lecture!' The other prisoners were getting restive. It was time the session came to an end and it was Ridley who was keeping them. 'The prisoners will keep silence!' The commandant's stick cut into the papers on the table beside him. Jim waited in the silence, then, at a look from the commandant, he scrambled to his feet and edged through the lines of prisoners to the front. There was an amused look in the commandant's eyes. Jim turned to face the prisoners.

'We are the victims of an Imperialistic regime,' Jim began. 'Our rulers are the wealthy factory owners who manipulate us like puppets. They say they want peace, but they don't. They want war, because in wartime, they can make more money. They tell us we're fighting for the freedom of the western world. But the west is not free. It's an illusion of freedom. That's all. The North Korean people are fighting for what they believe in. No one's trying to make money out of them. That makes them free. While we are being cheated, gulled, into fighting only to line the pockets of our capitalist masters.' Jim glanced at the commandant. He looked surprised but pleased. He inclined his head to one side as acknowledgement.

'Very good. A little simplistic, perhaps, but to the point. You may sit down.'

'Thank you, sir.' Jim bowed slightly, and ignoring the eyes of his fellow prisoners, made his way back to his place.

'You could all learn from Prisoner Ridley.' The commandant was almost smiling. There was a faint hiss and Jim fell, his body straddling across the sitting prisoners. The commandant pulled himself up sharply. No one helped Jim. But he got back on his feet, and made his place. His left elbow hurt like hell. He must've caught it when he fell. 'And now I have good news for you,' the commandant said. 'Your Red Cross parcels have arrived at the camp.' There was a murmur of approval from the men. 'Your commanding officers will come to the stores at 8 o'clock to receive them.' Then he turned on his heel and marched back to his quarters. The assembly broke up and, bubbling with excitement, the men returned to their huts.

Jim's arm was hurting. He rested his elbow in the cup of his right hand, and saw blood ooze through his fingers. Damn. How did it happen? What had he fallen on? His fingers explored the wound. There was something hard inside.

'Want me to take a look at that?' It was the English surgeon, Andrew Chapman.

'Thanks.' He started walking with the Englishman towards the sick bay.

'Sounded like you believed all that,' Chapman remarked.

'Good,' Jim replied. 'That was the idea.'

There was a pause, then Chapman went on, in a warning voice, 'The boys believed you meant it too.'

'Of course. You have to be convincing if you're going to fool the Chinese.'

Chapman nodded. 'Thought so. Only be careful. Some of our men don't like hearing . . . '

'Anyway . . . ' Jim cut in. 'Some of it's true.'

'You mean you *do* believe it?'

'Some of what they say's true. Some of it's not. Just like back home. We live in a world of half-truths, doc. It's dangerous to believe anything.' They stopped to salute a guard, then went into sick bay. Chapman inspected the wound, took a tiny pebble out of it with a pair of tweezers, then let Jim go. 'Aren't you going to cover it, or wash it out, or anything?'

Chapman shrugged.

'Want me to wash it out with dirty water?' Jim sighed. Point taken. 'I've not got any disinfectant.'

'The flies'll get at it,' Jim said.

'You'll be O.K. Better get back to work.'

Feeling shortchanged, Jim left the sick bay and got on with his job, breaking stones at the far end of the compound. After three days, Jim's arm hurt so much, he couldn't wield his hammer, and the wound smelt. It was going septic. He went back to Chapman.

Chapman looked at it, shrugged and said, 'You're O.K.'

'It's septic.'

'It needs the air at it. It'll clear up.'

'Didn't you get any antiseptic in the Red Cross issue?' Chapman shook his head. 'Well, I can't break stones any more,' Jim objected. 'I can't lift the hammer!'

'O.K. I'll get you onto another job. Right?' Jim nodded. He wasn't pleased. He was beginning to feel that the Englishman had passed judgement on him. Then he discovered what his new job was; digging the new latrines. Yes, Chapman had passed judgement, judgement and sentence. It was hot. Jim struggled with the shovel, his left arm aching at every movement. The stench of the old latrines was sickening. The flies buzzed round, bathing in the open wound. Hell, what was the English bastard playing at? Jim could lose his arm! He climbed out of the latrine, throwing back his shovel. A guard pointed a gun at him.

'Get back in!' he yelled. Jim indicated his elbow.

'Can't dig,' he said. 'Arm hurting. Wounded.' Suddenly Chapman was there. He had a word with the soldier, who dropped his gun. Then Chapman, turning to go, beckoned Jim to follow. Jim hesitated. What now? The Englishman beckoned again. So Jim followed the doc right back to the sick bay.

'I'm going to bind that up now,' Chapman said.

'Better late than never, huh?' Jim replied laconically.

Chapman smiled grimly. He wasn't giving anything away. He finished binding up Jim's arm. 'I want you to leave this on for a week, then come back and see me,' he said.

'What for? An amputation?'

'Just do as I say.' Jim sighed. He wasn't too sure about any of this. 'O.K. You can go now,' Chapman said. He wanted rid of him. There were other patients to see.

On light duties, Jim began to feel better. He didn't develop fever and his arm had stopped hurting. But this was surely a bad sign. Had it gone gangrenous? It smelt pretty off, that was for sure. Angry, he went back to sick bay and harangued the surgeon.

'Chapman!' Chapman looked up from a new patient. He had a mask over his face.

'Get out of here!' he shouted. Jim backed away, and waited outside. After a few minutes, the doc came out. 'What's wrong with you? I said come back in a week. It's not a week yet.'

'It's six days. I think I've lost the feeling in my arm, you bastard!'

'O.K. Let's take a look,' Chapman grabbed Jim's arm.

'Out here?' Chapman said nothing. He undid the bandage, and unwound it. With the dressing, came away a handful of maggots. Jim started retching and cursing. 'Very nice,' Chapman said, inspecting the wound.

'What do you mean, nice?'

'It's clean. Maggots have eaten all the dead flesh.' The doctor brushed off the remaining couple of maggots. 'They've saved your arm.' He went back into sick bay and brought out some clean bandage. 'We got some of this in the Red Cross issue.'

'I think I'm going to faint,' Jim said.

'Sit down, then,' Chapman smiled.

'I thought you thought I was a Commie bastard.'

'I know you did. And you're not. But you're not exactly pure brain-washed capitalist American either, are you?' Jim shook his head. 'So what are you?'

'I don't know. There's lies both sides. There's truth both sides. I guess I don't believe in anything but myself, any more.'

'Cynical little sod, aren't you?' Chapman commented.

'If you like.' Jim looked at the clean dressing. 'Thanks.' He nodded, then walked away, leaving Chapman to think whatever he damned well liked.

* * *

Thinking about Jimmy helped Eve. They'd had no news of him, but, watching T.V. from her sick bed, Eve could see the horror stories coming out of Korea for herself. American boys were involved in real suffering. So were the English, and the French and so on and so on. The whole Western bloc was fighting the Communist threat. For Jimmy's sake, for the sake of world peace, Eve had to swallow any doubts she might have, and support her husband one hundred per cent in his fight against Communism! She watched him as he got into the other bed, white toothpaste marks round his mouth. He looked tired. So many articles to write, so many people to see, on call the whole time. And he cared, John really cared about the issues, about the boys like Jimmy. And the war showed no sign of ending. Why didn't they just drop the 'A' bomb and have done with it? It'd put a stop to the last war soon enough! At least, that's what John thought they should do; drop the 'A' bomb on North Korea. John turned his back to her and grunted a good night as he switched off his bedside light.

'Good night, dear.' Eve called back. But what about those sheep in Nevada? All those people in Hiroshima? What about Jimmy? He was in North Korea! Eve didn't want the bomb to fall on Jimmy, even if it did put an end to the war, and save thousands of allied lives. John was a man. He could put the universal good before the personal. She honoured him for that, and was glad *she* wasn't in a position where she could influence government! You had to be really sure you were right before you stood up and made speeches, like John did. And he was sure. For John, black was black and white was white. Whereas Eve had a tendency to admit grey areas into her thinking. And grey areas were out of bounds. Either you were a Commie and black, or, you were a good American capitalist and you were white. There was nothing in between, like for instance a good Commie, or a bad capitalist. And, of course their side, the Americans, the U.N. Forces, never made mistakes, did they? The F.B.I. didn't make mistakes, did it? Even asking questions was wrong. If John knew what she thought sometimes, he would be so angry with her. I mean, why doubt? He didn't! The battle was joined. Doubts weakened the side. If he knew she doubted . . . ! But she kept her doubts to herself. She never even wrote to Vic or Danny to find out how they were. Not that John'd forbidden her to write, but that she didn't dare. For one thing, John might find out. For another, she might learn something she didn't want to know. John was snoring. Was he getting bored with her? He was so considerate of her condition, but, he was a man, he had his needs. Poor John. And there was she, doubting. She should be ashamed of herself, pull herself together, get well enough to get back on her feet and work at John's side! She had to rest. If only she could stop thinking! How was Victor? How was Jimmy? How was the baby waiting to be born? How healthy was her marriage? She reached for her herb tea and drank.

In September, when the weather was cooling, Eve was allowed out. She had grown so big, the doc had begun to think she was expecting twins. So he sent her to the hospital, where the obstetrician prodded and poked and listened to the noises in her womb, and then, putting the stethoscope in her ears, let her listen too. There were two heartbeats. Oh, if only John were here to listen! Two heartbeats! It was a miracle. God was good. She had lost one child; now, He had blessed her with two at once! Would they be boys, or girls, or one of each? As long as one was a boy, for John's sake, she wouldn't mind what the other was. Dying to share her news with someone who cared, Eve broke her self-imposed rule and wrote to Vic.

Three weeks later, Eve had a reply. Luckily, John was away on one of his research trips at the time, and Maria brought the letter in with the breakfast tray, leaving Eve to read it alone. The envelope was postmarked Chicago. As she opened it, a few newspaper cuttings fell out with the letter. There were a couple of cartoons, a picture of some musicians from Vegas days, who'd made a hit record, and one or two newsy articles. Glancing at the first one, Eve picked it up. Not that she was more interested in the article than she was in what Vic had to say, but because there it was in front of her, and it caught her attention.

'Insurance Companies to Sue Atomic Energy Commission.'

'Technicians at the Kodak Factory in Ontario have long been aware that their photographic production plant lies in the path of fallout from the nuclear testing site in the Nevada Desert, and after wasting film contaminated by fallout radiation, they have succeeded in persuading the Commission they are a special case, and entitled to advance warning of 'dirty bombs', the ones which produce the most fallout, so that they can avoid processing film during the likely period of contamination. But the casino owners of Vegas continue to suffer from shattered windows, and the farmers of Nevada continue to lose sheep, without any warning, at an alarming rate, either through sudden death or through the spontaneous abortion of lambs, and the insurance companies have to pay out. And now, an interesting case has cropped up, where one insurance company is actually threatening to sue the Atomic Energy Commission for damages. A test case like this could be very embarrassing . . . '

Eve glanced back through the article. 'Spontaneous abortions of lambs'. Were they saying then that the bomb made the sheep miscarry? Eve felt the first flutter of panic. She tried to bury it. She tried to stop thinking. The American nation needed the 'A' bomb to drop on the Communists, otherwise where would they be? The U.S.'d be ruled from Moscow before they knew where they were. And you can't say but that the Russians weren't doing tests, and making bombs just the same, and they couldn't be allowed to get ahead of the Free World, or the balance of power would be finished, and . . . well, it didn't bear thinking of. Eve

286

swallowed hard. So a few sheep suffered. So . . . ? There was the Universal Good to consider. She opened Vic's letter and started to read.

My Dear Evie,

Your letter was forwarded to me here in Chicago, where I now run a small club. 'Flamm's' in Vegas had to close, after an indictment for running a dirty joint. All trumped up, of course. First thing they tried was the old indecency rap. Of course it didn't stick. Imagine me being done for indecency? I only had a stripper on for a week, I never used mirrors, and you know what the other guys were doing in their clubs! Then, when the indecency bit didn't work, they started looking at my books. Well, they're clean as a whistle. But, they've got imagination these guys, I tell you! They worked out somehow that I'd fixed the machines so the management always won. Well, if I had, how come I was in cash problems? Doesn't make sense, does it? But then, sense doesn't come into it. Then they made up some cock and bull system that I was supposed to use, and that damn saxophone player, Vernon, he backed up their story! He said he knew the croupiers all played my system, but they'd never dare admit to it, because I'd have them trussed up and thrown into the Grand Canyon if they did. Would you believe it? The schmuck! Why do people like that do the things they do? I don't understand. Maybe the guy thinks I really am a Communist sympathizer. But even if I was, and you know I'm not, Evie, I don't hold with Communists, never have, but even if I was, I don't see that entitles anybody to persecute me and harass me and put me out of business! I'll be lucky if I keep *this* joint open! I mean, why don't they seek out the real troublemakers and conspirators in our society, instead of wasting their time on me? They're hot on my tail the whole time, the moonstruck stargazers!

Speaking of which, I am over the moon about the twins! Twins! I can't believe it! I'm very glad, Eve. I know you wanted it badly, and now you've got it twice over! Hope John's looking after you properly. It's a shame you've had so much worry it made you ill, risking them babies of yours. John should protect you from all that worry. It's a man's job to protect his wife. Tell him I said so! And laugh, if you can find anything to laugh about! It's the best medicine! I should know. I laugh all the time. I mean, if I didn't laugh, I'd cry! Hope you like the cuttings I sent you. Just some topical bits and pieces from up this way. I like the cartoon. That's one thing always makes me laugh in the mornings. I love you, Eve. I'm in bad shape here. I can't say otherwise. But, I love you. And I don't hold it against you that you had me give that break to that friend of yours at the club. I should have known better. But then, I'm just an old fool, an old sentimental fool. Take care of yourselves, all four of you.

Love, Vic

Eve put down the letter. Her heart was thumping. Greyness was invading her thought. Greyness pervaded her soul. Something was wrong. Something was very wrong. Nobody should hurt Vic Flamm! Tears stung her eyes. She wiped them away angrily. John had said, 'Better him than me.' But he didn't mean he'd dropped Vic in the shit, did he? He just meant, well, what he'd said! No. John was alright. But the F.B.I., Mr McCarthy, the Atomic Energy Commission . . . Lambs were being aborted because of the bomb. Eve'd bled. She'd seen a bomb go off. She'd been that close, she'd thought the world had come to an end. Then, she'd nearly lost her babies. Her hand slipped down her belly. There was a reassuring little kick. It was the first time she'd felt anything. The babies . . . one of them, anyway, was moving! She breathed a sigh of relief. She was crazy to worry. After all, she wasn't a sheep. Things affected humans differently from animals, and if there was any danger they'd surely have warned the American public, wouldn't they? Eve smiled to herself. She was just getting paranoid. Her babies were fine. And Vic . . . Vic was what? Unlucky? No. That wouldn't do. Vic was being persecuted and she knew it. There was something wrong. Her hand protected the bulge of her belly. But what could *she* do about the F.B.I.? She could tell John she thought things were getting out of hand. The F.B.I. was overreaching itself. But the very thought appalled her. John might get angry. He might do something awful. She'd been waiting for him to do something awful ever since they'd got back from Washington. He never had. It was as though that horrible part of him had died. And yet,

288

she still feared its resurrection. She had her children to think of. And of course, there was the Universal Good, whatever that was. Jimmy was a prisoner of war. That was the ony concrete fact Eve could hold onto. She was shaking. It was all too much. She needed something to calm her nerves.

When he came home, two days later, John was shocked to see the state Eve was in. She tried to cover up by unpacking for her husband, sorting his dirty linen, hanging his suits, folding and re-folding the unused shirts. She was making John dizzy.

'What's wrong, honey? You're as scatty as a roadrunner!'

'Nothing,' Eve said, too quickly. 'What on earth could be wrong?' Then he'd put out his arm, catching her in mid-run across the room, and stopped her short. She looked at him, scared and shaky.

'Hey!' he said gently. He pulled her in to him, and held her close. Immediately the tension went out of her body and she started to cry. 'This isn't just pregnancy nerves, is it?' Eve shook her head. 'O.K. Tell Daddy.' She looked up at him. His face was patient and kind and she felt she could trust him. He was her husband, after all. She was carrying his children. She ought to be able to trust him. She swallowed hard and buried her face in his chest, before speaking.

'Please, promise you won't be angry with me,' she said. She was quaking. He felt it, and he put a hand on the centre of her back, rubbing her, like a baby with wind.

'I promise,' he said. 'I won't be angry. What've you done? Have you overspent on the account?' She shook her head, face still deep in his jacket. 'O.K. What then?'

'I wrote to Victor.' She felt him stiffen.

'Vic Flamm?' he asked. Eve nodded. 'Well, I suppose you wanted him to know about the babies.' Eve nodded again. 'It's natural enough.'

'He wrote back,' she said. John said nothing. Taking her courage in her hands, Eve looked up at him. He was pale, and serious, but not at all angry. Absently, he raised his hand to the back of her head, and fondled her there. 'He's had a lot of troubles lately.'

'What sort of troubles?'

'People trying to put him out of business, for instance.'

'Want to show me the letter?' John's voice was restrained. He had promised he wouldn't be angry. Eve went to her handbag and took the letter out of the envelope, leaving the cuttings behind.

'Here.' She handed it over. 'I didn't know whether I should keep it. But . . . ' John said nothing. He was reading Vic's scrawling hand. When he'd finished, he folded it, struck a match, and burned the latter in the ashtray. Eve watched the flame grow bright, then die. All that was left was black ash. 'What do you think?' she asked.

'Poor guy's paranoid,' John said, laughing it off.

'Paranoid?'

'Yes! Seems to think there's a conspiracy against him! As if the F.B.I. had time to bother about small-time crooks like Flamm!'

'Vic isn't a crook!' Eve said sharply. Then she bit her tongue. She should watch her reactions. They were too quick, too strong.

'Any man who runs a club or a casino's a crook! It's the name of the game!'

Eve shook her head, and said, more softly, 'Not Vic.'

'You're too trusting, honey.' John smiled, and opened his arms for her. Cautiously she walked into them and allowed him to wrap her round, and hold her close again. 'Chicago's full of gangsters! The scare tactics being used on your Vic are typical gangster moves. Vic must've crossed somebody some time. Now he's paying for it. That's all.'

'But . . . '

'He didn't give any proof the F.B.I.'s behind it, did he?'

'No . . . ' Eve frowned, and looked across at the tray of ash. 'I don't think so . . . ' She wouldn't be able to check now.

'Well, then! The whole thing's either in his head or yours.'

'I've been a fool, haven't I?' Eve looked up at her husband, eyes wet and huge.

'Guess so!' John laughed. Then he hugged her very tight. 'Now, you've got to stop worrying. For the sake of those babies, if nothing else! I'm sorry Victor's having problems. But you know, honey, they'll be of his own making, whether he cares to admit it or not. And there's not a damn thing you can do about it.'

'Can I at least write back to him?' Eve asked.

'Don't think that would be a good idea, honey.' John's smile was sweet and compassionate. I'm sorry. But it wouldn't be good for my image if it got out my wife was corresponding with somebody who's mixed up in the underworld, now, would it?'

Eve shook her head. 'I suppose not,' she said.

'There now. Dry your eyes, dear.' Obediently, Eve took out her handkerchief and wiped away the tears. 'Ray's coming round at seven o'clock, take me to a ball game. Care to come?' Eve's heart sank. There was nothing she hated more than ball games. But she smiled bravely and nodded, to please him. 'Good girl,' John said. 'Fix your face, huh?' Eve fixed her face. She wished she could fix a drink, but she daren't. And when Ray came round, she was bright-eyed, pink-cheeked, strung-up, and ready for anything.

Ray was only just turned twenty. He liked ball games, but he didn't like hanging round afterwards, waiting for John to do his P.R. thing, especially when his only company was John's pregnant English wife, who merely thought of Ray as 'the office boy'. He lit up a cigarette and inhaled deeply. It wasn't as if she was full of interesting conversation or anything. Not with him, anyway. Maybe she thought herself too high and mighty to talk to the likes of him. He looked at her in the rearview mirror and took another drag. There were two hot spots on Mrs Ridley's cheeks. Neurotic dame! Ray sighed. No wonder John took off on them trips of his. Any man would. Why, the lady was the size of one of them hot-air balloons they sent up from Santa Fe. Idly, he visualized her, blowing up, fuller and fuller, till her face ran straight into her body, the hot spots, streaks of red, like stripes down the side of the great ball of her, and she floated off the back seat, through the sun roof, and up and up to the stars.

'What are you thinking?'

The balloon crash landed, and there she was back in the car, looking at him curiously through the mirror.

'Oh nothing! Nothing at all!' Ray smiled in an offhand kind of way.

'Can't be nothing. You were really staring at me. Do you know that?'

'Sorry, ma'am,' Ray said. Suddenly she wanted to talk, did

she? Oh well. That was O.K. with him. She was searching for another topic of conversation.

'I've never seen you smoke before,' she said. Ray looked at the butt of the cigarette thoughtfully.

'Don't usually smoke in public,' he said. 'But it's dark here. Don't mind, do you?' Eve laughed. What a silly question. Why should she mind?

'Course not,' she said. 'You must be a regular smoker, rolling your own, like that.'

'I smoke it when I can get it,' Ray said.

'Do they pay you so badly, then?' Eve was shocked. Ray stared at her, through the mirror. What was she getting at? 'Cigarettes are so cheap! Or is it just that you prefer an expensive foreign make . . . I must say, that smells like burning socks to me!'

Ray grinned. 'Oh yeah,' he said. 'This is very special tobacco. Like to try it?' He held the cigarette out to her.

'Me?' She was shocked at the idea. And yet, a lot of women smoked. She was tempted. It would be a chance.

'John doesn't approve of ladies smoking,' she said.

'Then I won't tell him.' Ray smiled.

'O.K.,' she said. Then she hesitated again. 'Just so long as it doesn't harm my babies.'

'No,' Ray said. 'Very relaxing, it is.'

'Good. That's just what I need!' Eve placed the butt between her lips and breathed in. Her head swam. For a split second, she felt sick, then she felt better again.

'Inhale deeply,' Ray told her, smiling like a Cheshire cat. Eve obeyed. His teeth turned into tombstones, glaring white in the semi-darkness. 'That's enough. Now just close your eyes for a minute.' Eve closed her eyes. She felt light, as if a weight was rising from off the top of her head, releasing pressure from her brain. It was nice. She took another drag. Then she started floating. Her smile spread across her cheeks. Ray was giggling. She opened her eyes, looked at him and started giggling too.

'I like this!' Eve said. Her voice sounded strange to her, at once far off and luxuriously close. Whose voice was it? Was it really hers? She looked up, through the sun roof, at the distant stars. Perhaps the voice really belonged to one of them Martians out there. Outer Space. Twinkle, twinkle little star . . . Eve started humming the tune, dragging on the cigarette from time to time, staring up at the sky.

Coming back to the car in a business-like mood, John was surprised to find his chauffeur and his wife in a dream. He sniffed the air suspiciously and gave Ray a look.

'You been smoking?'

'Sorry, Mr Ridley, sir,' Ray said, sobering fast. 'You were a long, long time.' Ray put the car in gear and Eve felt it float off down the street, like a U.F.O.

'Twinkle, twinkle, little star . . . ' Eve sang. John twisted his body to look back at her. Then he looked at Ray.

'You got my wife high on your smoke,' he whispered angrily.

'Sorry, sir. I thought with the roof off and the windows open, it wouldn't affect her, see.'

'It's good stuff that. I told you. You've got to treat it with respect. What if I'd offered a lift to somebody, huh? You've got to be more careful.'

'I'm sorry, sir. It won't happen again.' Ray was chastened. He glanced back in the mirror. Mrs Ridley's face had softened. She looked happy and when she looked happy, she was really pretty.

'Do you believe in the man in the moon, John?' Her voice drifted lazily from the back seat.

'No, honey. It's a lot of old baloney. And you know it,' John said. 'You'll feel better in the morning.'

'I feel just fine now, John.' Eve started giggling.

'Are you sure you didn't give her a drag?' John asked angrily.

'No, sir! I wouldn't do a thing like that, sir!'

'I hope you're telling me the truth.' John's voice was threatening. 'And you shut up, Eve!' he yelled at the back seat.

The balloon was well and truly pricked and it fell, crashing back to earth. Eve felt cold. Why was John such a killjoy? She sighed as the car glided through the streets back home and pulled up outside their fashionable adobe dwelling. Poor John. He had such a lot of responsibilities. The Universal Good and all that. She couldn't blame him for being a killjoy. What joy did *he* have? And he'd been so nice to her about Victor. Poor Victor. Eve was thinking about Victor as she stepped out of the car, bade Ray goodnight, and went inside. Poor Victor. She would have liked to have replied to his letter. She stared at the now clean ashtray sparkling in the light of the table lamp. She remembered how good Vic was, how clean, how straight. He was no crook. And if gangsters were getting at him, then couldn't John do something to help him? He was pouring himself a drink. She wouldn't get one. She was on the wagon. But that smoke was nice. She might take up smoking, on the quiet. After all, she'd never promised John she wouldn't smoke. She drifted into the bedroom and started to undress. She was still thinking about Victor, when, tired and dirty, she went into the bathroom and turned on the shower. It spluttered, spat out some water, then wheezed to a standstill.

'Damn!' she said aloud. 'Sooner you get on the City Government, the better, John!' she yelled back into the living room.

No, John couldn't risk getting involved in gangsters or Communists or anything like that. It'd make it difficult for him with the voters. Like Caesar's wife he had to be seen to be above suspicion. Mr Clean. Eve rubbed herself down with a towel and sprinkled talcum powder in every crevice. It felt a little better, anyway. Then she slipped on her nightie and got into bed. Poor Victor. She sighed. No. She mustn't write to him. It was a question of loyalty; to John; to the Universal Good. Not that Victor was bad. And it was funny how all his troubles had started after the F.B.I. business. John'd said, 'better him than me'. But she mustn't doubt. She really mustn't doubt. She mustn't. She prayed to God not to let her doubt.

John came in, at last. Silently, thinking Eve was asleep, he undressed and slipped into his own bed, putting out the light. After a moment, he heard her stir, and turn towards him.

'John.' She called in a little girl's voice. 'John. Hold my hand.' He rolled over, and stared across the gap between them. In the darkness, he could just make out her white hand. It was reaching for him. He took it in his own and held it. 'John,' she said. 'There's nothing to be scared of, is there? Tell me there isn't?'

'No, honey. There's nothing to be scared of.' John's voice was patient. He yawned. He tried to let go her hand, but she held on.

'Please, just keep on holding my hand, John.'

He kept on holding it. Then he dropped asleep, and with the first snore, he let go. Eve's hand trailed loosely on the floor between the beds. Poor Victor. But she didn't want to think about Victor. She didn't want to think at all. Thinking was a quagmire. It sucked you in and you went down and down, drowning in your own grey areas. But how to stop thinking? Her brain chattered on and on and on. She got up and made some herb tea. It made her drowsy, but it wasn't as nice as smoking. No wonder people got hooked.

Next day, Ray came round in his lunch hour. He looked furtive and scared.

'Mrs Ridley, I'm glad I found you in . . . ' he began.

'I hardly ever go out, matter of fact,' Eve smiled wanly. 'Why? What's wrong? You look like a frightened rabbit.' Ray nodded.

'Yeah. I'm scared. I'm sorry about last night.'

'Sorry?' Eve echoed.

'Yeah. I was playing a little game. That cigarette I gave you wasn't any ordinary cigarette.' Eve looked at him seriously. 'It was a joint. Dope.'

'Drugs?' Eve asked, amazed.

'You're very innocent, Mrs Ridley, I'll say that for you. You really didn't realize, did you?' Eve shook her head. 'Don't worry. Grass won't hurt you, or the babies. Only, please, Mrs Ridley, I beg you not to say anything to your husband. If he found out I'd given you a drag, he'd hit the roof. I'd lose my job! I mean, it's not that much, but it is work.'

'Don't worry,' Eve said absently. 'I won't give you away.' Then she frowned, put her head on one side, and asked, 'Where do you get that stuff?'

Ray hesitated, then replied, 'I can't tell you that.'

'I liked it.' Ray shrugged. 'And it really doesn't hurt you?' Ray shook his head. 'Then, do you think you could get *me* some?' Ray gasped. He hadn't bargained on this. 'Please, Ray. I need it to help me relax. John's out a lot and . . . '

'He'd smell it in the house. He'd know.'

'Oh.' Eve looked across the room at the drinks cabinet. Ray read her thoughts.

'Now don't do anything silly, Mrs Ridley.'

'I'm not silly, Ray!' Eve objected. 'I'm just bored and lonely and . . . well, I worry a lot.'

'O.K. I'll get you some stuff,' Ray agreed, and he was glad when he saw the smile lighting up Eve's face. Yes, she was pretty when she was happy. 'Look,' he said, 'I've got to get back now.

I'll bring you some round, when I can. Only, don't smoke it in the house or in public. Take a walk somewhere, huh?' Eve nodded and showed Ray out. 'And if anyone sees me here, I've come to take you shopping, O.K.?'

'O.K.'

Thanksgiving brought the first baby presents from the family gathered at The Lawe Top. They heaped the handknitted matinée jackets, leggings, and bonnets on the happy couple; two of everything. Eve glowed as she inspected each garment, oohing and aahing, and, obviously, feeling just wonderful.

'Married life suits you, Eve,' Lou observed, smiling. He glanced at Ella, who also smiled and nodded. 'And John, well, you do surprise me, I must say. I never thought you'd ever settle down to be the ideal husband and father.'

'Got to, Lou,' John said affably. He was sitting comfortably by the fire, a beer in his hand. 'My whole campaign rests on it.' The family laughed. Eve laughed too. She felt relaxed and happy. Her little habit had chased away all the grey areas, saved her from doubting her marriage onto the rocks, saved her sanity almost. When in doubt, literally, she just went for a bit of fresh air, and, far out of sight of the respectable folk of Albuquerque, she rolled herself a joint. She soon stopped thinking. The grey areas slowly turned pink, then rainbow coloured, then, afterwards, there was peace. Mothers should be calm. Maria'd said so. It's good for the babies. Eve's hand nursed her belly, as she sat, perched on the edge of a chair, eyes damp, looking at the little clothes. What with Sam's cast-offs and June's offerings from the charity shop, her layette was doing well. Babies sure brought out the best in people. Especially when they were twins. Why, John'd even got Ray on decorating their spare room for a nursery! There was going to be a fresco of Disney characters all the way across the wall, and Mexican mobiles hanging in the breeze by the window. Eve enjoyed watching Ray work. John seemed to trust him. In fact, Ray'd become almost like a member of the family. Well, his own was a long way off in Houston. She guessed he must be as lonely as she was. Watching Ella making apple turnovers, she wondered if she was lonely too. Ella glanced back and smiled. She'd changed. She'd become an American housewife, just like Eve had; at least on the outside. Was it just camouflage? Eve remembered that time in the barn, when she'd given up Lou to Ella and Ella had said Eve'd find somebody nice one day. Well, she had, hadn't she?

'Been up to Walpi lately, for any of your Indian ceremonies?' Eve asked. Nervously, Ella glanced at Lou, who said, shortly,

'Don't want another son of mine becoming a stranger.' It was true Jimmy'd become a stranger, to all of them. Was it the Hopis to blame? Well, if it was, he'd become a stranger to them too. After a while, when Lou'd forgotten the moment, Ella came to sit by Eve, and talk with her in low voices, the smell of baking turnovers perfuming the air.

'I still go home to my people,' Ella explained. 'Sometimes I take Sam, but Lou doesn't like it. Perhaps he's right. You have to be born one hundred per cent Hopi, to be a real Hopi, otherwise . . . '

'Still no word about Jimmy?' Ella shook her head.

'I don't suppose he'd write to us, even if they let him,' she said sadly. 'Don't mention him to Lou. It only upsets him.' Eve nodded. 'At least I gave him another son.'

Eve said nothing. It seemed such an odd thing to say, 'I gave him another son', as though Jimmy could somehow be supplanted. She sighed. She hoped she wouldn't be possessive of her children, rejecting them, when they asked for their freedom. Because that was surely what Ella'd done, whether she realized it or not. She was jealous. But no one could own anyone else. No one could tell anybody else what to think, or how to live their lives, could they? That was the American way. That freedom was what John and Jimmy were fighting for. Eve's face was serious. Ella misinterpreted.

'Are you and John really as happy as you look?' she asked.

'Do we look happy?' Immediately Eve was beaming.

'Yes. You do. I must say it surprises me. John's changed. I don't recognize him these days.'

'You sound suspicious,' Eve remarked.

'There's a saying, I've heard June use it, "Leopards don't change their spots".'

'Some do. In the winter. Their fur goes white,' Eve retorted sharply.

'That's just to camouflage them against the snow,' Ella said.

'What are you trying to do to me?' Eve's voice was low and

angry. 'Are you trying to upset me?' The Indian face gave nothing away. And to think Eve'd trusted Ella, had given up a man for her, had thought of her as a sort of a sister! Why, she stood there on her podium trying to let on she was better than the rest of them, and all the time, she was just jealous. That was all. Ella was jealous.

'Come on, you two! Stop your chattering there!' June was cutting up the pumpkin pie, ready for the table. The turkey smelt sweet. 'Clear those baby things up now!'

Ella helped Eve fold and pack each little garment, then the two women laid the table together, while John went out to fetch Jo and Sam.

Sam was riding on Jimmy's old pony. It wasn't as skittish as it used to be. The little lad was in no danger. Old Jo turned and looked at John, as he sauntered out of the house towards him.

'Table's laid,' John observed.

''Bout time,' Jo replied laconically. 'Belly thinks my throat's been cut.' Then the three of them went in to the feast.

*   *   *

The bell at Pyong Gang prison camp clanged the reveille, and Jim tried to move his legs. They were stiff with cold. Frost lay on the top of his thin Chinese blanket and the bare boards of the floor struck cold through the flimsy mattress. At half-past six the 'squawk-boxes' started up with their Red Army propaganda songs;

'Arise ye prisoners of starvation.
'Arise ye wretched of the earth . . .'

Jim lined up for a wash in the icy water, before a breakfast of rice and a potato. 'Arise ye prisoners of starvation.' It was Thanksgiving at home. Turkey and pumpkin pie. The saliva ran at the very thought. After breakfast, Jim joined the digging party on Boot Hill; graves for the prisoners who'd died in the night. There wasn't much on the bodies for the worms, Jim observed, as the chaplain did the honours, and the dead were rolled into their shallow graves. One of them had a burn mark round his neck. Spike Goldman, his name was. He'd mocked the Communist pamphlets at the discussion groups, the evening before. You shouldn't do that. It was rude to mock the host. So he'd been dragged off by the guards to an empty hut and roped up to the ceiling by his wrists. Then they'd tied one leg up, folding it against his back, tethering the rope round his neck. If he moved his leg he'd be bound to strangle himself. He'd been in there all night. He'd moved his leg. Poor bastard. 'Arise ye wretched of the earth . . .'

At ten-thirty the first indoctrination session of the day began. Jim sat cross-legged on the bare boards of the lecture hut, inscrutable as his captors. They might think they owned his mind. But they didn't. Jim was immune. He'd had experience of brain-washing before.

CHAPTER FIFTEEN

Eve went into labour five days before Christmas. It was a hard labour, being her first, and being as she was rather 'mature' for starting a family. There was talk of her having a caesarean section, but she didn't want that. Eve wanted to be alive to what was going on, and hear the first cries of her babies. So they held off, giving her painkilling injections, which anaesthetized the body and left the mind floating in space. Strange shadows came between Eve and the doctors and nurses. They scared her. She kept seeing the mushroom cloud that spun out of the explosion in the desert. It cast its gloom on everything. But there was no need to worry. Her babies had gone full term. They'd be alright, as long as she played her part. But it was hard to push, when you couldn't feel what you were doing. It was like pushing against a cloud, nothing real about it. Lying there, on her back, she could almost give up, drift off into a timeless sleep and just forget everything. But that wouldn't do at all. She fought against the temptation. She fought against the shadows. She asked the nurses if she could sit up, but they wouldn't let her. They could see what they were doing better, with her legs waving in the air. It was ridiculous. She felt an idiot. And to think her own mother had gone through all this for her! Poor Mam! If only Eve'd realized! Then, thinking of her Mam made her wonder what she thought about John and the babies. She'd finally got up courage to tell her mother she'd got married, by writing a note on a Christmas card. She'd have it, by now. Too bad if she didn't approve. At this moment, Eve felt too weary to care *what* she thought. 'Let her think what she likes! I'm happy,' she said to herself.

The doctor, seeing Eve smile inanely, got worried. He reached for the forceps. Eve saw the shining metal instrument and seized up.

'It's O.K., Mrs Ridley. Just you relax now and let us do the work.' Eve tried to relax. She wished John was there. But he didn't like mess, or, at least, that's what he'd said. Anyway, he was away, just now, on a trip to 'Frisco; newspaper business. Ray hadn't gone with him this time and had sent him a telegram, 'labour has started'. But there'd been no word back yet, so far as she knew.

'Now, give us a really big push, Mrs Ridley,' the nurse commanded. Eve did her best. The forceps went in. She didn't feel them. Then, after a lot of action behind the sheet, she saw her firstborn. The doc held it high up in the air, checking to see if it was alright. Eve peered at the red, slimy object. It was a boy. Its eyes were closed as if it were dead. Then the doc turned it upside down, clearing its passages, and the baby cried. Eve wanted to cry too.

'Is it alright?' she asked.

'Well . . . it's a boy, and it seems to have everything it ought to.' Staring at the child, Eve thought she'd given birth to both at once, without knowing it. She was seeing double.

'What's the other one? Is that a boy too?' she asked.

'What other one, honey?' the nurse said kindly. Then she was at her again. In went the forceps. 'Push, Mrs Ridley! Come on now. Let's have a big effort!'

Feeling like a baseball team, Eve pushed. Another red slimy object was pulled out of her and held high. Now she had four children. Her eyes were rolling, as she struggled to raise her head and look at them.

'This one's a boy too, Mrs Ridley,' the doctor said.

'So I've got two boys and two girls,' Eve said faintly.

'No, dear. Only two boys.' The nurse seemed pretty sure about it. Eve laid her head back, sighing.

'Whatever you say,' she agreed. Who cared any more? It was over. She could sleep. But they wouldn't let her. They were at her again, pounding her, pulling at her, forcing out the afterbirth.

'You can sleep soon, Mrs Ridley,' the doctor said. Then the nurse appeared at Eve's side, a baby on each arm.

'Want to hold them for a minute?' she asked. Eve smiled weakly as the infants were placed, one against each breast. Then she really started crying.

'Oh, I'm so happy,' she said. 'I'm so happy!' And everyone laughed.

'O.K. We'll just stitch you up now, and send you back to your room for a nice, long sleep.' The nurse was at her again, out of sight, on the other side of the sheet. Eve still felt nothing. Let them do what they liked. She was past caring. The babies were taken away. Her legs were let down, gently, one by one, and she was made decent. Eve's head was swimming. As she was wheeled out of the delivery room into the corridor, she wondered if she was really a chicken that'd just been stuffed, and was, even now, on her way to the oven. Then she told herself off. She really must take a hold on herself. Her thinking was going crazy. She was tired, that was all. They eased her gently onto her bed. She felt the cool sheets, groaned, and fell asleep.

June was there when she woke up. She was smiling, like she was really pleased. Eve tried to smile back. But she felt as though she'd been beaten up. She ached and she hurt.

'Who's a good girl, then?' June asked brightly.

'I suppose I must be,' Eve answered sleepily. Then she woke suddenly. 'Have you seen them, June? How many are there? Are they boys or girls? Are they alright?'

'Hey! Slow down, honey,' June said. 'You've got two healthy boys. Well . . . they've both got . . . '

'Oh God. Don't tell me.' Eve wailed, hands in front of her eyes.

'It's nothing. They can put it right soon enough.'

'Put what right? What is there to put right?'

'They've both got webbed feet!' June laughed. 'Where did you and John conceive those babies? At the bottom of a lake?'

She was laughing fit to bust. It gave Eve a headache. She felt

302

humiliated. Webbed feet? How was it possible? Was John a duck? Was she? The nurse came over and shushed at June. June was put out. She frowned, looking for another subject of conversation.

'What you going to call them?'

'We've not decided.' Eve didn't want to say, because they weren't family names and she knew June wouldn't approve.

'Seen the flowers?' June asked crossly.

'No.' Eve turned her head and saw a huge bouquet in the vase by her bed.

'They're from John. He says he'll be back tomorrow.' Eve was disappointed. She thought he'd've flown in the minute he'd heard he was a father.

'You mean, he isn't here?'

June shook her head. 'That's men for you! Always put business first.'

'I suppose so,' Eve said. Suddenly she was overcome by a tidal wave of weariness. 'Look, June, I'm really very tired now.'

'O.K. I can take a hint.' June started up from her chair. 'Ella sends her love. She says she'll be in tonight. She sent you some cologne to freshen up with.' June put the bottle on the table beside the flowers.

'Tell her I said thank you.'

'I will. Bye for now!' Then June was gone and the nurse was peering over Eve's bed.

'Can I get you a cup of tea, Mrs Ridley?'

'Oh yes!' Eve sighed with longing. 'And make it strong. Real English tea. Please!'

'Tell you what,' the nurse said, conspiratorially, 'I'll put in two tea-bags, just for you.' Then she disappeared. Eve wondered what time it was. Was it morning, or evening? She had no idea. But she was hurting. She knew that. Perhaps they'd bring her some painkillers with the tea. She hoped so. Webbed feet!

John finally came a couple of days later, and peeked at his sons in the little room alongside the ward. He laughed at the feet. But Eve didn't think it was funny.

'Just God's little joke,' the nurse'd said when she'd showed her. It only needed a minor operation to put it right, and otherwise the boys were fine, just fine! Eve was very lucky. She should be grateful. And she was. She stayed in the clinic over Christmas. It was restful. She needed it, and the babies did too.

'Tod and Peter had just as hard a time as you did,' the doctor explained. 'And we just want to run a few little tests on them.'

What tests? Eve wondered. They were supposed to be alright . . . apart from the feet. Eve sank back against her pillows, helplessly. They knew what they were doing. Better let them do it. What a funny Christmas this was! There were a few little presents for Eve to open on Christmas Day. The clinic gave them turkey and all the trimmings for dinner. They had crackers. They even had carols. And slowly the magic of Christmas got through to Eve. She told herself it was a good omen, to bring children into the world around Christmas time; the anniversary of the birth of Jesus. And somehow, thinking about that made her forget the webbed feet and everything, and just be glad. Then, on Christmas night, when they put the babies, one in each arm, Eve just lay there, feeling proud as Punch and full to overflowing with love. These were her very own children. She was the luckiest woman alive.

Vic'd seen the announcement in the paper, and sent a letter of congratulation. It unsettled Eve. It made her feel guilty for not having written to him. She loved Vic, in her way. Thinking about him brought tears to her eyes. She wanted him to come and see her babies. He'd be just like a real, doting grandfather, with his grey hairs and his warm touch. She missed him. He said he'd retired from business now. He'd bought a little log cabin somewhere, and was enjoying the fishing. It sounded nice. She hoped he was happy. She hoped he had enough money. But hope was all she could do. She wrote a note back to him, at his new address, congratulating him on his retirement, telling him about the babies. John would never know. Then, after she'd sent it, Eve started worrying. She'd promised herself, after they were married, not to do anything behind John's back. And now look what she'd done. She'd written to Vic, against his express instructions. On the other hand, she comforted herself that Vic'd said nothing about the F.B.I. in his letter to her, and she'd said nothing about the F.B.I. in her letter to him, and so, even if the letters were intercepted, they'd find nothing compromising in them. So, there was no real harm. Then, having satisfied herself on that score, she started thinking why it was she didn't trust John enough to tell him about the damned letter in the first place? A wife shouldn't have secrets from her husband. But then, John didn't tell *her* everything, did he? Not that she wanted him to. She'd be bored silly, if he droned on and on about all his business meetings and trips and projects of one sort or another. It was enough trying to keep up with his constant campaigning. The election was a long way off, but he never let up. He deserved to win. One day, John would be the President of the United States, she was sure of it. She'd be first lady, in designer suits and hats, her boys would play on the White House lawns and be photographed for *Time Magazine*. Well, you could dream, couldn't you?

Ray came in to see her. She was glad. He was young, full of fun news, and he brought a present of a lampshade for the nursery. It was shaped like a balloon, with a little basket hanging off the end of it.

'I got it last year at the Balloon Festival,' he said.

'Did you ever go up in a balloon?' Eve asked.

'Not yet. But I'm planning to, one day.'

'Sounds wonderful.' Eve projected herself mentally into a balloon, and soared over the mountains. It felt lovely.

'Maybe I'll take you!' Ray said.

Eve grinned. 'That'd be nice.'

Her next visitors were Lou and Ella. Lou soon got bored and wandered off round the clinic on the excuse they'd not brought Eve a present and he needed to find some candy. Ella was transported with delight over the babies. She hadn't heard about the webbed feet, and Eve was careful not to show them to her as she bent over the cot.

'They're asleep,' she warned, finger to lips. 'Better not move them, just now.' Ella understood and refrained, though her fingers itched to play with those little hands, and chuck the little chins.

'They look like John,' she said.

Eve laughed. 'I never heard such rubbish in my life. If they look like anyone at all, it's Old Jo!'

Ella had to laugh. She was right.

'The Hopis have a legend about twins,' Ella told her.

'I thought they might have,' Eve sighed.

'The Hero Twins are at the axes of the earth. It's they, holding on to the two poles, keeping the world rotating.'

'Well, they do a good job, Ella. Just so long, of course, as all these bombs don't throw us off beam!' Eve laughed a short, bitter laugh. The mushroom cloud had hung over her labour, and left its shadows in her mind. Grey shadows. Grey areas. She needed a joint. She shifted restlessly, feeling her stitches, and wincing.

'Perhaps your babies are a sign,' Ella nodded, like the all wise.

'They're a sign of double trouble!' the nurse said. She'd come to shoo Ella out. It was feeding time for the babies.

Eve loved feeding Tod and Peter. They soothed her, one at each nipple, the little gums working away, drawing the nourishment out of her. John'd wanted her to bottle-feed. He'd said breast feeding spoiled the shape of a woman's 'tits' and it would be a pity to spoil hers because they were so nice and girlish and small. But what were breasts for, if not for feeding babies? He had no answer to that so, for once, Eve had her own way, breast fed the twins, and enjoyed every minute of it. They were her world.

'My little ducks!' she murmured at them, after Ella'd gone, smiling and cooing, as they sucked and sucked her dry. She almost satisfied them and she was proud of that, for twins usually needed nourishment extra to what their mother could supply. The nurses were pleased. The doctor was pleased. Eve was pleased. Contentment prevailed. And then, Eve had to go home. It felt more like leaving home.

John moved into the spare room. He needed his sleep, working as hard as he did, and two babies took up so much time in the night, what with their feeds and their bawling. They exhausted Eve. She wished they could have Maria stay with them, but she had her own family to go home to, after all. Eve started to get thin and nervy. If only John would help. If only John would take some notice of her and the boys. But he was busy with the paper, and the campaigning and the business trips. She couldn't blame him for not helping. Not really. So, Eve worked hard at settling the boys down so that they slept through the night, and by the fourth month, she'd succeeded, and had her first full night's sleep. Then came the time for the operation on their feet and the short spell in hospital upset them. They came home restive, bawling again through the night, taking up all her time and attention. The house smelt of milk and wet nappies. It irritated John and Eve knew it. But what could she do? She consoled herself, wheeling the pram on long walks to the park, where she sat in a remote corner to smoke. She was becoming dependent on marijuana and she knew it. They said you couldn't get addicted, but she certainly missed it if she had to go without. Then she got so bad-tempered, even John noticed. And she did try to keep her husband sweet. One of the ways she tried was by doing her best to keep up with his election campaign. There was strong opposition to the incumbent city government as the city services creaked, groaned, and ground to a halt. They just weren't doing enough to accommodate the expanding population. But John was running on the 'United Albuquerque' ticket, that had promised to put everything right, and he was banking on winning. He put everything he had into it, and hadn't time or energy to spare for his family. Eve understood. It was the price she had to pay for being married to this charismatic man. She was proud of him. She would just have to bear up, knowing that, when the time came, she would enjoy the spoils and John would return to his former affectionate self.

In June, there was a lot of talk about returning prisoners of war. But the Korean prisoners released by the U.N. didn't seem to want to go back home. The North Koreans took exception to that, and there was no sign of American boys being released as a return gesture. There'd been no word of Jimmy. How long had he been prisoner? Eve couldn't take it in, really. It was beyond imagining what he must've gone through. John said they'd all been tortured, brain-washed, starved, and that the Geneva Convention had been totally ignored. And then, on the 27th July 1953, the cease-fire agreement was signed. It was to take effect at Midnight, and at midnight on the front, the soldiers of both sides lay in their dark trenches, wondering if the other side knew that they knew, they were supposed to stop fighting. A flare went up, then another, then another. They knew. It was over. At last, they could all go home.

When, finally, the camps were opened and the long lines of prisoners filtered back home, the sentimental hearts of the nation were opened to them. They were heroes. They were victims. They were good Americans. They tried to ignore those prisoners, who didn't want to come back to America, and stayed on, rebuilding North Korea. The poor things had been brainwashed, and the nation shouldn't let them dampen the welcoming spirits of the families awaiting the return of their valiant sons. The Ridley family waited, along with the rest, holding their breaths. Soon they'd know, was Jim alive or dead, or what? Then they heard he was on his way. Even John whooped with joy when the news came through. He wrote an article about it for the front page. After all, Jim was a symbol of what they'd all been fighting for, struggling for, believing in. He was America herself, tested, tried and proved true. The entire family, including Ernest and Clara, gathered at The Lawe Top to prepare a big celebration for the hero's return.

It was good fun, the whole family chipping in together. Eve, Ella, June and Clara cooked, while Lou and Jo looked after the ranch. Sam coloured in welcome home cards. With John's help, he made a 'WELCOME HOME JIMMY' banner, and then they set to blowing up the balloons. Eve loved to watch her husband with this little boy. He was so good with him! She could just see him, when the twins were older, the proud father, taking his boys to football, and everything. He'd be a wonderful father. Who'd have thought it?

Clara was very impressed. 'My, John's changed, Eve,' she said. 'And for the better! I take my hat off to you!'

Ernie, feeling redundant, wandered in and out of the kitchen, moaning, 'Nobody made such a fuss when *I* came home.'

But they all ignored him. He was just being Ernie, after all, and they needn't let it bother them. They were going to be all smiles when Jimmy came home. 'When he gets here, he'll want a ride round the place. See what we've been doing with the land!' (That was Ella.) 'When he gets here, we'll have to take him to the movies. He won't have seen one in ages.' (That was Eve.) 'When he gets here, he'll need a bath.' (That was June.) 'When he gets here, he'll need a new horse for checkin' them perimeter wires. They're in a pretty bad way.' (That was Lou.) 'When he gets here, I'll interview him for the paper.' (Guess who.) 'When he gets here, it'll be a lot easier on the ranch!' (That was Jo.) 'When he gets here, I think we should just sit him down quietly and sing him a hymn.' (That was Clara, of course.) 'When he gets here . . .' It was a phrase that opened most sentences. Every time they used it, they got a little bit more excited. And when, finally, the day of Jim's homecoming arrived, the Ridley family had never been more unified in its joy.

John and Eve, twins in arms, were sent to meet the returning hero at the airport. Jim looked thin, but bronzed and healthy. This was a surprise. They'd expected him to be pale and sickly. But, after all, looking healthy was something to be glad about, wasn't it? He greeted them distantly, looked in surprise at the babies, but asked no questions, then allowed himself to be led to John's car. Both John and Eve had been looking forward to having Jim to themselves on the drive back to Grants. But as soon as his behind hit the seat, Jim just closed his eyes, fore-stalling all conversation, and they were forced to drive to the ranch in respectful silence. They supposed Jim was very tired, and, for the first time, it occurred to them to wonder if the planned celebration wasn't going to be too much for him! Finally, the bumping on the road up to the ranch brought him round, and Jim opened his eyes. Eve turned to smile reassur-ingly. He didn't smile back. Her confidence was waning. And there they all were, standing in the yard, waiting for him. He seemed dazed by the reception. He didn't say anything about the banner. He just smiled faintly, rubbed Sam's head, and went in, to stand staring at the groaning table. In the silence that followed, they could hear the balloons, biffing against one another in the breeze from the doorway. Eve looked up at them fluttering on the ceiling. She wished she could hide them. They seemed so frivolously inappropriate. And then Lou spoke up awkwardly, a frog in his throat.

'Welcome home, son,' he said.

'Welcome home.' Clara kissed Jim on the cheek, like he was a visiting pontiff. For one awful moment, Eve thought she was going to genuflect.

'Welcome home, Jim.' June came forward and led him to his seat at the table. This was largely her offering. But he just stood

309

there, staring at the cakes and pies and jellies and all the other rich things they'd made for him.

'I can't eat any of this,' he said at last. 'Give me some plain rice, will you?' There was a stunned silence.

'Sure,' Eve said, covering the general embarrassment. 'His stomach's not used to rich food. We should have thought of that. I'll put some rice on.' Eve went to the larder to get started on it, but everyone else was staring at Jim. He was a Martian, unpredictable, dangerous. What would he do next? He eased himself round the table and went to sit in the chair by the fire.

'Commies gave you a bit of gyp, I suppose?' Old Jo's voice, sharp as a razor, cut the crap.

'Not really,' Jim replied. 'They treated us O.K.'

'Weren't you tortured?' Ernest asked.

'No.' Jim shrugged. Ernest's eyes were searching for the tattoos on Jim's arm, the bestial marks of pain in his face. There were none. The face was impassive.

'I suppose they tried to brain-wash you?' John asked warily.

'We had indoctrination classes,' Jim said. 'Reminded me of school, really. So long as you repeated what they'd said back to them, like a parrot, it was fine.'

'You mean, you had to chant Commie slogans?' Clara breathed.

'No. We didn't chant. We held discussion groups. You had to be careful what you said. That's all. What is this? The Inquisition?'

'Sorry, son.' Lou cleared his throat, and smiled expansively. 'I guess it's just that you knew what was happening to you, all the time, and we never did, and we'd like to share your experience with you.'

Jim snorted. 'You can never do that.' Then he saw the incomprehension and disappointment in their faces, and he was sorry for them. He sighed, and, making a great effort, looked straight at June. 'Is there a cup of coffee by any chance?' he asked.

'Sure.' June was pleased to have something practical to do. She poured him a cup, and they all watched as he put it to his lips. He sipped the coffee and picked the grounds from his teeth.

'Wonderful,' he said. 'I sure have missed the feel of those coffee grounds in my mouth, June.' The thin face cracked into a reassuring smile and they all laughed. Thank God, he was still their Jimmy underneath everything. The ice was broken.

'I suppose you'll be straining at the leash to get back in harness!' Old Jo rubbed his hands. 'It's going to be good to have a young man like you helping on the ranch again!' But Jim shook his head.

'I'm going to Yale,' he said. 'I'm going to study geology.'

The entire family gasped. Jo looked at Lou. Lou looked at Ella, Ella looked at Eve. Eve looked at June. No one said anything. Then, at last, John clapped his hands together, and made them all jump.

'Great idea!' he said.

'What do you mean, "great idea"?' Lou growled. 'What about the ranch?'

'The ranch is just what he's thinking of, isn't that right, Jim?' John asked. 'He's going to learn all about uranium and how to find it! And then we can all make our fortunes! Yes sirree!' John punched the air with his fist.

'No,' Jim said quietly. 'I'm not interested in mining. I'm interested in geothermal power. That's what I'm interested in.' John stared at him. Where'd the kid learned about that kind of stuff in North Korea? He grew suspicious.

'Sure you weren't brain-washed?' he asked.

'No. I wasn't brain-washed,' Jim answered. 'I've been interested in rocks a long time. I made my decision even before I went to Korea. But I had my twenty-first birthday there, and now I can tell you what I'm going to do.' He looked at each member of the family hanging on his words, as if life depended on it, then said, 'I'm going to renounce my claim to this ranch.' Eve drew in a long breath. So this was what he'd meant, that time by the corral. 'I've got my plans,' he'd said. He wouldn't tell her then. But now . . . 'I'm renouncing my inheritance, in favour of my step-brother, Sam here.' Jim nodded, smiling at the little boy. 'He's got Indian blood in him. He's attached to the land. Well, I love the land, but I'm not attached to it. I pulled out my roots long ago.' He picked some more grounds from his teeth. 'Can I have another coffee, June?'

June was hard pressed not to throw the stuff in his face. Was this what they'd slaved for, cleaning, baking, decorating and God knew what? She wanted to cry. Lou and Ella stood transfixed. Jo

311

was gaping, mouth hanging wide. Ernest and Clara had smug looks on their faces, as though they were just a little bit pleased. John was suspicious. And Eve smiled.

Driving back to Albuquerque in the car, John suddenly burst out laughing.

'The son of a bitch!' he yelled. The twins, asleep in the back, woke up and started crying.

'Who?' Eve asked anxiously. 'Jim?'

'Who else?' John snorted and shook his head, repeating, 'The son of a goddam bitch!'

'Don't be too hard on him,' she pleaded.

'Hard? I'm not being hard on him! John barked. 'I admire the bastard!'

'Oh. I see.' Eve was genuinely surprised.

'He's his own man. Doing what the hell he wants. He's lousing up *my* plans, but so what? You've got to hand it to him! He's the only one of them with any guts.' Eve nodded. She was smiling.

'I'm inclined to agree with you, John,' she said.

'The bastard!' John's hands were gripping the wheel hard, and he was grinning.

Before any of them had had time to get to know this new hard nut of a Jimmy Ridley, he'd gone. There were no goodbye celebrations. He just packed his bag, thumbed a lift and disappeared up the highway. There were a lot of unasked questions. They hung about the air of the ranch like ghosts. What had happened to him in the camp? Had he become a Commie spy? Were his natural emotions numbed by pain or something? Did he resent his own country for having sent him out there to fight and suffer? What had happened to that little Korean girl he'd thought so much about? Who was he anyway? Had they ever, any of them, ever really known Jimmy Ridley? Disconsolate, feeling somehow cheated, they picked up the threads of their lives. Clara and Ernie went back to 'Frisco, Jo and Lou got on with the work on the ranch. June cooked at the café in Grants, glad of the boom in uranium that brought in new customers. Eve got on with being a politician's wife.

She loved it. It was a whirl of social engagements, some of them fun. For John's sake, she kept up a good appearance, having her hair and nails done once, sometimes twice a week. Her wardrobe was bursting with dresses, suits, even a fur wrap. John was generous with his money. He wanted her to look nice. After all, she was an asset to his campaign. People liked her. They'd always said John Ridley was a good man, a charmer, he had brains, he had his feet on the ground and his finger on the city pulse, but he was cold. Eve made up for that. She was all woman, warm, healthy and natural as an apple growing on a tree. Being married to her proved he was alright. They made a good team. And when the twins were photographed on the front of a Santa Fe magazine, John's rating went up by six and a half per cent. John was over the moon.

'When we've sorted out the water shortage, honey,' he said to Eve. 'I'm going to build you a swimming pool in the back garden.'

Eve whooped with delight. Hollywood, eat your heart out. She had never been so happy in the whole of her life. She wrote to her mother, a eulogy on the subject of marriage, motherhood and moderate politics, dispelling the fears her mother'd expressed in her letter of congratulation. Life had never been better. Except for one thing. Eve's feet itched to dance. She had given up dancing, as a profession, on her marriage. It was part of the pact. But there was nothing to say she couldn't dance in a dance hall like everyone else, was there? With John, these days, all Eve ever got was a sedate shuffle round the floor, while the camera bulbs flashed. It was all very well but, sometimes, she would rather take the attention off her sparkling teeth and put it on her feet; let herself go, for once. Watching the kids rocking and rolling, while she and John sat smiling at the cameras in the ringside seats, the impulse to get up and join the youngsters became more than Eve could bear. Why, Ray was up and dancing with the best of them! There he was, throwing this girl around, like she was a drum majorette's baton. Of course, everyone thought they were marvellous. A space on the floor was cleared for them, and the other dancers stood back to watch while they showed off. Eve sighed. The girl wasn't very good; not really. Eve could do better, oldie or not. But, there she was, stuck on the sidelines, watching with the matrons. It was frustrating. It really was. The music ended. The band started in on the next piece, and the couples crowded back to the centre. Eve turned to John, to ask him if he'd care to get up and take a shuffle round the floor, but Sancho Mendez, from the opposition party, was creeping up on them. He had come to debate with John, and sitting by them, at their table, he put an end to all hopes of a good time. Eve was really fed up. Not only could she not dance, but she was going to be bored to death. Ray, coming back to the table, summed up the situation at once.

'Care to dance, Mrs Ridley?' he asked.

'Oh yes!' Eve replied enthusiastically. 'John . . .'

John frowned. He didn't like to be interrupted when he was scoring points.

'You don't mind if I dance with Ray, do you?'

John indicated that it was all the same to him, and, free as a bird, Eve skidded onto the floor with young Ray. It was a fast number. Ray started sedately, turning and twisting Eve like they were doing a Scottish reel. It was an unremarkable performance, which Eve found irritating. When was he going to get in the mood?

'You did better than this with her!' she complained in a loud whisper. Ray was puzzled. His eyes followed Eve's to the young girl, now sprawling in her chair and looking overheated. 'Come on,' Eve challenged him. 'Show me what you're really made of.' She did a triple spin, and sent the couple next to them flying.

'Have you been drinking, Mrs Ridley?' Ray asked anxiously. Eve pulled a face, and spun Ray round. It was enough. O.K. If that's how she wanted it, he would oblige. Then they started moving. The floor cleared as before. The band responded. It was getting hot out there. The cameras turned away from the debating candidates. John turned to see what was happening, and saw his wife's swirling skirt, as a camera flashed. There was nothing he could do, except look happy about it. He did his best. But, when Eve returned, sweating and happy, to her seat, he spoke to her through clenched teeth.

'Time we were going, honey,' he said. Eve was surprised. She opened her mouth to object, then saw the steel in her husband's eyes. She went cold. She picked her wrap off the back of her seat, and rose to go. The cameras flashed again.

'Come on, Mrs Ridley!' It was the reporter from the rival paper. 'Let's have some cheesecake. Huh?' John grabbed Eve's hand and steered her away from the table, and out of the club.

314

The valet brought the car, then, smiling and waving, they both got in, and John drove off.

Eve was quaking. John'd said nothing all the way home, but he'd skidded on his tyres, screeched round corners and pulled up so sharp in the driveway, she'd nearly gone through the windscreen. Now she sat where she was, staring ahead of her into the darkness, feeling a gaping hole inside her, and wondering how long it'd been there.

'Get out,' he snapped.

Eve got out, and hurried into the house before he could catch up with her. But he was quick. Soon as the door'd closed on them, he ran ahead of her, pushed her against the table, and smashed his hand across her face. Eve reeled back, falling painfully across the table edge. She could taste blood on her mouth.

'Slut!' he yelled.

The twins were howling in the nursery. Maria came out, white-faced, wondering what had happened. John saw her, dismissed her, and the maid, grabbing her chance, pulled on her coat and made for the door, with just one anxious glance back at her mistress. 'Don't you dare repeat what you've seen or heard in this house to anyone,' John warned. 'Hear me?' Maria nodded and the door closed behind her.

'I was only dancing,' Eve gasped, backing away from him.

'I saw your goddam suspenders!' John hissed. 'And tomorrow morning, the rest of Albuquerque's going to see them on the front page of the *Morning News*!'

'Oh no! I'm sorry. I didn't realize. Oh, John. I'm so sorry.' Eve started crying. It was obviously true. She *hadn't* realized.

'Silly bitch!'

'I'm sorry.'

'What do you think this is going to do to my campaign, huh?'

'I'm sorry.'

'I stand for decency in this town. Know that?'

'I'm sorry.'

'Stop saying you're sorry!'

Eve stared at him, eyes huge and dark, not knowing what else to say. Then, looking at him, so self-righteous standing there, while her cheek was hurting and her lips bleeding, she began to get angry.

315

'Anyway,' she said defiantly. 'It's not all my fault.'

'What the hell do you mean it's not your fault. Whose fault is it?'

'You wouldn't get up and dance with me.'

'Honey, I'm a damned cripple. And anyway, I was talking to Mendez!'

'You're always talking to somebody. Never to me.' John ran his fingers through his hair in a gesture of frustration. But Eve'd got the bit between her teeth. 'Sometimes I get the feeling I don't even exist. I might just as well be an android or something. After all, I'm only there to be photographed alongside of you, shake hands with the people you shake hands with, and make the kind of small talk you could programme a robot to do! But I'm real, John. I'm a woman. I need my husband. I need to be loved.' John stared at his wife, dumbfounded.

'I've given you everything,' he said. 'You've got kids, like you wanted. You've got clothes, jewellery, even a fur coat, for God's sake. What more do you want?'

'I know you're generous. But I need affection, John. I need you to talk to me sometimes, hold me in your arms, love me. Why, what kind of marriage is it? We don't even sleep in the same bed any more!'

'Oh, I see,' John said sarcastically. 'So suddenly we want sex, do we?' Eve looked away, embarrassed. 'So help me, you are about the most contrary dame I have ever come across!' He started stalking the room, from side to side, accompanied by the howling of the twins from the nursery. 'First you want it, then you don't. You know, Evie, the trouble with you is that you don't know what you *do* want!' Eve gaped. What kind of a Pandora's box had she opened up with her outburst? 'I play the gentleman for you and hold off, because I'm a considerate husband, and I know, you don't have to tell me, I know you want to be left alone. And I can understand that, while you're pregnant. After you've had a bad time giving birth and all. So I don't complain, though most men would.' He flung a glance at her. She was the picture of confusion. 'I mean, it's not as if you've actually encouraged me back into your bed, is it?'

'But, I thought , . . . I thought . . . .' Eve was floundering. Had he really been wanting her all this time, and held off because *she'd* been cold to *him*?

'You thought what? That I didn't have the normal feelings of any man? That I didn't want to make love to my own wife?' She stared back into his accusing eyes. 'Do you know how I've ached, these last months?' he asked. Eve shook her head. 'It's women like you encourage prostitution in this country,' he told her. Tears started in Eve's eyes. This was too much. 'Cold women.'

'I'm not cold,' she cried out.

'Prove it,' he said. He was waiting for her. Eve let down her shoulder straps and stood before him, naked. He smiled lightly, took her hand, and yanked her into the bedroom.

Next morning, as John had predicted, Eve was on the front page of the *News*. The caption read, 'Lifting the skirt of Decency!' Then came the write-up. 'And what do we find underneath? It is rumoured among the cognoscenti that Mrs John Ridley, wife of the Decency Candidate for United Albuquerque, has a drink problem. Did she have one over the eight last night at the Adobe Club? . . .'

It was a disaster. Eve wept over the breakfast table.

'What can I do to put it right, John?' she asked. John sighed, rocking back in his chair, sipping at his orange juice.

'Not much you can do. Let it blow over. Make sure it doesn't happen again,' he said. Then he looked at her, very hard. '*Had* you been drinking?'

'I haven't touched liquor since we were married, John. You know I haven't.'

'I don't know anything, honey. Do I?'

Eve felt very small, and extremely guilty. She looked at her husband, beseechingly.

'John, will you promise me you won't be angry?' she asked. He bit on the inside of his cheek, then nodded. 'I've not been drinking. 'Honestly,' Eve said quietly. 'But I have been doing something else.'

He waited while Eve swallowed hard, her heart thumping, as though it would break the walls of her chest. Then she said, 'I've been smoking marijuana.' Her ears blocked, so she couldn't hear. Her eyelids squeezed tight over her eyes, so she couldn't see. Any minute he'd hit her. Any minute she'd land on the floor. Seconds passed. She began to feel faint. She couldn't bear it any longer. She opened her eyes. John was still staring at her, a faint smile on his face. 'You're not angry?' she asked, amazed. He swung forward on his chair.

'Where did you get it?' Eve looked away. She hadn't bargained on him asking that. She couldn't tell on Ray. She shook her head. 'Ray?' John asked. He knew anyway.

Eve nodded. 'Don't be angry with him. It's my fault.'

There was a long pause. John was thinking. He started rolling his tongue round the inside of his mouth.

'I'm sorry, dear,' he said at last. 'He's got to go.'

'Go?' Eve was puzzled. 'Go where?'

'I've got to sack him, nincompoop!' he said. 'From the paper.'

Eve gasped. 'Oh no, John. Please don't do that. It wouldn't be fair. It wasn't his fault.'

'I've still got to sack him,' John said. Then he flung down his napkin, picked up his coat, and went into work.

Feeling like death, Eve struggled through the day. Maria, nervous and pale, was late arriving. She shook her head when she saw Eve's swollen lip.

'It's O.K.' Eve reassured her. 'I'm O.K. He's not angry any more.' Then Maria burst into tears and Eve had to comfort her.

'Remind me of my father,' Maria wailed. 'He was just the same!' Then Eve wanted to laugh. She didn't know why. She just wanted to. It was all so crazy. Only yesterday, everything had been fine, and today, the world had been turned on its head. As she listened to Maria weeping her way around the house with the duster, Eve lay on her bed, thinking. She must've been feeling dissatisfaction for some time, without knowing it. She had thought she was happy, and then, suddenly in the car, on the way home last night, she'd known she wasn't. Perhaps it'd all been for the best. Brought everything out into the open. There'd been so many misunderstandings. John'd thought . . . Eve sighed and looked over to his bed. Then she smiled, remembering the night before. He had been so passionate! She was an idiot. He was a good man. She was lucky to have him. But she was a liability. She daren't even go out because of what she'd done last night, everybody knowing, seeing her knickers on the front page of a rival newspaper! She wasn't worthy to be the wife of such a prominent man. And yet she was his wife. She'd borne his

318

children. She'd better pull up her socks and start coming up to the job!

Eve made John's favourite pasta meal that night. She plumped up cushions for him on the sofa, massaged his shoulders when he sat down against them, and brought him a drink. He loved it. So did she, in a way. She was dying to ask about Ray, but didn't dare. Then he went out, without her, to a meeting of the water conservancy committee, and she went to bed in her best night-dress, tried to wait for him, then fell asleep, exhausted by her own emotions. Next morning, feeling faintly disappointed, she was cooking John's French toast when he called her to come in and look at the paper. There she was, her photograph smiling from the front page. The caption read, 'Violator sacked!'

Eve sat in her chair with a thump and read on. John was clever. My God, was he clever!' She shook her head and looked at him with admiration. He grinned back. He'd made a public display of sacking Ray, accusing him of forcibly dragging his wife on to the dance floor and flinging her round with as much respect as you would show a dishcloth! It was typical of the disrespectful attitudes of the youth of today, and John Ridley, Decency Candidate, was not going to stand for it. This young man was going to be made an example of. Mrs Ridley was deeply dis-tressed, and bothered by a twisted ankle occasioned by the incident, was staying home to recover her health and her dignity, which had suffered greatly. The paper extended its sympathy to her. Eve laughed first, then looked sad after.

'What about poor Ray?' she asked.

'He deserves it. He's a drug peddler,' John pointed out.

Eve nodded slowly. It was true. She looked shame-faced at her husband.

'Do you know, dear,' she said quietly. 'For a while, I thought he was getting the stuff from you.' John roared with laughter and hit Eve lightly on the head with his paper.

The sensation soon passed over, and Eve's lip returned to its normal size, so that she was able to go out again and accept the commiserations of her peers. If anything, the incident had added to the reputation of this rising Albuquerque couple. John had capitalized on it perfectly. More and more, Eve was realizing she was married to a most enterprising and amazing man. Her cup ran over. Not literally, of course. She was still on the wagon, and now was having to do without her smokes. Jittery, feeling guilty about Ray, Eve sought release in charitable works among the poor Indian and Mexican population. One little boy she came across at the county hospital had sucked the poison of a rattlesnake from his mother's ankle and then fallen ill himself. This thin little waif was going blind, and his flesh, such as it was, had blossomed into huge blisters. The mother sat by the child's bed watching, miserably. Eve felt very small. Her boys were fine, healthy specimens. She had a lovely home, everything she wanted. And yet she'd got bored and wanted to show off in a night club and got somebody sacked. What the hell was she doing with her life? There was John working his butt off, trying to make the conditions of this town better. And there was she . . .

Every day her husband rose in Eve's estimation. But the little boy had done something to her. She started visiting him regularly. The blisters went septic after a while. Then they went gangrenous, and the surgeon had to slice bits off him. Eve helped nurse the kid, cleaning the sores, trying to smile and chat with him, to take his mind off his trouble, while the mother watched, letting the white lady do her work. Not that the boy joined in the conversation. He couldn't speak much English, but that wasn't the problem. He reminded Eve of Jimmy, come back from Korea. Suffering and sacrifice had lifted him to a different level somehow, out of the reach of someone like Eve. Then she felt a fool, chattering on, and she just sat by him and his mother till it was time to go. At home and out in the community, Eve began caring for, seeking out, the needs of others. John thought it was the raised skirt scandal that'd changed her, but it wasn't. Not really. It was the boy with the snake bite. After he'd died, she buckled down to some real hard work, sitting on committees, seeking out meritorious cases and fighting for them, but, most of all, supporting John's larger, civil struggles for the public good. Through him, Eve found a new and satisfying role in life. She thanked John for having led her to it. He was her idol.

So it was that as the year sped forward into 1954, Eve became increasingly involved in her committees and charitable activities. And she was to be seen, sitting on the platform, next to her husband, from factory, to university campus, to shopping precinct, to Indian village, to air base, wherever John could get an audience to listen to his speechifying. And he was good. He spoke mainly on services, and law and order. And law needed improving.

'Why, do you people know . . .' John paused and looked round the assembled technicians at the Sandia base, 'do you people know that, at the present rate of decline, by 1963 our police force will have dropped by a hundred and ten men?' He paused again. This audience was intelligent. It built bombs. It flew planes. It was a melting-pot of incomers from all parts of the U.S. 'Know how many men there are in the police force now?' John looked round the faces, his tongue rolling round the inside of his mouth. 'No?' There was an anticipatory guffaw from the back. 'Well, I'll tell you.' John conceded. 'There's just ninety-four.' The laughter rolled round the hanger. 'That's the kind of high security town you folks is living in,' he said, nodding and smiling. He let the tongues wag, murmuring against the City Government, then he shut them up again. 'Now you folks have got better things to do than worry about little things like sewers and water supplies and cops. I know that. I've been a pilot myself!' There was applause. 'Yes. I've been a pilot. That's how I got this leg of mine.' He slapped the crippled limb with the back of his hand. 'If it wasn't for this I'd still be going up there, punching a hole in the sky, chasing that goddam demon that lives up there . . . !' There was silence. He knew what he was talking about. He had them in the palm of his hand. His voice shook with emotion. 'There's times I'm mighty jealous of you folk. But I've got another sort of a job these days. It's not the sound barrier I've got to break down. Not now. It's the barrier of pig-headed resistance to progress!' His voice rose to a crescendo. He thumped his fist on the table in front of him. There was a sudden uproar of approval from the audience. But John topped them. 'It's the demon of self-satisfaction, in the face of poverty, suffering, delinquency, disease, and deprivation!' It was a near riot. John had manipulated their feelings, their thoughts, moulding them into one, and they were all for him. 'Are you people going to help me punch a hole in the present City Government?'

'Yes!' They all yelled back at him. Eve rose with the rest of them, clapping, smiling, tears rolling down her cheeks. John nodded and smiled in her direction. She shook her head in wonder as she walked towards him, put her arm through his and smiled for the cameras.

'I love you, John,' she whispered, still smiling out front.

'I know,' he said, patting her hand.

Then they both waved and took off in the car for the next assignment.

When the news came of Vic's death, John was very kind. He said Eve should go to the funeral, which was to be in San Diego, since that was where Vic's ex-wife and their children now lived. But Mrs Flamm wired her there was no point. Vic was Jewish. Women weren't allowed at the ceremony, and Eve didn't know the family anyway. So Eve had to be content with sending flowers. It wasn't enough. She felt she'd been left hanging in mid-air, incomplete. The day of the funeral, she left Maria in charge of the twins and took off in the car, driving north of the city up to Coronado. It was early spring. The leaves were sprouting on the trees, and the Rio Grande was full of water from melting snow in the mountains. She parked the car, and walked up to the ruins of the old Indian village. It was a nice place. Eve could see why the ancient Indians had wanted to live there. She pottered round the ruins, sticking to the paths for fear of snakes, and came to the Great Kiva at the far edge of the village. She'd never been in a Kiva before, though she'd heard Jim speak about them when he was small. Usually they were closed to tourists. But this one was no longer in use. She climbed the steps to the roof, and looked down the hole into the cavern below. She couldn't see much. She was standing in her own light. So, she decided to make the descent, by the rickety old ladder that'd been placed there.

When she got to the bottom, she was surprised to find how clean and light it was inside. The adobe walls were covered in paintings; bright yellow, black and white the figures, birds, signs and symbols; rust-red the tips of their weapons, their hands, and ornaments. Then, as she followed the pictures round the walls, Eve began to realize that they told a story. What it was, she couldn't guess. Jimmy could have told her. Perhaps even John. After all, he was supposed to be a sort of Indian brave! She made out a snake, lightning, water pouring on to the earth, a tree taking root. But one figure, faint, as though washed by time, drew her attention more than all the rest. She squinted at it, trying to make out what it was. It seemed to have wings. Or was it a cloak? She sat down on the little seat that ran round the wall, and stared at it for a while. She tried to imagine what it was like down there at night, the fire blazing, priests chanting. The Indians didn't allow the women in on their ceremonies any more than the Jews! Why was it women were always left out? It wasn't fair. Eve began to cry, sitting there; all on her own since it was long before the tourist season began. She needed to go to Vic's funeral. She needed to make it up to him for the neglect of the years since her marriage. She needed to show him she loved him. Somehow, she felt she'd lost out on a very important relationship, and now, sitting on this ledge, staring at a picture she couldn't make out, she felt unfulfilled. She sighed, got up, and climbed the ladder out of the Kiva into the sunshine. She stood there, some time, looking round the empty spaces, then made her way to the little hut where she hoped to find the john. She found it. She also discovered a museum in the making. In the shop, they had a book with photographs of some of the paintings inside. She flipped through it. It was nice. So she paid the monosyllabic desk clerk for it, and wandered out, down the path to the Rio Grande.

The view caught her breath. The river was gold in the light, so wide across, and the sky above so vast. Clouds gathered over the mountain head on the other side of the water; trees clustered on the river banks; scrub grew all around, like stubble on the chin of an unshaven man. It was beautiful; unbearably real. She had a sense of the aeons of time that had passed since the first Indians had made their homes on these banks. And this was supposed to be a new country? It didn't make sense. The newness had merely been grafted on the old and taken root, but not taken over, or fused with it. The old and new existed side by side, unaware of one another, like layers in a time warp. It was disorientating. It made her head buzz. She needed to sit down. Someone had thoughtfully provided a seat in the best vantage-point so Eve went to sit on it, staring over the flowing water. The wind lifted the pages of the book in her hands. She glanced down and saw the pale outlines of the painting she had seen in the Kiva. It had a caption underneath. It said, 'The Sun Father, wrapped in the robe of Mother Earth.' Eve's mouth twisted into a smile. The Sun Father. 'Our Father, who art in heaven . . . ' It always seemed to come down to that. She rose and looked at the golden water. Then she bent, picked up a handful of clay, and flung it hard. It fell, scattering, in the air, smattering the smooth surface of the river. Eve watched the rings pulsing strongly from the centres, growing weaker, then dying, and the river smoothing over the event, till it was as though it had never been.

Then she turned and went back to Albuquerque.

It had occurred to her earlier to question how Vic had died. But it was hardly the thing to ask the divorced widow, and there was no one else she could ask. Vic hadn't been so old. He was in his late fifties, that was all. But after the goodbye at the river, Eve had lain awake, wondering. She hoped he hadn't suffered. She hoped he hadn't been murdered. She hoped it didn't have anything to do with the F.B.I., or Communists, or gangsters or anything awful that human agents might have saved him from. Could John find out? No. Of course not. She wouldn't ask him. What was the point? Vic Flamm was dead. John was in the middle of an election. You have to get your priorities right. She flung herself into the last weeks of the campaign. And on April 6th, the Citizens Committee swept into office, taking John and a good many of the United Albuquerque candidates with them.

Everyone was delirious with joy. Good times were-a-coming! Eve felt so proud, as she watched her husband taking on the reins of responsibility in the city. Even the new Mayor was impressed.

'Your husband's made of the right stuff, Mrs Ridley,' he said. 'What's more, he's honest. And that's a rare commodity in these days.' Eve beamed with pleasure. She loved to hear her husband praised. It was her reward for loving him.

'He's a very caring man,' she told the Mayor confidentially. 'You know his voters come from all walks of life. Indians, Hispanics, Chicos, whites, but especially from among the younger folk. And it's the young people we have to look to for the future.'

'It sure is, Mrs Ridley,' the new Mayor agreed. 'We got to mould them into shape now! Education, law and order, welfare, we've got to get those things moved into the twentieth century in this town!' Eve nodded enthusiastically.

'The poorer sections of the community need more schools, Mr

324

Mayor,' she said. 'Are you going to do anything about that?'

The Mayor scratched his head. 'Trouble is, Mrs Ridley, it all takes money. Now if you had any ideas about how to raise any . . . ?'

Eve brooded on the subject for some time. Then she rounded up the wives of the elected representatives, and suggested they start a charity aimed at Pueblo children's welfare. The idea was well received, and Eve found herself at the head of a thriving, well-supported little organization that was able to influence city government through the husbands, influence the townspeople through the papers, and which began to spread rapidly, beyond the confines of Albuquerque. June and Ella each ran a weekly charity stall in Grants and Gallup respectively. And in 'Frisco, Clara started up a whole new group centred on the Church. The idea was taking off like a rocket. It took a lot of Eve's attention. John was now so busy, what with being on City Government, running a paper, and keeping up with his business ventures, that the two of them only seemed to talk on holidays. But they got along fine. After all, they were both working for the same thing, the Universal Good.

Three years into John's period of office, the Pueblo Children's Charity had become a major organization, recognized in five States. Eve was at the head of it, but it was taking its toll of her. The twins were now five, and full of beans. Maria couldn't be there all the time, and anyway, Eve wanted to give them more time herself, so she resigned from her position as secretary/chairman, and agreed simply to help with fund raising. Things weren't easy in that department. John was sympathetic.

'It's amazing, honey,' he sighed, 'in this wealthy country of ours, there just doesn't seem to be enough to go round.'

Eve shook her head. 'People are getting tired of charity stalls and coffee mornings and the like. They want something new. Something that fires their imagination. Know what I mean?' John nodded. 'Have you got any ideas, baby?'

John thought for a while. 'You need to cash in on something that's going on already,' he said. 'Something colourful, exciting, like a festival, and then talk the people that run it into letting you take part. Do a stunt or something.'

'O.K. So, what's going on this summer?' Eve asked.

'Well, there's the Balloon Festival. That's being held in Albuquerque this year!' Eve drew in a sharp breath. A Balloon Festival! Why, that would be marvellous!

'We could have a Pueblo Children's Balloon!' she cried. What an advertisement! Know who I can talk to about it?'

John smiled. 'Remember Ray?'

Eve frowned, then her jaw dropped.

'You mean, Ray, who got sacked?' she asked.

John nodded. 'Yeah. That's him. He's a big shot in the balloon business these days. He wouldn't miss a thing like that.'

'Where is he?'

'Based in 'Frisco. Why don't you let me talk to him?'

A suspicious thought crept into Eve's mind. It was strange how John knew about Ray, as though they'd stayed in contact. After all, what reason was there for John to see him? Business? Not the newspaper business, not any more. That only left . . . ' marijuana. Eve knew if she didn't utter this thought, if she let it lie there and fester, it would grow into a monster and eat her up. So she voiced it, then and there. 'How do you know where Ray is, John?'

'Why, honey, you don't think I'd just sack the poor schmuck and leave him to rot, do you? The whole thing was just a cover-up for *your* mistake. Now wasn't it?'

Eve nodded. She felt ashamed, not only for what had happened to Ray, but for her own suspicious mind. How could she doubt John?

'I see,' she said. 'So you've been watching over him, like a sort of godfather, have you?'

'Yeah. Something like that.' John smiled in agreement. 'I put up the capital for him to get started in the balloon business, and now he's doing well. He's got balloons up there doing all sorts of things; taking photographs for postcards, weather shots, experiments for the university, not to mention the way the whole thing's taken off as a sport. Folk love it. And I don't blame them.'

'Mmmm . . . ' Eve's eyes grew misty. 'It must be lovely up there, in the silence, above all your problems . . . '

'You could go up yourself. Take the kids,' John said. 'Do it as a stunt!' Eve leapt at the idea. It was wonderful! She kissed John

326

on the cheek and dashed off to tell the rest of the girls on the committee.

Tod and Peter were agog at the idea. Eve spent some time showing them pictures of balloons. She told them the history, of how some men had flown long distances in them, and how they worked, and everything.

'And are you going to go up with us, Mummy?' Tod asked. Eve nodded and hugged him close.

'It's going to be such fun,' she said.

'Better than learning to swim?' Peter asked uneasily, glancing at the pool out the back of the house. Eve laughed.

'Well, honey,' she said, 'it isn't at all the same sort of thing. I mean, you're not a bird. So nobody expects you to flap your arms about and learn to fly like one.'

'I'm not a fish, either,' Peter said, reasonably. Tod laughed at him. Tod was quite at ease in the water.

'Well it's just different,' Eve insisted. 'You stand or sit or something in a little basket, like that, look.' She pointed up at the lampshade in their room. Tod and Peter stared at it. 'And then a man on the ground lets go the rope, and you pull this pulley and a flame comes out to heat up the gas in the balloon, so it gets lighter, and you just gently float off into the sky.'

'Oooh!' Tod breathed. 'When can we go up in one?' he asked.

Eve laughed. 'In October. They're having the festival at the beginning of the month. Let's hope it keeps fine for us.'

'It's alright, Mom,' Tod reassured her. 'It never rains till November.'

October 4th dawned fair. There was a slight breeze, just right for ballooning. They had a light breakfast, listening to the news. The Russians had put a Sputnik into space!

'What's a Sputnik?' Tod asked.

'Oh, it's something in the sky that sends messages back to earth.'

'A flying saucer?' Peter's eyes were as round as one.

'No!' Eve laughed. 'Hurry up now. We'll be late!' She hustled the boys into their coats. It was going to be cold up there in the sky.

Eve had arranged to meet Ray at the festival ground but that was easier said than done. There were thousands of people there. She parked the car, and with Maria, set off across the wasteland towards the balloon site. Peter was crying. The whole thing scared him. There were so many people, crowds and crowds of them, all excited and yelling and pointing. Eve wished John could've come with them to help. It would have been good publicity for him too when all was said and done. But he'd been called to 'Frisco on business. 'If I don't keep my thumb in them pies, I won't be able to pull out any more plums, honey,' he'd said. She couldn't complain. She got her share of the plums and the boys wanted for nothing. So she let him go with a kiss and a sigh, and got on with it, as usual. But where on earth was Ray? It occurred to her to wonder if she would recognize him after all this time. After all, he might have grown a beard, or got fat, or something.

Someone let a balloon go early, for a joke. It had the word 'Sputnik' painted on the side. Everyone stared up at it, laughing, getting the joke, as it drifted, huge as a whale above ground level, floating across the heads of the crowd, ducking automatically.

'It's a lot bigger than our lampshade,' Peter objected.

Maria and Eve laughed. 'Of course it is, honey,' Eve said. 'How else would we all get into it?' Peter was staring up, head bent right back. Suddenly he swayed and tottered. Maria caught him as he fell. He was out for the count. Eve loosened his collar, and felt his forehead anxiously.

'He feels O.K.,' she said, puzzled. He opened his eyes, and looked at her blankly, then he shook himself and smiled. 'Are you alright, Pete?' Eve asked.

'He's just scared,' Maria said. 'Poor little child. He doesn't want to go up in the balloon. And I don't blame him.'

Eve sighed. 'If John was here he'd make him. But I don't know. We'll none of us go up in a balloon if we don't find Ray soon.'

Then Tod shouted out loudly, 'Look! Mummy! There's a balloon with a huge teddy bear on it!'

Eve followed the line of his finger. Sure enough, there it was, and when it turned in the breeze, they saw the lettering on the side. It said 'Children's Charity'.

'Come on!' Eve yelled. They all ran, scrambling through the

crowds and ropes and vehicles that were scattered across the site, and arrived panting, to see Ray wrestling with the rope, to the entertainment of several ladies from the committee.

'Hi!' Eve yelled.

He looked up sharply, saw her and smiled, pointing at the balloon. 'Like it?' he asked.

'Yes! It's marvellous!'

'Only thing is, I don't know how you're going to make money!'

Eve laughed. 'It's easy. Isn't it, ladies?' The ladies nodded their agreement. 'We just get people to sponsor us. That's all. Fifty cents a mile. The farther we go, the more money we get for the "Pueblo Children".'

'Great,' Ray said. 'Come on then. Who's going?' The other ladies shrank back, giggling. Maria shook her head and Peter hid behind her skirt. But Tod and Eve were willing.

'Is it a good idea to take a child up, do you think?' one of the ladies asked. Tod looked crestfallen.

'It's a children's charity,' Eve pointed out. 'Seems to me it's the only thing to do.' Everyone saw the sense of this, and Tod was a well-behaved little boy, so in they got, mother and son, full of excitement, tying their safety ropes round their waists, and waving as the journalists flashed their cameras. They were going to make a fortune for the charity and enjoy themselves enormously at the same time.

At last the moment of release arrived. Eve felt giddy with excitement as Ray got in the basket beside them, pulled on the lever and the flame flared under the balloon.

'Let go the cable!' Ray called. The ladies let it go, and for a second, the balloon hovered, inches from the ground. Then, as Peter looked up, his little face so serious that Eve had to laugh at him, the thing took off, and they were truly airborne. Tod yelped with delight, and threw his little hat in the air. It wafted towards the ground, and, looking down, they both saw Peter run out and catch it and wave back at them, holding it in his hand.

'I wish he'd've come,' said Tod.

'Yes. It's a pity he didn't,' Eve agreed.

'He's a scaredy cat,' Tod said.

'Not necessarily.' Eve smiled. 'It takes all sorts you know, honey.'

'Huh!' said Tod, manfully. Ray and Eve smiled at one another.

'Been a long time, Mrs Ridley,' Ray said, lighting a roll-up.

'Sure has,' Eve agreed. Then she pulled a wry face. 'I'm really sorry about what happened.'

'Don't be,' Ray assured her. 'I've done O.K. for myself. Might never have got into ballooning, if it wasn't for you.'

'I didn't have anything to do with that,' Eve said.

'No? Well, in a way you did. I was sacked from the paper because of you. Had to do something else. Making money and ballooning were about the only two things I was interested in, so . . . Your husband set me up. In more ways than one.' He laughed ironically. 'No, I'm grateful to you. I am really.' Eve shook her head and smiled.

'Life!' she said.

'Yeah. Here's to it!' Ray raised his roll-up and took a drag. 'Want one?' he asked, holding the end out to Eve. Eve hesitated. 'Just to show there's no ill feelings?'

'O.K. Just to show there's no ill feelings.' Eve took the roll-up, put it in her mouth and breathed deeply. It was wonderful.

'Here's to the first American Sputnik!' Ray said, taking the roll-up back and inhaling on it.

'Here, here!' Eve agreed. 'How come them Russians've got ahead of us?'

'Important thing,' Ray said. 'Important thing's to get a man up there!' Eve's head was back. She was looking up into space, floating like a bird. You could see the pale outline of the moon at the farthest end of the sky.

'Do you think anyone will ever fly to the moon, Momma?' Tod asked, following her sightline.

'Who knows, honey. But if they do, I sure hope he'll be an American. We don't want to have to look at a Russian moon up there, nights, do we?' Tod shook his head and looked down at the earth below.

'Momma, you can see our shadow on the ground. Look! Do look!'

'Not now, honey.' Eve sighed lazily. 'Momma's having a little rest.' Her eyes were closed. She was enjoying the sensation of the basket, swinging in the sky, so free and easy. Blissful.

Suddenly there was a yell. Eve opened her eyes to see Ray throw himself across the basket towards Tod. The basket swayed dangerously. Eve screamed. Tod seemed to be asleep. Eve grabbed onto his rope, but it came away in her hand. What had happened to it? He did nothing to save himself. He just slopped over the side of the basket, like tea out of a spilled cup. And Eve stood, her mouth open in a silent scream, watching him drift, drift, slowly down to earth.

CHAPTER SIXTEEN

The car was careering wildly across the road. In the back, Maria was holding tightly on to Peter. He was crying. His Mom'd gone crazy. She was at the wheel, and she was screaming at Ray, 'You didn't tie the rope right. It's your fault. You didn't tie the rope right.'

'What about you? Kid's Mom smoking on the job? That doesn't look very nice,' Ray yelled back.

'Ballooning's not my job. It's yours. It's your fault. You killed my little boy!' As Eve wailed, the car jolted off the road and onto the verge.

'Give me the car keys!' Ray yelled back. 'You're a crazy woman.'

'Yes. I am crazy. I must be crazy. I took my kid ballooning with a drug fiend.'

'Oh shut up!' They wrestled for the wheel. Eve put her foot down.

'You killed my little boy!' she screamed. Peter howled. Then Eve remembered he was in the back of the car and stopped yelling. But the yelling was a release, and when she stopped doing it, she started shaking instead.

The police took Tod back to the house in Albuquerque. They laid him out in the dining room. But Eve picked up the body and hugged it close. This was Tod, her son. She loved him. They tried to take him from her, but she wouldn't let them.

'Has anybody told Mr Ridley?' Maria whispered. Eve heard.

'Where's John? Where's my husband?' she yelled at the policeman.

'We've been trying to locate him, ma'am, but I'm afraid we've not had any luck. Not yet, anyway.'

'Tod needs him. You've got to find him.'

'We'll do our best, ma'am. Now don't you think your little boy could do with a rest? Why don't you put him down now.' Eve complied. She put the body back on the table and everyone breathed a sigh of relief.

'I love him,' she cried. 'I do. Honestly.' Then she thought of the other son. 'Where's Peter?' she asked.

'He's with the neighbour,' Maria assured her. She tried to persuade Eve to drink some herb tea, but she wouldn't. All she could think of was finding John. He'd know what to do. Ray was in police custody, being questioned. He'd killed her son.

She turned to the wall, crying out, 'Murderer!' and saw her own shadow there. She stopped crying and stared at it. Her hands reached out and touched it. 'Murderer,' she murmured.

'Who? Who's a murderer, Mrs Ridley?' the policeman asked.

Eve shook her head. 'It was an accident. Maybe Ray should've tied the rope better. I don't know. It's not my job. Maybe Tod was naughty and loosened it. He wanted to look out the top of the basket . . . I've got to go and find my husband.'

'You've got to have some rest,' Maria told her.

'Didn't the doc give her anything?' the policeman murmured.

'She wouldn't let him.'

And then Lou and Ella turned up. They came in, pale and shocked, not knowing what to do. Then they saw Tod on the table. Ella cried out and went to him, touching the cold face, the bloody head. Lou just stood there, staring at Eve.

'Don't look at me like that!' she yelled. 'It's not my fault.' Ella looked back from the boy to the mother.

'You can't stay here,' she said. 'Come back to the ranch with us. We'll look after you and Peter. We'll make the arrangements and everything.'

Eve fell into her arms. Here was comfort at last. The policeman laboriously wrote down the address.

'We got to know where you are, Mrs Ridley,' he said.

Eve didn't want to leave Tod, not even for a while. But Maria said she'd stay till Lou came back for him. Eve didn't like it. She had a fancy she might never see him again. Then Peter, back from the neighbour's, put his hand in hers. She felt the cool little fingers, wrapping round her own, and turned to look, confused, at her other son. He was so like Tod. He wasn't crying now. He was holding Tod's hat in his hand and Eve wondered, idly, how he'd come across it.

'Hallo, Mom,' he said.

'Hallo, Peter,' she answered.

'Don't worry, Mom. Tod wouldn't have felt a thing.'

Eve was about to ask 'How the hell would you know?' when she remembered Peter was just a little boy and doing his best. She bent to fold him in her arms, picking him up, perching him on her hip, and cuddling him, as they went out to the van and crowded inside.

'Are we going to the ranch?' Peter asked. Eve nodded. 'Will I be able to ride on White Cloud?'

'Maybe,' she said, tight lipped. She held her son close. This one wasn't getting away. She loved him. He tried to wipe the tears from her cheek, but there were too many. So in the end, he gave up, and just lay back against her, a warm, comforting presence.

Eve hadn't been to the ranch in ages. The uranium boom had brought a lot of traffic to Grants. Passing through slowed them down and when they reached the turning to Ambrosia, Eve barely recognized it. Where sage and rabbit brush had been the only vegetation, there now sprouted a plethora of road signs. They were in all shapes and sizes, and bore numerous announcements in ever bigger letters, as though they were trying to top each other. As the van stopped to let a wagon pass, Eve read them in amazement. 'Atomic Uranium Inc.'; 'Lisbon Uranium Corporation'; 'Muddy River Uranium'; 'Big Indian Uranium Corporation'; 'Continental Uranium Company'; 'Utek Exploration Co': 'La Sal Mining & Dev.'; and so on and on. Eve felt as though, like Alice, she'd gone through the looking-glass, and found herself in an alien landscape. Then the van squeezed through, past the wagon, and they started bumping up the little road. Eve stared at the drilling platforms, the washers, the lorries everywhere. The landscape was littered with them. But not at The Lawe Top. Nothing had changed there. They rattled into the yard, and June came out to meet them, wiping her hands on her apron. Her face was white. Soon as the van door opened, Peter was out and looking for White Cloud. Eve couldn't understand it. The child hardly seemed touched by the event. She allowed Ella to support her into the house, where she sat and took the coffee June offered her. Lou had gone back to Albuquerque to pick up Maria and the dead child.

But when he got there, Lou found the child had gone. It seemed a mistake had been made. Tod's body couldn't be released for burial. Not yet. There had to be an inquest and that meant there had to be an autopsy too. This was too much. Lou brought Maria back, and tried to explain it to Eve. She couldn't take it in. She just stared and stared in the silent kitchen. Then she started murmuring, nodding to herself.

'I knew it. I knew they wouldn't let me see him again. I knew they wouldn't.' Then the movement of her head changed, and she was shaking it, from side to side. They could hear Peter, out in the yard, talking to Sam. His voice was very matter-of-fact.

'I saw him, dropping out of the sky like a dead bird. That's how we knew where he landed. I knew it was Tod. I've got his hat. I always wanted it. Do you like it?'

They heard Sam's answering murmur of approval. Was this real? Was Eve going to wake up and realize she'd dreamt the whole thing?

'I want my husband,' she said flatly. 'I want John. I've got to find him.'

'The police are looking for him, honey,' June explained kindly.

Jo, looking very old and shaken, whispered, 'Has anyone told Clara?'

'Yes, Clara knows,' Lou replied. 'But Ernie's away doing his lay preaching. No one's told him yet.'

'Maybe Clara knows where John is,' Eve said loudly. Then she started getting her things together.

'What the hell are you doing, Eve?' Lou asked. He tried to stop

335

her, holding onto her arms. But she wrestled with him, and he had to let her go.

'I've got to find my husband,' Eve shouted.

'Better let her go.' It was Jo. 'She's better out of this for a while. Let her go and stay with Clara.' Silence hung in the air. Then Eve, busy as a bee, started organizing.

'I'll leave Peter here with you, Ella,' she said. 'Sam'll be good company for him. Take his mind off things. Maria'll help you, won't you, Maria?' Maria nodded enthusiastically, but she was worried about Mrs Ridley.

'You can't go on your own,' June pointed out.

'Why not?'

No one dared tell her, she was hardly in a fit state, out of her mind with grief or God knew what.

'Let her go.' It was Jo again. 'Clara can meet her at the airport.' He nodded slowly. 'We'll have to tell the police, of course.'

'I'll tell the police,' Lou said. 'After all, she's only going to find her husband. They're not going to object.'

Within three hours, Eve was looking out of the window at the shadows the plane made on the clouds.

'Momma, you can see our shadow on the ground. Look, do look!' She'd hear his voice calling to her for the rest of her days. She wept, her tears streaking the glass as she rolled her face against the window. The hostess was very nice. She sat beside her for a while, holding her hand. Then, when they got to Phoenix, they piled her into the next plane, and she went up again, arriving late in San Francisco to be met by Clara and Ernie, who had finally turned up.

'They found you,' Eve said to him.

'Looks like it,' Ernie said. 'We got the whole police department out looking for John.' They got in the car and Ernie drove into town.

'How did it happen?' Clara wailed.

'Don't start, honey,' Ernie commanded.

'I hear there's going to be a race to the moon,' Eve remarked brightly. Ernie and Clara looked at her. 'The Sputnik, you know.'

'We know,' Ernie said. He glanced at his wife. They might've warned them Eve was this bad. There were two hot spots on her cheeks.

336

'My dear,' Clara was using her sacred voice, 'Tod is in better hands than ours now. I know it's hard. But you have to learn to give him up to God's care.'

'Shut up,' Ernie said.

'I'm trying to comfort her, Ernie,' Clara warned.

'Do you think religion can give her comfort at a time like this?'

'Some lay preacher you are, Ernest Trevor,' Clara sniffed. 'I can't imagine what people would think if they heard you now, after all that spouting you do on the subject of surrendering to God's will and all.'

'She doesn't want to hear about God's will,' Ernie said bitterly. 'If there is a God.'

'What did you say?' Clara lashed the words at him.

'You heard.'

'Hypocrite!'

'I'm not the hypocrite of this family!' Ernie sniped. 'I never said I believed in God.'

'And you dare to stand in front of a church full of people in front of the priest and all, and preach? You'll burn in hell, Ernie Trevor!'

'Shut up.'

Eve, forgotten in the back seat, was happy to let them squabble. When they were squabbling they were leaving her alone. Thank God. (If there was a God.)

'Oh dear. Eve, I'm sorry. Please forgive us.' Clara had tears in her eyes. Her embarrassment at rowing in front of Eve was greater than her grief at her husband's declared atheism. 'I never even asked how the fund-raising went. Did the Children's Charity make a lot of money?' Eve thought she was going to be sick. Ernie looked at Clara as though he was going to kill her. She realized what she'd said, overcame her confusion, and smiled a hostess smile. 'I've given you your old room, dear,' she said.

This was not real. None of this was real. It couldn't possibly be real. Eve tossed on her bed. The sedatives weren't working. It was 3 a.m. She was dreaming she was awake. Any minute, she'd really wake, and everything would be alright. And yet there was a terrifying feeling of reality about what was happening to her. She put on her bedside light, and jumped at the shadow her arm made across the opposite wall.

'Momma, you can see our shadow on the ground. Look, do look!'

She had to find John. He would help her. Somehow, he would help her. She got up, dressed and went into the kitchen. Ernie was already in there, making coffee.

'Want some?' he asked. Eve nodded.

'Couldn't you sleep either?' she asked. Ernie shook his head.

'I hardly ever sleep these days,' he said. He passed her a cup and she drank. It gave her strength. At least the coffee was real.

'Is it true, you don't believe in God, Ernie?' she asked.

Ernie sighed, fingered the handle of his cup and said, 'I don't know. I keep hoping I will, one day. I used to. But . . . I seen such things. I don't know.'

'Why do you preach?'

'I don't know . . . I really don't know. I wish I did believe in God.' Eve said nothing. 'Do *you* believe in God?'

'I don't know,' Eve answered.

'There you are then.' For Ernie, it summed the whole thing up. 'Sorry about the kid,' he said. Eve choked. He patted her on the back and poured her more coffee. 'We're all victims, Evie. You and me, like all the rest of them. Sometimes I dream I'm a prisoner in one of them concentration camps. Did I ever tell you that?' Eve nodded. 'That's why I don't sleep.' He sighed again, then looked at her, his eyes sharp as needles. 'See, in this life, honey, either you're going to be the victim or you're going to be the other one. The aggressor. You've got to choose which side you're on.'

'That's a terrible philosophy.' Eve was sorry for the poor, tormented bastard. She took his hand. 'No one's ever understood what you went through, Ernie, have they?'

'And you think you do?' Ernie spoke resentfully.

'Not exactly.' Eve withdrew her hand. He was squeezing it too hard.

'I think I know where John is,' Ernie said suddenly. He was staring at her, with unblinking eyes.

Eve stared back. Then, clearing her throat, she asked, 'Where?'

'On a houseboat in Sausalito.' Eve thought she was going to faint. Only one person she knew lived on a houseboat in Sausalito. Ken Houlihan. She stared at Ernie. A grim smile stretched his lips, which were pale and thin.

'What's he doing with Ken Houlihan?' she asked quietly.

'In business together, I reckon,' Ernie said. 'Import–Export. Didn't like to tell the police. Wouldn't've done John any good if they'd seen him there. Might even've found evidence.'

'What sort of evidence?' Eve asked. 'What's going on? You've got to tell me, Ernie. I need to know.'

'Narcotics, I suppose,' he said lightly. 'I should think that houseboat's a busy little factory, making all sorts of goodies.'

'I don't believe you,' Eve said at last.

'See for yourself.' Ernie put his hand in his pocket, and pulled out the car keys. 'Here.' He handed them to her. She took them, put on her coat and left the house.

It was nearing dawn as Eve approached the quay where the artist community lived. She left the car on the street, and walked along the line of houseboats, looking for Houlihan's. And then she saw it. She knew it was his, by the photographs hanging out on the line to dry overnight. Other people had socks and underpants hanging up, but not Ken. The sun was rising now over the hills. She looked back at it. It just went on rising, day after day, without a thought for what went on on the earth, shining its rays on good and bad alike. She hesitated, jangling the keys in her pocket. Everything was so still, so silent in the early morning. Now and then a bird swept across the surface of the water, or a distant car started up, on the hillside back of the town. But mainly, it was quiet. It seemed a pity to disturb the peace, as she was surely going to do. She had to. She had to see for herself. She put one foot on the deck, and eased herself onto the boat. Ducking under the line of photographs, she eased herself towards the open door. Then, she descended the couple of steps down to the living quarters and saw her husband in bed with Ken Houlihan.

Rays of sunshine poured in through the dirty windows of the cabin. Two pairs of eyes were staring through the dust particles at the woman silhouetted in the door. Then Eve turned and fled, ignoring the shouts from behind. She threw herself back into the car, and started driving. Anywhere. Off the edge of the world maybe. Into another dimension. She drove on and on through the morning, down the coast and eventually found herself in San

339

Diego. San Diego. The name rang bells in her head. Something had surely happened in San Diego. She pulled up on the cliff top, and looked out to sea. Oh yes. Victor. Vic Flamm'd been buried here, a Jewish ceremony in this Roman Catholic spot. Didn't make sense. But then, nothing did. She got out of the car, and wandered to the edge of the cliff, to lean on the railings. The sea battered at the rocks below. It was a dynamic sea. Its energy clawed like an animal at the land. She had an urge to be near it. She hurried along the cliff, to the steps, and ran down them into the little cove, teetering over the jagged rocks, to stand straddled over a gap. Beneath her, the sea rushed in, and dragged out again, crashing against itself. It made her feel dizzy. She tore herself away, to sit on a stone at the water's edge. Slowly the dizziness subsided and the cold, numb feeling left her. The waves did the work, pulling the emotions out of her, dragging the tears from her eyes, and the howl from her throat.

'Dad!' she wailed into the wind. 'I want my Dad!' The sea responded, rolling towards her, sending its arms reaching out to take her, drag her off the rock, spray like hooks digging into her, claiming her. Then it pulled back, gathering its strength for another try. Eve lay on the rock, soaking wet and crying. Then a man's arm pulled her up, and back, away from the incoming wave. It was a battle between the sea and him. Eve fought against the man. It was John. John! Why was John here? What did he want?

'Get off me! Leave me alone!' she screamed. The gulls screeched in reply. But John shook her till her teeth rattled, and hauled her away from the sea. 'Bastard! Bastard!' she yelled. John gripped her by the arms. 'You're hurting me. Leave go!'

'What the hell do you think you're playing at?' he asked.

'Me? Me playing?' she croaked.

'Yes. You. What the hell did you mean by coming over here, spying on me?'

'I wasn't spying on you, you bastard. Do you know half the police force is out looking for you?' John went white.

'Bitch!' He spat in her face.

'I didn't set them on, John. They were looking for you because they thought you'd want to know about something that's happened. And when they couldn't find you, I came looking for you.' She was beginning to enjoy this. She knew she had a weapon. She paused, to savour the moment before she thrust it in. 'Your son's dead. Tod. He's dead. There was an accident . . .' John let her go. She reeled back and almost fell, then steadied herself, to see him, drunkenly staggering on the rock, shaking his head.

'I don't believe you,' he said.

'It's true!' she hissed. Then she started crying, remembering the child.

John just stood there, looking at her, shaking his head. 'How'd it happen?' he asked at last.

'Fell out of the damn balloon.' She started laughing, then hiccuped and cried again. 'Bastard!' she yelled.

'It's not my fault,' he objected.

'O.K. then,' she challenged him. 'Whose fault is it?' He didn't say anything. 'Bastard,' she repeated. 'Bastard, bastard, bastard.'

'Shut up!' he yelled. They stood, balanced on the rocks like a pair of drunken combatants. People were gathering on the cliff top to watch. He glanced up and saw them. 'For God's sake, let's get out of here,' he pleaded, but Eve wouldn't budge.

'I'm not coming with you,' she said.

'Honey . . .' Now his voice was soft, gentle. 'Honey . . .I'm sorry. I didn't realize you were upset.' She laughed wildly. 'I mean, I didn't know about . . . Tod.' He shook his head, then went on, 'Who told you where I was? Ernie?' Eve nodded. 'He shouldn't've done that. He knew. He shouldn't've done that. Why'd he do such a thing? The poor bastard must be twisted.'

'*He's* twisted!' Eve rejoined. 'And I thought you were only into drug peddling!'

'I can't help my nature.' John shrugged.

'What would the good folk of Albuquerque think if they knew, huh? Their Decency Candidate, a pervert who makes his money from drugs?'

'Keep your voice down, honey.'

'Why?' Eve laughed. 'I want to shout it from the house-tops. You're a cheat, John Ridley. You cheated me. You cheated the town. You cheated your own children. You cheated Vic . . . You cheated everybody, you bastard!'

'Everybody cheats, honey,' John said softly. 'It's the way of the world.'

'You fought your campaign with dirty money,' she said bitterly.

'You lived it up on that dirty money, Eve. You enjoyed it. You can't say you didn't.'

'I didn't know!' she wailed.

'Come on . . . ' He made a move towards her. She stepped back. She was close to the rock edge. He stopped. 'Come on, honey. It won't seem so bad, once you get used to the idea. Think of the good I've done. I've built them schools you wanted in the pueblos, stepped up the welfare, mended the leaking sewers.'

'Mend your own sewer!' she spat.

But he ignored her and went on, 'I couldn't have done any of that if I hadn't got into power. And I'd not have got into power without the money to back me up, would I?' She stared at him. He believed he'd done right. He really did. 'Now, I want to go on doing that good work,' he said. 'And I need you by my side to do it, honey. Together, we can help so many people . . . '

Eve started laughing. 'You're not on your podium now, John. And if the Mayor hears about this, you never will be again.'

'Why pick on me? Everybody does it! It's just they don't get found out!' Eve stared. Who was this man? Did she know him? 'Come on, honey. Blame the system, not me.'

'You killed Vic Flamm.'

'How?' John was at a loss.

'You put the finger on him. The F.B.I. did the rest.'

'Honey, Vic Flamm died of cancer!' Eve was visibly thrown. How did he know? Was it true? But she didn't care to admit her ignorance.

'You and your kind drove him to it,' she said lamely. John capitalized on a weak moment.

'O.K. I'll make a deal with you,' he said. 'Help me to expose the evils in our society, Eve.'

'Can you hear yourself, John?' she asked, incredulous.

'Once I'm in a position of real power . . . '

'Over my dead body.' Her jaw was set firmly. 'I'm going to divorce you, John.'

'You can't,' he said.

'Watch me.'

'What about Peter?' It was John's last card. 'You've got to stay. For his sake.' Eve sat on a stone. She was silent. After a while, he came and sat beside her. She made no move to stop him. 'You

342

can't let him down, honey.' John's voice whispered in her ear. 'You love him, he loves you. He needs his Momma and his Daddy. Especially now Tod's . . . ' He was going to say 'dead', but he finished, 'gone'. Eve started crying. He put his arm round her, but she shook him off. He wasn't getting away with it that easy. 'You made me what I am, Eve,' he said. She looked at him blankly. 'You gave me the power to rise. You did, honey. Without you, I'd be nothing.' She looked with horror into those frank, charming, boyish eyes. 'Now you've got the chance to reform me. Huh? If you stand by me . . . ?' He watched her. She watched him. Had she really created this monster? Was he her doppelganger? Was he her mirror image? Her shadow?

'Momma, you can see our shadow on the ground. Look, do look!'

'No,' she said at last. 'It won't do Pete any good to be brought up on lies.' She stood, awkwardly. The wet cloth of her skirt clung to her legs. They felt cold and stiff. 'No,' she said. 'I'm finished with you.' She staggered across the rocks towards the cliff. He jumped up and grabbed her hand, pulling her back.

'Please!' he said. 'Please, Eve! Don't divorce me!'

There was a frightened look in his eyes. For a second she almost sorry for him. Then she wrenched her arm away, and climbed the steps up to the cliff top. The little crowd moved to let her pass. She hardly registered their presence, but looked back to see John, sitting, head in hands, on the rock. The ocean had pulled away from the land, and was waiting for the man to go.

When Eve arrived back in Grants, another surprise awaited her. The autopsy had revealed something unexpected and she was asked to call in at the police department to find out what it was. Feeling weak and shaky, Eve sat facing the doctor over his desk.

'Did you know your son was very ill, Mrs Ridley?' he asked. Eve shook her head. 'Well, he was.' The doctor sighed. 'It might be some consolation to you to know that his death probably saved him from a lot of suffering.' Eve shook her head. What was the man saying? 'He had leukaemia, Mrs Ridley. Cancer of the blood.' Eve's brain ricocheted inside her skull. 'Are you O.K., ma'am?' Eve dropped her face onto her hands, and sat very still. 'Are you O.K., Mrs Ridley?' the doctor repeated more loudly. Eve raised her head and nodded bleakly.

'There's times,' she began, in a broken voice, 'there's times, I think I've gone up in one of them rockets, and landed on another planet. I'm not living in any world I know, that's for sure.' The doctor nodded sympathetically. 'You don't know the half of it,' she told him. 'If I wrote down what's happened to me lately, nobody would believe me.' She got up, ready to go.

'Inquest's Thursday,' the doctor said. 'I don't foresee any real problem. Maybe a slap over the wrist for the balloonist. Lose his licence probably. That's all.' Eve nodded and left the office.

Jimmy Ridley took time off when he heard the news, and turned up at the Coroner's Court on the day of the inquest. He sat at Eve's right hand. She was grateful. The rest of the family were sitting behind, as though dissociating themselves. Then John arrived, and took his place on Eve's left. He kept trying to catch her eye, but she wouldn't play ball and when the session started and he reached for her hand, she wrenched it away from him. The business was got over quickly, to spare the grieving parents, and a verdict of accidental death was brought in. The coroner looked compassionately down on the white-faced mother and the nervous father.

'You can start your lives over again,' he told them kindly. Then they rose. The coroner retired and it was all over. The cameras flashed as they left the courtroom, John sticking like a limpet to Eve's side. They'd appear together on the front page of his newspaper, 'United in Grief', but Eve didn't follow John into the family limo. She took Jim's arm, automatically accepting his offer of a lift. Trusting Jim came naturally. Alienated, like her, from the family, not caring how things looked, only how they were, he was the one person on this earth Eve could possibly want to be with just now.

When they were moving, she told him, 'I'm going to divorce John, you know.'

Jim nodded. 'What about the kid?' he asked. 'Pete. How's he taking things?'

'Who knows?' Eve sighed. 'Who ever knows with kids? I try to think how I'd be in his situation, but . . . kids never react the way you expect.'

'No,' Jim said. 'What are you going to do?'

'I don't know. It's a mess. I don't see the family welcoming me into their embrace at The Lawe Top. Do you? After all, I'm divorcing the illustrious son of the house, and the shit is surely going to fly.' She laughed bitterly. 'There's nothing for me in Albuquerque. The very thought of Clara and Ernie makes me feel sick. Vic's dead. And Danny . . . ' She sighed. 'I turned my back on Danny a long time ago. When I think how I stood in judgement over him!' She shook her head. 'What the hell was I playing at?'

'Do the family know?'

'They know I'm going to divorce John. They don't know why.' Eve smiled. 'Had you any idea he was into drugs trafficking?' she asked.

Jim took his eyes off the road to glance at her. 'Did you?'

'I guess I didn't want to know,' Eve said finally. 'But I do now.'

'What's the grounds going to be?' Jim asked.

'Adultery, with one Ken Houlihan,' she said. Jim almost crashed the car. Then they both laughed.

'You wouldn't do that,' he said, when the laughter had died. 'Would you?'

'Try me.' She grinned back.

'What about Peter? How's he going to feel, when he grows up, and hears about it, as he surely will?' Eve said nothing. She stared through the windscreen at the other car, just ahead. 'And what about custody? Is John going to fight you for that?' Eve didn't know. 'You've got a lot to work out, haven't you?' Jim said, as they turned up the road to the ranch.

'I guess I have,' Eve sighed. He parked the car but Eve sat on, looking across the yard at the old house. 'And I can't see me working it out here.' Jim lay back, hands behind his head, thinking a while.

'I've got some vacation time owing me,' he said. 'Suppose we go off, lose ourselves in the wilderness for a while?' Eve turned her head to look at him.

'Are you sure you want to?' she asked. Jim nodded. 'I'd like that, Jim,' Eve said quietly. 'I really think that would help.' She started opening the car door to get out. But Jim didn't budge.

She looked back in surprise. 'I'm not coming in,' he said. 'Anyway, I've got to get back to Los Alamos tonight. I'll sort things out with my boss, and ring you, huh?' Eve nodded. 'Be in touch.'

Eve got out of the car, and watched Jim turn it round and make off back down the track to the main road. She wished she could have gone with him, then and there. But there was Peter to think of.

It was awkward having John and Eve in the house at the same time. June was sure they'd make it up. Tragedy would bring them together. Tragedy always brought people together. But it didn't bring Eve any closer to John and June didn't understand why.

'I mean, what's he supposed to have done?' she asked Eve. Eve shook her head.

'You'll know soon enough,' she said. And June could see John was scared. What had that little English bitch got on him? She closed ranks. She whispered in her brother's ear and Jo started giving Eve the cold shoulder. Lou watched in confusion. He didn't know what to make of anything. He was shocked by the boy's death. They all were. It was beyond him how it could have happened. And John was obviously in a state about it, so why was Eve having a go at him? Surely she should be standing by him at a time like this? Only Ella was sympathetic.

'I never liked John,' she said, shaking her head. She couldn't do much to help Eve, in the face of family hostility. But she seemed to feel responsible somehow. So she said she could take in Pete, at least for a while. At least while Eve went off and sorted herself out. 'It's no trouble,' she said. 'He makes a nice playmate for my Sam. They get on fine.'

Eve was grateful. 'Don't let John take him away, will you?' she warned.

Ella shook her head. 'I don't suppose he'd try.'

'It won't be for long,' Eve assured her. 'I'll get set up somewhere, and then . . . '

'Sure,' Ella nodded. 'You have a nice holiday. Do you good.'

'When's Tod coming back?' Pete asked, as he watched his mother packing. Eve was puzzled. Pete'd seen his brother fall out of the sky. He knew he was dead. And now he was asking when he was coming back! She glanced at Ella, who shrugged. Best not to say anything.

'I don't know, honey,' Eve smiled. 'Now will you be alright here, for a little while, till Momma's found us a new home?'

'I suppose so,' Pete said. 'Are we not going to live at our old house any more?' Eve shook her head. 'Not never?'

'Not never,' she said firmly.

'They haven't got a swimming pool here on the ranch,' Pete pointed out. 'I won't be able to go on with my swimming lessons.'

'No,' Eve agreed. 'That's true.'

'Great!' He grinned. Eve laughed. Kids! She picked him up, hugging and kissing him till he resisted, then she let him go, and took off into the hills.

It was getting late in the year for a trip up the mountains. As the car left Cuba and started to climb, Eve saw the first signs of snow. Soon the good surface petered out, and the road turned into a narrow track. They sure didn't like folks visiting Los Alamos, she thought! She was scared. She held her breath as she turned the bends between the rocks, passing the lumberjacks still out felling trees on the mountainside, her tyres slipping in the mud till, having climbed for a couple of hours, she at last reached the little river where Jim had his log cabin. There was smoke coming out the chimney. Her heart leapt at the sight. Thank God he was there ahead of her. He came out to greet her, dressed in jeans and a thick coat.

'I like your hideout,' she said. He took her inside, fed her with hot soup and roast rabbit, and they had a game of cards together, sitting by the log fire, with a beer or two, before settling down for the night.

It was the first decent sleep Eve'd had in weeks. She woke early, to the smell of coffee and frying eggs.

'You'd make somebody a good wife,' she shouted from her bunk.

Jim laughed. 'That's what I'm afraid of.'

'What do you mean by that?' Eve asked curiously.

'Nothing.' Jim wouldn't be drawn. 'Come on now. Rise and shine. We've got to get moving early.'

'Where are we going?' She shivered as she pulled the bed-clothes back. It was a frosty morning.

'A long, long ride,' Jim said, smiling.

'Horse ride?' Eve was immediately enthusiastic.

'Aha,' Jim said. 'Well, some of it's horse ride.'

347

'Stop fooling.' Eve laughed. 'And tell me where we're going.'

'Mystery tour.' Jim thrust the plate of eggs at her. 'Enjoy your meal.' Eve grinned and ate, as though she hadn't eaten for days.

Jim's jeep made short work of the track down the mountain. He was a good driver and he didn't need a navigator either. Eve found herself dropping off, as they drove on through the day, past Farmington and Shiprock, the great stone eagle that guarded the way to the ancient Indian lands. They stopped off for a meal in a roadside café, only to move on again, in companionable silence through the afternoon. They had supper in Utah, at a motel, and Eve went to bed early, leaving Jim to amuse himself. It was as though she had sleeping sickness. She was sleeping heavily, long dreamless sleeps, and next morning, Jim had to knock loudly on her door before she'd wake.

'It's a beautiful morning,' he yelled through. 'Come and have your breakfast. We've got to get moving.' Eve shook herself like a dog, showered, dressed, and joined Jim in the restaurant. 'Feeling better?' he asked. Eve frowned. She had a headache. Her head felt like somebody'd hit her with a mallet. Jim smiled, and let her drink some coffee.

'It's funny this,' she said at last. 'It's like having breakfast with a stranger.' She looked at him, and he looked back, his face impassive as usual. 'I hardly know you, do I?' Jim smiled and shrugged. 'And yet, we're both of us outcasts!'

'Suppose so,' Jim agreed. 'In a way.'

'Where are you taking me?'

He thought for a minute, then spoke up. 'I'm taking you on a sort of pilgrimage, through sacred Indian lands.'

Eve frowned. 'But I thought you'd given up on all that,' she said.

'I never said there wasn't something in it.'

'I don't understand.' Eve shook her head.

'You will,' Jim told her. 'I'm hoping you'll find yourself in these places, same as I did.' Eve looked at him for a long time.

At ten in the morning, Eve had her first glimpse of Monument Valley. She'd seen it on the pictures of course but it wasn't the same as actually being there, experiencing it. She started singing, as they drove on down the valley, singing with joy. She had

348

never seen anything so extraordinary, so beautiful, so raw, in all her life. These rocks surely didn't stand on the same earth as England, did they? It didn't seem possible. And when Jim stopped, and they got out of the jeep into the silent, windy landscape, Eve felt as though she was walking through a cathedral. Jim didn't say anything. He let her wander for a while, looking at the rocks, taking snaps. Then she got back in the jeep and they took off again, driving south, until finally the valley was behind them. Eve was exhausted. She felt wrung out, peevish, and didn't know why.

'Where are we stopping for the night?' she asked crossly, as they drove on into the blank wilderness.

'Right there.' Jim pointed to a huge rock, just ahead on the roadside. Eve squinted to see what it was. Finally, Jim drew up on the patch of ground opposite. Eve climbed out of the jeep and looked across the road. It wasn't one rock. It was two. They were monolithic, and looked for all the world like a pair of elephant's feet. 'That's just what they are,' Jim told her. Eve wandered over to the rocks, and touched them gingerly, as though expecting some sort of shock from them. Trust Jim to know a place like this. She started stroking the feet and found she was smiling. Then the tears started pouring down her face, and she knelt on the ground, holding on to the feet, crying. Jim watched from the other side of the road, silently. After a while, she got up again, and walked back towards him. Her tiredness had slipped away. Her face was glowing. It was as though something had gone out of it. He nodded and started putting up a tent. They were going to camp.

It was the most beautiful night of her life. A crescent moon hung in the starry sky, as Eve huddled round the fire, wrapped in her sleeping bag. No one passed by on the road. They could've been alone in the world, except for a coyote screaming in some far-off creek. It was peaceful, sitting opposite Jim, as he stared silently into the flames of their fire. He felt her looking at him, and glanced up. She was smiling. He smiled back.

'Thought you'd like it here,' he said.

'I do. Don't know why. I feel as though the years have just rolled off me and left me a child again.' Jim nodded. He didn't want to talk. Talking spoiled things. So she got up, pulling the sleeping bag round her, and walked across the road to the shadowy forms of the great stones. Touching them again, she felt comforted, safe, forgiven. 'Forgiven.' The word was like lightning. 'Forgiven!' Why? What had she done? An uneasy feeling crept over her, and she ran back across the road to Jim, startling him as he sat, silent, by the fire.

'What's wrong?'

'I don't know. I just felt . . . Jim, do you like me?'

'Sure,' he said.

'But you don't know me.' She sat close to him, hanging on his opinion.

'I like you instinctively,' he said.

'Why?'

Jim reluctantly gave up his silence. She needed to talk. So he turned his attention to her, considering her anxious eyes.

'Because I think you're a good woman, at heart,' he said at last.

'I let my child die.' Eve's voice was harsh. 'I killed my own child.' Jim said nothing. He continued looking at her, till she couldn't take it any more and turned her eyes to the less searing light of the flames. She had condemned herself. And she was right to condemn herself. She had killed her first child, by wishing it dead. It had bled away from her onto the street. And now she had killed her second child. Something in her rejected her own children and sought their destruction. She saw it so clearly now and she was filled with horror at herself. 'I don't understand,' she said aloud. 'I loved Tod. I love Pete. I love kids. Why?' Jim said nothing. She turned to see what was in his face and saw nothing, neither judgement, nor sympathy, only watchfulness. 'I set up a charity for kids, for God's sake! Why would I do that if I hated them?' Then she answered her question. 'Guilt?' Jim shrugged. He thought for a minute and reached into his inside pocket. He brought out a photograph, and held it in the light of the fire. The picture was faded, but Eve could see it was a little Korean girl. 'Who's that?' she asked.

'Kid I got to know when I was out there.'

'Yours?'

Jim shook his head. 'Orphan. Picked her up after a bombing raid, delivered her to a place in Seoul. Used to go see her a lot. Then I was captured by the Chinese. When I got out, I tried to

350

find her again, but the country was in uproar. Don't know what happened to her. I often wonder. I guess I loved her in a way.'

Eve bit back her tears. 'Thanks for showing me,' she said.

'Kids are tougher than we think in some ways, and more fragile in others.'

'What am I going to do about Pete?' Eve asked. Jim was putting the picture back in his pocket book. 'I'm scared. I love Pete. I don't want anything to happen to him.'

'Why should it?' Jim asked.

'Something in me,' she said, 'wants to destroy him.'

'I don't believe that.'

'No. It's true.' Eve spoke forcefully. 'It's as true as I'm sitting here. I've got something inside me, some bit of me, that's destructive.' The coyote screamed again, far off. Eve jumped, looked round, then settled again. She was silent for a very long time. 'I think I saw it in San Diego,' she said at last. 'It was when I knew the truth about John. For the first time, I looked at him, and I thought, that's why I married him! I mean, because I *knew* he was a bastard. I recognized something of myself in him. I'd tried not to see it, I'd convinced myself he was a good man, even a great man. But I knew really.' Jim drew in a long breath, studying Eve, before he spoke.

'Obviously, in marrying John, you gave your own shadow form, so it had the power to destroy you.' Eve went cold. 'What is your shadow?' he asked. His eyes were calm, still, as though he expected her to know.

But she stared at him blankly. 'I don't know,' she said. 'Do you think I need psychiatry?'

Jim laughed. 'No,' he answered. 'I think you're doing pretty well all by yourself.' Eve laughed too. 'I'd say you're no madder than most people. In fact, if it's any consolation, probably a good deal less.'

Eve lay back on the earth, and looked up at the stars, breathing deeply.

'Do you know?' she said, 'I feel so much better!' Jim grunted. It came as no surprise at all. 'I do like this place.' Now she was chattering. 'I used to be really scared of the land . . . I mean, here in America. It's so huge and raw, as though God made it only yesterday. You feel as though dinosaurs were roaming through here this very afternoon.'

351

'There's some dinosaur tracks up Tuba City,' Jim said. Eve laughed. 'True. I'll take you to see them, if you like.' Eve sighed.

'Yes,' she said, after a pause, 'there's definitely something about this land. It reminds you that life's good. At rock bottom. Literally,' she chortled. 'I guess the rot set in with the dinosaurs. And then the humans came and really messed things up.'

'Hopis tried to stem the tide,' Jim said. Eve turned to look at him. She wasn't sure if she dared. She had a feeling the subject was taboo. Then she asked, all the same.

'Why did you turn your back on the Hopis?'

Jim drew in a deep breath. He shuffled a bit, settled, then said, 'I'd learned all I could learn from them. They're very wise people. They're in touch with real things. But they aren't free. Not any more. They've made a sort of strait-jacket out of their religious ideas. It's the same with anything, religion, politics, you name it. Once it becomes a system, it's finished. Because you end up not using it, but being used by it. Your own ideas become your strait-jacket. See?' Eve nodded. 'You brain-wash yourself really. I mean everybody's brain-washed to some degree or other.'

'Do you believe in Communism?' Eve asked outright. It was a question John had often asked. He shook his head. 'What do you believe in then?' Jim pointed at his own heart. 'I see.'

'In the end, it's all there is. You've got to stay free inside.'

Eve thought for a while, then, sadly told him, 'I don't think I ever was free. Not even inside. Not even when I was born.' Jim said nothing for a while. He leaned forward and fed some twigs onto the fire. Eve watched him curiously. 'Is that why you cut yourself off from your inheritance, Jim? To free yourself?' Jim nodded slowly.

'It was a burden. I wanted to do other things.'

'What *are* you doing, Jim? Or is it top secret?'

He laughed. 'No. Not everything we do at Los Alamos is secret, you know. I'm just working on geothermal power. That's all. Using the natural energy of the earth peacefully.' He laughed softly. 'Do you know one of the greatest ironies?' Eve shook her head. 'The place they built the first atom bomb, Los Alamos, well, it's perched on the edge of one of the biggest dormant volcanoes on this earth. God's nuclear arsenal.' He laughed loudly. 'I don't know how they had the nerve!' Eve started laughing too. Then she realized what Jim had said.

'You said "God".'

'Mmm. Yes. I did,' Jim admitted.

'You believe in God then?'

'Depends what you mean by God.'

'Stop it,' Eve reprimanded him. 'What do you mean by God?' Jim considered for a while. Then he looked up at the stars, back at the fire, and patted the earth with his hand.

'It's whatever's behind all this. It's whatever's the energy in the volcano. It's what's in here.' He pointed at his heart again, and then at hers.

'What about my . . . "shadow"?' Eve said quietly. She found she was near to tears. 'What's that?'

'I guess it's whatever sets itself up as the opposite of all this.' He looked at the sky, the fire, and touched his heart again. Eve sobbed, just once. 'At least you've seen it,' Jim comforted her. 'It's more than most people ever do.'

'Why me?' she asked. 'Why have I got a shadow?'

CHAPTER SEVENTEEN

Riding through Canyon de Chelly in the late autumn sunshine, golden leaves from scattered trees drifted slowly in the dead air. Instinctively Eve's eye slid from the tree tops, up the canyon walls, to the distant brim of this enclosed and silent world, known only to the Indian; then down again, her eye passing dwellings hewn high in the rock centuries before to rest once more on the trees, and the leaves, falling at last on the river bed. The rains were late. The horses could still pick their way up the Canyon, through the rivulets and lakes. But, in a week or two, the Canyon would be closed, its floor a rushing river. As Jim led the way round the bend, to the place where the Canyon forked, a little dog came rushing at them, snapping at their heels. It was a terrier, a pet. It seemed anachronistic in this lost world and yet the Indian in his hogan, watched T.V. He was human too. They skirted the straggling herd of cattle, ankle deep in water, and turned to pass into the Canyon del Muerte.

Golgotha: stone skulls staring eyelessly down from the heights of the Canyon tops, watching the strangers pass. Almost a century before, Kit Carson and his men had rounded up the Navajo, and then pursued them into this, their chosen world, killing all their stock, then laying siege, as they hid out in their high caves out of the white man's reach. There, as winter came, the Indians slowly starved and froze to death, rather than surrender. The stone walls darkened and seemed to close on Jim and Eve as they rode further into the Canyon. The silence deepened. The sense of being watched became more acute. Yet Jim rode on, looking back only to check Eve was still behind. Seeing her anxious face, he pulled up, waiting, while she continued to his side.

'Creepy, isn't it?' Jim laughed.

'I keep thinking of those murdered Indians,' Eve said. 'I feel responsible.'

'Why?' Jim was surprised.

'I'm white.' To Eve it was obvious.

'So?' Jim asked.

'Of course. I'd forgotten. You probably identify with the victim.'

'Why on earth would I do that!?'

Eve looked at him; this little boy, now grown into a man. Did she have to remind him of his very name?

'White Eagle.'

'I'm called Jim Ridley,' Jim corrected her. 'And I don't identify with anything.'

'How do you manage that?' Eve snorted.

'It's the only way to live.' Eve sighed. She didn't understand. 'Hungry?' Jim dug a bar of chocolate from his pocket, split it, and offered her half.

'Thanks.'

Immediately the little terrier reappeared. Eve threw him a piece of chocolate. He gobbled it up, then stood there, wagging his tail, waiting for more.

'That'll teach you,' Jim laughed.

'No more. Good dog.' The dog yapped at Eve. 'Go home now.' It yapped again. Eve shook her head. 'What do I do?'

'Ignore him. He'll give up and go away eventually.' Jim looked up the Canyon. 'Want to go on?' Eve shook her head.

'No. Not up there. It's sinister. Like going through a grave-yard.'

'O.K. We'll start back,' Jim agreed. It was all the same to him. Side by side the horses walked on, Eve deep in thought. And soon they'd passed out of the Canyon del Muerte back into the golden Canyon.

Eve breathed more easily. She took a sidelong glance at Jim. He looked no different. The place hadn't affected him.

'What difference did it make, do you think? Being brought up half Hopi?' Eve asked curiously. Jim sighed, and thought for a moment.

'I suppose it helped in Korea. Self-reliance was the key to survival. Out there we all had to be Indian braves. I guess the training helped some.'

'Is that all?' Jim looked at her blankly. 'Don't you think it's made some difference to your outlook on life? In general?' Jim shrugged.

'What is, is. At the moment, your horse needs to drink.' Eve slipped off the animal's back and stood by while it lowered its head and drank calmly in the cool stream. The terrier was rushing hither and thither, wanting them to go on. Eve smiled to herself. She wished she was more like the horse and less like the dog. 'What's the joke?' Jim asked, climbing down.

'I'm not going to tell you,' Eve said, laughing. Jim looked slightly uncomfortable. She was surprised she had been able to undermine his aloof self-sufficiency so easily. He slapped his horse irritably on the behind, sending it to join the other. 'Have you not got a girl?' Eve asked suddenly.

Jim jumped, as though he'd been stung. 'Why?' he asked brusquely.

'Well . . . I should think you'd rather've brought your girl friend on a camping holiday like this, than me. I'm almost old enough to be your mother.'

'So?' he asked.

'Don't be like that!' Eve objected. 'Have you got a girl friend?'

Jim sucked in his cheeks, snorted, then turned his head to look at Eve, an amused expression in his eyes. 'I'm not like John, if that's what you're thinking.'

Eve blushed, and stuttered, 'It wasn't what I was thinking.' Suddenly she felt upset. 'I'm sorry. I shouldn't pry, I suppose, but you're being so kind to me. And to be honest with you, I find kindness weighs rather heavily.'

'You think I'm not getting anything out of this trip?'

Eve shrugged.

'Something like that.'

'You're wrong.'

'Good.' But Eve was not satisfied. 'Would you mind telling me what?'

'You're good company,' Jim said. 'It's nice to be able to share these places.' Again, Eve wondered why Jim didn't bring some girl with him, instead of her. 'A girl friend would have to be something very special to share this.' Jim answered her thought and walked away, towards the cliff wall to study some petroglyphs; horses, men, a snake, the swastika, primitive dwellings etched into the stone like the drawings of cave dwellers. She wanted to know what they meant, but somehow daren't ask. Seeing him, a silhouette against the pale stone wall, Eve recognized who Jim Ridley was; a man; a real man; the first real man she had ever known. And she was too old for him. The admission was bitter inside her. Her gall rose in her throat and when Jim turned smiling to her, he saw that her face was transfigured with pain. He stopped, frozen to the spot. She shook her head and turned away. But he was concerned for her. He didn't know what she'd thought and felt. So he ran after her.

She shook him off, crying, 'Oh don't. Don't. Please. It's cruel.' She was sobbing violently. He took her shoulders in his hands, anxious and concerned.

'What is? What's cruel?'

'Nothing.' She didn't dare tell him, but as she looked at him, through her tears, he saw the truth written in her eyes. His hands fell from her sadly. 'What am I going to do with the rest of my life?' she cried.

Jim shook his head. 'Why ask me? The answer's inside you.'

'I'm scared of what's inside me.'

'All the more reason to face it.'

'Do you know how smug you sound?'

Now he'd rejected her, she wanted to goad him for her wounded pride.

'I'm sorry,' he said. 'Shall we get going?' The horses had finished drinking and were standing waiting for them. The little terrier, head cocked, watched them. Eve laughed in spite of herself.

'Yes. Let's get going.' She swung onto her horse, and started off down the Canyon, followed by Jim and the little dog, who didn't leave them till they were back at the lodge at the Canyon's mouth.

The Indian stable lad took the reins as Eve jumped down and started walking. Jim paid, patted the dog, and caught up with her.

'Why are you angry?' he asked.

'I'm not angry,' she replied sharply. 'You should get a girl friend, you know. It might humanize you.'

'Humanize me?' He was amazed at the implied insult.

'Yes,' she snapped. 'Humanize you, you smug little prig.'

Pulling off her gloves, Eve wrenched open her room door, went in, and slammed it shut behind her. Jim stood, staring at the door, a look of amused surprise on his face. 'Humanize him?' Did he need humanizing? He smiled to himself. Maybe she was right. But he hadn't met the girl to do it.

Eve leaned back against her door, crying. She had never felt so humiliated in all her life. Here she was, a middle-aged mother of . . . a middle-aged mother, falling in love with a man nearly half her age, who obviously thought of her as someone to be pitied and patronized and babied. She swung onto the chair in front of the dressing table. Her image reflected back at her, angry and *middle-aged*. Yes. What a sight she looked, with her hair all over the place. Automatically she started tidying the stray ends, then stopped, wondering who would admire her when she'd finished. Who would care whether she looked nice or not? Jim obviously judged a woman on a quite different level from other men. He was not interested in appearances. And what was she but superficial? Her inner voice told her now that she was worthless, ugly, no one would ever want her again, and she laid her head on her hands and howled.

When she'd finished crying, nothing had changed. Crying hadn't altered her opinion of herself, or altered anyone else's opinion, come to that. It was physiological. She'd finished crying simply because she'd run out of tears. Now what? Her reflection showed the same angry, middle-aged woman, only now looking rather blotchy and red in the face. She had better pull herself together and do something constructive. What? Suddenly she ran to the telephone and roused the operator. She wanted to talk to her son, Peter. He loved her. She loved him. That was all that mattered now.

At last they got through, and Ella answered.

'He's fine,' she told Eve. 'He had a fainting fit a couple of days ago, but he's alright now.' A worm started chewing at Eve's heart. Peter, fainting? He'd fainted once before, at the balloon festival.

'Did you call a doctor?' Eve asked.

'No. He's fine now. June said it was "his age".'

'June would,' Eve said angrily. There was a pause at the other end of the line. 'I'm sorry, but I think it would be a good idea to call a doctor,' she said.

'If you want.' Ella obviously didn't think it was necessary, but she could understand the mother being anxious in the circumstances.

'Yes. I do want,' Eve said. 'I'll call again tomorrow.'

She put the phone down, heart pounding. Tod and Peter were twins. Tod had leukaemia. Both had been exposed to radiation from the bomb, two days old, in her womb. Horror rose like a fountain, gushing into her understanding. Leukaemia was a form of cancer. Vic had died of cancer. What had she done? What had they all done? She fell onto the bed, hiding her head in the coverlet, unable to face the daylight that filtered through the curtained window. Only today, in that beautiful place, that canyon of golden memory, she had played with the idea of love. What was she? Was she a whore, that she had to seduce a young man, a young man who had befriended her as no one else had? And all the time her own son . . . ! What was she thinking of? Was she really like this? Eve sat up suddenly. She saw her reflection in the mirror, some way off. She saw her reflection and she saw the shadow she made on the wall behind her. She looked at it for a long time. What was the darkness she cast about her? How could she find out?

Cold, Eve stirred herself to shower and dress, ready for supper. She really must pull herself together and act her age, whether she liked it or not. What was her age? Had the last twenty years passed her by? Had she got older, but no wiser? She dug a sensible dress out of her case, and put it on, much as a warrior might put on a coat of armour. Then she got out the war-paint and applied it, precisely. She was going to have supper with her young nephew. Adjusting herself in the glass, she began to laugh. She had caught herself out, acting again. She shook her finger at her reflection.

'Oh no, you don't,' she told herself. 'Act your age, but don't act.' It sounded wonderful. But she hadn't a clue how to carry out her own advice.

Jim was as amused as Eve was by the change. They shared a bottle of wine and giggled a lot.

'I'm sorry about what happened in the Canyon,' she said.

'What did happen?' Jim asked. Eve looked at him, sobering with every second. Was he teasing her? Was he testing her? He dropped his eyes.

'Sorry,' he said. He looked at her again to check her reaction to his apology. She looked so vulnerable, he wanted to kick himself. She was right. He needed humanizing. He was ashamed.

'I phoned the ranch tonight,' Eve said at last. He waited for her to go on. She swallowed hard, trying not to cry. Was it the wine, he wondered, guilt at leaving Pete, or had something happened? 'I think Pete's ill,' she said. 'He fainted.'

'Lots of kids faint.'

'Jim,' she appealed to him, 'do you know the early symptoms of leukaemia?' He stared at her. 'They're twins. The morning after we got married, John and me, we went up into the hills, and we watched a bomb go off. I saw it . . . ' Her mind recreated that drawing of the light, into a darkness that was anti-light, anti-life. 'You kept in touch with Vic, didn't you?' Jim nodded. 'He died of cancer . . . I'm right, aren't I?' He nodded again. 'Have you any idea what sort of cancer he had?'

Jim cleared his throat. 'I can find out,' he said.

Eve nodded. 'I wish you would.' She bit her lip hard to stop herself crying. 'Jim, I'm scared.' He grasped her hand and held it hard. There was no suggestion of boy meets girl, only of compassion in face of deadly danger.

Eve arrived back at The Lawe Top two days later. The doc had been and hummed and hahed and said he didn't see anything wrong with the kid and hospitals were scary places when you were young, and didn't they think they were making a big fuss about nothing? But Eve was not satisfied. Pete seemed tired to the point of lethargy. He didn't even want to ride White Cloud any more. He just hung onto her with his fists, and looked at her from his pasty white face. Eve turned right round, and drove the kid into Albuquerque to hospital. She wouldn't budge till she'd seen a specialist. She ranted and raved, she waited and pleaded, and finally, realizing who she was, or rather who her husband was, a specialist was found for Mrs Ridley.

After a short examination, he smiled and said, 'I'll keep him in for a couple of days, check his blood for you, if that'll reassure you, ma'am.'

Eve nodded. She'd got what she wanted. As her little boy was wheeled away from her she let out a sob. He looked back, waved lightly, and she thought her heart would break. She didn't want to go back to the house in Albuquerque. She didn't want to go back to the ranch either. So Eve checked in at a hotel. That night, she phoned Jim in Los Alamos. He had found out about Vic. Vic had developed a thyroid tumour, a form of cancer apparently related to radiation exposure; as was leukaemia. Eve was not surprised. In a way, she felt strengthened by the news. At least now she knew, or thought she knew. And in a couple of days, when the tests came in positive, and the specialist told her her son had the disease, she took it calmly. There was hope. They might cure him or, at least gain a reprieve. And so the long course of treatment began.

Unable to pay hotel bills on the slight income she received from John, Eve sought out a small flat, near the hospital. It wasn't up to much, but it didn't need to be. She spent most of her waking hours at Pete's side, as they changed his blood, drugged him, and tested him. She held his hand, she read stories to him before he slept, she brought him treats. Maria visited, and sat on the opposite side of Pete's bed, throwing reproachful glances at the mother over the counterpane. Maria didn't understand this divorce business. A husband and wife should stand together at a time like this. What was Eve thinking of? But she didn't say anything. Sometimes Ella came and, as Pete got better, she brought Sam too. It made a change. Just seeing Sam brought the colour to Pete's cheeks. He asked after White Cloud, and the sheep, and Old Jo, and the hens, and it seemed to do him no end of good. John came too, making a great show of visiting his sick son, courting sympathy, reporting himself in the newspaper the next day. It made Eve sick. Then, after a while, Pete was allowed out. By now it was early March '58. The snow still lay thick on the mountains, and Jim had to put chains on the jeep to take them up to the log cabin. But it was great when they got there. They had a real holiday, tobogganing, skiing, making snowmen and so on. Eve cherished the moments. She adored to watch Pete with Jim. There were no shadows between them, in this high place, up the mountainside, where the light shone clear and white. Eve wished this time could go on forever. But the lawyers were busy, down in the city.

John was trying to make out Eve was an unstable character. Her testimony was half-imagined. She'd been addicted to drugs, had had an affair with Ray and had compromised his career with her left-wing friends in the entertainment business. Anyway, she was English. Surely the court weren't going to take any notice of her, were they? Houlihan swore blind he'd never had relations with John, and the police were short on evidence so far as the narcotics racket was concerned. Why, the little lady was just trying to cast a slur on the most illustrious career of this great New Mexican politician. And why? Well, it was as plain as the nose in your face: money, of course. Eve was gunning for a good settlement.

Spitting fury, Eve told her lawyer to tell John's lawyer she didn't want any of his damn money, all she wanted was her child.

Then came the worst blow of all. The lawyers were casting doubts on Eve's suitability as a mother. Hadn't she let the other son fall out of a balloon? Accident or not, it should never have happened. By this time, Pete was back in hospital. It was a scheduled visit, but it depressed Eve when she took him in, said goodnight, and left him, to go back to her lonely apartment. She sat on the bed, listening to the traffic in the street, watching the lights scan the walls of her room, and brooded. She began to question her own suitability. What were they doing, John and she, wrangling over a sick little boy? Maria was right. He wasn't a piece of cloth they could tear in two, after all. He was a human being. He had feelings. He had rights. And what if John, without knowing it, had spoken the truth? Maybe Eve wasn't cut out to be a mother. Her heart ached at the thought. She loved Pete. She adored him. He was all she had left. He was her life. Why, she'd grown up because of him. But wasn't it enough to ask of a child, that it should help its parent to grow up?, she thought bitterly. There was something in her, she knew, that had rejected the first child, conceived of her union with John, had wished it dead. So it had bled its life away into the gutter. And it was true, she blamed herself for Tod's death. What if, deep down inside her, that shadow was also plotting Pete's end? Suddenly she was filled with horror. Why, it had already started to do so. Two days after the twins were conceived, they had been exposed to death rays. Wasn't radiation the cause of Pete's illness? She hadn't realized at the time . . . and yet, unconsciously, something in her had prompted her to go purposely to watch, celebrate even, the most destructive weapon man had yet created! It had been John's idea. But wasn't he her shadow too? Sitting on her bed, in the apartment, Eve dropped her face into her hands and cried in anguish. She was going to have to give up her only surviving child, for its own sake. And then, anger filled her again. Give him up? To John? No! If she wasn't fit to be a mother, John surely wasn't fit to be a father!

She called on Jim. He came down from Los Alamos and met Eve in a fast food bar near the hospital. He thought Pete had taken a turn for the worse and was ready with comfort. He watched her, as she handled a hamburger, hands shaking.

'Jim?' she asked at last. 'They aren't going to let me take Pete out of the country, are they?'

Jim was surprised. 'Could be a problem,' he said. 'Why?'

'I was thinking . . . I really ought to go home, you know.' Jim said nothing. Mentally he was trying to catch up with her.

'Why?' he asked, at last.

'I've got so much to sort out,' she said. 'Jim, I don't know who the hell I am. It's crazy. I'm over forty, and I'm as mixed up as a kid of fifteen!'

Jim shrugged. 'How's going home going to help?' he asked.

'If I've got something in me . . . something . . . well, not very nice, I guess it must've come from somewhere.'

'Stands to reason,' Jim acknowledged.

'The best place to start looking's in your own roots, don't you think?'

'Guess so.'

Eve took a deep breath, then went on, 'And until I've sorted myself out, I don't trust myself to be a good mother to Pete.' Her voice had gone shaky. Jim looked at her in surprise. 'But I don't want John to have him.' She bit her lip. He watched her struggle against the coming tears. 'Do you think Ella would care for him? Just for a while? Just till I've sorted myself out?'

'She might, yes,' Jim agreed. 'Kids get on well with her and young Sam. Nice stable sort of background. Yes. It might work.'

'Thanks.' Eve was obviously relieved.

'But what about the kid?'

'I don't know. He's so little. I wouldn't leave till he was better, of course. He *is* getting better, you know!' Jim nodded. 'I mean, I'm lucky. I am really. I do still have a son. And I want the best for him. It's just . . . at the moment I don't think I can give him the best. And I know John can't. So I want to ask you a favour.'

Jim sucked in his cheeks, and his eyes got that amused look again. 'What favour?' he asked.

'I want you to be Pete's godfather. I want you to watch over him, look after his interests. And most of all, I want you to talk John into letting Ella bring him up at the ranch, without interference.' There was a long pause. Jim watched a girl throw a half-eaten burger and an empty Pepsi carton into the bin, then swing the doors open and go out into the street. He watched her pass by the window. When she'd gone, he turned back to Eve and said,

'O.K., I'll see what I can do.'

Relief at having arranged things so well soon turned to sorrow. That night, Eve lay in bed, in her apartment, watching the car lights scan the walls of the room, questioning her own motives. Was she doing the right thing by Pete? Was she really concerned to do the best for him; or was she avoiding her responsibilities? How could she tell? Only time would supply the answers.

On condition Eve change the grounds of the divorce, John agreed to her suggestion for Pete. The public washing of dirty linen was to be avoided. It was better for the kid, anyway. And when Eve told Pete he was going to live at the ranch for a while, he whooped with joy. Apparently it was what he'd secretly been wanting.

'We'll have nice times, Mom,' he told her enthusiastically.

'I won't be there, honey. That's the only thing.' It was the fly in Pete's ointment. But it was only a fly, or so it seemed. Perhaps he just didn't understand. Or perhaps he didn't care that much. Or perhaps he was being kind to Eve. However it was, he accepted the deal without making a big thing of it. 'Where will you be, Mom?' he asked.

'In England, honey. It's time I went back to see *my* Mom. She's your grandma, you know.'

'How long will you be away?'

'I don't know. It's just a visit.'

'Will I see my grandma one day?' he asked.

'Maybe.'

It was a nice thought. It warmed Eve, and when she got back to the apartment, she was feeling a little less hollow than usual. But there was a letter awaiting her. It was from home. It was in Jack's hand. He never wrote to her. Eve was filled with terror. Her Mom was dead. It was the last dirty trick God could play on her. And He'd done it! The bastard! She was crying before she read the note. Then she stopped crying. She read the message again.

Dear Eve,

I am writing because your Mam is up to her ears in funeral arrangements. Your Auntie Hester died last week in the institution. It was a nasty business. She cut her own throat. Apparently there was blood all over the place. I pity the poor warders. Anyway, it's over for her now, poor woman. Your Auntie Maisie seems pretty upset about it, though your Mam's coping well, as usual. I thought I'd write, partly because we've not heard from you for such a long time, and partly because, well, I thought you'd like to know. A letter from you, right now, would help Maisie and your Mam quite a lot. They always like to get your news. Only the other day, your auntie was moaning on, because she hadn't seen any new pictures of the twins for such a while. They are her great-great-nephews, you know. It means a lot to her. So, if you get the time, drop us a line, love. We always like hearing from you.'

Jack

Hester Beattie. Eve turned her mind back to the visit at the institution, and remembered the poor, tormented woman. Jack was right. At least, hopefully, she was out of her misery. Then she remembered what her mother'd told her about Hester's birth. 'Not that it affects you, pet,' she'd said. But didn't it? She belonged to the same family tree. Way back, they shared the same roots. If one branch was diseased, didn't the others feel it? Perhaps, even the branch line in the States? That was a long time back, and yet, didn't they all share the same blood? Didn't the shadow of their ancestors haunt the tree?

PART THREE

September 1958

'The sun is coming through the window now. Oh, Lord, what a heavenly light.'

'Gordo' Cooper astronaut. Orbited the earth twenty-two times
(May 15th 1963)

CHAPTER EIGHTEEN

Jack met Eve at Newcastle Central Station on an afternoon in late September. The sun, low in the sky, blinded them, till they'd crossed the sparkling River Tyne into Gateshead, and turned east onto the Shields road. There was an air of celebration in the air because of Eve's return, but with it, a feeling of mystification.

'You're a bit late for the funeral, if *that's* what you came for,' Jack said.

Eve smiled. 'No. I didn't come for that. I was going to come anyway. Even before I got your letter.'

'Oh.' Jack nodded, one eye on the traffic. 'That's nice. To what do we owe the honour?' Eve hesitated. Immediately, Jack sensed trouble. 'There's something wrong, isn't there? You can't kid me, lass.'

'Lass!' Eve laughed. 'You sound almost Geordie.'

'I should do, after all the years I've lived here!' He threw her a smile across the wheel and started showing off his accent, singing, 'Dance for your Daddy, my little laddy, dance for your Daddy, when the boat comes in . . .'

'I can't call you Dad,' Eve blurted out, interrupting him.

'I know,' Jack sighed.

'It's funny, but you feel more like a benevolent uncle to me.'

'Well! That's not so bad!' He was quite pleased. 'I'll settle for that!'

369

'Good.' Eve eased back into her seat, watching the road. Things had changed a lot since she'd last been to Tyneside. The place was dirtier, noisier, full of traffic. Jack was having quite a time working his way through it. 'It's funny,' Eve pondered. 'I know hardly anything about you. I mean, Davey, my stepfather I suppose he is really, I know about him. I knew where he was brought up, and who his mother was and everything, because I was brought up there too. But you . . . ? Where were you born? Who were your parents?'

'Million dollar question that.'

'Oh I forgot. You're an orphan, aren't you?'

Jack laughed. 'At *my* age?'

'Well you don't suddenly sprout parents just because . . . your hair's gone grey,' Eve said kindly. Jack smiled at her, grateful for the indulgence.

'Do you know, Jack.' Eve spoke as though she knew what she was talking about. 'I think you're lucky.' She looked at him, her jaw set, eyes hard. 'You're free of all obligations to the past . . . to your ancestors and so on.'

'You call that lucky?' he asked. Then he sighed. 'Oh well, the grass is always greener, I suppose.' Then he added, 'But you know, Eve, your ancestors are always with you, whether you know who they are or not. You carry their message around with you, in your genes.' It was his turn to look at her. Then someone hooted a horn and, harassed, Jack turned his attention back to the road. 'At least you know where your problems come from. *Me*? I'm a mystery book.'

Eve was silent for some time. She wanted to cry. No one got away with it. Not even Jack Scott.

'I'm sorry I was hard on you, Jack.' She sounded choked.

Suddenly, Jack made up his mind and pulled in at a little transport café on the left.

'Let's have a cup of tea till the traffic's died down, eh?'

He was switching off the engine. Eve nodded, but she wasn't so sure; now she'd have to look Jack in the eye. She got out of the van and followed him into the café, where he ordered two teas. Dark brown, English tea, it flowed, stewed, from the pot. You needed sugar in it, to mask the bitterness. She let him stir some in and sat opposite, at a formica-topped table.

He threw her a chocolate biscuit, and she ate it hungrily. He watched her, waiting for her to speak; frustrated because he daren't ask her what was wrong again.

'I've made a proper mess of things, Jack,' she said at last, staring at the sugar left in the bottom of the cup.

'Oh aye?' Jack encouraged.

'Honestly!' Eve laughed, daring to look at him, for a second. 'You sound *so* Geordie! I can't get over it!'

'*Honorary* Geordie, me,' Jack grinned. She couldn't stand his look. She turned away, watching the other customers. Then, slowly her face crumbled, and she looked down at her cup again. Jack put out his hand to touch hers and, without looking at him, she grasped it hard.

'I've made such a mess of everything.' She was crying. She felt a fool. Other people would see. Jack pulled out a hanky and let her blow her nose hard. 'I don't know how I'm going to tell my Mam,' she went on. Then, at last, she looked at him. 'It's a long story,' she warned. Jack looked out of the window.

'Traffic's still bad,' he said, smiling. Eve smiled back.

'O.K. Here we go, then. Once upon a time . . .' she joked. And she launched into her story.

When she'd finished, Jack, slumped in his chair, looked like he'd been hit by a bomb. He was shaking his head in disbelief.

'Why?' he asked. 'Why you, Eve? You were such a go-getter, such a bright spark. What happened to you?'

'Don't.' His words echoed her own bitterness. And her own was enough.

'What do you want to do now?' he asked, leaning forward to take her hand again.

'I don't know. I don't want to think about it, yet.'

'What about Peter? The little lad needs his Mam.'

Eve shook her head. 'I don't know if I'm up to it, Jack.' She couldn't control the tears. They kept on falling, and she shook them off her cheeks like raindrops.

'Of course you are!' Jack said.

'No.' She was trying to say something. He wished he could help, but he had no idea what it was. 'Jack . . . ?'

'What?' Jack looked down, hoping that by averting his gaze she'd find the courage to speak her mind. But she hesitated and, looking up again, Jack glimpsed a shadow crossing her face. 'Tell me, Eve,' he pleaded. 'I'd like to help, if I could.'

Eve struggled to spit it out. Finally, shame-faced and embarrassed, she said, 'There's something in me. I don't know what. But it turns everything I touch to . . . it's the kiss of death, Jack.'

'Stop that talk!' Now he was angry.

'I've got to sort myself out, before I decide what to do about Peter.'

'You may not get the chance,' Jack said bitterly. 'The bastard'll probably get custody. I mean, you've run off and left your son.' In spite of herself, Eve sobbed, burying the sound in Jack's hanky. 'Face facts, love. That's how it'll look to the American courts.'

Eve nodded. In her heart she knew it. But she could' only repeat, 'I've got to sort myself out. That's all I know.'

'Can I get your another cup of tea, pet?' The woman from behind the counter, drawn by the dramatics, was dying to sympathize. Eve shook her head.

'We'd better get going,' Jack said, smiling his thanks and extricating himself from the seat.

'Yes,' Eve agreed. 'They'll wonder where we've got to.'

'Thanks very much.' Jack nodded courteously to the woman, and the pair went out to the car park.

Eve slipped into the seat beside Jack, feeling vaguely like a schoolgirl caught playing truant. The feeling surprised her. She tried to shake it off. But Jack was angry.

'Kiss of death, my arse!' he spat. He put the van in gear and drove back onto the road.

'It's true!' Eve shouted. 'Whatever I do, something goes wrong. And it's not because fate's picking on Eve Lawson, either. It's something inside makes it happen!' Jack was silent, listening. He put his hand against the mirror, blocking out the dazzling sun.

'Well, whatever it is, you don't get it from me,' he said at last.

'I can't keep running away, Jack. Because, in the end, I'm just running away from myself. That's why I came home.' Jack nodded slowly. He was thinking of Eve's mother, Frances. She'd tried to run away, just the same. And he'd brought her back,

back to the shop, Shields and the family. Eve used to condemn him for it. She said he'd ruined her Mam's career.

'So, you don't blame me any more?' Jack asked.

'Jack! I never blamed you!' Eve was aghast.

'Liar,' Jack said quietly. Eve was trying to remember. She nodded.

'Yes. I did. I blamed you for the whole mess. I thought it was your fault Mam went with my . . . with Davey Lawson, and I ended up being brought up by another man. But, maybe . . . maybe it wasn't your fault at all. Maybe it's just . . .'

'There's never any point blaming anybody, our kid,' Jack said. 'What is, is. That's all. We've got to forgive and forget. Make the best of it.'

'Well, after the mess I've made, I'm in no position to cast blame on anybody else, am I?' Jack snorted. You had to admire her honesty.

'Just hold your horses, Eve,' he advised. 'If you're not careful, you'll swing the opposite way and get into an orgy of blaming *yourself*. And that's not going to help, either, now is it?'

'No.' Eve was shaking her head, crying and smiling at the same time. 'You're not so bad, Jack. Know that?'

'The accolade!' Jack laughed. But he was pleased all the same. 'By the by,' he said, 'before we get home, you should know we've got visitors.' Eve looked at him. 'Hester's daughter, Anna, and the grand-daughter, Elizabeth.'

'Still here?' she asked. Jack nodded. 'But the funeral was ages ago, surely?'

'Still here.' He sighed, then grinned impishly. 'Maybe you'll be the incentive to send them packing.'

After helping Jack in with the luggage, Eve's brother, Os, and his wife, Mary Jean, got back to their work in the shop.

'I'll see you later for a nice chat,' Mary Jean whispered. 'There's plenty of folk to look after you, just now.' And she was right. The back kitchen was full to bursting. Eve sat on her suitcase, winded at the reception.

'This is George, Os's son. You remember him?' Frances hadn't given Eve any welcoming embrace. She seemed flustered, even embarrassed. She behaved as though undecided whether to treat her as a mere guest, or a member of the family. Equally awkward, Eve took George's hand and shook it. The lad was thin, dressed in a tweed jacket, hair cut short back and sides, old-fashioned.

'Hallo, Auntie Evie,' he said, backing away.

'To think you were a little bairn, when I last saw you,' Eve said, smiling and nodding. At the mention of 'bairn', a frown appeared on her mother's face, telling Eve the dreaded thought had occurred. Where were Tod and Peter? Where was John?

'I've got some swotting to do.' George, still backing off, fell against the side of the door, winced, then turned and disappeared up the stairs to the office.

'Nice lad,' Frances said. 'He's studying for his "Ordinary National Certificate", you know.'

'That's nice.' Eve smiled, wondering what on earth the 'Ordinary National' was. Then a tornado flew in from the yard. It was Maisie Beattie, seventy-six years old.

'Eeeh, why didn't anybody tell me?' she gasped. 'I was pegging out the washing!' She fell on Eve, hanging on her neck. 'Eeh! Eeh!' she said. It was all she could manage. But the wet eyes and the innocent smile said it all. 'Welcome Home'. It was the first real welcome Eve'd had. She kissed her aunt gratefully on the cheek.

'Hallo, Maisie,' she said. 'Jo still asks after you, you know.' Maisie giggled and, overcome, plonked herself in a chair, drying her eyes on her apron.

'And you remember Anna?' Frances pointed out the pale woman, sitting in the best chair by the fire. Eve smiled politely and ignored the limp, extended hand. She might have forgiven her for being so bossy last time she was home, but she hadn't forgotten it. 'And Elizabeth?' Frances continued round the room. Eve smiled.

'You were a baby . . . doesn't time fly?' The clichés covered a gap. What could you say about a teenager, dressed all in black, eyes outlined in black, black hair sticking out like a haystack?

Elizabeth pulled a mock smile, and asked, 'Are you real?' Eve was thoroughly taken aback. 'Only you look like you've stepped off the front page of a glossy mag.'

It was not a compliment. Elizabeth returned to her doodling. Stuck for a response, Eve glanced at the doodle on the back of the

374

envelope. It was somehow threatening. At once, Elizabeth covered it with her hands.

'Sneak previews are not allowed,' she said.

'She's very intelligent for fifteen, you know,' Anna intimated. 'She's going to college.'

'She? Who's she? I am not the cat's grandmother,' Elizabeth reprimanded. Anna shrank back into silence and Frances looked desperate. She wanted to ask where the twins and John were, but it didn't seem polite. The polite thing would be to take the guest up to her room, but . . .

'Eeh, I don't know where we're going to put you, our Eve!' Fran said, looking in dismay at the huge suitcase her daughter was sitting on. 'We've not got a room spare.' Then, to her relief, Frances thought of a way to ask the difficult question without seeming to ask. 'It's a good job you've not brought John and the twins . . .'

Eve laughed, awkwardly, avoiding the difficult answer by saying, 'Well, I don't mind a sleeping bag on the kitchen floor, if it comes to it!'

'We can surely do better than that!' Aunt Maisie stared pointedly at Anna and her daughter Elizabeth who, between them, had commandeered the two attics.

'Yes,' Jack coughed. 'Can't Elizabeth bunk in with Anna? Then our Eve could have Elizabeth's room.' Anna looked as if she'd been shot. She was scared of her daughter. She couldn't get near her, literally. Her hair was back-combed till it stood out like a lavatory brush, taking up far more room than it ought to. It wasn't natural.

'I'm sorry, Jack,' Anna said. 'My nerves just wouldn't stand it.' Anna took out her handkerchief. 'I need my privacy, after all I've been through.' Then she started sobbing. 'My poor mother, left to languish in an asylum, uncared for by anybody, till in despair she took her own life.'

'I beg your pardon!' Frances bristled like Elizabeth's hair. 'But I beg to remind you, Anna, that I visited your mother in her institution, every week, without fail, which is more than you ever did!'

'That's right,' Anna squealed, 'rub it in!'

'Stop whining, Mum,' Elizabeth said sharply. 'Grandma carried out the existentialist philosophy to its logical conclusion.

Suicide. Personally, I respect her judgement. I mean who wants to go on living in a world with the bomb?'

'Shut up, Elizabeth!' Frances snapped.

Elizabeth shrugged, and went to languish in the back yard. Nobody understood her. They all thought she should be like George. Normal. God! They'd all grown older and older till they were past it. George'd been born past it. The great useless twit! She sighed, and lit a French cigarette, hoping the generation on the other side of the gap would see her through the kitchen window and try to stop her.

But the family was far too preoccupied with Eve to think about Elizabeth's minor peccadilloes. Where was Eve's husband? Where were the twins? Why had she not mentioned them?

'Stopping long?' Anna asked in a tremulous voice.

Eve shrugged and smiled brightly. 'Depends on how I like it,' she said, jumping off her suitcase.

Now Frances was really worried. She glanced at Jack. He knew something, she could tell. She'd ask him later.

'Well . . . for now . . . I do think Elizabeth might go in with you, Anna,' Frances said. 'Jack . . . would you go out and ask her, please?'

Jack gave his wife a sour look, but did as he was bid. He was the only one who dared. He opened the door to the back yard and looked out. Elizabeth turned and blew a smoke ring at him. He coughed. 'Get your things out of your room, miss!' he barked. 'Now!'

Elizabeth sat where she was, smiling slowly. 'I will if you ask nicely, Uncle Jack,' she said. Jack made a strange noise. It sounded like a hiss. But perhaps it was 'please', because Elizabeth sauntered in, and said airily, en passant, 'I think it's time we went home, to London, Ma. I've got to get back to my studies, anyway.'

As Elizabeth escaped up the stairs, Anna was taken by a fit of the shakes. 'Oh God help me,' she cried. 'God help me. Doesn't anybody care?' Eve exchanged a glance with her anxious mother.

'I hope you won't find us boring, after America,' Frances said politely.

Eve spluttered, then burst out laughing. 'I think I'll go and help Elizabeth,' she answered.

Elizabeth was busy taking her posters down from the walls. She rolled each one up carefully, secured them with elastic bands, and then started shovelling her clothes, willy-nilly, into a plastic bag.

'They'll get creased!' Eve objected.

'So what?' Elizabeth retorted.

'Don't you like nice clothes?' Eve was dismayed. This was beyond understanding.

'Not particularly. You know it's just not natural to look as good as you do. If you ask me, you need help to reshape your entire image.' Eve sat on the bed, watching, as the girl stuffed skirts, jeans and jumpers in, one after the other. 'I'll help you, if you like,' Elizabeth volunteered.

'I like the way I am,' Eve said. 'But I think *you* like to shock.'

'Think what you like.'

'Thanks. I will.' A note of accord had been struck. Eve capitalized on it. 'What are you studying?'

' "O" levels. I want to go to art college. Unless I go to the Sorbonne, of course.'

'Oh yes. Now I remember, your mother was very good at painting.'

'Chocolate box stuff,' Elizabeth sneered.

'Was it? Oh. I wouldn't know, I suppose.'

'No. I don't suppose you would.'

Back in her place, on the wrong side of the generation gap, Eve floundered searching for touchstones. Her eye lighted on the great wooden statue in the corner. Ganesha. There He was. Who'd brought Him up from the shop? Elizabeth? That young lady had certainly made her presence felt in the house!

'Isn't it time you were back at school?' Eve sounded rather more like a maiden aunt than she would have wished, but Elizabeth didn't seem to notice under the pressure of other, more important stimuli.

'Of course it is. You tell my mother that!' she lectured. 'She doesn't want to go back to London, to be all on her own with me!'

' "On her own?" But . . . what about your father?' Eve asked. 'Where's he?'

'You're very rude, aren't you?' Elizabeth stopped packing, to stare at her.

'*Me*?' Eve was dumbfounded.

'Yes. You. I mean, I don't ask where *your* father is, do I?'

Eve gasped. That was below the belt. 'You don't pull your punches, pal, do you?'

'It's better than being a hypocrite!' Elizabeth snapped.

Eve thought better of challenging the assumption. This was obviously a case for stepping in feet first.

'So where *is* your father?'

'Bunked out. Gone to live with some councillor woman on the G.L.C.'

'I see.' Eve took a deep breath, before the next question. 'Does Mam know? Frances?'

'Course not. *My* Ma couldn't face telling her. She's a coward. She thinks a woman's nothing on her own.'

'And you don't?' Eve asked hopefully.

Elizabeth caught the change in Eve's voice and looked at her carefully. 'Where's your husband?' she asked.

'I'm divorcing him,' Eve said.

'Good. Men're weak creatures. Not worth bothering about if you ask me.' Eve smiled, shaking her head. 'I'd've thought *you'd* agree with me, at least.' Elizabeth seemed put out.

'I don't know what to think,' Eve said. Actually, she was thinking of Jimmy. If what Elizabeth had said was true, then he was an exception to the rule.

'So, you're staying then. I mean this isn't a little hol then straight back to the jolly old States, is it?' Elizabeth asked. Eve was panting under the assault.

'No. It isn't a "hol", as you put it.'

'Look. I'll tell my Ma. She listens to me. I'll tell her we've got to go home. This is your place. O.K.?'

'That's very generous of you.' Eve was genuinely impressed.

'It's not such a big deal. I hate it here anyway.' Elizabeth shrugged, and crashed out of the room. She was going downstairs to the kitchen. Eve's heart jumped. Was she going to tell her now? She shot off the bed and followed her down, but she was too late. Elizabeth was in full spate. Eve gesticulated wildly, but she took no notice. It seemed nothing could stop her.

'Ma,' she was shouting at the whimpering creature in the armchair. 'Ma, we've got to go back to London. Auntie Evie's divorcing her husband. That means she's back here for good. It's not just a visit like you thought. You've got to be sensible for a change. There's not room for all of us, is there? So, pack your bags.'

Eve thought her mother was going to faint. Frances gaped, looking from Elizabeth to Eve then back again.

'Is this true?' she asked. Jack was holding his head in his hands. Maisie, in the middle of mangling a sheet, kept on saying 'Eeh, eeh!' over and over, till her finger got caught and she yelped.

'I was hoping to break the news more gently,' Eve reprimanded Elizabeth, who was looking far too pleased with herself.

'Is it true?' Frances asked. Eve nodded. 'We've never had a divorce in the family.' Jack helped his wife to a seat. She looked very pale. 'And what about the kids? Tod and Peter?' Eve bit her lip. How to tell her mother her grandchild was dead?

'You know, I did write. I did write to tell you Peter was ill.'

Frances nodded. 'Yes. But he's better now.'

'Yes. But he's better now.'

'Yes. *He* is. But . . . Well, Tod was ill too. He was going to die anyway. But . . . there was an accident.' Frances gasped.

'Tod?' Eve nodded. 'He's dead?' Jack put his hand on her arm. This wasn't the time. Eve was too much on the defensive.

'He was going to die anyway, Mam. He had leukaemia.'

'*Peter* didn't die of it!' Frances pointed out sharply. Her mother was too quick on the draw. Like Anna, Eve wanted to say, 'Don't rub it in.' But she didn't.

'Well, anyway. Peter's staying at the ranch for the time being. Till things are sorted out.'

'How can you hope to sort them out over here?' her mother asked.

'Because, Mam,' Eve shouted, 'things are not quite as simple as they may look to you!' Elizabeth darted her aunt a look of sympathy, and Eve surprised herself by returning it. Each had recognized a kindred spirit in the other. But, to Elizabeth's disappointment, Eve immediately backed down. 'I'm sorry, Mam.'

'No. *I'm* sorry,' Frances said. 'You must be . . . You must need . . . Oh God.' Then she started crying.

Elizabeth yanked her mother out of the easy chair. 'Come on, Ma. Let's get you out of the way for a bit,' she said. Anna, for all her apparent weakness, fought her daughter off, lashing out at her viciously. 'Please, Ma,' Elizabeth warned.

'We're in the way here.' On her high horse, Anna rose and marched out of the room upstairs, followed by Elizabeth in the role of prison warder. Out of sight, Anna started protesting that she didn't know what the youth of today was coming to.

'No respect!' she yelled at the top of her voice.

'Do you mind keeping your voices down? I'm trying to work here!' George cried desperately from the first floor landing.

'And that includes you!' Anna jabbed her finger at him, and he flung himself out of the office, down the stairs, into the kitchen, to be faced by a mayhem of weeping women. He rolled his eyes, wrenched open the door to the shop and found escape with his parents.

'Are Os and Mary Jean still in the shop?' Jack asked.

'Must be;' Frances replied. 'And it's long past closing.' Jack opened the door. The perfume of chrysanthemums wafted on the air, covering the smell of boiling onions. Eve and Frances wandered in after him.

'It's nice and quiet in here,' Eve said, looking round at the old wooden drawers and counter, the old battered buckets brimming with flowers.

'It shouldn't be,' Os said, shaking his head. 'That's business, though.' Another worm was wriggling out of the woodwork. Eve didn't want to know. There were far too many of them.

'Why didn't you come in the back and join us?' she asked.

'We didn't like to,' Mary Jean said sheepishly.

'I don't blame you.' Jack was laughing. 'I wouldn't mind moving into the shop. Lock stock and barrel. It's a haven of peace after being in there.' He indicated the house behind.

'It's not funny,' Frances snapped. Os went to the door, turned the notice to 'CLOSED' and pulled down the blind.

'Would you not like to bed down in here, Eve?' Jack continued his joke. Eve smiled. She was looking at the space where the statue should be.

Upstairs, Anna screamed loudly. 'I am not having that thing in here!'

'Here we go again!' Jack sighed.

He and Eve pounded up the stairs to sort things out. Anna and Elizabeth were in the hallway, on either side of the statue of Ganesha.

'I wouldn't give it house room!' Anna spat.

'Well I like it!' Elizabeth insisted.

'Look,' Jack intervened, trying to sound reasonable, 'it's got to go somewhere . . .'

'I don't mind if you leave it in *my* room,' Eve volunteered. Elizabeth, Anna and Jack stared at her. 'If nobody else wants it,' she added.

'O.K. You can have it.' Elizabeth let it go, and Jack helped Eve cart it back into the bedroom.

'Better you than me.' Anna was whining. 'That thing gives me nightmares.' Anna retreated into her bedroom, and started complaining again, almost at once.

'And you're not having them, either!' she said. 'I don't know! Other girls have Elvis Presley and Cliff Richard on their walls, but not you. Two old men, like that! I mean, who are they?'

'Albert Camus and Jean-Paul Sartre, if you really want to know, Ma,' Elizabeth explained patiently, as she sellotaped her Buddha poster up beside them.

'She wants to take French for "A" level. If she ever gets that far,' Jack whispered.

'Oh. I see,' Eve whispered back. Then she grinned. 'Do you know what? I like her.'

'Elizabeth?' Jack rolled his eyes to heaven.

'Yes. Honestly. *She'll* not let the buggers get her down!' Jack snorted. 'You'd better go back to Mam. She was looking terrible. Tell her I'm sorry.' Jack nodded, and reluctantly left his daughter to get on with her unpacking.

The old room felt like home. It was funny that. But it did. In fact home felt like home, which it never had before. Eve was wondering why, when she opened the top drawer of the chest, to put her undies in, and found the battered old book she'd flung across the floor more than a decade before. She pulled it out and took it to the bed, where she lay on her side and opened it up. Oh yes, she remembered now. It was the story of the brothers, Ganesha and Kartikkeya; how their parents, Shiva and Parvati, had said that the first son who returned home, after going round the earth, would be married. Kartikkeya had hurried off to do their bidding, but Ganesha had stayed at home . . . Eve glanced at the statue in the corner of her room. It was true. Ganesha had always been at home. At least, in her home. While she, like Kartikkeya had gone off. Anyway. Back to the story. Eve flicked through the pages, remembering. Ganesha had simply walked round His Parents, because, as He said, They *were* the entire earth. Whereas, and this was the point where Eve had thrown the book across the room, 'He who leaves his parents at home and goes on a pilgrimage incurs the sin of their murder.' Eve frowned and sighed, looking up from the book. What on earth did it mean? 'Incurs the sin of their murder?' Perhaps reading on would enlighten her.

'Then Shiva and Parvati praised their son, Ganesha.

'O, son, you are a supreme soul, and your thoughts are pure. What you have said is true and not otherwise. What has been done by you, shall be done by anyone. We have honoured it. It shall not be altered now.'

After saying thus, and appeasing Ganesha, the ocean of intelligence, they resolved to perform his marriage. After some time, the noble Ganesha begat two sons, one of each of his two wives. But while Ganesha was enjoying his happiness, the second son returned, after circumambulating the earth. Learning what had happened, the infuriated Kartikkeya went to the Krauncha mountain, though forbidden by his parents, saying, 'O parents, I shall not stay here for even a moment, when deception has been practised on me.'

O, sage, he went away, saying so. And ever since that day, he remains a bachelor. His name bestows auspiciousness in the three worlds. It dispels all sin, is meritorious, and confers the sanctity of celibacy.'

Eve put the book down, and sank her head on to the pillows. So, that was it. Because she'd gone away, she was condemned to celibacy, was she? While Os enjoyed his wife and son, she was alone. But like Kartikkeya, Eve didn't think it was fair. Had God built unfairness into the system, then? Life wasn't fair. It was true. She stared across the room at the statue. Had she shared Kartikkeya's fate? Had there been a husband waiting for her here all the time? And had he married someone else, while she'd been round the earth? She shook herself and went to put the book back in the drawer. She was tired, battered by emotion and exhausted by too much thinking.

'Eve!' It was her Mam, knocking on the door. 'Eve? Are you asleep?' Eve opened the door. Her mother stood awkwardly on the threshold. 'Supper's ready, if you want some.' Suddenly Eve put out her arms and Frances grabbed at her, hugging her close. 'I'm sorry, pet,' she said. 'I'm sorry you've had such a bad time. I never liked him, you know.'

'I know,' Eve said. 'I let myself in for it. There's no one else to blame.' They looked at one another for a moment. Eve thought her mother looked older. White hairs grew round her face, like a frame, in contrast with the red hairs behind. 'I love you, Mam,' she said.

'I know, pet.' Frances sniffed back her tears.

'It's nice to be home.'

'Is it?' Frances snorted, then sighed. 'I don't know . . . ' Eve felt a moment's panic before Frances smiled and said brightly, 'Come on. Supper's getting cold.'

They were eating in the dining room, for a change. At first Eve flattered herself it was in her honour, then she realized it was actually because the kitchen table simply wasn't big enough. There was a stranger sitting on Os's left. He rose, as Eve entered the room.

'Oh, Eve,' Os said. 'This is David Jackson. Do you remember him?' Eve shook her head and smiled a greeting. 'You have met, I think,' Os continued rather too formally.

'Oh yes. We've met,' David said, nodding. Eve looked blank. 'I was in the same regiment as your brother, Eve. I was here when you and your husband paid a visit home during the war.'

'Oh.' Now she remembered. She looked at Os. Os grinned.

'Aye. That's right. The night I belted him. As a matter of fact, David here held the bastard down while I did it.'

Eve burst out laughing, and the laughter spread round the table, till even Elizabeth was smiling sardonically down at the green dragon that curled its tail round the rim of her bowl. But while the general laughter died, Anna's continued on, shriller and shriller. Everyone stopped and stared.

Frances, waiting to serve the soup, fell against the sideboard, Memories crowded in on her; those dragons in the plates; green dragons with red and gold fire coming out of their mouths, prowling through the family dinner service. It had been a present from her grandfather, George Beattie, to her grandmother Jane, on the occasion of their anniversary. Seeing it for the first time, Jane had taken leave of her senses. She had rushed from the table, crying, down the stairs, through the shop, and into the street, to be trampled under the horses' hooves. Frances had been a little girl then. But she remembered the blood, the dragons, and her grandma's screams.

'Mam, are you alright?' It was Eve. She'd risen from the table and come to her mother's side, while the men saw to Anna. Jack's hand swung smartly against the pale cheek. Anna gulped, coughed, then whimpered, rocking to and fro.

'I know you all think I'm no good,' she said. 'I know you all think it's my fault, but what could I do, living in London? I mean Henry needed his teas got ready for him, after work and everything, and now even he thinks I'm useless. All those teas I got for him, and now, Oh God, he says I'm not a proper woman. He says she's more of a woman than I'd ever be. Well I hope they rot in hell, the pair of them.'

'What's this?' Frances asked. Eve glanced at Elizabeth whose tongue was rolling in her cheek.

'I think Anna's just let the cat out of the bag,' Eve said.

'What do *you* know about it?' Frances asked.

'Elizabeth told me. Her Dad's walked out on them. He's gone to live with another woman.'

'Dear God.' Frances sighed and sat in Eve's seat at the dinner table. Anna was gushing forth, like a tap with a worn washer.

'I hope they rot. And they will. God will thrust them into the jaws of hell. For the proud shall suffer and the meek shall inherit the earth. I own half this shop, you know.' Sharp as a needle, Anna's eyes darted round the assembled family. 'It's my inheritance, and my daughter's after me.'

'That's right, Anna,' Mary Jean said, helping her to rise. 'Why don't you go and have a little rest now.'

'There's no rest for me. No rest for the wicked. And we're all wicked. Our parents ate of the forbidden fruit and we shall suffer to infinitude.' In this vein, Anna continued as she left the room, escorted by Mary Jean, her voice droning on, up the stairs.

'My God,' said Frances. 'She gets more like Hester every day.'

'Fran!' Jack gave his wife a warning look. Elizabeth was still at the table, head in hands. She lifted her face to look at Frances. Frances flushed. Eve came to the rescue.

'Elizabeth, what your aunt means is just that your Mam's been badly affected by your grandma's death . . .'

'She was "affected" before!' Elizabeth cut in. 'That's why Dad left home. She was driving him crazy!'

'But she's got worse . . . ?' Frances queried.

'Yes. I suppose she has really,' Elizabeth said.

'Surely your father's responsible for her. He should be looking after her!'

'I don't think Mam'd let him. She's scared of him. I mean she's scared of me as well. Actually, she's scared of everybody. And when she's scared she gets nasty.'

'Anna?' Frances and Jack exchanged a look.

'You don't believe me?' Elizabeth asked. Then she said casually, 'Wait and see.'

'I think the world's gone mad,' Frances said.

'You've only just noticed?' Elizabeth drawled, as she left the room. David Jackson's stomach was rumbling. He coughed to cover it.

'I'll put out the soup, shall I?' Frances said in response. But when she turned to it, she realized it was stone cold. 'Damn!'

'Come on, Mam. I'll take it down to the kitchen and heat it up.' Eve took the tureen away. 'Maisie, will you help me set the table down there? I think we might as well give up the grandeur and be comfortable.'

Maisie rushed to comply. Frances looked after her daughter, astonished. She'd only been back one afternoon, and she'd taken over already.

'This isn't my home any more, Jack,' Frances said, as the remainder of the dinner guests left.

David spent the rest of the evening in the office with George, going through his A.C. theory. George had failed it in the summer, and still couldn't make head nor tail of it.

'David's an electrical engineer now,' Os explained. 'Works on the grid. He's at the Control place in Chester le Street. It's very kind of him to come and help our George out the way he does.'

'What's George want to be?' Eve asked.

'Electrician. You can get a good job on the N.E.E.B.'

'If he passes his exams,' Frances said drily, as she poured the tea.

'He will!' Mary Jean assured her irritably. 'He works hard enough. He's bound to.'

'Doesn't always follow, pet,' Os sighed. 'He's worried sick about them. I know that. And if he fails this time, they'll not give him another chance.'

'He could always work in the shop,' Eve said. 'I mean, I suppose you will retire one day, Os.' Os sighed. A look passed from him to Mary Jean, to Frances, to Jack, and on to Maisie.

'Let's have a hand of gin rummy,' Maisie said brightly. 'Take our minds off our troubles, eh?'

'Some of them won't go away,' Frances muttered, as Maisie shuffled and split.

Sleepy old England, eh? Eve chuckled, as she lay in bed that night, half-asleep, listening to the muttering from across the corridor. Poor Elizabeth. Perhaps the child could sleep in her room for a while. But how long was 'a while'? Apparently, there was no home for Anna and Elizabeth to 'go home' to! Eve sighed. Anna was obviously ill. She needed help. Why, if she lived in the States, she'd've been sent to a shrink long ago. Had she inherited the weakness from her mother, Hester? Hester; Jane's daughter. Eve's eyes sprang open. Hadn't Jane Beattie committed suicide too? What was in store for that poor girl with the hair? Her father'd deserted her. Her mother was crazy. No wonder she'd turned existentialist! It was enough to drive anyone to Sartre! Those posters; James Dean, Camus, and *who* was Jackson Pollock? Elizabeth was only fifteen. How could she hope to cope? Eve felt very sorry for her. She was fast developing an urge to take her under her wing. Someone had to. Sleepy old England, eh? Well, England was 'where it was at' right now! No doubt about it!

Unwilling to go back to London and a life without Henry, Anna allowed Frances to telephone her father, Tom Fairbairn. Could he take his daughter in? Frances asked.

'What sort of state's she in?' Tom asked warily.

'Well, she's nervy, you know . . .'

386

Tom sighed. 'I see,' he said. There was a long pause. 'Well, I am her father. So, the responsibility falls on me. But, I'll tell you one thing, Frances,' he said, 'at my age, I cannot be expected to cope with a teenager as well.'

'No, Tom. I see your point. Look, if Elizabeth's father can't have her back in London, I'll see if the family will have her here.' Tom sighed with relief, and resigned himself to receiving his daughter on the next train.

'It'll be a nice holiday for you, Anna,' Maisie said kindly, as she helped her pack.

'Huh!' Anna snorted. 'I'm not daft, you know. I know what's going on. You're all trying to get shot of me. Just like Henry. You all think I'm no good, don't you?' Then, of course, she cried.

'No, no,' they all lied. Elizabeth had locked herself in her room. She wouldn't come down, not even to see her mother off. Anna was cut to the quick but some travel pills had sedated her. So there were no tantrums and she left, more or less docile, in the florist's van, the same way Eve had arrived a few days earlier.

'My, don't people come and go quickly round here?' Eve observed, remembering the land of Oz.

'What, pet?' Frances asked, startled.

'Nothing. Just a line from an old film,' Eve said.

'I'd've thought you'd have had enough of your Hollywood dreamworld,' her Mam said curtly.

'Oh I have. I have,' Eve agreed. 'But dreams can be prophetic, you know?'

'What do you mean?' Frances was blushing. Eve looked at her, surprised.

'I didn't mean anything,' she said. 'But perhaps I've accidentally put my finger on something. Have I?' Frances bit her lip and got on with making the dinner. Mary Jean was busy in the shop, so Eve went upstairs to ponder what her mother might have up her sleeve, and sort out her clothes at the same time. Her wardrobe was perfect for the lifestyle of a politician's wife, but it really didn't suit the unemployed status of a shopkeeper's daughter! Most of them would have to be put in mothballs.

But, when she reached the top of the stairs, Eve was surprised to find that the door to her room was wide open. So was Elizabeth's. Smelling a rat, Eve hurried in, and found Elizabeth joyfully stamping and wiping her feet on an assortment of designer suits and dresses which had been strewn about the floor. Eve hurtled across the room, throwing herself, screaming, at Elizabeth, who fell backwards, yelling in agony.

'Oh God! My arm! I think I've broken my arm!'

'Think yourself lucky I haven't broken your neck!' Eve screamed. She was standing over her, fists clenched.

'Oh, for God's sake, cool it!' Elizabeth was trying to sound casual while scurrying to the far side of the bed, out of harm's way. 'I was only trying to help,' she drawled. 'I mean, now, at least you can wear them without looking stupid.'

'Thank you very much!' Eve blustered.

'Well, what were you going to do with them? Put them in mothballs?' Elizabeth was absently rubbing her elbow, when Eve started towards her, looking vindictive. Immediately Elizabeth doubled up in pain. 'Oh God, I'm in agony,' she cried. It was a terrible truth that Eve couldn't hit a girl when she was down. She hesitated, her rage made impotent. If only Elizabeth hadn't been right about the mothballs. It was the worst blow of all.

'Someone needs to teach you a lesson, my girl,' Eve said, slumping on the bed.

'You hurt me,' Elizabeth whimpered. Eve gave her a sidelong glance. She wouldn't put it past this one to be putting it on. 'But you're right,' Elizabeth said quickly, seeing her ploy had been too transparent for the sophisticated American, 'you're right. I do need to be taught ever such a lot. In fact, I'd be very grateful, Auntie Evie, if you'd help me sort things out with the local school. I suppose I do have to attend the local school? I'm dying to start lessons again and nobody else seems remotely interested in my education.'

Elizabeth was busy hanging up Eve's clothes as she spoke. And, before she knew where she was, Eve had agreed to go with her to see the head of the grammar school.

The head was not a 'sophisticated American'. He was a very nice man, who tended to believe what he was told. And Elizabeth easily persuaded him she was an offer he couldn't refuse. Laudably anxious to continue her studies without delay, and her scholarly abilities having such merit, Elizabeth was allowed to start, before the formalities had been gone through, the following Monday morning. So it was that, dressed in the wrong uniform, she turned up at South Shields Grammar, three weeks into the winter term. She wasn't nervous, or scared, and as for the uniform, well, she liked to be different. She put it about that her deserted mother was far too poor to afford a new one, and her relatives were only keeping her on sufferance as it was, so she could hardly ask them to cough up. In a way, it was true. Anyway, the head swallowed the tale, hook line and sinker. He informed the staff they all had to lean over backwards to make allowances for poor, highly-talented, extremely intelligent, Elizabeth Strachan. With any luck, she'd do them proud. She was a catch. The ambitious head was busily creating a rosy picture of her future, as possibly the first pupil from the school to enter Oxbridge. She might even get an Exhibition, throwing even more glory on his school. He rubbed his hands with glee, and started a regime of catching up for her, which, in fact, was a thinly disguised attempt at cramming.

Elizabeth didn't mind. In fact, she rather liked all this attention. And she enjoyed learning too. Not that she went along with all this Latin and Greek. She had no intention whatsoever of becoming a Classics Scholar. Nor did she intend to specialize in Ancient or Modern History, which was another suggestion that had been made to her. No. Art remained her goal. Of course she could, if she was very lucky, get onto a Fine Arts course at university. Elizabeth considered the idea. It gave her access to all the art materials she wanted. But considering the matter was all she did. And while George bussed it three nights a week to Sunderland Tech, struggling for his 'Ordinary National', Elizabeth queened it in the art room at South Shields Grammar.

In November, Khrushchev requested the allies to withdraw their troops from Berlin, Elizabeth had her birthday, and Eve received her first indication of the settlement with John.

The news came in a letter from her solicitor. John was not happy about the idea of divorce. He was not happy at all! In fact, he had decided not to go along with it. Deeply distressed, Eve slopped her tea into her saucer, and swallowed down a sob. Everyone noticed, but pretended not to have.

'Don't let the bastards get you down,' Elizabeth whispered in her ear, as she left for school. Frances threw her a dirty look. So Elizabeth patted Eve on the arm and went out singing. George gave Eve a wide berth, as he edged round the breakfast table on his way to work, and Frances escaped into the shop, to help make wreaths with her son and daughter-in-law, leaving Jack to pick up the pieces.

'Bad news?' he asked, as he poured the tea from Eve's saucer back into her cup.

Eve nodded. 'He won't give me a divorce.'

Jack raised his eyebrows and sat down, sighing. 'Well, it doesn't altogether surprise me,' he said. 'It would be detrimental to his political career, wouldn't it?'

'He wouldn't have one, if I exposed him.'

'Have you proof of any misdemeanour?' Eve shook her head. 'You do realize, don't you, that whatever you said would come across as the vindictiveness of an estranged wife, and nothing more?' Eve sobbed, and threw the letter down. 'It's not fair, I know. But that's how it is.'

'You know what the bastard's doing?' Eve cried. 'Jim told me. He sent me a cutting from the local paper. John is actually running a newspaper campaign against "fags"; you know, "homosexuals". Damned hypocrite! How can he do it?'

'He's clever. I'll say that for him,' Jack said. 'Diverts attention from himself, you see.'

'I wish . . . I wish . . .' Eve blustered helplessly.

'He'll trip himself up one of these days. Mark my words,' Jack said.

'I'd like to think you're right.' Eve blew her nose, and wiped her eyes.

'So . . . what are you going to do?' Jack asked.

Eve picked up the letter again, reading over the suggestion made by the solicitor. 'He's prepared to make a separation settlement. He's being quite generous, actually.' Eve hated to admit it. 'He's offering me a lump sum. Quite a lot. And access to Peter, any time I like, just so long as I leave him domiciled in the States with Lou and Ella.' She passed the letter over to Jack.

He read it carefully. 'It sounds reasonable enough. For now,' he said, looking up at her.

'What do you mean, "for now"?'

'Well, it suits you really, for the moment. I'd say you'd be wise to accept.' Eve was about to blow her top, but Jack ploughed on. 'Later, when you've had a chance to make your own way, you can sue for divorce. When you're in a better position to offer Pete a home, for instance.' His face assumed a wry expression. 'You might get married again!'

As expected, Eve spat furiously in response. 'I'm not completely stupid!' she said.

'Stranger things have happened, love,' her father told her. 'Don't bank on being single for the rest of your life.' With that, he got up and went to take Maisie her morning tea in bed. Eve watched him go, uneasily. She had to do something, that was for sure. She couldn't just scrounge off her family for ever more, and she certainly wasn't getting married! But what could she do? Teach dancing. That was about the top and bottom of it. She looked at the letter again. It was a lot of money. She looked hard at the mantelpiece, wondering how much it would cost to buy and refurbish a studio. It was an idle thought, but one which took root in her mind. She made a tour of the estate agents, and scanned the newspaper ads. There were already one or two dancing classes in Shields but none in the centre of town. If she could only find a place on Ocean Road, for instance, she might make a go of it. There was an old church hall for sale, down near the Marine Park. Eve went to see it, once, twice, and sat at the kitchen table, drawing plans, to see if, somehow, she could afford to give the hall a decent dance floor, and, at the same time, convert the rest of the accommodation into a flat, for herself and eventually, Pete.

The enterprise caught Elizabeth's imagination. As David Jackson took George through his A.C. theory upstairs in the office, Elizabeth and Eve sat downstairs, drawing up plan after plan, working out budget after budget.

'I could come and stay with you, Eve,' Elizabeth mused. 'I could help you run the dance school, and I daresay Uncle Jack and Auntie Frances would be glad to be rid of me.'

Eve smiled. 'You'll be off to university before long, I should think,' she said.

'Not for another couple of years. I've got to do my "A" levels

391

first. Unless, of course, I go to art school.' Eve glanced up sharply. There was a playful look in Elizabeth's eyes.

'You silly cat. You'd do it just to spite everybody, wouldn't you?' she said.

Elizabeth laughed. 'Not you, Eve. I would never spite you.'

'I'm glad to hear it,' Eve said drily.

'I've entered for an art competition, you know,' she said. This time, Elizabeth was serious.

Eve stared at her. 'When?'

'Oh, six weeks ago. The results aren't for ages yet. Don't tell anybody, will you?'

'Why ever not? I should think you'd want them all rooting for you!'

'Good God no!' Elizabeth was horrified. 'Supposing I didn't win? They'd never let me go to art school then.'

'Are you serious about this art school business?' Eve asked.

'Maybe, maybe not,' Elizabeth said airily. Eve nodded slowly. Obviously Elizabeth's seriousness depended on the results of this competition.

'Are you going to tell me any more about this thing you've entered?' she asked.

'No,' Elizabeth laughed. 'If you could see your face!'

'Elizabeth Strachan, there are times I could murder you,' Eve said. But she was smiling, in spite of herself.

David and George came down in search of a cup of tea at nine o'clock. George looked 'proper pasty', as Maisie put it. She offered to make him some Ovaltine, while she was getting her own. But George declined the offer and got stuck into some of his mother's chocolate cake instead.

'You'd think he had worms, wouldn't you, David?' Elizabeth said. David Jackson was taken aback. He blustered for an agonizing second, and was rescued by Eve.

'Don't be so rude, Liz,' Eve said. Elizabeth cringed at the 'Liz', as Eve knew she would. 'And it's Mr Jackson, to you.'

'Oh I don't mind . . . ' David said easily, as he slipped into a chair. 'I feel almost part of this family.' Elizabeth smiled slyly.

'I bet you'd like to be, wouldn't you, David?' she said. David laughed awkwardly, then went silent. Eve was furious. She glared at Elizabeth, who lolled her tongue round her mouth, and, looking very pleased with herself, leaned across the table to him. 'You've never been married, have you, David?' she said breathlessly.

David coughed, then replied, 'Well, Elizabeth, as a matter of fact I have.'

There was a shocked silence. Eve almost dropped the chocolate cake, which she was hiding from George, in the larder. 'My wife died. She was run over by a bus.' Elizabeth burst out laughing. She lay, sprawled across the table, shaking helplessly. Then, in spite of herself, Eve started up. Then George choked on his chocolate cake, and David, protesting, 'But it's true, honestly, it's true, she did!', started laughing too. 'It was going to Two Ball Lonnen!' At this news, Eve and Elizabeth screamed with delight, and Os, putting his head round the door to see what was going on, was mystified to hear David Jackson apologize, saying, 'Well, it *was* a long time ago Vera died, Os.'

'How's your A.C. theory coming on, son?' Os asked, hoping to change the subject.

'I don't understand a word of it, Dad,' George replied.

At this, they all howled with laughter, all over again, and, shaking his head, Os retired thunderstruck to watch T.V. in his room.

Christmas came and went. Anna came, but never went. Eve hated every minute. She didn't have money to buy presents, so she altered some of her 'posh clothes' to fit Frances, Maisie, Anna and Mary Jean, and, after racking her brains for weeks, hit on the idea of giving Elizabeth a cheap cigarette-holder for her Christmas box.

'Don't tell anybody, mind.' Eve warned the delighted Elizabeth, who kissed her warmly on the cheek.

'It's the best present I've ever had,' she said and presented Eve with a large painting of herself. Eve looked at it for a long time.

'Do I really look like this?' she asked anxiously.

'It's your essence I paint,' Elizabeth explained.

'My essence,' Eve nodded slowly. 'No wonder I've got problems.'

'It's one of you I sent for the competition. I call it "Fracture".'

'Oh.' Eve decided not to ask what it meant. 'Heard the results yet?'

Elizabeth shook her head and put her finger to her lips.

The pair went for a walk on Christmas Day, leaving the rest of the family to doze in front of the circus, on T.V. It was a bright, crisp day. The sun was almost white, and glanced off the sea in a display of flashing lights. It sent Elizabeth delirious with delight.

'I mean, how would you paint that?' she asked. 'It's alive!'

Shading her eyes from the glare, Eve smiled to see the young girl reaching out to the sun.

'You should see the landscape of New Mexico and Arizona. Everything's red, rosy red. It's like the place's been burned by the sun. You'd paint some pictures there!'

'I wish I could go.' Elizabeth's head turned sharply. 'Don't you wish you could go back?'

'I wish I could see Pete. I wish I knew if he was missing me,' Eve blurted out.

'Haven't you heard anything?'

'Yes. I got a card from Ella. She said he's fine. Perfectly well. Perfectly happy.'

'There you are then. What are you worried about?' For Elizabeth, everything was simple.

'How do you suppose I feel, knowing he's *not* missing me?'

'Oh! I see!' Elizabeth hung her head in shame. 'Aren't I thick? I'm sorry, Evie.' She threaded her arm in Eve's, and Eve responded, exposing still more of her wounds.

'He's my son. I love him. I . . . I want him to love me back!' she cried. 'I mean it's reasonable enough, isn't it?'

'Mmm . . . ' Elizabeth mused. 'It's a heavy scene, children. Personally I've decided not to have any. I mean, who wants all that heartache? All that responsibility? Anyway, I think it's positively criminal to bring a child into this world. I mean, what sort of a future is there?'

'Thanks for the sympathy,' Eve said bitterly.

'Sorry!' Elizabeth smiled. 'Come on, Evie. Cheer up. David's coming tonight and there's a special of "Hancock's Half Hour". You know you like that. You can cuddle up together on the sofa and watch it.'

'Stop it!' Eve laughed in spite of herself. 'I have no intention of doing anything so stupid!'

'Well,' Elizabeth said. 'If you don't want him, I'll have him. Personally I rather go for older men.'

But, in any case, David Jackson failed to turn up on Christmas Night. Too many people had put on too many ovens to cook too many Christmas turkeys all at the same time and overloaded the grid. So he was stuck, in Chester le Street, doing overtime.

Eve was pondering the idea of going back to America just to see Pete when, late in January, George having passed his Ordinary National Certificate, Os announced he wanted to sell the shop. They were all gathered, in the dining room, for a special celebration tea. Maisie had made a cake, with 'Congratulations George' piped on the top in pink icing. And, of course, David Jackson was present, as honoured guest. He sat, pink-cheeked with pride at one end of the table, while his pupil, George, sat looking bemused at the other.

'I still don't understand A.C. theory,' he said.

'Never mind, George,' David comforted him. 'You made them think you did.'

'Will you be applying for jobs now, George?' Anna asked. 'Away from home?' She was hopeful of another room falling vacant in the house.

'Oh, you don't apply for jobs, Aunt Anna,' George told her. 'You just go on their list. Then they write a letter, inviting you to be interviewed for any job you're qualified for. It's automatic, like.'

'Oh, I see,' Anna said. But she didn't see, and she hadn't got the answer to the most important part of her question. 'So, em . . . will these jobs be in Shields, then, George?' she asked.

'Not necessarily,' he told her. Anna brightened. It was then, as though to put paid to her hopes of a permanent residency, that Os exploded his bomb.

'Well,' he said, 'now our George's got a career, I don't see any point in hanging on to the business.' There was a long silence. Nobody had understood what he'd said, so Os went on to clarify. 'I'm going to sell the shop,' he said.

'Over my dead body!' Anna shouted.

'Who'd buy it?' asked Elizabeth.

'You might well ask,' Frances commented. Eve was thunderstruck. It had never occurred to her that the shop might, one day, pass out of the family.

'You can't,' she gasped. 'Can you?'

'I don't see why not,' Os said. 'Mam and Dad've got no objection, so . . .'

'But where'd they go?' Eve asked.

'As a matter of fact,' Frances said coyly, 'Jack and me've been offered a nice little council bungalow at Marsden. It'd be a lot easier to run than this miserable old place, and we'd be near the sea, and Cleadon Hills, and that.'

'What about Maisie? Eve objected.

'They've offered me one too,' Maisie told her. 'A single person's bungalow, in the next row. Eeh, it'll be nice to be independent again.' Poor Maisie. Years before, she'd sold her precious flat to buy tickets to America, so Eve could try her luck in Hollywood. It'd been more of a sacrifice than Eve had ever allowed herself to realize. And now Maisie was to have a home of her own again.

'I see,' Eve said. 'Well, I'm very glad for you, Maisie.'

Eve's voice caught in her throat, and when she looked at her Mam and Jack, it was with accusing eyes. She'd come home to them. She'd made it up with Jack and she'd thought they'd developed a real relationship at last. In fact, she'd come to rely on Jack being there. And now, they were both deserting her!

'Well, I'm sorry to put a spoke in the wheel,' Anna was saying. Eve struggled out of her own thoughts, and tried to catch on to the proceeding argument. 'I'm sorry and all that. But Os has simply no right to sell the shop.' There was a general outcry. 'Do I have to remind this family that half the business, half this house, actually belongs to me?' Anna pointed out. There was a silence. 'And after I die, my share'll pass on to my daughter, Elizabeth here.'. Elizabeth laughed, almost putting Anna off her stroke, but not quite. 'And what are you laughing at, miss?' she shrieked.

'Oh, Ma,' Elizabeth drawled, 'I don't want the bloody shop!'

'Language!' Anna protested.

'You can sell the place any time you like, as far as I'm concerned, Uncle Os,' Elizabeth said, ignoring her mother.

'Thanks very much,' Os replied courteously.

'Of course . . .' Elizabeth inclined her head coyly to one side, 'I wouldn't say "no" to my half in cash . . . after you've sold it, of course.' Everyone smiled slowly, everyone but Anna, who looked as though she was about to blow a gasket.

'Sounds fair enough,' Os agreed. 'What do you say, Mam? Dad?'

Both nodded and grunted approval.

'That's settled then,' Elizabeth said.

'It is not settled!' Anna shouted. Remembering the hysterics on the last occasion they'd met in the dining room, everyone tried to calm her down.

'I do think we should refrain from argument. After all, this is meant to be George's celebration tea,' Maisie reminded her.

'Don't blame me, Maisie,' Anna said. 'I didn't bring this sale business up, did I?' Self-righteous approval made her lip quiver and they all thought she was going to cry.

'It's alright, Auntie Anna,' George said, his mouth full of egg and tomato sandwich (his favourite since his very first birthday tea). 'I'm enjoying myself anyway.'

'Heartless brute!' Anna burst out crying, after all. 'You've all had it in for me, and for my mother, right from the start. If you ask me, it was you lot sent her mad in the first place. You drove her to it. Just like you're driving me!' A sigh passed round the table. 'Here we go again.' And Anna, wound up like an old gramophone, went on and on, till, finally, Os said,

'Well, I'm going to sell our half-share. Get what I can for it. So put that in your pipe and smoke it, Anna Strachan!'

'Nobody'd buy a half-share!' Frances objected.

'Yes, they would,' Eve said quietly. They all looked at her. What had it to do with Eve? 'I would, for a start.'

Even Anna stopped crying in the general astonishment.

'But . . . why, pet? You don't want this place round your neck!' Frances pleaded. 'You've got some money from your settlement, I know, but that's for *you*! It's to make a new start in life! You don't want to waste it on this dump!' Frances was near to tears. She'd seen her daughter brought low, she didn't want to see her driven under.

'Don't worry, Mam,' Eve assured her. 'I wouldn't keep it as a shop.' Slowly light began to dawn. 'As you all know, I've been looking for suitable premises to turn into a dance studio for some time. Well, none of them's worked out. I've got some money, but not enough to do what I want with. But, if I was to buy only half the worth of this place, I'd actually be left with enough to do the conversion!' Frances and Jack were nodding.

'It's ideally placed. I mean, it's central, and it's right opposite the Queen's Hall. What better advertisement for a dance studio? Anybody going to the dances at the Queen's would only have to look across the street and they'd know where to come to improve their rumba, wouldn't they?'

'It's a great idea.' Jack was smiling.

'What about *my* share?' Anna said.

Eve's voice was businesslike in reply. 'Well, Anna, you're only a sleeping partner as it is. What difference does it make to you whether the family business is a shop, a dance studio, or a fish and chip emporium? Eh?' There was no answer.

Anna sat silent, apart from the odd sniff. She felt sure she ought to disapprove, but couldn't think of anything to disapprove of.

'You've got her!' Elizabeth was victorious. Then her expression faltered. 'What's going to happen to me?' she asked.

'You could stay on here, if you liked,' Eve volunteered.

'Great! I could help run the dance school and everything!'

'We'll see.' Eve smiled. She glanced at Os and Mary Jean. It wasn't the right moment to ask, not with Anna present, but what were they going to do?

Late that night, with Elizabeth's plans for the new studio strewn over the kitchen table, Eve was sitting drinking tea with Os, when she said,

'Os, you must have had some plan in mind . . . for you and Mary Jean, I mean . . . ?'

Os shrugged. 'Mam said I could have the money to set myself up with. But what doing, I don't know.'

'You could work for me . . . ' Eve suggested tentatively.

Os snorted. 'I can't dance for toffee, man!'

'I don't mean as a dancing teacher, Os! I meant . . . well, the business side. You've had experience of keeping books and marketing and so on. I'm going to need somebody to do all that.' Os frowned. He couldn't see himself working for a dancing school, and yet what Eve was saying did make a sort of sense. 'You could continue living here, you and Mary Jean, just like now. There'll be plenty of room. What do you say?' Os said nothing for a while, then he nodded slowly.

'I'll think it over,' he said.

He talked it over with Mary Jean, that same night. Next

morning, he took Eve quietly aside, in the shop, and told her he was willing to give it a try. Eve could have jumped for joy. From being an outsider, she had gravitated to the centre of the family. She was approved and respected, in her own country. And, once the papers were signed, Eve's status improved further. As a woman of substance, she gained new identity, and with it, a sense of her own, growing, inner strength.

But when, at Easter, Jack, Frances and Maisie all began packing for Marsden, and George left to become a linesman in Hexham, the feeling of being at the centre was somewhat dissipated. Elizabeth too watched the general exodus with dismay.

'Whatever happened to the extended family?' she asked.

'Never mind,' Eve consoled her. 'The builders'll be in soon. It'll be easier with fewer people around.'

'I'm afraid you'll have to manage without me,' Anna informed her apologetically. Eve tried hard not to look pleased. 'I'm afraid my nerves wouldn't stand all that banging and hammering and what not. And anyway, my old Dad needs looking after. He's not as young as he was, you know.'

Poor Tom. Eve couldn't help feeling sorry for him. She knew who would be looking after who. But when Anna suggested Elizabeth go down with her, to spend the Easter holidays, and see her grandad, Elizabeth was panic-stricken.

'Eve needs me, to keep an eye on the builders,' she objected. 'After all, I did draw up the initial plans. And I do have a vested interest in the business, don't I?'

This latter argument held sway with her mother, who grunted, then agreed to let Elizabeth stay. But once Anna was out of the way, Elizabeth began joyfully packing her bag.

'Where are you going?' Eve asked indignantly. For answer, Elizabeth produced a letter. It was an invitation to attend the prizewinners' function of the young artists' competition in London. Elizabeth had won second prize.

'Just think, Evie,' she said. 'Everybody'll be looking at a picture of you!'

Eve didn't know whether she was pleased or horrified. If she remembered correctly, the picture had been called 'Fracture'. She shook her head in disbelief.

'You really are good then,' she said, at last.

'Looks like it,' Elizabeth grinned.

'But why didn't you go and stay at your grandad's? *He* lives in London!'

'So does my father,' Elizabeth pointed out. 'With the woman from the G.L.C. They've asked me to stay. I'm going to go with them on the C.N.D. march to Aldermaston and everything. What an Easter this is going to be! Ban the bomb! Ban the bomb!'

'I get the picture!' Eve sighed. 'But I thought your father had deserted you, orphan Annie!'

'Well, actually, he only deserted Ma. Only don't tell her, will you?' She winked.

So it was, that when the builders finally arrived, only Eve, Os and Mary Jean were present to see the old place ripped apart. They tore out the shop fittings, then the kitchen, then they pulled down the dividing wall between the two, and, leaving the balcony hanging, as if in mid-air, took away the old stair from the shop floor to the office above. To Eve, it felt as though they'd actually pushed the walls of the old house farther apart, leaving new space in which to breathe and live. She slept, as on a cushion of air, aware of the house, suspended, floating on its, as yet, unmaterialized future. And when, next morning, she came down, before the builders had arrived, she was transported by the sunlight that was pouring in through the naked windows.

CHAPTER NINETEEN

A year brought remarkable changes both in Fowler Street, and in Eve. It had galled her, when she'd realized she would have to get English teaching qualifications before setting up her studio, and it had taken nine months going through the motions, learning each syllabus and passing the exams. But she had to do it. If Elizabeth could get nine 'O' levels, Eve could manage to get what was surely a matter of form, the papers to prove she could do what she'd been doing anyway, for years! For it was to be a top drawer studio, attracting pupils from all over the north-east. They would win medals, trophies, championships, go on to star in West End shows, dance at Sadlers Wells and appear on T.V. But this was all in the future. First, pupils had to be found and then they had to be trained. Eve knew it would be a labour of love.

But, as the year progressed, the upstairs slowly turned into two flats, one for Os and Mary Jean and one for Eve, with, of course, Elizabeth as lodger. It proved a cosy, manageable arrangement, which they all liked. The office remained more or less the same, though new wallpaper and paint brightened it, and plants hung over the balcony, trailing green fronds that wafted like weeds in the air from the open windows below. The whole of the down-stairs was exposed now, and its wooden floor, a real sprung dance floor, reflected light like a glassy pond. The old counter wall was mirrored, with a barre running from end to end, and a white spiral staircase led up to the balcony and the cloakroom. The spiral staircase had been Elizabeth's idea. Eve had thought it wildly romantic and entirely out of place. But Elizabeth had been right to insist on it. It was a focal point. It added style, and it took up far less space than all those old stairways, one from the back kitchen and one from the shop, both gone now. It had left room for the cloakrooms too. The dressing rooms, male and female, were downstairs in the cellar, which was now dry (more or less), having been tanked up, and lined with wooden boards for warmth. Seats ran along the walls, with hooks above, and the floor was covered in cheap carpet. The place was a dream come true. All it needed now was pupils.

Os prepared to launch his long-prepared advertising campaign for the autumn term, which was to start in the second week of September, and Eve paced the polished floor of the dance studio, biting her nails. What if nobody came? What if she'd spent all that money for nothing? It didn't bear thinking about. She chased Os from pillar to post, demanding results like yesterday, driving him crazy. But it was only July. She had to be, what Eve was not, patient.

'Have a holiday, Sis,' Os told her, 'while you have a chance! As a matter of fact, I've heard the Costa Brava's very nice. David Jackson went last year. Shall I ask him to get you a brochure?'

Eve scowled at him. What *was* he suggesting? Tossing her head, she went up to her flat. Elizabeth was watching T.V.

'Sh!' she hissed as Eve came in, moaning about Os. The American rocket launch was on its last count-down. Eve stood watching the little numbers flash in the corner of the T.V. screen, and, to her surprise, felt very excited. Then the moment came for the blast-off. The whole rocket disintegrated, collapsing onto its own launch pad.

'Oh well, try, try again,' Eve said.

'Damn,' swore Elizabeth. 'I was hoping we'd have a glass of sherry to celebrate.'

Eve smiled and shook her head. 'I can't afford sherry,' she said. I don't know. Os seems to think I'm made of money. He wants me to go to the Costa Brava for a holiday!'

'Good idea. Can I come?'

'No! If I had any money, I'd go to the States, to see Pete. He's growing up without me.' Eve was surprised to find herself near to tears. Elizabeth looked at her sympathetically.

'Os's right. You do need a holiday. You could always come to London with me. Dad and Myra'd love it. I've told them lots about you and they're very impressed.'

'*What* have you told them?'

'Only the truth.'

'What truth? I wasn't really a big star, you know.'

'No. No. They're not interested in any of that! They're interested in the fact you actually witnessed some of the Nevada tests!'

Eve's mouth dropped open, then she shut it again. Why should she be surprised? After all, which was more important, dancing at the Bowl, or witnessing the explosion of an atomic bomb? She laughed ironically and shook her head.

But Elizabeth persisted. 'They are, you know! In fact, they're rather surprised you haven't come on any of the rallies.' She gave Eve a quizzical look. 'Why haven't you?' Eve sighed and went to the kitchen to make some tea, but Elizabeth followed her doggedly. 'Look, Evie, we're hoping to plan a big gathering, Trafalgar Square or somewhere, this summer. Not a march or anything. Maybe a candlelight vigil. So it wouldn't be exhausting, but it's a chance to stand up and be counted. Why don't you come?'

'I don't think so,' Eve said. 'It's not for me.' She was watching the kettle.

'6th August. To mark the anniversary of Hiroshima. Do you know how many survivors've ended up with cancer?'

'Stop it, Liz,' Eve warned.

'You can't just bury your head in the sand! We now know radiation causes cancer, and yet we're still making bombs! We're even thinking of setting up nuclear reactors to make electricity! Imagine nuclear reactors all over Britain, time bombs ticking away. Sooner or later, devastation! David told me, it's the new thing. The C.E.G.B. . . . .'

Eve rounded on her, shouting bitterly, 'My sons had cancer. You don't have to preach at me.'

Elizabeth stared at her. She'd known the boys had been ill. She even knew it had been cancer, but she'd never connected it with the bomb. She went cold from head to foot, then flung her arms round Eve in an impulsive gesture of compassion.

'Oh, I'm sorry. I'm sorry. I'm so stupid.'

'It's O.K. Forget it,' Eve said. 'And don't think I don't approve of what you're doing . . . the marches and so on. I do. Somebody's got to do it. Only, not me, please. I've had my fill of politics one way or another. So . . . ' She held Elizabeth away from her and looked at her tear-soaked face. 'You go on marching, and shouting, getting arrested if need be. The future's in the hands of the young now. Go to it. And do a better job of it than we did.'

They hugged one another as the electric kettle boiled and boiled and finally blew its back out.

But after Liz had gone down to London, the place seemed so empty. Os was out, drumming up business a lot of the time, and Mary Jean spent her day potting geraniums and doing up tubs for the back yard.

'Makes it look nice,' she said. And it did, but it bored Eve rigid. She looked over the accounts, again and again, trying to work out a way to afford the trip west. But there was so little money left, and they needed a cushion. Then a letter came from Jim. As usual, he had enclosed newspaper cuttings, and this time as they fell out of the envelope, Eve's heart jumped. 'Councillor in Drugs Racket', was the headline that met her eyes first. She read on, racing over page after page, report after report, the best from the Albuquerque locals, where the scandal of Councillor John Ridley was second only to the sighting of yet another U.F.O. in the vicinity of Sandia Mesa. The news items seemed equally improbable. After all this time, was it really possible John Ridley could be exposed and brought to trial? Eve was smiling as she turned to Jimmy's letter. He was urging her to come over and start divorce proceedings proper. Once the association with Ken Houlihan was out, public sympathy would swing her way and she would be sure to get custody of her son.

So, throwing caution to the winds, Eve drew out her last few hundred and blew them on a restricted period ticket to the U.S. She had never flown the Atlantic before and she arrived before she'd got used to the idea of going.

Jim met her at Albuquerque airport and took her up to Santa

Fe, where he now had a bungalow. Unfair as it seemed, the family at The Lawe Top irrationally blamed Eve for John's humiliation, and so she wasn't welcome among them. But Eve *was* welcome in the city, where she was remembered for her charity work. A lot of people were behind her, many of them John's former victims and associates.

'I never liked him,' the Mayor told her, shaking her hand. What was it about this man that reminded Eve of her mother? 'You were far too good for him, Mrs Ridley. You going to make your home here now?'

Eve shook her head and smiled. 'Once I've got my son back, I plan to make a new life for us at home in England,' she said.

The Mayor wiped his eyes. 'Sad loss,' he said. 'Why, didn't you make a lot of money for the Children's Charity doing ballooning marathons or something?'

Eve swallowed hard, but kept smiling. She had to do her own P.R., and the Mayor knew the best lawyer in town.

Eve had a fortnight. Jim had taken time off to help her, and went with her to see the lawyer. The divorce was not going to be a problem, and, in normal circumstances, custody of Pete would be automatic. But Eve was proposing to take her son out of the country; and the family at the ranch had been looking after him for some time. So, it wasn't as straightforward as it seemed. Suppose the family objected? It could turn out to be a long-drawn-out struggle.

'Of course, it would be easier if you were intending to remarry, Mrs Ridley,' the lawyer said, looking from Jim to Eve, then back again. Jim blushed and stared out of the window. Eve pursed her lips.

'I've no marriage plans, at the moment,' she said.

'Pity, lovely-looking woman, like you,' he simpered. Eve glared at him. 'Well, not to worry. We'll do our best.' The lawyer smiled with sudden confidence. 'As for access to the child, you know you have every right to see him. If they won't play ball, I suggest you just go along there and insist. And if there's any trouble, why you just tell me. Then we'll see what we can do about it.'

'I'll go,' Jim said, as they walked out into the summer heat. 'We could take him up to the mountains for the weekend. They can't object to that.'

'You've still got the old cabin?' Eve asked.

'I live there, in the summer. It's handy for work, and much cooler.' He threw her some dollars. 'Get yourself a cab. I'll see you at the bungalow later.' Eve nodded and, heart beating much too fast, she went back to pack.

The heat of the afternoon had left a haze over the city and a grey, blue streak floated on the horizon as the sun began to set in the red sky. And still there was no sign of Jim and Pete. Eve sat at the open window, staring out, thinking about her son. Flesh of her flesh. Why was she afraid of him? What was she afraid of? Something inside her fought against him. The shadow? She snorted. Maybe she should take analysis. Get her own childhood out of her system. She'd made it up with Jack, sort of. But had she made it up with Davey Lawson? He'd brought her up, believing, as she had, that he was her natural father. And Eve'd put up with his drunkenness, his maudlin talk about the first war, his nightmares and screams in the dark. Then she'd found him on Remembrance Sunday . . . She felt disgust at the memory, quickly followed by compassion. He had destroyed himself as surely as Aunt Hester. It was the same sort of shadow that had followed them and now followed her, trying to pass itself on, through her, to the next generation. The sins of the fathers . . . it went all the way back to Adam and Eve; sins carried on the tide of history. Eve's throat ached with unshed tears, and her fists clenched against it. She couldn't let it happen to her son. Why must his innocence be shrouded by the sins of the past? What had Jack said? Something about it being in you, even if you didn't know where you came from. You carried the message of your ancestors round in your genes. Yes, that was it. No escape. But there had to be. There must be. She had to find it. A car door slammed and Eve jumped. They had arrived.

Pete cautiously followed Jim into the darkened room and saw his mother at the window, her face red in the light of the setting sun. She was smiling sweetly. He stood looking at her for a while, then, as her arms opened for him, he dutifully walked to her and allowed himself to be cuddled. Eve knew she was holding on too tight. She could feel him pulling away, but she wanted to hold him forever.

Then he started crying. 'I want Ella,' he said. 'Where's Ella?'

'You'll see her Monday,' Jim promised. 'Don't worry.' Eve felt a pang of jealousy. He was her son. Why should he prefer another? But she was being stupid to think like that and she knew it. She gave him his present, an English toy fire engine. He was pleased with it. He stopped crying, said thank you and took it out into the garden.

'Does he remember me?' Eve asked.

'Sure. Give him time. He's just confused, that's all,' Jim told her. He took her hand and squeezed it hard. The gesture acted like a trigger. Eve burst out crying and flung herself into his arms.

Pete remembered the log cabin from when he was ill. He brightened up, soon as he opened his eyes next morning and saw where he was. He had grown plump, and his sturdy legs ran all over the place. But he usually ended up in the river, where he splashed and laughed like any little boy, looking back to check if the grown-ups were watching him. And they always were. They sat, side by side, drinking in the sweet, mountain air, and talking, talking, talking.

At night, when Pete was asleep, Jim lit the kerosene lamp and they listened to the radio, and talked, and Jim brought out his photographs. Outside, the breeze lifted the branches of the trees. The leaves rustled hypnotically, as they went through the pictures one by one. Jim and the boys at Los Alamos. Jim and Louise at a jazz festival. Jim and Louise eating hamburgers. Jim and Louise . . . Who was Louise?

'Oh, just a girl I know,' Jim said, shrugging.

Eve teased him. 'She looks pretty. Nice smile.'

'She looks pretty. Nice smile.'

'Uhuh,' Jim agreed.

'I think you're pretending not to care,' Eve said.

'No. I do care. Matter-of-fact, I've known Louise a long time. Since school days. She's wild. Always was. Kind of woman who likes to own a man. You know?'

'I've seen it,' Eve agreed. 'Bloodsuckers!'

Jim grimaced, then laughed. 'You're right. That's just what she is. And I'm prize sucker. I guess I must love it.'

'You deserve better,' Eve reprimanded him.

'Yes, aunt,' Jim said. Eve was furious at the 'aunt', and hit him.

'I don't want to see any more pictures of her,' she said. She was only half-joking.

'Would you rather see me married to some nice Indian squaw?' Jim teased, producing photographs of himself with several Indian ladies, smiling en masse coyly at his side. 'Ella approves of these.'

'Do *you*?' Eve asked. Jim grinned.

'They're very nice. This one's doing a law degree just now.' Eve gaped. 'Your prejudices are showing,' he said.

'I'm sorry. I thought they must be all . . . well . . . they don't exactly respond to progress, do they?'

'She's an exception.' Jim smiled, but Eve's attention was distracted by a picture underneath. She pulled it out and stared at it.

'Is that you?' she breathed. It showed a young man with a rattlesnake in his mouth. The head swung one side, the tail the other, and he held its middle in his teeth.

'Yes,' Jim said. 'That was taken last summer at the Snake Dance.'

'I suppose it's had its poison sac removed or something . . . ?'

'No,' Jim said casually. 'But they're harmless, if you treat them right. In fact, they're beautiful creatures. Have you ever watched them move?' Eve shivered. 'You know the snake's a symbol of wisdon and spirituality? You've only to look at the Hindu religion to see that. It's an image of kundalini; the power of conscious spiritual evolution. *And* it's a symbol of healing. It is! Comes from the Greek. You see, most people think of the snake as evil, but it depends how its power's used. Knowledge on its own is dangerous. It has to be tempered with wisdom. Now we know it takes wisdom to deal with the snake, because, if we don't treat it right, it turns round and bites us. But any great power's like that; a curse or a blessing. It's up to us. Nuclear power's the same. We better not misuse it.' Eve was thinking of Elizabeth and her C.N.D. rallies. Jim was thinking of the Hopis. 'I took Sam and Pete up to the reservation for the Snake celebrations . . . just as tourists, you know.' Eve gave Jim a suspicious look. 'Don't worry. Like I told you, I'm finished with all that Hopi stuff, but it doesn't mean I'm against it. I haven't rejected what they taught me. I've just sort of digested it, and passed on.' He paused, looking at the picture with the snake. 'Pete was fascinated. He likes snakes.'

'He would!' Eve sighed and shook her head. 'Do you think he'd take to life in England?'

'Only one way to find out,' Jim said.

Eve was looking at the photo with the snake. 'Can I keep this?' she asked.

'Sure. Why do you want it? I thought it gave you the creeps.'

'I know somebody who'd like to see it!'

'O.K. Take it. I really don't mind.'

The weekend flew and before Eve knew where she was, Pete had gone back to the ranch, there'd been a last-minute interrogation by the police, a last visit with the lawyer, and she was at the airport, waiting to go.

'Soon as the papers come through, I'll bring Pete over,' Jim promised. Eve was crying. Jim thought it was because of Pete, but it wasn't just the leaving of her son. It was all sorts of things. She was, in fact, finally grieving for her marriage. She'd been too angry before, and anyway, there'd been too many other things to grieve over. But now, she realized that a whole phase of her life had ended; her marriage, her career, her relationships with the American cousins, June, Jo, Lou, Ella, Clara, Ernie. It hurt her that none of them had showed, not even to see her off! It seemed Jim was the only member of the family she could actually rely on! Dear Jim. As she turned to wave goodbye, she saw him, standing, smiling, waving back, and in that moment she knew she loved him. Louise whatever-her-name-was was no good for him. He deserved much, much better! Eve gave one last wave and one last look, cherishing the memory of that smile which was to warm the cold, lonely journey back to the new life, waiting for her in England.

Elizabeth was already home from London when Eve returned to Fowler Street. She was goggle-eyed, staring at the box.

'They're making another attempt at sending up a rocket!' she said.

'Who? The Americans or the Russians?' Eve asked.

'The Americans!'

'Come on the U.S.A.!' Eve yelled. Then she went into the

kitchen, desperate for a cup of tea. She took the kettle over to the sink to fill it, but found the sink was full of flowers. Eve looked at them, wondering if jet lag had made her see things. Pink roses. It was too good to be true. She touched the cellophane. They were real alright. She put the kettle down and searched excitedly for the card in the bouquet. It said, 'Welcome home. All the best, David Jackson.' Eve filled the kettle, then went into the sitting room to see how the rocket was doing. They were on final count-down.

'How was the rally?' she asked.

'Oh, it didn't happen,' Elizabeth replied without looking at her. 'They're going all out for a really big one next year. By the way, you've got six dancing classes fully booked for next week.'

'Six?!'

'Isn't that enough?' Elizabeth asked.

'Fancy a sherry?' Eve grinned. The rocket shot a few feet into the air, then collapsed back onto its launch pad, in much the same way as Eve collapsed onto her bed with sheer exhaustion.

When she woke, it was three in the morning. She got up and made herself some coffee, then started to unpack. She'd unpacked her suitcase, and had started on the flight bag and the second cup of coffee, when Elizabeth wandered into her room, bleary-eyed with sleep.

'What time is it?' she asked, yawning.

'Just gone four. Sorry if I woke you.' Elizabeth sat on Eve's bed, watching the things come out of the flight bag. 'Want some coffee?'

Elizabeth nodded and reached for Eve's passport, hoping to have a laugh at her photo. But as she picked it up, a couple of snapshots dropped out onto the floor. She reached down to rescue them. One was of Pete. He was a solid little lad, grinning his head off, proudly holding up a huge tree branch, and looking for all the world like it was about to topple him over. She smiled and looked at the other one. It was the photo of Jim with the snake hanging in his mouth. She gasped, and ran into the kitchen with it, shouting,

'Eve, who's this?'

Eve glanced at the picture. 'Jimmy. Jim Ridley. You know. The one who works at Los Alamos.'

'Wow!' Elizabeth looked at the photo again, shaking her head in wonder. 'That's really primitive, man!' Eve snorted and put the coffee in the mug. 'Isn't the snake a symbol of virility?'

'Honestly!' Eve shouted. 'You of all people!'

'I'm not a prude, you know.' Elizabeth defended herself.

'No. But you're intelligent. Or at least you're supposed to be!'

'Freud said . . .'

'Freud wrote a load of nonsense! If you ask me, he had more hang-ups than his patients!'

'Evie,' Elizabeth said admiringly, 'I never realized you knew so much about psychology!'

'All Americans know about psychology. All the rich ones, anyway. It's a national pastime!'

'I see.' The kettle had boiled. Elizabeth poured it for herself. The roses were still in the sink. 'Aren't you going to see to your flowers?' she asked.

'I expect so. Eventually,' Eve snapped.

'They're lovely. So romantic,' Elizabeth mocked.

'You have them, then!'

'Ooh thanks!' Elizabeth bundled them up, and started looking for a vase. 'So Freud's out then, is he?' she asked, her head, deep in the cupboard under the sink.

'According to Jimmy. Jung's the coming thing.'

'Jung? Who's he?'

'He worked with Freud for a bit, then left, to follow his own path. You saw him on T.V., last year, in "Face to Face". Remember?'

'Oh!' Elizabeth nodded. 'He was a nice old bloke! I wish I could meet him.'

'Why? Thinking of undergoing analysis, are you?'

'Why are you so angry?' Elizabeth asked, emerging from the cupboard. Eve sighed and shook her head. She didn't know.

'I'm tired,' she excused herself.

'Then go back to bed!' Elizabeth said. Suddenly she thrust the flowers into Eve's arms. 'I don't think I should have these. They're meant for you.' Eve sighed. But Elizabeth had found a vase, so Eve obediently put the roses, one by one, into the water. 'Lovely,' Elizabeth approved, when she'd finished. 'Now, go back to bed. Mmm?'

Eve shook her head, staring at the roses. 'I couldn't sleep. I think I'll go for a walk instead. Get some fresh air.'

Elizabeth watched Eve pull on her trousers and a jumper, then slip her feet into her sneakers. She was like an electric eel, all sparks and tension. Maybe she was nervous about the new term at the studio. Maybe she was upset about leaving Pete. Maybe she was in love! Or maybe all those things. It was understandable. Elizabeth would have to make allowances for her. She yawned and started back to her room.

'Have a nice walk,' she said.

Eve watched the door close behind her, then ran downstairs and out into the street.

The sun was just beginning to rise over the sea. Eve ran down the lane towards it, as if towards the fulfilment of a dream, but fearing she wouldn't arrive in time. Then she climbed the dunes, walls of sand giving under her feet, falling back, then, clambering on again, hands gripping the cutting grass, till at last, she stood, panting, at the top, king of the castle, looking out over the wide ocean. And then it happened. Orange, the giant globe floated up from under the sea, lighting the world. And Eve danced in its radiant beams, alone, on top of the dunes, like an Indian brave preparing for war.

Drunk with sea air, Eve returned to Fowler Street and a day's work. It was exciting, starting up the school. She had two ballet classes, one modern musical, one tap, and two ballroom classes to prepare for, and then, of course, there'd be private lessons to fit in too. She went through the pile of records by the radiogram, and talked Os into wiring speakers high onto the studio walls, one at each end of the room. She answered the telephone and booked three more pupils. Soon she'd have to start another class. She even laid out a tray of resin for the dancers' feet. And then the signpainter came to change the sign on the front window. He painted out 'Jack Scott. Florist', and painted in 'DANCE STUDIOS. Prop. E. Lawson.' After that, all Eve had to do was wait for Monday. It was the hardest thing of all.

But Monday came, the first ballet class was given, studio badges were issued to be sewn onto wrap-overs, and compliments were received. The compliments grew as the weeks wore on. Mothers approved. Girls got the feeling they were learning 'proper' ballet, like at proper stage schools, and were awestruck. Adults at the ballroom classes enjoyed the stimulus of Eve's enthusiasm, her quick observing eye and clear explanations. All had ambled shabbily in, and gone away feeling they had better pull their socks up. A third ballet class was soon introduced to accommodate extra demand and two more ballroom classes, crowded into Saturday mornings. Ballet girls learned to do their hair neatly in buns. Ballroom dancers learned to polish their shoes. And slowly, the clientèle rose to the level of the establishment that served them. Eve smiled on it all. Elizabeth teased her by buying her a cane, so she could pretend to be a 'ballet madame' whacking the erroneous legs of her students. But soon she too was taking part in lessons. She started learning modern musical, helped demonstrate jive for the ballroom class and, accompanied by the ever-willing David Jackson, learnt a paso doble, which she thought 'wild' (and so did he). It wasn't wild enough to stir Eve.

Another rocket left the launch pad at Cape Canaveral, only to nose-dive back to earth in seconds.

Then Eve started a weekly social dance over the road in the Queen's Hall. Jack and Frances came. To them, especially to Frances, it felt very strange. She'd dreamt of going to dances in this place. When she was little she used to look out of the windows over the shop, and watch the grand ladies, wrapped in furs, going up the steps into the Hall. She used to stare longingly, through the glass, into the ballroom on the first floor, entranced by the gorgeous ladies waltzing under the chandeliers, wishing she could be one of them. Her grandfather, George Beattie, founder of the shop, had used to cater for the buffet suppers at the Queen's, and arrange the flowers for the do's. There used to be banks of them, bordering the stairs, festooning the grand entrances, gracing the tables. And now, the flowers were absent, and the buffet consisted of a beer and a bag of crisps from the bar. But Frances was here all the same, in her best frock, waltzing under the dusty chandeliers, and looking out of the window of the Queen's Hall at the lighted windows of her old home. It was as though she'd walked through a mirror, to become one with the world on the other side. And her daughter had arranged it. Trust Eve.

413

Frances and Jack watched her doing the demonstration dances with David Jackson. He was a big man, but light on his feet, and he knew how to hold a lady. His hand was firm in the small of Eve's back and he was proud to partner her.

'Does she know he's in love with her?' Jack asked his wife.

Frances sighed. 'Why ask me? Our Eve's part of the new generation. They don't believe in love, do they? Just sex!'

'If you're right, they're in for a bonny shock,' Jack said drily.

'I thought our Eve'd had enough shocks.' Frances watched David whisk her daughter expertly off the floor, to enthusiastic applause. Then Jack offered Frances his arm, and they strode boldly into a tango.

The fourth rocket attempt exploded in mid-air. They were all getting used to the disappointments. Dreams of space travel were fast fading from the consciousness, and hope was fading in the heart of David Jackson. He had asked Eve out many times but she always refused on the grounds she was far too busy. If she wasn't taking lessons, she was making dance frocks or giving an extra shine to the floor that Mary Jean had already polished perfectly.

'You have to eat,' he told her. 'Let me take you out for a meal after the class on Friday.'

'She likes Chinese,' Elizabeth told him, as she peered over her 'A' level French book. Eve gave her a look, so Elizabeth smirked back.

'I was thinking of something more on the lines of duck à l'orange and a good bottle of wine,' he said, smiling generously. Eve loved duck, but she didn't want to encourage David.

'I'm on a diet,' she said.

'You could just have a crisp green salad with it,' he pleaded.

'Go on,' Elizabeth urged. 'Duck's very lean.'

'It is not! It's the fattest meat there is!' Eve objected.

'They do steak,' David tempted.

'There!' Elizabeth said. 'You've got her. Well done, David!'

David blushed furiously. 'Why don't you just shut up and let me do things my own way!' he shouted at her.

'Yes!' Eve agreed. 'Mind your own business, our Elizabeth!'

414

'*Our* Elizabeth!' Elizabeth mocked the Geordie. 'As a matter of fact, if I wasn't minding my own business, I would be trying to stop you eating meat at all. I mean, you know what they say. We are what we eat. Like eating pork makes you a . . .'

'I see,' Eve interrupted acidly. 'You'd rather we all turned into limp lettuce leaves, would you?' Elizabeth raised her eyes to heaven. The older generation really didn't understand a thing. 'What I mean is, eating meat is primitive,' she explained patiently.

'Oh? I rather thought you *liked* the primitive!' Eve exploded. Elizabeth looked puzzled. She was racking her brains to find the reference but she didn't make it. 'Never mind,' Eve sighed.

'So you'll come on Friday? After the class?' David pursued. Eve groaned. But Elizabeth was following her own line of argument.

'Actually, it depends what you mean by primitive and civilized, doesn't it?' she said. 'I mean, to me,' her voice assumed an archness, 'to me, solar energy and wave power are a far more civilized form of energy than nuclear-generated electricity. Don't you think, David?'

David went pale and sat down. 'There's a lot of arguments both ways,' he said sadly. 'If we can make our reactors safe . . .'

'If!' Elizabeth squealed. 'That's a big "if"!'

'Alright, alright . . .' Eve was leaving the room. There was washing up to do in the kitchen. David would have liked to go and help, but Elizabeth held him captive.

'You know, it really makes me angry,' she said. 'I mean how you people in the C.E.G.B. can fool yourselves with arguments about being economically viable and so on . . .'

'I never mentioned being economically viable,' David pointed out. 'But, while we're on the subject . . .' The discussion continued, getting nowhere, till Elizabeth brought forth the argument that man was basically evil, as proved in *Lord of the Flies*, and really shouldn't be in charge of the world at all; the only hope being, that man would seek and find Nirvana, and disappear as into a black hole, as soon as possible, thereby saving the beautiful earth for the birds and the bees. Mercifully, David hadn't read *Lord of the Flies* and Elizabeth agreed to postpone the rest of the discussion until he had. At last, he was allowed to limp, tail between his legs, into the kitchen. Eve looked up from chopping the onions and smiled.

'Who won?' she asked.

'Why's she so angry?' He was genuinely puzzled.

'All the kids are. It seems to be the new trend. And I don't blame them. We've made such a mess of things. I'm angry too.'

David looked at her steadily. 'With me?' he asked.

Eve jumped, surprised. 'You? Of course not. Don't be so stupid! Why should I be angry with you?'

David flinched, then felt relieved, then became anxious again, wondering if it wouldn't be better if she *was* angry. At least it would prove she had *some* feelings for him. Whereas, at the moment, the message that was coming across was sheer indifference.

'What does Elizabeth believe in?' he asked. 'I got rather lost. I mean, one minute she wants to save humanity, ban the bomb and so on, and the next, she thinks we all ought to disappear down a black hole and leave the good earth for the animals.' Eve laughed.

'I think she's a sort of Nihilist with humanist tendencies, if that's possible,' she joked. He leaned against the draining board, and sighed. He still hadn't got an answer out of Eve about Friday, but he didn't dare try again.

'Is it worth coming all the way over here, from Chester le Street, just for an argument with Elizabeth?' Eve asked.

'I keep hoping I'll get something else,' David said. Eve nearly chopped off her finger. The blood ran into the onion and she winced at the stinging pain from the wound. Quickly, David grabbed her hand and stuck it under the cold water tap.

'Have you got some plaster?' he asked. Eve nodded at a drawer. 'Keep it under the stream of water,' he instructed. Then he pulled open the drawer, and untidying the contents, discovered the plaster, which had been at the front all the time.

'Men!' Eve jeered. David smiled apologetically, shoved the drawer back, without tidying it, cut a piece of plaster, and after drying and inspecting the wound, placed the plaster on Eve's finger. 'Very good,' she said.

'I love you,' he answered, then blushed helplessly.

'No, you don't!' Eve laughed, and went into the office to go through accounts with Os.

The fifth rocket did nothing at all for a few seconds, then popped its cork.

And then, at the end of January, N.A.S.A. sent a chimp up into space. So it *was* possible! Excitement bubbled. Elizabeth, preparing for her 'A' levels, skived off school in February to join the C.N.D. rally in Trafalgar Square and came home jubilant, because twenty thousand people had turned up. There was hope. The human race *could* turn back from the brink of destruction. It could do anything, even fly to the moon, if it wanted! Elizabeth, dressed in black, was filled with joie de vivre. Meanwhile, Eve was preparing her dancers for the Easter competitions at the Heddon Hall. It was to be her first public display, and she had to do well if she was to increase her reputation. It took all her energy, coaching the children, while Mary Jean instructed the mothers in how to do the costumes, and a pianist was added to the overheads. David felt left out. Exhausted with travelling to and from Chester le Street, he gave the courting a rest. But Eve found she missed him. Angry at her own perversity, she drove her dancers on. And then, when Elizabeth was in London with her father and Myra, the dancing school entered the annual Heddon Hall competition. It might be small fry on the national scale, but for Eve's studio, it was an important landmark.

Os and Mary Jean accompanied Eve on the morning of the first day. They were all dry-mouthed, pulses racing, as the tiny tots started their routines, feet jingling on the shiny floor, piano jingling on the platform behind. Eve remembered the pianist she'd had for her Hollywood test, and smiled. Nothing changes. The same, tired rhythms. You could almost hear him thinking 'Well, it's not Rachmaninoff, is it?' What did he care? But the kids cared. So did their mothers. And so did Eve and Os and Mary Jean. They smiled encouragement as the child faltered, waiting for its turn to do its tap solo, its sequinned top hat falling to one side, its bow tie too tight, its socks wrinkling under its feet. They were sweet really. That is, when they weren't being obnoxious little show-offs! Eve clapped the seven-year-old from Billingham after her masterly rendering of 'Putting on my top hat'. The child's feet had been sharp and clear on the floor, and Eve sought out its teacher to talk to her, striking up a friendly acquaintanceship. You never knew when it might come in useful. Eve's own pupil came third in the section. Not bad, for a start. At least the studio was keeping its end up. Then came the ballet solos. One girl from Stockton was breathlessly good. Eve watched her, imagining how she would develop. She was a real dancer! A professional in the making! A ballerina. Eve was almost jealous. She herself had never been as good as that at the classical stuff and there was nobody on her books now as talented. She gritted her teeth. She would have a pupil like her, one day. She'd show them. To her delight, her own girl came in second, better than Eve'd hoped.

And so the first day wore on into the second, into the song and dance, and the national dancing, the duets, the troupes, and even the acrobatics. And, at the end of it, Eve's studio had won two trophies, and fourteen medals, three of them gold. Also, she'd made some good contacts. Janet Cook from Stockton was going to send her a pupil who was moving up Eve's way. She'd been dancing for five years. It was a windfall. At last Eve had an experienced pupil to build on.

When she came home, Eve found two letters waiting for her; both postmarked the States. One, in an official-looking envelope, was from her solicitor. She ran up to her flat, and opened it, heart pounding. The divorce had come through and she'd been given custody of her son. The satisfied feeling of the day gave way to jubilation. She ripped open Jimmy's letter and scanned it quickly. Sudden emptiness followed. Pete was back in hospital. Nothing serious. Just a check-up. No need for Eve to come over. Jimmy would write again in a couple of days, when the results were known. Still in her coat and hat, Eve sat staring at the unlit fire. She could hear Os and Mary Jean chattering downstairs about the excitements of the day. She couldn't go down and spoil their mood. Anyway she didn't want to confide in them. Os was her brother, but they'd been brought up as strangers and there was still a barrier between them. No, it was Elizabeth Eve needed. She hadn't said so at the time, but she'd been disappointed Elizabeth had gone off to London rather than stay and support her in the competitions, and now she missed her. Her mind drifted automatically to David. She could phone him. But what could she say? 'I need to cry on your shoulder?' He'd be thrilled, of course, but . . . no! All the same, it would be nice to hear his voice . . . anybody's voice, really. What could she say? She could ask him how he was. She hadn't seen him for ages. Was he losing interest? The thought piled in on her already-shattered emotions. She was finally, irrevocably, divorced. She looked at the piece of paper and began to cry. It was as though somebody had cut a knot in her heart. It might be good for her, but it hurt like hell. And now Pete . . . one step forward, two steps back. That was life. He would be alright, wouldn't he? Eve sobbed, then pulling a hanky from her coat pocket, blew her nose hard. Why cry over that bastard? David Jackson was much nicer than John ever could be. And yet, silly cow, she just didn't want him. He was too nice. That was the trouble. No backbone! No. She wouldn't phone. It wasn't fair on him. She'd only be using him. Leading him on . . . and Eve didn't do that sort of thing. She thrust her hanky back in her pocket and hung up her coat. What she needed was a drink. She poured herself a sherry, tasted it, threw it out, poured a scotch, smelt it, then remembered the old days. So she made herself a cup of tea instead, and wrote her reply to Jimmy. She would have to find a nice card to send Pete. How old was he now? Nine next Christmas. He was growing up without her.

Elizabeth dashed home from London, her face flushed with excitement.

'I know,' Eve said. 'The Russians've got a man in space. Yuri Gagarin.'

'That's not all,' Elizabeth told her.' 'Something *much* more important happened. I've got a provisional place at the Slade.'

'What's the Slade?' Eve frowned.

'Oh honestly, Evie! It's the top art college in the country. Well, one of them anyway.' Eve stared at her, her eyes filled with tears.

'But I thought you were going to Girton?' she said. Elizabeth guffawed.

'I wouldn't be seen dead at Girton. Newnham's a bit more trendy, I suppose, but I don't want to go to Cambridge anyway. I don't want to hide myself away in cobwebbed academia!'

'Does the school know?' Eve asked. Elizabeth giggled.

'They don't even know I've applied for art college!' Eve's jaw dropped and Elizabeth, sensing her disapproval, was peeved. 'I thought you'd be pleased for me,' she snapped.

'Oh, I am. I am,' Eve enthused unconvincingly.

'My Dad's ever so pleased,' Elizabeth boasted. 'So's Myra. Actually, it was Myra got me the interview. A friend of a friend of hers is an artist.'

'Oh. *I'm* pleased too,' Eve said, nodding a lot.

'Good.' Elizabeth smiled. Then she stopped smiling. 'You're not, are you?'

Eve sighed, then laughed and sat down. 'The trouble is, I've become middle-aged,' she said. 'When I was young, I was just like you. I suppose I'd hoped you'd get into something more secure than art and painting and so on. After all, taking the Oxbridge entrances only means one more year at school, and . . . !'

'*Only!*' Elizabeth rolled her eyes in horror.

'Yes. Only. I mean, don't you see, with a good degree behind you, you could have security while still going on to . . . '

'Nothing's secure with the bomb around!' Elizabeth reminded her.

'Yes. You're right.' Eve smiled, then gave up. 'I am glad for you. Really. If it's what you want, I wish you the best of luck.'

'Thanks. It's really a good idea, you know. I'd hate being academic. I've got a creative sort of mind. It balks at institutions.'

'I don't get on well with institutions either,' Eve said ruefully.

'You run one!' Elizabeth objected. 'And very well, so I've heard!' She was referring to the competition. 'I'm sorry I couldn't be there,' she said more softly, taking Eve's hand in her own. She looked at the hand and kissed it gently. 'I had these interviews, you see. Slade, Central School, the R.C.A. I'd have been there, rooting for you, otherwise.' Eve's face softened, and she took the girl in her arms. They hugged close.

'Congratulations,' Eve said.

'And congratulations back,' Elizabeth replied.

Elizabeth and Eve had been like two girls, flat sharing. But now Elizabeth was going away a year earlier than expected, Eve felt panic rising. It took her by surprise. She hadn't realized she'd become dependent on the relationship with Liz. And why had she? By living with a young girl, allowing youth to rub off on

420

her, hadn't Eve successfully evaded her responsibilities? This had not been her intention! After all, she was not on the threshold of life, as was Elizabeth. Not any more! Eve had done it all. She'd already travelled the world, exploring its possibilities, and come home to find herself again, to climb into her own shoes, grown large enough to fit them. And yet, she'd allowed herself to be once again duped by herself into simply not growing at all! Bemused by Eve's irritable mood, Elizabeth went out dancing at the 'Downbeat Club', leaving Eve to cry alone in her bedroom. She was so vexed at herself! How could she have been so stupid? So blind? How could she have allowed herself to be distracted from her own path? Let Elizabeth go on hers. Eve must, really must, walk on her own! So she told herself. She sniffed, dried her eyes and looked at herself in the mirror. The sun, shining through the windows, reflected back at her, dazzling her eyes, so that she saw only the rainbows of light refracted in the bevelled edges of the mirror. She blinked, then looked again. She hardly saw herself, but, beyond the rainbows, in the corner of the room behind her, she saw the statue of Ganesha, darkened by her own shadow.

Elizabeth came home that night to find Eve's door locked against her. She frowned, then knocked lightly.

'Who is it?' Eve's tired voice answered her.

'The milkman. Don't be so daft. Who do you think it is?' Elizabeth asked. 'Are you going to let me in, or are you doing something sordid in there?' Eve wrenched open the door.

'Don't speak to me like that,' she snapped. Elizabeth put her hands up as if to ward Eve off.

'Sorry,' she said. 'Hey, what's wrong?' Eve shook her head and went to sit on her bed. 'Look, I'm sorry I didn't tell you I had an interview for the Slade, but . . .'

'That's not what upsets me, Elizabeth.' Elizabeth looked at her through wet eyelashes.

'What *has* upset you then?' Elizabeth asked.

'I'm growing old!'

'You?!' Elizabeth laughed.

'No. That's not it, either.' Eve couldn't explain; not even to herself. 'I'm going to be so lonely when you've gone,' she said, at last. Elizabeth warmed to the admission. She bounced onto the bed beside Eve and threw her arms round her.

'But you'll have Os and Mary Jean . . . and . . . ' she said, archly, 'there's always David Jackson.'

'Huh!' said Eve. 'He's no good to *me*! I'd eat him for breakfast!' Elizabeth snorted with laughter.

'Oh well. There'll be somebody along soon!' she said. It was easy to say that when you were young, but Eve knew better.

'I got my divorce,' she said. Elizabeth took a deep breath.

'I see,' she said. 'And now you discover you still love him?'

'Good God, no! What a stupid thing to say!' Elizabeth sighed. Eve was certainly mixed up just now. She would have to be very patient with her. 'Look . . . Pete's ill again. At least . . . '

'No! Oh, Evie, I'm sorry!' This was genuine sympathy. This was something Elizabeth could understand.

'Well, he's gone back into hospital for a check-up, anyway.'

'Are you going over?' Elizabeth asked.

'Jim says not to. He says he'll keep me in touch with what's going on. But . . . ' Eve started crying. 'I was hoping he'd fetch Pete over for the summer holidays. I thought he might even stay for good.'

'Who? Pete, or Jimmy?' Elizabeth joked. Eve glared at her but didn't answer.

'I'm so lonely,' Eve said again. Elizabeth hugged her for a while, then fetched her some warm milk before going to bed. Poor Eve. She'd had a rotten life. If there was only some way she could help.

The following Saturday, David Jackson turned up for the modern ballroom class, complete with shining shoes.

'Thought you'd given it up,' Eve said coldly.

'Been a bit busy. You know how it is.'

Eve gave him a look. Was he taking a rise out of her? But his innocent face said not. David Jackson wouldn't take a rise out of anybody. Since Elizabeth was now busy swotting for her 'A' levels, the class had an odd man out and Eve was forced to partner David herself. He thought it was his birthday. But his hopes that Eve would ask him up for a cup of tea afterwards seemed unlikely to be fulfilled. She was brisk and business-like, with him as with everybody, and, if it hadn't been for Elizabeth, emerging bleary-eyed from her swotting, he would have had no excuse to hang on at all.

'How's it going?' he asked her casually, as she swung her leg onto the barre and stretched it.

'Oh God, it's awful!' she replied. 'I'm steeped in Georgian politics. They're disgusting.'

'Oh dear,' David sympathized, watching Eve from the corner of his eye. She was sitting on the spiral stairs, counting up the takings. 'I missed my usual partner.'

'You're joking!' Elizabeth protested, wide-eyed, and her leg dropped from the barre with a crash that made Eve look up. She saw David give Elizabeth a huge wink. Then, he looked over his shoulder to make sure it hadn't been seen, and found Eve's eyes glued to them. He blushed furiously. Eve put down the box of money and walked over to them.

'Elizabeth was just saying I ought to get out more,' she said.

'Was I?' Elizabeth asked. 'Oh yes! I suppose I was!' she added hastily.

'And she knows some lovely places to go to,' Eve smiled coldly at Elizabeth, who was gaping at her in amazement.

'Oh?' David took the bait like a hungry fish. 'Perhaps *we* could check them out, Eve.'

'*What* lovely places?' Elizabeth asked warily.

'Well, there's that Downbeat Club of yours, for a start.'

'*That's* not lovely!'

'*You* seem to like it,' Eve pointed out.

'Yes, but . . . ' Elizabeth stuttered.

'It's good enough recommendation for me,' Eve said. 'Isn't it for you, David?'

David nodded enthusiastically. 'It certainly is. Do you need to be a member?' he asked.

Elizabeth saw her escape, and came in quickly. 'Yes! I'm afraid so. Sorry.'

'Well, that's alright. Elizabeth can take us. Can't you, Elizabeth?' Eve said. 'Members can always take in guests.'

'Can they?' Elizabeth said weakly. Eve and David nodded.

'Well, that's settled then. We'll all go together.' Eve swanned off, leaving the other two gaping.

'What are you going to do for the rest of the afternoon?' Elizabeth asked sulkily. David shrugged. He didn't really want to go back to Chester le Street, only to have to come all the way out to Shields again. 'You'd better come up.' She started towards the stair, but he hung back. 'It's no good waiting for *her* to ask you!' It was true. He pulled a wry face and followed her, knowing he'd feel like an interloper once in the sacred flat.

At eight o'clock, Eve, Elizabeth and David piled into David's car, and drove into Jarrow. It was a part of Shields Eve hardly knew. It consisted mainly of the docks, a few old terraces, still left after the war, and the new housing estates, which were sprouting everywhere. It was not normally what she would have thought of as the centre of cultural life but Jarrow was where the Downbeat Club had its being, and that was therefore where they were going. Elizabeth was silent, as they drove along.

'Cramping your style, are we?' Eve asked.

'No. It's not that. Well, not *only* that . . . ' Elizabeth replied. 'It's just . . . well don't you think you're a bit overdressed?'

She glanced at the sequinned top and the frou-frou skirt of Eve's frock, showing underneath her coat. But Eve only laughed.

'I'm certainly not going out dancing in a tight black skirt and polo neck jumper, like you!' she said.

'You'll gas everybody with your hair lacquer,' Elizabeth objected.

'Talking of lethal weapons,' Eve went on, 'where did you find those false eyelashes? They look like the spikes on the town hall railings!'

David's heart was down in his boots. He had a feeling that this evening was going to be, was meant to be, a disaster.

The entrance to the club was down a dark alley, in a large warehouse. The upstairs windows were mostly blacked out, but an eerie blue glowed from behind them, and a dull thudding sound that might pass for percussion was coming from inside. Elizabeth's step quickened as they entered the alley. Was it from excitement or fear? Eve wondered. When they arrived at the door, she knocked on it heavily six times. It opened slightly and a tired voice said, 'Card?'

Elizabeth thrust her card into the darkness. It disappeared for a few seconds, then was thrust out at her again. She took it back and said, in a hopeless tone, 'There's a couple of people want to come in with me as guests.'

'O.K.' said the tired voice. 'We're not that busy yet.'

Obviously disappointed, Elizabeth stepped back and allowed David and Eve to enter the club.

At first, both were utterly confused by the black shapes moving in the bluey darkness. Smoke hung everywhere, obscuring the view, and the crushing sound of soulful jazz numbed the brain.

'Where's the cloakroom?' David whispered to what he thought was Elizabeth. A strange pair of black-lined eyes stared up at him, and blinked. 'Where's she gone?' He turned to Eve, who shrugged. 'I feel like I'm in an aquarium,' he said. Elizabeth had disappeared. It was clear she had disowned them.

'I think we'll have to do without cloakrooms tonight,' Eve said. David sighed, and as she looked at his hurt, angry face, Eve found herself almost relenting. 'Well, David Jackson, that'll teach you and our Elizabeth not to conspire against me.'

'Conspire?' David's voice rose above the minor key of the club, and black heads slowly turned to look at them. 'It's the first time I've ever heard an honest bit of courting called conspiracy,' he hissed. He gripped her tightly by the arm, manoeuvring her into what passed for the middle of the dance floor. 'Well,' he said. 'Now we're here, I insist we stay and enjoy every minute!' He put one hand on her back and held her hand with the other. 'May I have the pleasure?' he asked, and launched into a fox trot, which continued, independent of the music, on one spot.

It was like treading water. Slowly, Eve began to giggle. In the end, she was helpless, and stood shaking beside him, looking up at his angry face, till he gave way and started laughing too.

'O.K.,' she said. 'You win.'

Then he pulled her close, and they swayed cheek to cheek like everyone else, till, when the music stopped, and the black shapes moved on, Eve and David were left exposed, his white shirt purple, her sequins glinting wickedly in the gloom, locked in an embrace.

Next day, at breakfast, Eve tried to fend Elizabeth off by making snide remarks about the club.

'Call that dancing?' she said. 'Mind you, I can see why no one bothers. Move one step and you're in danger of falling over a dead body. The place is like a bloody mortuary!'

'You seemed to find some life in it,' Elizabeth replied sarcastically. Eve blushed. She'd asked for that one, and she knew it.

'Well, I hope it teaches you not to interfere in my life,' she said pompously.

'What do you mean, "interfere"?' Elizabeth asked, hurt.

'Don't try to tell me you *didn't* ring up David Jackson and tell him I was lonely, because I *know* you did,' Eve spat.

'Sorry, I'm sure. I was only trying to help.'

'Well, your efforts failed. O.K.?'

'You do surprise me,' Elizabeth said. 'From where I was standing, in the crowd, I thought it was rather successful really. When're you seeing him again?'

Eve was about to speak, when there was a knock on the door. Elizabeth jumped up to answer it and let David in. Both were smiling fit to crack their cheeks. Eve scowled back.

'Why are you both looking so pleased with yourselves?' she objected. 'It's all too much for a Sunday morning!'

Elizabeth and David exchanged a look, and she poured him a cup of tea, before discreetly leaving the room.

Eve couldn't look at David. It had been alright in the dark, but in the cold light of day she felt so embarrassed she didn't know what to say or how to behave or anything.

'I thought I might drive us out to Barnard Castle for the afternoon. It's a lovely day. Sun's shining . . .'

'Barnard Castle's miles away!'

'Well, where *do* you suggest?'

'I don't know . . . we could go up to Hexham to see our George.'

'Sounds grand,' David said, drinking his tea. Honour was satisfied. Eve could pretend to herself this was not a romantic jaunt but a dutiful family visit and, at least, it got her out with him. Elizabeth watched them drive off, from the upstairs window. She smiled to herself, satisfied, put on an Elvis L.P. and started in on Jacobean history.

Pete's tests showed a low blood count but the doctors put it down to anaemia rather than returning cancer. It was a great relief, although they were loath to let him go too far from the hospital, wanting to keep him under regular observation for some months yet. 'Better safe than sorry,' Jim said in his letter.

'Just hang in there. We'll soon be over, and, maybe for good.'
The mixture of good news and procrastination made Eve like a
jangling wire, and she needed David's quiet attention like the
piano needed tuning. So she let him take her out again the next
weekend. They went up to Bolam lake, where she fell in love
with the swans. It was the start of a long, hot summer.

And on May 5th, the first American successfully rocketed into
space.

427

CHAPTER TWENTY

In July, Eve and David enjoyed the bluebells in Plessey Woods, and Kennedy, a rather dishy young man, according to Elizabeth, got the nomination for the American presidential election. In August, Eve and David strolled on Bamburgh sands, C.N.D held a rally in Hyde Park to commemorate the bombing of Hiroshima and twenty thousand people turned up, Elizabeth among them. Then, the Russians built the Berlin Wall, and Elizabeth got her 'A' level results. She'd got four 'A's' and the jubilant school, preparing to cram her into the Oxbridge entrances, were shocked to discover she had no intention of ever going back to school again, but was asking for a reference for art college instead. Then suddenly, Elizabeth changed her style. Raiding Eve's wardrobe, she began dressing herself in multi-coloured, multi-textured garments, which were never meant to go together. Eve watched bemused, as she raised the hem of one of her old designer dresses, then proceeded to make a bolero with the vast chunk of cloth she'd cut off.

'It looks ridiculous,' she told her. 'Not to mention disgusting. And you're bound to catch cold, exposing yourself like that.'

'Art students are the designers of tomorrow, Eve,' Elizabeth explained. 'I know it looks strange to you, but soon, everybody's going to be wearing their skirts this short.'

428

'*I* won't!' Eve blustered.

'Then you'll have to wear trousers. It's the only alternative.' She sighed, surveying herself in Eve's mirror. 'There's something missing.' Suddenly she dived into her handbag and pulled out the cigarette holder Eve had bought for her two or three Christmases before. She posed with it, then checked back with Eve.

'I didn't know you still had that,' Eve said. 'In fact, I haven't seen you smoke for ages.'

'Gauloises leave such a nasty taste in the mouth,' Elizabeth said. 'What I really need is some pot!'

'It's not all it's cracked up to be,' Eve said quietly. Elizabeth almost swallowed the cigarette holder.

'What? You know about pot?' Eve nodded. 'How do you know? You haven't actually smoked any, have you?'

'I smoked it for a long time,' Eve sighed.

'It must be great being high!' Elizabeth was sitting at her feet like a devotee before a guru.

'No,' Eve said bitterly. She was remembering the balloon. '*Momma, you can see our shadow on the ground.*' Eve put her head in her hands, and waited till Tod's voice faded, then she looked down at the girl, who was still looking up at her, wistfully.

'You're really experienced, man,' Elizabeth said in awestruck tones.

'Yes,' Eve agreed. 'But not all of it's been good.'

'Why? I mean, I've heard pot doesn't do you any harm. I've heard it's easier on the system than alcohol!'

'That's true,' Eve agreed. 'But, you know, when you take something like pot, or anything really, you give away a part of yourself. Maybe at the time, when you're in pain, or bored, it feels good, like its an unwanted bit of yourself you're getting rid of. And, yes, you do sort of float, everything looks brighter, different, more alive somehow. It's like being drunk, only nicer. But . . . still, you *have* given something away. You're not in control any more.'

'I think that's great,' Elizabeth said. 'People should lose control! It's when things happen!'

'They sure do,' Eve agreed sadly. She looked at Elizabeth, considering whether to tell her, then said, 'I was smoking pot when Tod fell out of the balloon.'

'Oooh!' Elizabeth felt a frisson on her spine. 'Poor Evie. No wonder you went off the stuff!' Then she got up and started gathering the clothes she'd been trying on. 'Wait till I tell Myra you've smoked grass!' She was smiling broadly.

Eve saw Elizabeth off at Newcastle Central Station. The girl was ready for anything and everything. God help the world and God help her. She only hoped they could cope with one another. Then, she turned back to Shields, and wrote a long letter to Jimmy.

'I'm really worried about the younger generation,' she wrote. 'They seem to be throwing all caution to the winds. I know we were a bit wild when we were young, but these young people seem so unafraid, so unaware of the dangers. Perhaps, when you come over, you can talk to Elizabeth and warn her. She might listen to you . . . '

In the winter of 1961, Jack Scott had a heart attack, and Eve, who had already lost one father, was beside herself at the idea of losing the other. It wasn't that she saw a great deal of Jack, but knowing he was there made all the difference. He was like her backbone, always behind her, never seen. Life without him seemed impossible. She rushed to the hospital with Os, to find their mother, Frances, sitting waiting in the corridor. Crouching at her side, Eve took hold of her hand. It was freezing cold.

'How is he, Mam?' she asked tearfully. Frances sighed, and shook her head slowly.

'One minute he was drinking his tea, and looking at the paper. He got excited about Kennedy being elected, you know. Said it was the dawning of a new era and all that. Then, the next, he was keeling over, clutching his chest. Eeh . . . ' Frances dabbed her eyes. 'It was awful. I didn't know what to do for the best. I ran out into the street, and the woman next door came round. Mrs Willett. She's a nurse. Eeh, she was marvellous!'

'And how is he now?' Eve asked.

'They tell me, if he gets through the next few days, he stands a chance.'

'How big's the "if"?' Os asked.

'Your guess is as good as mine,' Frances replied. 'I don't think they'll let you in to see him, love,' she said, as Eve drifted to the doors of the unit. Disappointed, Eve contented herself with looking through the glass. She saw Jack, lying on a high sort of bed, more like a stretcher really, all wired up. His eyes were closed and he looked very pale and vulnerable. It made Eve want to cry. Her throat ached so much, she thought it would burst. This was her father; her real father. Would she ever talk to him again? Would she ever be able to tell him she loved him? She turned away quickly, biting her lip, trying to swallow down the tears. Frances gave her a watery smile, then rose and took her in her arms, hugging the daughter, while the son, Os, in his turn, looked through the glass.

That night, in Fowler Street, Eve couldn't sleep. At three in the morning, she gave up trying and put on the light. She stared at the statue in the corner of her room without really seeing. Her mind was on Jack, Pete and Tod: '*Look Momma, you can see our shadow on the ground.*' She started crying. So much had been lost; so much good love; spent, wasted, like blood pouring from an open wound. Eve shook her face free of tears and registered the statue. She blinked. She looked at Ganesha again. She thought she saw a snake, coiled round His waist! She blinked again. Yes. She was right. There was a snake. But she hadn't seen it before. What did it mean? Perhaps Jack knew. Jack! Why had she squandered her love on worthless shadows? Why had she squandered her life on useless trivia, on business and travelling, dashing hither and thither, and failed to learn from her own father? She had failed to love him! But she would, if Jack recovered . . . if Jack recovered!

Next morning, Eve was allowed to see him for a few minutes. He was awake and smiled wanly, glad she'd come.

'I came yesterday, but you were asleep,' she told him.

'I sleep a lot,' he said.

'It's good for you. Very healing.' He nodded slowly, but the movement cost him great effort, and a tear squeezed out of the corner of his eye. Wiping it away with her handkerchief, Eve thought her heart would burst. 'Dad . . . I . . . I . . .'

It was all she could get out. But it was enough. His face creased, as though in terrible pain, and for a moment, she thought she'd killed him. Then he sobbed, like a child, and said, 'I love you, pet.' She took his hand, tugging it, but afraid for him.

'You mustn't upset yourself. That's the best thing . . . please, Dad, promise me, you'll rest now. Get better! Please, get better!' He nodded and sighed, closing his eyes. He was falling asleep.

Eve sat on, her eyes darting back and forth between his now peaceful face and the monitor where a green light bleeped the rhythm of her father's heart. It was steady. She hadn't killed him.

Christmas came and went. Elizabeth came and went with it, enlivening Jack's bedside with tales of the Slade. She was obviously enjoying every minute of it. But she exhausted him and he was glad when she'd gone. And then, at last, the specialist said Jack could go home. Fresh air and gentle exercise were recommended and Eve was glad to do her share, wheeling him out, and then, as he grew stronger, escorting Jack down to the sea at Marsden. He loved the cliff path, but he hankered to be nearer the water; so, one day, David Jackson drove them all up to Marsden Grotto, where a lift took them down the steep cliff face to the sands below. It was Frances' favourite haunt and she berated David soundly for preferring any other place on earth.

'I don't know why you've got to go so far on the weekends!' she told him. 'When you've got all this here!'

David smiled apologetically, his eyes resting on father and daughter, as they walked on, slowly, ahead of them.

'Eve likes travelling,' he said.

'Oh I don't know,' Frances replied. 'I think she's settled down a lot. Don't you?'

The question was a challenge and David knew it. He coloured slightly but said nothing. He hadn't asked Eve to marry him. He'd thought about it often enough, but something always stopped him. He felt that somehow, Eve might take a proposal as weakness. He could almost hear her sharp retort, 'What's the matter with you, David Jackson, that you need a woman to hold your hand? Can you not stand on your feet, eh?' Courting Eve was like negotiating barbed wire. Getting entangled would be nice, if it wasn't for the barbs. And yet, he knew she liked him. They got on well, bumbling along merrily together. Frances was eyeing David quizzically, waiting for his answer.

'I don't know, Mrs Scott,' he said, at last. 'She's got a wild streak in her, has your Eve.'

'Isn't that what attracts you?' she said. David grinned.

'Aye. You might be right at that,' he said.

'Then what's wrong?' she insisted. But Frances knew what was wrong. David didn't have the answering streak of wildness, or if he did, he didn't know about it.

The tide was out, so Eve and Jack walked on to Marsden Rock. It was huge, stranded on the beach, as though the tide had parted it from the mother cliff. Looking at it, Eve was suddenly reminded of Elephant's Feet, where she and Jimmy had camped and talked about the shadow.

'Dad?' Eve asked. She had stopped walking, so he stopped too, and waited for her. 'Why does Ganesha have a snake round his waist?' Jack pulled the rug close, to keep out the biting wind.

'I don't know,' he said. 'I believe, in India, when a baby's born, they tie a thread round its waist. I think it's a sort of symbolic umbilical cord, tying you to God. But why in Ganesha's case, the thread should be a snake, I don't know. The snake's a very mysterious sign. It sheds meanings, like a real snake sheds its skin. A lot of the Hindu deities, including Shiva, Ganesha's father, are seen with snakes. Maybe it's a sign of their power. Have you heard of Vishnu?' Eve shook her head. 'Well, Vishnu's a God who rides on an eagle in one of His incarnations. But between times, when He's waiting to be reborn, He sleeps on a huge snake, called Shesha. "Vish" actually means light. So, every time He's reborn, Vishnu casts a different light on the world, taking it on, quite literally, to a new stage of enlightenment.'

'Dad, how do you know so much about India?' Eve asked. Jack was staring beyond the rock, out to sea.

'I used to know an Indian once,' he said. 'I met him in the war. The first war. He was called Vijay Ridley.' Eve's head swung round in surprise. 'Yes,' Jack went on, 'he was an Anglo-Indian. But he was, as you rightly guessed, a sort of relative.' His voice strained to be casual and Eve got the sensation she was stepping onto a minefield, when she asked, 'What happened to him?'

Jack moistened his lips, then taking his courage in his hands, he looked her straight in the eye.

'I killed him,' he said. Eve was puzzled.

'You mean he was on the other side? A Nazi?'

'No,' Jack answered. 'I killed him because he wanted to come up to Shields and make trouble.'

'You mean . . . you murdered him?' Eve was horror-struck. Even John hadn't stooped to murder.

'He was Robert Ridley's son,' Jack told her. 'The son of your great-grandma's brother.'

'You're standing there, telling me you murdered a man?'

'Yes!' Jack snapped.

'How? I mean, how did you kill him?' Eve asked. 'I mean did you shoot him, or what?'

'I pushed him in the way of a shell, if you really want to know.' Eve drew in a deep breath. Jack was showing signs of distress. His breathing rasped on the cold air, and his face was pinched. 'I told your Mam . . . but, well, Os doesn't know . . . '

'I won't tell him,' Eve said quickly. 'It's alright. Keep calm. Don't upset yourself. I'm sorry I . . . I'm sorry I reacted so . . . Don't upset yourself.'

'You blame me, don't you?' Jack's eyes pleaded with her. 'Please don't blame me,' they said. Eve shook her head quickly. She was afraid he'd have another heart attack on the spot.

'How can I blame you?' she said. 'It's not so different to Tod falling out of the balloon really, is it?'

As soon as she'd said it, she wished she hadn't. It might have reassured Jack, but it worried Eve. After all, she wasn't guilty of murder, was she? Was she? An accusing voice echoed through her mind, a voice that had been shut up, and now, because of Jack's confession, had been let out to torment her.

'There's a world of difference, love,' Jack said warmly. 'Tod's death was an accident. Vijay's only looked like one. Not that I blame myself.' Jack shook off the guilt. 'I did what I thought was right, to protect my family. All I'm afraid of's the blame of other people . . . people I love.'

'I don't blame you, Dad.' Eve wanted to be finished with a conversation which was doing neither of them any good. 'I told you. I'm in no position to blame anyone. But . . . ' She looked at him, wondering if he could take it. 'What I want to know is, what you thought you were protecting your family from?' Jack breathed slowly, steadying his heart. Then he sat on a rock, before attempting to explain.

'Vijay told me his father had been very harsh to him. Robert

434

Ridley left England, under a cloud, accused of stealing money from the shop. But apparently he felt he'd been treated unfairly, and had been angry ever since. He took his anger out on Vijay, and Vijay, in his turn, wanted to get his own back on us, the English family who had hurt his father. Apparently, Robert was so embittered he'd turned his back on England altogether. He'd converted to Hinduism, married an Indian woman and had children by her, vowing never to return to England ever again. In fact, he became Indian, and the man I killed was one of his sons.'

'So it was Vijay who told you so much about India?'

'He started me off, but I found most of it out for myself. I was curious, I suppose. I wanted to know what I'd missed. You see, when someone dies, they take part of the jigsaw with them, and you can't quite make out the whole picture. At the time, I was afraid of seeing it, but now . . . ' Jack was near to tears. He'd said he didn't blame himself, but it wasn't true. Guilt had driven him to discover all he could, trying to fill in the picture puzzle, after he'd destroyed one of its key pieces.

'Who brought that statue of Ganesha over from India?'

'That was a present for your grandma's wedding. I don't know who sent it. But I do know it was shipped from India, years and years ago.'

'Could it have been Robert?' Eve asked.

'Who knows?' Jack sighed. 'Anyway, I was telling you about the snake, wasn't I?' At once, and, as though escaping from his memories, Jack warmed to the story. 'Once upon a time . . . ' He smiled, as he began. An answering smile flickered across Eve's face, but she was only half-listening. 'My father killed a man,' she kept saying to herself as she watched him spinning the old legend. 'My father killed a man. And I'm no better than he is.'

'Once,' Jack was saying, 'when the demons were getting too much for the gods, Vishnu told them to take a mountain as a stick, and a snake as a rope, and churn the sea of milk. The gods had to use the help of the demons to hold on to the snake, pulling it at the head and pulling it at the tail, churning the mountain to and fro in the sea. The churning was so great, they almost drove the mountain right through the earth, and the snake suffered so much, pulled this way and that, that it spouted out enough venom to poison the whole world. Luckily for us Shiva drank all the poison, burning His own throat, but saving the earth. Then, at last, out of the churning sea, arose a number of gifts. I can't remember all of them. But Shiva took the crescent moon, and there was a tree of paradise, which perfumed the entire earth. And then, of course there was Vishnu's wife, Laxshmi, the beautiful Goddess of Prosperity, who rose, fully formed from the sea of milk, sitting on a lotus. She was crowned with flowers, and the sacred elephants who support the earth poured holy water over Her. Last of all there was Dhanvantari, doctor of the Gods, who bore in his hand a vessel containing the ambrosia of immortality. The demons snatched it from him but, by a trick, Vishnu got it back, and the Gods drank it, becoming strong enough to drive all the demons away.'

'The churning sea sounds like an end of the world myth.'

'Well, I suppose it *was* the end of one phase; but the beginning of the next.'

'And in between, the snake sleeps,' Eve said.

'Yes. Till, at the right moment, it starts churning up the waters . . .'

'So the snake's a sort of power.'

'Yes. Available to Gods and demons, apparently.'

'But I still don't know why Ganesha wears one round his waist,' Eve persisted. Jack's eyes misted, as though remembering something from a long time ago and then he murmured, in a voice that was barely audible, 'The shadow of the elephant . . .'

Eve turned sharply to look at him. 'What did you say?' she asked.

' "The shadow of the elephant." Your great-grandfather's last words. I'll never forget them.'

'What shadow? What did he mean?' Eve's voice was urgent. But Jack shook his head.

'I think it was something to do with Hester . . . and Anna.'

'And Elizabeth,' Eve filled in. Jack nodded.

'You know what your Mam thinks . . . ?'

'She told me; when I went to the asylum with her; she said Hester was born of incest.'

'It's just a guess.' Jack shook his head sadly. 'If Vijay had come home, if I hadn't killed him, we'd probably know the truth. But that's the shadow, I reckon. Hester's birth. The sins of the fathers . . .'

'But . . .' Eve was puzzled. 'Why did Great-Grandfather call it the shadow of the elephant? I mean, you told me once, that Ganesha was Lord of Innocence, like Jesus.' Jack nodded.

'Yes. Light of the world.'

'But, if He's the source of the light, how can He cast a shadow?' Eve asked.

Jack turned to look at her and smiled slowly.

Suddenly they were startled by Frances. Turning to look, Eve saw her laughing at David. He glanced up at Eve, at once, and waved. He didn't seem to mind being laughed at. Eve waved back. 'You'll like Jimmy,' she said to Jack. 'You've got a lot in common. I should think you'll natter on till dawn, or the cows come home or something, once you get together.'

'When's he coming over?' Jack asked. Eve shrugged.

'Still waiting for the all-clear from the hospital.'

'Pete'll be alright,' Jack comforted her. 'I recovered. So will he.' He touched her hand, and Eve shivered. He was cold as ice.

'Dad! You're freezing! Why didn't you say? Come on. Let's call in at the Grotto for a brandy. Warm you up!' She hustled him out of the biting wind, and into the smoky confines of the pub at the bottom of the cliff.

'What were you laughing about?' Jack asked.

'Oh . . . I was trying to take a rise out of David here.' Frances grinned. 'But he wouldn't bite.'

'Yes,' Jack observed, smiling at David, who was getting in the drinks. 'He's very even-tempered, isn't he?'

David cringed. Eve looked anything but pleased. To her, he knew, 'even-tempered' was damning with faint praise.

'Are you alright, Eve?' Frances asked. 'You look really peaky.'

'Fine.' Eve smiled brightly, but Frances wasn't taken in. She looked curiously at Jack. What had they been talking about?

For Eve, putting a face on things had never been harder, and when she got home from the outing, she sent David away, locking herself away in her flat, thankful to be alone.

'What's wrong?' David had asked. 'Can I help?'

She had felt almost sorry for him, but she couldn't have talked to him, anyway. He was a man. And at this moment, Eve hated men. They were all deceivers and murderers of one kind and another. How had her mother put up with hers all these years?

Eve'd known there was something wrong with him. And she'd been right, hadn't she? What could be more wrong than murder? And somehow, the bastard had made her love him! He'd got under her defences, and even had her calling him 'Dad', before telling her, all casual like, he'd killed somebody! What did he expect her to say? 'Oh, is that all, Dad? Think nothing of it?' Typical! Of course, it was the heart attack that had done it. The bastard had probably had it on purpose, just to soften her up, before putting the knife in! Men! It was unbelievable! Surely before you forgave somebody you were allowed to know what you were forgiving them for? She sat on the edge of the bath, watching the taps gush, and the foam rise on the surface of the water. And with the foam rose new thoughts; thoughts about Tod. 'It's not so different from Tod falling out of the balloon, is it?' But that *was* different. That'd been an accident; like the mushroom cloud had been an accident. She hadn't known it was dangerous. She wasn't to blame. She pushed the thoughts down under the foam, and drowned them in a torrent of soap bubbles and fury against Jack Scott.

After a few hours' sleep, Eve woke, soaked in sweat. The day before was still bright in her memory, the impetus of Jack's story continuing in her head, like the wheels of an upturned cart spinning round and round and getting nowhere. She sat up in bed, and switched on the light. But the room and its contents seemed less real than her own thoughts, which possessed her like a demon, driving her against herself, telling her, she was no better than her father. She'd said so herself. The words had just popped out, as truth had a way of doing. And yet, her good angel answered, she hadn't meant to kill Tod. She really hadn't. Yes, but she had neglected to watch over him. She hadn't listened to his warning. '*Momma, you can see our shadow . . .*' She'd been shown the truth at Elephant's Feet. 'In marrying John, you gave your own shadow form, so it had the power to destroy you.' Now there was no John. But the shadow remained. It welled up out of her unconscious, and stood behind her, waiting for its chance to act, to speak, to live through her. And if she wouldn't let it? Why, it would turn on herself. Was there no way out? She looked at the statue. 'The shadow of the elephant.' But His was not the shadow . . .

Eve shivered. The sweat had gone cold on her. She needed her dressing gown. So she threw back the bedclothes and tried to climb off the bed to get it. But she was stiff. Her spine and legs hurt. Every joint had pain in it. She rubbed her hips and knees, then managed to roll off the bed. She must have got a chill on the sea front. She hoped Jack would be alright. Perhaps a cup of tea would help warm her up. She went into the kitchen and put the kettle on. She made a whole pot without thinking, and drank down one cup. Such a waste. If Elizabeth had been there, she could've taken her some. Eve would certainly have liked to talk to somebody. But who? She checked her watch. It was far too early to phone anyone anyway. She couldn't go back to bed, so wandered aimlessly down the stairs, past Os's flat, and stood looking over the balcony into the studio. Perhaps a work-out would do her good. She switched on the light and went down the spiral. But she was caught by the mirror. There she was, forty-odd, hair dishevelled, pale with lack of sleep, in a damp nightie, and an old dressing gown. And she ached all over, as though she'd been dancing non-stop ever since she was born.

As the year wore on, and Jack grew stronger, Eve tried to put the shadow out of her mind. But every time she felt a twinge in one of her muscles, or a joint ached, it brought it all back. And the more the shadow came back, the harder she worked to put it out of her mind.

'When a dancer gets older,' she explained to Os and Mary Jean, 'she has to work twice as hard to keep in training.' So she drove herself on through the year, driving her dancers on with her, promising them the big competition in Newcastle if they did well at Easter. And when they did, and the chosen few went on to the more prestigious event, Juliet Rochester came up trumps, and carried off the senior ballet championship for the Lawson Studio. It was a moment for champagne. There wasn't a dance teacher in Britain hadn't heard of Evie Lawson by now. New pupils flocked in so fast that Eve could hardly keep up with them. And she was grateful. The busier she was, the less time she had to think. But sometimes, Jack caught her looking at him, with a question on her face. And he knew what was on her mind. Then one Sunday, when they were out walking on Cleadon Hill, he asked her.

'Evie, spit it out,' he said. Eve was startled. She blushed and stuttered. 'Go on,' he insisted.

'Alright.' Eve couldn't look at him. 'It's about Vijay Ridley.'

'I thought it might be,' Jack answered. 'Well?'

'Did you know what you were going to do? Kill him, I mean? Or did it just happen out of the blue? I mean, like it happened in spite of you?' Jack thought seriously for a moment.

'I'm not sure,' he said. 'I certainly hadn't planned to do it. It just happened. It was like a part of me knew it was going to happen, and was only waiting for the moment, but *I* didn't know. Not till I was doing it . . . '

'Yes,' Eve said slowly. 'I understand.'

'More than I do!' Jack snorted, then laughed. 'But I'm glad. I thought you were holding it against me.'

'I was,' Eve said. 'But it wasn't you that did it.' Eve was looking at Jack's shadow. It lay round his feet like a dark pool, and when he moved, it moved with him. 'I love you, Dad.' Eve reached across the shadow and kissed her father's confused face.

'I'll never understand women,' he laughed. 'When are you going to fetch me somebody sensible to talk to? Like that Jimmy you're always on about?'

It was a sore point.

'The mountain is going to come to Muhammad,' she wrote to Jimmy. 'I'm coming over in the spring. Soon as the competition season's ended. I want to see how Pete's getting on, for myself.' And Jim wrote back.

'Hold your horses, Evie. Pete's had the all-clear. And I promise, I really promise, we'll be in England in the spring.' It sounded like the promise of paradise; wonderful, if it were only true. But the world was on the brink of war, nuclear war. Kennedy, 'that dishy young man', had called Khrushchev's bluff over Cuba and the cold war had suddenly turned hot. Jack was filled with the fervour of an old war horse.

Elizabeth didn't know whether to be scared silly or smug. 'I knew this would happen,' she kept saying, on the phone from London.

'Elizabeth, this is a reverse charge trunk call. Please don't waste time, saying "I told you so"! What do you want?'

'I've got glandular fever,' she said. 'Well, suspected glandular fever, anyway. I'm coming home to be cosseted.'

'What?' Eve exploded. 'Why don't you go to your father's? Let the amazing Myra look after you? Or can't the G.L.C. spare her?'

'It'll probably only be for a couple of weeks,' Elizabeth said. 'I mean it's only suspected. And you surely don't begrudge me a couple of weeks, when the world's about to end, do you?'

'Oh really! You've only just got back to college!'

But when Eve saw Elizabeth at the station, she was sorry she'd been unkind. She looked pale and exhausted, and she moved slowly, dragging her little bag as though it was lined with lead. Eve pecked her cursorily on the cheek.

'Give me that,' she said. 'How did you get it?'

'I bought it in a market in Soho,' Elizabeth told her.

'Not the bag, you twit! Glandular fever!'

'They say you get it from too much kissing.' Eve gave her a sharp look which made Elizabeth giggle.

'*Have* you been doing too much kissing?' Eve asked.

'Only a teensy weensy bit of kissing. Little kisses. You know. To keep in with the gang,' Elizabeth replied casually.

'Now, Elizabeth,' Eve began as they got into Os's van, 'you're an attractive girl, and . . .'

'I know,' Elizabeth said. 'You don't have to worry, though. I'm into careers, not boy friends.'

'I'm glad to hear it,' Eve said sternly. 'Men are far more trouble than they're worth.'

'Even David?' Elizabeth asked innocently.

'Even David,' Eve snapped. Elizabeth sighed.

'I thought you two were hitting it off,' she said.

'David's a weed,' Eve told her.

'Yes. But a nice weed,' Elizabeth replied.

Elizabeth mooned around the flat for the first week, too tired to do anything but watch T.V., while Eve rushed through the days, as usual, teaching classes and private lessons, going through accounts with Os, and dashing off to see her mother and father whenever she could. She left the care of the 'suspected' invalid largely to Mary Jean, who enjoyed every minute of it. But Elizabeth was bored. She had too much time to think, and apart from nuclear war, the only subject worth thinking about at the moment was Eve's love life.

'I know what your problem is with David,' she drawled. 'You're avoiding sex, Evie. I think you're hung up.'

'Rubbish,' Eve replied. 'And I wish you'd change the subject. The needle's got stuck!'

Then Elizabeth started singing 'Wooden Heart', pretending to be David, and they ended up laughing. Things looked a little more lively, when Cousin George came home on the weekend. He was a strapping lad now and loving every minute of his time on Hexham District. He downed milk by the pint, drinking it straight from the bottle, like a man. But he was so blatantly healthy, it made Elizabeth feel tired again. And when he told her she was a nice bit of talent and would she come out with him for a drink and a bit of a dance and maybe even a bit of a snog, Elizabeth shrank into the sofa, pleading continuing illness.

'Now who's avoiding sex?' Eve sniped.

'I thought you wanted me to avoid sex,' Elizabeth retorted.

Disappointed, George went back to Hexham, and Elizabeth entered her second week of convalescence.

She was feeling stronger by now, and had started to work. In the evenings, after classes were over, Eve would join her in the sitting room, to watch telly, while Elizabeth sketched. She loved drawing trees. She drew forests of them, poplars, pines, planes, beeches and ancient oaks. Their huge trunks and boughs seemed to ripple with muscle, like the limbs of men, striving to reach away from the earth up to the light. But Elizabeth's trees were no trees of paradise. Her trees had lived, far from Eden, among mortal men. They had become knotted, twisted and gnarled, till their bodies were as complex and tortured as a knot of serpents. They were haunted trees.

'Like them?' Elizabeth asked, smiling up at her. Eve's expression of distaste surprised her. 'What's wrong?' she asked. 'Don't you think they're any good?'

'Oh they're good alright,' Eve said. 'Very good, in fact.' Elizabeth thrust the drawing at her.

'You can have it, if you like. Unbirthday present.'

'Thanks very much,' Eve said. 'Especially since you forgot my birthday this year.' She put the sketch in her bedroom, and came back to make some tea. She didn't want to talk about the trees.

They made her uneasy. In fact, she didn't want to talk about anything. But Elizabeth followed her into the kitchen and insisted on chatting.

'You know, Evie,' she said idly. 'I almost wish they *would* drop the bomb.'

Eve turned on her in horror. 'That's a terrible thing to say!'

'Well,' Elizabeth explained. 'It would get it over with, wouldn't it? I mean, look at the world! I mean, it's not a fit place to bring children into, is it? What sort of future is it for them?'

'It's just as well you *do* feel like that,' Eve said briskly.

'Why?'

'Because you're obviously not cut out for motherhood, are you? I mean, you're not exactly the mother earth type!'

'No! Thank God!' Elizabeth said, laughing. 'The very idea of babies turns me off. Actually . . . you're not exactly the mother earth type, yourself.' Eve's face collapsed suddenly. 'Hey! I'm sorry. I didn't mean . . .'

'No. No you're right,' Eve said. 'I'm not. But that doesn't mean I don't care about my kids . . . I love Pete very much. I loved Tod too.'

She was thinking about the shadow. Jack had one. She had one. Shadows made you do things you didn't want to. And if you stopped them, they turned against you and destroyed you. Perhaps everyone had a shadow. Elizabeth too . . .

Elizabeth was a branch from a haunted tree. The serpent had entered the Garden long ago and because of the knowledge it had tempted them to, the unthinking innocence of the first man and the first woman had been replaced by self-consciousness so that, knowing the difference between good and evil, those Children of God lost their Eden and found themselves living instead in a world of haunting shadows; eternal conflict within and without; always good struggling with evil, like enemy twins, locked in one womb. But the memory of Eden remained like a distant echo in the minds of the sons and the daughters of those firstborn beings and they began seeking the way back to the place where good and evil would finally be resolved and made whole again. Peace. That was Eden. Perhaps, one day, a serpent would lead them?

. . . 'Maybe you're right,' Eve said briskly. 'Maybe the world isn't a fit place, and we're not fit parents. I mean, it's not exactly the Garden of Eden any more, is it?' Her face was taut, as she looked at Elizabeth.

'You've never had it so good,' Elizabeth said slowly.

'You could have fooled me,' Eve replied. 'What in heaven's name is going to happen to this world?'

'If it survives,' Elizabeth reminded her.

CHAPTER TWENTY-ONE

Khrushchev backed off, and for the moment, the earth was safe. Shesha slept and the hero twins at the polar axes kept the globe rotating gently on its diurnal course. Elizabeth went back to college, while Eve waited impatiently for the spring, and the return of her son. But as the year turned into 1963, Eve became increasingly nervous. David's constant attentions threatened her. He seemed to feel he had a claim on her now. And when she went to see her parents or Maisie, they all asked after him, as though he was a sort of appendage. She was also very keyed-up about seeing Pete again. Would her son remember her? Did he still love her? Did he blame her for Tod's death, or for their separation? And then there was Jimmy. It was a long time since she'd seen Jimmy. Had he changed? Had she? She looked at herself in the mirror. Eve looked young for her age. Everybody said so. But why was she getting so worked up? The trip would probably be postponed again. There'd be some reason Jimmy and Pete couldn't come. There always was. She sighed and tried to prepare herself for disappointment. In his last letter Jimmy had said he'd grown a beard. She couldn't imagine it. Horror of horrors, had he turned into a beatnik? Then, after all the waiting, Eve was taken by surprise. Earlier than expected, towards the end of February, Jimmy sent word he and Pete were on their way.

Eve did her best to put David off. She didn't want him driving her to the airport, but he insisted. He insisted on being present at all family occasions when, really, they didn't concern him at all! Eve resented it. She'd looked forward to Pete and Jim coming for so long. It had been such ages since she'd seen them, and she wanted those first few minutes with them alone. Was it so odd? And was David really so insensitive, he didn't know when he was in the way? Or did he, like the rest of the family, think of himself as a necessary appendage, like a handbag? She was fuming as she made up her face, ready for the trip. She spilled powder on her dress, and had to change. Pulling the dress over her hair disarranged it. Everything was a mess. And it was all David's fault! Eve's smile was strained by the time David called to pick her up. He was not so blind or insensitive that he didn't notice, but he put it down to nerves, saying to himself she was bound to be strung-up. She was seeing her son, when all was said and done. So, instead of reacting angrily when Eve bit his head off, David was extra nice. And the nicer he was, the more irritated Eve became. Until by the time they reached Newcastle airport, Eve was as taut as one of David's high tension cables. You could see the sparks coming off her.

And then, when the car was parked and they were standing, waiting at the barrier, they discovered the flight had been delayed. David put a brave face on it, and suggested they find a cup of tea. And for an hour and a half they sat, hardly speaking, drinking cup after cup of stewed brown mud. By this time, even David was getting nervous. He was on night shift and he hadn't had any sleep yet. He kept looking at his watch.

'You didn't have to come!' Eve reminded him. But she couldn't send him away now. His car was the only form of transport available. So, they were stuck, waiting. And then another delay was announced. Forty minutes later, they crawled to the barrier. And suddenly, she saw them. She couldn't believe her eyes. They were here. They were actually here at last.

She saw Pete first. He was so big, and looked so much like his father, it took Eve's breath away. Whereas Jimmy, she hardly

446

recognized him in his beard. His lean form had filled out, and he strode forward with the gait of a lumberjack, rather than that of an intellectual. He raised one of the suitcases in greeting. Eve waved back. Then he inclined his head to the little boy and said something. The boy looked at Eve with dark unsmiling eyes, then waved tentatively. Suddenly, unable to wait any longer, Eve ran towards them. Jim dropped the cases, and opened his arms, taking her and Pete into their wide circle, crying, laughing, and kissing one another, till even Eve was sated. Embarrassment followed, as they stood back from one another, and smiled, and nodded, and strived to think what to say.

'How was the flight?' Eve asked nervously. 'Oh sorry. Stupid of me. You were held up. You must be exhausted.' Pete was staring at her silently. It gave Eve the creeps. 'Do you want anything at the cafeteria? Or would you rather go straight on home?' She remembered David. He was their lift. But, looking round, she couldn't see him. For a moment, she panicked. Where had he gone. Had he just 'buggered off' and left them to it? But . . . he wouldn't, would he? Not David? And, of course, he hadn't. He was leaning against a wall near the exit. He was yawning his head off. He hadn't had his sleep. Eve felt a pang of guilt and started hurrying her charges towards the door. 'I think maybe home would be a good idea. Come on.' She tried to take Pete's airline bag from him, but he wouldn't let her and pulled against her. Surprised, she glanced at Jim. 'Strong, isn't he?'

Jim laughed, and picked up the two cases. 'Who's this?' he asked. He was looking at David who was now standing right behind them. Eve introduced him and Jim dropped the cases again to shake hands.

'I've heard a lot about you,' David said. But obviously Jim had heard nothing whatsoever about David, and Eve was desperately trying to explain him away as a friend of Os's.

David drove them all back to Shields, then took off again, straight away, without waiting for so much as a cup of tea. If he was lucky he'd get his head down for an hour or so before the shift started. He crashed the gears as he took off and he didn't look back to wave at Eve who was standing waiting by the door. The crashing gear set her teeth on edge. Why be so angry about losing his sleep? It was his own fault. She hadn't asked him to drive them. He'd insisted on it. Typical of men. They always blamed the woman. She went in, shutting the door on any further thoughts of David, and got on with the more important task of settling in her family.

The first evening was dreadful. At first, Pete wouldn't talk at all. Eve and Mary Jean plied him with the presents they'd got; Dinky toys, toy garage, even train set. But Pete didn't seem to think much of anything. He rolled the odd lorry cursorily across the carpet, then sat sighing in a corner. He asked for the T.V. to be put on. But he couldn't make out what anybody was saying.

'They all talk funny,' he said. 'And you all talk funny. Even Mom.' He glared at Eve, who decided her son was probably just tired, and should go to bed.

'It's been a long journey, love,' she told him. 'You need to rest now.'

'Yeah,' Jim agreed. 'I'm tired anyway. You know, Pete, it's later than you think.'

'I know all about the time change, thanks.' Pete's face was stiff with resentment.

'My. Aren't you turning out to be the clever little boy.' Eve's smile was tight. 'Come on . . . I'll show where you're to sleep . . .' She held out her hand, but Pete refused to take it. He stood, legs apart, close by his uncle.

'Where's Uncle Jim sleeping?' he asked.

'He's going to sleep downstairs. In my brother Os's flat. I'm afraid there's not room for both of you in mine.'

'Who else'll be in this apartment, besides me?' Pete asked warily.

'I will.' Eve smiled, her hand was still extended, waiting. But Pete was adamant.

'I want to sleep near Uncle Jim,' he said.

'Come on, boy. Don't be tiresome!' Jim said, picking up his bag to follow Mary Jean downstairs.

'I want to sleep with Uncle Jim!' Pete shouted.

Everyone stopped to look at him. The little face was pale and set. The hands were clenched hard at his side. Mary Jean and Os looked helplessly on as Eve moved forward to take her son's hand, and coax him gently.

'Come on, honey. He'll only be downstairs. And you've got me here. There's nothing to be afraid of.'

'I want to sleep with Uncle Jim!' the child repeated.

Swallowing pride and hurt feelings, Eve smiled bravely. 'Would you mind, Jim? Just for tonight?'

Jim shook his head and sighed. 'He can have my bed. I could sleep on a clothes-line, I'm so tired. Come on, Buddy.' He jerked his head in the direction of the door. The little boy picked up his bag and ran out, as though escaping from a den of wolves.

The evening being so curtailed, Eve was left at a loose end, unexpectedly alone. She cried a little bit, then brushed the tears away, cleared the dirty china and the crumbs, and made the place ready for breakfast. Tomorrow was another day. Pete and Jim would surely rise bright and shining in the morning, and she'd better be ready for them. She smiled as she broke the eggs in the bowl ready for the French toast they liked so much, and wondered whether they'd like to go down to the sea if the weather was nice. They could maybe take a boat out, and have traditional English fish and chips in a café on the sea front. Yes. They'd like that. And so would she. By the end of the day they'd have that feeling of togetherness back again, see if they wouldn't. So, comforted, Eve went to bed early, and slept soundly, to rise with the lark, and sing as the fat sizzled in the pan.

'Smells good,' Jim said, as he breezed in. His eyes were fat from heavy sleep, but the strain had gone from them.

'French toast,' Eve said. 'Thought it'd make you feel at home.'

'Thanks. It's appreciated,' Jim told her, sitting at the breakfast table. 'By the by, it's a nice place you've got here, Evie. Me and Pete went down to explore this morning. Nice studio.'

'Yes.' Eve smiled. 'Where is Pete?'

'Oh . . . he had a boiled egg, Mary Jean gave it him. Woke early, you see.'

'Oh.' Eve tried not to show her disappointment. 'I thought we might go out for our first day. What do you think?'

'Anything you've got planned's O.K. by me.' Eve smiled at him. Dear free and easy Jimmy.

'I'm so glad you were able to come,' she said. Jim rocked on the chair, patting the sides like a tom-tom, and grinning back at her. 'How many toasts?' He put up three fingers. 'Glad to see you haven't lost your appetite,' she said.

After breakfast, Jim and Eve picked Pete up from downstairs, and ran out into the street to catch a trolleybus. Pete immediately rushed upstairs to the top deck, and clambered over the front seat to look out.

'Hey! This is great!' he shouted. He looked back, caught Eve's eye, and smiled at her, before he even knew he was doing it. Eve sighed with relief. Thank God for trolleybuses, she thought, as she and Jim sat in the seat behind him. And when the bus conductor came round, with his hat and his ticket machine and his little clippers, Pete's eyes almost popped. 'I want to buy the tickets,' he said to Eve.

'O.K.' She gave him the money, and told him what to say. Then he watched the conductor putting the money in his leather pouch, fetching out the change and then punching out the tickets.

Pete giggled with delight, especially when, afterwards, the conductor said, 'Kyou.'

'What's he mean, "kyou"?' Pete asked.

'Thank you. It's a quick way of saying it,' Eve whispered.

'Kyou! Kyou!' Pete mimicked, laughing. The conductor ruffled the scallywag's hair, before passing on up the bus, shaking his head and, to Pete's delight, saying 'Kyou' every time he gave someone a ticket. Then, when they finally had to get off the bus, there was the joy of swinging down the stairs, as the bus jolted dangerously, throwing Pete against the rail, and then he had to rush to ring the bell so it would stop in time. Everything amused him, even the sea fret, which billowed in, and made Eve shake her head about boats and sea trips.

'Please. I want to go in a boat. Please, Auntie Momma,' he said. Half-amused at the auntie, half-hurt by it, Eve gave in. She realized she was probably crazy; and as they sat in the little rowing boat, Jim at the oars Eve and Pete side by side in the stern, she knew she'd been crazy. It was wet and cold. Jim had his cagoulè hood up, but his face was raw by the time they'd got out between the twin piers of North and South Shields and reached the choppy waters of the North Sea.

'I don't think we should go into open water,' Eve said, alarmed.

'Please,' Pete whined. Eve shivered. Water was dripping from the sides of her umbrella onto their legs, and she felt cold. She was wishing she'd brought a thermos flask with her. But it was too late for wishing now. 'Please, Auntie Evie,' Pete said. Eve bit her lip. What had happened to the 'Momma'? 'Please, I've got my fishing rod and everything. I could probably catch enough fish for our dinner tonight, if we can only go out to sea.' Eve sighed and looked at Jim, who was resting on the oars. He laughed.

'Tell you what. I'll take us out as far as that buoy out there.' They looked beyond him. Eve saw a distant buoy bobbing in the waves. It looked so far out. Pete saw a round thing, very close. Both sighed.

'O.K.,' they said together. And Jim started rowing.

It took twenty minutes to reach the buoy, by which time Eve was shaking with the cold, and so was Pete, though he refused to admit it. He got out his fishing line and threw it over the side of the boat. Jim winked, and pulled a hip flask from his inside pocket.

'Thank God,' Eve said, as she took a swig. 'I think you just saved my life.' She smiled ruefully and turned to Pete. 'Caught anything yet?' she asked him a hundred times, till, at last, he got a bite. The excitement was too much for all of them. Eve jumped up. Pete scrambled to the edge of the boat. The whole thing rocked and Jim yelled. But it was too late. They had come adrift from the buoy and one of the oars was floating off into the distance.

'Sit down!' Jim yelled. 'For God's sake, sit down, will you? I've got to get that oar!'

'I've got to haul in my fish!' Pete yelled back.

Eve sat in the middle, trying to keep the boat balanced, helplessly watching the oar drift further and further away. Jim was leaning out, trying to catch hold of it, and almost fell in, so Eve held on to his hips, but he still couldn't reach. And then, Pete hauled in his fish. It was a mackerel. A good sized mackerel at that. Eve congratulated her son, then using the one remaining oar, tried to steer them in the direction of the lost one. After half an hour, they gave up. The question now, was how to get back in with only one oar. The answer was, it took a long, long time. They kept their spirits up singing sea shanties, led by Eve. 'Bobby Shaftoe' was favourite. But, at last, they arrived back at the quay, paid the boatman for the lost oar, and walked rockily over to the nearest café. That cup of tea had led Eve home, through the fret, like a beacon. When she drank it, Pete laughed at her, because her nose had turned into one. It was glowing redder than Rudolf's.

'What an adventure!' Pete said, launching into his fish and chips with obvious relish. 'I think I like England, after all.' Eve exchanged a glance with Jim. That 'after all' said a great deal.

Opening the mackerel up, Eve found it was full of maggots. She threw up, wrapped the fish in newspaper, and slid out round the corner to the fishmonger's. 'The things I do for love,' she thought to herself as she slipped back in, a replacement fish hidden under her coat, and tip-toed past Os's flat, where Pete was still telling Auntie Mary about his great adventure. Then she cut and cooked the fish, serving it up for tea, as the greatest delicacy ever eaten in Fowler Street, a mouthful per person.

That night, Pete went down to sleep in Jim's room again. Eve longed to stop him and say, 'Sleep up here tonight, close by your Momma.' But she thought better of it. Nice and easy does it. She was wooing back her son. But she did go down, to hug him good-night. And he was asleep before she'd left the room.

'How'm I doing?' she asked, as she went back up.

'Fine. Just fine,' Jim said. Then she told them all about the fish, and they roared with laughter before settling down to a hand of cards, a bottle of cider and some crisps. It was homey. In fact, Jim thought, the atmosphere was not so very different from the log cabin back home in the Santa Fe mountains. Though of course, outside, the scenery was rather different. Then, at ten o'clock, Os and Mary Jean retired downstairs and, yawning, Jim decided to follow suit. Eve was a little disappointed. She'd hoped to have a talk with Jim on their own. But she could see he was tired. All that rowing, she supposed. So she said goodnight, pecked him on the cheek, and let him go.

Next day, Eve took Jim and Pete into Newcastle on the train. She found a bus conductor's costume in one of the big stores, and managed to buy it secretly while Pete was watching the toy trains with Jim. Pete grizzled a bit because there weren't any hamburger bars to eat at at lunch time, but he enjoyed his ice cream, and was content to let Eve go, while he and Jim went round the science museum together. Eve was sorry to leave them but there was a class she really couldn't cancel. Easter was nearly on them, the competitions were looming again and she had a reputation to keep up. Mary Jean, who was helping make costumes as usual, took on herself the task of cooking supper that night, and so, everything under control, and everyone occupied, Eve felt free to get back to her teaching.

The class was Grade Two ballet, made up mostly of girls of around eight or nine. Many of them were entered either as solos or duets in the competition and so had dances to practise after the normal barre and floor workout. So, at half past six, when Jim and Pete came home, they were still at it. The arrival of the strangers caused quite a stir. Jim looked wild and handsome, and the mothers, sitting round the edges of the dance floor, couldn't keep their eyes off him. But it was Pete the little dancers were interested in and Eve had to do a lot of shouting and clapping of hands to keep their attention. When, at last, the music stopped, deeply embarrassed, Pete was allowed to walk through the studio behind Jim, up the spiral and out of sight. For him, it was like being made to walk the plank; agony.

'I don't like dancing,' he complained, as he toyed with his sausage and mash that night.

'Have you ever tried it?' Eve asked, slightly offended.

'No!' he shouted. 'Dancing's for girls!'

'There's lots of good men dancers,' Eve told him.

'It's those tights put you off,' Os observed. Mary Jean giggled.

'What's he mean?' Pete asked.

'Nothing,' Eve answered and gave her brother a hostile look. 'You have to be really strong to dance, you know, Pete,' she said. 'Someone like Nijinksy, who could jump higher than anyone else, has to be amazingly powerful.'

'Who's 'jinsky?' Pete asked. Os and Mary Jean laughed and clapped. 'Is he famous or something?'

'You could say that,' Eve replied drily.

'If he's not a footballer, Pete wouldn't know about him,' Jim told her.

Eve took it like a philosopher, saying, 'Boys will be boys, I suppose.' Then she laughed and added, 'And a good thing too! Hey, I've got you a present!' Then she rummaged in her bag and brought out a big box. Pete tore it apart and oohed and aahed like children are supposed to when they get something really nice.

453

'You've hit jackpot, there, Evie,' Jim told her, as they all watched Pete putting on his plastic pouch, his felt hat, and slinging his ticket machine over his shoulders. 'Why, it's even got a little thing to punch holes in the tickets.' And that was that for the rest of the evening. Pete organized the dining chairs into lines, and had them all sitting as if they were on a bus, then bossed them about mercilessly, going 'ding ding!' to start and stop it, throwing people off for being a nuisance, and saying 'Kyou' as often as possible. That night, Eve was the first to yawn. Her son was thoroughly exhausting!

The next day was Saturday. Eve woke late, still feeling rather tired, and went down to Os's to join everyone there for breakfast. Pete had on his conductor's uniform already. Eve told herself to wait for it, it would be coming sooner or later, and sure enough, as Mary Jean poured the milk onto Pete's cornflakes, he said, 'Kyou' and giggled joyously. Eve yawned and rubbed her eyes.

'What's the matter?' Jim whispered. 'Flagging?'

'I'm just not used to it any more,' Eve said. 'I'm a working woman these days, you know. And I've got two ballroom classes this morning. Would you like to join in? I'm sure I could find you a partner.' Jim shrugged and laughed.

'I don't think ballroom's really my scene,' he said. Another disappointment. But Eve told herself she didn't mind and if Jim wanted to take Pete off somewhere, it was probably a good thing. In the end, he went with Mary Jean on the trolleybus, in his conductor's uniform, to try the life out of the poor, complaining real-life conductor, who was only trying to do his job on a Saturday morning.

David Jackson turned up for class as usual. Eve smiled her greeting and repeated her thanks for the lift earlier in the week. He seemed a little stiff, Eve thought, as they demonstrated the latest cha-cha steps together, and he was holding her a little close, whenever he got the chance. She had to prise herself from him at the end of the last dance, and smile her goodbye, as he stood, dancing pumps in hand, waiting after the class.

'How are the guests?' he asked.

'Fine,' she replied.

'Out, are they?' he asked.

'Yes,' she answered.

454

'Good,' he said.

'Yes.' She smiled and went up the spiral stairs. To her annoyance, he followed her. Half-way up, she looked back, in feigned surprise.

'I er . . . do usually get invited up for a cup of tea,' he said, trying to make a joke of it.

'I'm sorry, David.' She was laying on the charm with a shovel, but it didn't make up for the coldness underneath. 'But you do see, don't you, that things are just a weeny bit hectic just now?'

Then, the street door opened, and Elizabeth slunk into the studio. Eve froze.

'Well, don't all say "welcome", at once,' Elizabeth drawled.

Eve swept past David onto the studio floor to confront her. 'What are you doing home? It's not your holidays yet, is it?'

'Suspected . . .'

'Glandular fever . . .' Eve filled in for her. 'I see. Too much kissing again?' Elizabeth winced at the sarcasm, and smiled over Eve's shoulder at David, who was dancing attendance in the background. 'Anyway, you don't usually come home for Easter at all, these days. You usually stay at your father's in London, so you can go on the rally. Why aren't you there?'

'Because, Evie, I didn't want to miss the transatlantic visitors, did I?'

'Oh, I see. So, this "suspected" glandular fever of yours is largely convenient, mmm?'

Elizabeth smiled winsomely and let David take her bag upstairs to the flat. Eve glared after them. They had each gained entrée for the other!

To Eve's annoyance, David stayed on, upstairs, in her flat, talking to Elizabeth, while Eve battled on with extra lessons for competitors all afternoon. By five o'clock, she was thoroughly exhausted and rather cross. No one had done a thing in the flat. Dirty cups and mugs littered the kitchen. Elizabeth's clothes were strewn across the corridor, after a dress parade which had David in stitches. Elizabeth had been showing her new metallic dress. Eve snatched it up to tidy it away, and cut her finger. She swore, put on a plaster, then got on making the supper.

'Are you staying?' she asked David.

'If I'm invited,' he answered.

''Course he is,' Elizabeth said. So Eve peeled some extra

455

potatoes and tried to think of novel ways to spin out five chops for seven people.

'Are you still vegetarian?' she asked Elizabeth.

'Well . . .' Elizabeth considered the matter. 'I don't know. What do you think?' Eve spluttered with exasperation.

'At the moment, you being vegetarian would suit me rather well!' she said.

'O.K. Fine. I'm vegetarian,' Elizabeth said easily, then swanned off to her bedroom to put on her make-up.

Jim and Pete had been back for an hour. But they'd stayed downstairs talking. Eve could hear their laughter coming up the stairs. Thank God for Os and Mary Jean, and a chance to mend her temper before supper. David helped in the kitchen, cutting up the cabbage and peeling the apples for the pudding, and Eve softened towards him.

'Why are you so nice?' she asked, as they set the table together.

'I don't know. Just comes naturally,' he smiled, glad the ice had thawed, at last.

'You'd make some woman a good wife,' she observed. David hesitated, then recovered himself to smile as she looked up at him, and said, 'Table's looking nice. I'll go and call the others.' He leaned against the back of a chair, gritting his teeth, and was still there when Jim and Pete poured in.

'Hi.' Jim held out his hand and David took it, shaking it warmly. 'Feel as if I'm seeing you for the first time, Dave. I guess I was a bit tired at the airport.'

'That's alright,' David said. 'As a matter of fact, so was I. I was on night shift at the time.'

'Oh. What do you do?' Everyone was taking their places at the table, and Eve was dishing out supper. Chops, new potatoes and peas for everyone else; Yorkshire pudding, potatoes and peas for Eve and Elizabeth.

'I'm a control engineer for the C.E.G.B.,' David said.

'Hey. That's interesting. I'm kind of into energy myself. Geothermal.'

'That's so much more ecological. Don't you think?' Elizabeth stared at the guest.

'Who are you?' Jimmy asked.

'Oh. Sorry.' Eve almost dropped the plate on Jim's lap. 'This is Elizabeth Strachan. She's a sort of cousin of mine.'

456

'Actually, if you really want to know,' Elizabeth said coyly, 'I'm Evie's aunt.' There was a stunned silence, then David laughed.

'What do you know?' he said.

'Well, I *am* her senior in ancestral terms, anyway.' Then she whispered loudly across the table at Jim. 'Eve takes a lot of looking after, you know. The younger generation and all that . . . why, heaven knows what these two . . .' she indicated David and Eve, 'would get up to, if I wasn't there to chaperon them.' Everyone laughed but Eve.

'And what do *you* do?' Jim asked.

'I'm an art student. Isn't that outrageous?' Elizabeth breathed.

'She's supposed to be ill at the moment,' Eve explained. 'Glandular fever. It's the latest adolescent disease.'

Elizabeth pouted at the 'adolescent', as Eve knew she would, but turned the tables, adding in a sultry voice, 'I'm told it comes from too much kissing.' She pouted her lips at Jim, who flushed and laughed uproariously,

'I can't believe she's from the same stock as us!' Jim said. 'No, I just can't believe she's a Ridley!'

'Why not?' Eve asked.

'I don't know. She's just . . . just . . . so . . .'

'Outrageous.' Elizabeth filled in for him.

'You said it, sister.' Jim smiled. Pete issued Elizabeth with a bus ticket and punched a hole in her sleeve, then sat down to look at the puny chop on his plate.

'You sure have small animals in this country,' he complained.

After the meal, everyone went downstairs for coffee, leaving Eve to clear up. David wanted to stay and help her but she insisted he join the others.

'I'll be fine,' she said. 'I get through it quicker on my own.' But she was angry all the same. Why was it she was doing all the work, while everyone else was having all the fun? And yet, she knew she wasn't being quite fair. Only something was eating her and she wasn't quite sure what. She tried hard to put herself in a happier frame of mind. She shook her shoulders to relax them and she practised smiling. But, by the time she went down, everyone'd split into groups and she didn't quite know where to fit in. Pete was telling Mary Jean and Os about the Indians and making quite a lot of it up as he went along, whereas David, Jim and Elizabeth were arguing vehemently about ecological forms of energy. Eve hovered between the two groups uncertainly, ending up in neither.

'How can you work so close to Los Alamos and not feel strongly one way or another about nuclear energy, Jim, I shall never know,' Elizabeth sniped.

'How do you know I don't have strong feelings on the subject?' he retorted.

'Alright. How can you work there at all?' she asked.

'I'm not working on nuclear stuff,' he reminded her. 'Like you said, I'm into ecological energy.' David snorted and earned a glare from Elizabeth.

'David thinks the only future's nuclear,' Elizabeth sulked.

'I don't say that. We've still got enough fossil fuel to keep us going into the next century. It's after that I'm worried about,' David explained.

'Solar power!' Elizabeth said the words like they were a war cry.

'It's O.K. for heating swimming pools,' Jim said. 'But, David's right, we've got to find something else to take the place of fossil fuels, and soon, if we don't want the world littered with nuclear reactors.'

'Wave power?' Elizabeth suggested.

'Seems a pity. The oceans are so pretty.' Jim smiled softly, and his smile took the steel right out of Elizabeth. She seemed to drop at his feet, softly, like fallen petals. Slowly, she smiled back, and David, sitting between them, felt suddenly uneasy. 'All the same,' Jim spoke as though Elizabeth were the only person in the room. 'I think it's great you protest and march and so on the way you do.'

Elizabeth found it necessary to clear her throat before she answered.

'I expect I'll be going on the Aldermaston march again this Easter. Why don't you come along?'

Jim hesitated for a moment. His face had clouded, and as he looked away, he considered the far-reaching effects such an action could have on his life and career. Then he looked down at her and said, 'I'll think about it.'

Disappointed, Elizabeth pursued him, 'Don't just think about it. Do something. You can't sit on the fence all your life.'

'You may be right at that.' Jim sighed and took her hand, stroking it absently. 'But I've got to make sure that when I make my protest, it has the maximum effect.'

Elizabeth stared at him, speechless for the first time in her life. David, catching Eve's eye, smiled ruefully. But Eve didn't smile back. She couldn't. She was trying too hard to keep down the tears.

Next day, they were all to go to Marsden, so that the grandpa and grandma could meet their grandson at last. Eve fussed over her son till, exasperated with her, he flew off the handle and went to sulk in Jim's room.

'She wants me to wear a tie!' Pete complained.

'And what do *you* want to wear?' Jim asked.

'My bus conductor's outfit, of course.'

'Of course,' Jim replied. 'I'll talk to her for you, shall I?' Pete nodded glumly and sat on Jim's bed to await the result of negotiations.

Jim found Eve in a state. Elizabeth had pinched her nicest dress and was wearing it herself.

'What's wrong with that tinfoil thing you brought with you?' Eve demanded. 'You thought it was the best thing since sliced bread, yesterday!'

'I just want to wear something softer today,' Elizabeth explained. 'More feminine.'

'Well, wear something of your own. Does it have to be mine?' Eve glared.

'But I haven't got anything feminine of my own,' Elizabeth whined. 'Unless I wear my hippy things, and you know what Aunt Frances thinks of those.'

'Ooh, you're impossible,' Eve said, stomping back to her room.

Then Elizabeth saw Jim on the stair, smiled hesitantly, and swished away into her bedroom to listen, as Jim knocked on Eve's door, went in, and started pleading the case for the bus conductor.

'He's young,' Jim said. 'You've got to let young people live.'

Eve didn't argue. And before you could say 'Jack Robinson', Jim had come out again, gone downstairs, and Pete was happily punching holes in the lavatory paper.

'Doesn't she look nice?' Mary Jean approved, as Elizabeth did a twirl on the stair, prior to departure.

'Sure does,' Jim agreed. Eve, in her second-best dress, emerged unnoticed. Vexed to tears, she bit her lip as they drove along the road to Marsden.

'Nice guy, that David fellah,' Jim observed. He was smiling. Eve smiled back.

'Yes, isn't he?' Her voice was cold and formal. Jim shrugged and turned to Elizabeth, who was sitting like a lady, hands clasped on her lap. Butter wouldn't have melted anywhere near her mouth.

When they arrived at Marsden, the first thing Maisie said was, 'Eeh, doesn't our Elizabeth look smashing? Eeh!'

'She's supposed to be ill,' Eve observed.

'*I've* been ill,' Pete said seriously.

'We know,' Frances told him.

'I've been *very* ill,' he said.

'We know that too,' Jack said.

'What's wrong with you, pet?' Maisie asked Elizabeth sympathetically.

'Oh, I don't know. I just feel tired all the time.'

'*I* felt tired all the time too,' Pete told her. 'You've probably got what I had.'

'Leukaemia?' Elizabeth squeaked.

'They take away all the blood from your veins and put new stuff in.' He whispered. 'I think they give the old blood to vampire bats.'

Eve prodded her son in the back to shut him up.

'Where's David?' Frances asked, to change the subject.

'Why? He doesn't come with the furniture!' Eve snapped. 'He's on shift for all I know. I'm not married to him, you know!'

Jack and Frances exchanged a look, and Pete, who had been ignored for three seconds, started punching holes in the table cloth. Reprimanding her son, Eve cast a sidelong look at Jim and Elizabeth. Moonstruck stargazers! She wanted to cry with vexation, and took it out on Pete.

'You're acting like a spoilt child,' she said, confiscating the clippers. But, as she knew very well, it was she who was behaving like the spoilt child, not her son.

460

Jim hadn't agreed to go on the march but he did agree to go with Elizabeth down to London for Easter. Pete, alarmed at the idea of being left behind, insisted on going along. They would see the sights, Tower of London, Buckingham Palace, London taxi cabs!

'Why don't you come too, Evie?' Elizabeth asked. 'I'm sure Myra'd find room for everybody!' But Eve had a dancing school to run, and the competitions were a week away. She couldn't. So she let Os drive them all into Newcastle to catch their train. She'd see them in a couple of weeks. But a lot could happen in a couple of weeks, and in the following days, Eve found herself going round in a 'complete tizz', as Mary Jean told her sharply.

'Eve,' she said, hands on hips, 'I don't know what's got into you. You're shouting at the children, snapping at their mothers and driving us all half-crazy. Maybe you need to take some time off. How about after the competitions, eh? There'll be nothing to stop you then. Go away somewhere. Get some fresh air. Enjoy yourself!' Eve burst into tears. 'Whatever's wrong with you?' Mary Jean asked, astonished. 'Is it the change?' Eve yelped with rage and stamped her foot.

'I'm not *that* old!' she said.

'Yes, you are.' Mary Jean had never been cowed by a tantrum, especially when it was interfering with her cleaning the changing rooms.

'Alright! Alright! I am!' Eve admitted. 'But it isn't that. It really isn't!'

'Well then what is it?' Mary Jean shouted back helplessly.

'I'm in love!' Eve yelled.

There was a stunned silence, then Mary Jean raised her duster to her lips and burst out laughing.

'Oh. Is that all?' she said.

'What do you mean, "all"?' Eve snapped.

'You're going on like a daft teenager, and there's really no need! I mean, why don't you just marry him and be done with it?' Mary Jean went on in a matter of fact voice. 'Your Mam likes him. Your Dad likes him. He's steady. Got a good job. He's Os's best friend. And he thinks the world of you. What more do you want?'

Eve stared at her, unable to speak. Mary Jean was thinking of David. But Eve didn't dare tell her who *she* was thinking of. She felt a hot flush rise up her spine and knew that that wasn't 'the

461

change' either. It was deep embarrassment. She had almost given herself away to Mary Jean. But, worst of all, she had given herself away to herself. There was no escaping it. She *was* behaving like a teenager. 'In love', if you please, and with a man who was young enough to be her own son! Eve gulped down a sob, and choked. Mary Jean banged her sympathetically on the back. Marriage was a big step, after all. She understood Eve might be nervous of it, especially when it was the second time around.

'Yes,' Eve said aloud. 'I think I'll take your advice. I'll go up to Marsden after Easter. See Mam and Dad.'

'Good idea!' Mary Jean switched on the Hoover, and started doing the changing room floor. The business was out of her hands, thank God. She could rely on Jack and Frances to talk some sense into their daughter, and Mary Jean had work enough to do, keeping this place spick and span.

The two days of the competition took a lot out of Eve. She had to be all things to all people. She couldn't even go to the ladies without someone following her and wanting to know how they'd done, whether it mattered they'd lost their sequinned bow and if the dance floor wasn't too slippy or the pianist too fast. But, finally, by Sunday night, it was all over. As usual, Eve's studio had done well. But no one bothered to uncork the champagne. Success was taken for granted. The trophies had disappeared with the successful pupils and Eve was left with nothing but the props and the sheet music, to pile into the van after Os and Mary Jean.

'I'm hungry,' Mary Jean said. 'I could just fancy some chips.'

'We'll call in on the way home, if you like,' Os answered.

'Tut,' Mary Jean sighed. 'They won't be open. It's Sunday.' But chips weren't what Eve wanted anyway. She wanted celebration; she wanted the sparkle put back in her life, before she got too old to enjoy it.

'Are you too tired to go out?' Eve swung round. It was David Jackson. He'd come up, unnoticed, behind her. She smiled.

'No. The night is young,' she answered. He tipped his hat to Mary Jean and Os, who winked back, then led Eve away to his own car, parked round the corner. She heard Os's van take off, and slipped gratefully into David's comfortable saloon.

'Oh, this is nice.' She groaned, rubbing her aching legs. 'I've been on my feet all day. Where are we going?'

'Surprise,' he answered, letting in the clutch. 'How did you get on?'

'Pretty well, really. Won most of the things we expected to.'

'You don't sound all that pleased about it,' he observed. 'I mean, if it was me, I'd be over the moon.'

'I am. I am really,' she said. 'It's just . . . I did it last year and the year before, and nobody seems that impressed any more, including me.' The car was purring along the road to the coast. 'I mean, there's nowhere to go now. Juliet'll probably get into the Royal Ballet School. She might even go on to be a star, but, I don't suppose I'll get the credit for it. I'll still be here, running the old studio, year after year.' David said nothing. He just listened, trying to understand. 'I miss dancing, you know. I mean, doing it myself,' she said. 'I used to let off steam that way. Now . . . well, there's a lot of steam built up inside, and no way out.'

Suddenly, as they came out from among the houses, she saw the sea. It was like a golden ribbon in the late sunlight. She gasped with pleasure. 'Isn't it lovely?' David parked in the cliff-top car park above the grotto, and they got out, to stand looking at the ships coming and going from the port of Tyne.

'Jim's right,' Eve said. 'The oceans *are* too pretty just to lock up and use as energy.' David slipped his hand into hers and squeezed hard. Eve stiffened, panic stricken. Never, in all their times together, had David taken hold of her hand, except to partner her in a dance. Next thing, he'd slip that hand round her waist. She knew it. She tried to pull gently away, but his grip was strong, and she didn't want to make a scene. Then, he turned his head towards her, and she knew he meant to kiss her. He hadn't tried that since that time at the beatnik club. Eve was still looking steadfastly out to sea. She felt his warm breath on the side of her head, closer and closer. Her hair began to tickle with his nearness. Then suddenly, unable to bear it any more, she turned, as if to speak to him and banged her cheek hard against his. Wincing, he let go her hand, and held onto his nose.

'Sorry,' Eve said, 'I can be very clumsy for a dancer.' David smiled bravely. 'Where are we going, David? Go on. Tell me.'

'There's a dinner dance at the Crown. I thought you might like to go,' he said.

'Lovely!' Eve grinned. Suddenly, David made a dive for her mouth. He planted his lips on hers and kissed her. Stunned, she received the kiss without struggling, then, as he grew in confidence, his lips warmed and melted into hers, taking her into a deep embrace. Afterwards, he pulled away, smiling victoriously. But Eve was distressed. She had responded to him. She knew she had. But she shook her head.

'What's wrong?' he asked.

'I . . . I feel like a tart,' she answered.

'You're crackers,' he laughed. Eve pouted. 'Alright, if it helps, you can always agree to marry me,' he volunteered, still confident and proud of himself.

'You don't understand,' Eve said. 'I'm sorry, David. I'm very fond of you.' Then came the inevitable 'but'. 'But, you see, I'm in love with somebody else.' David frowned.

'Who?' he asked, puzzled.

'If you can't guess, I'm not telling you,' Eve replied, turning away. But he took hold of her arm and pulled her back.

'This isn't a guessing game, Eve,' he said. 'You've been leading me on for the best part of three years now. Who the hell are you talking about?'

'Jimmy.' Her voice was scarcely audible. His eyes grew rounder and rounder. His mouth dropped open in amazement.

'I don't believe you,' he said. 'You're having me on.'

'I am not having you on, as you put it,' Eve said pompously. Suddenly David raised his hand and struck her hard across the face. 'Well, you should be, you stupid bitch,' he said. He was walking off towards the car.

'Wait for me.' Eve scurried after him. But he was too quick for her. He was in the car and had started the engine before she'd reached him. 'David . . . ' she shouted as the car jerked forward, 'don't leave me here!' He stopped and wound down the window.

'There's a taxi service available in this town,' he said. 'Why don't you take *them* for a ride! At least they get paid for it!'

'David! I'm sorry! I didn't mean . . . !' She was standing in the dim light of the car park, bawling like a child. He sat, looking at her for a moment, then said,

'Give me a ring when you've reached puberty! O.K?'

Then he drove off, leaving her speechless with shame and rage.

Next day, Easter Monday, Eve went down to Marsden to see her Mam and Dad. She was dreading the usual question, 'Where's David?' Or, as it was sometimes phrased, '*How's* David?' But her Dad had been poorly with angina, and was a bit 'pale round the gills' as her mother put it. So, forgetting the usual formalities, they just sat in front of the telly, watching whatever came on and drinking tea laced with brandy.

'I need it for my heart,' Jack explained, winking. Eve thought she needed it for hers as well, though she didn't say so. And she was grateful for the distraction of the T.V. It saved her from having to talk, and it saved her parents from looking too closely at her face. 'You wear your heart on your sleeve, pet,' her mother used to say to her. Well, she couldn't take their questions or their sympathy just now. *If* they offered any sympathy, that is. They might just laugh, and tell her it was her own fault, which would be even worse. The C.N.D. march was on the news. There were as many as a hundred thousand people protesting this year, according to the organizers. Fran, Jack and Eve all strained to see if they could make out Elizabeth in the crowd, and in spite of herself, Eve found herself mentioning Jimmy.

'I wonder if she got Jim to go on it,' she muttered.

'Never!' her mother said. 'He's got more sense. Anyway, he wouldn't take Pete! It wouldn't be right. I mean, anything could happen! And somebody's got to look after him. They can't all march off and leave him.'

'Doubt if Myra'd stay behind for him,' Jack observed. 'She's a career woman, her.'

'I don't know,' Eve said cagily. 'I think if Elizabeth was dead set on it, Jim'd do anything. She's got him eating out of her hand.'

Frances and Jack looked at Eve, then at each other.

'Oh no,' Frances said, at last.

'Oh no, what?' Eve asked.

'Do you remember, years ago, I had to split up our Os and Anna . . . ?' Eve nodded.

'It might be alright in this case,' Jack said. 'Elizabeth seems

465

normal enough.' Frances laughed ironically. 'Well, all the kids're round the twist these days, I grant you, but, she's not neurotic. I mean like Anna was at her age.'

'Like mother, like daughter,' Frances warned.

'You don't know that,' Jack objected. 'And anyway, Jim and Elizabeth aren't all that closely related. Just sort of distant cousins. I don't see it matters so very much.'

'All the same,' Frances said. 'If they had kids . . . It wouldn't be fair on them.' Listening, Eve felt something grow inside her. It was a sort of dread.

'Does Elizabeth know?' she asked.

Jack and Frances looked at her.

'Well, I've not told her,' Frances said. Jack just shook his head. 'Somebody should, though.' They were both looking at Eve. Eve grew pale, and drank some more 'tea'.

'Liz doesn't want to have kids,' she said.

'Accidents happen,' Frances told her. 'Forewarned is forearmed.'

'I suppose it wouldn't do any harm,' Eve said slowly. Then Maisie came back from a walk and broke up the discussion to talk about her rheumatism.

'*I've* had a lot of pain lately,' Eve said.

'Where?' The other two women pounced on the symptom.

'Oh, in my legs, hips, knees.'

'Could be arthritis,' Maisie said, shaking her head.

'At my age?' Eve was alarmed.

'Well,' Maisie told her, 'it was asking for trouble, pet, spending all that time in the desert getting your oils dried out, then coming back to this cold, damp climate.' She was shaking her head like a messenger of doom. 'And you're just the age to be starting it.'

Annoyed, Eve retorted, 'Fat lot you know about it Auntie Maisie!'

It was unworthy of Eve to take it out on poor old Maisie, and she knew it, but the gall was rising so fast in her, she hadn't time to check it before it spewed over the nearest victim.

'Sorry,' she sighed.

'I got that about the oils from a magazine.' Maisie blew her nose defensively and helped herself to some 'tea'.

Eve was in a fever when she got home. She wasn't used to

466

drinking brandy in the daytime and it had given her a headache. She took some aspirin and lay down for a while in her room. The house was quiet. Os and Mary Jean had gone to Hexham to see their son. Everybody else was in London, probably sticking plasters on their blisters by now, Eve thought. Elizabeth would be the heroine of the hour, at least in Jim's eyes. Jealousy rose inside her like foam in a rabid dog. It was a horrible feeling. Eve wasn't used to it. She'd never been host to the green-eyed monster before. But she was now. There was no getting away from it. It wasn't fair. Jim was the first real man she'd ever met. She'd fallen for him years ago, in the Canyon de Chelly, while the golden leaves fluttered down to the flat, dry, riverbed. The high walls rose straight up, as though they'd been cut by a knife, and that dog had followed them . . .

She wiped away her tears. Well, she was lucky to have known Jim at all, she told herself. She should count her blessings. I mean, what would he want with a rheumaticky old woman like her? She rubbed her hip. It was really hurting. These rheumatics had started after she'd found out about Jack and Vijay, hadn't they? She eased herself into a sitting position and tried to remember. The bedside light threw her shadow across the curtain. Shadows. They made you do things you didn't want to. And if you stopped them, they turned against *you*. She rubbed her leg absently. Elizabeth had a shadow. The sins of the fathers had brought a curse on their descendants, the tortured descendants, Hester, Anna and now . . . Not Elizabeth's fault, poor thing. But the shadow was there. She'd inherited it, and sooner or later it would make itself known. She had to be told. She was an intelligent girl. By her own admission she didn't want children. And it wasn't fair on Jim. If he got serious about her, and then . . . No. Eve had to tell her. Somebody had to. She couldn't ask it of her Mam and Dad.

The Thursday following Easter, Jim, Elizabeth and Pete all came home. As soon as she saw them, Eve knew something was afoot. Jim and Elizabeth were bubbling with a secret happiness that made Eve's heart ache. She tried not to show her chagrin, chattering on and on, telling them all the news about this pupil and that pupil, and how well they'd done in the competition. And then, when she'd exhausted that topic, she smiled at the couple who were, by now, looking as glazed as the chintz covers of the sofa they were sitting on, and asked, 'How about you two? How did you get on?' Then very quickly, before they could answer, 'Did you go on the march, Jim?'

Jim shook his head.

'No,' he said. 'Myra thought it was "inadvisable". Especially as I'm an American citizen. Why, if I got my name on your MI5 list, I might never get back into this country!'

'Oh dear!' Eve looked at Elizabeth who was sitting demurely in a floral print dress, bought for her by Myra. 'See where your hare-brained ideas might have got you?'

'Don't worry, Evie. Jim's taking me in hand.' Elizabeth grinned, and looked at him. Eve's heart lurched. 'He's even got me to agree to go on from fine art to architecture. Imagine me designing actual buildings! The mind boggles!' Jim laughed.

'Why don't you tell her?' Pete asked suddenly. He was sitting on the floor, tearing a newspaper into strips.

'Tell me what?' Eve asked brightly, looking from Jim to Elizabeth.

Then Elizabeth moved her right hand from over the left, and showed the sparkling diamond on her engagement finger. Eve thought she was going to faint. Jim was apparently deeply engrossed in his hands, which were practising 'Here's the church and here's the steeple . . .' and didn't so much as glance at Eve, as she oohed and aahed said how pleased she was. He didn't dare. So at last, Eve spoke to him directly.

'When did you ask her?'

Then he had to look at her. 'Oh . . . ' Jim said awkwardly, 'we were in the Tate Gallery at the time . . . looking at a Turner.'

'I'll never forget that picture till the day I die,' Elizabeth said. 'It was a view of the Thames.'

Jim took her hand and kissed it, then looked straight at Eve.

'I don't like Turner,' Pete sulked.

'You're a cretin,' Elizabeth told him.

'I don't like cities either. I like farms best.' This was too much. Eve's face fell, and suddenly she looked very lost. Jim kicked the little boy at his feet. 'Ouch,' Pete said. Then he realized what he'd done, and looked up at Eve to say, guiltily, 'Sorry, Momma. It's just I miss my horse and the kids at school and that sort of thing. Grown-ups are really boring, you know.'

'Yes. I suppose we are,' Eve said. 'And I don't suppose Jim and Elizabeth had much time for you, with all their courting.'

'That's not fair!' Elizabeth shot out of her seat in indignation.

'I'm sure you did your best,' Eve said quickly. Jim was still holding his fiancée's hand. He pulled her back into the seat, and put his arm round her.

'Sure we did. Didn't we, Pete?' he said smoothly.

'Yeah. You were O.K. I suppose. Jim and me went to the zoo while the rest of them did their march thing. And we found a hamburger place. London's a bit ahead of South Shields.'

'I expect it is,' Eve said. 'When are you thinking of . . . er . . . "tying the knot"?' she struggled to ask. Elizabeth grinned at Jim and he grinned back. They looked a proper pair of charlies, Eve thought. 'Why don't you do it here?' she suggested suddenly. It was the last thing she wanted and the first that came to mind.

'Could we?' Elizabeth asked. Jim didn't seem so sure.

'Your father might want us to get married in London,' he pointed out.

'But that would have to be a register office ceremony, and I want a white wedding,' Elizabeth said, starry-eyed. 'I want a veil and satin shoes, and a three-tiered wedding cake with silver horse shoes on it, and I want church bells ringing when I come out!'

Jim laughed. He was obviously pleased. 'You forgot the bridesmaids,' he said. Elizabeth looked hesitantly at Eve.

'Eve could be matron of honour. If she'd like to, of course.'

Eve gulped, and managed to smile. 'Thank you, Liz,' she said as graciously as she could. Then Jim got a look on his face, and Eve knew what was coming. He was going to ask if David would be best man.

'Do you think David would agree to be best man?' he asked. Eve gritted her teeth. 'Or would it be better to ask Os?'

'I think Os, don't you?' Eve answered. 'And when's it all going to be?'

'Well,' Jim shrugged. 'If it's going to be here in England, it'd better be soon! I'm due back in the States, end of May.'

'A May wedding,' Elizabeth breathed. 'It's so romantic.' She lay back against the sofa cushions, delirious with joy.

'And where're you going to live?'

Elizabeth and Jim spoke at once. 'In the States,' Elizabeth said. 'In England,' Jim replied. Then he smiled. 'Well, matter of fact, we'll just see how it works out, when Elizabeth's qualified. See, I might try for a job over here. Transfer my interests to reviving the Midlands oilfields . . . something like that.'

'I see,' Eve said. 'Well, I wish you luck.' She looked from one to the other, smiling, and they didn't know why they felt so uneasy. 'There's the rest of the family to tell yet,' Eve reminded them. 'Are you going to phone, or what?'

'Let's go down to Marsden now!' Elizabeth pulled her fiancé off the seat and fell over Pete, who yelled angrily.

In a little over a week, Elizabeth was to go back to the Slade. Jim had decided to go down with her, and check out the job situation, as Eve had kindly offered to take care of all the wedding arrangements. Pete wanted to go too. He was fed up with Shields, and anyway, he'd left his hole-puncher thing at Auntie Myra's and he couldn't possibly go back to the States without it. Eve asked him if he was sure he *was* going back to the States but he got so upset at the idea he might never see his horse again, Eve let it drop. She and Jim would have to have a long talk about things, later.

Meanwhile, desperate to keep up a front, Eve took Elizabeth for dress fittings, helped her decide on flowers, booked the church, the organist, and the reception, and at night, when everyone else was asleep down in Os's flat, she helped Elizabeth draw up the invitations list. They had drunk half a bottle of wine between them, and Elizabeth was mooning over the invitations, the date, May 15th, neatly printed on each card. Eve was racking her brains trying to think who really couldn't be left out.

'I love these invitations,' Elizabeth said idly, stroking the embossed silver of the print. 'They're so lovely. Nobody ever had a nicer wedding than mine's going to be. And it's all thanks to you, Eve.' Eve showed her the new name she'd added, and Elizabeth, chin resting on hands, stared at the list. 'You haven't put down David Jackson,' she said.

'That's true,' Eve replied.

'Why not?' Elizabeth was staring at Eve. She blinked suddenly. 'Come to think, I haven't seen David since we got back from London. You haven't had a row, have you?'

'Yes, as a matter of fact, we have,' Eve replied curtly.

'Lovers' tiff, I suppose. Me and Jimmy had one of those. And all because I wanted another cream cake. He said I'd get fat. But

470

I told him I burned off more calories in one day than he could consume in a million years. Then he told me not to be so impossibly inaccurate, and I accused him of being pedantic, and . . .'

'I see,' Eve said. 'How interesting.'

'What was *your* row about?' Elizabeth asked generously.

'Nothing,' Eve answered.

'Well, you'll be able to make it up all the more easily, won't you? Ring him now. Go on.'

'Don't be stupid,' Eve snapped. 'It's after midnight.'

'O.K. Have another glass of wine. Drown your sorrows,' Elizabeth said, pouring it out. Eve took the glass, raised it to her lips, then put it down again.

'No. I've had too much already,' she said.

'Don't mind if I have one?' Elizabeth asked.

'Be my guest.' Eve was playing with the corner of the list. 'Have you thought about . . . you know . . . I mean, there's clinics now. You could go on the pill. I've heard that's one hundred per cent safe.'

'Oh dear. Are you going to tell me about the birds and the bees now, Auntie?' Elizabeth asked, blinking outrageously.

'No,' Eve replied, curling up the paper, and uncurling it again. 'Only, you did say you didn't want to have children, didn't you?'

'Well . . . ' Elizabeth sighed, 'that was then. I don't know. I'm beginning to think the world's not such a bad place after all.' She giggled and hiccuped.

'Elizabeth . . . ' Eve began. 'Look, I wish it wasn't me who had to tell you this, but somebody has to.' Elizabeth frowned and tried to focus on Eve more clearly. 'You see, the reason I want you to think about contraception's just that, well, when you know the facts, you may decide you still don't want to have children, no matter how rosy the world looks.' Elizabeth stared blankly at her. Eve sighed, and put the paper down on the table. 'Do try to concentrate, Elizabeth.' Elizabeth saluted, tried to rest her chin on her hand, missed and banged it on the table.

'Sorry. I'll try,' she said, composing herself.

'You know your mother . . . '

'Slightly,' Elizabeth nodded.

'I'm trying to be serious, love,' Eve said. 'This isn't easy, you know. Look, I'll come straight to the point. And for God's sake

471

try to take it in. There is some mystery surrounding your grandmother's birth.'

'Goodness!' Elizabeth cried. 'Don't tell me it was an immaculate conception!'

'Quite the opposite, if you've finished blaspheming!' Eve snapped. Elizabeth was looking at Eve, and in her eyes Eve saw light slowly dawning.

She sat up straight, and asked, without a trace of flippancy, 'What mystery? What are you talking about?'

Eve swallowed hard, then went on nervously, 'Your Auntie Frances and Uncle Jack believe she was . . .'

'Oh!' Elizabeth smiled. 'I get it. Illegitimate! How romantic. Don't tell me great-grandma had her out of wedlock. What was it? An affair?'

'Yes,' Eve answered. 'With her brother.'

There was a stunned silence. Elizabeth was trying to take it in, through a fog of wine and romantic delirium.

Finally, she asked, shakily, 'You mean, they committed incest?' Eve nodded. 'And my grandma was born as a result?'

Eve nodded again, then added, 'We don't know for sure. But it certainly looks like it. And anyway, it's not worth taking the risk of having children. I mean Jim's only a distant cousin, I'll admit, but he is family, and in this case, too close for comfort.' Elizabeth was shaking. Her face had gone pink, and she was looking down at the floor.

'Does he know?' she whispered, without looking up.

'I don't know. I don't think so,' Eve said.

'Don't tell him. Please, don't tell him.' Elizabeth spoke quickly. 'I'd hate him to know.' Then she looked directly at Eve. 'Promise me, you won't tell him.'

Eve looked away, then back again, then shrugged. 'If it's what you want. But . . .'

'Don't worry. I'm not going to marry him.'

For a second, Eve felt real pleasure, then immediately, shame.

'But . . . you could still, as long as you didn't have children . . .' she encouraged.

'No.' Elizabeth shook her head. 'Jim wants kids. He adores Pete, you know. He doesn't want to leave him here when he goes back to the States. He wants a son of his own. And if I can't

472

give him that . . . ' She started crying, as though her heart would break.

Eve took her in her arms. Standing over her, hugging her close, she murmured, 'Oh God. What have I done? What have I done?'

'It's not your fault, Eve,' Elizabeth comforted her.

'I needn't have told you. I could have just let you marry him and . . . '

'You couldn't. If I'd found out later, I'd have felt I'd cheated him. And what about the kids? The son Jim really wants? I mean, I know what happened to grandma, the asylum and everything, and my Mum's not exactly . . . Oh God. What's going to become of *me*?'

'I'm sorry. I'm sorry,' Eve cried. 'Please forgive me. Please. I was jealous!' Elizabeth pulled away and looked at Eve.

'You mean, it isn't true?' she asked. 'The incest and everything?' Eve couldn't meet her eyes.

'It is true. At least . . . talk to your Uncle Jack about it. He used to know your great-grandpa very well. He knows all there is to know. He might be able to help you.'

'I couldn't.' Elizabeth took Eve's face in her hands, and looked straight into her eyes. 'Only tell me you haven't made this up, Eve? Tell me, please?'

'I wouldn't do that, Elizabeth. I'm not a bad woman . . . ' Eve sobbed and the two held one another for a long time. Then Eve, seeking a ray of hope, said, 'I wish you'd talk to Jim about it. I'm sure he'd understand. He'd still want to marry you.'

But Elizabeth would have none of it.

'No. I feel dirty. I feel . . . I've got to come to terms with this thing first,' she said. 'I need a few days to myself. I need to go away. Don't worry. I won't be gone long.'

Next morning, Elizabeth announced she was going straight down to London.

'I want to look for a flat,' she said. 'It'd be so much nicer for us, Jim. Don't you agree?' He shrugged and said if it was what she wanted, it was fine by him, but why shouldn't he come too? He could help her look. Elizabeth smiled playfully. 'No,' she said. 'I want to do this on my own. Show you I can be really grown-up.'

He grinned at her, pleased. 'O.K. Have it your own way.'

'I'll phone as soon as I've got a place,' she told him. And within the hour, she'd gone.

Eve carried on making wedding arrangements, hoping Elizabeth would ring and say she'd got over her fright and would Jim go down and talk it out and everything would be fine again. But she didn't ring. After four days, Jim rang the Strachan house. Myra didn't know where Elizabeth was. She hadn't been in touch since she'd come down to London; if she'd come down to London. Perhaps she was staying with one of her friends from college? But Jim was worried, and so was Eve. Then, on the sixth day, a letter arrived. It was for Jim. Jim stared at the letter for a long time, then handed it to Eve, who read it with trembling hands.

Dear Jim,
I'm sorry to do things this way, but I can't go through with the wedding. I suppose, like you said, I'm just not grown-up enough. Well, anyway, I've decided to try to grow. I joined a group of people who are all really keen on spiritual things and so on, and they're going to India, at the end of this week. I've decided to go with them. It'll be really exciting. We'll be camping when we get there, and living à la native. I've talked to the Principal at college and he said I could take a year off if I wanted. He's been really nice about it. Well, I'm sorry I've caused so much trouble. Please say so to Evie and everybody. But I suppose it's better to find out now than later, isn't it? You should be grateful to me really. I've probably saved you from a fate worse than death! I do care. I even love you. Honestly. But perhaps you won't believe me.
T.T.F.N. and S.W.A.L.K.
Elizabeth

'I'm sorry, Jim,' Eve said, tearfully, handing back the letter. 'I really am. I had no idea she was going to do *this*!' And she burst out crying.

'All the arrangements . . .' he muttered.

'Look,' Eve touched his arm gently, and pleaded with him, 'Why don't you go down there. I'm sure you could find her before she goes and . . . and you could persuade her . . . I know she loves you.'

'No.' Jim shook his head. 'I don't think so.'

'She does!'

Jim looked at Eve. She was desperate.

'Hey! It's O.K.,' he said. 'Elizabeth needs time to find herself, I guess. Everybody does. I had it. You had it. Why shouldn't she? Maybe later . . . I don't know.' But his expression was hopeless. A few minutes later, the phone rang. It was Elizabeth's father, ringing from London. Jim took the call. They had just had a letter too. He agreed at once to go down and talk to them.

'Can I come?' Pete asked, when he heard. Eve stroked his head gently. 'I think Uncle Jim needs me,' he explained with an instinctive stroke of genius.

'O.K.,' Eve agreed. 'Just for a while, huh?'

Pete raced to pack his bag. He was going to get his hole-puncher back. It was all he could think about.

'You know what?' he said gaily as Jim piled their bags into the van, 'I could let you use all the bits from the punched holes for confetti, if you like.'

'Thank you,' Eve said. 'That's very thoughtful of you.'

Then she waved them both goodbye.

Eve hadn't wanted Jim to marry Elizabeth. Well, she'd got her way, and now she'd have done anything to put the clock back. Jack and Frances comforted her, telling her she'd done the right thing. Elizabeth had to know the truth as they knew it, and her going off the way she had, was proof of an unbalanced personality, if ever there was proof! But to Eve, it was cold comfort. She didn't want Jim now. He was far too young for her. She could see that. What had blinded her before? What had made her so stupid? Her own vain ego? Or was it the shadow, trying to make trouble as usual? As for Pete, he didn't want her, not really. He wanted Jim and Ella and his pony and the ranch and big hamburgers, but not Eve. So she'd let him go back to the States with Jim. She'd see him again. He'd probably be over every summer, if the money ran to it. And when he was older, he'd have the choice of two worlds, the old and the new. It was better this way. But Eve felt lonely and wondered what it had all been for. Must've been something.

May 15th, the day Jim and Elizabeth had planned for their wedding, came and went. Nothing more had been heard from

Elizabeth. No doubt they'd get some zany card from Timbuctoo or somewhere one of these days. Eve switched off her bedside light and lay back against the pillows. Lonely. She turned her head to see the dark shape of the phone by her bed. Not now. Maybe tomorrow she'd phone him. Tomorrow. A breeze strained at the curtains in the window. She'd closed them to keep out the draught from the open window. But now, as she lay in the stuffy room, not sleeping, she wanted it. So she got up again, and swung the curtains back. A gust of air caught her throat. She gulped it down. It was a beautiful night; a night for honeymoons. She looked up at the stars. Something was moving up there. A plane? Then she remembered 'Gordo' Cooper, circling the earth in his satellite. She smiled up at the twinkling craft that was speeding across the sky. Jim and Pete must've already seen it, as it flew over New Mexico, and soon, perhaps Elizabeth would look up, see the crescent moon lying on its back, and think of the man hurtling starlike across the Indian skies towards a new day, and a new sunrise. But Eve was here, at the centre; still. She turned her back on the starry sky and saw her shadow on the wall of the room. She walked towards it, and opening her arms to embrace the shadow, found it was no longer there.

THE TURNING TIDES

Valerie Georgeson

'Nobody has the power to keep me from you but you yourself!'

Cathy Straker is still a young child when her beloved father is lost at sea. All but penniless, she and her mother move into her aunt's teeming Dockside home.

All seems lost, but Cathy becomes a vibrant and beautiful young woman. She soon charms wealthy, kind-hearted Gilbert Stoddard and they determine to marry.

Then on Cathy's birthday, their celebrations are joined by a striking handsome blond Norwegian sea captain and she knows she cannot yet make such a promise. Torn by her conflicting emotions, still loving Gilbert, she yet knows that they must part . . .

In the best tradition of Catherine Cookson, set against a vividly realised background of early twentieth-century-Tyneside, THE TURNING TIDES is a memorable and poignant story of loss, betrayal, loyalty, love, and of Cathy who, eager for all that life offers, must come to terms with the promise and heartbreak of life itself.

FUTURA PUBLICATIONS
FICTION
0 7088 2698 9

HEARTS AND FARTHINGS

Beryl Kingston

LONDON IN THE 1890s . . . a foggy city bustling with activity and bubbling with Cockney repartee.

To this alien world comes Alberto Pelucci, an early immigrant from distant Italy, dreaming of adventure and romance. Adventure enough is the verminous room of his first night's stay in London, but romance seems more rewarding when the shy Alice accepts his hand. Only on their wedding night does he realise that his bride will never share his passion for physical pleasures.

And so when Alberto meets Queenie Dawson – exuberant, sensuous star of the music halls – his ordered new life is flung into turmoil . . .

HEARTS AND FARTHINGS: the heart-warming saga of a man torn between two women, and of children born in the last, bittersweet days before the war that should have ended all wars.

FUTURA PUBLICATIONS
FICTION/SAGA
0 7088 2976 7